Acclaim for Janny Wurts' *The Wars of Light and Shadow* series

"Wurts is an accomplished builder of worlds, scenes and characters through well-chosen detail, with an ear for dialogue and an eye for realism-her shipboard scenes, the battling street mobs and the reluctantly taxed merchants are exemplary. Though not yet up to Tolkien or Jordan, Wurts is getting there, and fast."—*Publishers Weekly*, Starred review

"The author's attention to detail and her skill for creating memorable heroes and villains lend a sense of immediacy to a tale of epic battles and great betrayals. For most fantasy collections."—*Library Journal*

"Wurts is in fine form here, providing endless twists and turns of plot and an artful complexity that is marvelous to behold."—*Booklist*

"With each new book, it becomes more and more obvious how important Janny Wurts is in contemporary fantasy. She writes as if the genre *matters*. It does, and she is one of the reasons it does."—Guy Gavriel Kay

"The gift of Janny Wurts is that of a true artist: intense, driven, passionate. She takes no prisoners, offers no quarter. This is powerful, gritty fantasy at its very best, full-bodied and bloody. Her characters come out changed-and so do her readers."—Jennifer Roberson

"Intricately woven of tragedy and hope, faith and betrayal, Curse of the Mistwraith never pits pure Evil against obvious Good but instead explores the haunting complexities of both—a rare achievement."—Melanie Rawn

"Janny Wurts writes with astonishing energy. Both in the scale of the stories she tells, and in the scale of emotions with which she fills those stories, she aims high; and she tackles the challenges at a white heat. Just when you think she's gone as far as anyone can go, she raises the stakes."— Stephen R. Donaldson

"Janny Wurts's Alliance of Light is a fascinating story, full of twists and turns and mind-stretching events. I'm delighted to recommend PERIL'S GATE as a grand fantasy on a truly cosmic scale. Readers will be enchanted."—C.J. Cherryh

"Janny Wurts builds beautiful castles in the air; also wonderful hovels in the dirt. From high-born to low, prince to peasant, and mage to barbarian, every detail of this accomplished world-builder's books is thoroughly imagined and vividly rendered. You can open the cover, and walk right in."—Diana Gabaldon

"Janny Wurts writes, not surprisingly, like the finest artist and illustrator that she also is. Using words like paint she builds up layer upon layer of convincing detail and rich description creating an overall fantasy texture that demands, and rewards, the reader's best attention."

"As in reality, few people in Janny's novel think they are real villains, they just believe that what's best for them is best for the world. Of course, the reader will form their own conclusions, though as with watching the delightfully convoluted science fiction television series *Babylon 5*, it's best not to grow too fond of your own opinion because you may have to change it!"—*Australian SF News* (Thyme Edition #127)

"The novel is fantasy on an epic scale, featuring the ambitions of kings and the machinations of sorcerers and enchantresses, the tale taking place in a world with its own millennia of history, and yet it is more subtle than much of its genre, being written in a style that is both elegant and sensuous. Descriptions of locations and interiors are lavish and evocative, while major and minor characters leap vividly from the page,"—*BSFA* #210

"Janny Wurts does a great job managing to keep both the two main characters and a lengthy cast of supporting characters fresh and realistic. She also continues to do a wonderful job at contrasting the elements of light and shadow in the characters and the plot elements of the story as it unfolds"—Wayne MacLaurin

"Traditionally the dark child would be the villain, but under Janny's pen we come to see each brother as flawed."—Stuart Dunnion (Eastern Daily Press)

Traitor's Knot

Books By Janny Wurts

To Ride Hell's Chasm

Sorcerer's Legacy

The Cycle of Fire Trilogy
Stormwarden
Keeper of the Keys
Shadowfane

The Master of Whitestorm
That Way Lies Camelot

The Wars of Light and Shadow
Curse of the Mistwraith
Ships of Merior
Warhost of Vastmark
Fugitive Prince
Grand Conspiracy
Peril's Gate
Traitor's Knot

With Raymond E. Feist
Daughter of the Empire
Servant of the Empire
Mistress of the Empire

Janny Wurts

Traitor's Knot

The Wars of Light and Shadow

Fourth Book of the Alliance of Light

Meisha Merlin Publishing, Inc.

Traitor's Knot

Published by Meisha Merlin Publishing, Inc.
PO Box 7
Decatur, GA   30031

Editing by Stephen Pagel
Copyediting and Proofreading by Sara and Bob Schwager
Interior layout by Lynn Swetz
Cover art and interior illustrations and Copyright © 2004 by Janny Wurts
Cover design by Kevin Murphy

ISBN: Hard Cover   1-59222-081-9

ISBN: Soft Cover   1-59222-082-7
ISBN 13: Soft Cover   978-1-59222-082-3

http://www.MeishaMerlin.com
First MM Publishing Trade Edition: September 2006

Printed in Canada
0 9 8 7 6 5 4 3 2 1

For Diane Turner,

close friend, sister spirit —

with profound gratitude for returning the "two penny lecture"

at just exactly the right moment.

Acknowledgements

A story of this size and scope cannot be done without helping hands at every stage. Thanks are due to a number of outstanding people—who already know who they are—but I will mention them, anyway.

Jeff Watson, for generous assistance with technology wonders.

Andrew Ginever, Betsy Hosler, Jana Paniccia,

Alan Carmichael, Gale Skipworth,

Sara and Bob Schwager, Jane Johnson.

The Meisha Merlin crew:

Stephe Pagel, Kevin Murphy, Lynn Swetz.

Two others, with gratitude that surpasses words:

Suzanne Parnell and Larry Turner.

Never last, Jonathan Matson, my husband, Don Maitz,

and not least, my mother, Roberta, who's read all of them.

Contents

Border of Rathain and Melhalla

If feet that marched the earth to war
could count their wounds by steel,
and blood that scorched clean ground in gore
could speak in words that feel,
the cry would ring forevermore
for mercy and repeal!
—MASTERBARD'S LAMENT FOR
THE WIDOWS OF DIER KENTON VALE
ARITHON s'FFALENN, THIRD AGE YEAR 5652

I. Wayfarers

INSIDE THE KITTIWAKE, randiest of the dockside taverns in Shipsport, two hunted men were unlikely to find the space for anonymous privacy. Raucous sailhands and sweaty stevedores jammed every nook, accosted by swindling tricksters, and the steamy blandishments of the whores. Rumors and gossip spread faster than plague. If the venue posed risks, Dakar, the Mad Prophet, need only eavesdrop to learn that the merchant brig, *Evenstar*, had weighed anchor from Tharidor and resumed her run down the eastshore last fortnight.

"Well, what did you expect? We're a month overdue." Fionn Areth shoved back from the trestle, chafed raw. One shout from a sailhand might see him exposed. The wide-brimmed hat just acquired from a riverman scarcely masked his striking, sharp features and black hair. The prospect of extending their journey for two hundred more leagues, over roads mired to mud by spring thaws, would but worsen his already desperate straits. "We should be leaving. Now."

Yet the spellbinder stayed planted in mooncalf complacency. Slumped in his uncivilized, travel-stained jerkin, a pitcher of beer tucked in hand, Dakar crossed his mud-caked boots at the ankles. His stout bulk stayed wedged between a soused party of chandlers and a tattooed longshoreman amused by two doxies, who both vied for a perch in his lap.

Their giggling raised Dakar to soulful envy. Lacking the coin to indulge his male itch, but with no dearth of copper for drinking, he tugged his snarled beard. The cinnamon strands now showed silver roots. He would soon be gray-headed. The legacy of his trials on Rockfell Peak: a harrowing entanglement in Fellowship magecraft that five brimming tankards still failed to erase from recalcitrant memory.

Already busy demolishing the sixth, Dakar swiped foam from his mustache. His jaundiced attention refused to acknowledge the anxious companion across from him.

Fionn Areth's impatience exploded. Above the taproom's racketing noise, he let fly in his broad moorland accent, "If *Evenstar*'s gone, then where in the name of thrice-coupling fiends do we go to seek news of your master?"

Heads turned. Laughter, dart games, and ribald conversation faltered at the teeming trestle. The Kittiwake's roisterers were always impressed by the prospect of a picked fight.

A fool's move, to draw notice, since the subject just broached involved a despised royal fugitive. The towns feared Prince Arithon of Rathain as a sorcerer who practiced fell rites and dark magecraft. On suspicion, his associates were likely to burn, condemned out of hand as collaborators.

"Want to visit Sithaer's eighth hell without setting foot out of Shipsport?" Dakar gripped his tankard. He gulped down the contents, then topped up Fionn Areth's half-pint. "Drink," he urged, hoping the young idiot would take the safe hint and succumb to a glassy-eyed stupor. "Trust me on this! You don't want to risk disrupting the peace. The shoreside magistrate's got a dungeon more wretched than anything you saw back in Jaelot. Spring tides flood the cells farthest down. You haven't touched misery until you've languished neck deep, with hordes of rats scrambling onto your head to save themselves from a drowning."

"Given the untrustworthy company you keep, should I be surprised that you've sampled every Ath-forsaken jail on the continent?" Fionn Areth shoved the filled vessel aside. "As for Sithaer's favors, I'm not getting sotted. Keep on as you are, and your fat skin could be stewed into soup grease right where we sit!" The moorlander caught hold of Dakar's moist wrist. "I'm using the good sense my grandame taught the goatherd. Will you haul your arse up and get out of here?"

By now, intrigued onlookers shouted for bets. Coins flashed, to the patter as someone made odds on which brawler was going to swing first. Here at the Kittiwake, fisticuffs and mayhem were counted as prime entertainment.

"Young fool!" the fat spellbinder snarled. Now jostled as enthusiasts totted up wagers, he nursed his pitcher and, with sullen deliberation, refilled his dry tankard. "I'll wring your neck, you dirt-stupid Araethurian, before I move even one step." Ignoring the whores, who stopped kissing to crane, and the growl from their displeased patron, Dakar nattered on. "Press me further, yes, beware! You'll see trouble on a scale you can't possibly imagine. Enough to make a verminous sinkhole seem blithe as a nursemaid's picnic. Now, shut your mouth. Sit on your temper and swallow the beer set in front of you."

"Damn you to Sithaer before I take a drop," Fionn Areth retorted.

The rabid pack of gamblers shoved back to make space.

Dakar shut his eyes. He sucked a martyred breath. Then in one lightning move, he elbowed erect and dumped his brimming tankard over his tangled head.

The runoff doused the longshoreman, to earsplitting shrieks from his harlots. They hiked up scarlet petticoats and fled. Their swain's irate bellow clashed with the clerks' howls and rattled soot from the Kittiwake's rafters.

Dakar freed his captive arm. While the trestle skidded, upsetting the pitcher and smashing two lightermen's dinner plates, he skinned through the clerks' snatching grasp and used his tankard to parry the stevedore's battering fist.

Crockery shattered. Fragments pelted over the dicers crammed elbow to elbow on the seat just behind.

Yelling murder, and unnaturally quick for a stout man grown tight on the Kittiwake's twopenny brew, Dakar ducked a dockworker's left hook. Then he lost his balance and sat. The brute's knuckles hammered into the clerks' outraged charge. The leading one crashed with a bloodied jaw, and flattened two of his fellows. Their thrashing upset the adjacent trestle. Bowls and hot chowder went flying. The four brawny fishermen deprived of their meal unsheathed flensing knives, screamed, and plunged in. Their vacated bench upset with a bang, toppling a drunk, who bowled into a circle of overdressed merchants. Lace tore; spilled food and spirits rained over fine velvets. The outraged peacocks redoubled the noise, bewailing their despoiled finery.

Trapped in the breach, Fionn Areth clambered upright. Disaster overtook him. Bedlam exploded like froth on a pot, and the Kittiwake's taproom erupted.

Tankards sailed. Broth splashed. Elbows and fists smacked against heaving flesh. Beneath the soaked tits of a gilded figurehead, an agile pack of sailhands laid into their neighbors with marlinspikes, knucklebones, and clogs. Their sally encountered the longshoreman's kin, who had leveled a trestle for use as a ram. Card games whisked airborne. Stew bones and cutlery showered the brick floor, stabbing toes and tripping combatants. Three prostitutes scuttling for cover went down, then another man, who became mired in their skirts. Their squeals drew the lusty eye of a galleyman, who dived in to lay claim to the spoils. While the landlord at the tap screeched threats and imprecations, the three heavies the Kittiwake employed to toss drunks at last stirred themselves to take charge. Brandishing cudgels, they waded in, dropping bodies like beef at a knacker's.

By then, Dakar had vanished, swallowed into the battering press.

Fionn Areth found himself trapped, all alone, mashed against the rocked edge of the trestle. The burgeoning riot cut off his escape, a riptide that raged without quarter. The Kittiwake's brawlers were a Shipsport legend, vicious with drink and seething with the age-old bad blood between galleymen and blue-water sailors. Crews seized on the chance to hammer their rivals. Enraged coopers shied bottles at all comers, while a reeling topman snatched lit candles from the sconces and flung them at random targets. Sparks flurried and ignited a puddle of spirits. Beset by fire and windmilling fists, the Kittiwake's strongmen yelled to summon reinforcements. The cooks, the potboys, and two muscled butchers burst out of the kitchen, armed with bludgeons and cleavers. Their vengeful flying wedge suggested an experience well primed for this afternoon's frolic.

At risk of being crippled, or knocked senseless for arrest, Fionn Areth grabbed the rolling pitcher as a weapon. But the body he slugged was a knife-bearing rigger, who whirled around, swore, and accosted him. His sally was backed by his ship's bursar, and another sailor swinging a belaying pin.

Fionn Areth fell back on sword training, ducked the club, and used a guarding forearm to parry the wrist of the dirk-wielding assailant. The slash missed his gut and, deflected upward, the follow-through skewered his hat brim. He snatched, too late. The snagged felt whisked away. Bareheaded, and wearing the flawless, spelled features of a notorious criminal, the moorlander panicked.

His last feckless brawl had sent him to a scaffold, mistakenly condemned as a sorcerer. A blade through the heart, followed by fire would give the most stalwart man nightmares.

Haunted by dread since that narrow escape, Fionn Areth ducked in blind terror. He dodged the swift stab of a marlinspike, desperate. Unless he recovered the hat, now impaled on the point of a maniac's dagger, he risked being falsely arraigned once again as the most wanted felon on the continent.

No one would believe the fact he was innocent. The uncanny likeness he wore was too real, a permanent imprint aligned by the wiles of the Koriani enchantresses. They had altered his face, then played him as bait. Their crafting was seamless: even his mother presumed the change was no less than his natural birthright. His late capture in Jaelot might have seen him dead for the deeds of his lookalike nemesis.

Arithon Teir's'Ffalenn, known as Spinner of Darkness, was too well renowned for obscurity. His horrific record of wanton destruction had dispatched fifty thousand armed men, sworn to serve the Alliance of Light.

"Furies take Dakar for a witless wastrel!" Fionn Areth gasped, sorely beset. Both marlinspike and dagger thrust in concert to maim him. He dodged the first, caught a gash on his forearm. His dive for the hat ran afoul of the brute with the cudgel dispatched to clear out the taproom.

Fionn Areth crumpled, glassy-eyed and raging, into the dark of unconsciousness.

Roused by the throb of the bruise on his head and the stinging slice on his forearm, Fionn Areth groaned, limp and queasy with vertigo. Spinning senses revealed a small, paneled chamber, lit by a clouded casement. The fusty air smelled of ink and hot wax, while an old man's voice stitched through his fogged thoughts, gravid with accusation.

"…same pair wrecked the Kittiwake's taproom before, in the company of a known smuggler."

Someone unseen cleared his throat and replied in the sonorous drone of state language.

While the debate sawed onward over Fionn Areth's head, he absorbed the fact that he slumped facedown, cheek pressed to a battered table. Iron manacles circled his wrists, which were draped like dropped meat on his knees. Somewhere nearby, a quill nib scraped.

He tried to sit up. The effort spiked fresh pain through his skull, jogging the memory of terror. Where else could he be but in a magistrate's custody? His despair was confirmed by the crack of a gavel, then a man's bitten phrase, that the miscreants' infractions were anything but a moot point.

While Fionn Areth mustered the shaken breath to assert his abused state of innocence, Dakar's unctuous speech intervened.

"Captain Dhirken passed the Wheel years before you took office. Lord Magistrate, the past charge was not left outstanding. Yes, her crew wrecked the Kittiwake. But the damages were settled in full at the time, paid off by the singer responsible."

Fionn Areth shut his eyes. *This was Shipsport, not Jaelot.* His panic still haunted with visceral force. The nightmare repeat of prisoner's chains *could not* be happening again. Through rising nausea, he tried to protest. "But I wasn't th—"

A kick rapped his ankle. He gasped and shoved straight, snatched the swimming impression of a vaulted ceiling above a railed dais. There, a number of corpulent, robed men sat arrayed in stern judgment against him.

"Shut up, you fool!" Dakar hissed in his ear. "Handle this wrong, and we're dog meat." To Shipsport's gathered tribunal, he temporized, "This time, to our sorrow, we haven't the coin to pay fines for disorderly conduct. We can't make amends to the Kittiwake's landlord, beyond our respectful apologies."

"Well, sorry's no recompense!" The stout table jounced as the tavern's graybeard owner thumped an indignant fist. "I've suffered enough of your hot air already to bore me past Daelion's Wheel! The last time, your friend played his lyranthe for handouts. He sang, forbye, like a silver-tongued lark! Caroled until every last mark cleaned his pockets, and bedamned to your pleas that you're penniless." To the magistrate rapping his gavel, he railed, "My taproom's in shambles! My son broke his arm. I demand satisfaction. Grant the Kittiwake use of the bard's talent for one month. The house takes his proceeds until the debt's paid, with the extra for punitive damages."

The town clerk waggled his pen in remonstrance. "The accused in the dock broke the peace, don't forget! Shipsport's coffers are due a steep fine for their act of civil disturbance. These charges must be met beforetime."

While the magistrate stroked his suet chin, and the spring's nesting wrens cheeped in the eaves outside, Fionn Areth stirred to a sour clank of chain. "But I don't—"

Dakar jammed an elbow into his ribs, then spun lies with pressured invention. "The bard has a head cold. Can't sing a note. Force him to try, his sick croaking is likely to rile your patrons past salvage. You said yourself, the Kittiwake's crowd likes to toss inept singers through the window. That won't meet your fees, and my friend lies at risk of suffering a crippling injury."

Truth and impasse; the magistrate smothered a yawn. The victimized landlord glowered, arms folded, while the clerk licked his thumb and flattened a clean sheet of parchment. "Hard labor, then? Incarceration? Public whipping? The brawling was started without provocation." He tapped the scroll bearing the transcribed statement. "Disrupting the peace calls for a harsh sentence."

Shipsport's magistrate laced his prim knuckles and delivered the final verdict. "The accused have no money. Therefore, the bard will perform until the debts to the town and the tavern are discharged." He silenced objection with the superior glare he reserved for the low-class condemned. "No reprieve!"

"I won't sing for any man!" yelled Fionn Areth, a mistake: his broad grasslands vowels displayed no congestion. "Not for a penny, not for struck gold, and not ever for settling damages over a riot that I didn't start!"

The Kittiwake's landlord stared down his beak nose. "Upright men don't keep the company of smugglers."

Since such shiftless character was the s'Ffalenn bastard's legacy, the slung mud was going to stick. By luck alone, none of Shipsport's officials connected today's face with the infamous Master of Shadow. Draw undue attention, and some sharp-eyed busybody might come forward to point out the oversight.

Fionn Areth slumped in the prisoner's dock, cowed by his fear as the steps of due process saddled him with the arraignment.

Experience taught him the futility of argument. His just plea would only fall on deaf ears and earn him a savage beating.

"You dare the impertinence of claiming to refuse?" The magistrate flicked a glance toward his clerk, then granted the case his sharp quittance. "Call back the guards to remove the offenders. Lock them in the dungeon on bread crusts and water till the singer sees fit to change heart."

The dungeon in Shipsport outmatched even Dakar's revolting description. Floodtide clogged the drains with green slime, coating the floor with decomposing shellfish, strained through the wracked straw and stranded kelp. Fionn Areth gagged on the nauseous stench. Too miserable to curse the rough handling of the wardens who hauled him into confinement, he sagged as they bolted his manacles to a chain spiked in the sweating stone wall.

Head tipped forward, shoulders hunched to avoid the damp masonry chilling his back, the Araethurian squeezed his eyes shut. The pound of his pulse split his skull to white agony. To make matters worse, the Mad Prophet had burst into a fit of inebriated singing. The cell had an arched ceiling. Within closed confines, his racket raised echoes fit to drive the dead to screaming torment.

Oblivious, Dakar belted on through a ballad expounding the exploits of two whores, a blind cobbler, and a goat. Cuffs from the guards failed to silence his noise. Dakar grunted, undaunted, through his tone-deaf rendition of the repetitive chorus.

"He's sloshed to the gills on the Kittiwake's rotgut," the long-faced turnkey observed. Anxious to leave, he jangled his keys. "If you bash him unconscious, he'll just wake back up. I say, let him bide. Locked in without recourse, his wretched companion is going to be driven insane. He'll either pay up the charged fine for relief, or he'll kick the brute's bollocks clear through his throat. If such doesn't kill him, the muttonhead jape won't be left in a fit state to breed."

Dakar widened his brown eyes, unfazed. Limp as a roped walrus in the hands of the guards, he forced them to tow him up to the ring to fasten his prisoner's shackles. As they wrestled the bolts, puffing vile curses, his chained posture proved no deterrent. Dakar followed the ballad with warbled, scurrilious doggerel extolling the virtues of gin.

"That's it!" snapped the turnkey, ears plugged with his thumbs. "The tide floods apace. Tarry much longer, and we'll have wet boots." He fidgeted until the last guardsman filed out, then clashed the grille shut on the miscreants. His malicious grin flashed by the glare of held torchlight as he secured the rusty lock. "Enjoy the Lord Magistrate's sweet hospitality!"

The squelching tread of officialdom retreated, plunging the cell into darkness.

Fionn Areth stifled his impulse to shout. The icy air settled like a batt of inky wool once the upstairs portal banged closed. The reek of sea rot and urine overpowered, as the flow of fresh air was cut off.

A large insect scuttled over the Araethurian's scraped wrist. His jerk of revulsion clanged the fixed chain, and his curse snatched the break between choruses. "May the furies of Sithaer's eighth hell plague the day that your dam spread her knees and gave birth!"

Through the hitched pause to recover his breath, Dakar chuckled. "You might as well sing along with me, bumpkin. Stay cheerful, you won't have to think overmuch, or listen to the skittering wildlife."

"Damn you for a sot!" Fionn Areth lashed back. "Without your loose habits, we wouldn't be dangled like carrion, nose to nose with the starveling rats."

"Ho!" Dakar whooped. "Starveling rats! That's poetic." Buoyed to euphoria by the Kittiwake's ale, he nudged his companion's ankle. "Know this one, do you?" He plunged into another obscene recitation, at a pitch fit to mangle the eardrums.

"Shut up!" Fionn Areth kicked back, cleanly missed, and clunked his head against the wall with a yelp of anguished frustration. "Just how are we to get out of this fix? They think I'm Athera's Masterbard! In truth, I don't sing any better than you. If you're going to insist that we work off our fine that way, the Kittiwake's roughnecks might as well batter us straight to perdition right now. Better I give my consent to such madness, before we pickle in this cesspit, drowning in rat crap and seawater."

"Well, practice a bit first." Dakar hiccoughed in brosy hilarity. "Might as well test your talent before we're marched out to get diced by a mob of drunken sailhands."

"You should care, numbed as a dolt on cheap beer," Fionn Areth cut back in ripe sarcasm.

"Actually, I'm not," Dakar confessed, his blurred whisper nearly lost in the darkness. "For the record, at least, I'm uselessly pissed until after the tidewater rises." Louder, he added, "Sing, damn your hide. Howl like a monkey, or warble in counterpoint. If you don't, the pesky warden might decide to withhold our ration of bread crusts. The last thing we need is some ham-handed grunt trying to drag us back upstairs beforetime."

"What!" Fionn Areth jerked his sore wrists in a balefire flash of amazement. "Refuse the chance to get out of this place? You're off your head! Gone moonstruck, and truly."

"Skintight on beer, but not crazy," Dakar insisted with owlish gravity. "I thought, since we're here, you should savor the experience. The odd, swimming varmint who might perch on your head will be offered the gift of survival. Far more than a rat might see benefits."

Past hope of holding a sane conversation, Fionn Areth lapsed into stiff silence. Besotted whimsy could not reverse the gravity of his current quandary. He felt no pity for the doomed rats, though the shut door blocked their way to the stairwell. Not as long as he languished in chains, bearing a criminal sorcerer's features.

Dakar was no use. Unfazed by the threat, he filled his lungs and resumed bawling singsong nonsense. The cold grew no less. The stink stayed oppressive. The herder from Araethura cursed the short length of the chain, which would not let him clasp his hands to his aching head. While he sat, chewing over his circling fears, the news from upcoast moved apace: word already spread, that the Master of Shadow had escaped from the Mayor of Jaelot's close custody. The men-at-arms dispatched in his pursuit had been lured over the Skyshiel Ranges and into the wilds of Daon Ramon Barrens.

In darkness, the graphic accounts spurred fresh terror: of townborn blood spilled by savage design; eyewitness tales of shadows and haunts bringing death on the Baiyen causeway; of men lulled to sleep by the singing of stones and frozen to glass under moonlight. Everywhere, Arithon's name inspired fear. If Dakar gave short shrift to the doctrine that claimed Rathain's prince was a demon, today's episode of manic debauchery destroyed the last foothold for trust.

Fionn Areth snarled a frustrated oath. Although Arithon Teir's'Ffalenn had risked capture to spare him from the horror of Jaelot's scaffold, the Mad Prophet's assertion the deed sprang from sound character only made the surrounding facts seem the more ominous. Today's truth spoke too loudly: when the passes reopened, no more wearied men straggled in upon starving, lamed horses.

The first hardy caravan to descend from Eastwall had described the emergency muster at Darkling. Bloodshed had dogged Arithon's heels at each step. By command of Avenor's high priesthood, Alliance troops had unfurled the sunwheel banner and marched upon Daon Ramon. They had not embarked on the campaign alone. At Narms, no less than Lysaer himself had gathered a veteran company. His cry to arms also raised the standing troops trained by his steward at Etarra. Both forces had converged on the snow-clad barrens, to wage the Light's war against Shadow.

Until breaking ice reopened the northcoast, and the trade galleys hove in from the west, the eastshore towns held their uneasy breath, as yet unaware that a crushing defeat had shattered Lysaer's combined host.

Licked by the trickle of rising water, young Fionn Areth had no choice but to hang his trapped fate on a prayer. "Merciful maker, let the ice hold the north passage closed for a while longer."

A trained seer, Dakar knew the Spinner of Darkness had survived the Alliance assault. He would not divulge his liege's location. That sore point piqued Fionn Areth's suspicion and tightened his queasy stomach. No platitude eased him. Not since the hour the Mad Prophet broke his last scrying, stunned into unyielding silence. He refused to speak of Prince Arithon's plight, even sunk in his cups at the Kittiwake. Desperately determined to carol himself hoarse, perhaps needing to smother the nag of his conscience, Dakar stayed deaf. He would not acknowledge the scope of his peril, allied to the Master of Shadow.

A goatherd who lacked arcane talent could do nothing but thrash out his worries alone.

An hour passed; two. The well of the tide crept across the stone floor. The kiss of cold water seeped through dry clothes, then like slow agony, deepened. Soon the pool lapped at Fionn Areth's tucked ankles. The flood stirred the vermin, who quested forth upon tentative, pattering feet. Every fraught effort to kick them away brought him vengeful nips from sharp teeth. The misery mounted. Dakar's filthy stanzas had devolved to gibberish, touched here and there by the oddly placed line, lilted in cadenced Paravian.

Distempered and ill, Fionn Areth lost patience. Curses did not stop the rodents that clambered over his shivering skin. The sea rose, inexorable. Soon immersed to the waist, he fought chattering teeth, while the scrabbling rats became frantic.

"Fiends plague you, Dakar!" Fionn Areth jerked his chin left and right, but failed to dislodge the wet creatures that nosed at his ears. "Can't you shut your mouth? Maybe fashion a bane-ward. Anything to send these fell pests to oblivion!"

Yet the rats' splashing struggles and shrill squeals could not dampen the madman's racketing choruses. He sang without letup, each quavering line of botched meter an insult that mangled intelligence.

"Oh the sun brings us cherries, then ripe red berries,
oat sprouts make malt whiskey, while the barley king whispers,
Praise for the bees and the willow trees,
Seed for the birds and grass for the herds,
Sweet grapes love spring rain, t'an li'arient, Lu-haine!"

The emphasis set on the name at the end served Fionn Areth scant warning. The closed cell became charged. Hair rose at his nape, while his skin puckered into sharp gooseflesh. Not being chained, the rats squeaked and bolted. They splashed helter-skelter in panic. A knifing breeze that moaned down the stairwell, the discorporate Sorcerer drawn by Dakar's summons, arrived with the force of a silenced thunderclap.

If darkness still reigned, its texture had changed, filled by that ineffable presence.

Fionn Areth recoiled. *He wished to be anyplace else in Athera.* The affray with the Mistwraith's prison at Rockfell had shown him the reach of Luhaine and the Fellowship's power.

"Wards!" Dakar pealed in jagged hysteria. "Set them now! Koriani enchantresses are seeking the goatherd, and I can't stand them off any longer!"

"Done," Luhaine answered, mercifully brief.

Fionn Areth shut his eyes, braced for a blast of scouring light, or a purging release of wild energies.

Nothing happened.

The slosh of salt water did not abate. Apprehensive, the Araethurian cracked open one lid. Stillness remained, laced by a nexus of withering, cold air and a living awareness not to be gainsaid.

"Rats," Luhaine qualified. "They gave their consent and carried the spells to lay down my guarding circle." Fixated on Fionn's repressed jerk of startlement, he bristled, "What did you expect, goatherd? A flare of crude conjury? Such a beacon would have been grossly misplaced where the utmost of finesse is needful."

"What enchantresses? Where?" Fionn Areth accused. "I saw no women but shameless harlots when Dakar's lunacy rousted the Kittiwake."

"Be quiet, Fionn! Koriani spellcraft was the reason I tipped the damned beer on my head in the first place." To the Sorcerer, not drunken, the Mad Prophet said, "Then you knew the accursed witches were after him?" His slurred speech in fact the sapped mark of exhaustion, he complained, "For my pains, then you might have come a bit sooner."

"Your goatherd is not a blood prince of the realm," Luhaine pointed out, miffed. "To strike a clean balance, you did have to ask. Even then, my act stands on tenuous ground. I could not defend, but for Arithon's ill-advised pledge to spare a crown subject from injustice." Met by Dakar's crestfallen silence, the shade of the Sorcerer tempered his censure. "Though you need not have waited for use of salt water to mask your cry of intent."

The Mad Prophet's sigh echoed off dripping stonework. "Well, you're scarcely the sort to choose congress with rats." Chain clanked as he shifted, trying to ease the strain on his manacled wrists. "Last I saw, Luhaine, you hated their ornery nature worse than the plague."

"I don't enjoy rats," the Sorcerer admitted. "Although Koriathain please my sensibilities far less, our Fellowship is critically shorthanded. Next time you cry out for help in a crisis, we may not be able to answer."

"What's to be done, then?" Dakar appealed, racked by his galling frustration. "Shipsport's dungeon can't keep us protected." He need not press his point: once the brutal news of the Alliance's losses traveled the eastshore trade routes, Fionn Areth's unnatural resemblance to Arithon would turn into a red-hot liability. "We've missed our planned rendezvous. *Evenstar*'s already weighed anchor and sailed on her scheduled run south."

Luhaine subsided to stilled cogitation, as much to measure the rigid distress behind Fionn Areth's stark quiet. "You'll have to change plans. A sea berth's unwise."

Fresh off the docks, even the backcountry goatherd was forced to the same grim assessment. Every ship bearing flags of town registry flew the gold sunwheel of the Alliance. Aboard such a vessel, amid Arithon's pledged enemies, the young double could all too easily find himself hung from the mainmast yardarm. Yet lacking the natural defense of salt water, a spellbinder's skills risked being outmatched by the quartz-driven snares unleashed by the Koriani Order. Until the pair reached warded walls at Alestron, Fionn Areth's contested freedom was bound to remain under constant siege.

Begrudging the ice water freezing his bollocks, and ambivalent toward the powers of sorcery, the beleaguered herder buried his fears behind his uncivil suspicion. "You'd rather we came to grief on the road?"

Luhaine had the grace not to rise to offense, though the chill in his silence rippled the brine, and the Mad Prophet hissed through his teeth.

"I don't like rats, either," Fionn Areth lashed back, tired of being a bone in the jaws of a deadlocked political conflict.

The stillness stretched, filled by the slosh of the tide. The Sorcerer's presence stayed, a poised force welded into obsidian air. The truth kept its cruel edges: Arithon Teir's'Ffalenn would never have been forced into flight through Daon Ramon, if not for Fionn Areth's obstinate wish to align with Lysaer's Alliance. The Light's war host would have had no hazed fugitive to chase and no fresh round of slaughter to lay at the feet of the man they called Spinner of Darkness.

Justly reviled by the uncanny weight of the Fellowship Sorcerer's displeasure, the Araethurian flushed with embarrassment. No use to lie, or to pretend his deliverance by Arithon's hand had not torn his youthful ideals to raw wounds and conflicted loyalty.

Thrown out of his depth, Fionn Areth clung yet to his obdurate, grasslands honesty. He dared not rely on the spellbinder's word or place trust in the doings of Sorcerers. The s'Ffalenn prince himself had yet to account for the criminal charges against him. Until guilt or innocence could be resolved, Luhaine must respect the unquiet fact: that the straightforward cut of country-bred cloth could not reconcile a stance that had plotted a cold-blooded massacre.

Though he drowned, gnawed by vermin, Fionn Areth would as soon run his steel through Prince Arithon's heart. While he lived and breathed, he would not embrace the dread choice of abetting dark magecraft.

"Boy, you grant me no opening to respond," Luhaine pronounced at due length. "Your grounds for safe conduct must still rely on the oath Dakar swore to appease his Grace of Rathain. Remain in the spellbinder's company, and the shield of crown justice will provide you with shelter. Leave, and all ties become forfeit."

"I can't stand down the Koriani Prime Matriarch alone," Dakar appealed in trepidation. "My defense wards won't hold. The instant the tide ebbs, we'll be stripped and hung by our heels like a brace of skinned rabbits."

Luhaine's leashed presence revolved, unperturbed. "Then you'll have no choice but to show their trained scryers precisely what they expect."

"Cast me off in surrender?" Fionn Areth cried, shocked. "Your crown prince risked death, first!" Despite his ambivalence, the meddling Koriathain had wrought the bane that unraveled his destiny in the first place.

"Fionn, be quiet! You won't be betrayed." Too short and fat for his tether of chain, Dakar wrestled the pain of racked joints, and pursued harried converse with Luhaine. "Yes, my fit of erratic behavior disrupted their spelled sweep of the Kittiwake's taproom. But now we owe fines. We can't lose their probes by seeding a wild rash of bar brawls. What do you actually suggest?"

"Give them the whoring wastrel." Luhaine's pause carried a poison simplicity. "Would any celibate circle of women, rigidly scrutinized by their seniormost peers, play the role of voyeur to keep pace with unsavory company?"

"Sithaer's coupling fiends!" Dakar gasped, half-strangled. "Oh, please, let them try!" The order's initiates were female, after all, with most of them blushing virgins. The calm state their scryers required for trance could scarcely withstand the raw onslaught of vice, with its bestial range of sensation. The spellbinder whooped, his eyes leaking tears. "You know, I could wreck those prim ladies through drink!"

Quartz crystal would magnify his drunken stupor. Even an experienced circle must falter, hazed out of focus as their snooping seeresses threaded their watch sigils through him.

"Give them debauchery," Luhaine agreed. "Who would waste breath to comment? For you, rank indulgence is not out of character. The distortions such excess will spin through your aura can be made to mask my wrought binding to shield Fionn Areth."

"Well, you'd better not fail me," the Mad Prophet said, tart. "Wasting hangovers hurt, not to mention, my access to conjury is going to get pissed straight to shambles." Undone that way, he would be incapable of even the small cantrips to cure his myopic eyesight.

Luhaine stayed unmoved. "The stakes could go far worse for your charge, if Prime Selidie learns that you've balked her will by asking for Fellowship backing."

"I'll bang myself witless," Dakar said point-blank. Before Fionn drew breath, he doused the inevitable protest. "The witches had you swear an oath of permission over the Skyron aquamarine. That tie has kept you in peril since the moment Prince Arithon snatched you from Jaelot. The Koriani hold on your life might turn out to be revocable. If so, you'll need the trained help of an embodied Fellowship Sorcerer. Or else find your way to a Brotherhood hostel, and risk the chance you can beg Ath's adepts to call down a divine intercession."

"If indeed, they would extend such relief," Luhaine temporized, "and provided you arrived with your freedom intact to ask for the grace of their sanctuary." The nearest such haven lay too far removed from Dakar's planned route to Alestron. "Very few supplicants who petition receive the fruits of exalted, wise counsel." The Sorcerer gave that faint hope his crisp closure. "You can't sustain such a pilgrimage, herder. None pass the threshold to enjoin the high mysteries who walk with an unsettled heart."

"Should I argue mixed feelings?" Fionn Areth attacked. "By Alliance tenets, *which might pose the truth*, your Fellowship's practice is tainted. The Light's doctrine also holds that Ath's Brotherhood is corrupt, suborned by the powers of Darkness."

Luhaine's presence recoiled.

"Forgive backlands ignorance!" the Mad Prophet cried. "Leave Rathain's crown prince his preferred right to answer this."

Yet Fionn Areth lashed out, goaded on to brash fury. "I don't need—"

"Shut up, you dolt! The bright powers of Athera are not Lysaer's enemies, no matter who taught you to fear them." Dakar leaned forward,
jerked breathless as his manacled wrists wrenched him short. "Luhaine, for
pity! Respect the constraints of my bond to Prince Arithon." The spellbinder's
appeal gained a frantic, shrill edge, as the hair on his skin stabbed erect. "You
know the young fool has a vicious tongue, and no semblance of manners
when he's been terrified."

"An apology would be civil," the Sorcerer snapped, vexed. "If the cant of
Avenor's false priesthood held truth, your yokel would no longer be using the
blameless air to support his ungrateful opinions!"

"For Arithon's sake, don't deny him your help," Dakar begged with
strained dignity.

"Help?" Luhaine huffed. "I'd sooner converse with a Sanpashir scorpion.
At least they don't sting before they are threatened, and they are soft-spoken
and gracious."

"Once, I was the harebrained scapegrace," Dakar entreated. Warned that
his charge might open his mouth, he dispatched a kick, underwater. "Luhaine,
for pity! Grant me the favor. The delay from your summons to Rockfell Peak
is what cost us our safe passage on *Evenstar.*"

"There are limits." Yet the missed rendezvous with the brig scored a point
that could not be dismissed. For the harrowing service just given to spare his
strapped Fellowship from a crisis, the Sorcerer chose to unbend. "I can't ease the
constraints," he admitted, begrudging. "Technicalities cloud your present awareness. Fionn Areth bears a life debt, acquired at birth. Elaira yielded that tie under
oathbound duress to the power of the Koriani Council. Her retraction might
free him, with Asandir's backing. But at present, your lump-headed moorlander
can't ask that choice, or be traumatized by anyone's act of grand conjury."

Though the cresting tide surged through the cell in black currents and
immersed the chained prisoners chest deep, Luhaine's summary canceled the
needful alternative. "My colleague cannot spare the resource, just now. Nor
have I the leeway to chase after an ingrate stripling as nursemaid. You'll have
my warding as far as Alestron. From there, take to sea aboard *Khetienn* forthwith. Wring what refuge you can from blue water."

To the bumpkin, inflamed by his feckless ideals and his suicidal confusion,
Luhaine discharged his last word. "Dakar must escort you to safety himself.
The wards that will hide you are spun through *his* aura. By your will, mark my
warning particulars carefully! I can't grant you a guarded shred of autonomy
under my Fellowship's auspices. Woe betide you if you should ever stray from
the side of your oathsworn protector."

"Luhaine, wait!" Teeth chattering, Dakar shouted to stem the rushed breeze
of the Sorcerer's departure. "What of the fee imposed by the Kittiwake? Hold

back! Shipsport has passed sentence, and we haven't the coin to defray the clerk's fine or meet the landlord's exorbitant damages."

"You do now," corrected the Sorcerer's shade, his fading voice thinned to asperity. "The magistrate's clerk will find an entry that states the fine's paid in full in the morning. Farewell!"

The chained prisoners were abandoned to hollow darkness, scored through by the lap of salt water and the resurgent chittering of swimming rats.

"Is he gone?" Fionn ventured, his rage drained away to threadbare exhaustion.

Dakar cursed in spectacular, rough language until he ran short of breath. "Yes, Luhaine has left us. Bad cess to your yapping grasslands insolence! Now we get to soak through a miserable night. Don't try another damned *word* or believe this! I'll leave your scared arse as chained bait for the witches and watch Shipsport's vermin feed on your carcass!"

Late Spring 5670

Binding

The town of Erdane's formal banquet to honor the Divine Prince's return from his arduous campaign against Shadow had been planned as an effusive celebration, until the moment of Lysaer s'Ilessid's opening statement. Hushed anticipation welcomed his entry. Resplendent in the sharp glitter of diamonds, his state presence on fire with white-and-gold thread, he delivered the list of shattering losses that outlined a vicious defeat. Beyond words for sorrow, he retired at once. His wake left behind a stunned silence.

The lean companies from Etarra encamped by the south wall were not the advance guard, transporting the critically wounded. In harsh fact, no more troops would be marching home, bearing accolades, honor, and triumph.

Hours later, the impact still rocked the guests who lingered in the mayor's palace: news that Arithon, Spinner of Darkness, had escaped beyond reach through the entry to Kewar Tunnel. Everywhere else, that formal announcement might ease the impact of tragedy, even offer resounding relief. The renegade Sorcerer, Davien the Betrayer, had fashioned the maze that lay beyond that dread threshold. The foolish who dared to venture inside did not survive the experience.

Yet Erdane possessed more accurate knowledge concerning the powers of Fellowship Sorcerers. Here, where the archives had not been destroyed with the overthrow of the high kings, breaking word of the s'Ffalenn bastard's evasion was received with sobering recoil.

The terse conversations exchanged in the carriage yard became a trial on Sulfin Evend's taut nerves. Despite the biting, unseasonable cold, guild ministers decked out in jewels and lace seemed to pluck at his cloak at each step.

"My Lord Commander of the Light?" The latest petitioner plowed in, undeterred by the field weapons and mail worn beneath the Alliance first officer's dress surcoat. "What are your plans? Will the Divine Prince regroup his defense in the east?"

"I don't know," Sulfin Evend demurred. His hawk's features turned from the blasting wind, he unhooked the merchant's ringed fingers. "Too soon to tell."

"The entrance to Kewar should stay under guard." The insistent courtier still barred the way, unscathed by the war veteran's impatience. "Did the Prince of the Light leave no company in Rathain to stand watch over the portal?"

"Had anyone stayed, they'd be dead to a man!" Sulfin Evend barked back, since his tied hands on that score rankled sorely. Although tonight's bitter weather still gripped all of Tysan, to the east, spring thaws mired the roadways. Ox trains would labor, slowed to a crawl, with Daon Ramon rendered impassable. Meltwaters now roared through the boulder-choked vales, too engorged for a safe crossing. Supply would bog down in those forsaken notches, riddled with uncanny Second Age ghosts, and enclaves of hostile clan archers. "I won't post my troops as bait to be murdered. Our toll of losses has been harsh enough without risking more lives to stupidity!"

As the guildsman bridled, Sulfin Evend cut back, "That ground is reserved as Athera's free wilds, and deep inside barbarian territory."

"Your bound duty is not to eradicate vermin?" a fresh voice declaimed from the sidelines. "Our gold fills the coffers that arm your men! To what use, if you pack them up and turn tail each time the chased fox goes to earth?"

"Good night, gentlemen!" The Alliance commander shoved through the last wave of inquirers, pushed past his last shred of patience. Too many fine officers had died on the field. Left in sole charge of demoralized troops, he found his resources stretched far too thin. Erdane was a stew of insatiable politics, both council and trade guilds riddled with clandestine infighting, and colored by the entrenched hostility held over from past resentment of old blood royalty. The Lord Commander preferred not to billet the men here, worn as they were from the last weeks of a harried retreat. Yet his bursar lacked ready funds for provision, and troop morale was still fragile. Tempers ran too ragged to risk quartering the company at large in the countryside.

Beside the Master of Shadow's escape, Lysaer's regency faced pending crisis: each passing day raised the specter of famine, as the unnatural, freezing storms rolled down from the north and forestalled the annual planting.

Yet since the Blessed Prince had wed the Lord Mayor's daughter, a strategic refusal of this town's hospitality became a social impossibility.

Sulfin Evend outpaced the overdressed pack at his heels, stamped slush from his spurs, then mounted the stair from the carriageway. Admitted through the mayor's front door, he endured the butler's imperious inspection. He stood, steaming, for the liveried boy who removed his sunwheel cloak, and sat for another, who buffed his soaked field boots until he was deemed fit to tread on the mansion's priceless carpets.

Their service was gifted no more than a copper. The shame was no secret: the Alliance treasury was flat strapped. If the town's ranking ministers were all jumpy as jackals, expecting appeals for new funding, the mayor's sleek staff accepted their token with the semblance of deferent charm.

"Your Lordship," they murmured. "Enjoy a good evening and a sound rest."

Sulfin Evend stood up, a whipcord lean man with dark hair and pale eyes, and the well-set, alert bearing that bespoke a razor intelligence. Hanshire born, and the son of a mayor, he showed flawless courtesy, inwardly knowing he dared not trust Erdane's cordial reception too far. Secret brotherhoods still gathered inside these gates. Practitioners of magecraft and unclean rites lurked in the crumbling tenements by the west wall. Tonight's wealthy sycophants spurred his concern, as their flurried whispers and rushed, private dispatches widened the breach for covert enemies to exploit.

The Alliance commander climbed the stair to the guest wing, decided on his response. He would stand his armed guard in the Divine Prince's bedchamber, and be damned if the mayor's pretentious staff took umbrage at his distrust.

His intent was forestalled by the royal equerry, who had obstinately barred Lysaer's quarters.

"You'll admit me, at once," Sulfin Evend demanded. "I'll have the man whipped, who says otherwise."

"The Divine Prince himself." The equerry's nervous distress emerged muffled, from behind the gilt-paneled entry. "His Blessed Grace is indisposed. By his order, he stays undisturbed."

That news raised a chilling grue of unease, fast followed by burning suspicion. Lysaer s'Ilessid had often looked peaked through the weeks since the campaign ended. Aboard ship across Instrell Bay, his Blessed Grace had scarcely emerged from his cabin. The retirement seemed natural. Each widow and grieving mother would receive a sealed writ of condolence from the hand of the Light. Over the subsequent, storm-ridden march, Sulfin Evend had not thought to question the hours spent addressing correspondence in the shelter of a covered wagon. Yet if Lysaer was ill, and masking the fact, the cascade of damages ran beyond the concept of frightening. A man hailed by the masses as a divine avatar dared not display any sign of a mortal weakness in public.

"You will admit me!" His mailed fist braced against the locked door, Sulfin Evend surveyed the latch, an ornamental fitting of bronze the first hard blow would wrench from its setting. "Open up, or I'll come, regardless."

No man in the field troop defied that tone.

Wisely, the equerry chose not to risk scandal. "You, no one else." He shot the bar with dispatch. "The mayor's staff was led to understand that his Exalted Grace was overjoyed with the welcoming brandy."

Sulfin Evend slipped past the cracked panel, at once enfolded in blanketing warmth, expensively scented by citrus-polished wood and beeswax. As the nervous servant secured the entry behind him, his tactical survey encompassed the loom of stuffed furnishings and the gleaming, shut doors of the armoires. The room's gilt appointments lay wrapped in gloom, the resplendent state finery worn for the feast long since folded away in the clothes chests. By custom, one candle burned on the nightstand: the Prince of the Light did not sleep in the presence of shadow or darkness. Amid that setting of diligent neatness, the lit figure sprawled upon crumpled sheets stood out like a shout of disharmony.

Every nerve hackled, the Lord Commander advanced. The frightened page who minded the flame abandoned his stool and jumped clear. No stammered excuse could dismiss the harsh truth: Lysaer's condition had passed beyond indisposed. Nor had drink rendered him prostrate. Lifelessly white as a stranded fish, a torso once muscled to glorify marble lay reduced to skeletal emaciation.

Horrified, Sulfin Evend exclaimed, "How long has your master been padding his clothes?"

"My lord," the boy stammered. "His Divine Grace swore us to silence."

"Blazing Sithaer, I don't care what you were told!" Sulfin Evend strode forward. He tugged off his gauntlets, snatched up the pricket, then bent to assess the shocking extent of Lysaer's condition. The porcelain-fair profile on the pillow never stirred at his touch. The icy, damp flesh was not fevered. Alarmed, the Alliance commander raked back the disordered gold hair. No reflex responded as he pried back the flaccid, left eyelid. The unshielded flame lit a glassine, comatose stare, and a pupil wide black with dilation.

"Answer me now! How long has his Divine Grace languished like this?"

The equerry quailed before that steel tone. "My lord, we don't know when this wasting began. Grief would blunt the appetite, one might suppose, so soon after the loss of a son."

That honest uncertainty seemed reasonable, since the train of personal attendants initially brought from Avenor had all died in the course of Daon Ramon's campaign. Sulfin Evend shoved back the rucked coverlet and continued his anxious survey. The prior disaster did not bear thought, against this one, sprawled senseless before him.

"Do you actually fear someone poisoned him?" the equerry ventured from the sidelines.

Sulfin Evend said nothing—just thrust the candle back toward the page. "Hold this." While the whipped flame cast grotesque shadows about him, he grasped Lysaer's arm. Unnerved by the grave chill to the limp wrist, the Alliance commander held out in grim patience while the light steadied, and unveiled the dread cause of the malady.

Up and down milk pale skin, in recent, scabbed cuts and old scars, Lysaer wore the telltale marks of a man being leached by the dire magics of a blood ritual. Sulfin Evend leashed his stark fear. The nightmarish course of this sapping addiction scarcely could have occurred under Lysaer's informed self-command. Nor would such a complex and dangerous binding be invoked by rote or the lore of a fumbling novice.

"Those scabs aren't infected," a new voice declaimed. The prince's long-faced valet had emerged from the closet where he kept his pallet. Barefoot, still plucking his livery to rights, he padded up to the bed.

The Lord Commander waved him back, wordless. Peril stalked here for the unwary. Bearing a taint of clanblood in his ancestry, he owned a birth-born talent, if an untrained one. Though that unsavory history was nothing he wished to make public, he had little choice. Erdane's mayors had burned the mage-gifted for centuries. Since that policy was also held in force by the Alliance of Light, and the sealed mandate of Tysan's regency, no initiate healer could be summoned here without causing political havoc.

Exposed to risk, uneasily aware that his lack of knowledge laid him open to an untold threat, Sulfin Evend ran a tacit, spread palm above Lysaer's livid wounds. Eyes closed, he sounded the range of awareness outside his immediate senses. The horrid grue all but crawled up his wrist, as his seeking hand ruffled across what felt like a chill flow of wind, ripped with tingles.

Beyond question, an arcane influence was draining the Blessed Prince of his vitality. Worse, the debilitating tie was entrenched to the point where a recovery might lie beyond reach.

Sulfin Evend addressed the hovering staff, dangerously level and low. "First, how often does his Divine Grace undertake the foul ritual, and next, where are the knife and the bowl?"

Blank stares from the servants; Sulfin Evend met their stone-walled quiet with fury. "Don't pretend you don't know what I speak of! Your master has cast his life into jeopardy, and I won't stand down until you give me a straight answer."

"But my lord," protested the equerry. "His Blessed Grace said not to"—which words clashed with the valet's shrill dismay—"but my lord, he can't die! As the avatar sent here to put down the Dark, how dare you imply he is mortal!"

"Avatar or not, he can still cross Fate's Wheel!" Sulfin Evend smoothed the slack hand on the sheets. Distaste turned his lips as he lifted the other, which still wore streaked stains of dried blood. "Here! See the proof? Our liege may be blessed with unnatural longevity, but he can't sustain if he's been enslaved by dark practice. Or are you sheep, too awed to see that he's skin and bones? Before your eyes, he's bled himself white! For all we know, the vile rite has been feeding some sorcerous cabal that's hell-bent to destroy him!"

Consternation wrung gasps from the pair of servants, while the page boy looked sick unto fainting.

"Oh, yes! Believe it," Sulfin Evend cracked to their stupefied faces. "Did you think Avenor's high-handed Crown Examiner could sweep the length and breadth of the realm executing born talent and not draw a wolf pack of powerful enemies?"

"Merciful Light!" cried the valet, aggrieved. "His Exalted Self claimed he was scrying in search of the Master of Shadow to secure our defense against Darkness."

"That's doubtless the lure that first saw him entrapped." Raw with disgust, and taking due care not to sully his hands, the Lord Commander resettled the bloodied limb on the mattress.

Lysaer's unresponsive, comatose state whipped him to freezing despair. Had the High Priest's acolyte, Jeriayish, not died on campaign, the Alliance commander would have flayed the skulking creature skin from bone, here and now: for hindsight suggested that the priest's rites of augury had opened the access to engage this fell binding. Whether through slipshod practice, or by darker design, the dire plot would not originate there. *Someone* insinuated into Avenor's inner council wished Athera's Divine Prince reduced to a puppet-string power.

The equerry was speaking. Sulfin Evend refocused his wits and insisted, "Excuses don't matter. Stop dragging your feet! I can do nothing at all if you can't fetch the bowl and the knife that Lysaer used for the ritual. No! Don't touch them!" He barely quelled his imperative shout, as the page boy scrambled to fling up the lid of one of his master's clothes chests. "Such objects are unclean and unspeakably dangerous. Lend me a silk shirt to wrap them."

A fraught interval later, the Alliance Lord Commander braved the night in a borrowed servant's cloak, an anonymous shadow bound for the unsavory district flanking Erdane's west postern. Crystalline frost crunched beneath his boots. Under the gleam of spring's constellations, the unseasonable chill cut his exposed skin like a scourge. Sulfin Evend slipped past the gray-on-black timbers of the shuttered shop fronts and crafthalls. At each skulking step, his left instructions chased through his circling thoughts.

"Guard him! With your lives, do you hear? I'll send up my captain to stand at his door, and this time, no one comes in!"

No words could settle his harrowing dread. The alley he sought would be hidden from sight, guarded by ward since Avenor's harsh interdict, which outlawed the practice of talent. As ranking commander of the Alliance war host, Sulfin Evend knew he risked his life simply by showing his face here.

He pressed onward, regardless. The artifacts he held bundled inside one of Lysaer's silk dress shirts left him no rational alternative. His rapacious profile masked under his hood, Sulfin Evend closed his eyes and edged forward. One blind step, two; his third footfall raised a crawling chill. The eerie sensation surged through his boot sole, chased up his spine, and prickled his nape into gooseflesh.

Sulfin Evend kept his face averted and cautiously unsealed his sight.

The town gate loomed ahead, alight in the glow of the watch lamps. To his right, a narrow, nondescript archway opened into rank darkness. Sulfin Evend resisted the urge to use more than peripheral vision. If he tried, the uncanny portal would vanish, not to reappear without use of initiate knowledge. He sucked a deep breath. Braced by a courage as dauntless as any demanded of him on a battlefield, he turned away from the main thoroughfare and plunged through the queer, lightless entry.

Darkness and cold ran through him like water, then as suddenly fell away. He found himself in a squalid back alley, little more than an uneven footpath overhung by ramshackle eaves and sagged stairways. The prankish gusts jangled the tin talismans of *iyat* banes, a dissonance that seemed to frame uncanny speech as he picked his uncertain way forward. The ground-level tenements were shuttered, but not locked. Here, the prospective thief was a fool, who ventured without invitation. Sulfin Evend picked his way forward, the chink of fallen slates underfoot driving vermin into the crannies. The stairway he sought had carved gryphon posts, a detail he was forced to determine by touch, since no lamps burned in this quarter. No wineshop opened its door to the night, and no lit window offered him guidance.

By starlight, Sulfin Evend mounted the stair. The creaking, slat risers bore his weight sullenly, no doubt inlaid with spells to warn away the unwary. Against quailing nerves, he reached the top landing, just as the door swung open to meet him.

"You've come to the right place," said a paper-dry voice. Backlit by a glimmer of candleflame, a wizened old woman in rags beckoned her visitor inward.

Heart pounding, skin turned clammy, Sulfin Evend understood there would be a price. Nonetheless, he crossed over her threshold.

"You've been expected," the crone stated as she fastened the latches behind him.

Sulfin Evend believed his surprise was contained, until her crowed laughter said otherwise. Hunchbacked and ancient, she spun to confront him. Eyes blinded with cataracts picked at his thoughts as thoroughly as any dissection. No coward, he resisted his urge to step back as her seeress's talent unmasked him.

"What did you expect?" she admonished, not smiling. "You come to consult, have you not? Would you rather have met with a charlatan?"

He bowed to her, managed not to sound shaken as he named her with careful respect. "Enithen Tuer. Rightly or not, I have come to the only place where I might seek help within Erdane."

"I know why you've come," said the crone, fingers tucked in her mismatched layers of fringed shawls. "Years, I have known. So many long years, that I am left weary with waiting."

Her clipped gesture offered a rough, wooden chair.

Released all at once from her piercing regard, Sulfin Evend sat down as she bade him. Her attic was tiny, shelves and tabletops jammed with balled twine and strange leather sacks, filmed with dust. Wrapped in the fragrance of drying herbals, smoke, and stale grease, the Alliance man-at-arms huddled under his cloak, afraid to disturb the unnerving items clutched in his awkward grasp. "What do you require to lend me your services?"

"No coin." Enithen Tuer shuffled to the hob. Her stumpy feet were bound in frayed flannel, and her fingers, chapped rough as a ragman's. She snapped a flint striker to give him more light. "There is peril in this. Are you prepared? Can't be turning back once you've chosen." Eerie, milk eyes surveyed him, unblinking, while the tallow dips hissed on the mantel. "Be aware, warrior. The cost will test and try you. If you are weak, you'll be broken."

"What cost, old woman?" Struck cold, Sulfin Evend suppressed his impatience. "I don't care for riddles or the drama of veiled threats. A man that I speak for lies dying."

But Enithen Tuer would not be rushed. Her uncanny awareness seemed to press like a blade against the raced pulse at his neck. "Beware who should carry your heart's pledge, brave man. The wise would walk softly, and rightly so. Lysaer s'Ilessid has been declared outcast from the terms of the Fellowship's compact." The crone sensed his start; nodded. "Ah, truly, then you do understand what that sentence means."

"Explain anyway." Unnerved by the pitfalls that might arise from the folly of a presumption, Sulfin Evend dropped pride. "My sources at Hanshire might not have been accurate."

Enithen Tuer decided to humor him. "For breaking the sureties sworn by the Sorcerers, your prince's license to inhabit this world is revoked. His fate will be ruled by Paravian law. All the worse, for the trouble you carry tonight. As a man disbarred, Lysaer can't ask for the grace of a Fellowship intercession."

"But the Paravians are vanished!" Sulfin Evend shoved back his hood, ruffled as a jessed hawk. "Should I fear the old races' absent reprisal? There are other powers abroad on Athera. Perhaps I should present my liege's appeal to the Order of the Koriathain."

The seer raised frosty eyebrows. "Would you indeed?"

Sulfin Evend steadied his rankled poise, aware all at once he was bargaining. "Their oath of debt might give me the more lenient terms." The sisterhood had chafed for thousands of years under the yoke of the Sorcerers' compact. Surely, in the breach of Paravian presence, they would extend arcane help if he asked them.

Enithen Tuer gave that prospect short shrift. "Koriathain will not treat with the powers that currently shadow your prince. Why else, worthy man, did you come here? After the scandal that destroyed your grand uncle, surely you recognized Lysaer's malaise as a blood-bound tie of compulsion?"

Sulfin Evend could not mask the straight fear that shot through him. "How I'd hoped not. You're certain?"

The crone tucked bowed shoulders. "Sure enough." She seemed suddenly tired as her gesture encompassed the objects swathed under his cloak. "The items you carry will show us which faction."

"No!" she exclaimed, arresting his move to unveil the unpleasant contents. "Not so fast! Never, without wards of protection where such a cult has engaged active workings!" Porcelain eyes glinted, nailing him down with the force of their occult regard. "I, too, must demand my due reckoning for this service. Will you bear the cost and the consequence?"

Her swift, stabbing finger forestalled his response. "I will help. But know this, young man. You bring me my death. The moment I opened my door to admit you, that forecast outcome was set. I have waited to go, for years longed for the day I would greet the turn of Fate's Wheel. What are you willing to pay in exchange? Would you give your heart, if I ask, or the last breath in your lungs? Will you stand firm, and risk all you hold dear to salvage the life of your master?"

The Alliance Lord Commander said, threadbare, "Anything. I must. The s'Ilessid prince carries my life debt."

"Then shoulder your fate." The crone bent to one side, and snatched up the blackened spike of the fire iron. "You are a loyal man, Sulfin Evend. There lies your strength and your downfall."

"Enough caterwauling emotion, old dame." Eyes like chipped slate matched that ancient, blind stare. "How do you want your pledge satisfied?"

"Set down your burden," the seeress replied. "Then, if I can, I will ease your straits, but after you've sworn a *caithdein's* oath to the kingdom."

"Here? *In Erdane?*" Prepared to unfasten the knots on the bundle, Sulfin Evend shoved upright, his brows arched with fierce incredulity. "That's a perilous folly, since the Fellowship Sorcerers have already appointed the post to a reiving forest barbarian!" This was insane precedent, set alongside the fact that the Lord Mayor would subject any man who dared to revive the old forms of crown charter law to a branding, followed up with a public gelding.

"Folly, is it?" The ancient wheezed through a breathless laugh as she heaved herself to her feet. Fire iron in hand, she stumped over the carpet and fetched a slender birch rod from a hook. "How little you know of your bloodline, young man."

Sulfin Evend clenched his jaw, head turned as the crone touched the wood stave to the floorboards. She began scribing a series of interlocked circles, her swaying steps moving widdershins.

"I won't hear this," he stated. "I can't. I'm aligned with the towns!" The witch had to know: he was a mayor's son by birth. The duties invoked by his Alliance office ran counter to all that Tysan's *caithdein* must stand for. "I'm not free to swear you an oath to the land. My rank as commander of Lysaer's war host has already claimed my pledged loyalty."

The old woman ignored him. She sealed the last circle, invoked a charm that puckered her forearms with gooseflesh, then hefted the iron and flicked back the silk that covered the ceremonial artifacts. Dingy glow from the dips brushed the bloodstained bowl, with its dark band of incised ciphers. The horrid, black knife, with its slender bone blade seemed to drink the available light.

Enithen Tuer gave his vehement protest a sorrowful shake of her head. "Then bear the cost of your pride, foolish man. The ones you oppose steal the living and usurp their identities." As Sulfin Evend turned pale, the crone nodded. "Yes." She flipped the shielding cloth back into place without ever touching the contents. "They are necromancers. Unopposed, they will suck off your prince's vitality. When he is weakened enough to succumb, they'll replace him with another, long-dead awareness. To have any hope of standing against them, you must invoke the latent heritage of your bloodline."

"My ancestress, the Westwood barbarian," Sulfin Evend snapped, startled. "Damn my forefather's unbridled lust! You claim to know who she was?"

Enithen Tuer settled cross-legged on the rag rug by the hearth. Her marble eyes remained fixed ahead, as though the far past had been written across the murk of her spoiled vision. "The first Camris princes were seated at Erdane. Their ancestress declined the honor of founding the lineage of Tysan's high kingship, did you know that?"

At Sulfin Evend's vexed breath, the crone nodded. "Oh yes. There are records the vaults under the palace have lost. The Fellowship did not compel your first forebear. They would not, by the Law of the Major Balance. When their second choice, Halduin s'Ilessid, gave his willing consent to enact the blood binding for his future heirs, Iamine s'Gannley accepted his plea to stand shadow for that authority. She became the steward for Tysan's throne. Her descendants have kept that tradition, unbroken, for well over five thousand years."

"Ancient history, old woman. This has nothing to do with me," Sulfin Evend broke in. "Nor does it bear on the life of my prince."

"It has everything to do with your threatened prince!" the crone contradicted him, curt. "In your generation, the old line of the Camris princes has devolved into three significant branches. In primary descent is Maenol s'Gannley, oathbound as Tysan's *caithdein*. He has answered the Fellowship's call for an heir. One branch, until this generation, bore the title of the Erdani earls, until its recent, importunate offspring established himself as unworthy. The other, descended matrilineally, is your own."

Sulfin Evend might have laughed for the evil, sharp irony. With his father now standing as Mayor of Hanshire, and his uncle, Raiett Raven, as Lysaer's acting chancellor to secure the absentee mayorship at Etarra, his immediate family wielded the axe blade of Alliance power. That set them in direct opposition to s'Gannley, as dedicated enemies of the clans. Unless, of course, the preposterous tale was founded on senile fancy.

"A fine theory," he said in scorching relief. "I might have believed you, had my great-grandame not been taken captive in Westwood."

Enithen Tuer nodded. "She was there for her wedding. Her name, do you know it?"

Sulfin Evend was forced to concede he did not. The infamy was part of the family legend. The woman had left a blank line in the register, when his great-grandsire had forced her to wife.

"Now you'll hear why. She was Diarin, Emric s'Gannley's first daughter. The clanborn blood enemy of Lysaer s'Ilessid is none other than your distant kindred."

That news fell like a blow to the chest. Strong man though he was, his heart missed a beat: for why else should the Koriani enchantresses have pursued their strangling interest in his father's offspring? Moved to slow rage, Sulfin Evend said tartly, "Old woman, which of my two bollocks would you take for your offering, that my prince might regain his autonomy?"

"Your oath," said Enithen Tuer, not gently. "Sworn now, on your blood and then repeated in the presence of a Fellowship Sorcerer. You must promise to journey to Althain Tower, where you will seal tonight's pledge in completion."

"No man could reconcile what you demand," Sulfin Evend blazed back.

The seeress stared him down. "One path must be taken. I have foreseen. Some day fate will force you to choose which of two loyalties you will sacrifice. The land does not bear a blood-sworn oath lightly. The powers you invoke will be greater than you, and they will not treat with duplicity. You will stand before them, stripped naked, young man. Heart, mind, and body, you will be bound true. No way else can I give what you ask for."

Sulfin Evend returned her glare, anguished. "Demand something different! My own life, if you must! I cannot consent to dishonor."

The crone watched him, saddened. "Then go. Abandon the life debt you owe to s'Ilessid. Walk away loyal, and do nothing."

Yet he could not. Should Lysaer be suborned by a necromancer's cult, the power at risk was too dire to unleash on an unsuspecting populace. The seeress had weighed the fiber of his character and measured him down to the bone. "Then fetch out your knife, and be quick, old witch. You have saddled me with the reckoning."

Late Spring 5670

Errand

The unseasonable cold lingered on through the spring, blustering off the Bittern Desert and whistling over the stark bastion of Althain Tower, set amid the sere and frost-scoured hills. The tightly latched shutters rattled and creaked. Yet no influx of draft winnowed the candle in the snug chamber on the fourth floor. In the beleaguered lands to the west, this isolate haven remained: the tempestuous gales born of misaligned lane flux were not granted license to enter.

The quarters where Sethvir of the Fellowship languished stayed sealed to inviolate calm. There, the wax light burned straight and true, as flame must, in the presence sustained by the white robed adepts of Ath's Brotherhood.

Here, where tranquility reigned absolute, the frail fulcrum that balanced the fate of the world trembled, poised, at the brink of disaster.

When Paravian presence had ebbed from the land, the Fellowship Sorcerers had shouldered the task of guarding Athera's mysteries. Heir to the last centaur guardian's gift of earth-sense, Sethvir provided their eyes and ears and much more: if he foundered now, the core balance of the planet would shift. The forces of expansive renewal would shrink, and the spiral would sink into entropy. Ath's initiates had extended their constant attendance ever since the Koriani Prime's insane bid to seize power distressed the flow of earth's lane flux. Although that imbalance was swiftly restored, the disruption deranged an array of spelled boundaries, including the ungoverned wells of raw chaos constrained by Athera's grimwards.

That black hour at midnight, while the wick burned serene, the most critical of these had been rededicated. Three yet remained, with the Sorcerers' resources strapped to the verge of paralysis.

Sethvir kept the crippling vigil at Althain. Day to day, moment to precarious moment, he endured, while the insurgent trend of town politics moved apace to exploit the lapse of the Fellowship's oversight. No colleague owned the breadth of vision to counterbalance the triplicate breach. The slow burn of stressed wards consumed him, relentless, while Asandir braved the perilous work in the field, realigning torn ciphers and weaving the boundaries back to their former stability.

Sethvir lay prostrate to mask the stressed pain that leached at his innate vitality. Drawn flesh over bone, his stilled face seemed winnowed beyond substance, and his form, wrought of gossamer spirit light. The ivory hands tucked over the coverlet seemed naked without their archivist's spatter of ink stains.

Tonight, as the lane tides surged toward solstice, Sethvir's office as Warden of Althain demanded active use of his earth-sense. The adepts on watch as he asked for assistance numbered an even six.

Four were arrayed at the cardinal points to protect his weakened aura. Two more steadied a pane of polished obsidian, Sethvir's preferred tool to reflect the impressions garnered from current events. The combed fall of his beard streamed over his chest, scarcely stirred by his shallow breathing. His farseeing eyes remained closed. If the tension pinching his parchment lids seemed the sole sign of his living awareness, he did not stint the demands of his task.

The images that unreeled like smoke over glass stayed meticulously clear as an etching…

…in the mountains near Eastwall, an auburn-haired enchantress lays a quartz sphere aside, while her mind rides a daydream in longing search of a black-haired, green-eyed man…who, in a place far removed, looks up from an opened book and smiles an affirmation. "Soon," he assures, as her tender thought touches him. "Brave heart, I'll fulfill my sworn promise to meet you…"—while far to the south, riding the turquoise swells off the Scimlade, a blond-haired captain on an ocean-bound brig paces over her tossing decks, for not knowing the same man's location…while elsewhere, another clad in the nine-banded robes of the Koriani Prime Matriarch nurses her fire-scarred hands and commands an avid circle of scryers to search for the selfsame spirit…

Beloved, or friend, or inveterate enemy, all would find their desires deferred: Arithon Teir's'Ffalenn seemed content to extend his earned sanctuary in the caverns beneath Kewar's mazes.

Without judgment, Sethvir recorded. The male adept on station at south glanced up in concern at his counterpart, on guard at north. "He's drastically weakened. Much longer's unwise."

She inclined her hooded head in response, the silver-and-gold threadwork stitched into her mantle glinting through the hazed light of her presence. Her hands moved, gently cradled the Sorcerer's head, and touched reverent thumbs to his brow. "Sethvir is aware. His senses are tracking a formative current that demands his listening attention."

In the dark glass, meantime, the sequential ripples sown by Arithon Teir's'Ffalenn flowed one after the next, unobstructed.

...as in Halwythwood, alone, a younger girl weeps, and bitterly curses the name of the prince whose enemies destroyed her father... then that image dissolved, to another, *showing a fat prophet and his dark-haired charge, asleep in the brush by the fringes of Atwood...*

That instant, a static spark cracked across the polished face of the glass. The image sheared off, and re-formed to another: a view focused with the exquisite detail invoked by the blaze of true magecraft.

...in the close gloom of a candlelit garret, a fighting man worn whipcord lean from campaign stands naked inside a scribed circle. At his side, a bent crone whispers quavering cantrips and calls the four elements to guard point!

Sethvir's eyes snapped open, their cerulean depths as vacant as fired enamel. "Luhaine!" His whisper carried an imperative edge, and his gaunt hands locked on the coverlet. "Luhaine! You are needed! Go to Erdane, at once! Our pledge to protect an old friend has come due."

Yet the summons, once sent on the flicker of thought, today lacked the force to imprint the stream of the lane flux.

"He'll need to use quartz." The adept at the Sorcerer's feet moved forthwith. Though by nature, he would not raise power to affect the way of the world, on request, he could fetch and carry for the infirm. Beyond the scarlet carpet, he delved into an ambry tucked in an embrasure that once had served as an arrow slit.

"The clear point," Sethvir prompted, his voice gravel rough. "The one charged last week in the midday sun, that's wrapped up in fleece and black silk." He shut tortured eyes as the unpolished crystal he required was laid into his anxious hands.

He cupped the base, traced its contours in welcome, while candlelight flared through its streamered veils and fired the shimmer of rainbow inclusions. As the stone warmed and awoke to the Sorcerer's touch, he acknowledged its conscious presence. A flash of joy answered. Moved to a faint smile in response, Sethvir lifted his trembling grasp and puffed a soft breath to charge the front-facing facet. Then he placed his thumbs overtop and aligned his determined awareness.

The quartz matrix imprinted his patterned thought, amplified his intent, and recast its frequency as a beacon. Sethvir's appeal rode the magnetic tides and ranged outward, bearing summons to his distant colleague...

Far southward, gusty winds spattered rain on the glass of the firelit hall where the crowned sovereign of Havish kept late hours in council with his weatherbeaten *caithdein*, Machiel, and three other seasoned advisors. The handpicked foursome were not known for soft words. Under King Eldir's ringless, broad hands, the tally sheets lately compiled by the clerks showed the wear of a tactical chart spread for a siege. Machiel had a crossbow disassembled on the table. His mood eggshell brittle, he oiled and scoured the rust from the trigger latch, while his neighbors in their spotless brocades observed, walleyed, caught in the breach.

Yet the enemy confronting the restored realm of Havish wielded no concrete weapon.

As the imbalanced weather kept its savage grip, the sown crops were struck cold in the fields. The rich, coastal lowlands fared no better, as frost left the ground, and the driving storms drowned the farmsteads under sheet-silver puddles and ice melt. Swollen rivers were raised to boiling flood. Seagoing galleys were forced to stay battened, snugged to moorings within sheltered harbors. The roads were awash, soaked to bogging mud, and the looming specter was famine.

Eyes gritted red from a sleepless night, King Eldir slouched in his lion-carved chair. A large man whose presence might not seem imposing, his square chin wore steely filings of stubble and a plain circlet contained his tousle of fading brown hair. The realm's scarlet tabard had no jewels or gold thread. His sleeve cuffs were bare of embroidery.

In words just as blunt, he addressed a point of vacant air by the window nook. "Our straits are grim, Luhaine. If we can't charter blue-water ships and skilled captains, the reserve stores we have can't be shifted an inch." His irritation sprang from the exasperating fact: the best crews under sail in rough waters were associates of Arithon s'Ffalenn, whose name was political disaster.

Eldir ran on, his intent features tracking the vexed breath of air, now riffling dust from his tapestries. "If, as you say, the rains won't cross the Storlains, then Havistock's harvest won't fail. But word's in from Quaid. The passes to Redburn are still choked with ice. Mercy on us, the inhabited countryside's devastated. Tomorrow, I'll be faced with reports that more children are wasting away from starvation!"

The discorporate Sorcerer paused in response, his florid style turned painfully clipped. "That's not why I've come. Your treasury's not wanting. You can hire more deepwater vessels. If you're uneasy in bed with his Grace of Rathain—"

"That choice of alliance could start a war!" Machiel interrupted, busy hands scraping the firing pin.

Luhaine lost patience. "We already have a war! I'm here to help you stay clear of it!" To the High King, he added, "If you balk at liaison, then learn by example: Prince Arithon trained his captains by recruiting the cream of Eltair Bay's smugglers."

"It's his navigators we need, not his damnable sly habits!" the Minister of Trade ventured sourly.

"So who needs to know?" snapped the spokesman from Mornos. "Men with esoteric knowledge can be kept under wraps."

"Who could guarantee their unsavory characters?" The upright, prim chancellor forgot his ribboned cuffs and folded angry forearms on top of the oil rag. "Would they change their stripes for a starving babe, do you think, when the same breed of henchmen cut throats in cold blood for the Master of Shadow's assault at the Havens?"

"That's enough!" Luhaine's outburst shook the floor with an ominous, subsonic vibration. "Let us not sully facts with irrelevant hysteria."

Eldir stared back with unswerving brown eyes. "Should I be surprised? The one accursed name always saddles us with trouble. In fact, why have you come, Luhaine?"

Machiel remembered, by his disproving glance: the last unsought message from a Fellowship Sorcerer had plunged the royal court into mayhem, playing host when Arithon Teir's'Ffalenn had required sanctioned oversight for the ransom of Lysaer's first, ill-starred princess. As the pause hung, the *caithdein* broke in, sarcastic, "Don't tell me the poisonous rumors are true? That Lysaer's *second* wife has gone missing?"

Luhaine's disembodied quiet stunned the air to suspended intensity.

Machiel unleashed a studied string of expletives, while the councilman who guarded the venues of trade leaned forward with fired agitation. "Dharkaron Avenger's Five Horses and Chariot! An outbreak of plague couldn't sever our rotten relations with the Alliance port towns any faster!"

King Eldir's jaundiced calm remained fixed, even dangerous, as he challenged the Sorcerer's silence. "Are you here to tell me an estranged royal wife will be scratching at my door and begging for sanctuary?"

"No one knows what Lady Ellaine will choose," Luhaine responded with acid delicacy. Tired of breaking Sethvir's packets of bad news, he would not give way and temporize. The straight possibility the princess might look south for safety could destroy the last, frayed thread of accord between Havish and Tysan. Strained relations, on top of the ravages of famine, were going to rattle Avenor's choleric ambassador harder still. "Served with timely warning, you can field the problem with diplomacy. I remind your Grace: the lady has borne a living son to s'Ilessid. Since she won't realize her status under charter law, she could be advised of the fact she's entitled to ask our Fellowship for assistance."

Before the harsh point was argued, that the Sorcerers might not have a free hand to answer in time to forestall repercussions, Machiel interrupted. "But Lysaer's son passed Fate's Wheel. Got himself scorched to heroic cinders by a Khadrim, so we heard." Never fully at ease within walls, the forest-bred steward retrieved the crossbow stock and used his skinning knife to ream out the quarrel slot. "We were led to understand that breaking news of the tragedy was what caused his mother's crazed flight in the first place."

"Not exactly." The Sorcerer's shade whisked over the patterned carpet, fanning groomed heads and lace and riffling the coals in the grate to a sullen flare of heat. "Prince Kevor's still alive. An arcane recovery, not yet widely known." Now poised by the mantel, Luhaine's presence all but bristled the air into hoarfrost. He required to say more. But today his fond penchant for diatribe was cut short as a hammering gust battered into the latched glass of the casement. The draft that seeped through stalled his windy voice and engendered a freezing silence.

A crowned high king attuned to all four of the elements, Eldir stood up. Braced short by his move, the wiser councilmen stilled, while Machiel shivered outright and ceased his idle fuss with the workings of dismantled weaponry.

"Spare us!" Eldir cracked. "If it's bad news for Havish, tell us quickly."

Across the wrenched pause, Luhaine's shade stopped cold as the urgent summons dispatched from Althain's Warden exploded across his awareness…

…in Erdane, amid crawling shadows in a cluttered attic, a strong man stands naked within a raised warding and lays a flint knife to his wrist. His swift stroke enacts the ritual cut. As the flow of let blood wakes a flash of raw light, his shocked outcry reflects an anguished note of betrayal.

"Oh yes, my fine man," whispers Enithen Tuer. "You have in fact consecrated that knife's arcane properties. A binding act, born out of necessity, since that blade alone will enact your primary line of protection! Now listen well: here are the words you will swear, sealing your oath unto your dying breath, or take warning! You will fall to a hideous fate that's far worse, and suffer the eternal consequence…"

Luhaine recovered himself, jaggedly frantic. The dropped thread of his audience closed with a rush that distressed those who knew his staid character. "If the bereaved s'Ilessid mother should chance to make contact, she's best left to believe that her royal son perished."

"Ath's Grace, Luhaine!" The king's shout chimed through the complaint of cleaned steel, as he slammed his closed fists on the tabletop. "Don't ask this! I can't! The very idea's a straight cruelty!"

The Fellowship spirit whirled in tight agitation, scattering maps and requisition lists, and setting goose quills to flight like chased leaves. "Not in this case! Had young Kevor died, he could not be any more lost to her!"

Machiel's granite features went pale. "Dharkaron avert! A wicked turn, if the boy's in fact fallen to necromancy!"

"Mercy! No! Not the young prince," Luhaine cracked as he spun in pained haste toward the casement. In actuality, that threat confronted the boy's *father*, a horror too dire to contemplate. Forced away in the face of the High

King's stressed adamancy, the Sorcerer flung back on departure, "Trust us, your Grace! In compassion, I ask you to heed Sethvir's counsel! I can't tarry to explain. Another crisis is breaking in Erdane, and I must go at once to attempt intervention!"

Late Spring 5670

On Death and Banishment

In the dark, musty garret, the knife that had served as her protection now gone with a loyal man to spare his prince, the ancient seeress encounters the moment foreseen as her hour of death: inside the spent lines of her guarding circles, she is whispering banishments, to no avail; the insatiable ring of cold specters close in, sucking her failing vitality…

At Avenor, Cerebeld, High Priest of the Light, takes uneasy pause to blot his brow, then smooths his rich robes, descends to the wardroom, and accosts Avenor's elite palace guard, "I want another three galleys sent out! More patrols. Sweep every roadhouse and country inn. Or how will you laggards respond when the Divine Prince holds inquest over the fate of his errant wife…?"

One moment shy of disaster, Enithen Tuer's locked door becomes breached by a gust that bursts into scouring light; and devouring shades scatter, as Luhaine of the Fellowship wraps the dying old woman in veils of blue fire and calm: "Peace, my dear. I will hold you, secure. Let your brave spirit cross over Fate's Wheel in safety…"

Eastern Tysan

II. Excision

Three hours before dawn, Lord Commander Sulfin Evend returned to the mayor's palace. Rumpled and chilled, his rapacious mood fit to stamp an impression in pig iron, he bowled past the butler with four trusted officers, on the pretense of holding a war council. His party mounted the carpeted stair in a muffled thunder of boots. Their stubbled faces and ready steel brooked no protest as the Lord Commander set them on guard in the anteroom of the state guest suite.

"I'm going inside. No one follows! You'll prevent any servants from leaving." His wolfish review permitted no questions. "Whatever you hear, whatever you think, I rely on you to stand firm. No one, I don't care who, or what rank, will cross over this threshold behind me. If I don't reappear to relieve you by dawn, your orders will proceed as follows: set fire to these chambers. Burn the contents, untouched. Let nothing and no one attempt any salvage until this whole wing has been razed to the ground! Am I clear?"

Shock stunned the men silent. Lest they bid to question their commander's sanity, the senior officer requisitioned from Etarra spoke fast to quash stirring doubt. "He's testing our nerve, you limping daisies! The Prince Exalted's beyond that shut door. Do you honestly think the immortal Light born as flesh could be harmed by a paltry house fire?"

Still hooded, and masking the burden he carried under the folds of his cloak, Sulfin Evend doused the conjecture. "Hold my line! On my word, if you fail, we shall see the day evil triumphs." Forced to the grim crux, he tripped the latch and slipped into the royal apartment.

The closed air within was stuffy and dim, cloyed with the herbs the distraught valet was using to sweeten the closets. At the commander's arrival, he abandoned his fussing, while the officious chamber servant shot to his feet, and the page boy napped on in an overstuffed chair, snoring beside the lit candle.

Against the appearance of indolent normalcy, the unconscious man stretched on the bed lay ivory pale, and too still. Lysaer's blond hair gleamed on the tidied pillow, shadowed beneath the rich hangings. Devoted hands had tucked away his marked limbs, then raised the satin-faced coverlet up to his chin to lend the appearance of natural repose. Past one surface glance, the fallacy crumbled. The imperceptible draw of each shallow breath was too sluggish to be mistaken for regular sleep.

Sulfin Evend shoved back his hood. Hard mouth pressed to a line of distaste, he flung off the cloak, which still reeked of clogged smoke from the seeress's fusty attic. Then he shed his swathed bundle on a marquetry table and addressed the fidgety staff. "Roust up the boy. Then, get out, every one of you." Jet hair disheveled, a steel gleam to pale eyes, he forestalled the least opening for argument. "My armed men will not allow you to leave. You'll have to bunk down in the anteroom."

The scared servant shook the logy page to his feet, hushed his grumbling, and steered for the doorway. The valet did not stir a finger to help. Gangling arms clasped, his gray hair fashionably styled above his immaculate livery, he stuck in dapper heels and refused.

Sulfin Evend met that obstinacy with frightening resolve, an uncompromised fist closed over his sword grip, and his unlaced, left sleeve flecked with bloodstains. "Stand clear!"

"Someone should stay," the gaunt servant insisted. "Whatever foul work you intend to commit, my master will have a witness."

"That's a damned foolish sentiment, and dangerous!" The Alliance Lord Commander crossed the carpet, cat quick, prepared to draw steel out of hand. "You have no idea what vile rite's to be done here. Nor have you the strong stomach to last the duration."

"I daresay, I don't," said the man with stiff frailty. "Nonetheless, I will stand by my master."

Shown threadbare courage in the face of such trembling fear, Sulfin Evend took pause with the blistering glance that measured his troops on a battle line. Then he sighed, moved to pity. "Why under Ath's sky should you ask this?"

The valet swallowed and shuffled his feet. His manicured hand gestured toward the bed. "For too long, I have watched something evil at work. You are the first who has dared to react. If your trust proves false, then I fear nothing else. His Divine Grace may be saved or lost. If I share in his fate, come what may, I will know that one steadfast friend remained at his shoulder."

"Have your way, then, but be warned: I'll have no interference." Sulfin Evend released his weapon, his level, black eyebrows hooked into a frown as he moved past and snapped the curtains over the casements. "Fail me there, or breathe a word of loose talk, and I'll have your raw liver for a league bountyman's dog meat. What you've asked to observe can't be done clean, or dainty. If you lose your nerve, or if I fall short, this room's going to burn, taking everyone with it. My captains won't pause, or shirk the command. Leave now, and I won't fault your bravery."

The valet backed a step, rammed against the stuffed chair, and sat as his spindly knees failed him. "This time, the command not to speak is a blessing," he said, in a quavering voice.

Sulfin Evend had no second to spare and no words to acknowledge such staunchness. Dawn approached, far too quickly. Fingers flying, he stripped off spurs and boots. His surcoat came next, then the corded twill jacket that had masked his mail shirt at the feast. His studded belt clashed onto the pile, followed by his baldric and several sheathed daggers. Stripped to gambeson and breeches, he crossed the chamber and peeled back the carpet. Somewhere downstairs, a kitchen dog barked. A door banged, and a shrill voice berated a scullery maid for returning late from a tryst. Sulfin Evend bit back a harried oath. The household servants were already stirring, no favor, in light of the trial lying ahead.

He built up the fire. Without the oak logs, he used only the birch, split into billets for kindling. As the flames crackled and caught, hot and sweet and fast-burning, he rifled the nightstand, set the filled washbasin onto the floor, then cracked open the curtain and whacked the bronze latch off the casement. He used the snapped fitting to stub ice from the sill. The chips were dumped in the bowl, where they melted, settling a fine sediment of gritted soot and caught mortar. Hefting the iron poker, he crouched by the hearth and hooked out a smoldering bit of wood. Both coal and hot metal were doused with a hiss, then laid, steaming wet, on the floorboards.

Pinned by the valet's dubious eyes, the Lord Commander plucked the wax candle from its pricket. Stuck upright, it joined the array on the floor. Snatched light cast his movement in fluttering shadow as he stripped off his gambeson, then advanced to the bed.

He tore off the blankets. Lysaer's nightshirt was sacrificed, next, yanked away from his wasted frame with a snarl of ripped cloth and burst laces. All but unbreathing, the victim remained slack and pale as a day-old carcass. Careful, so careful, not to brush against skin with even a glancing touch, Sulfin Evend jerked the tucked sheet from the mattress and bundled his stricken liege into his arms.

Lysaer weighed little more than a parcel of sticks. His golden head dangled. Poked from the racked linens, his bare feet showed blue veins like the crackled glaze on antique porcelain.

Sulfin Evend ignored the valet's incensed glare, for what must appear callous handling. Enithen Tuer had been adamant concerning her detailed list of peculiar instructions. Charged not to skip steps, the commander knelt. He spilled the Blessed Prince in a naked heap on the stripped surface of the parquet. Vulnerably thin, his muscles were wire, the joint of each bone pressed against parchment skin, and each cadaverous hollow a pool of jet shadow.

No life seemed in evidence, beyond the reflex as the ribs rose and fell to the draw of each shallow breath.

The lit profile alone kept its heartwrenching majesty, pure in male beauty as form carved in light, envisioned by a master sculptor. Sulfin Evend shrank away from sight of Lysaer's face. Already savaged by inchoate dread, he refused to give rein to the rending grief that suddenly threatened to unman him. Braced against worse than the horrors of war, he swathed his grip in a wrapping of sheet and tugged the seal ring from Lysaer's limp finger. The sapphire signet was cast aside, a tumbling spark of scribed light as it fetched up against the rucked carpet. Still shielding his hands, Sulfin Evend grasped Lysaer by the wrists and tugged his yielding frame on a north-to-south axis. The arms he extended out to each side, at right angles to torso and shoulder. He straightened Lysaer's bare legs from the hip and arranged a cloth yard of space at the ankles. A towel scrounged from the bath pillowed the unconscious man's head.

Lastly, the wadded bedsheet was burned. While the flames in the hearth consumed the spoiled cloth, Sulfin Evend addressed the valet. "Move your chair. Turn your back. You can't watch what happens. Whatever unpleasantness follows, you can't help. My life, and Lysaer's, will hang in the breach until this foul rite is completed."

The old servant bridled, outraged protest cut off by the officer's ice water eyes.

"I don't have better remedy!" Gruff with dread, Sulfin Evend fought to master the requisite note of authority. "If harm overtakes us, you'll have to trust that the powers that wreak ruin will be none of mine. The last steps will be harrowing. You can't intervene. Stop your ears. Use a blindfold if you can't keep your nerves in line through the worst."

The valet reversed the cumbersome chair. Shivering, he reassumed his perched seat, then fussed his sleeves smooth from habit. "If you lie," he said, "if you darken our world with the death of the avatar given to save us, I will watch you burn with a sword through your heart, I so swear by the grace of the Light."

Sulfin Evend shoved erect, scalded to running sweat in the glare from the dying fire. "As I am born, if I have misjudged, my own captain will do that work for you."

Past chance to turn back, Sulfin Evend retrieved his wrapped bundle from the tabletop. He laid it alongside the poker and basin, then slipped the seeress's knife from his waistband and discarded its deerskin sheath. The stone weapon was hung from a thong at his neck. Lastly, he peeled off his breeches and hose. The ritual of excision required him barefoot. Since the act of unbinding would invoke a working of air, he could not wear metal, even so much as an eyelet. Stripped down to his smallclothes, Sulfin Evend sucked a sharp breath, wrung by a spasm of gooseflesh.

He knelt at last, swallowed fear, and shoved back his soaked hair, then picked the knotted cords off the bundle. The first layer held numerous ceremonial items given by Enithen Tuer. Beneath, still masked by the fabric of Lysaer's purloined shirt, were the unclean clay bowl and the bone knife, wrought to waylay the spirit by the dark workings of necromancy, then raised active by acts of blood sacrifice. Sulfin Evend left those covered objects untouched. The seeress had assembled two packets of herbs. One, he emptied into the fire. Laced in the fragrance of sweet-burning smoke, he ripped open the other and spilled the contents into the basin. Next, he took up the quill from the wing of a heron, long and gray as a blade, and whispered the Paravian word, *An*, for beginning.

Power spoke through Athera's original tongue, a tingle of force that sharpened his gift of raw talent. Brushed by the lost echoes of an ancient past, before mankind had trodden Athera, Sulfin Evend clamped down on the ancestral instincts that whirled his mind toward a blurred haze of vision. He focused his thought to define his intent, then drew the circle of Air with the feather and arranged it, point outward, at east. West, he painted the circle for Water with a finger dipped wet in the basin. Birch charcoal, soaked cold, scribed the circle for Fire, beginning and ending at south. North, he laid the iron poker, also with the point faced out. The last ward, for Earth, must be written in blood, using the tip of the seeress's flint knife.

Now committed past help, Sulfin Evend gripped the obsidian handle and cut the dressing off his marked wrist. The blind woman's instructions rang still through his mind, their cadence exactingly wary. '*You will make the last circle, beginning at north. Reopen the wound that you made to swear oath. The rite bound you to the land for a term of life service. Used rightly, its virtues will answer.*'

Sulfin Evend traced out the glistening red line, for the fourth and last time surrounding himself and the comatose prince, stretched naked as birth on the floorboards. Then he recited the time-honored words that called the four elements to guard point.

'*The necromancer's victim will regain his awareness, about now,*' the elderly seeress had cautioned: and Lysaer had. His sapphire eyes were wide-open. His pupils, distended, were bottomless black, and his limbs, bound in iron possession. First focused by pain, the Divine Prince encountered the horrid discovery that he was utterly helpless. Deadened nerves denied him the power to move or cry out in furious protest.

'He will feel the halter of power laid on him, but not recognize you as his savior. Stay vigilant, young man. Set one foot awry, displace any of your circles, and all your protections lie forfeit. Fail here, and you will fall prey to the uncanny forces that bid to break through. The necromancers whose binding is threatened will strive to reaffirm their disturbed ties of possession. You stand in their way, your work seeks to defy them. They will strike you down, if a slipshod step shows them the least little sign of a weakness.'

Lysaer would be terrified. His irate stare reflected no less than the racking shock of betrayal. His most-trusted field officer surely appeared in league with a shadow-sent sorcerer.

Unwilling to suffer that stark, anguished gaze, forbidden to speak the one kindly phrase that might mend a broken confidence, Sulfin Evend ripped the silk hem of the shirt into strips. Wedded to his unassailable purpose, he knotted a cuff around each of Lysaer's slack wrists. Then he bound each slender ankle in turn. He soaked the dried sea sponge the seeress had given, and using the cloth to avert a chance touch, washed every last patch of bared flesh with the herbal brew in the basin. He had no time to make his ablutions tender. Lysaer s'Ilessid lay supine throughout, unable to offer resistance. His birth gift of light would not rise through the bindings laid down by the knife-cut circles.

The defenses were holding firm, a backhanded blessing: even minor instruction in arcane knowledge would have allowed Lysaer to snap the stay set on his will. No such knowledge informed him. Bitterly helpless, shamed beyond pride, he suffered the cavalier handling. Those gemstone eyes burned with a cognizant rage that would have raised scorching light on a thought, and blasted his tormentor down to a cinder.

Silenced by the demands of the ritual, Sulfin Evend could ask for no leave; could not for decency's sake beg understanding or forgiveness. He gathered the four copper nails from the seeress, then the granite stone pried from her hearth. His heart closed to mercy, he pierced the tied knots in the cloth and fixed his liege's cuffed limbs to the floorboards.

Lysaer's outrage drilled into his turned back as he hammered. Sulfin Evend held steadfast. The seeress's dry voice instructed from memory, 'You must break the bowl, next. Ah, no! Foolish man, you will never unwrap it! Those sigils incised on the rim channel power. Harm could strike at you, through your unshielded vision, or worse. The unclean powers engendered by necromancy might open a portal within your defensive circles. Keep the bowl veiled. Use the stone. Crush the clay through the cloth. Now, be warned. The act will cause pain, for the resonance of shed blood on that vessel will harbor far more than residual spellcraft. As the sigils are shattered, their forced bond will release. The matrix that shackles the spirit will break, and Lysaer will feel the unpleasant shock as it happens.'

Sulfin Evend braced his nerves. Rock in hand, black hair soaked with sweat, he groped through the masking layer of cloth and sorted the ugly contents by feel. Then he aimed for the bowl and brought the rock down with all of his war-hardened strength.

Pottery smashed with a muffled thump, and Lysaer s'Ilessid screamed. High and thin as a wounded rabbit, his keening note sawed the stark fabric of silence and extended beyond all endurance. Aching, Sulfin Evend crashed the stone down again. Blow after blow, he hammered into the cloth, and pulverized the burst fragments. Lysaer whimpered and cried. He howled in agony. Contorted spasms racked his splayed form. His back arched. The ties that entrapped him tore his fine skin, as his vibrating heels drummed the floorboards.

Horrified, Sulfin Evend pressed on. Lysaer's distress would not ease, while he faltered. Reprieve could not happen before he enacted the full course of the banishing ritual. His hand shook. His eyes blurred with tears. He exchanged the stone for the black-handled knife, and rinsed the blade in the basin.

Enithen Tuer had warned of worse yet to come. Back in her attic, Sulfin Evend believed that she mocked him. Now all but unhinged by the force of his pity, he realized she had exhorted him out of heartfelt compassion.

A wiser man might have listened and walked free: more than a life debt attended this balance. Yet the choice of that moment was forfeit, and the hour too late to turn back.

Sulfin Evend lifted the flint dagger point over his liege's navel. Lips sealed, throat locked, he cut swiftly. The small flesh wound welled scarlet: the indented scar that once tied the cord to the mother filled and ran with the blood of the child. Sulfin Evend pronounced the birth name of his prince, then phrased the Paravian invocation for prime power. He capped his appeal with a plea that was mortal, common to all of humanity.

"I demand this man's freedom! By right of birth, by right of life, by right of spirit, by the right of the undying light that sources his greater being, let him reclaim the pure truth of his wholeness. He is, himself, sovereign, alive by free will."

'*You will then cut the cords,*' Enithen Tuer had instructed. '*By your born talent, one by one, you must feel them. Leave the one you will find at his brow! You must not touch that tie! If you slip, brave man, if you strike that last bonding, even by chance, you will do worse than destroy the victim you have set your very self at risk to preserve. Not only would you bring yourself under attack, you would call forfeit Lysaer's first claim to autonomy. His will would be lost, forever enslaved through your act to the undying web of the necromancers.*'

Sulfin Evend cleaned the stained knife. Left hand raised, fingers spread, he sounded the space above Lysaer's straining body with testing intent. Where he detected the invisible threads of resistance, he slashed the stream of energy crosswise with the black flint. At each cut, the air thrummed with vibrations past the range of his natural hearing. Lysaer shuddered and cried. Tears streaked down his temples. He recoiled, flinching, as though each encounter that disturbed the cords left him burned. Sulfin Evend barred his torn heart. Beyond mercy, he quartered the prince's stretched flesh, up and down, across the torso, at each ear, and over the crown, then down every strained limb. Each methodical pass, he nipped the bands of spelled energy, however small and fine.

Dumb exhaustion set in, then shivering nausea. Sulfin Evend persisted, while Lysaer's sobs dwindled. Long before the finish, the flesh he worked over subsided to a flaccid chill. Taut skin shuddered and streamed poisoned sweat, while the pounding pulse in the stretched veins of the neck raced as though the victim was set under torture.

Sulfin Evend swiped back his drenched hair. Thread after thread, he tested and sundered, until only the last tie remained. By then, Lysaer's breathing was broken and harsh, beaten down to the verge of extremity.

'*You may think your liege is near death from shock*,' the seeress had said of this jointure. '*As you love life, if you care for his spirit, I charge you not to be fooled!*'

Set back on his heels, Sulfin Evend regrouped. Weariness racked him. Every nerve in his body felt sickened. The hearthfire had subsided to a bed of dull coals, painting the chamber in textureless shadow. Inside the cut circles, the close-woven air seemed as the walls of a tomb, rippled with sullen heat and cloying with blood smell, wet charcoal, and herb smoke. The single man, striving, sensed the trembling web of the cult's powers coiled tight through the gloom. Sweat burned through his lashes and scoured his eyes, and fear coiled cold in his vitals. Come triumph, or ruin, the dread crux was upon him.

Direct touch at this stage could not be avoided, a pitfall of consummate danger. Enithen Tuer had told him, unflinching: the salvage he staked his life to complete was all but predestined to fail.

'*There is no recourse*,' she explained, unequivocal. '*The necromancers snared Lysaer by willing consent. Consciously, he must revoke their foul hold. Your prince has to wield the knife by his own hand. His free choice alone can release the last binding.*'

Sulfin Evend braced for the final contest. Straddled across Lysaer's helpless, stripped body, he reached for the left wrist to slice away the silk binding.

'*Your loyal heart will lay open your defenses*,' the wise old seeress had cautioned. '*Since the first moment you severed the auric streams tapped by the cultists to siphon vitality, you will have unsealed a self-contained line of spellcraft. Touch the victim, and the imbalanced conduit will affix to you. Until the remaining cord is destroyed, your strength will be drained to replenish Lysaer. Each moment thenceforward will sap you, brave man. Your prince will revive, and you will diminish. With no effort at all, the bound victim might bring the enemy's work to completion. He need do nothing more than outlast you.*'

Sulfin Evend had met her concern with his fixed choice to go forward. '*I'll trust Lysaer's innate gift of justice will lend me the opening to prevail.*'

Yet words were not action. No stringent warning prepared: first contact ignited a welter of pain.

Hard resolve could not reconcile the chain-lightning jolt that slammed through mind and senses. Hurled headlong into vertigo, Sulfin Evend reeled, cut adrift, as the explosive shock flayed his awareness. On blind fear, he grappled. The parasitic evil that leached life and breath could bring him down just as fast as the rush of arterial bleeding. He could not pull back. The die had been cast. Mulish courage was not going to save him. Lysaer would be lost for his fatal mistake: the spelled creature whose savage, blue eyes reviled him would never accept a clean death, far less comprehend the chance of a self-claimed redemption.

Tonight's ruin would seed a future of ashes.

The paragon who wielded the power of Light would become a puppet, possessed by the will of reanimate shades. His suborned majesty would destroy the very Alliance whose cause was to banish the oppression of Shadow and tyranny.

Sulfin Evend locked down his jagged scream. Beyond help or resource, he cut the silk restraining his liege's left hand. Pain slowed his reflexes. With humiliating ease, Lysaer's bone-slender wrist twisted free of his sweaty grasp.

The commander deflected the fingers that jabbed at his face. War-trained to fight, he discarded the knife. A feint, a wild snatch, and he snapped a fresh hold. His two-fisted grip bore down on Lysaer's forearm, while the spells of the necromancer sucked at him like a lamprey and snapped his live tissue to agony.

Lysaer bucked under him. With one wrist and both ankles still constrained, there should not have been any contest; except that vile craftwork fueled his manic strength, and likewise sapped his beset opponent.

"Your treason won't take me," Lysaer gasped, enraged.

Whipped to tears, panting through lancing pain, Sulfin Evend could not snatch the resource for answer. Without words, against hope, he must mend shattered trust, before the fell forces his meddling had unleashed drained off his life and claimed both of them.

Where muscle failed, he used leverage and weight, jammed the murdering fist to the floor. He knew where the nerve ran, and jabbed, as he must. Through Lysaer's snarled curses, Sulfin Evend bore in. He matched that incensed blue stare until the wrist that he savaged went limp in his ruthless grasp. He groped, one-handed, recovered the knife.

Fury whipped through his liege's taut frame. Sulfin Evend grappled drawn wire and steel. He held on, while faintness sucked at his balance. His stomach felt yanked inside out, while his hands and feet came unraveled and dissolved into substanceless air. Every skilled art of war, all his tricks of infighting, ebbed away under roaring vertigo. Rushed witless, he fell back on expedience, and gouged a knee into Lysaer's exposed groin.

The prince curled, caught short by the cruel restraints. The pinched breath in his nostrils passed, whistling.

He gasped, while his officer hefted the knife. Grainy flint blade, and sweat-printed obsidian handle: the weapon seemed made for no purposeful good.

Yet its foreboding appearance could not compare with the obscene shard of knapped bone that Lysaer had used to enslave himself. The Lord Commander leveled the dagger before his liege's racked face. Reeling, he waited. Through surge upon surge of debilitating torment, he held on until those gemstone-blue eyes showed the flicker of restored comprehension.

Moving slowly, he reversed the keen edge, then laid the stone handle in the slack fingers of Lysaer's pinned hand.

He relaxed his grip slightly, sensed the impulse to kill, and locked his fist down once again. If the venomous, stinging pain was receding, a numbing fog now invaded his being. Sulfin Evend battled its deadening lethargy. He would persevere; even failing, he must. He released his clamped hold on his liege's bruised forearm.

Lysaer's fingers, too willing, stayed clenched on the knife.

Wrung to reeling faintness, Sulfin Evend tried release.

The blade dived for him, glittering. He parried with his forearm, felt the grazed burn of flesh meeting flesh. His instinctive counterresponse proved too brutal: Lysaer's hand released, skating the weapon in a clattering spin over the wax-polished floorboards.

Sulfin Evend hurled sideward, pinned the flying blade before its slide escaped the protective circles. Hard-breathing, his raced pulse a roar in his ears, he battled his upended senses. Despair struck: *he was not going to rally*. The hesitation as he tried to regroup would only sink him, unconscious. He rolled again, used deadweight to bear Lysaer backward. Lose his hold now, and the other, bound arm would wrestle free of the silk wristband.

Couched on straining flesh, gut-winded and sick, Sulfin Evend placed the haft of the knife into Lysaer's slack palm once more. The wrist he crushed to submission was scuffed raw, congested with bruises from brutal handling. Beyond pity, the commander grappled his ebbing strength. Each second he succumbed, Lysaer rebounded. The next strike of the knife would be lethal. Exposed beyond recourse, Sulfin Evend locked stares with his liege, all the mute will in him pleading. He forced the awareness that he foresaw his own murder. As his grasp weakened, he stood down, unresisting, while his loosened hand grazed in an unvoiced apology over the welted scars marking the length of Lysaer's forearm.

The ritual joined in the circle still ruled him. Sulfin Evend sensed the imprint of his own touch. He recorded each unpleasant, tingling snap, as his fingertips grazed the healed lesions. Lysaer felt the sting also. Hazed into recoil, he *must* know the intrusive sensation was nothing natural. The man in him had to acknowledge the queer, creeping wrongness that suffused his intimate flesh. If his s'Ilessid lineage ran true, he would respond through his forebear's gift of true justice.

The demand of the ritual disallowed speech. Shoved hard against the last rags of awareness, Sulfin Evend mimed the cut through the air that would sever the tie set by necromancy. Propped, shivering, on his spread hand, he pointed to Lysaer's damp brow, then repeated the gesture, just short of disturbing the unseen cord that rooted the source of vile conjury.

Strapped logic could not find a second approach. Win through, or fall woefully short, the commander could do nothing more. Crouched on his tucked heels, he waited.

The knife thrust at his leg. Sulfin Evend flung himself clear. Design, or plain accident, as he sprawled, his bent elbow rammed into Lysaer's exposed thigh. The blow shocked the nerve. While his liege moaned in spasm, Sulfin Evend dragged himself back upright. Reeling, he caught the freed forearm. Again, badly trembling, he hefted limp weight and laid Lysaer's slack knuckles in place. The dropped knife seemed beyond him. Twice, he fumbled before he managed to capture the obsidian grip. Rocked by shuddering gasps, he pressed the weapon back into Lysaer's clasp.

By then, the hardened blue eyes showed recovery. Taut fingers closed. The flint edge of the blade jittered red in the hellish glare of the embers.

Light-headed, unmoored, Sulfin Evend owned no last stock of resource. He braced, streaming sweat, racked hoarse by the rush of his breathing. Throughout, the victim of necromancy watched him, deadly and poised as a predator.

Naught else could be done, except tip back his chin, shut his eyes, and invite the quick strike to the throat.

Caithdeinen offered their lives to test princes, if no other means lay at hand.

Stung by that edged truth, the doomed man might have laughed, had the irony not robbed him of dignity. Chance ruled the moment, as he embraced his fate in sacrificial surrender.

Through that last, drawn second, while risen darkness choked down swimming vision, Sulfin Evend tracked the pattern of Lysaer's forced breaths, brokenly rising and falling. His own chest ached to bursting. Every joint hurt. The spurred beat of his heart stabbed pangs through his breast, while his ears rang with the memory of his own voice, swearing the timeworn oath by which every sanctioned prince of the realm had been tested. He clung, while life trembled upon the snapped thread of a mad prince's forgotten mercy.

Crippled, exposed as bait for a necromancer, Sulfin Evend felt the cold ribbons of sweat stripe his back through fast-fraying awareness. He measured the acid-etched stir of the air, as Lysaer firmed his grip on the knife. No coward, the commander opened his eyes and welcomed the stroke that would take him.

The aimed point of the dagger snatched short in midair. Sulfin Evend stared full into Lysaer's face, while the tears he could no longer contain spilled and ran down his cheekbones. His terror could not be masked, or his pity, sustained in the locked stare between them. He bowed his head, waited, and again sensed the move as the knife settled trembling. Razor-edged flint pressed the side of his neck.

Sulfin Evend lost his will to move. Resigned beyond even wrenching despair, he could no longer endure the crazed light in his liege's eyes. Nor would he reason with suborned insanity. Undone by weakness, trembling with terror, he swayed under the dissolving pull of the spells. At the last, the frail stay that kept his upright posture was the bruised and tenuous trust he owed for the discharge of life debt and service.

The blade moved. Sulfin Evend lifted his chin, just in time to see the black knife drop down. The stroke followed through and slashed across the last binding, rooted at Lysaer's forehead.

An electrical snap sheared the air. Pain followed. The tearing onslaught as the spell sundered arched Lysaer violently upward. The knife left his contorted grasp and flew wild, while Sulfin Evend ripped in a cramped breath and gasped the Paravian word, *Alt!* His scraped whisper finished the ritual, one split second shy of disaster.

Then the hurled knife crossed the fourfold line of the circles. Dimmed hearing rushed back, shot to crystalline focus. The embers in the grate seemed the blaze of a holocaust, and the chamber, hurtfully solid enough to confound the overstrung senses.

Yet the peril was over.

Sulfin Evend felt the crushing weight of dissipation lift away. Retching, still dizzy, he raised his marked hands and caught Lysaer's thrashing head. If his strength was spent, he could still lend support. Weeping, he could muffle Lysaer's fraught screams against his shoulder and chest.

"Here!" he pitched his hoarse command toward the chair, where the valet presumably still kept his vigil. "Fetch dry towels and a blanket."

As the commander's battered awareness slid back into focus, he flexed his left hand and picked at the knots confining Lysaer's right wrist. Holding the Blessed Prince propped upright against him, he let the valet assist with the cloth that collared the bone-slender ankles. Then he waited, recovering, as towels were brought, one thoughtfully soaked in cool water.

"Make up the bed," Sulfin Evend ground out, while a competent touch wrapped the prince's flushed forehead in soothing folds of wet cloth. "I'll help attend to his Exalted Self. He is freed, but not likely to stay conscious."

"You don't look much better," said the servant, distraught. He shuddered, exclaiming, "Merciful Light! Just what manner of foul apparition did you banish?"

The Alliance Lord Commander stared back, battered blank.

Wordless, the valet struggled with his wrecked poise. His large hands were shaking, and his chattering teeth hampered his stumbling speech. "There were *things*, icy cold, crowding outside that circle. Unearthly, ill spirits, and Sithaer knows what else."

"You didn't bolt," Sulfin Evend pointed out.

The prince's serving man brushed off the praise. "His Blessed Grace has been unwell for some time. What else could I do, except stand by your word, that those horrors were sent here to claim him?"

"Well, they failed!" Jabbed to vicious distaste for the fact he could not subdue his own trembling, Sulfin Evend realized the prince had gone limp. The gold head lolled, hot and damp, on his shoulder, while the skin cut he had made at the navel dripped blood with sullen persistence. "Your master's ill, now. He requires our cosseting. Meantime, I don't wish to burn for a sorcerer's workings in Erdane! We've got this chamber to set back to rights. No one must see what's occurred here."

While the anxious servant took charge of Lysaer, Sulfin Evend untangled his legs, stood erect, and forced his unsteady feet to bear weight long enough to rub out the spent circles. Next, he recovered the spoiled silk that contained the bowl shards and bone knife, scrounged up a coffer, and dumped out its load of state jewelery. After he had secured the ill-fated bundle under lock and key, he toweled himself dry and wrestled back into his breeches and shirt. The valet was no slacker. By then he had the unconscious prince bathed and groomed, and installed in warmed comfort on the bed.

Lysaer himself remained senseless throughout. Until he roused in his collected, right mind, his keepers could do nothing more than watch and guardedly wait.

As the windows were thrown open to dispel the herb smoke and the rug was spread over the scuffed flooring, the valet exchanged a tenuous glance with the Alliance Lord Commander. Neither man spoke. The next trial was inevitable. Until Lysaer recovered, they would have to fend off the mayor's house staff, and worse, the inquisitive pressure applied by Erdane's ambitious officials.

For that, Sulfin Evend chose to rely on the battle-trained wits of his field captain. "No one else will come in," he assured the stressed servant. "There's not another damned thing we can do but try our utmost to maintain appearances."

Wrung out and tired enough to fall down, the Alliance Lord Commander left Lysaer's bedside and unbarred the shut door to the antechamber. No help for the fact he looked washed to his socks; raked over by the avid, curious eyes of the men under orders to keep vigil till dawn, he could but hope that the room at his back revealed nothing more than the brushed gold head of divinity, lying at peace on the pillows.

Still alert, his ranking officer stepped forth, expecting the word to stand down.

Sulfin Evend spoke fast to stall questions. "Send everyone back. The crisis is over. We're into convalescent recovery, but for that, the prince must have quiet." He finished his orders in a lowered voice. "The page and the chamber servant must stay here in seclusion. I won't have them abroad to spread idle talk. Let your day sergeant assign that detail. He's capable. You are not excused, meanwhile. I plan to sleep here in Lysaer's close company. This door remains tightly guarded, throughout. Not so much as a rumor slips by you. Have I made my needs understood?"

"No one comes in?" Honorably scarred from a dozen campaigns, the grizzled veteran flushed with dismay. "Plaguing fiends, man! I've no glib tongue, and no stomach for mincing diplomacy."

"That's why I need you." Sulfin Evend returned his most scorching grin. "If the petitioners get testy, let them try your sword. Since when has the Grace of Divine Blessing on Earth been required to answer to anyone?"

Dawn arrived, pallid gray. Light through the fogged casements spat leaden glints on the mail shirt and sword, still draped on the chest by the armoire. Its unflinching candor also traced the gaunt face and dark hair of the Lord Commander, who watched at the bedside with steely, light eyes. Aching and sore, awake by the grace of a tisane mixed by the self-effacing valet, Sulfin Evend watched the new day expose a divinity no less than mortally fallible. Left burning with questions he had no right to ask, he guarded his charge with the dangerous calm of a falcon leashed to the block.

Morning brightened. The watch bells clanged from Erdane's outer walls. When the rumble of cart wheels racketed echoes from the cobblestone yard by the kitchen, the Blessed Prince still had not stirred. For the first time that any man could recall, Lysaer s'Ilessid slept soundly past the hour of sunrise.

Westward, the velvet shadow of night was just lifting in Tysan's regency capital at Avenor. There, Cerebeld, High Priest of the Light, attended his custom of daybreak devotion. A florid man with a dauntlessly focused intelligence, he sat, knees folded in meditation, the drape of his formal robes like sunlight on new-fallen snow. Four alabaster bowls on the altar before him contained his daily offering: of clear water, sweet herbs, and a wool tuft infused with volatile oils, commingled with a drop of pricked blood just taken from his lanced finger. Now immersed in deep trance, he waited for the ecstatic communion with the Divine Prince of the Light.

Yet this morning, the contact never arrived. No distinctive presence invoked his true visions. Cerebeld received nothing, while the minutes unreeled, and the flood of cold fear filled the vacancy.

"My Lord, my life, why have you forsaken me?"

No answer followed. Only an empty and desolate silence that reduced him to anxious distress.

"My Lord!" he appealed, shaken. "How am I to enact the work of your will?"

Aching, Cerebeld hurled his mind deeper. He extended his awareness through the limitless void, but no bright power rose up to meet him.

Instead, something *other* stirred out of the dark. Alone, driven desperate, Cerebeld embraced the encounter that, after all, was not threatening or strange, but offered his name back in welcome.

Then the rapture struck in a welling, sweet wave, as always. Cerebeld shuddered, swept up in sublime content, as he had each day since his investiture.

He surrendered. Swept under, he shivered and gasped in the silken rush of a pleasure that ranged beyond reason. The moment of joined exaltation sustained until sunrise, then peaked, and faded away. The High Priest at Avenor tumbled backward, recalled to himself. Ahead, he faced the dull framework of duty: petitions from councilmen, and charitable dispositions, and the ongoing difficulty posed by an absent princess, still missing.

Cerebeld opened his eyes to the shearing, intolerable pain of his solitary awareness. He arose from his knees. No witness observed him. The oddity passed without pause for question that, today, the Prince of the Light had not spoken.

Late Spring 5670

Wakening

On the unsteady moment when he had sworn his guest oath, the Prince of Rathain had not realized the extent he would need to rely on Davien's hospitality. The safe haven offered within Kewar's caverns gave his exhausted faculties time to recoup from the devastating trials of the maze. Soon enough, he encountered the unforeseen changes stitched through his subtle awareness. After years of blank blockage, the healed access that restored his mage-sight required an interval of sharp readjustment.

Arithon Teir's'Ffalenn was not the same man who had crossed Daon Ramon shackled by guilt and the horrors of loss and bloodshed.

Nothing was as it had been. With each passing week, he encountered the odd rifts shot through his initiate awareness. His waking thoughts tended to stumble without warning, unleashing a mind-set that was not linear. The least supposition, no matter how trivial, might touch off an explosion of thought. He saw, perhaps, as the Sorcerers did, in vaulting chains of probability. The sudden shifts became disconcerting. Overcome, seated at breakfast one day, his inward musing upon his borrowed clothes showed him vision upon vision, overlaid.

Arithon viewed himself, using knife and needle to shorten his oversize sleeves; then observed Davien, who could sew as well as Sethvir, poking fun at his sailhand's stitching. In future imprint, he watched as he was offered a green-velvet tunic edged with ribbon and emblazoned with the leopard of Rathain. That raised his hackles. The jolt of his visceral rejection became an electrical force, impelling him into chaos...

...even as he thrashed to recover himself, Davien laughed again, *while his unruly mind raced on and leaped to reframe his adamant preference: of simple, dark trousers and a loose linen shirt. Unreeled thought patterns streamed past all resistance. Left no* choice, except to close down his mage-sight, Arithon tumbled back into the confines of his five senses. Even as he wrenched himself back in hand, he heard echoes: *the loom in a weaver's shop, and behind that, like crystalline imprint, the singing of countryfolk, pounding raw flax into fiber...*

Reoriented, gripping the edge of the table, Arithon sat, hard-breathing and deeply disturbed. He clung to the moment: as though the smells of bread and honey and fresh fruit could reweave his form out of something more solid than air.

Across the breakfast nook, an inquisitive Sorcerer regarded him, arms folded and dark eyes amused. "My shirts are too large?" Davien raised his eyebrows. "I've been remiss? I'm expected to see you reclothed in state?"

"If you're offering, I'll take plain linen," said Arithon. "The simplicity would be appreciated. It's the cloth of my mind that won't cut down to fit."

Davien suppressed laughter. "Not if you try to cram yourself, wholesale, back inside the same vessel. You have much more than outgrown your past, Teir's'Ffalenn. I daresay the puzzle enchants me."

Fast enough, this time, to checkrein the surge of another spontaneous trance, Arithon reached for the bread knife. He buttered a crust, as though that one act might anchor the spin of turned senses.

"You can't live, shut down," the Sorcerer prodded.

The faintest of smiles bent Arithon's mouth. "I can't starve, overset by unbounded visions. That would demean your hospitality." He bit into the morsel and regarded the Sorcerer, who watched him, each move, with tight focus. "I intrigue you that much?"

Davien found the jam jar and shoved it across the table, unasked. "Wrong word. You amaze me. But that's the least point."

Arithon set down his bread crust. "Why do I sense this discussion is verging on dangerous?"

"Words are dangerous," Davien agreed. "Thoughts, even more so. That's why, when mankind first came to Athera in need of a haven, I stood opposed to the compact."

"Your one vote, cast against your other six colleagues." Arithon accepted the preserves. "That fact is on record at Althain Tower, and truly, I'd prefer you kept out of my mind."

Davien's interest expanded. "You read into my history?"

Arithon regarded the enigmatic being before him, wrapped in the fiery colors of autumn, with a wolfish, lean face and the shadowed eyes of a creature that had lived for too long by sharp wits. "I saw enough to realize you wished to guard against the horrid expedient, should the terms of the compact break down."

"Expulsion, before enacting humanity's extirpation from Athera," Davien summed up with steel-clad dispassion. "You believe what was written?"

In fact, the historian had condemned Davien's stance: that twenty thousand refugees should be left to perish, before risking the reckless endangerment posed by the acts of their future descendants.

"The suppositions on paper were damning." Arithon retrieved his knife, slathered his bread crust, then halved the unseasonably ripe peach set before him. "Doubtless your own words cast a different light. I don't think you rejected compassion."

The Sorcerer blinked. "I voted to replenish the refugees' supplies and send them onward, before risking the potential abuse of Paravian territory."

"Send them on, to what fate?" Arithon said gently. *"Frightened, in darkness, what would they find, but more fear and more darkness to hound them? What world will they desecrate, in their sore desperation? What innocent life might be trampled? Send the refugees elsewhere, and we will have disowned the problem, as well as washed our hands of all hope of a reconciled solution.""*

"You quote Ciladis." Davien reclaimed the jam, thoughtful. "Once, our Fellowship was that frightened, that dark. No. We were darker. Without the drakes' binding, we would have gone mad when first we encountered the Paravians." Bread slice in hand, the Sorcerer expounded, "You have traversed Kewar. How much suffering did you lay on yourself before you awakened and recognized that guilt is deadly, and empty, and profitless?"

"The touch of a centaur guardian uplifted me," Arithon allowed. "Without that grace, I would surely have perished."

Davien's dark eyes flicked up and bored in. "You say? Then who admitted the centaur in the first place? Teir's'Ffalenn."

Arithon's gaze turned downward, abashed. He could not disown himself; not again. The infinite presence that had touched and absolved him of itself demanded self-honesty.

"Whose will broke the wards on the maze?" Davien pressed. "You plumbed your self-hatred and demanded your answer, prince. Then you followed up with the courage to acknowledge your own self-worth. There is your grace. You are my fit weapon, to champion the cause of humanity."

Arithon's knife slipped through his nerveless fingers. He stared, transfixed and horrified. "The Mistwraith's curse is mastered, Davien. Its hold upon me is not ended!" When no reply came, he said, tortured, "Your *weapon?* You expect me to salvage the compact and drag humanity back out of jeopardy?"

Davien's answer came barbed. "I expect you to live out your life, Teir's'Ffalenn. To make choice in free will. That you have endured Kewar's maze, and survived, has well fashioned you for your destiny. You have broken the mold and stood forth on your merits. Mankind's hope of survival will come to rely on the consequence. Either way."

The ominous ambiguity behind that soft phrase smashed Arithon's tenuous hold on awareness. He perceived the forked path of his resolve in simultaneous split image: either he would rise to assume royal heritage, and rule with intent to heal the eroded tenets of the ancient law. Or he would adhere to his preference, and abjure his born charge, and let Rathain's royal lineage die, crownless.

The irony cut with piercing clarity: how readily he might force Paravian survival by enacting the lawless alternative. The curse wrought through his being might slip even his most vigilant grasp. He might err out of weakness, or misjudge the impact of his active or passive presence. Such forceful power as he carried might in fact precipitate the last crisis that brought town politics to sunder the compact. The dread consequence of that course was not revocable: the Fellowship of Seven would be charged to eradicate mankind from Athera, ruled as they were by the terrible binding set over them by the dragons.

Aware of Davien's regard, which acknowledged his shocked grasp of the vicious train of repercussions, Arithon shivered, bone deep. "No one should dare try to fathom your motives," he addressed the Sorcerer point-blank.

"Inside the Law of the Major Balance, our Fellowship cannot determine your future," Davien corrected with acid clarity. "Before that fixed truth, my motives are moot. For the ending, on our part, is certain. We are bound to our fate. Paravian survival will be enforced, since our Fellowship has not found the means to break the binding the great drakes laid over us."

Understanding unfolded, a wounding epiphany. "Would you try?"

The Sorcerer did not respond to that question.

Caught in the breach, the man who was Masterbard surveyed the being before him. Davien stared back, his black eyes intense. He was not smiling. The shifting patterns of his inner thoughts could not be read in the depths of his silence. His driving restlessness could only be sensed, pattern upon pattern, behind entangled pain that was not caprice; and a genius vision whose brilliance was such that it would not brook any fixed boundary.

Arithon was first to lower his gaze. After meeting a centaur guardian, just once, he could begin to sense the grave weight of the Fellowship's intangible burden. How could man or sorcerer wish to live in a world so darkened, it might forfeit the esoteric gift of the Paravian presence? Which binding tied the heart with more fierceness: the blood charge of the dragons, to stand guard at all cost; or the bright exultation of the harmony that walked, living, in the form of Athera's blessed races?

One dared not, in this case, press for answer.

Yet as Arithon curbed that line of reeling thought, Davien crossed his arms, prosaic. "Ciladis would willingly speak on that point, if you should ever chance to encounter him. Whatever he might say, the primary issue was never in doubt. Paravian survival is paramount."

Arithon valiantly picked up his bread crust. "It's the pernicious question of *mankind's* right to upset the balance that enables this world's greater mysteries. That is what fractured the Fellowship's unity."

Unblinking, unmoving, Davien stated outright, "That is also what threatens the compact."

Arithon regarded the Sorcerer, hard braced. "I am mortal, and human, and initiate to power, and cursed by Desh-thiere's geas to seek violence. Therefore, I also embody the potential of the wanton destruction you speak of, but on the grand scale. My doom in the maze could have simplified things."

"You survived, in complexity." Davien grinned outright. "Cursed or not, you are also the living exception." His confounding nature seemed to find delight in the quandary of razor-edged paradox. "Proved fit to rule, and honest enough to acknowledge your conscience. Have you a gambler's addiction for risk? You have set yourself to cast the one loaded dice throw. How will you choose, Teir's'Ffalenn?"

"Not to kill." The words, lit to burning, hung on the air with an oath's indelible clarity.

Davien leaned forward, detachment quite gone, and his face pared to riveted intensity. "The most dangerous path, and the most difficult, my friend. Strive for that, and the Mistwraith's curse will be left no other avenue except to destroy you."

The warning struck Arithon with splintering force. A barrier snapped. Inside him, the tissue-thin veil of reason gave way. Torn across by the scale of future event, strung through an obstacle course posed by his own sequence of cause and effect, he experienced a cascade of scalding awareness that unmoored the center pin of his being.

Sight hurled him too far: the course that abjured violence with such visceral need must inevitably carry a terrible, wide-ranging impact. Arithon reeled, eyes newly unsealed. Each decision he weighed engendered a seed, which leaped, branching, into sets of probable outcomes like an unfolding tienelle vision. His senses opened *in all directions*, tumbling him into an uncontrolled state of bewildering simultaneity. Cast beyond the frail shell of his flesh, he became as a light beam split by a prism, shattered headlong down the posited avenues of overlaid future projection.

He perceived with a clarity that scattered him, until he lost himself into the infinite.

"You could use a crystal to anchor your focus," Davien stated, bridging the chasm with words. The Sorcerer in his wisdom did not use touch. Compassionate restraint stayed him, and respect for crushed dignity, as his guest folded against the tabletop, sickened with vertigo, and fighting nausea as his body rejected the upset frame of its balance. "I don't recommend this, since you would not live self-contained, but create your stability in codependency."

Jaw locked, running sweat, Arithon gasped back, "There are, of course, precedents?"

Davien's mercuric chuckle implied more than wry sympathy. "Oh, my wild falcon, there are not, in this case. The path you now walk is uncharted. You must find the way to temper your gifts."

Recognition followed, provocative, that a facet of Davien's piquant interest desired to witness the ongoing experiment.

At the earliest, right moment, the Sorcerer did rise. He rounded the table and closed a firm hand upon Arithon's shoulder, steadying him back erect. The contact soothed down his unsettled aura, for the roiling sickness subsided.

Davien added, in dry and astonished rebuke, "You are a s'Ahelas scion gifted with farsight, and wakened. How novel, that you should be shocked or surprised. You are suffering visions in multiple overlay?"

"Prismatic conscience," Arithon agreed, still enraged. Too plainly, he could not temper the backlash set off by his loss of stability. Nor could he quell the riled suspicion that, like the skilled surgeon, the Sorcerer had lanced the latent pressure of his unconstrained talent deliberately. Cornered too deftly, he had to acknowledge the scope of his savage predicament. "The full range, from horror to exalted redemption."

"I thought so." Davien's smile turned wicked. "Oh, I thought so! My wild falcon, you have found flight. Now you must master the currents. Know this: each of the futures you see holds a driving thread of intent that is personal, and quite real. Those probabilities that are dim, you must defuse by withdrawing your stake in their outcome. Those that are bright, you must align and nurture. Choice will prevail as you focus. You will redefine the depth of your mastery. But to do so, you must constantly sharpen your self-honesty to discern. Each moment demands that you build on your strengths. You can no longer afford the false haven of hiding behind your shrinking weakness."

No course remained but to integrate the altered perceptions until their wild force could be reconciled.

Arithon leaned upon Davien's strength, eyes shut, his strained face white to the bone. "Just don't expect me to finish the meal," he said, taxed to desperate humor. "If I try, at this stage, no doubt I would slight your exemplary turn of kindness."

Late Spring 5670

Resolve

Still dazed by exhaustion, Sulfin Evend snapped out of a catnap at noon, disoriented by the sight of a ceiling adorned with vines in gilt paint. He stirred, encountered the bed, just adjacent, and Lysaer's opened eyes fixed upon him. The Lord Commander punched the overstuffed chair that embraced him and straightened his aching posture.

Dawn's pall of overcast had scudded away to unveil a sparkling morning. The clean linens threw off a dazzling glare, making the royal face propped on the pillows seem wrapped in a fine haze of light.

Braced to field autocratic resentment, Sulfin Evend met an expression of collected serenity that first stopped his breath, then forced him to scrape at his gritted eyes to mask his unguarded emotion.

"You try a man's nerves, unrelenting," he managed, the moment his tight throat released.

Lysaer's regard remained unabashed. "I won't ask. If my Crown Examiner at Avenor might wish to burn you for achieving my redemption, the rumors will only raise eyebrows."

"Hackles, more like," Sulfin Evend snapped back. "Don't try that again. The bit player won't stand the repeat performance."

No move rustled the pillows, but the smile that threatened suggested a self-conscious chagrin. Then, said with unflinching care, "The dead priest, Jeriayish. Did his fell work with the scrying entrap me?"

Sulfin Evend chose unsparing words in reply. "His filthy blood ritual permitted the groundwork. But he was no master of dark arts, or necromancy.

That kind do not show themselves, under daylight. The priest would have been no more than a link in a clandestine chain of suborned tools."

Lysaer closed his lids. "I feared as much, as I pondered the quandary while waiting for you to awake." The fine hands on the coverlet again wore the ring bearing Tysan's star-and-crown blazon. The seal was now paired with the diamond setting incised with the sunwheel of the Alliance. The glitter of gemstones stayed nailed in stilled light, as Lysaer pronounced with edged clarity, "Good men died in Daon Ramon. Their loss, at my order, has surely fueled someone's unscrupulous plotting." The burning eyes opened. "There won't be redress, until judgment is done."

"You can't dream you'll fight necromancy," Sulfin Evend gasped, shocked. "Do you know what I risked to achieve your release? We are lucky to be here, breathing and free! There are horrors abroad in this world that even the Fellowship Sorcerers handle with wariness. I would die before watching the price of such meddling. You have no concept to measure the evil you might raise through your blindside ideals and bullheaded ignorance."

"More than innocents have been thrown into jeopardy, drawn by the Light into slaughter." At rest on the pillows, Lysaer said, unequivocal, "I cannot stand down. Not since an invested acolyte was involved! The integrity of the Light can't be compromised."

Undercut by a horrid, gut-sucking fear, Sulfin Evend refused to give pause through the stir, as the Blessed Prince signaled his valet to serve sorely needed refreshment. "Fool! Challenge that, and you're baring your idiot neck to the knife! If your priests are corrupted, you will have to disown them! All their works are now suspect. You don't know, in your absence, how deeply their claws have been sunk into Tysan's crown council."

Shown no break in that regal, unwavering calm, Sulfin Evend unsheathed his temper. "Don't put on your airs, prince! You are no god, to call down the Spear of Dharkaron's vengeance on a cult whose foul webs have been spun for thousands of years under the cover of darkness."

Lysaer's response came brisk, through the clink of porcelain as the valet doled out honeyed tea. "You have known such corruption exists, before this?"

"Mercy upon me, I surely have not." Unthinking reflex let Sulfin Evend take the cup pressed into his rigid hand. "There are nightmares too vile. Madness lies on the black side of witchcraft. The wise talent steers well clear of that morass. Respect such restraint! There are fears you can't counter through mortal awareness. Lacking the discipline of initiate mage training, no unleashed emotion is harmless. The entrapment of active attention is real. The slip of one random thought, made unguarded, can invite the fell things that poison the mind."

"Is this your best counsel?" Lysaer said, bleak. "To tuck tail and hide without ever putting the question?"

"Yes." Sulfin Evend sipped at the scalding tea, shameless in his need to chase off the creeping, deep chill of alarm. "Abandon Avenor. Revoke your sanctioned connections at once. Buy your war host the arcane protection it lacks, and relocate to your reinforced stronghold at Etarra."

"Retreat without salvage?" Thin hands moved and locked, and now the pale jewels sparked to the simmer of outrage. "That's a brutal remedy, and a coward's expedience, to leave the botched brunt for others to bear."

"I did try to warn you," Sulfin Evend said, too weary to steer the discussion away from disaster. "Again and again, I begged you to consider a basic arcane defense." His stance had invoked Lysaer's wrath before this, despite every logical argument, that forged weapons could never eradicate sorcery, and troops sent to battle against invoked spellcraft could not survive without any shielding bulwark.

"I was badly influenced," Lysaer stated. Harrowed still by the winter's unconscionable string of defeats, he did not mask his face, or offer excuses to deny the horrific burden of full culpability.

Sulfin Evend lost his breath. The last thing he wished was a stripping confession. Still raw with rancor, he might strike out, or inflict a worse cruelty, given his liege's torn nerves and wretched state of convalescence. He gulped down more tea to constrain his tried patience. "Your Grace, I am earnest. You must seek protection. Walk softly and watch whom you bind as your ally. Erdane is a dangerous stew of old intrigues. I cautioned you once, and will say yet again. Beware of the factions who offer you gold without an apparent agenda."

"Such ones work for necromancers?" Even wrung by remorse, Lysaer's probing thrust stayed dispassionate. "Then why should such ill-starred, slinking creatures stand in support of the Light?"

Sulfin Evend shut his eyes, fighting lassitude. "They want what you want," he said with brute candor. "Break the Fellowship's compact, kill off the clan bloodlines, and eradicate the free practice of sorcery from Athera. Once that's done, initiate knowledge is sundered. Nobody's left with the masterful force to oppose what steps in through the breach."

Lysaer's response seemed oddly removed, as though his voice dimmed into distance. "What about the Koriathain?"

"The witches won't become the implacable enemy of such powers until the moment they've ceased being useful." Sulfin Evend slid his emptied cup on the side table. His fingers were shaking. The valet's bitter brew had done nothing at all to lift his clouding exhaustion. "As long as the order's active enmity ties up the Fellowship's hands, none of the black cults will touch them."

Lysaer's inquiry continued, a relentless assault that pummeled against flagging faculties. "Ath's adepts?"

"You know they won't practice outside of their hostels." Sulfin braced, prepared for rebuttal, since he had never spoken against Lysaer's entrenched belief that Ath's Brotherhood worked in league with Shadow.

Yet needling contention never arose. Lysaer lay quiet, if not actively hostile, at least choosing the threads of his arguments.

Chin propped on his fists, but resistant to the overpowering need to ease his numbed feet with a bolster, Sulfin Evend marshaled his strayed thoughts and qualified. "Some scholars suggest if this world falls to entropy, the Brotherhood will simply fade from Athera, much as the Paravian races have done since the Mistwraith encroached on the sunlight."

"My valet can undress you," Lysaer said, all at once crisply smiling. "Will you save trouble and grant him permission before you pass out in a heap?"

Caught with his head drooping, Sulfin Evend snatched up short. The room spun around him. Porcelain rattled as he jammed his arm on the table to salvage his sudden, swayed balance. "What have you done, prince!" But his slurred voice already affirmed the fact that the drink had masked a remedy potion. "I don't recall giving any man leave to dose me out on valerian."

"Sleep," murmured Lysaer. "You look pounded to pulp. The least I could do was to grant you relief from a duty too harsh for the asking. Let go and rest. The matter at hand can be left to wait until you've made a recovery. As well, my friend, we'll fare best by appearance if you play the one fallen sick."

Sulfin Evend awakened to someone's hand, urgently shaking his shoulder. The fragrance of expensive soap let him know he had not been returned to the field camp. His eyes felt stuck with horse glue, and the coverlets were stifling. He pushed off the valet's bothersome fingers, snapped a curse, and shoved erect in a nest of down pillows.

He was in Lysaer's bed. It was daylight. His sinews felt slackened to caramel, and every bone in his body seemed recast in lead. "Damn you for meddling," he said in gruff fury.

The Divine Prince sat in the stuffed chair by the bedside, immaculately dressed. Lace cuffs masked his wrists and shadowed his rings, and a sumptuous white doublet smothered everything else up to his clean-shaven chin. The impact was one of forceful, pale elegance, composed as a sword blade in ice. "The soporific you drank was too weak to lay you out for as long as you've rested."

"How long?" croaked Sulfin Evend, then swore with invention to learn he had slept the day and night through, and lost most of the following morning. "Why didn't somebody waken me?"

"Somebody has." Lysaer's prankish smile and arched eyebrows almost concealed the bruised shadows left by his ordeal. "You are *meant* to be ill. Why disturb the felicitous appearance?" Still seamlessly talking, he encouraged the valet, who, undaunted, bore in with a razor and basin. "The fibbing gets tiresome. I don't have your field captain's knack for singeing language, or your uncle Raiett's charmed gift for dissembling diversion."

"Raiett doesn't lie. He evades, that's his secret." Sulfin Evend shoved back his rat's tangle of dark hair, scowling to fend off the servant. "I don't care for charades. What's changed?"

Succinct, Lysaer stated, "I need you awake." His piercing assessment suggested far more, as he watched his Lord Commander seethe with clenched fists amid the rumpled billow of bedclothes. "Are we not under threat?"

Blue eyes locked with inimical steel gray, and Sulfin Evend attacked first. "Liege, you shouldn't be upright."

"Appearances are everything," Lysaer amended. "You're in that bed, sick, upon my direct orders. The Mayor of Erdane is due momentarily. He's expecting an audience. I suggest, for time's sake, that you let my valet do his work to make you presentable. Or not, of course. You may stay looking furious and degenerate, as you wish."

The accents of refined Hanshire breeding clashed with a phrase borrowed straight from the barracks. His hawk's profile livid, Sulfin Evend concluded, "I don't fancy another man's mincing hand, gripping cold steel at my throat."

"Well, I don't care for strewn lather spoiling my bed," Lysaer said with disarming delicacy. His nod summoned the valet. "You'd make a poor job. One look, and you'd notice. Your fingers aren't steady. Allow you the razor, you'd rip your own veins without someone's outside assistance."

Pinned as the valet raked back his loose hair and fingered his chin with light expertise, Sulfin Evend clamped his jaw in offended forbearance.

"I do realize, today, that I owe you everything," Lysaer stated point-blank.

No rage could withstand that aimed barb to the heart. Given the accolade of absolute trust, Sulfin Evend suffered himself to be handled. Combed, shaved, and tucked back like an invalid under perfumed sheets, he endured the ignominy as the Mayor of Erdane was ushered in by no less than the same callow page. Insult to injury, the rabbit-faced chamber steward also manned the anteroom door. Both had been restored to their posts, a folly too late to redress on the verge of a royal audience.

Already, Lord Mayor Helfin plowed in, a heavyset man who had married into his wealth. Curled hair, a clipped silver beard, and pouched features wearing a strawberry flush reflected his choleric temperament. His quilted velvet clanked with jeweled chains, a threat to the ornate furnishings. While the steward hopped after him, rescuing candlesticks, he encountered the sangfroid glimmer of Lysaer's state dress and diamonds.

Hot water crashed against glacial ice. Erdane's mayor took the padded chair the valet had set to receive him.

The Light's avatar, Prince Exalted of Avenor, inclined his head and ceded his gracious permission to speak.

The mayor's chest heaved. "I have received a letter in my daughter's hand, the first since her marriage that was not set under the seal of your regency secretary."

The Alliance commander looked on, unsurprised by the floundering pause. The magisterial elegance seated, coiled, in pearl silk, had a way of peeling even an honest man's nerves.

"She has fled Avenor?" Lysaer said, as though some sixth sense informed him. Habit sustained that colorless tone. Not the eyes, focused with the same, fearsome intensity last seen on a windswept night in Daon Ramon: when, from breaking news of a son's tragic death, the Divine Prince had been incited to close in and attack the small force defending the Master of Shadow.

The deployment had launched a disaster. Every man standing had been burned alive, with Sulfin Evend left as the last, living witness. Chilled where he lay, he watched the mayor's bluster lose force.

"For fear of her life, Ellaine's fled into hiding," he admitted at cringing length.

No move eased the tension, no whisper of lace issued from the man in the chair.

The mayor moistened dry lips.

Before he spoke further, Lysaer bore in, furious, his majesty unimpeachable. "Ellaine is my wedded wife, and the mother of the child who was the crown heir of Tysan. Tell me this. Who has dared threaten the Princess of Avenor in her own home, under the Light of my justice?"

The mayor flushed crimson. "Your own crown council, who also arranged and paid for her predecessor, Talith's assassination." While springing sweat matted his fur collar, he delivered the raw gist. "My daughter has seen documents, under Cerebeld's seal and signature, stating the name of the marksman who fired the crossbolt. Ellaine's testament, as proof, arrived in the pouch of our courier from Quarn. He rides routine post, and doesn't know where on his route the letter was slipped into his dispatches."

A detail had changed: illness, perhaps, slipped the mask of cool sovereignty. After an unremarked little silence, Lysaer's stopped breathing resumed. "Cerebeld?" he said, glacial.

Lord Mayor Helfin wisely said nothing.

One royal palm turned. The fingers snapped, causing the bystanding servants to startle. "I'll have your state scribe draw up the indictment. Now!" cracked the living voice of Divine Light. "Be very sure of your evidence, my Lord Mayor. A sentence of treason does not carry an appeal. Upon your daughter's unimpeachable word, I will expose the truth. The trial will be public. The party responsible will be arraigned as a criminal. He and all who have served as collaborators will be put to death under the law. You will tell my commanding officer immediately, and say where my wife has sought shelter."

"Her writing doesn't mention her whereabouts," the Lord Mayor said, panicked. More than Avenor's commander of armies had moved him to blurt out, appalled, "My Blessed Prince, you didn't know!"

"That my vested high priest has sanctioned a murder?" Lysaer's rebuke stung like balefire. "Do you think so little of the cause that I ask men to die for? I am no tool of politics, no weapon of factions that kill innocents in clandestine secrecy. Where is my wife, Princess Ellaine?"

Afraid, the Lord Mayor shook in his seat. "She hasn't told anyone her location. Her letter implied her earnest belief that your son also died by design. Blessed lord, I beg you, forgive her! How could the princess have known that your orders were not behind the criminal acts of your high council officers?"

Through a searing, drawn moment, flames crackled in the hearth. Dumb wind rattled the casements. Then Lysaer said, "I will read Ellaine's letter."

The Lord Mayor of Erdane fumbled into his doublet. The creased sheet he surrendered had been made from pulped rags, unbleached for workaday commerce. The ragged, left edge might have been torn from some wayside inn's string-bound ledger.

Lysaer settled the document in his lap, to a flashfire glitter of rings. "Your amazement demeans all that is wholesome," he responded, his voice chill as the gleam on a sword blade. "As of this moment, every household resource you have has been requisitioned by the Light. My officers will spend every coin in your coffers to secure the life of your daughter, who is my princess. She is not your prestige. Nor is she my callous possession, to be discussed like a string of dropped pearls." The rebuke gathered force, shame distilled to bleak venom. "No mercy! Those who have threatened her may ask for no quarter, whether or not she is brought home unharmed." Lysaer ended the audience. "My Lord Mayor Helfin, you have leave to go."

Laid raw, the fat townsman slammed to his feet. He stamped out in a rage that would empty his treasury, if only to protest the ruthless slur just dealt to his family pride.

As the door banged shut with hammering force, Sulfin Evend shoved straight, to applaud. Lysaer's statecraft was masterful. This superb play would replenish the coffers left emptied since Daon Ramon Barrens.

Yet Lysaer's expostulation cut across his commander's sardonic praise. "Leave!" The word smashed the composure of his hovering chamber servant. He jumped, with the page boy hard at his heels. The valet hesitated, and found himself curtly dismissed by a summary gesture. The man went, contrite. In the emptied, cold room, light gleamed on blond hair: the Exalted Prince had tipped his head to rest against the high back of his chair.

Sulfin Evend was left to try tacit address. "My liege?"

The imperious face turned. Eyes wide, pupils distended with vacuous shock, Lysaer's unseeing gaze encompassed the ranking retainer his royal orders had installed in the bed.

He had no words in him, to dismiss this last witness, no strength left, to constrain his deep horror. He crumpled, undone by his heartsore grief. His forehead rested upon his closed fist, while the tears welled and spilled, soaking the fine, thread lace of his sleeve and spoiling priceless white velvet.

"She had your love," Sulfin Evend said, his gravel-rough pity subdued.

"My joy," Lysaer gasped. "All my joy. Ended, I find, by an ambitious animal who had her dispatched by a thug with a quarrel." Not Ellaine: his deceased *Talith* had moved him to agony. Pushed straight, rings trembling, he collected himself and considered the rest of his family. "What have I created under the sun, that corruption has twisted into a force that would slaughter a woman and child?"

"Ambition serves power," Sulfin Evend said, harsh. The lives burned to cinders in Daon Ramon Barrens *even still* kept him haunted beyond equanimity. "You were never Ath's sword, to see into small minds."

"I will have to be, now." Lysaer's blue eyes stayed direct, still wide-open to turbulent grief, and a revulsion that stopped thought to witness.

Sulfin Evend threw off the bedclothes. Naked, he strode over the rug, wrenched open the armoire, but found only rows of white-satin sleeves, and marmalade silk, cut for banquets.

"I will have my weapons and armor returned." He stood planted, uncaring that he had not a stitch of cloth on him. "This foolish pretense is over. I am not sick, and you are not god sent, and your Talith was surely cut dead by a faction whose backing is rooted in necromancy. The cultists are secretive. They are powerful enemies. You have no trained knowledge, and less overt power, to withstand their black spells and vile practice. I have not just risked my life, or set my spirit in jeopardy, to watch you destroy all you have built for a woman who's seventeen years in the grave. You must not return to Avenor! On my sword, if you try, I shall stop you."

Lysaer was too depleted to rise from the chair. Yet the stare he returned raked with scouring contempt. "How dare you imply I should run for your sake."

"For all our sakes," Sulfin Evend said, wild. "Now, what have you done with my clothing?"

"You don't have the requisite power to stop me, with your breeches and sword, or without them!" Rushed, Lysaer appended, "I am not ungrateful. I trust you to leave, if you fear your life's compromised. Your possessions are there, in that chest. You may dress and take arms at will. Shall I date and sign your discharge today? Or will you deign to accompany my retinue, and maintain your post through the journey I'll make, by way of the south road, to Hanshire?"

Which insufferable dismissal at last insulted Sulfin Evend's intelligence. "You can't haze my nerve, that way."

Violent as a winter-lean wolf, he flung open the clothes chest, but found he could not stop listening. The proposal to take the roundabout route to Avenor at least showed a shred of good sense. The strongbox, as well, was sequestered and safe. The thoughtful valet had left that dread charge discreetly wrapped in his field cloak.

All brisk business, the Lord Commander snatched up his breeches. "You'll need Hanshire's backing if you're set to pursue this. Also, the records found in the sealed vault underneath of Erdane's library. If the mayor is convinced to make free with those, he'll do so at sword point, and not one bit for the love of his missing daughter."

Gratitude restored the hint of a smile before Lysaer spoke, without adamancy. "I must go back. A conspiracy has tainted my council at Avenor. Far more than my wife and child have been haplessly set in harm's way. I created this government! Its soundness of principle is my avocation. As Tysan's regent, the challenge is mine, to restore a just rule. I will not rest, nor will your sword, until this rot has been exposed and cut out."

"Then you had best pray that Dharkaron Avenger will forgive your rank arrogance and drive his Chariot at your right hand. Naught else can save you." Sulfin Evend's dark head vanished in twill, then reappeared, recent grooming undone. He hooked up his mail to a jangle of rings. "You won't have my sword right away, mercy on you." His glare lost no edge as he ducked to slither the field armor over his shoulders. "I'll have to do my sweet best to advise, then rejoin you by galley after the ice breaks."

"This is not resignation." Lysaer smiled then, clean sunlight on snow. If his eyes shone too bright, the embarrassment escaped notice.

Sulfin Evend sat, busy with hose, boots, and spurs. "Help me find grace! I ought to be drunk, to be acting so feckless. I have an errand I have to run first. The bone knife that enslaved you must be destroyed."

Lysaer need say nothing. His point had been won. Wrung limp, he regarded his depleted hands and the letter caged lightly between them.

Sulfin Evend stood up. As he snatched in nettled haste for his baldric, his sideward glance settled and sharpened. He moved with dispatch after that, hung his scabbard, and wrapped up his discourse forthwith. "Liege, I'll be calling your servants to set you in bed. Then I'm making rounds of my war camp. After two days, I expect to find shambles. Once my officers have orders, I'm taking the best horse in your father-in-law's stables. Don't ask where I'm bound. Your vaunted principles assuredly won't stand it. If I come back unscathed, and if you're not waiting in state at Hanshire with every fit company we have at your back, then yes. By all means. Give my written discharge into the hands of my family."

Dressed and fully armed, the Alliance commander bowed before his liege's chair. "Guard yourself well," he murmured in parting.

Silence answered. Lysaer had passed beyond conscious awareness. The discovery yielded a poisoned advantage: a sane intervention was possible, now. Act upon spurious opportunity, and Sulfin Evend might strip the false tissue of the divine cause. He might break the course of his sovereign's willed future, through informed mercy and the brute force of his vested command.

Lysaer slouched in the huge brocade chair. His senseless hands lay loose in his lap, tucked over the desperate words of a wife he had played as a painted game piece. Yet the hardness that drove every inhumane choice was not written into the man. Careworn to exhaustion, exposed in the artless sleep of an all-too-human fallibility, the magisterial presence that had stood off Erdane's mayor should have seemed reduced to its thread of mortality. Instead, the brazen commitment just spoken lost its overtone of brash arrogance.

The raw courage behind Lysaer's resolve caught Sulfin Evend like a fist at the throat.

"Mercy on you," he whispered, and spun on his heel. Too proud, too heart-torn to break trust with such naked vulnerability, the Alliance Lord Commander retrieved the wrapped strongbox and fled headlong from the room.

Too late: two sworn oaths and the contrary grain of his honesty pursued him beyond that closed door. Peace had been destroyed by the conflict of loyalties now branded into his skin.

Late Spring—Summer 5670

By Land and by Sea

While dark cultists regroup from their surprise setback, and a secretive liegeman rides out of Erdane, Sethvir of the Fellowship faces dilemma: with no available help from the field, and no remedy for his invalid weakness, the necromancers who bid to suborn Lysaer's rule might yet rip the compact apart at one stroke...

Beating to weather against the stiff winds that presage the turn of the season, Feylind, who captains the merchant brig *Evenstar*, drives her vessel around the cliffs at Sanpashir, then wears ship, checks her yards, and plows a white streamer of wake toward her home port of Innish...

Trail-weary and silted with summer's thick dust, a lone clansman breasts the hills of Caith-al-Caen; just past summer's eve, he crosses the ancient Paravian way, and slips into Halwythwood, bearing the first confirmed news from the north concerning the Prince of Rathain...

Mathiell Gate - Inner Citadel - Alestron

III. Citadel

While storm followed tempest, and incessant rain lashed the western king-doms to deluge and mud, the lands east of the Storlain Mountains enjoyed a golden, mild summer. The light breezes pranked and whispered through the forested wilds of Atwood. Gusts skimmed through the fringe of the East Halla farmsteads, and riffled like billowing silk through the grain fields that bordered the coastal lowlands. The trade roads were dry, and forage was plentiful, which caused the Mad Prophet a cracking irritation.

Since Luhaine's deliverance from Shipsport's magistrate, his temper was not resigned. Denied the sharpened, fit edge of his talent by his forced re-gime of loose living, Dakar suffered a tipsy journey on foot, plagued by pounding hangovers and hay fever. This morning, with the heat a feverish blanket around him, his tight skull was played like hammer and tongs by tortuous fits of sneezing.

The easy living left Fionn Areth too much time for his badgering ques-tions. "I thought you said East Halla raised mercenaries, not crops," the young man ran on. "I've seen no army. Only cud-chewing cattle, defended by nothing but grasshoppers."

"So you're meant to think." Dakar pressed a handkerchief to his livid nose. "Look again. That's not a byre, and those aren't windmills, and for the sweet tits Ath puts on a virgin, keep your hat on your head, and your foolish hand off your sword hilt!"

Fionn Areth grinned, his brown cheek flecked with the light that scat-tered through his straw hat's brim. "We'll be spitted like geese at a field shoot?" He had noticed the arrow slits; the looped apertures for crossbows;

then the sinister fact that, beneath timber sheathing, the croft buildings were stone, built two spans thick and recessed with galleries for arbalists.

"The s'Brydion have a dagger set into their fists when the midwife cuts the cord at their birthing. They get dandled by fathers who wear mail shirts to bed, and are blood-suckled on the arts of warfare." Dakar rolled red eyes sideward. "You'll see soon enough. There's the citadel."

"Where?" Fionn Areth craned over the shoulder-high corn, tasseled and droning with insects.

"There." Dakar pointed. "Don't act cocky. The lookout's seen you. He'll have counted that blade at your belt, first of all. At the gate, they'll already know the coin worth of your buckles and buttons."

A winkle of light flared through the sea haze, banked above the horizon.

Fionn Areth stared, enchanted. A moment's search, and he made out the outline, gray overlaid on a palette of slate: the high teeth of stone battlements, seemingly cast adrift above the shimmering scarf of the barley fields. "The watch surveys the road, do you say? Just how, in that steam bath of mist?"

"Are you simple?" Dakar honked noisily, veiled in the dust thrown up by couriers and drays returning unladen from market. "We've been under their eye from those windmills, since dawn. The signals are passed on with mirrors."

Footsore from the iron-hard ruts, Fionn Areth pressed on toward the stronghold of the Duke of Alestron, whose clan family, Arithon s'Ffalenn had once said, were *'warmongering lions who judge a man first by his armament.'*

They reached the walled citadel in the slatted shadows of late afternoon. Perched on its promontory above the sea, the massive, tiered bastion of Alestron reared up like a cliff face, its flint stone notched with arrow slits, and its mortar glittering with embedded glass. From the soot shade under the outer gate, beneath the teeth of its massive twin portcullis, a man would be flattened by the inbound traffic before he could count even half of the murder holes.

"I feel like a seamstress's pincushion, already," Fionn Areth murmured in awe. Shown what the duke's men considered a guard's standard issue of weaponry, he added, chilled, "Or I should have said, collops and mince. Do these folk have any enemies left alive with the warm bollocks to breed offspring?"

"If they didn't, they'd thrash up some more in a heartbeat," Dakar said. "They're wont to pick fights like starved wolves dumped fighting mad into a cur pack."

For him, the steep, switched-back road past the gate carried too many damnable memories. The last time he had called on the lord of Alestron, he had come on an errand for Sethvir, with Arithon of Rathain made the butt of a personal plot laid as a double cross. Even after twenty-six years, Dakar winced at the outcome. S'Ffalenn cunning had defanged his set trap. Without intervention from a Fellowship Sorcerer, Dakar would have seen himself spitted on the venom of s'Brydion vindictiveness.

Today, escorting Arithon's shapechanged double, he sweated by turns, clammy dread superseded by his eagerness to see Fionn Areth receive his long-overdue comeuppance.

"They don't like besiegers, I see that much," the young man allowed. Just as anxious to give the spellbinder his brisk quittance, he turned his admiring regard to the gate barracks, and the brick bailey just visible through the portal, where the guard checked arms for the watch change at sundown. "Where should I go to sign with the field troops who fight for the Alliance of Light?"

"A trained swordsman like you? March with the foot ranks?" Dakar's sidelong glance showed contempt.

Fionn Areth drew himself up, his pleased surprise at the compliment stifled behind a thick scowl. "The day sergeant could have told me," he insisted, dodging a wine tun rolled by a boy in a stained-leather brigandine, "where I should go to sign on the rolls as an officer."

Dakar tucked a strategic cough behind his fist. "They would not," he said, eyes watering from stifled laughter. "This is Alestron. Charter law rules here, and promotions to rank go by merit. However," he said, snatching his companion's sleeve, before he ducked back toward the barracks, "if you wish to be seen as more than a green recruit, you could come along to the upper citadel. I might present you in person to the reigning s'Brydion duke."

Fionn Areth stopped short, almost run down by a wagon filled with crates of squabbling chickens. Oblivious to the carter's oaths and the blizzard of down dusting over his hat, he said, "No! You're damned to the dark as a minion of Shadow! In such company as yours, I'd likely be lopped into mincemeat the moment you opened your mouth!"

"You think so?" Dakar's grin widened. "More likely, my friend, I'd be cut dead for standing next to your face. You're so blissed at the prospect of killing for glory, you've forgotten whose features you're wearing?"

Fionn Areth flushed. "Well, maybe I'm thinking I'd be better off if somebody else introduced me. Your name's too well known, for a certainty."

"By all means," the Mad Prophet mocked. "You can try. But without my credentials, I'll tell you now, you won't pass the gate to the inner citadel."

"And you can?" Fionn Areth marched onward. "Show me a marvel I can believe, like a chick from an egg-hatching donkey!"

"I'm the apprentice spellbinder to a Sorcerer. Charter law answers to crown justice, and, grasslands idiot, no offense to your ignorance, crown justice upholds the compact *as granted* by the grace of the Fellowship of Seven." Smug as a swindler, Dakar sidled into an alley with a steep, twisting stair, without pause to see if his mark followed. "The s'Brydion will not only receive me, they'll provide board and bed, and a bath with a willing maidservant."

Fionn Areth raised his eyebrows, prepared to retort. But Dakar's wheezing seemed cruelty enough, as the ascent robbed him of breath for dignified speech.

At the top, disgorged on a road like a cliff rim, they passed through another wall, and another gate, this one more heavily guarded. Here, a plank bridge spanned a vertical ditch, with keep towers on either side. The streets beyond snaked up the promontory, overhung by slotted-wood hidings. These had murder holes also. The unwary traffic moved underneath, drowned in a blue gulf of shade. Footmen and carriages, horsemen and drays breasted the seething press. Squeezed into the slot of another close, Fionn Areth realized the craft shops and houses were built chockablock, their fortified facings pierced with notches for bowmen.

"S'Brydion don't like besiegers," Dakar agreed, puffing to recoup his wind where a matron's herb pots soaked up a thin slice of sun.

Upward again, they passed the rock springs and the cisterns; then the chopped turf of the tiltyards; another barracks and armory, attached to a smithy. The heat wafted through the crossbuck door smelled of charcoal, and the clangor of hammers was deafening. Fionn Areth stepped, crackling, over curled shavings, whisked on the breeze from the cooper's shacks; dodged a boy rolling rims to the wheelwright's. Higher, three muddy children tugged a squealing pig on a string, past a fat woman who scolded. Pigeons flew in flurries of slate wings, and gulls perched, white, on the cornices. They passed the brickmaker's kilns, and the steaming vats where the renderers stirred fat to make yellow soap, and a sweating girl boiling fish glue. Dakar puffed a complaint that his chest would split, and asked for a stop at a wineshop.

"Only one glass," he promised. "It's our chance to take in the gossip."

Fionn Areth sat in a dimmed corner, his hat brim pulled low, while a man who made rivets flirted with the barmaid, and others with sword scars shot dice. In the streets, he had noticed that most men bore the marks of campaigns; or else the s'Brydion sergeants taught their recruits with sharpened weapons.

"This whole town's a war camp," he murmured to Dakar, as they paid up to leave.

The comment earned him a mooncalf glance. "It's a wasp's nest," Dakar amended, then belched into his hand. "I thought you would feel quite at home here?"

They climbed again, past dormered houses, then another deep ditch, and a wall notched with razor-toothed barbicans. The gatehouse held embrasures for ballistas, and a sand arena contained the full-scale array of a field camp. Horsemen were at practice, and other men, stripped, were perfecting the aim on a trebuchet.

"You will notice, there's been no standing timber for five leagues," said Dakar. "If an attacking host wishes to assault with siege weapons, it must import the timber, then cross that naked valley by ox carriage. Plenty of time for that monster, there, to hammer such toys into matchsticks." He finished with wine-scented gravity. "You don't want the s'Brydion clan for your enemies."

Higher, they climbed, past stables and commons, while the swooping rooks wheeled in the salty gusts whisked off the channel inlet. They sheltered in a doorway as an armed troop clattered by, drilled to a cutting edge of obedience. The captain who led them had eyes like his steel, sharpened and ruthlessly wary.

"There, just ahead." The Mad Prophet panted. His wave encompassed two high towers, and a slit in between, which glowered down over a cleft like a quarry. The gulf was spanned by a thin, swaying bridge suspended on cables and forged chain. "That's the Wyntock Gate to the inner citadel. Here's where the war host that sacked the royal seat at Tirans was broken, then crushed, in the uprising over five hundred years ago. They say the ditch, there, ran knee deep in blood at low tide, with the heaped fallen seething with ravens and vultures." Overhead, there were such birds, now, circling high on the air currents. Dakar mopped back his screwed hair and shoved off toward the bridge. "They bring up dray teams and supply wagons by winch from the sea gate, and now, the defenses get serious."

The approach took them through another set of twinned keeps, pierced by a narrow, cobblestone ramp, pitched too steep for a cart. Planks had been laid, ribbed with nailed strips. The wood had been gouged into slivers by horses shod with screwed caulks.

"In war, they will unshackle the span of the bridge, then take up the planks and sluice down this causeway with grease," Dakar said. "Foot troops can't pass then. See those embrasures? That's where the archers lie back and slaughter each wave of attackers at leisure."

"They don't advance under frameworks and hides?" Fionn Areth asked, breathless.

"They try, and they burn like a torch." Dakar added grimly, "Look up."

Overhead lay a spider work track of forged metal, where an iron cart bearing boiling oil, or pitch-soaked batts could be dumped to scorch any force pressed against the meshed gate.

At the top, stopped by hard men with bared steel, Dakar gave his name. "He's with me." A jerk of his chin set the sentries' cold glance sweeping over Fionn Areth. "My surety," the Mad Prophet informed them, then said, "We're expected. If you don't wish to trouble the duke or his brothers, Vhandon or Talvish can speak for us."

The man in charge grinned, his helm polished over the scratches of veteran service. "Brave man, you say my lord's family knows you? Better pray, if they don't. The two captains you mentioned will vouchsafe your identity, or else you'll soon be greeting the rooks who clip the dead eyes from your carcass." He surveyed them again, lingering over Fionn Areth's plain sword and blunt hands. "Go across. Since I don't know your faces, expect that you're going to be challenged."

The watch officer stepped back. High overhead, someone yelled, "It's a maybe?"

The sentry nodded. Another man must have dispatched a signal, for torchlight winked in smart reply from a mirror in the far keep.

Past the narrows of the Wyntock Gate, goatherd and prophet stepped onto the bridge, whose gouged planks heaved under their load like sea rollers. The steel links of the chain pinched a swatch of snagged tail hair.

"They can't cross a horse here!" Fionn Areth protested, clenched sick by the irregular, bucking sway and the creak of taut cordage beneath him.

"They do," Dakar rebutted. "Specialized light cavalry and stronghold couriers, the animals are ridden or led over one at a time." He paused, queasy, as a raven soared down the ribbon of shade cast by the span underneath them. "The animals are trained as sucklings beside their dams. Legend holds the original mares were handpicked, starved for water, then lured over to drink under a blindfold. You don't," he finished, "presume the impossible with s'Brydion. Foes who have tend to rue the experience."

Several dizzy steps later, clued by the lack of disparaging comment, the Mad Prophet appended, "If you're going to be sick, don't try running back. They'll have a spanned crossbow sighting you from behind, and an archer apiece, stationed in the towers ahead of us. Longbowmen ready to skewer your heart, and mine, if the first marksman happens to miss."

Fionn Areth swallowed. He disliked windy heights. "They're that good?"

"Better." Dakar mopped his brow in relief as they neared the pair of squat keeps, each housing the massive drums for the windlasses, which required twenty stout men to turn. They set foot at last upon secure stone, buffeted by the freshening wind, and surrounded by darting cliff swallows. The upper fortress reared up beyond, with the eyrie vantage of more drum towers and lookout points, each with streaming banners painted in sun against the clear, lapis zenith.

"The Mathiell Gate," Dakar stated. Before the forged grille, six sentries in scarlet-blazoned surcoats stood ground with mailed fists and poised halberds. "It's a corruption of the Paravian, *mon-thiellen*, for 'sky spires.'"

More guardsmen in plain armor lurked in the sallyport, armed to the teeth, and with no trace of slackness about them. Two others, clad in stud brigandines, advanced to issue the challenge.

Dakar stated his name, then used Luhaine's, concerning an issue of sanctuary. He added much more in Paravian, several times stating Prince Arithon's formal title of Teir's'Ffalenn.

"You don't match the description," the gate captain snapped, while his men-at-arms responded to doubt with instantaneously lowered weapons. "The Mad Prophet is said to have ruddy coloring. Your pelt looks dyed, and a poor job at that."

Dakar sighed over the silver roots of the hair grown in since his ordeal at Rockfell. "That's the price of my service to a Fellowship Sorcerer. Would an imposter try such stupidity?"

The sentry's sharp glance flickered to his companion. "Hat off, you!" he rapped with impatience.

Fionn Areth obliged without turning his head, still mollified by the view. The massive, lower fortress lay spread out below, clutched like a bezel around the ducal council hall, with its craft shops and gabled houses a jumble of lead roofs and slate, descending in steps to the valley. Beneath the chain bridge, the first combers swirled in scallops of green, flooding in from the tidal rip in the estuary. At the periphery, the double take of chagrined alarm passed unseen, as the gate sentry noted black hair and green eyes, then the sharp-angled set of his features.

"Dharkaron's glory!" the watch captain gasped, low-voiced. "Here I thought you'd brought me a yokel." He wheeled, cracked an order to the halberdiers, then slipped through the grille and bolted uptown at a jangling sprint.

Dakar, smiling, murmured a laconic phrase to the man who remained.

The gate sentry now stood rigidly smart, and answered with punctilious deference. "Someone's already fetched Vhandon and Talvish. Naturally, now, they'll serve as your escort. The wait's just a courtesy. Our watch officer will have gone on ahead to inform the duke of your arrival."

The herdboy from Araethura overheard this, impressed. Faced forward, he jammed on his straw hat, while Dakar touched an arm to forestall an untoward exclamation. "Patience. We'll be warmly welcomed."

As the grasslands-bred hothead this once minded decency, the Mad Prophet stifled his pique. The problem with bear-baiting Arithon's double: the artless creature provided no sport.

The recent arrivals were closely observed from an overhead vantage in the right gate tower. Two heads bent close to peer from an embrasure, one close-cropped and gray, and the other flaxen. Granite strength set in counterweight contrast to a dancer's mercurial quickness, the ill-matched pair of retainers surveyed the two men held up at the bridgehead.

"Merciful death! Did you look at that hat!" Vhandon burst out in amazement. Normally the more restrained of the two, he lapsed back into thoughtful silence.

"Yon's not himself," Talvish agreed. His narrow features hinted at laughter, while his clever fingers danced a tattoo against the battered stone coping.

"The stance is all wrong. That sword's not Alithiel. What I see is a flat-footed bumpkin who's maybe experienced at skipping through cow clods?"

"The rescued double," Vhandon surmised. Stolid frame planted, arms crossed, he was frowning, soot eyebrows shading creased sockets. He resumed in the rural drawl of East Halla, "If the bait from the Koriani trap's been brought here, then where under the Fatemaster's almighty eye is his royal Grace of Rathain?"

Talvish grinned like a weasel. "Shall we go down and find out?"

For answer, Vhandon poked his spike helm through the siege shutter. "Pass them! They're known to us."

The gate sentry detaining the arrivals waved back, and Dakar, glancing up, shouted a pleased phrase in Paravian.

"Tal, damn you, wait! Stop and listen to this!" Vhandon's blunt grip trapped his fellow's wrist, halting the rush for the stairwell. "The Mad Prophet's brought us a parcel of joy! The child's a goatherd who believes all the mummery, that Duke Bransian's allied with the Light."

"You say?" The taller blond chuckled with rapacious delight, then cracked his knuckles to limber his sword hand. "My beer coin says the duke's brothers will spit him."

Vhandon's frown vanished. "And mine says, Bransian will get his lambasting blade in before them."

"Ath!" Talvish plunged for the landing, snorting back laughter. "The duke might, at that. It's a squeaking tight call."

A fleeting glance was exchanged in the dark, as side by side, the retainers who were life-pledged to serve Arithon descended to wring the Mad Prophet for news.

Whisked at brisk speed through the shaded, tight streets of Alestron's inner citadel, with the two men-at-arms padding like predators after him, Fionn Areth was shown through an iron-strapped door, into the bowels of a drumkeep.

"Up there," said the blond, whose leopard's glance absorbed everything, and whose narrow lips did not smile.

The sturdy partner with the reticent face held his stance.

Parted from Dakar, assigned to these veterans, Fionn Areth stifled his questions. He shoved back his straw hat and set about climbing stairs.

The swordsmen trod after him, matched. The feat should not have been possible, the breathless goatherd thought sourly. Their differing frames should not have been able to stride in such seamless tandem. Distempered by the time he was granted a guest chamber, Fionn Areth closed the door on his disconcerting armed escort. Faced about, he bumped into a liveried page, sent to help with his bath and his dress.

"No." Flushed scarlet, Fionn Areth jerked his thumb toward the doorway. His scowl would have credited the Prince of Rathain, as he dispatched the fellow outside.

The room had no rug, no tapestries, no ornaments. A bronze-bound clothes chest sat beside a low table bearing a basin, and a close stool, shoved underneath. The bedcovers were linen and beautifully woven, with a weapon rack waiting at hand's reach. The bronze tub had massive, lion ring handles, and was already filled and steaming. Fionn Areth stripped and washed, pausing a moment to admire the towels. Hair dripping, lips pursed in a tuneless whistle, he hooked up his grimed hose to wipe down his baldric and scabbard.

Still naked, hands busy, he heard the door gently open. He wheeled, but found no one there: only a clean pair of boots and a pile of folded clothing.

Sword in hand, he advanced. His nonchalance frayed into a desperate silence as he surveyed the offering he was expected to wear.

The garments themselves were no less than royal. Fionn Areth fingered the silk shirt, nipped and darted with a gentleman's cords and eyelets, and finished with silver-stamped studs. The matching hose were too narrow and short. The emerald doublet was exquisite, but left him terrified the rich velvet would fingerprint if he touched it. Worse, it fastened over the left shoulder with buttons and cord, adorned by a black sash braided with silver, then a belt, and a studded baldric whose fastening required a bewildering set of chased buckles.

Fionn Areth dropped the shirt, his calluses catching on satin facing and sleeve ribbons. The boots were too small. Knuckles pressed to his temples to forestall a headache, he stopped trying to number the rows of frogged silver buttons.

He had been ten times a fool to have done away with the servant.

"Pox on the finicky habits of greatfolk!" Wiping damp hands on his shivering flanks, he assaulted the problem, aware he was going to be late.

By the end, Fionn Areth faced the racking decision of whether to leave his blade behind on the bed. The scabbard provided was too narrow and long. Presented before a duke who loved war, he was going to make a bungling impression bearing a weapon that banged at his ankles. Bothered to curses, the Araethurian hiked up the hose, gave a rankled jerk on the doublet, then buckled on his sweat-stained baldric and minced toward the door.

His testy jerk flung open the panel. On the other side, experienced faces impassive, were the two men-at-arms appointed to stand as his formal guard.

"Please follow," said the lean one with overdone elegance. He spun on his heel and plunged toward the stair, doubled over with suspect sneezes.

Fionn Areth regarded the grim-faced henchman who, politely, intended to follow. "I won't stand being mocked," he snapped under his breath.

The older man looked him once, up and down. His pale eyes flickered over the disaster of snarled cords, mishooked eyelets, and crumpled sash, dragged askew by the blotched leather harness, which hung the dead-serious set of the sword. "Of course not, stripling. A pity we're late. You might have sent Talvish for a doublet that fit, not to mention a suitable scabbard."

Flushed, Fionn Areth dug in his heels. But the fellow's mailed fist clapped down on his shoulder with uncompromising camaraderie. "On you go. The cooks here are war-trained, and apt to pitch fits if the duke's honored guest doesn't show at the banquet."

The feast took place in a vaulted hall, located above a gallery with bare floors, evidently used for sword training. Twilight was falling. Led in from the gently darkening streets, pricked by the first flare of watch lanterns—that, by Alestron's immutable custom, would be snuffed by full dark, to preserve the night sight of the lookout—Fionn Areth was shown through an oak-beamed entry. He stumbled, wide-eyed, past walls arrayed with collected blade weaponry. Hustled upstairs, he was propelled by Talvish's firm hand into a dazzle of candleflame. There, he paused blinking, while the ongoing conversation tailed off and stopped, and the strapped door boomed shut behind him. As his sight read-justed, his panicked glance showed that his honor guard had pulled back. Iso-lated in front of Alestron's best blood, Fionn Areth squared his shoulders and pulled himself straight, hitched short by the treacherous trunk hose. The dan-dyish garment was inches too short and threatened to skim off his hips.

Since a courtesy bow would invite a disaster, the Araethurian made the best of the awkwardness. He dipped his chin in salute toward the glittering persons before him.

"Daelion's bollocks!" a deep voice said, awed. "Dakar! What have you brought us?"

"A masterworked piece of Koriani spellcraft." The Mad Prophet was already wedged in a stuffed chair, within easy reach of a carafe. A goblet of wine rested on his crossed knee. "The young man was shapechanged to match the Master of Shadow as the bait for a plot that was foiled. May I present to your lordship and brothers, Fionn Areth, lately from Araethura?"

"He doesn't fill Arithon's boots, that's for certain," someone else quipped from the sidelines.

Fionn Areth assayed an ungainly step forward, creaking in the tight boots. His sight had adjusted. Before him, broad as a shambling bear and seated backward astride an oak chair, the imposing fellow in front had to be the reigning Duke of Alestron. He wore no jewels. The only costly glitter upon him was the high polish of chain mail, worn under the faded scarlet and gold of an old-fashioned heraldic surcoat. A beard that, in youth, had flamed like a lion's, had grizzled to iron gray. He had eyes like steel filings, a face of lined leather, and the bastard sword cocked back at his heels could have spitted a yearling calf. "Guest welcome, young man," his deep voice resumed, "from the s'Brydion of Alestron."

The duke's bulk was shadowed by two more gray-eyed men. Large-boned, and wearing their piebald hair in a clan braid, by stance and expression, they seemed alike as two wolves culled from the same litter.

"My brothers, Keldmar and Parrien," said the duke, his arms folded over the back of the chair and his avid gaze still fixed on the Koriani's made double. "My mother's sister's son, Sevrand, the heir next in line for the title."

The successor who nodded, beer tankard in hand, was a broad-shouldered, tawny-haired giant, also armed. He lounged by the window seat, propped on an arm strapped with bracers, a targe and a shortsword slung on his back.

The duke inclined his head to the left. "There stands my last brother, Mearn."

Youngest, not yet gray at the temples, the sibling just named proved to be a whip-slender version of the rest. His preferred taste embraced a rapier, but disdained the encumbrance of armor. His narrow wrists were encircled with lace, and his taut, balanced body wore tailored style, tastefully set rubies, and a doublet trimmed with gold ribbon.

Exposed before that spare, pleated elegance, and surrounded by men who wore blades like jewelery, Fionn Areth felt coarse as an unfired brick. He swallowed, then ventured through the expectant stillness, "I am honored to be here, your lordships."

Duke Bransian's eyebrows lifted a fraction. Steel-clad knuckles pressed to his shut lips, he clashed a quelling fist on his chair, overriding Keldmar's and Parrien's simultaneous bid to offer rejoinder. "The women will be joining us for the meal, along with the rest of the household." The duke finally smiled. "Meanwhile, we were pressing Dakar for news. Be welcome and join us, and make free to say how we might make an honored friend comfortable."

"There is nothing I require," Fionn Areth declared stiffly. After his host's crisp, clanborn accents, the twang of his Araethurian origins spun drawled echoes to the farthest corner of the room.

"Nothing?" Mearn advanced, to a light-footed rustle of lawn. "But then, you shall entertain us."

"The goats didn't teach him to make conversation," Parrien said. He pulled his dagger, balanced the tip of the blade on his thumb, and set the steel spinning with a deft flick of his forefinger. "Or did they?"

His seeming twin, Keldmar, laughed into the breach. "Words, is it? That's mockery, man. What use has this fighting cock got for hot air? That's a nice enough sword, despite the gross scabbard." Disturbing gray eyes bored into the guest. "Is that blade sharp, child?"

Fast as echo, Parrien launched a rejoinder. "Never mind sharp! Can he use it?"

Keldmar considered. "Maybe. But I'll stake you my next turn on watch that Sevrand can best the young rooster, even sunk in his cups."

"That's lame!" Mearn cut in. "Sevrand's no contest!" At close quarters, now, he paced round the victim, then saw fit to amend his assessment. "Except for the boots. That could even the match. But is that a sufficient handicap, do you think, to the beer Sevrand's swilled since the watch bell?"

"No such foolery," Dakar said with sidelong relish. "Fionn's not come here to make casual sport. Actually, he longs to enlist, and hopes you'll consider his prospects as a field officer."

"Does he!" The duke shoved erect off the back of his chair. "Do you presume, young man, you've the skill and the nerve for it?"

"By Ath!" burst in Keldmar. "He can scarcely get dressed!"

"Oh? You oafs would measure a man by his looks?" Parrien moved, snake-fast, and recaptured his twirled dagger without shifting his attentive stare from Fionn Areth. "Does he actually think he can meet the requirements?"

Dakar shrugged, sipped his wine. "I made him the promise I would provide him the chance to speak on his own merits."

"No," Mearn declaimed. "No question about it. Another ten minutes wearing those boots, he'll be too crippled to stand for a demonstration."

Fionn Areth shouted to make himself heard in the tumult. "I would beg leave to try!" As quiet descended, he ignored the precarious state of his hose, and bowed from the waist to the duke. "My lord, I should like nothing better than to be tested for mettle. I am not inexperienced. If I fall short of Alestron's high standard, I beg to enlist with your foot troops. I'd be willing to train for as long as it takes to win my fair chance for promotion."

"Enough!" The duke glowered to quell his pack of brothers, then joined Mearn for a closer inspection. "We have an earnest young man who's a guest. He's declared himself to have fighting potential. Let's hear out what assets he brings us."

Fionn Areth drew in a lungful of air. While he groped for the words to begin, Mearn lost patience. Ablaze with a wanton, mercuric energy, he started to circle, dizzy as a moth at a lamp. "Do you write?"

"No," said Fionn.

"Recite poetry? Ah, don't bother, boy, to open your mouth. With that hayseed accent, certainly not. Do you paint? Play music? Raise beautiful flowers? No time, I see. What *do* you do, then, *a'brend'aia* with the nanny goats?"

"*What?*" Fionn Areth did not know Paravian.

Mearn's pause extended. His level brows lifted. "Must I translate?" he taunted. "You don't speak in fair tongues?"

Before the goatherd could rise to that bait, a faint cough from the sidelines. "The term means 'dance,'" the Mad Prophet said, owlish.

Fionn Areth raised his chin, dazed by the suspicious awareness of something gone over his head. Determined, he leashed his temper. "We breed them quite otherwise."

"No doubt you do." While his three brothers watched with rapacious amusement, Mearn moved again, pricking with words. "I see by your hands that you've never dyed cloth. You don't spin. You can't weave, you won't mix straw clay for bricks. You've not rowed in a galley, though you might have dipped water, or maybe cooked swill, or dumped slop for the rowers. *Perhaps* you've done that, though I doubt such. Despite the fact that nice doublet's too tight, your shoulders are slim as a maiden's."

As Fionn Areth's hazed fury notched higher, Mearn slapped his forehead and turned a glance of discovery upon the crowding ranks of his brothers. "Oh, now I have it! How did I miss seeing? Those lovely buttocks, those melting, sweet haunches! And those *wrists!* Fit for kissing. He's some fat pimp's runaway *prandey!*"

While Sevrand choked and exhaled sprayed beer, the victim flushed crimson, nipped by that gadding tone to recognize mortal insult.

Five pairs of gray eyes, and Dakar's, of brown, waited to see how he would choose to react.

A brief pause ensued.

Confronted by suspended expectation, Fionn Areth ventured a thin challenge. "You called me a name, sir?"

"He did," murmured Keldmar, leaned forward with bloodthirsty interest.

Mearn pattered on in venomous delight, "Oh, that." He fluttered his lashes. "My tender child, are you so inexperienced? Or didn't you *listen?*"

Parrien provoked, grinning, "He's from Araethura! He doesn't know the Shandian gutter name for the painted boys they geld with hot knives to serve twisted filth in the brothels."

Fionn Areth snarled out an inchoate syllable. Then his hand moved, and his sword, which was sharp, leaped with a practiced shriek clear of his scabbard.

Mearn danced back, laughing, as steel darted to spit him. "Oh, brothers, he fights!" Whipped back by the lunge, his rich doublet glittering, he smiled throughout, and kept talking. "The manikin fights, and most prettily even with his drawers skint down to his knee joints!"

Fionn Areth bore in, furious, to a shrill shredding of silk, which, obliging his tormentor, had slithered to hobble his boot tops. Mearn bounced out of range to a mocking gleam of gold ribbon. The sword whickered through air, and narrowly missed. Fionn Areth overreached, and his tight doublet tore, to a jingling shower of sprung buckles.

"Look out!" howled Parrien, bent double, tears streaming. "He's giving us the strip show of his young life!"

97

As Dakar scuttled clear to secure the carafe, Mearn kicked the table into the goatherd's advance. Filled goblets gushed and tumbled onto the carpet. Glass shattered, crunched to slivers as Fionn Areth charged ahead in his misfitted boots.

"Enough!" Duke Bransian waded in and slapped down a mailed fist. The goatherd's struck weapon hit the floor, clattering. A page boy who descended with towels dodged the flying blade. As though he mopped up after brawls by routine, he bent to sweep glass and blot puddles.

Fionn Areth, hazed wild, stood in the wrecked shreds of his clothing, rubbing his shocked wrist. He looked up. And up; while from his muscular height, the Duke of Alestron glared down at him. "Stripling, you haven't a babe's self-control, to wipe your smeared arse with a napkin."

The Araethurian glared back, hornet-mad, and possessed of a desperate dignity. "Then teach me. I'll learn." While Bransian's auger gaze bored him through, he plunged ahead with bravado. "I'll serve. I'll black boots. I'll do anything you ask. Only let me sign on to your troop rolls. Let me march under Alestron's proud banner to take down the Master of Shadow."

The pause was electric.

"*What?*" whispered Mearn.

"Kill Arithon," said Fionn. "That is why I came here."

At that, the whole room exploded: every man standing rushed forward and pounced. Fionn Areth was milled down by a flurry of mailed blows, knocked bloody and flat, then spread-eagled. Three brothers s'Brydion gripped him, wrists and ankle. His right leg was crushed under the gray-haired man-at-arms, while the blond one poised a dagger over his heart, and the duke's bastard sword pricked at his windpipe.

Only Sevrand stood rearguard, tankard in his left hand, and his bared blade bent at a menacing angle toward the Mad Prophet's nonchalant back. "Have you brought us an enemy?" he challenged, dead earnest.

"Irons!" snapped Bransian. "We'll know soon enough after *this* wretch is put to the question."

"No!" Dakar yelled across spiraling uproar. "That boy's under Prince Arithon's warding protection!"

"You didn't say this!" Keldmar bellowed, fast echoed by Parrien's accusation that the prisoner was a slinking spy for the Light, and why didn't Talvish set to with his knife and gut the cur here on the carpet. "I'll do the work and unravel his tripes, if you're sniveling, spit-licking squeamish."

"You didn't say he was Prince Arithon's charge," Keldmar interjected, "Why not?"

"Yes," Parrien echoed, "Why not? Just why shouldn't we flense him to crow bait right now?"

Mearn's manic laughter rang through crowding heat. "It's not obvious? I think Dakar's been clever. The ingrate who's wearing a friend's royal face requires a sharp lesson in humility."

The irons arrived, clinking, in the care of a house steward, who also was fit as a mercenary. Capable hands snapped them over pinned limbs.

Fionn Areth spoke, strained by the sword point pressed to his throat. "Where are you taking me?"

Bransian spared no sympathy as his shaken prisoner was hauled by the scruff to his feet. "West tower dungeon," he declared forthwith. "The irons stay locked. Under Arithon's bond of protection, you say?" At Dakar's nod, the Duke of Alestron stepped back, "Then his Grace had better collect his goods, quickly. I don't care fiend's get if the wretch rots in the dark till the rats pick him down to a skeleton."

"The tower guard's apt to spit him," Mearn warned, his evil smile still in place.

Parrien's agreement chimed in lightning fast. "A shove on the stairs, or a slip with a knife. I'd do that, myself, there's enough provocation."

"You're turncoats!" Fionn Areth gasped, faint with shock as the hold on him viciously tightened, and someone's badgering blade nicked through skin. "Traitors gone over to Shadow!"

"We are Arithon's men," said Duke Bransian, complacent. "And my brothers are right. You're a damned idiot with a tongue that the breeze flaps to every fool point on the compass. Leave you to yourself, you won't last an hour. Sithaer, without help, I doubt we can get you out of my sight without somebody hasty pinning your liver up on my wall for a trophy!"

At Dakar's concerned glance, the duke finally smiled. Still murderously vigorous, he had all his teeth. "Don't worry, man. He'll have Arithon's feal backing. Vhandon and Talvish will serve as his wardens. Let them handle the puppy as they see fit, and keep him breathing against all comers."

"That's rich!" Keldmar whooped. "We'll take bets to see who winds up bloodied first."

"Or better," Parrien attacked with bright relish. "A thousand royals on whether Vhan or Talvish is willing to die, defending a priest-sucking goatboy."

Summer 5670

Last Homecoming

Of nine Companions who marched with their Earl's war band from Halwythwood, eight had held the blood-soaked ground in Daon Ramon and broken the net of Alliance forces that had closed on the Master of Shadow. Five were killed in the red slaughter on the field. A sixth succumbed during rearguard action, defending a ragged contingent of scouts as they slipped through the lines and took flight. Cienn, who was seventh, was dispatched for mercy, by the knife of a steadfast friend. The eighth, single-handed, had been charged to defend the s'Ffalenn prince through a desperate retreat to the Mathorn Mountains.

Against odds, alone, he survived to return.

Braggen came south and entered the forest on foot to avoid leaving tracks for the headhunters. He crossed the north fork of the River Arwent in the heat of high summer and paused to trap a black fox. As he intended, his smoke fire to finish the cured hide drew the clan scouts who watched over the downlands near Caith-al-Caen. News was exchanged, and directions.

Under the regal crowns of the oaks, the warm air scarcely trembled. The fragrance of greenery clung thick as glue, shafted with sun through the heat haze. In the shaded glens, the deer drowsed through midday, fawns asleep while the does stamped off flies. Braggen slipped on his way, his step just as furtively silent, and his strapping frame lost in the brush.

Worn lean from the trail, he arrived at the s'Valerient chieftain's encampment in the lucent glimmer of twilight. He carried the pelt slung over his shoulder and the black brush strung at his belt.

The pack of clan children discovered him first. "Look! It's Braggen! Braggen's alive! Another Companion is back!"

Like starlings, they descended, calling his name. Their eager hands plucked at his clothing. He tousled heads, fended the boys off his knives, and detached the girl toddler before she wore the caked mud from the last stream he had forded.

No welcoming crowd of adults came forward. No one mentioned the loss of his clan braid.

Instead, given space out of mourning respect, two men were sent by the watch. They arrived unaccompanied, armed and dressed in the fringed, forest leathers that carried no other adornment. The expected, tall figure was slightly ahead, with the other sturdy and short, striding fast through the failing light. The children all scattered. Left standing alone, his heart heavy in him, Braggen confronted Sidir, and after him, Eriegal, whose round face was no longer merry. "We are four. After us, of fourteen, only Deith is still living."

Deith, who had not gone with the war band, but remained in Strakewood, holding the tenuous ground in Deshir since the massacre at Tal Quorin that had savaged a whole generation.

Now, the other survivors were fallen. Against crushing numbers and impossible odds, their lives had been given as well, to win their prince free of Lysaer's massed assault on Daon Ramon Barrens.

Braggen, who was not a demonstrative man, bent his close-cropped head, overcome. "I knew there were deaths. Just how many, the scouts would not tell me."

Grief closed his fists against helpless pain. Then Sidir caught him, gripped his massive frame close, and Eriegal embraced him also. Braggen wept with these two, whose lot had been hardest to bear: their doomed earl's command had asked them to stand guard for the children and families in Halwythwood. Of them all, the bravest and best had been spared to advise the heirs chosen to inherit the s'Valerient titles. Barach, not yet twenty, was now Earl of the North, and clan chieftain ruling Deshir. Young Jeynsa, a hot-tempered and rebellious seventeen, must swear her oath and stand as *caithdein* to the crown of Rathain.

Eriegal stood back first. His crooked smile broke through as he tipped his fair head to bear-bait the comrade, whose return was a gift unexpected. "You've hacked off your hair, man? Whoever she was, she must have shown you a rousing performance to have filched your braid as a keepsake."

"We were certain the Fatemaster had passed you for judgment," Sidir added, gruff. "Since you're not maimed, we're right to presume the knife work was yours, not a townsman's?" The same height as Braggen, but spare and long-boned, he lost none of his quiet dignity through the moment of desperate emotion. "Come in. You'll be starving. Better expect you won't get any sleep until you've satisfied Feithan's questions."

Braggen gripped the fox hide, too nerve-racked to eat. He had dreaded this meeting with the earl's widow for the better part of three months. Now the hour was upon him, he pressed the question. "What of Jieret's successors?"

Eriegal hooked fretful hands on his antler-bossed belt. "Barach will come once the runner's informed him. He's out on patrol with the archers."

"And Jeynsa?"

The two Companions exchanged a taut glance. Then Sidir murmured, "You'll see."

Flanked by his peers, Braggen crossed the encampment. Since the return of the Prince of Rathain, increased persecution by headhunters had redoubled an already rigorous security. No open fires burned after dark. The Companion passed through the lines of dimmed tents, then ducked into the balsam-sweet shadows of the central lodge.

The hide flap slapped shut, and Braggen stopped cold. Trophy hide on his shoulder, scarred hands crossed on his sword pommel, he stood speechless, while Sidir lit a pine knot in a staked iron sconce, and Eriegal dodged to avoid being mown down by a tiny dark woman clad in leathers.

"Braggen!" Quick as a sparrow, Earl Jieret's widow stretched on tiptoe and brushed a kiss on his bearded chin. Her black-and-silver hair still wore the s'Valerient clan braid. Bound by a deerhide fillet, her brow showed a crease of stunned disbelief. Then her brown eyes spilled over with tears. "Ath Bless! You've returned. We thought—ah, no matter!" Ravaged by grief, but as tirelessly vital, she embraced every part of him she could reach, then hammered his broad chest until his ornery nature relented, and he sat on a grass-stuffed hassock.

The taciturn Companion offered up the rare fox pelt.

"Who told you?" Feithan whispered, overcome yet again. She raised the silky fur to her cheek. Eyes shut, she thanked him. Steady in his silent support, Sidir stood at her back, while Eriegal dragged up a second hassock. She gave way and sat. "You have news? It can wait. You're aware, we've lost Jieret."

Braggen nodded. "I knew." He found all speech difficult. "Prince Arithon was blood-bonded. His Grace told me he sensed the High Earl's crossing at the moment that spirit left flesh. But we were already past Leynsgap, by then. I cannot say how my lord fell."

"We were told," informed Sidir. Enough time had passed, he could force his tone level. "Luhaine of the Fellowship brought word back to Halwythwood. He said, further, that Arithon Teir's'Ffalenn had survived, and that his enemies could no longer reach him. But the Sorcerer would not answer our questions or disclose our liege's location."

Braggen glanced down, marked hands laid uncertain before him.

Where Sidir's grave tact preferred space, Eriegal flared to impatience. "Ath, you're too quiet. You know where his Grace is! Is that why you're shorn of your clan braid, for shame? *Braggen, where did you fall short?*"

The accused Companion snapped up his chin, bitter. Against precedent, his anger turned inward. "I did not fail in my charge! As a man with no other skill but the sword, I stood ground at my prince's shoulder. I could, and I did, defend him with weapons. But I am not made as his chosen *caithdein*. I was not fit to stand in the breach and challenge his adamant spirit."

"What happened?" pushed Eriegal. "Where did Arithon go to seek refuge?"

Braggen stood in a rush, with Feithan beside him, her small hands caging his fist. "Peace! All of you! This was Jieret's lodge, and he would not have your contention."

And trembling, Braggen was first to back down. He turned from Eriegal's leashed accusation, and with a dignity no man had seen, eased the earl's widow back to her seat. Then finesse deserted him. "My lady, on my word of honor, the truth: I cut off my clan braid at need, in order to pass through the lines as a townsman. Now it's my right to know. What happened to your husband in Daon Ramon Barrens?"

While Sidir pressed long fingers over closed lids, and Eriegal watched, white, Feithan looked up at the man who overshadowed her, savage and raw with resentment. She told him. "Jieret was captured by Lysaer's Lord Commander of the Alliance armed forces. He was wounded, Luhaine said, and not handled kindly. Yet he was kept alive. His enemies thought to use him as a hostage to bring the Teir's'Ffalenn back to heel."

"Ath's mercy!" gasped Braggen. "For Jieret's *life*? Defend us! For that, the s'Ilessid pretender would have flushed Arithon from cover."

Sidir bared his face, and found grace at last to lift the burden from the brave woman now sorely bereft. "Jieret knew that, as well. He found resources no other *caithdein* has tapped. The Sorcerer told us he achieved true greatness, and opened a gateway into the mysteries through his sworn tie to the land. Signs and wonders were shown to men on that night. Lysaer's war host was paralyzed, unable to fight. They could not be made to regroup until Earl Jieret received a sorcerer's two-fold death, first by a sword through the heart, then by immolation with fire."

"The hand on the blade was Lysaer s'Ilessid's," Eriegal added with wretched clarity. "Our High Earl met a dog's end, without succor. Now, tell us the fate of Prince Arithon."

Pale to the lips, Braggen backed up until his huge frame bumped against the center pole of the lodge tent. There, he braced, at a loss for retort. His fellow Companions held their wary ground, well aware he was wont to strike out when cornered.

Yet Braggen gave them no whisper of argument. His volatile fists stayed locked at his sides. "Grant me the presence of my acting clan chief. Also Rathain's appointed *caithdein* since, in this life, I can scarcely bear to repeat what will have to be said."

Feithan arose. Silent and quick, she fetched wooden cups and a bottle of cherry brandy. Eriegal woke out of his bristling distress. He took Sidir's urgent hint and left to bring Jeynsa, who had yet to make timely appearance.

Nothing remained except to wait, with Braggen's raw nerves wrapped in the lodge tent's familiar, close shadows. Though he had a wife and a daughter, kept safe, in the northern wilds of Fallowmere, this place was as much a home to him. Head bent, he breathed in the pitch scent of resin, underlaid by the fragrance of leather and goose grease and the wax used for weatherproofing the camp gear. The summer furnishings seemed as they always had, except for the absence of Jieret's sword and the dearth of scouts coming and going. The encampment had been three-quarters stripped of its fighting men, blood-bought cost of a crown prince's freedom.

None too soon, the pent silence shattered, cut across by a male voice, declaiming, overlaid by a woman's vituperative anger. The lodge door flap cracked open, careless of the light, and Jeynsa strode in, still raging.

Brows pinched into an iron scowl, eyes like chipped flint, she encountered the motionless presence of Braggen, and stopped. Her vivid regard raked him over. From cropped head to scraped boots, she missed only the foxtail melted at one with the shadow.

Her opening was hostile. "Did you cut your hair out of protest as well?" Against the stunned stillness, she raked back the hacked bangs that remained of her shining brown hair.

Eriegal moved, shut the door flap, then caught her arm. "You have no shame!" Despite his dumpy stature, he manhandled her subsequent, wildcat wrench. Curbed, she stood glaring, hard-breathing and heedless of the deep bruise her clamped wrist was going to show later.

His voice level, Sidir explained from behind. "She cut off her hair rather than suffer the formal ritual of her investiture."

Braggen stared, horrified. "Girl, you did this to avoid receiving the pattern of the *caithdein*'s traditional clan braid?"

"We're a perfect, matched pair, as you see," Jeynsa sheared back. "Why'd you cut yours?"

"That's enough!" Feithan plowed Eriegal aside to confront her daughter. "No get of mine is brought into this world to insult clan heritage under this roof! Apologize, Jeynsa! Right now."

Strapping at seventeen, with her sire's tough strength clad in scout's knives and leathers, the girl towered over her mother. Nonetheless, her eyes dropped. Smoking with banked defiance, she spoke the rote phrases, then perched against the board trestle. To Braggen, she said, "You have news of my father? Don't trouble to report. *I know how he died.* By Sight, I stood witness. No reason, and no blooded prince under sky could justify how he suffered!"

Struck breathless, Braggen appealed to Sidir. "What's she saying? Ath's own mercy. The High Earl was tortured?"

"Worse." Jeynsa spat on the packed earth floor, while the brand dipped her drawn features in carmine. "He was mutilated, degraded, cut dumb, and drugged. Did you know, when they finished, they threw his charred skull to be mauled in the teeth of the tracking dogs?"

"He was gone by then, and you know it!" Feithan's composure withstood the cruel pressure. "Luhaine swore you his oath that your father was raised beyond pain when his spirit crossed over Fate's Wheel." Upright, arms folded, she drew a fierce breath. "But that's not why you won't forgive him. Be honest! You hate what happened because Jieret held true to his oath as *caithdein*. He died, and died well, for this land and his prince. You reject the willed choice of his crossing because of his triumph, that dared come before his own family."

"What's to forgive?" whispered Jeynsa, while the tears welled and spilled. "Not Father! It's the crown prince who left him that I would cry down for Dharkaron's redress."

Braggen shoved off the center post. "Prince Arithon's will had nothing to do with this! Jeynsa! I was there." Helpless anguish broke through, as, after all, he spoke out before Barach arrived to share witness. "Your father broke orders. As *caithdein*, by right claim of precedence to the realm, he rejected Prince Arithon's instructions. *I was to have been the one sacrificed to Lysaer.* Jieret was your liege's choice to return, safe and sound, to this hearthstone."

"I don't believe you," Jeynsa gasped, unappeased. Her glimpsed sight of the fox brush roused more galling venom. "I still see the sword fall. Every night, I smell the stench of the pyre. My father's heart's blood runs red through my dreams. He had no tongue, and no voice, beyond the wretched sound Ath gave an animal."

"That's quite enough, Jeynsa!" Sidir thrust forward; yet Braggen, like rock, only shuttered his face with blunt fingers.

"I will tell you this much," he said, muffled, then lowered his arms, unutterably altered. "I heard our prince beg. I listened to his appeal to Earl Jieret. His Grace used words that no man I know could possess the stern fiber to refuse. Naught but one. Out of love, this prince's *caithdein* held firm. When I tell you what our liege risked to spare Rathain's royal bloodline, you will realize: Arithon was forced upon Earl Jieret's mercy. As the man sworn to preserve our crown heritage, your father rejected his liege's bared will. There is no fault, and no blame for what happened. No reason, past the needs of this kingdom, that have robbed us all without quarter. As the last standing witness, I promise: none suffers more for the death of your father than the prince now left burdened, and living."

A soft sound, to the left, as Sidir responded. He gathered Feithan's slight form as she swayed, lent the shield of his shoulder, while Jeynsa uncoiled and rose to full height, untamed as a wounded lioness. "Then where is his Grace? Why is he not here? Why are you and Luhaine sent to speak in his place?"

Braggen's stripped attention stayed on her. "His Grace couldn't," he said, numbed. "To evade Lysaer's war host and escape certain doom through the madness of Desh-thiere's curse, Prince Arithon claimed refuge by entering the maze in the Mathorns."

"Kewar!" Sidir was rocked.

Eriegal stared, aghast, while Feithan pushed straight, and Jeynsa, wild with malice, burst into jagged laughter. "Oh, how apt! The score of his blood debts shall kill him, no doubt."

But it was Sidir whose grave intellect interpreted Braggen's strained face. "His Grace hasn't died, has he?"

The Companion shook his head, anguished. "In fact, he survived. I've been charged to bring word by the Fellowship Sorcerers. The Prince of Rathain withstood the harsh challenge. His Grace is fit, and still sane."

"And?" whispered Eriegal, as the pause grew prolonged.

"Barach should hear this," Feithan broke in.

Yet Jeynsa's merciless, challenging stare impelled the reluctant answer.

"The last living blood of Rathain has been granted sanctuary, embraced by the old code of guest welcome. His haven is Kewar, and his host is no less than the Sorcerer, Davien the Betrayer."

"A fine, abrasive pair they will make," Jeynsa snapped. "I wish I could be there to watch the fur fly as they tear each other to ribbons." She spun and stalked out, just barely careful to mask the light as she pushed through the door flap.

The shocked quiet lingered, a speechless abyss: the last survivor of Rathain's royal line remained with the renegade Sorcerer. Davien, whose incentive had fomented rebellion, raised the towns, and broken the rule of the high kings over five hundred years ago.

Against cracking tension, Eriegal moved, crossed the lodge, and rescued the forgotten tray of refreshments. Braggen accepted the brandy thrust into his hand. Then he watched, brooding, as Feithan was coaxed to a seat on Sidir's dauntless insistence.

She looked frail as cut paper, though her hands, bare of rings, did not tremble. As Eriegal poured a cup for her, Braggen spoke with a tact he had never possessed. "No, lady. You will not apologize for Jeynsa's behavior."

"Her defiance is setting a terrible precedent." Feithan sighed. "Ath knows, we've all tried. I can't make her listen."

"Prince Arithon will handle her," Sidir assured, the wing of white in his hair a moonlit patch against darkness. His words offered hope. Of the four who remained, he knew the prince best, having shared the harrowing campaign in the mountains at Vastmark.

Braggen knocked back his drink. Yet no fire in his belly could warm his heart. He had too much to say: the uneasy details that had allowed Arithon Teir's'Ffalenn to evade certain death inside Lysaer's closed cordon. The Companion who had partnered his Grace must choose whether to disclose the last words exchanged between prince and sworn liegeman, and whether to reveal the tenacious desperation behind Earl Jieret's terrible sacrifice. Until Barach arrived, and while Feithan regained her composure, Braggen sat with his forehead laid on his fist. Quiet, among friends, he wished he was numb. The trophy foxtail stayed tied to his belt, promised but not delivered to Jeynsa by the father lost in Daon Ramon. Who had broken the heart of his youthful successor because he had commanded another to stand in his place and, inevitably, had not come home.

Summer 5670

Home Port

The merchant brig, *Evenstar* sheared into Innish, crammed with barrels of dried orange peel, Elssine steel, and candied peaches from the orchards of Durn. She was warped to the dock, while the shore factor's stevedores called ribald comments, half-naked in midsummer heat. They waited, observing with ferret-sharp eyes, while the brig's well-disciplined crew raised her hatches to unlade her hold.

Yet the slim, blond captain who incited their best gossip had already gone, whisked ashore from the anchorage by the oars of a lighterman. While her first mate settled affairs at the wharf, Feylind rushed up the stairs to her brother's office, a garret room set above the tenements and shop fronts overlooking Innish's harbor. She found the door locked. Scarcely pausing for expletive, she hammered the oak panel.

"Fiark! I know you're in there!"

Her brother's voice answered, nonplussed, through her racket. "No, Feylind. Don't bother. I'm not going to burst myself arguing, and you're sailing upcoast beyond Shand. There is famine. I have signed the lading bills to send succor. The shore warehouse already holds your next cargo. My secretary's primed with the tax-stamped documents, at the customhouse to receive you."

Shut out in the musty dark of the corridor, Feylind howled a filthy word through her teeth.

"Beans," her twin spoke back in rejoinder. "Also salt pork in barrels, dried corn, and flour. Spirits and wine—because of rains and flooding, the low-country cisterns have become uselessly tainted. Children have sickened. You'll be carrying medicinals. Oh yes, and some nets of fresh limes, dropped by fast galley from Southshire."

Feylind smiled like lightning unleashed. Captain to a crew of twenty, all male, she unslung her boarding axe and let fly. Molding and varnish smashed to uncivil splinters as she razed off the outside latch.

"Feylind, you maniac!"

The lock turned with alacrity. Sunk steel was wrenched from its setting as Fiark jerked open the mangled panel. Feylind immediately began her next stroke. As the door swung wide, the raised blade topped its arc. She snapped her wrists; changed its falling trajectory.

The haft left her hands, and the edged helve impaled in the rim of her brother's desk. Quill pens fluttered airborne. Stacked ledgers toppled. Piles of correspondence disgorged their lead weights, and sluiced in white sheaves to the floorboards.

Fiark's fair brow relaxed. Immaculate in his dark velvet and pale lawn, he sized up his twin sister's strapping, tanned arms, and the sailor's slops she wore hacked to frayed threads above bare feet and neatly turned ankles. His sigh masked a smile. "After the scars from your hobnailed boots, today's flourish is scarcely significant." He met her eyes, of identical blue. "You are not sailing east. King Eldir needs a skilled captain, and *Evenstar's* the only bottom we have with no dicey political strings on her registry."

"Bugger that, with a goat," Feylind said, furious. "You can kiss your High King's landlubbing arse! Give him your mouthful of sweet consolation, because I am not sailing to Havish."

"I will not start a war!" Fiark snapped. "And dare spew that filth to King Eldir's face, he'd have your tongue for guttersnipe insolence."

Feylind hooked her chapped thumbs in her belt. "You know *who* missed his backup rendezvous at Alestron."

Her volatile change in subject need mention no name. Fiark shut his eyes, only half in forbearance. "Ath, you're obsessed." Then, "Yes, I was aware." Without pause to tidy the wreck of his desk, he reached for his key, closed and locked his breached door, and valiantly called for a standoff. "Since the taverns at this hour are too hot for arguing, we'll discuss the matter at home?"

"Yours?" Feylind said. "Not Mother's."

Fiark grinned. "She won't give up trying to put you in skirts? Or are you concerned that your language will finally hound the poor lady to drink?"

Feylind laughed. "It's the subject we're hellbound to discuss. *His* affairs. If she overhears us, she'll have a nerve storm. Last time I spoke of his doings in her kitchen, she doused me down with a milk pail, then just about dinged me unconscious."

"Using what? Her straw basket of sewing silk?" Fiark needled sweetly.

"Sithaer's raving furies, nothing so kind." Feylind pattered down the dim stairway. "Mother gives the impression she's fifty and frail. But raise her temper, we're more alike than you know. She went for my nape with her flatiron."

"To keep you in the house? And it worked?" Fiark burst into unbridled delight. "Is that why you're packing your boarding axe? Ath, I wondered. After all, you're not dressed to repel panting suitors."

"The ones who pant get my boot in their teeth." Paused under the arch at the outer arcade, a flamboyant, slim figure stamped against the glaring noon sunshine, Feylind paused. Her freckled face sobered. "With Mother, you don't get the grace of a warning. I swear I saw swimming lights for a week, with a bump fit to rival a peacock's egg."

In the cool, whitewashed kitchen with its azure tiles, the light fell like rippled water through roundels of glass. Feylind sat at ease at the trestle, a robust toddler astride her bent knee. Summer had bleached the child's hair from its dark brown to the mixed hues of pulled taffy. His flushed face resembled his pert mother, while the blue eyes that surveyed the ship's captain, beyond mistake, favored Fiark.

"That's not a toy," Feylind murmured, prying curious fingers away from the hilt of her rigging knife. "Just haul on my earring. There's a fine little man." She grinned as the wife laid out fruit and pale wine. "My son's aboard ship?"

"And your daughter." The neat woman smiled. "Tharrick took both of them. They were wrecking the peace until they could visit their father."

Feylind raised her eyebrows, head tipped to forestall the mauling yank at her earlobe. "They saw the flags on the customhouse?"

"Flags! They know the lines of a ship and her sail rig," Fiark corrected from the sidelines. "The boy's been begging for months to ply his hand at the oar as a lighterman."

The wife sat beside him, perhaps to revive the exhausted admonishment, that long since, Feylind should have wed her first mate.

"Don't start," Feylind warned. "The randy goat's already married to *Evenstar*, besides." Her strong hands set down the squirming child, then unsheathed the disputed blade and began to dismember peaches. "Our boy's too young for the lighters, as yet. He could run errands for the chandler's, if he's keen. You don't mind them underfoot?"

"Shore rats." Fiark grinned. His elegant, buckled shoes were propped up on a chair seat. Fair-skinned, but without his sister's lined squint, he leaned back with his collar and doublet unlaced. "You'd have them on *Evenstar*'s deck? The sea's in their blood, there's no question."

"To mimic my sailhands' randy habits?" Feylind chuckled. "Not on your life. I'd set them a ruinous example as a mother, forbye. No. The pests can stay safe in the nursery with yours." She pinned her brother's sapphire stare. "Since, after all, I am not bound for Havish."

Fiark's pigeon of a wife shoved erect and bristled. "You promised! No language!"

Feylind shrugged. "That's up to Fiark. He doesn't need to provoke me with reasons to go back on my given word."

"In fact, I must." Her brother lunged. Faster than his rich clothing suggested possible, he snatched his son short of his clamber up Feylind's knee. At his nod, the mother whisked the wailing child out. "We're going to argue in earnest, I see."

"Argue!" Feylind glowered like a shark, regretting the axe left behind in the garret office.

Fiark's brows were set level, now, as their need to mince pronouns was discarded. "Feylind. There were setbacks. Arithon never reached Eltair's coast. His escape plan from Jaelot met failure." He told the rest quickly. "His Grace is safe, but holed up in the Mathorns."

That Arithon was now the guest of Davien was a fact far too volatile to reveal, given Feylind's impulsive temperament. In no mood to try her with subtle explanations, Fiark waited, intent.

When his sister said nothing, he caught her wrist. "Feylind, his Grace is safe! I've had confirmed word by fast courier, through Atchaz. Dakar and the rescued double are also secure with the s'Brydion at Alestron. That's a milk run, damn it! A coastal lugger and a hired crew of fishermen can collect the pair, and *Khetienn* can be flagged down for an offshore rendezvous."

Feylind stared, drained under her seagoing tan. "Leaving Arithon landbound? Merciful death. I can't bear it!"

"For now," Fiark stated. "The idea is his choice. I can't cross his royal will on the matter, and neither can you."

When his twin swallowed, anguished, he held his breath, hoping that somehow good sense would prevail.

"The weather's not canny." Uncomplacent, Feylind squared her shoulders. "They say it's done nothing but dump rain in the west."

Fiark released his sister's taut limb. Sympathy, from him, would destroy her tough strength. She had not married, as both of them knew, because her unswerving devotion tied her heart to the cause of the Crown Prince of Rathain.

She stirred finally, stabbed the knife into a melon, and folded her arms at her breast. "Why couldn't his Grace have made me the acting captain of the *Khetienn?*" she whispered in plaintive longing.

Fiark need not answer. The reason was self-evident: Feylind was bound as master to an honest brig because Arithon Teir's'Ffalenn had sworn his royal oath not to set her at risk. Once, years ago, a female captain had been killed, mistakenly condemned as the Master of Shadow's associate. The trumped-up charges had been an act of spite, inflicted by frustrated enemies.

"You would break his heart, sister," Fiark said, a quiet truth. Day by day, the Alliance's influence strengthened. The network of correspondence he handled was becoming increasingly dangerous. "You will sail for Havish. There are people suffering. Even as we speak, the *Evenstar*'s being loaded to relieve them."

Feylind reached out and halved the melon, first sign that she might capitulate. Yet her truce held razor-edged warning. "There will come a time when the promise his Grace swore to our mother will not be enough to restrain me."

Fiark released the pent air in his lungs. His smile was calm, and his eyes, very bright, as their minds at last reached concord. "On that day, if it comes, and if his Grace requires your sniping interference, you'll cast off your hawsers and sail with my wholehearted backing." At her laughing breath, the trade factor who masterminded Arithon's shoreside affairs let his guarded worry evaporate. "You didn't doubt?"

"Never you," Feylind stated. Aware she was hungry, she attacked the hacked melon. "Though I wonder sometimes, watching you mince about with your gentrified manners, and your pompous velvets and lace. Let's see how you manage when Mother grabs for her iron and brains you for keeping dishonest company."

Not chastened at all, Fiark replied in the fishing village vernacular of their childhood. "Leave mother to Tharrick. It's the wee snip I married who's the more apt to snatch her pothook and geld me for agreeing to your feckless risks."

Summer 5670

Incursions

When the Fellowship Sorcerer Kharadmon appeals to Althain Tower for help to curb an invasion of free wraiths that threaten Athera, Sethvir must defer the request, since Luhaine cannot leave the Peaks of Tornir before restraining the Khadrim who fly and slaughter the caravans bearing relief supplies into Camris...

Snapped awake from a vivid nightmare, the acting steward of Etarra, Raiett Raven, discovers the priest dedicate of the Light lurking next to his bed and muttering queer lines of incantation; "A guarding ward to defend against Shadow," the robed man declaims, brazenly insisting the irregular intrusion should not merit an instant expulsion...

Daybreak at Avenor, in distant contact with the same Etarran acolyte, High Priest Cerebeld receives the private sequence of passwords to access Raiett Raven's established network of spies; immediately after his morning devotions, he applies that suborned resource to his thwarted search after Lysaer's runaway princess...

Crown Territory of Havish

IV. Refuge

Once Lysaer s'Ilessid recovered his strength, he applied his state influence with muscular will and accessed the vault housing Erdane's old records. The moldering texts he perused showed how narrowly close he had brushed with disaster. A friend's desperate courage had spared him, unscathed. If that depth of loyalty warmed his cold days, his icy resolve only hardened.

As Prince Exalted, for the common trust, he would see such dark works cleansed from the face of Athera.

Past solstice, as the flooding rains scoured the fields, and the north winds howled unabated, he took the rote steps that must guard his onward journey to Hanshire. He learned to frame lines of intent by clear thought and to bind his innate autonomy through affirmations. Fear gnawed him to doubt. The power of his naked word felt inadequate as he tired, and the vivid freight of his own memory closed in. Distorted faces sometimes appeared to gibber and leer from the shadows. He memorized Paravian cantrips to stave off the menacing nightmares that shredded his sleep in the chill hours past dark.

On sobering terms, Lysaer saw where his pride had led him to blinded folly. Sulfin Evend's insistence on arcane defenses had never been empty advice. While the Blessed Prince held his council in diamonds and silk and received the reports from his couriers, the cultists who coveted his influence would not rest. Lysaer brooded less on Shadow and sorcery and more on the treason that stalked his state hall at Avenor.

He answered correspondence and leaned without mercy upon Erdane's treasury to regroup his campaign-shattered companies. When the roads dried, and the drays could be moved for supply, he was hale enough to wear armor and sword, and ride, surrounded by the handpicked cadre of guards Sulfin Evend had detailed to attend him. Protected at night by herb-scented candles, he began his staged journey to Cainford, and thence to a borrowed manor at Mainmere. There, his officers mustered new recruits. Lysaer placated trade ministers, heard the blustering Mayor of Barish, and arranged for state galleys to transport last year's surplus grain stores. As Tysan's regent, he invoked martial law to ease shortage as blighted crops failed from the damp.

If folk blamed the weather on the Master of Shadow, no voice arose to gainsay them. Lysaer dispatched his idle troops to mend washed-out roads, and offered his powers of Light to cure the cut hay threatened by billowing rain clouds.

While affairs on the mainland trod their mundane pace, the Lord Exalted sweated in his sheets each night. He resisted the acid-sharp prod to seek after the Master of Shadow. He paced, drained hollow, and assayed no more scryings, though the craving urge racked him like recurrent thirst. The gray months slipped past without any word of the half brother sequestered under the Mathorns.

Arithon himself seemed content in retreat within Davien's impregnable sanctum. The caverns beneath Kewar blurred dawn and dusk. The underground deeps spoke of silence and dark, and the wisdom of timeless reflection. Stone measured itself, tuned to the magnetic spin of the earth, a spiral carved by orbit around a star, which itself trod the harmony of the grand dance amid the white whirl of a galaxy.

A man attuned to the depths of those mysteries might lose the boundaries of himself. For days, sometimes weeks, Davien disappeared on odd errands and left his royal guest unattended.

Rathain's prince did not object to the solitude. The radical shifts that rode his awareness made even light conversation too difficult. Since complex thought also unchained the wild reflex that invoked his matrilineal talent, the books in the library were too steep to assay until he had reforged his quietude. Arithon began by reviewing the disciplines learned as a child novice. The exercises of mind and body, precise arts that eased contemplation toward the resharpened focus of mage-sight, let him plumb the new depths unveiled in the wake of his ordeal in Kewar. He encountered the patterns that sparked his rogue farsight and gradually learned not to tumble into the scattering current.

As though veils had been torn from his inner senses, his vantage point straddled the volatile interface between mindful will and expansive thought. Activity prompted reaction too suddenly. Emotions exploded with juggernaut force. Arithon found refuge in the blindfold repetition of sword forms using a practice stick. He slowed down his movement until he was able to fuse the balance between his mercuric inner senses and the encumbrance of his earthbound flesh. He progressed. Atonal sound let him test each vowel, then each pitch, until he understood the flowering charge awakened by note and by cadence. Since music invoked the octaves beyond eyesight with overpowering vividness, he tried poetry. The result, more often than not, lit and burned him. The lyrical joy in Ciladis's verse could drive him unconscious with ecstasy. As his eye tracked the beautiful script, unfolding in ancient Paravian, he sensed the power and force in each word *and saw their structure* as ruled lines of infinite light.

The snug chamber where Davien housed his collection was a haven of carpeted silence. Carved shelves lined with leather-bound books towered over the wrought-iron sconces. Arithon sat, curled in a stuffed chair, while the architecture of the lost Sorcerer's thought refigured the frame of his mind. He bathed in that radiance. Touched by grace that showered the air into sound, and refined form to exalted geometry, he embarked on a waking dream that trod the far landscape of the grand mystery beyond the veil.

Arithon shivered, lifted dizzy; overcome. He paused with closed eyes, *and still saw.* The cry of raw light poured through his skin and sang in the depths of his viscera. Beyond hearing, the Sorcerer's art struck the heart like the shimmering peal of tuned bells.

Immersed in harmonics, wrung speechless with ecstasy, Arithon could not have been more ill prepared for the voice, charged with hatred, that spoke from the air at his back. *"We are well met, brother."*

Exposed, wide-open to mage-sight, Arithon recoiled out of the chair. The book tumbled, forgotten. Before it had thumped in a heap on the rug, he mapped the invasive presence: the electrical touch of an auric field that matched the imprint of his half brother.

Hackled, the Master of Shadow met Lysaer, who faced him over the edge of a drawn sword. No shielding space spared him. No thought might respond. The curse of Desh-thiere awakened like chain lighting. Enmity surged to throttle free will, a ruthless fist in the gut.

"No!" In the drowning, split second before reflex forced violence, Arithon snatched back lost discipline and tuned his mind to the chord once raised by Paravian singers to Name the winter stars.

Grand harmony snapped all chains of compulsion. The ungovernable impulse to murder checked short, leaving him trembling and weaponless. Light bolt or sword must take him defenseless: the blue eyes fixed upon him held murder. Still, Arithon sustained his adamant choice. Shielded in sound, he suppressed the brute drive of the Mistwraith's geas and did not lift his hand to strike out.

The next second, the fair form in front of him shimmered. Live flesh dissolved, undone by a tempest of subtle light. The auric field changed, shifted upward to frame another pattern of frequency. Blond hair became a roguish tumble of red locks, laced through with silver-gray. The wide shoulders lost their elegant white velvets. Reclothed in a jerkin of sienna leather, the frame of the intruder become ascetically thinner and taller. The Sorcerer, Davien, stood in Lysaer's place, his baiting stare devilish, and his smile a satisfied tiger's.

Arithon bit back his explosive curse. Nerve-jangled, he stepped backward, turned his chair, and sat down. "That was extreme," he managed, unsteady. His hands stayed locked to subdue helpless trembling. "Another test?"

"Perhaps." The speculative glint in the Sorcerer's dark eyes implied otherwise.

Arithon released a shuddering breath. "Your books stood at risk," he said mildly.

Davien's smile vanished. "Did they, in fact?"

"I wouldn't rush to repeat the experiment." Three months had changed little: Arithon was far too guardedly wise to expect he might sound this Sorcerer's deeper motives.

Davien's curious nature kept no such restraint. "I thought you should harden your reflexes." He surveyed his guest. The informal shirt, tailored breeches, and soft boots clothed a wary poise, and the wide-lashed, green eyes were anything else but defenseless. "You don't care to ask why?"

Arithon stared back in mild affront. "Whatever's afoot, didn't you just peel my nerves to prove I could handle it?"

The Sorcerer laughed. He spun on his heel as though to pace, then vanished from sight altogether. The instantaneous transition was unnerving, from embodied man to ephemeral spirit. As closely as Arithon had observed the phenomenon, he still gained no whisper of warning. Trained awareness yet showed him the Sorcerer's presence: a pattern of energies fused with the air, just past the limit of vision.

"You may not thank me, now," Davien stated, nonplussed. "Later, you'll realize you'll need every edge to secure your continued survival."

But Arithon refused to rise to the bait. Instead, he retrieved the dropped book, smoothed mussed pages, and traced a longing touch down the elegant lines of inked script. "Ciladis was a healer?" he inquired point-blank.

"Beyond compare." Davien permitted the sharp change in subject. "I have copies of his notes, and his herbals. Are you asking to see them?"

"Begging," said Arithon. "Is it true, that small songbirds flocked in his presence?"

"Near enough." The chill that demarked the Sorcerer's essence poured across the carpeted chamber. An ambry creaked open. "Here. The texts you will want are bound in green leather. Of us all, Ciladis was the least shielded. More than finches found joy in his presence."

Davien's essence hovered a short distance away. When Arithon made no immediate move to accept the offered volumes, he added, "No traps, no more tests. Where the memory of Ciladis is concerned, the deceit would be a desecration. Any knowledge he left is yours for the taking."

Arithon considered that phrasing, struck thoughtful. "Your use of past tense was what caught my attention." Then he added, "Though you don't think your missing colleague is dead."

"No." Davien moved, the fanned breath of his passage too slight to displace the flames in the sconces. "The bindings laid on us by Athera's dragons transcended physical death. As you've seen."

The pause lagged. Moved by bardic instinct, Arithon stayed listening.

Then Davien said, "It is not spoken, between us. But the fear is quite real, that something, somewhere, may be holding Ciladis in captivity."

The beloved colleague: who had searched for the vanished Paravians and who had never come back. Since that disappearance cast too deep a shadow, Arithon again shifted topic. "I do realize I can't stay in hiding, indefinitely. Nor do you act without purpose, even if your style of approach might be mistaken for devilment."

Davien rematerialized, no trick of illusion. This time, he wore boots cuffed with lynx and a doublet of autumn-gold velvet. Beneath tied-back hair, his tucked eyebrows suggested uproarious laughter.

By contrast, his answer was tart. "There are factions who would play your quandary like jackstraws."

"The Koriathain have already tried," Arithon agreed without blinking.

"Would I take the trouble to harden your nerves for that pack of hen-pecking jackals?" Davien showed impatience.

And Arithon felt the grue of that sharpening ream a chill down to the bone. "Now you imply they're no longer alone in their chess match for royal quarry?"

"Were they ever?" Davien's manner shaded toward acid bitterness. "The compact permitted mankind to seek haven on Athera. By its terms, subject to Paravian law, the Fellowship could not limit the freedom of consciousness. Therefore, well warned, we let in the dark fears. Such things always come with the narrowed awareness that is inherent in human mortality. The imaginative mind can be dark or light. Its storehouse of terrors can spin shadow from thought. These will find fallow ground, on the fringes, and there, the compact as well as the dragons' will binds us. Our Fellowship must continually stand watch and guard. No easy task on a world where Paravian presence demands that the mysteries remain expressively active!"

Again, Arithon sensed the subliminal chill. "You don't fear for me, but my half brother?" As silence extended, the thin breath of cold worked its invidious way deeper. "Show me."

For he did understand: if Lysaer's convictions fell to ill use as a tool, Deshthiere's curse could become a weapon of devastating destruction. "Who else wants to play us on puppet strings?"

"My library might offer you certain suggestions," said the Sorcerer, in glancing evasion. "Though I can assure in advance that you won't find such things written in the fair hand of Ciladis."

Yet Arithon had little choice but to place the implied warning under advisement. He knew well enough: the stays just established to checkrein his farsight were too tenuous, still, to withstand an unexplored threat. "If there's news, you can tell me," he informed Davien.

The Sorcerer's parting smile was wolfish. "You cede the permission? Pray you don't regret, Teir's'Ffalenn."

Through the following weeks, Arithon pursued rare texts on healing. Discoveries there prompted a deeper study of Athera's flora and fauna, then more texts on lane tides and fault lines. He studied fish, maps, and the astonishing arcane insights revealed in a folio stuffed with Sethvir's patterns of geometry. As promised, the Sorcerer who sheltered him brought updated word of outside events. Arithon was informed of Dakar's and Fionn Areth's safe arrival at Alestron, and of the pressures of famine harrowing lands to the west. In snippets of vision, shared with an eagle, he saw the *Evenstar* sail, laden with stores of relief grain dispatched for Havish.

If the aftereffects of the equinox grand confluence had enriched the fields in the east, other developments sprung from the event had whipped up a storm of fresh discord. Aware that whole buildings and walls were left torn to havoc by the cresting of harmonic lane force, Arithon received Davien's updated views: of skilled masons raising new fortifications and founding temples pledged to the Light. On the hazy north plains, under brass sun, the summer's recruits sweated in training. He saw old talent burn. A fresh wave of acolytes flocked to serve Lysaer's cause, both as oracles and itinerant priests.

All this, in the east, fell under the masterful sway of the advisor installed to rule Lysaer's interests at Etarra.

"Raiett Raven is no friend to the clans," Arithon commented, after a poignant, stiff silence. He sat, peg in hand, and one foot set in a looped wire, keeping tension, while his deft twist of the wrist wound a new lyranthe string. The day had finally come. His host had just granted him use of an instrument to try the altered wellspring that sourced his masterbard's talent.

"A wise distinction," Davien allowed. Poised under candleflame, he stood with arms folded over a brushed leather jerkin. His boots showed spoiling traces of mud, and one sleeve wore a scatter of burdock. "You've suspected the man's not Lysaer's panting lackey?"

Arithon looked up and unhooked the scored wood of his winding peg. "That one's eyes are too clever. He'd have noticed my actions haven't matched the ideological agenda. I wonder what actually drives him?"

Davien did not answer.

"No." Arithon coiled his shining, wrapped wire, then reached for the spool on the table. "I'm not interested in taking an excursion outside to find out."

The Sorcerer laughed, short and sharp. "Wait too long, you'll be fielding a holy war."

"With no cause to be found?" Arithon measured out six spans in length, used a knife, and nipped off the fine-grade silver. "Troops will lose their edge, speaking foolhardy prayers on their knees."

"No cause?" Davien shrugged. "My dear man, Raiett's a snake in the grass. He will make one."

"Not with yokels, still sparring with padding and sticks." Unperturbed, Arithon finished stringing the borrowed lyranthe. When at due length, he perfected the tuning, the Sorcerer had departed.

But the undertone troubling the recent discussion struck notes that snapped like live sparks from the musician's strings.

A wily statesman with a clever network of spies would not lack for resource to support an armed conflagration: a royal wife gone missing and a dead heir at Avenor would become reason enough for unrest.

Arithon passed the afternoon, absorbed by the glory of watching his spun lines of melody key the unseen octaves of light, now unveiled by the healed invocation of mage-sight. Made aware of the pulse thrumming from the low registers echoed back from the polished rock floor, he sensed the slipstream of time, aligned to the dance of the season. Fully restored to initiate mastery, he reaffirmed his intent to honor Earl Jieret's bequest: that one day he would forge the blood-binding promised to the s'Valerient daughter in Halwythwood.

The next morning, the strung lyranthe was set aside for more books, heavy tomes inscribed in the fine, flowing runes of the Athlien Paravians. The beings the Sorcerers called sunchildren, more than any, knew the mysteries encoded in air and fire. Arithon studied the properties of the energy sprites, named *iyats* in the old tongue. He listened through crystals to songs sung by whales, and explored older things, recorded in the pictorial symbols the dragons had used before Athera received her awakened gift of actualized language.

The black volumes bound under iron locks, and kept on warded shelves, stayed untouched. Nonetheless, the uncanny awareness pursued him: like a dousing of ice water poured down his back, Arithon sensed that the Sorcerer urged him to ask about those, first of all.

Outside of Kewar, summer yielded the harvest. The trees turned and wore the penultimate glory of autumn, except in the west, where the scouring rains lashed their storm-tossed, stripped branches. The High King's restored capital of Telmandir fared no better under the onslaught. Candles burned behind the steamed glass of the casements to lift the drear damp of the gloom. Outdoors, the harbor heaved like pocked lead, the beaten sea swells surging in without whitecaps. The sluicing downpour and the hammering breakers made a trial of unlading a ship.

Feylind stood on the puddled boards of the wharf, shivering, while the streaming water seeped down the caped collar of her oilskins. The merchant brig *Evenstar* lay warped to the bollards, while swearing deckhands fought the jammed hoist. Others wrestled the wind-lashed tarps, chapped raw by gusts that foreran a cruel season, come early. The miserable work was already behind schedule when from shoreside, Feylind heard the crash. Shouts slapped off the misted facade of the waterfront. Whatever had gone wrong, the king's customs keeper would be watching from behind his steamed glass, with his parcel of ferret-eyed clerks.

The captain's oath could have reddened the coarse ears of the longshoremen, now clumped into a distempered knot surrounding the stopped wagons. The risk of wet grain sacks, and losing damp cargo to rot shortened tempers: arms waved, and accusing voices entangled in argument razored through the pounding rain. Since the customs keeper's officers would wait for a riot and damages before drenching their heads to take charge, a ship's captain who wished to leave on the tide had no choice but chase after the dock crew.

Grumbling, Feylind wrung the sopped tail of her braid and sloshed shoreward.

A slop taker's cart had snarled the thoroughfare. Misfortune compounded by inconvenience, the ungainly vehicle also blocked off the bridge leading down from the palace. The impasse was not going to clear in a hurry. A split wheel hub had dropped the afflicted axle amid a mess of snapped spokes. The brimful barrels in the canted wagon now leaked under the tailgate, streaming ripe sewage into a street momentarily due to receive no less than the High King himself. Filthy weather would not deter the royal preference. His Grace of Havish would personally seal the bills of lading, and so nip the temptation of shifty dockside officials, who might stoop to blackmarketeering in a shortage.

The blistering insults surrounded the fact that no man wished to shoulder aside the broken-down vehicle.

"You'll shift your pissing load, yourself, damnfool boy!" howled the overseer to the carter, who stood, reins in hand, by the steaming draft mule in the traces. "Won't catch us doing your stinking job for you! We aren't being paid to handle any lowlife's haulage o' jakes."

"By the curled hair on the Fatemaster's bollocks!" Feylind yelled. "Why hasn't some nit gone aboard and asked for a block and tackle?" Heads turned, bearded and flushed, while the argument spluttered and died.

Feylind shoved into the sheepish press. "While you stand here, ankle deep, my deckhands are left twiddling their puds in the hold! They can man a capstan and winch this hulk aside. Move out! Smart! I'll rip off your bollocks before I watch you bunglers start fisticuffs over a muckheap!" As the slackers peeled out, the captain's invective switched target to the sopped figure clutching the headstall. "You! Get that sorry donkey out of the shafts before I decide to press-gang a new hide for the trusses on my main yardarm!"

The cowled head turned. Beneath ingrained dirt, the graceful features were no boy's. One glance of the wide-lashed, distrustful eyes made Captain Feylind take pause: a heartbeat to realize she confronted a person in desperate trouble. Before thought, she raised a piercing whistle and summoned her trusted first mate.

No customs keeper's sluggard, he came at a run, a solid presence arrived at her back that warmed through her sopped layers of oilskins.

"Handle that mule," Feylind told him, point-blank.

Years at her side, blue eyes bright with humor, he took over the reins without question. Feylind's grin shared her gratitude. Then, as the drover moved to sidle away, she latched on to wet cloak and dragged the stumbling creature into an alley beyond sight and earshot.

"Don't even try," Feylind said through her teeth, as her catch drew breath to cry protest. "I realize this mess you've arranged was no accident."

The woman stopped struggling. Tense, snapped erect, she sized up the ship's captain without cowering. Her eyes were rich brown as the gloss on an acorn. Fear, or deep-set cold, had started her trembling. Yet authority and intelligence showed behind her exhausted bravado. "I'm sorry for your inconvenience. But I have dire need to address his Grace, the High King of Havish."

Her accent was north westlands, townbred, and cultured. Feylind sized up fine hands that belonged to no slops woman, though the skin looked the part, cracked raw by her noxious profession. Alive to the perils of dockside rumor, the brig's master veered away from conjecture. "All right. But not here. Will my ship's cabin serve?"

The woman hesitated.

Afraid she would bolt, Feylind tightened her grip. "Don't be a braying ass! There's no man in my crew who can't keep his mouth shut."

As the woman's strained features showed panic, Feylind swore. "You want the ear of Havish's king? Then listen, lady, whoever you are! Hang on his stirrup, and all the whores in the district will share your misfortune. By tomorrow, you'll be the news in the mouth of every drunk sailhand. His Grace won't have sympathy. He detests subterfuge. Won't stand one moment for subtlety, either. Never mind this pissing downpour, you stink, ripe as a damned slave broker's privy!"

The woman blinked, shamed. "You're no friend of the Alliance?"

Feylind released her iron grasp and wiped her smeared palms on her breeches. "Damned well not! Canting bigots! I'm going belowdecks where it's dry to have tea. If you don't mind the fact I don't pack skirts, at sea, you can borrow clean clothes, if you want them."

"Bless you, yes." The strange woman put aside wariness, near tears for the refuge just offered. She trailed Feylind's stalking tread to the wharf, while the eagle who observed with living gold eyes watched unnoticed from a perch on the customhouse cornice. Head turned, fixed as the gargoyles who glared, chins on fists, right and left of its hunched silhouette, the raptor tracked the two women until they had boarded the brig.

An eye blink later, it vanished...

...to reappear farther north, soaring over a stream, where storm wrack had backed up the flood. The eagle alighted on a dead-fallen limb, snagged in the rush of dammed water. There, he shook sodden wing feathers and preened. The thrusting shove as he hurled airborne again dislodged the dead branch, and the rain-swollen current took charge. Balked water found opening, surged, then roared through as the impedance crumpled and gave way.

The eagle's flight followed the foaming, brown crest racing in due course downstream. A small ford became temporarily impassable, and a travel-worn rider who sought passage was forced to make camp, before crossing. His curse at the delay carried on the worlds' winds and glanced through the mind of Sethvir.

As the eagle veered east, the Warden of Althain flicked back a caustic reproof above range of audible hearing.

'*Meddler!*'

The eagle fluffed its crest, eyes gold as hot sparks. The thought returned was not avian. '*You would rather have that man ride to your tower doorstep with no help at hand to receive him?*'

Sethvir's retort came, sarcastic. '*You can hear through the rings of the Radmoore grimward?*'

Had Davien been formed as human, he would have laughed. As eagle, he screamed as he rose on the frigid winds of high altitude. '*I hear the mourning dreams of Haspastion's living mate. Asandir will be returned to your side in five days.*'

The subsequent silence was sudden and deep, engraved on the ethers with startlement.

Experience honed Arithon's wary awareness, refining his listening senses. Yet no boundary ward he wrought, set in air, served him warning when Davien chose to steal up on him. The Sorcerer slipped past such defenses at whim. No subtle shift foreran his uncanny arrival. Arithon leaned at last upon prescience: came to recognize the fleeting, ephemeral suspicion that *something* alive was listening over his shoulder.

Brushed by that whisper of premonition, Arithon closed a volume of Paravian ballads, transcribed during Cianor Sunlord's reign. "You've been sight-seeing, again. Is the news so unpleasant? The spin of the world will scarcely falter if I don't share the plodding details."

Davien appeared at ease by the hearth, cut in outline against the brass grilles that covered the shafts drilled for ventilation. His goldenrod cloak was adorned with black knotwork, gently ruffled by the whisper of draft. By contrast, his russet-and-gray hair seemed tumbled by an intransigent wind. "Your half brother's in Taerlin, bound west by slow stages. A conspiracy in Avenor will keep him preoccupied. But not long enough, Teir's'Ffalenn."

Arithon traced the embossed spine of the book held in hand, his angular features hardened to adamancy. "I won't ask."

"You must." Unsmiling, Davien chose not to mock. "The impact might well invoke your sworn oath."

Already tense, Arithon turned pale. "Which one?"

Davien advanced to the edge of the agate table, set next to the prince's chair. "You shall see for yourself, Teir's'Ffalenn." His citrine ring burned as flame through the air as he traced a circle on the polished slab. Seen by the extended perception of mage-sight, his touch ignited a line of white light.

Within the scribed round, stone spoke to stone: the mineral matrix of agate dissolved, revealing a view inside a seamless rock chamber. Arithon glimpsed a closed well of granite, and a dark pool, encircled by ring upon ring of fine ciphers. Water rippled over the characters, releasing a charged mist of electromagnetic force. The play of raised energy twined in rainbow colors that shimmered like boreal lights against darkness. Then a falling droplet struck the still pool. Circlets of ring ripples fled, unleashing a pristine, clear vision, and more: the distinctive pungence of ship's tar and varnish, sea spray, and salt-dampened wool...

King Eldir of Havish arrived without fanfare, his solid frame an imposing presence that crowded the snug stern cabin aboard the merchant brig *Evenstar*. Past the cramped threshold, he peeled his wet gloves and swiped back his dripping hair. Eyes gray as the storm beyond the streaked glass fixed at once on the stranger installed on the cushioned seat by the chart table. All else seemed in order: bills of lading awaited, alongside a trimmed quill and ink flask. Not one to dismiss an uneasy detail, the High King held his ground and stayed standing. "What have you brought us, Captain? A foundling cast up by the sea?"

"*Evenstar* ships cargoes, not hard luck passengers," Feylind demurred where she leaned, arms crossed by the gimbaled lamp.

The blanket-wrapped presence of the woman defied that impression: the bare feet tucked under her loose trousers were raw, and her diffident voice faintly trembled. "I came by land, your Grace." Still damp, she pushed back masking wool and unveiled a crimped spill of brown hair, gently salted with gray. Careworn eyes of a liquid, doe brown watched the royal stance, wary.

King Eldir decided her reserved poise did not match the menial callus that ingrained her small hands.

His held silence demanded.

The woman made haste to explain. "Captain Feylind has lent me the use of her cabin to spare the embarrassment of importuning your favor out in the public street."

The king's steel gaze flickered, a wordless query redirected back to the *Evenstar*'s master.

"Your Grace, I have granted the privacy of my ship. Nothing else," Feylind clarified. "If you care to listen, the lady has come a long and perilous distance seeking a royal audience."

King Eldir advanced to the chart table, then bent his head under the encroaching deck beams. No servant attended him. Only his taciturn *caithdein* stood guard in the companionway, close behind. The court clerk would be detained outside, strategically snagged by the mate concerning the matter of a mislaid tally sheet. By now aware the delay was no accident, the king tossed off his soaked mantle. Beneath, he wore no regal tabard. A badge with Havish's scarlet hawk blazon was discreetly sewn onto his sleeve. His plain leathers were cut for riding. The fillet that gleamed on his brow was thin wire, with the ruby seal upon his right hand the only royal jewel upon him.

He seated himself, his eyes on the woman who filled sailhand's clothes with the grace of a birth-born courtier. "My lady, you have asked for my ear. Be assured, at this moment, you have it."

This crowned sovereign's demeanor did not overwhelm, or bate the breath like Lysaer's blinding majesty. Buoyed by a bedrock patience that appeared willing to wait, the petitioner wasted no words. "Your royal Grace, I have come here to beg Havish for sanctuary."

Eldir held her pinned with his level regard. "Under whose name?"

"I prefer anonymity, your Grace. With good reason. My life has been threatened."

The caught flame of reflection in the gold circlet stayed steady, unlike the bald *caithdein* behind, whose wary fingers closed on his knives. "Who has threatened your life, lady?"

She swallowed, uncertain, now unable to mask the tremors of her breaking terror. "The regency of Tysan," she whispered.

"I see," said the king. Yet, he did not. The surprise that flared within those gray eyes was sudden and wide as new morning. "Lady, do you have proof?"

When she nodded, King Eldir commanded his *caithdein* without turning his head. "Fetch Ianfar s'Gannley. At once!"

At the woman's bounding start, he moved, caught her wrists. Fast as she set her hands to the table, he arrested her thrust to arise.

She protested, rattled. "Your Grace! I have asked for your ear with no outside witness at hand!"

"Princess," said the king, stripping pretense away, "where you are concerned, there can't be anonymity! The young man I've summoned is the named heir of Tysan's invested crown steward." As her courage deflated, he qualified swiftly. "We observe the old law, here. By royal charter, Avenor's business is his. That is as it must be, or are you not Ellaine, wife of Lysaer s'Ilessid?" He released her, and waited.

When she sat, as she must, or go her way destitute, his commanding baritone gentled. "Accept your clan spokesman. He is ally, not enemy. For Havish to shelter you would be grounds for war. Your safety can't be bought through bloodshed."

Machiel's shout filtered back through the strained pause, shortly broken by running footsteps. An energetic man clad in the king's livery burst in, breathless and scattering raindrops. He was a strapping fellow in his late twenties, come into the grace of his stature. His fair hair was bound in an elaborate braid, and his eyes, dark as shadow, missed nothing. He bowed to the king, fist on chest, as the clans did, his flushed features keenly alert. "Your Grace?"

King Eldir referred him to the woman huddled under the blankets, in borrowed shirt and sea breeches. "She is Lady Ellaine." As the clan liegeman's eyes widened, the king qualified, his choice of state language precise. "She has come here in appeal against an injustice, claimed against the pretender's regency at Avenor."

The clansman recovered himself, faced the woman who sat opposite, then bowed, fist to heart. To his credit, her dress and rough hands did not merit more than a curious glance. "Ianfar s'Gannley, my lady," he announced in flawless address. Then he smiled. "As a mother who has borne the blood royal of Tysan, freely ask of my service, as heir to my cousin's title."

Ellaine regarded him, taken aback. His accent was crisp as a forest barbarian, and yet, no trace of contempt or antipathy moved him. Accepted in fosterage to Havish's court, Ianfar seated himself with aplomb, then deferred, as was right, to crowned sovereignty.

The High King was swift to make disposition. "My lady, the tenets of charter law must apply, here. Entrust your proof to the hand of s'Gannley."

The parchment she produced was stained, and still damp, the seal's wax cracked from rough handling. "This was smuggled out, sewn into my garments," Ellaine apologized as she extended the unsavory document.

"Best take her seriously," Feylind declared. "The lady worked her way here since last winter, earning a slop taker's wage in a refuse cart."

"To the sorrow of my cousins," Ianfar said as the soiled parchment changed hands. "The news of her hardship does nothing but shame us." He flipped open the folds, jarred to bitterness. "You could have appealed to the clans for help, lady. Your court at Avenor has misapprised us."

"As my husband's confirmed enemies?" Ellaine burst out, incredulous. "Or is your cousin not Maenol Teir's'Gannley, who has formally sworn that Lysaer is an imposter, with his life declared under forfeit?"

Ianfar flattened the parchment on the chart table, flushed with affront, and not smiling at Feylind, who had moved to brighten the wick in the gimbaled lamp. "Maenol is that same man. The history occurred before your current marriage. Did you know he made his lawful appeal to s'Ilessid, to challenge false claim to crown title? That just inquiry provoked an infamous reprisal! For as long as our people live under an edict of slavery, my cousin has no choice but to stand in his place as the throne's oathsworn shadow."

Eldir intervened to smooth hackles. "The *caithdein* must serve for Tysan's rightful successor, not Lysaer, who was never sanctioned by Fellowship authority. Charter law is explicit. Earl Maenol is the voice charged to guard the crown's unbroken integrity."

Ianfar bent his flax head to examine the document. As he perused the opening lines, the High King watched the clansman's demeanor shift from tense to aghast. Prerogative stayed him; he withheld his royal counsel, waited motionless, until the binding signatures with their row of wax seals had been recognized. As father of three sons, with this one raised to manhood among them, Eldir must not flinch for the horrific burden thrust upon Maenol's heir lest he risk the innocent blood of his realm. The aching pause hung, until Ianfar straightened, and affirmed the most desperate thread of his fear.

"The lady cannot be sent back to Tysan. If she goes, her life could be far more than threatened." Ianfar finished, with leveling force, "This document outlines the terms for a murder, and confirms every rumored suspicion. Your Grace, Avenor's regency is corrupt and involved in criminal treason."

Eldir sighed. The light flickered, scoring the gouged lines of sorrow that tightened his mouth. "Lady Talith, I presume?" His regard measured Ellaine. "Your predecessor was not driven to suicide for an unpleasant political expediency?"

"Suicide?" Ellaine bristled, sparked to regal outrage. "The former princess was brought down by a crossbolt, fired by a killer whose hire was arranged by Avenor's high council. I can't be certain they acted alone, though my heart tells me Lysaer is innocent. Talith's premature death scarred him, cruelly."

"We're not speaking of that sort of venal corruption." Ianfar tapped a seal at the base of the paper. "This," he said, sickened. He appealed to Eldir, ripped to horrified dread. "Your Grace saw fit to warn my cousin, long since. Lord Koshlin is the suspected affiliate of a necromancer, and at work for years, cheek by jowl with the appointed high priest who governs the trumped-up regency in Lysaer's absence…"

Within Kewar's library, the Sorcerer Davien raised his forefinger. The image called in from the ship's chart room flicked out, while he fixed Rathain's crown prince with wide-open eyes and a hunting cat's fascination. "Do you need to see more, Teir's'Ffalenn?"

"To realize that Feylind's endangered? I do not." Bristled enough to stay stubbornly seated, Arithon matched the Sorcerer's challenge. His expression revealed nothing. But the ringless, fine hands on the book were no longer relaxed. "Are you implying a lawful appeal to the Fellowship on Ellaine's behalf won't bring help?"

"Can't," Davien stated. "Sethvir lacks the resource. No colleague is left free to answer."

Unwilling to test the abstruse intent behind Davien's voluntary exile, Arithon said, "Then King Eldir can't deal. He won't risk open war, as he must, if he dares to grant Lady Ellaine his sanctuary. This event is ongoing? Then you already know the sure outcome."

"Your mind is too sharp, prince." The Sorcerer would leave a pause dangling to provoke, but not trifle with cruel games of intellect. "There's only one pertinent fact left unsaid. On Ianfar's behalf, Mearn s'Brydion once signed the Teir's'Gannley his oath of binding protection."

Arithon mapped the logic. "Therefore, the *caithdein*'s young heir must take charge of Ellaine and appeal for an offshore passage. *Evenstar*'s handy. Feylind won't resist. She has a true heart. My half brother's renegade wife has no last option, except to sail east. Where else would she appeal for safe harbor, except at the citadel of Alestron?"

Davien tapped his shut lips with a restless finger.

Arithon mused on, stirred beyond grim interest. "Why show me that scene in the first place? Don't claim you had any bleeding concern over my standing promise to shield Feylind. What is your stake in the *Evenstar*'s welfare?"

Davien's image whisked out, his response tossed back as he drifted past the fireplace. "What do you know about necromancy, Teir's'Ffalenn?"

"Enough to raise all my hackles at once." Arithon tracked the Sorcerer's presence, alarmed, though he clung to his bent of grim humor. "I thought you claimed Luhaine would haze you to Sithaer's dark pit, should I sample the vile rites written into your collection of black grimoires?"

"Not mine," Davien corrected, precise. "The author of those volumes pitched a roaring fit when he noticed his horrid memoirs had been stolen."

"That was your light touch?" Arithon grinned, then laughed outright at the subsequent, mortified silence. "Or no. More like Sethvir's pilfering, I see."

Davien's answer rebounded from the arched alcove framing the doorway. "What couldn't for conscience be shelved at Althain Tower must naturally be bundled up and sent here." The chill that comprised his essence flowed out through the door latch, as always ahead of his mocking last word. "If you don't fancy the unpleasant reading, I suggest that you visit my armory. The wise prince in your shoes would lay aside music and revisit an heirloom Paravian sword."

"Alithiel keeps her edge with no help from me," Arithon said, his peace shattered. Though practicing forms with a stick kept him fit, the mere thought of touching war-sharpened steel moved him to blistering vehemence. "If I had any reason to crack a black grimoire, the temptation would likely arise from my sore need to curb your nefarious meddling."

Autumn 5670

Obligation

The visitor who reined up at Althain Tower was a lonely speck upon the windswept downs of Atainia. Morning by then was almost spent, lidded under a raced scud of storm cloud. His horse blew steam in the frigid air as the rider dismounted, stripped both saddle and bridle, then hobbled the gelding to graze. Head bared to the tumbling gusts, he removed a locked iron box from his bedroll, and confronted his grim destination.

Few men, standing under the spire's bleak shadow, would not tremble and wish themselves elsewhere.

Sulfin Evend proved no exception. Although the sky forepromised a drenching downpour, he would gladly have turned his back. His binding pledge to the blind seeress in Erdane now seemed an errant act of insanity, no reason not to turn tail and run south, fast and far from this desolate wilderness.

Fear rooted his feet. Lysaer's endangerment posed too dire a threat to abandon the purpose that brought him. Sulfin Evend gazed upward, chilled bone deep. High overhead, the leaden gleam of the roof slates loomed through the masking mist. A raven's croak floated downward. Wind snaked through the tasseled grass, snarling over the lichened summits of the Bittern wastes to the north.

"Avenger's black pox on the doings of mages!" the townsman snapped, and pressed forward. His reluctant step crunched on the diamond frost that still clung to the flanks of the hollow.

Sulfin Evend's distrust of the Sorcerers was direct; all his prior experience, confrontational. Having once been ensnared by Asandir's spellcraft and forced to watch his company of lancers die while entrapped in a grimward, he still suffered the harrowing nightmares. The Fellowship would scarcely welcome the man sworn to rank as the Alliance Lord Commander.

Arrived on the cracked slate at the entry, Sulfin Evend found the outer grille raised. The ancient, strapped portal was also unbarred, its array of geared chains and counterweights a stitched glint of steel under an inside flicker of torchlight. Nobody waited beside the spoked windlass. Past the oppressive gloom of the sallyport, the far gate had been wedged back, as well. No Sorcerer lurked there: only the wind fluted dissonant notes through the black gaps of the murder holes.

Sulfin Evend faltered and stopped. If wards had been set, he sensed no prickle of gooseflesh. Althain Tower stood open before him. The invitation lent no reassurance. He edged forward. One step, two; he paused again. Every nerve strained, he breathed the scents of dank stone and oil, the aromatic resin of pine smoke underlaid by the taint of burnished chain. He assayed a third step.

Nothing happened.

A gust flapped his cloak, making him start, and setting the torch flame winnowing. The fourth step would see him under the gate arch, no wise move. A man raised to recognize the rudiments of spellcraft should be loath to cross over any sorcerer's threshold.

"You have two choices," a voice pronounced at his back.

Sulfin Evend whirled, hackled. A tall, straight figure cloaked in indigo wool blocked the pathway behind him.

"Go back, and leave all your questions unanswered. Or step forward and accept our hospitality." Silver hair tumbled free as Asandir pushed back his hood. "I will not presume to advise you, either way, since you have already tested the nature of the peril you carry."

Sulfin Evend wrestled his outright fear. "You!" he gasped, strangled. "Why not take me captive, as you did the last time?"

Asandir raised eyebrows like bristled, black iron. His tarnish gray eyes never flickered. Silent, he waited for his town visitor to make up his uneasy mind.

Retreat would require a step *toward* the Sorcerer, a sly fact Asandir used to his unsavory advantage. Sweating with terror, Sulfin Evend forced speech. "After my abduction in Korias, no word you might say could establish your good intentions."

"Even the truth?" Asandir tucked his fingers under his sleeves, a pretense: the morning's damp cold should scarcely pose one of his kind the least moment of inconvenience. The voice, crisp and light, was impervious steel. "False son of s'Gannley, no prayer to the Light spared your life that day on the Korias Flats. Your deliverance from that grimward was done by my hand, despite what you chose to believe for the sake of convenience."

"Liar!" Hanshire arrogance instinctively bridled. "I am no son at all, to s'Gannley."

Asandir's amusement was wild as wind. "Are you not? As you stand there, all pride and quick temper, you are breathing proof of your matriarch's ancestry. Go or stay by your merits. I shall not intervene. After all, your promise was not made to me, and Lysaer s'Ilessid rescinded our Fellowship's protection when he cast off the terms of the compact."

Shocked to hear that fact reconfirmed, and with incontrovertible finality, Sulfin Evend mustered the rags of his courage. "You'll swear to my safety?"

"Swear by what?" Clipped to impatience, the Sorcerer said, "You are the spearhead for the Alliance's war host! Do you presume to think we might have common ground?" For an instant, perhaps, his cragged features seemed touched to an elusive sorrow. "Did you know you were never at risk from our Fellowship? My promise is only a word, by your lights. Even still, Sulfin Evend, you have it."

A keen strategist, the commander wrestled the ironic challenge: a retreat at this pass would reject the Sorcerer's spoken integrity; and also repudiate the blood pledge he had made at Erdane to Enithen Tuer.

"Men die for promises," Sulfin Evend allowed. "What is a life in the hands of your Fellowship?"

"More than words." Asandir tipped his head toward the entry, his chisel-cut face bemused enough to seem friendly. "Inside, if you dare, you'll find out."

Sulfin Evend braced his rattled nerves, faced about, and crossed over the tower's threshold. The Sorcerer followed, his close presence mild and his footstep light as a ghost's.

If the Hanshire-born visitor regretted his choice, no chance remained to turn back. Asandir laid brisk hands to the windlass and secured the outer defenses.

As the thick doors boomed closed, drear daylight replaced by the fluttering torch, the Sorcerer's frame was thrown into relief. Sulfin Evend observed, too wary to be undone by disarming impressions: how the capable hands that cranked the oiled chains were raw with recent burn scars. If the Sorcerer's face appeared gaunt, or the spare frame beneath masking wool seemed hard-used, even haggard, his vast power remained unimpaired. The warding he raised to secure bars and locks drove his guest to a shudder of gooseflesh. Sulfin Evend had watched spellcraft being invoked all his life, by Koriathain who resided at Hanshire. The only working he had seen to rival Asandir's seamless touch had been an awareness half-sensed: an impression left as a whisper in stone, laced through the stairway fashioned by Davien the Betrayer at the entrance to Kewar Tunnel.

Asandir locked the drum of the windlass and straightened. "The defenses kept here are an obligation made to Athera's Paravians."

Startled to find his unspoken thought answered, Sulfin Evend said baldfaced, "You can't still believe the old races exist."

This time, as the Sorcerer retrieved the torch, his fleeting grief could not be mistaken. "They exist." He moved toward the last set of fortified doors, passed through, and attended their fastening. "If the Paravians had died, our years of trial would be over, and our most cherished hopes, crushed by failure."

The last bars were seated, the pin latches secured. Beyond, the last barrier was no defense, but a pair of ornamental panels, leafed in chased brass, which cut off the draft through the murder holes. Their varnished wood moved to Asandir's touch, slid wide, and unveiled a vista of dazzling splendor.

Sulfin Evend stepped into the Chamber of Renown, with its ranks of exquisite, stilled statues. First to draw his eye, the centaur guardians lifted their antlered heads, winding their dragon-spine horns. Unwitting, the man gasped, incredulous.

His scarcely suppressed recollection exploded: of the creature that had once stepped, alive, out of legend last winter in Daon Ramon Barrens. The unsettling memory would not be denied, when overcome, he had witnessed an immortal grace that had driven him to his knees. Through the awestruck aftermath, he had dismissed the event as a dream.

Until now, in cut stone, he faced the echo of that towering majesty, and more. This time, the centaurs' stern sovereignty saw completion, placed amid the threefold matrix of the harmony Ath Creator had gifted to ease the sorrows that troubled the world. Now, Sulfin Evend beheld the strength of the Ilitharis Paravians, partnered by exquisite beauty. Exalted form spoke in the purity of tossed manes, and high tails, and in the stone hooves of the unicorns, dancing. Their wide-lashed jade eyes and slit pupils of jet reflected the essence of mystery. In captured grace and shimmering delicacy, their carved presence suggested a tenderness to freeze thought and unspin mortal senses. Amid their lyric, arrested pavane, the sunchildren clustered, blowing their crystalline flutes. The sculptor had captured the sublime joy and delight on their elfin features. Their radiant merriment made the very air ache, suspended in stark, wistful silence.

The Alliance Lord Commander stopped, lost his breath; felt the wrench as his heartbeat slammed out of rhythm.

He stared speechless with wonder. Then his eyes brimmed. Tears dripped unabashed down his chapped cheeks and splashed the rough cloth of his collar.

"They still exist," Asandir repeated, steadfast. His saving grasp captured the metal-bound box, before his visitor thoughtlessly dropped it.

Sulfin Evend scarcely noticed his clamped grip had loosened. His long-standing distrust could not be sustained, not here, swept away by what stood unveiled in commemorative glory before him. In the moment, Asandir's bracing touch offered a balm for stunned nerves, while his obdurate will gentled the mind through the reeling shock of its weakness.

Left unmoored, the man could do little but lean if he wished to remain standing upright.

For grief pierced into a shattering pain, that the light of such majesty should have walked in the world, and been lost, dimmed into abandoned forgetfulness.

Sulfin Evend bent his head, masked his face, crushed down by the force of his shame. "We are desolate," he murmured, ripped wretched by honesty. "How does your Fellowship bear our foolish insolence, that most of human-kind does not spare time to realize, or far worse—that we blind ourselves with rank arrogance rather than acknowledge such overpowering greatness?"

"How does man or woman bear cold, death, and ignorance?" Asandir finished the grim thought himself. "Because they must, and for no other reason. To do any less would cast away hope, deny truth, and declare that caring and peace have no meaning within Ath's creation."

Sulfin Evend permitted the moth-light touch that steered him on and guided his way up the stairwell. Led into a carpeted chamber and installed in an antique chair, he managed to sit and brace his elbows upon a polished ebony table.

There, he endured until the raw fire of his anguish burned itself down to embers.

He blotted his cheeks, finally. Aware of himself, and embarrassed for his bruised dignity, he looked up and encountered the Sorcerer, seated across from him.

Wax candles lit Asandir's cragged face. Two ages of weather had chiseled those features down to their gaunt frame of bone. The eyes, reflective as light on a tarn, gazed into places no man had gone.

Sulfin Evend caught himself staring; and Asandir, with an unlooked-for calm, permitted that uncivil liberty.

Observed at close hand, the Sorcerer's patience seemed nothing less than formidable. An unquiet shadow, or some ravaging horror had been the force that annealed his tenacious endurance. Behind his stark power, which wore no disguise, Sulfin Evend sensed more: the lurking spark of a wistful joy, and a dauntless strength tempered by what was in fact an uncompromised well of serenity.

"People have reason to fear you," the Lord Commander insisted, but quietly.

Asandir did not move. "They fear their beliefs." The question followed with disarming mildness. "Have I caused you harm?"

"Not yet." Sulfin Evend glanced away. A pot of spiced tea steamed on a tray. Someone thoughtful had included a cheese wedge on a plate, brown bread, and bowls of raisins, nuts, and dried apples.

"Sethvir insisted you'd be tired of game." Asandir already cradled a brimming mug, infused with the rich scent of cinnamon. The scatter of burns first observed at the windlass, unnervingly, seemed to be fading, the blisters reduced to rose pink against a lacework of older scars.

Again, Sulfin Evend averted his sight, only to become overawed by the details of his surroundings. Heraldic banners covered the walls, offset by a massive fireplace with black-agate pilasters. The Lord Commander identified the star-and-crown blazon of Tysan, then the silver leopard on green of Rathain, and left of that, the scarlet hawk of Havish, adjacent to the purple chevrons of Shand. The golden gryphon of Melhalla no doubt hung at his back. The inlaid chair that supported him had served as a royal seat for far longer than the Third Age. Before man, this room had hosted the sovereign grace of Paravian rulers, whose names and deeds framed the heroic legends of the early First Age ballads.

The King's Chamber at Althain Tower had heard Halduin s'Ilessid swear his blood oath of crown service. Here, Iamine s'Gannley would have stood witness, assuming a charge still borne by an heir who now skulked in the wilds of Camris.

Weighed by that past, and distressed by his errand, Sulfin Evend remembered the ironbound coffer, mislaid since the moment he had witlessly lowered his guard.

"Your burden is safe." Asandir tipped his head toward the mantel. There the coffer rested, still locked. He moved one hand, but did nothing more than reach for the teapot. "You look like a man in need of refreshment. Or will you hold out as the victim of nursery tales, which warn against sharing food or drink with my Fellowship?" The glint of a smile came and went as Asandir filled a mug, then pushed the honey pot across the table.

Eyebrows raised, the Sorcerer waited again. When Sulfin Evend left his offering untouched, he shrugged. "Crumbs won't harm the ebony."

Then, as his visitor failed to relax, the Sorcerer checked a sigh of incredulous, caustic impatience. "Mother of mercy! The tea is quite normal, imported from Shand, and whatever plain fare we set before guests, the food is by no means ensorcelled."

With that, eyes half-lidded, Asandir lifted his own steaming vessel and sipped.

Sulfin Evend managed the semblance of courtesy, stirred unsteady fingers, and spooned out a dollop of honey. "My nurse was more graphic." He talked to forestall nervousness. "She claimed that your Fellowship tore the hearts out of babies and ate them."

"Raw and still beating?" Asandir helped himself to some raisins. "Not particularly pretty, to stand accused of a practice that in fact is not ours. Such an unclean death is actually used by cults of black necromancers in their rites of initiation."

Sulfin Evend choked on his tea.

Brilliant as mercury lit by a spark, the Sorcerer's eyes sharpened. He passed a cloth napkin, and added, contrite, "Did you not come here to inquire on that subject?"

After a cough to clear his closed throat, Sulfin Evend admitted, "I had expected to broach the matter with Sethvir."

Asandir savored his tea, frowned a moment, then hooked back the honey for more sweetening. "Sethvir has a scar as long as your arm that was left by a necromancer's knife. His patience is short where their works are concerned. For myself, I've spent too many years in the field to waste undue time over niceties. Will you hear my straight warning? The faction you've roused is un-speakably dangerous. Leave Tysan. Travel under my ward of protection, live your life, and never turn back."

Despite gnawing doubt, Sulfin Evend held firm. "I can't do that."

"Then make no mistake. Your brash bravery is not wisdom!" When Lysaer's officer withstood that sharp censure, the Sorcerer broke off, grasped the cheese knife, and began to slice bread.

"I made a promise to Enithen Tuer," Sulfin Evend revealed at due length. "Would you send me off with a meal and no hearing?"

Asandir pinned his guest with steel eyes. "You might as well eat. The dan-gers you're bound and determined to face aren't going to forgive any weak-ness. Your nerves falter now? Then rethink your position. The works of the death cults are by lengths more ugly than the unfounded whispers you've heard concerning our Fellowship."

That said, the Sorcerer folded a chunk of cheese into the bread, took a bite, then shoved the filled plate toward the opposite edge of the tray. "I know how it feels to spend months on the road. Don't try to pretend you're not hungry."

Thereafter, the Sorcerer tucked into his meal. He did not look up. Nor would he respond to polite conversation. Sulfin Evend was left watching. Need triumphed, eventually. Soon after, the tray was emptied of food, and the bread loaf, demolished to crumbs.

"That's better." Asandir stretched and arose. He fetched goblets and a decanter of cider from a carved hutch, then served himself and Sulfin Evend.

As the cut crystal-glass was placed before him, the Hanshireman bridled. "Do you think me a fool? I did not journey here to have my tongue loosened with drink!"

The Sorcerer regarded the pale amber liquid, unoffended. "Sethvir does brew strong spirits when the mood takes him." He sampled the cider, then looked up, brightened to an incongruous spark of hilarity. "What threat from me are you guarding against, Sulfin Evend *idna cou'wid en tavrie s' Gannley?*"

A son brought up by the Mayor of Hanshire had the schooling to translate the Paravian, which meant, *'fourthborn who denies a Named heritage.'* "I won't let you bait me," Sulfin Evend replied.

Asandir settled back, looking suddenly worn. "By all means, have things your way. I merely hoped a difficult discussion would go easier if you were not saddle worn, or strung-wire taut with distrust. As I've taken delicate steps to point out, *I am not your judge.* Nor am I your misguided master's executioner! I will not support pretense. If you won't hear my counsel, why else are you here?"

Evasion was not possible. "I made a vow to Enithen Tuer that I would swear a blood oath under Fellowship auspices."

"That requires my consent." Asandir spun the crystal between his deft fingers. "A *caithdein*'s invocation binds a tie to the land. Do you understand fully? You are asking my sanction to stand moral ground as a high king's conscience, and the s'Ilessid you serve is most vilely cursed. The Mistwraith's set geas is what drives his war against Rathain's *lawful* crown prince. Not shadows. Not evil. Not moral cause. This is the bare truth. Are you ready to own that your campaign of slaughter is a manhunt for a spirit who is blameless?"

Sulfin Evend raised his cider, defiant. "I survived the fires of Lysaer's madness on the field in Daon Ramon Barrens. I watched him kill as a person possessed, then torment himself in the aftermath. I have seen through the lie he plays out as self-sacrifice. While his heart is imprisoned beyond reach of pity, your Fellowship has named him as outcast."

"With great sorrow," Asandir interjected. "Lysaer chose, despite our urgent advice." The fingers poised on the stem of the goblet kept their forceful calm. "Do you realize what you ask, Sulfin Evend of Hanshire? Your sworn bond must set you at odds with your family. It will splinter your integrity as Alliance Lord Commander. Understand clearly: a binding made here cannot supplant Maenol s'Gannley. Nor will it lend you any false grounds to pose Lysaer as a prince at Avenor."

"I bled and pronounced the vow once in Erdane," Sulfin Evend shot back. "Do you imply that my act held no consequence?"

"Enithen Tuer would not err, in that way. Make no mistake, foolish man. You were bound, well and truly. *But not under terms of old charter law, and not under our Fellowship's formal endorsement.* A binding made here will command your true self. The accounting for that will extend beyond flesh, and could even endure after death."

Sulfin Evend held braced through a shuddering chill, as an icy wind blew on his destiny. "If I do not stand firm at Lysaer's side, who else will? In all of Athera, where can he turn?"

"Do you think to redress the flaw in his character?" Asandir waited.

"No." Sulfin Evend swallowed. "I can't. Lysaer's web of subterfuge is too seamless. Everyone who gets close is in awe of him. Who else can provide a staunch voice of reason, or act with a conscience outside the reach of the cursed forces that drive him? Will your Fellowship stand aside while his last shred of principle is stamped out by the hideous usage of necromancy?"

"Our hands have been tied by Lysaer's free will," Asandir rebuked, unequivocal. "The priest, Jeriayish, also bided his time. He was a mere pawn, but a clever one, careful to instill his cult's compulsion when his victim was weak. That opening was snatched when a lane imbalance claimed all of our Fellowship's resources. Rest assured, the problem shall be addressed. You need not stay involved in the outcome."

"You will intervene to spare Lysaer from threat?" Sulfin Evend challenged point-blank.

"We must act to curb necromancy in its most extreme forms," Asandir allowed. "Its practice abrogates the most basic terms of the compact."

"But not this time?"

The Sorcerer sighed. The hands that had crowned the original high kings now rested flat on the tabletop. "If Lysaer should fall victim to the Kralovir, the gray cult, the power its practitioners might seek to wield through him could compromise the very heart of Athera's deep mysteries."

"You would execute him," Sulfin Evend gasped, shocked.

"We do not kill!" Asandir snapped, emphatic. "Do you understand the abomination you face? If Lysaer succumbs fully, he'll be worse than enslaved. Something other than dead. The rites the cults practice do not leave soul or spirit intact. We are sadly left to release what remains. The devoured husk must be burned in white fire to put an end to a horrific misery. Stay at Lysaer's side, you might risk the same fate."

Sulfin Evend leaned forward, roused as a mantled falcon. "I will swear oath." He raised his glass and tossed off the spirits as insistent proof of his trust. "Lysaer spared my life, once. I owe him this much."

"Lysaer saved you from nothing," Asandir reasserted. "You are free, Sulfin Evend. Walk away from this place under my warded protection."

Yet no entreaty displaced the Lord Commander's fixed stance. The Sorcerer regarded him one taut moment more. Then he emptied his glass, and accepted the burden laid on him with a sigh of hard-set resignation. "Very well. As you wish. What can be done, will be. Fetch down your locked box. You'll allow me to deal with the contents?"

"Freely." Sulfin Evend stood up. Anger steadied him as he retrieved the strapped coffer, then unhooked the chain he wore at his neck and surrendered the key to the Sorcerer.

Asandir placed his fingers against the top one brief second, then turned the lock. He flipped up the lid and touched the wrapped contents. His mouth tightened, as though contact pained him, even through veiling silk. Then he said, "Do you wish to step out?"

Returned to his chair, about to sit down, Sulfin Evend checked sharply. "If I stay, do I stand in jeopardy?"

"No." The Sorcerer did not elaborate, but incanted a phrase in actualized Paravian. As the knots binding up the sacrificial blade loosened, he slipped off the silk and snapped a fist around the knife's handle as though he took charge of a striking snake. His left forefinger and thumb grasped the bone blade, and ran, hard, from hilt to tip. Light flared. Air screamed. Through rushing wind, a child cried out in piteous pain. An old man's voice wailed for reprieve. A young woman wept, and something else sobbed in shrieking, soprano agony.

Head bowed, Asandir gripped the vibrating knife. His tall form seemed wrapped in scintillant light. Through tumultuous noise, he gathered himself and began speaking. Names, Sulfin Evend realized with cold horror: a long list, recited one after the next, with a glass-edged, imperative clarity.

The wailing gained volume, keened into a hideous, tormented cry that first raised the hackles, then threatened to freeze mind and heart.

Asandir turned the knife, point down toward the earth. Then he clasped his left fist at the haft, firmed his grip, and drew the blade through. The sharp edge slit his flesh. Blood ran. Fire bloomed. Droplets pattered onto the ebony table and dissolved, smoking, into white light, within a chamber that seemed suddenly darkened and crawling with shadows.

Inky ribbons of force unfurled from the bone blade. As the power awakened and, called by blood sacrifice, snaked out to claim a fresh victim, the Sorcerer's person came under attack. His arms, his broad shoulders, then his face and head were bound up, then swallowed by those blighting streamers of darkness.

Cramped to nausea, Sulfin Evend reeled. He snatched a bracing grip on the chair back. While he steadied himself, the room dissolved through a burst of blinding, unbearable brilliance. Asandir spoke a word that razed through the turmoil and caused the stone table to ring like a bronze bell. The pure tone shattered thought, undid human reason. With a start, the Hanshireman realized the voices had all fallen silent. No more fell winds howled. The queer lights were gone. Only the commonplace candleflames burned in their metal sconces.

The knife lay, clean and ordinary, on the stone table. Asandir was stanching his opened left hand with the sleeve of Lysaer's erstwhile dress shirt. "You found that unpleasant?" The Sorcerer glanced up. His scalding stare blistered. "I beg you, go. Don't try to meddle with necromancers. Their doings lie outside all mercy."

Speechless, Sulfin Evend sat down. Sick and shaking through the aftershock, he watched the Sorcerer unwind the stained silk. Asandir's hands seemed quite normal. The fresh wounds on the fingers and palm had already closed and healed over. Naught remained but the seam of a livid scar. Beneath that, his workaday callus was marked across and across: older weals, thin and shiny white, their accounting too many to number.

Asandir smoothed down his cuff. He reached for the cider, refilled his glass, then slid the bottle toward Sulfin Evend. "You will bury that knife," he instructed as he eased his dry throat. "The blade was cut from the bone of a girl child's thigh. Her name was once Enna. Her parents believed they had apprenticed her to an upright woman who worked for the weaver's guild as a yarn spinner."

Sulfin Evend managed a shuddering breath. "You will take my oath?"

Asandir sighed. "I must." He retrieved the cleansed knife, gently laid it to rest in the box, shut the lid. "As you said, we have no one to stand guard for Lysaer. I have a simple request, in return. Are you willing?"

The Lord Commander straightened. "What do you ask of me?"

Settled back with his cider, Asandir tucked away his scored hand. "You carry a stone knife from Enithen Tuer, given for your protection. I ask you to accept my direct warding instead, since an object could be easily lost or misplaced. The stone knife may help to guard Lysaer, as you wish. But when the day comes, if you rout the works of the gray cult from Avenor, and clear the foothold they seek at Etarra, then—"

Sulfin Evend shot straight. "Etarra!"

"Oh, yes." The Sorcerer leaned forward. He pressed his guest's hand around the stem of the goblet with an almost ephemeral touch. "Drink, foolish man. You've established your bravery. Cerebeld has been a cult puppet for years. He dispatched his priests to three cities in the east, and your uncle Raiett is already shadowed by the same peril."

Pale to the lips, Sulfin Evend raised his glass, amazed at how quickly Sethvir's strong cider burned off his deep-seated nausea. "I'll give what you ask." Prepared for a blood price, a geas, or some demand for a difficult sacrifice, the Hanshireman held braced for the worst.

Asandir smiled. The expression showed tender sweetness and sorrow, and quite transformed his gruff face. "Take the knife given you by the seeress and, at your earliest convenience, return it to its rightful owner."

"Who might that be?" Sulfin Evend asked, disbelieving. "Do I know him?"

"Her?" The Sorcerer shook his head. "She is the elder of the Biedar, a desert tribe found in the Black Waste of Sanpashir."

Autumn 5670

Game Pieces

While falling leaves and frosts clothed the north in carnelian and gold, edged with diamond, amid the milder lands to the south, the day's early heat streamed through the high colonnades of the ancient hospice at Forthmark. The Koriani Seniors who attended their Prime Matriarch were obliged to wait in the glaring sun of the courtyard. Yet unlike her three sisters, Lirenda was powerless to shed her stifling formal mantle. While sweat trickled down her nape, and her layered skirts clung to her humid ankles, she could not unclasp even one tight button. Chin held high, she was powerless to protect her pampered complexion or raise her hand to relieve the prickle of heat rash inflicted by dampened wool.

No reprieve lay in sight. The courtyard's stone walls, with their uncanny carvings, blocked the breeze from the snow-clad peaks. Shaded under the overhang, Selidie Prime sat enthroned in a high-backed chair. Her purple mantle draped in pristine folds, the hems stitched with sigils of copper. Beneath pinned gold hair, her aquamarine eyes offset a delicate, doll's face. Exquisite in beauty, her deformity jarred: bundled in linen, her maimed hands lay like clubs on a cushion placed in her lap.

Tragic center of the morning's activity, the most skilled of the hospice's healers bent over the Prime's ravaged limbs. They fussed and conferred, in no rush to finish the delicate task of removing their enspelled bandages.

While the ranked seniors waited, constrained to patience, Lirenda fumed in forced stillness.

A more terrible fate could not be conceived to crush pride and dismantle ambition. Fallen from power and privileged position, Lirenda suffered, consumed by trapped rage, her favored title stripped from her. Through the months since she fell under punitive sentence, she fed on her well of balked hate. Though she still owned the knowledge of an eighth-rank initiate, her punishment denied her autonomy. Snared by the sigil of obedience sealed through the matrix of the Great Waystone, Lirenda could not move or speak without a direct command. Kept like an item of valuable furniture, she existed now as a precision tool at the beck and call of the Matriarch.

Unlike the witless ones, stripped as blank husks, Lirenda suffered the corrosive torment of her unimpaired intelligence. Day to day, she endured, her most basic needs enslaved to one voice, that her flesh must obey without question.

She could not speak, though the pretense ongoing before her scalded her very blood. She must watch each move as the sigils for reversal, destruction, and regeneration were dissolved, one by one in succession. The polished quartz stylus dipped, flashed, and cut, a moving light in the healer's deft hand. The meticulous work would be tiresome: each eddy of tied energy must be recaptured in crystal, then given release and dispersal. Close handling of such contrary forces required deep concentration. One slip, or one misplaced stroke might easily sever a finger. With unflagging courage, the hospice healer blotted her brow. A skilled assistant answered the Prime's breathless complaint, then offered a posset to numb her gnawing pain. Slowly, the fine gauze bandages were snipped, then unwound with tender care.

Lirenda chafed as the rest of the farce was played through. She seethed to witness each hopeful, faked phrase the Matriarch spoke to her underlings. For this warped creature who sat wearing the mantle of prime power well knew of the gaps that existed between the restorative spells and a resident spirit that did not match the auric matrix of her youthful body. Today's exhaustive effort must fail. The same as it had, week upon week, since the Matriarch's arrival four months ago.

Immersed in their dangerous, intensive labor, the best healers at the order's command still believed they might cure their Prime's ruined hands. Lirenda stayed powerless. She could not divulge the unsavory secret: that Selidie was a being possessed by the unscrupulous shade of her predecessor. The irony scalded, that *Morriel* sat there, a smug, changeling crone, reembodied as a slender sylph.

The last layers of the dressing were eased away to a cry of dismay from the healer. For of course, the contracted claw fingers remained frozen amid their scarred calyx of wrecked bone and tissue.

Selidie said no word to ease the distress. Forthmark's most skilled talent exclaimed with bent heads, then faced their defeat with hushed deference. The thin silk mitts were retrieved and slipped over the Matriarch's ghastly infirmity.

"Next week," the Prime ordered. "You shall try again."

143

"Your will, Matriarch." The healer dared not argue a direct command, or protest today's thankless dismissal. Oathbound to obedience, she wrapped her instruments, while her assistants swept up the cut shreds of bandage and bundled them for disposal. The group curtseyed and filed out, leaving Prime Selidie enthroned in her chair.

Such towering confidence should have raised hackles, had anyone present possessed either authority or courage to try inquiry. Yet Prime rank of itself granted total immunity. The sole voice that might have denounced the vile crime had been crushed by that tyranny, then silenced. As Selidie surveyed the seniors awaiting her needs in the courtyard, Lirenda alone had the sense to be frightened, aware as she was of the ruthless mind behind that peremptory glance.

"I want Fionn Areth," the Prime opened at length. "He has been left at large for too long. I require him taken back in hand and placed under our order's protection."

The peeress wearing the fourth band of red rank responded with veiled trepidation. "By your will, Matriarch, your command shall be served, though with all due respect, the boy is still kept under lock and key inside warded walls at Alestron. We lack the duke's confidence, and the merchants we hold under our sworn oath of debt have not succeeded in buying his ransom."

"This could change, shortly," Selidie said, crisp. Where, as Morriel, she would have dispatched subordinates with an impersonal snap of her fingers, now, her change of persona compelled her to address them by name. "Marisette! Prepare an array for a grand scrying. Lirenda, take charge of my keys and fetch the Great Waystone from the compartment beneath my state chair." On afterthought, she added, "You look hot. If you like, my page can take charge of your mantle as you let yourself out."

Reduced to a miserable, subservient gratitude, Lirenda swept out on the errand. By the time she returned, shrouded jewel in hand, Forthmark's skilled seeress had completed her protective chalked circles. The quartz sphere for her scrying had been aligned to receive the Prime's influx of tuned spellcraft.

Lirenda placed her wrapped burden in the Matriarch's lap. Under orders, she had to kneel on the tile, then set up the shielded tripod with its forged ring of containment. Next, her fingers were needed to untie the jewel's silk wrappings. She unfolded the cloth, taking desperate care not to graze the perilous contents. The bared presence of the order's great amethyst puckered her skin with unpleasant chills. Worse torment still, she sustained the dazzling proximity of its powerful presence as she used shielded touch, and seated the sphere into its cradle.

Longing seared her to obsessive desire. To be this close to the penultimate might of the order outmatched every concept of cruelty. Lirenda steamed, become little more than the acting hands for a position that should by due right have been hers. A helpless slave, she stepped clear as ordered, while the onlooking seniors took position to one side, and the active seeress settled herself into trance. Then the usurping Prime leaned forward and rested her brow against the faceted jewel. The southern air chilled to ice as she woke the dire force of the Waystone's focus.

Lirenda sensed the harrowing flux of stirred energy as the great amethyst engaged. She shuddered to its contrary tides of charged malice as its matrix was tuned and locked into submission. Once the stone's wayward forces were bound, firmly under the Matriarch's command, Lirenda was asked to enact the sigils to connect the grand focus to a smaller quartz sphere, preset by the seeress for scrying. Harnessed as thoroughly as the massive amethyst, she must act in strict concert, her neat, puppet gestures entrained with the Matriarch's invocation.

When the poised sigils meshed, a thread of hot light burned through the stilled air, there and gone, as the paired crystals equalized their resonance.

"Now," said Prime Selidie.

The seeress invoked her high art, made the dedicate vessel to her Matriarch's will.

A saffron streak of sunshine speared through the quartz sphere. As the image resolved fully, the need to empower the Great Waystone became obvious: this scrying bridged an expanse of salt water, prying into the gloom of a ship's cabin lit by the checkerboard glare from an open hatch grate. Further, the vessel carried a powerful protective talisman: the view came through scattered with flecks as the cipher warding the hull diffused the imperative of the Prime's sigils. The specialized training of Lirenda's lost rank let her interpret the signature of the lane tide and divine the ship's eastbound course, southwest of the Cascain Islands.

"Merciful grace!" murmured Forthmark's titled peeress. " I never knew such a potentized scrying could be done in an ocean setting!"

Selidie's secretive lips framed a smile. "The *Evenstar* has carried our tag for some time. We had a ship's chandler on our rolls. He discharged his due debt by embedding our wrought-copper sigil under her sheathing when she was careened."

The elderly senior showed dismayed interest. "The merchant brig bearing an Innish registry that's been shipping relief to the west? Don't say her mission hides covert motives."

"Listen, you'll see," Prime Selidie responded. "The ship's records might appear spotlessly clean. But her captain has been a loyal supporter of the Master of Shadow since childhood." A direction to Lirenda fine-tuned the array of sigils. The increase in power, upstepped by the Waystone, pressed the air into palpable tension. The scene in the quartz sphere flickered to life and unveiled two figures engrossed in a scathing argument...

* * *

"…won't put in at Innish, to try would be madness!" Feylind's long braid flicked like rope in the shadow, to the adamant toss of her head. "A ferreting customs keeper's forced inspection could land us in trouble over our heads!"

Her first mate's remonstrance bounced back, through the irritable clomp of his sea boots. "Because of our passenger? Sithaer's deathless fires, Captain! The crew isn't partial. They'd see your live contraband thrown off for bait before they would sail to Alestron without putting in for provisions. We'll be down to stale water and salt beef with maggots. Run out of spirits, besides, you'll see your best sailhands swim for Shaddorn's brothels the moment we wear ship to round Scimlade Tip!"

"Oh, 'Captain,' is it? Formal title, but no respect for my orders?" Feylind chose a word she had learned in the stews rousting laggards. "The bullheaded crew on this hulk is well paid. They'll use their brains, not their bollocks!"

"You say?" Before she launched into the rest of her tirade, the mate grinned, caught her close, and pinned her mouth under his challenging lips.

Wrung breathless, half-laughing, Feylind wrenched free. "That ploy isn't going to soften me, this time." She pushed him off, only to find her body assaulted more thoroughly. The hand wound in her shirtfront jerked her to a stop. Two buttons tore loose. She was bare underneath. "Alestron," she gasped, as her mate cupped her breast. He kissed her again, and through the busy interval, expertly began to unbreech her.

"What about your twin?" Neat, sun-browned, and sculpted with muscle, her longtime lover tasted her ear, then her throat. "Fiark will gut you if you break a schedule that's been kept as dependable as the turn of the tides."

"Fiark can howl himself inside out—"

Smothered again, Feylind pounded the mate's back as he lifted her onto the berth.

"Stop biting," he grumbled into her neck. "This tub stops at Innish, as scheduled. The runaway woman can be dressed up in slops. Hands chapped like that, and scrubbing a deck, she wouldn't be given a second glance." A pause, a heave, and a burst of soft laughter. "Feylind, you wildcat, why not just give in and enjoy this!"

Her reply emerged muffled from behind his broad chest. "Randy stud horse! Why don't you give up? I won't forget how we dumped standing orders to transfer a specific party of hot fugitives onto the *Khetienn*, offshore."

That persistent subject engendered a sharp pause. The mate rolled onto his back, Feylind caught against him, her slender waist fanned by the crimped gold of her braid, which, rifled of its tie, came undone. "Dharkaron's Spear and Black Horses, woman! Will you never let loose? Fiark will have dispatched a fishing lugger long since to sail that bunch out to rendezvous."

Feylind slugged the blanket beside the mate's ear. Her man never flinched, only shifted his shoulders and kneaded languorous fingers into her nape.

"He didn't," Feylind retorted, though with less heat. "Dakar hates fishing boats, and the rescue in Jaelot was a Koriani game piece. Did you know that the witches spellcrafted a grasslands goatherd for bait? He's said to look like Arithon's double. Dakar's too wily to play loose with that quarry. I'll lay you six coin weight, gold, to a toss in the sheets, that the spellbinder will have stayed stranded in port before entrusting his charge to a bought captain and a strange vessel."

"Here's my toss in the sheets, and without your pestering contest," the mate murmured, complacent. His grin flashed in the gloom, then vanished again, to nibble another sweet patch of flesh.

Feylind gasped and recoiled, just once. Then she flushed and subsided against him. "I'll show you exactly what you can toss..."

"Oh?" Her man tucked her close as tenderness crumbled down her resistance. "Keep your gold, minx. I'll make you a bargain better than that. Stop at Innish, as scheduled. I'll back your case against Fiark. You'll have that east-bound cargo you're craving—"

Feylind squirmed, caught his shirttail, and jerked the cloth over his head with indulgent pleasure. "One bound for Alestron, you randy goat. Or trust me, the next time you cozen me this way, I'm likely to reach for my rigging knife and put an end to your shameless distraction..."

Selidie snapped a wrapped hand across the Waystone, cutting off the entrained thread of the scrying. The quartz sphere went dark. While the heart of the amethyst glimmered with sullen needles of light, idle and still perilously active, the Matriarch addressed the hospice peeress. "If *Evenstar* puts in at Innish, you will carry out my orders. Review our books for oaths of debt. I want a port exciseman to call for an impoundment, and a cooper that swims to access that brig in the course of her cargo inspection. The marked sheathing strip we have under the hull shall be augmented with a sigil of tracking. I will create the new ciphers, myself. They will be tied, but inactive, and shielded to be overlooked by the Fellowship's spellbinder."

The Forthmark peeress clasped fretful hands. "We may not have an exciseman on the Innish rolls. What then?"

Selidie stared back, unblinking. "You will get one."

The peeress stiffened. Uneasy with the implied demand to use duress, she glanced away and attempted to hedge. "You can't guarantee that your doctored brig will finally reach port at Alestron. Or that, once there, Dakar and your targeted quarry will be available to go aboard."

"If *Evenstar* sails east, we'll stand prepared." Selidie raised her imperious chin, her dismissal including the seeress.

Through the rustle of skirts as the circle disbanded, the peeress strove one last time to relieve her distress. "Wouldn't we be wiser to let the young double go? He's least apt to see harm if he stays among Arithon's active associates."

"We will leave no loose ends!" Stilled in her chair, aligned with the roused Waystone, the Prime forced the subject to closure. "Fionn Areth owes a binding life debt to our sisterhood. As Lirenda's feckless creation, would you insinuate we're not responsible for safeguarding the course of his future?"

The Forthmark peeress bent her knee and curtseyed in contrite obeisance. "Your will be done, Matriarch. You shall have your two men and your plan to waylay the brig."

Lirenda fumed, left alone with the Prime, who had just served her with a vicious, backhanded betrayal: Morriel *herself* had sanctioned the act of Fionn Areth's transformation. Forced to stand in the disturbing coronal discharge thrown off by the active Waystone, Lirenda could raise no word to defend the implied burden of her disgrace. Instead, all her skill and initiate knowledge were put to ruthless use. Since the Matriarch was crippled, the ill-set chain of sigils for *Evenstar* must be framed, here and now, by her captive hand.

The cipher was not beyond reach of her expertise. As an eighth-rank initiate, Lirenda had no equal within the order, excepting the Prime, who alone had survived the ninth test. When Selidie dictated the central pattern, Lirenda realized at once the design was too powerful: this chained sequence would do more than straightforward tracking. The outer ring of characters was sequenced for summoning, in force and limitation attuned to shape what seemed an insidious trap. Prime Selidie intended to recover Fionn Areth. Yet Lirenda could not escape the intent as the last layers of strung energies were appended. Methodology forced the surprise revelation: the runes for lawlessness, excess, and chance twined through the squared sigil that was used for binding stray *iyats*.

No fool, Prime Selidie noted her comprehension. Alone, without witnesses, the usurper could not resist a self-satisfied smile. "We'll call down a storm of fiends at the moment of my choosing. The spellbinder has a known weakness, there. His feckless emotions will never cope. Risk of damage must turn *Evenstar*'s course back to shore, where an Alliance ambush will be lying in wait. The brig will be boarded, and we'll snatch our prize. More than one, to be sure. The Fellowship's still tied hand and foot, knitting grimwards. Who will come to answer Dakar's cry for rescue?"

Lirenda could not comment. Obliged to stitch sigils one after the next, helpless as any other trapped pawn played into Selidie's design, she could not escape sensing the unspoken afterthought: that Fionn Areth's recovery was, in fact, nothing more than a surface distraction. The true target behind today's ploy would be the blond-haired captain who carried Prince Arithon's sworn bond of protection.

Feylind and her brig, Lirenda would have gasped for the bold revelation. For Dakar's predicament was certain to draw the Teir's'Ffalenn away from his impregnable refuge in Kewar.

The underlying motive dangled almost within reach, that a second round of stalemate could be broken. If the Master of Shadow came into the open, initiate Elaira would be compelled to resume the lapsed burden of her Prime's directive. She would have no choice but to leave her sanctuary in the hostel of Ath's Brotherhood, and pursue her deferred involvement with Arithon's close affairs.

Selidie's next instruction disrupted the thread of Lirenda's rapt speculation. "Add the quadrangle runes of chaos, then close out the sequence with *Alt*, but specifically leave the cross on the stave open-ended."

The Matriarch watched with half-lidded eyes, while the hand of her pawn fashioned the sigil with its incomplete rune of ending. The result would leave the spell's pattern stable, but dormant, until the hour Selidie willed its completion. Secretive, silent, the Prime wielded the order's supremely powerful gemstone, while raised power flowed into the work of Lirenda's subordinate fingers.

Yet under the mask of those porcelain-fair features, the usurper's control was not perfect. When the last cipher was scribed, and the ritual incantation released the charged might of the Waystone, her glance flashed like a stalking predator's.

Lirenda knew that expression, had witnessed the same ferocious intensity when the past Prime had plotted her vicious double entendres.

'What else?' raged Lirenda, scalded by a frustration that hammered the closed walls of her mind. *'What else is afoot, you unscrupulous imposter?'*

The sly intrigues of this Matriarch spanned a millennium of machination. Some snare of artful subtlety would be lurking to trip the s'Ffalenn bastard. A covert entanglement far more invidious than the traditional threat of a binding made in recompense for Koriani services, that, by surface appearances, Elaira had been sent to extract.

No clue suggested what pitfall awaited the crown prince that Prime Selidie wove her wiles to entrap.

Lirenda seethed, impotent, as the Matriarch's sweet treble remanded her to the role of a servant. "Veil the Waystone, at once. Then send for my pages. They'll fetch pen and paper, and the lap desk from my chamber. You'll write my correspondence, while the cook's boy brings sweet cakes along with my morning tea."

Autumn 5670

Dispatches

Closeted with his chancellor to address the influx of devotees from Avenor who come seeking converts to follow the Light, King Eldir of Havish adds the sealed parchment bearing Princess Ellaine's witnessed statement and a copy of the proof that condemns Lysaer's false regency at Avenor, saying, "I realize the errand is dangerous, but this missive must reach Tysan's *caithdein*, Lord Maenol, by way of the clan scouts who stand guard in Caithwood…"

When a network informant sends a reliable report that Lysaer's errant wife has boarded an eastbound ship for Alestron, High Priest Cerebeld relays orders to his acolyte at Jaelot: "You will approach Duke Bransian s'Brydion as the Light's envoy, and acquire hard evidence of his collaboration in Princess Ellaine's abduction…"

In the black deeps of the void between stars, hard-pressed by a ravening horde of free wraiths and facing the threat of a redoubled assault by a new wave just arisen from Marak, the Sorcerer Kharadmon unleashes a cry of distress to warn Sethvir, back at Althain Tower…

Althain Tower

V. Convolutions

Asandir abandoned his uneasy town visitor in Althain Tower's first-floor guest suite, closed the door on a promise to return in the morning, then bolted at speed up the unlit stairwell. The sky past the arrow slits now showed scattered stars. Yet if the gusts blew, scoured clear after rain, another storm brewed past the rim of the world that threatened a large-scale invasion. The Sorcerer ascended two stairs at a stride, impelled by the force of raw urgency.

Scarcely twelve hours returned from a grimward, with no chance for rest or recovery, he faced another breaking disaster.

A glimmer of gold light glazed the King's Chamber landing, two levels above. Since the torch set burning for Sulfin Evend's arrival had long since spent its fuel and gone out, this light was sourced by a female adept clad in the white cowl of Ath's Brotherhood.

"Another swarm of free wraiths from Marak, I've picked up the damaging gist." As Asandir's hurried pace brought him abreast, she fell in at his side, unruffled as he continued his clipped accusation, "Sulfin Evend's a s'Gannley descendant with the latent gift of his great-grandame's precocious talent. He sensed the impacting distress in your call! Since no one has time to soothe his raw nerves, you might have thought to come down for me."

The adept touched his sleeve in tacit apology. "In fact, I could not without causing more harm." The Alliance doctrine already held that Ath's Brotherhood practiced fell craft, hand in glove, with 'Shadows' and Fellowship tyranny. Her presence at Althain would appear to confirm that wrongful and dangerous impression.

"I respect your concern," Asandir all but snapped. "But that man down-stairs has too sharp an intelligence for me to waste a moment with less than the truth. Dead set as he is to pick quarrels with necromancers, he'll have to learn fast that you, and I—and Arithon Teir's'Ffalenn—are anything but his enemies."

Up the rough granite stair, past the fifth level's locked double doors, Asandir's deerhide boots made no sound. His purposeful focus through the ascent stirred the adept to alarm. She said, "Sethvir expected you would kindle the third lane beacon."

The Sorcerer maintained his cracking fast pace, with speech crisp as glass tapped by iron echoing in the chill darkness. "If I light the beacon in summons, Luhaine would be pulled out of Teal's Gap before he could finish the bindings to curb the Khadrim." A corporate Sorcerer required five weeks to reknit the wardings that held the Sorcerer's Preserve. As a shade, Luhaine had to invoke tedious steps to safeguard his unshielded presence. The labor he shouldered would take that much longer and expose him to far greater danger.

Asandir rushed the next flight, still expounding. "Traithe's raven would sense the lane's summons, as well. Should I let him worry? He's too far away to respond. If Davien changed heart and decided to help, surely before now he'd have troubled himself to lift some of the strain off Sethvir!"

Gold ciphers flashed; the adept turned her hooded head, startled. "You can't mean to respond to this crisis alone!"

Asandir passed the eighth landing, still climbing, and breathless enough to sound irritable. "Call Luhaine to go? I can't sanction the choice. Not with Lysaer in jeopardy. We cannot afford to strap another sorcerer's resources off-world indefinitely."

Stopped, appalled, the adept stared as they reached the ninth-floor thresh-old, and Asandir checked his stride to fling open the door. Beyond, the eyrie chamber that held Sethvir's library lay silted in gloom under starlight. "You realize I can't intervene in support of your reckless choice!"

"As you wish, naturally." The Sorcerer's shadowy form swept ahead. His haste raised eddies of book-scented air, and flicked dust from the sheaves of the quill pens stuffed in their crocks atop the carved ambry. The ebon table was already bare, cleared of its cached stacks of books since the onset of Sethvir's prostration. "Go or stay," said Asandir, unequivocal. "I will enact what is necessary."

The adept clasped tight hands, her censure kept silent: the Sorcerer's intent to slip free of his body, then fare into the void without posting safe oversight was no less than a lethal risk. Kharadmon had been sheared, live spirit from flesh, caught short in the same adverse circumstance.

Too rushed for precautions, Asandir tossed back a pressed explanation as he rifled a cupboard and withdrew a brazier of black iron. "The trace imprint of the spell that attracted these wraiths was a working of mine, made in partnership with Sethvir. I share the permissions that frame it." Still talking, he assembled the antique tripod at the center of the stone table. "Where Luhaine and Kharadmon could only react in defense, I can enact a direct intervention based on the right of my authorship."

The adept did not leave.

Sethvir's herb stores yielded a braid of dried sweetgrass to ignite the brazier. Asandir filled the pan, then looked up, his glance hidden steel under the shrouding of darkness. "Marak's wraiths are voracious. They consume by possession. With Athera imperiled by three deranged grimwards, our Fellowship cannot possibly field an assault. If we tried, we would certainly open the chance of provoking a large-scale invasion."

Outlined by the pricked glimmer of stars shining beyond the latched casement, Asandir scrounged for a sliver of chalk amid the odd caches of snail shells and the pebbles with mica that Althain's Warden had collected to amuse visiting crows. Then he swiped the layered dust from the tabletop and ticked off the cardinal points to frame a passive circle of warding. His hand did not shake. The straight line of his brows, the taut cleft of his mouth were the mask of a man who seemed heartless.

The adept, who read auras, saw the unshielded spirit. Asandir's inner nature held caring so fierce, the deep flame of it seared without surcease. She crossed over the threshold. The subtle, stirred light that moved with her presence brushed the Sorcerer's peripheral awareness. He checked, raised his head. The focused restraint behind his mild glance could have melted fixed stone with compassion.

"I might be bound by the will of the dragons," Asandir said. "This does not make me a puppet. Your grace is the exalted gift of Ath's peace, and not suited for sordid conflict. Leave here. Do as your given nature requires, and stay on your path with my blessing."

She smiled. "I would sing in sorrow for the greed of your wraiths, but not share in your action to bind them."

Her dusky complexion lost in the gloom, she presumed, and clasped the Sorcerer's wrist. He was as lean as the wind itself, all strong bone and wire-strung tension. "Have you done more than eat, since your working to stabilize Radmoore's grimward?" she chided. "No sleep, not so much as a catnap? Then I will stay, and keep watch for your health."

Asandir touched her knuckles to his forehead in salute. "Brave one," he murmured. "The trial of these times are a burden on us all. I'm heartened to have you beside me." Eased free, he bound his closed circles with runes to rein the beacon into containment. Then he asked due permission, invoked the four elements, and tuned his established rapport to channel the lane flux through the brazier.

The herbs flashed alight, releasing a plume of sweet smoke. Their kindled spark blazed on without fuel, a searing point of indigo blue that notched the Sorcerer's cragged features with creases. Asandir hooked a chair and sat down. Against the looming backdrop of bookshelves, the sliced gleam of gilded Paravian lettering demarked his gaunt silhouette. He laced his competent, large-knuckled hands. Eyes closed, without ceremony, he bent his silver head and settled into deep trance.

Ath's adept took position beside him, quiet hands laid on his shoulders. Their broad strength was as bedrock. Asandir's auric field wrapped her, dense as the fires of a star. The intimacy of close contact laid bare the painfully volatile paradox: the breathing vessel that housed his vast presence was most fragile, a living tissue of flesh and bone no less than mortally vulnerable.

The adept resisted the cry of her fear. Poised at the crux, she saw far too clearly as Asandir stepped into the breach. For Athera herself had been left wounded by the wanton acts of the dragons. Ath's gift of love, sent in redress, had been the Paravian races; and the Fellowship, who stood as the drakes' chosen champions, were appointed to protect the resonance and safeguard the heart of the mysteries that sustained them.

A misstep tonight might tear the fabric of a world, unspinning its expansive existence. If Asandir failed, the penultimate truth in Athera's weave might be dimmed, lost to the pain of entropic separation, destruction, and sinking darkness. If the mysteries withered, the conclave of Ath's Brotherhood could not hold open the gateways or maintain the exalted discipline of their mastery.

Peacefully as sunlight cast through a pool, the adept sent her calm reassurance. *'Keep your strength. Hold the line.'*

She experienced the moment, as the Sorcerer balanced himself into a state of stringent harmony. Mind and will, emotion and thought were centered into alignment. Embodied consciousness became condensed to a pinpoint that hung the poised axis of power: Asandir bridged the liminal threshold *between* the strictures of order and chaos.

The deft instant passed. The adept sensed his auric field lighten, then spin away, while the etheric awareness mooring his spirit unreeled like dropped thread behind him. Then the lane beacon blazed into adamant brilliance. Now immersed in its current, the Sorcerer inducted the raw charge he needed to fuel his journey.

Amid her listening calm, the adept sensed the caught echo of Asandir's experience. Merged into the singing magnetics, his being became at one with the flow that guided the migrating birds, then the convection of winds raising the static charge for a storm front. He absorbed the cold hands of the desperate poor, gleaning the overlooked grain from the fields, then the silenced pounce of an owl, and the squeal of the mouse in its talons. He knew the pinched hunger of families in Dyshent, and the misery of clansmen serving in chains on the galleys snugged under a town breakwater. He was a caravan camped by a road, while oxen grazed under starlight; then the dissonance of crystallized water, warped out of true by the discharge from Scarpdale's torn grimward. The current there bespoke Sethvir's bright pain, holding the desolate span of what fast was becoming a rampaging breach: Asandir endured the horrific ache and passed on by, as he must. Farther south, the ancient circle at Telmandir brought him the laughter of King Eldir's sons. Clan lodge fires burning in Elkforest braided into the silent bleeding of trees cut down for charcoal at Deal. The Sorcerer felt the delvings of miners who broke rock for tin beneath Lithmere, and rolled as the surf, slamming the shingle at Earle; he was icy water, and the schooling of fish, then misted cloud, billowing under the new risen moon.

Althain's lane beacon intensified as the Sorcerer drank in its cascading stream of wild energies. The change struck too fast: one instant the adept felt Asandir's essence, nestled into Athera's magnetics. Then the brazier flickered, divided, as the Sorcerer launched in departure. Cold blue as a star, the spark resteadied and blazed, a detached beacon behind him.

Asandir traveled the icy void without anchor. Into unshielded territory, endangered by questing wraiths, he dared not carry his rapport with the lane's flux. He fared outward adrift, dropping all but the ephemeral memory of the clay shell left at Althain Tower.

The adept steadied her breathing and curbed her raced heartbeat. Apprehension would serve no purposeful good. For where the observer constrained to five senses might dimly sense hostile cold, and the emptiness of deep vacuum, the stream of the Sorcerer's unleashed presence would discern vistas beyond. Asandir would reencounter himself, mirrored in the upper registers. Shifted into vibration and light, his trued self would be redefined: in music beyond hearing and color beyond sight, he would rejoin the grand spectrum that sourced Ath's creation.

That siren call could unstring the mind. Even the self-aware spirit might run mad with desire to embrace the sweet ease of surrender. Against the thundering chord that *was* life, unveiled as exalted glory, Asandir had no more than spare will, and the hard-set choice of endurance. The dragons had bound him. The warp thread of his life had been precisely matched to the weft thread spun by their dreaming. Summoned with such clarity, his nature must answer. Irrevocably, fate had wedded his destiny to the cloth of Athera's existence. If he lost his grip, or let go of himself, there would be no route back, except through tormented insanity.

Braced for the course of a steadfast vigil, the adept tracked the tuned pulse of the Sorcerer's life chord and committed herself to patience...

An adamant presence hurled outward across the vaulting dark of the deep, Asandir touched against the protective matrix laid down by his discorporate colleagues. The construct gave him the reference point to leap over the distance at speed. Spelled wardings rang like a cascade of tapped chimes as he answered the challenge and passed, clean as a needle through silk.

Onward, he pressed. The crystalline voices of stars braided song all about him. Ahead, if he reached, he could sense Kharadmon, weaving a convolute string of evasions. The inventive working strung a web of entanglements to delay the first influx of marauding free wraiths.

Asandir allowed that contest wide berth. Even the most shielded contact with his colleague invited the chance of disaster: if such an encounter drew glancing notice, conflict would be joined. The pack that nipped at Kharadmon's heels would turn, with the tenantless husk of the body at Althain posing an irresistible gambit. The tenuous tie between spirit and flesh would lead back to Athera and provide the ripe opening for hostile possession.

The field Sorcerer had no choice but to pass Kharadmon by and hold to his unswerving purpose. With the planet behind no more than an azure chip inset against velvet darkness, his reference became the whisper-thin trace of the trees, a remnant left by the defunct spell once created to call his colleague home from an ill-fated survey of Marak. That cold, icy world had succumbed and died, overrun by the wraith-riddled fogs that had also sourced the Mistwraith's destructive invasion. To the famished horde, cut off at South Gate, the rich life on Athera remained as a prize to be ravaged by relentless conquest.

Asandir made his way without disturbing the imprinted energies the old spell had scribed through the ethers. If he ranged too near, the wraiths already in progress and tracking might sense him. More than agile opponents, they could slip between time. To evade their keen senses, the Sorcerer upstepped the frequency of his being until he rode the carrier wave of harmonics, octaves above solid matter. Awareness without form, he sailed the vast deeps, whirled in the black flame of the untamed glory that existed before ordered creation.

Here lay his danger: streamed through the very essence of joy, cradled by power to absolve every grievance, Asandir knew a pure exaltation that acknowledged no pain and no boundaries. Marak's wraiths, Athera—the binding charge of the dragons—seemed dwindled to insignificance.

The ties that sustained vital flesh became both prison and leash, an encumbrance the self-aware spirit might snap as identity thinned and faded.

For that thread to endure, the Sorcerer must renew his attention from moment to moment. The very act denounced his full Name. Each reaffirmation cut like a betrayal as, steadfast, he refuted the core of all knowing that cherished his greater existence. Asandir suffered a hunger of spirit that transcended all cares of the flesh. Beguiled, then claimed by the might of Ath's mysteries, he drifted, while a whisper arose to sustain him.

Far behind, so very far, the Sorcerer still sensed the echo of peace set forth by Ath's adept. A spirit entrained by free will and high mastery, she expressed the grand dance while still holding to human form. Her stance extended him gentle reminder: of the body and the frame of intent left behind at Althain Tower. The drakes' legacy caged him in danger and hardship; separation and pain, that knotted his heart to the fate of a world, sliced sharp and deep as old agony.

Asandir chose.

The residual spell cast its faint, shining line across the black well of the deep. From his point of raised vantage, through force of bared will, he could trace the course of its reduced vibration. He sensed the wraiths also, knew them by the flat tang of their avarice and their driven, voracious hunger. He hurled his awareness farther out into the dark, searched until he encountered a space where the spell's inactive path was untrammeled. There, he wrenched the frame of his consciousness back into dimensional space. He arrived, tightly shielded. Since a whisper of presence would draw the free wraiths who currently quested in crossing, his deterrent must be worked in stealth, and at speed.

No use, simply to annul his permissions, or use a forthright rune of banishment. The original conjury was impressed in the memory of Athera's live trees. To impose straight will on their dreaming consciousness, or to refigure the remnant as anything else but a tie of regenerative expression would be an invasive violation. The staid grace of a forest did not comprehend choice. Its tidal cycle of being did not recognize destructive intervention. A tree did not act; it simply *was*, a reflection of placid tranquillity.

The Major Balance demanded exacting integrity. What could not be ended must be reworked within the strict frame of harmonic alignment.

Asandir engaged help from a distant, hot star, one that possessed no fair, spinning worlds to entice the ravenous wraiths. Its gifted fire fashioned half of his remedial warding: a loop of geometry, hard-edged and impenetrable knit into a circle expressed in both darkness and light. From the gap of the void and the stuff of shaped energy, he welded opposition into pure balance: birth and death annealed in the cyclical spiral understood by the language of trees. In consummate mastery, the Sorcerer bound the opposing forces through the torus of time, without end and without a beginning.

The effort taxed him. Unlike his colleagues who existed as shades, the concentration required to engage his craft must be enacted in dual awareness. Asandir dared not waver, or slacken his grasp on the contrary forces he handled. One strayed thought, for a fractional second, would dissipate the energy field that sustained his untenanted body.

If he misstepped, so far out in the void, Ath's adept could not extend her power to save him.

Asandir sealed the primary layer of his conjury, aware the foundation he created was vulnerable. Should any Fellowship colleague or adept with initiate knowledge succumb to a free wraith's possession, *all* that he fashioned could fall to misuse and violation.

The Law of the Major Balance was a stricture graced on permission, not a limitation based upon force. Its restraint was enacted by choice of free will, without imposing fixed bonds or control. Its wisdom sprang out of living awareness, not a rote rule, or formulation. True order was not subject to knowledge, but arose from the deepened awareness that sprang from coexistence in unified consciousness. Used without due care for consent, the rarefied power the Sorcerer wove could be turned to harmful intent. A pattern of creation in symmetrical balance *must also* encompass the means to warp, and imprison, and destroy.

Whole power entrained the hoop of all being and did not deny the constrictive face of its nature.

Asandir wrought knowing he could not enact the least set of punitive protections. Not without sullying the dire symmetry of existence and admitting the stasis that seeded all entropy.

He closed the last rune, worn thin by his labor. Peril confronted him. The new, active matrix now must be conjoined with the ghost imprint of the old homing spell. The surge of live power as he welded the link could not be masked, since the bias of the earlier working had never been meant to impede. Its primary design was a homing call, fashioned to welcome the weakened, strayed spirit, and assist swift return as a carrier.

At the instant the new conjury aligned with its matrix, the defunct structure would refire, and react once again as a wide-open conduit.

Asandir took swift pause, scanned backward, and measured the flesh left at Althain Tower. His breathing and heart rate were slowed, not yet damaged by creeping exhaustion. Beside his stilled form, steadfast as flame, the adept maintained her calm vigilance. The Sorcerer took ruthless stock, as he must. Once he committed, his straits became sealed as his action flagged the wraiths' notice. Outside of his body, he would be raw bait, and starved for fresh prey, they would come for him. He must close the last rune and slip clear on the instant before his reserves were expended.

Schooled to know his own strength, already tested against the bittermost limits of hardship, Asandir struck with surgical speed. He tapped the older spell's structure, reclaimed his personal permissions, and renewed their validation within an exact flash of thought. He sensed the wraiths also. Their quickened interest woke an insatiable drive to consume the intoxicating power contained in his essence.

Despite dire necessity, the Sorcerer dared not rush. Constrained to subtle delicacy, he adjusted the old spell's continuity. The pulse of changed energy shifted the imprint, there and gone, as a flicker. He damped what he could, reduced his touch to the barest ephemeral signature. Unmasked and vulnerable for the duration, he seamlessly joined his new crafting into the stream of the structural remnant. He sealed each connection with intricate care, aware of his enemies, closing. Wraiths converged on two fronts: hordes from teeming Marak as well as the pack on his back trail, raging under his colleague's defense. The trace of the homing thrummed under Asandir's touch, plucked like a strand of taut wire. An echo bounced back: Kharadmon's startled cognizance, fired to sharp response, as his colleague redoubled his effort to snag back the free wraiths' converging attention.

Asandir dared not pause for acknowledgment. If that saving help eased the pressure on one flank, the side facing Marak had no ally. As long as his work kept the spellcraft unsealed, Athera lay open to invasion. Each second, wraiths seethed from the ice-bound waste. They rushed the connection, mad with sentient hate and beyond every power to stem.

Asandir wove his craft, lightning-fast, sure as granite, even as the homing spell trembled and flared. He marked the approach of the descending swarm, foresaw critical deficit, and, at raw need, expanded the reach of his resource. That resharpened focus took all that he had. Given a narrowed, split second to finish, he shouldered the risk under fullest command. His body would suffer, but only as long as the moment he needed to lock the last ciphers to forestall attrition. He must take the chance that he could wrest clear in time to salvage the anchor that grounded his absent spirit.

In that crucial split second, the adept's brilliance dimmed. Asandir sensed that change. Forerunning prescience detected her influx of clean power, dispatched through his aura, and flung down the breached cord in a gesture of unconditional reinforcement.

His raw instinct screamed warning. Disaster would follow!

He reacted before thought, slammed the rune of closure over his *almost* complete structure. The construct would stand, flawed, subject to decay. That loss had no remedy. Time had run out. Asandir whirled clear of the free wraiths' starved rush. He twisted his being outside the veil, rejected the stream of the prime life chord dispatched by the adept *as it happened*. Snapped back inside of his damaged flesh, sprawled in the chair back at Althain Tower, he cried out as the pain of shocked nerves whirled him dizzy.

Asandir was granted no space to prevaricate. A seizure ripped through him. He quelled the convulsed muscles; unsealed stinging eyes, burned his own life force at reckless need, and shoved back his wheeling faintness. Through needling agony, as his impaired auric field whipped through imbalance, he encountered the adept, tumbled slack in his lap, with her cheek pressed over his heart.

"No," he grated. "I refuse you! This is my clear right!" He raised shaken hands, cupped her face, and stared into her opened, stunned eyes. "You will not diminish yourself to assist me. Dear one, no. The charge of the dragons was never your burden!"

"My gift," she corrected, her whisper all pain. Tears wet her lashes, then spilled over. "Such pride hurts, that you should refuse me."

Asandir held her secure, while his pulse raced, too ragged. His breathing ran rough, as though he had sprinted a marathon. "What pride?" he gasped. "Did you not know? Your act invoked the drakes' binding upon me."

Her dismay touched him sharply, though she did not speak.

The Sorcerer sat, very still. He engaged a deft thought, used the spark of the brazier to recharge and burn clear his stressed aura. When he moved, he absorbed her jagged distress; but not her tears. There, he had no strength. If he wept for this, the break would destroy him. "Oh, yes," he murmured, then stroked the damp hair that escaped from the crushed back cloth of her mantle. "Even so. The burden I carry can't sanction your sacrifice."

As adept, she must bow to the source of his sorrow: *Athera's mysteries could not sustain the loss if the grace she embodied within breathing flesh should be dimmed to a less-than-exalted expression.*

"No," Asandir whispered. He moved leaden arms and gathered her close, while her anguish soaked his rough mantle. "No. With the Paravians lost, we can't spare you."

The adept shifted in protest. "Your work—"

"Incomplete." The admission carried no rage, and no judgment. "The wraiths are delayed, and the crisis, deferred. That grace of reprieve is sufficient." The shared grief stayed unspoken: had he not returned to deny her, the remnant spell line would now be fully secured. The closed conjury *most likely* would not have cost the last spark of life in his body.

"Such risk as you shouldered was not to be borne." The adept raised her hand and traced over the seams quarried into the Sorcerer's face. "Never say you weren't worth the cost of my effort."

Asandir could not answer, aware as he was that the library chamber was no longer private. Three male adepts now surrounded his chair, waiting in expectant, grave silence.

He gave his consent.

The white brothers moved in, still without speech or censure. They supported their distressed colleague, then eased her weight from the Sorcerer's lap. Constrained by his own formidable dignity, Asandir endured, as he must. "You have been here at Althain Tower too long," he informed them in soft apology.

The elder among them tipped his hood in salute. Since no word could encompass what had just passed, he helped as the others bore up their colleague and tenderly ushered her out.

For she was unimpaired. The blaze of her light remained brilliant; unsullied. Yet how narrowly close she had come to reducing the glory of her initiate state of high mastery. Asandir bent in his chair, brow rested upon the trembling clench of his knuckles. At the last, none but he knew how sorely he had been tempted to accept the unpardonable gift of a high adept's act of sacrifice.

By midnight, the lane beacon at Althain Tower was extinguished, with the deserted library left under starlight. Bathed, changed into a soft, dark blue robe, with his silver hair damp on his shoulders, Asandir settled into a stuffed armchair, pulled up beside Sethvir's bed. The Sorcerers were private. The adepts had left a lone candle burning, while two spirits locked by the blows of adversity shared a rare moment in conference.

The gilt glow lit the Warden's opened eyes, limpid and clear as a dawn sky viewed through a crystal.

An interval passed without attempt at speech.

Then Sethvir said, "You made a right choice."

Asandir shifted broad shoulders, to a rustle of horsehair stuffing. More than careworn, he looked wrung sick with exhaustion. "That does not make me feel any less like a murderer."

The wraiths were curbed, but not thwarted. Further, Marak's hordes had been roused. Over time, as the incomplete warding decayed, Athera would hang in a state of worse-than-redoubled jeopardy.

"You've bought a reprieve," Althain's Warden insisted, his scraped whisper that much more determined. "The future's not set. At the first opportunity, we'll restructure the flaw in that warding and make an end of the problem together."

Asandir stilled his impulse to hammer a fist into the moth-eaten chair arm. Once the grimwards were rededicated, he could turn his hands to many a critical task left unfinished. Yet ahead of the urgent work waiting in Lanshire, he had Sulfin Evend, downstairs. While the hiss of the candleflame sweetened the air with the fragrance of melted beeswax, his thoughts ranged the dark, where eyes could not see, and fixed on the pulse of men's fears.

"Where is Lysaer?" he asked presently. "What safeguards is he taking, have you seen?"

"You should sleep," Sethvir whispered.

The field Sorcerer did not answer. Silence reigned, except for the restless wind, sweeping the bare crests of the fells outside. The candle burned lower. Sethvir closed his eyes. Frail as a thread of unreeled silk, he expelled a reluctant breath. "Very well. Though you won't be pleased by the bent of the knowledge extracted from Erdane's library."

Asandir raised his eyebrows. "Not the Gray Book of Olvec."

"That and worse," Sethvir grumbled. "They've unearthed the whole pile of scrolls on the known genealogies as well."

*   *   *

Lysaer s'Ilessid, called Divine Prince, was said to be ensconced in the seaport haven at Capewell. The fact was whispered about in the taverns, and debated in the cozy, private salons of the rich. Yet where merchants bemoaned losses, frustrated by commerce slowed to a crawl by the savage weather, the outlying crofter whose barren fields languished was forced to endure the pinch of privation and scarcity.

In town, the Light's Prince Exalted might succor the weak, and comfort the disaffected. But the workingman who built his house with his hands, and who lived by his sweat in the Korias Flats watched his family grow gaunt with despair.

The traps set at need had long since claimed the last of the summer's importunate young hares. A father come home empty-handed again did not expect to encounter a white horse, tied up with six outriders' mounts in the churned-up mud of his yard. Amid lashing rain, the gold-stitched bridles and sunwheel saddlecloths gleamed blindingly spotless and bright.

However improbable, the visitation was real. The simple man blessed by the royal avatar's presence could not offer a traveler's hospitality. Shamed to the quick by his poverty, he could do no more than creep with embarrassment across his own threshold.

The smells struck him first: of hot sausage, and cinnamon-spiced mead, and the fragrance of newly baked barley cakes. Afraid he was dreaming, he heard the music of his youngest child's squealing laughter. The man shed his soaked mantle and made his dazed way into a kitchen transformed by the startling brilliance of candles. His rough trestle was crammed with strange faces: imposing men wearing sunwheel surcoats and a self-assured air of cold competence. Yet their gleaming mail and spired helms were thrown into eclipse by the fair-haired figure in scintillant white, on fire with gold ribbon and diamonds.

Divinity perched on the stool by the hearthstone. Such magnificence should have seemed displaced amid the rough setting. The rude board walls, and mortared stone hob of the farmstead glorified nothing.

Yet Lysaer s'Ilessid displayed no airs. His gilded head bent in artless collusion with the crofter's tiniest daughter. Clad in muddy rags, her drawn cheeks like paper, she clung to his upraised knee and clamored to tug at his rings.

The father stood, stunned, his breath stopped in his throat, as the white-clad avatar looked up. The attentive clarity in his blue eyes could have pierced a man through to the heart. Despite his lordly bearing, the speech that followed was not condescending. "Please forgive the fact we've arrived, unannounced."

The crofter stared, tongue-tied. He had no grace, and no courtesy to fit the astounding occasion.

Lysaer's ease was effortless. He scooped the ragged child into his arms and passed her off to the wife as though the best part of his privileged life had been spent dandling mannerless toddlers. The little girl wailed, grubby fingers still straining to snatch at the shine of his jewelery.

Lysaer's smile held laughter. Burned into the air by a beauty that scorched the senses like fire and ice, he wrested off his largest diamond setting and handed the ring to the child. "See that she doesn't spoil her teeth by gnawing the stone from her dowry."

Then, as though magnanimous gifts had no strings, he confronted the stupefied crofter.

"He's asking for Edan," the wife blurted, afraid. Two years past, in agonized grief, they had dedicated their older daughter to the Order of the Koriathain. Better, they felt, to lose her alive than abide the risk that her gift might draw notice from Avenor's Crown Examiner.

The crofter swallowed, defiant. "Edan's a man grown. Come of age, this past year. Neither I nor the wife can speak for him."

Lysaer s'Ilessid missed no small cue. His smile stayed woundingly genuine. "A party come to make an arrest does not bring food, or leave diamonds. Your young man is quite safe. He will choose for himself. Withhold his consent, and I'll leave you in peace. Your child keeps the ring, since it pleases her."

In a croft crammed with men wearing chain mail and swords, that statement seemed beyond reason. More than gemstones flecked that form in starred light. The crofter reeled, his breaths rushed too fast, and his fists clenched with sweating terror.

"Sit down, good fellow." Lysaer strode forward. His warm, steering grip eased the crofter's stunned frame past the grinning sprawl of his outriders, and into the better chair by the fireplace. "No father should weigh his son's lot in soaked clothes, on the misery of an empty stomach. Your wife's told me that Edan's out mucking the barn? Then bide your time. Let him finish his chores. You'll have enough time to measure your feelings and question my motivation."

The elegant creature moved on and perched a casual hip on the trestle. The rough plank might as well have been a throne, the way his regal bearing still blinded. The crofter found even the simplest speech painful. "What brings your exalted self to us, asking?"

"You can't guess? Because Edan's a sensitive." Those sapphire eyes stayed direct, though the answer entailed an explosive disclosure. "The Light is calling for talent to serve. Your son's gift will soon be sorely needed."

"Why?" The question burned. Grief for the lost daughter was still too raw to broach the sore subject, headlong.

The wife was less reticent. "Your Crown Examiner burns talent!"

"My Crown Examiner guards against misuse that harms innocents," Lysaer corrected with unflinching candor. "He destroys the potential minions of Shadow, wherever such pockets of depravity exist. And they are widespread.

I carry firm proof: an evil faction has made inroads against us. Corrupt men who ply the dark arts have poisoned my regency at Avenor. I'm bound by realm law to see justice done. Would your son stand up with a handpicked few? The most gifted among them will receive training to fill the seats of high office. The Light's cause will not pander to wealth or ambition! I would have staunch young blood at my back to lend oversight in my absence."

"He will go," said the crofter. "For that honest cause, we will spare him."

The wife dropped the spoon in the kettle with a clang. "You're that certain?"

Yet in a starved household with no crops to harvest, the change of fortune offered an unparalleled gift of opportunity. "Let him go, Vae. Where better? You know in your heart, wishful thinking won't make him a farmer."

The wife bent her head. She would have to agree. What prospects could the young boy expect among neighbors who distrusted talent? Sworn to Lysaer's banner, Edan would no longer be shunned. Nor would he be tempted to fall into wrong company and undertake harmful practice.

"He will go to the Light," the crofter repeated. Over the bounty of the hot meal, he heard through the Divine Prince's straightforward terms. When the boy came in, redolent of the cowbyre, the grant of consent had become a formality.

One had but to look at his young, unmarked face: the avatar's presence struck the living spark that ignited to incandescent resolve.

The sunwheel outriders arose and moved out to collect the horses tied up in the yard. They mounted Edan on a fine, dappled mare, while the family he would leave sonless behind him was signed onto the rolls by the hand of Prince Lysaer, himself. They received the sealed parchment, promised a dedicate's crown stipend that would keep them in comfort for life.

As the glittering cavalcade clattered through the sagged gate, and the cruel wind blew the cold rains of a premature winter, the wife blotted tears for her departed child, now destined for wider horizons. "How did those men find us?"

The crofter hugged her stooped shoulders, just as fiercely inclined to weep. "Need you put such a question, or give way to doubts? That creature who chose him was god sent."

Late Autumn 5670

Sword

Immersed in a physical exercise learned at Rauven to sharpen reflex and balance, Arithon stood, eyes closed, in the peculiar little six-sided chamber that centered Kewar's private library. Each wall was cut by an open arch. The portals led off into separate rooms, filled floor to ceiling with books and scrolled maps, and bronze cornered chests crammed with arcane paraphernalia. Davien's tastes were eclectic. His fascination with architecture infused all his works. In this place, the domed ceiling amplified sound with precise and unnerving clarity.

Rathain's prince had not lit the sconces. Amid absolute dark in that windowless place, the time might have been night or day. A mage-trained awareness could discern which was truth. The spiraling whisper of Athera's magnetics ran through the matrix of mineral, and plant, and also the human aura. The touch of sunlight made mountain rock speak.

Outside of Kewar, the first blush of daybreak fired the snowfields in carmine and orange.

Inside, immersed in velvet silence and dark, Arithon Teir's'Ffalenn exercised body and mind. He anchored his breathing to the cycles of sky and earth. In disciplined form, through a dancestep range of movement, he precisely aligned his etheric awareness.

Sound acquired an expanded clarity, and light, a purified brilliance. The dark was not featureless, and silence was not still. The master initiate moved through the forms, enraptured and wrapped in the expanded glory of mage-sight.

The queer shape of the vestibule allowed no mistakes. Its properties magnified every flawed thought as well as each snagging distraction. Yet

Arithon had chosen the site out of preference. The vexing enhancement of untoward noise made his solitude the more difficult to breach without warning. Immersed in the web of subtle perception, he first sensed a rearrangement of air, as though the element suddenly became *more*. Chameleon-like, the effect disappeared the moment he plumbed for the source.

He stopped trying. Ruffled, he paused with closed eyes: and so captured the faintest, smoke bloom of movement that no material senses might capture. A ripple of warmth touched against the smoothed veil of his aura, and his Sorcerer host stood before him, two practice sticks gripped in his hands.

Davien's censure was arid as he accused, "You're losing your edge."

Arithon smiled, eyes open and mild. "Am I, in fact?"

Davien did not answer. Wrapped in pitch dark, he tossed one of the sticks, hard.

His targeted victim fielded the catch. The slap of the wood against his bare flesh rattled the stilled air with echoes. Warned by sharp instinct, Arithon also parried. The ferocious crack as the sticks collided destroyed the last vestige of peace. In darkness, reliant on subtle mage-sight, the Master of Shadow was compelled to match the challenge of Davien's latest caprice. Strict schooling sustained him. The responses required for blindfold sparring had been practiced to ingrained reactions since childhood. Attuned with the subtle aspects of self that extended the range of perception, he rose to meet Davien's fast-paced assault. He had stayed fit. His body moved with the grace of a tiger, sustained by an effortless balance.

Where the expanded reach of his gifts might slip his grasp and whirl him into the slipstream of prescience, Arithon stayed centered. He constrained his willed focus, pushed back the rogue trance state that unveiled the blurred imprints of what *might be*. Trained breathing steadied him. The sticks cracked and slid, each blow met and turned in the *actual* frame, born from the ephemeral moment as choice and willed movement begat consequence.

Arithon deflected each whistling strike, his faculties stretched to the verge of that heightened awareness. Davien did not play by predictable parameters. A success never passed uncontested. Behind the straightforward sparring with sticks, there would be the arcane twist that must press mental wit, and vault the intellect to imaginative acuity.

Braced for such tricks, Rathain's prince was not stunned by surprise when his parry in form failed to block the Sorcerer's descending riposte. Two-handed style came naturally as breath. As his stick encountered no clash of impact, his left hand already responded. Arithon caught the hammering swing of the wood. The opposing blow slapped into his opened palm. He locked agile fingers and captured the stick, informed by the sting that a miss or a fumble would have bruised his unpadded shoulder.

Davien said, from the darkness, "Where's your trust, Teir's'Ffalenn? Don't you think I could have recouped a missed blow the same way I evaded your parry?" He stood; calmly countered the wrenching twist, just tried with intent to disarm him. "You should heed *all* my free words of warning, my friend. I didn't try you with a bared sword."

The rejected suggestion to visit the armory had not been met with complacency.

Arithon kept his fierce hold on the contested stick, too wary to fall for distraction. "Why should I rush to pay court to a weapon whose purpose is blood and destruction?"

The wood left his grasp, dissolved away to nothing. The wall sconces ignited at the same instant. Flame light unveiled the Sorcerer's expression of unabashed provocation. "You might test that presumption."

Rathain's prince lowered his foolishly empty fist, his smile tried to edged humor. "First tell me why you think that I should."

Davien laughed. "That would be unsporting. Nor will I apologize for disrupting your privacy. *Evenstar*'s beating the narrows to Alestron. Three days from now, she'll reach the s'Brydion citadel and drop anchor as the slack tide turns."

"Lysaer's errant wife cannot be my concern." Lightly clad in dark hose, a loose shirt, and soft boots for wearing indoors, Arithon was a study in crisp black and white, except for his eyes, which drank in the light like sheared tourmaline. "One princess bagged like caught game was enough. Let this one sharpen her claws and her wit on somebody else's forbearance."

An even head taller, the Sorcerer posed the more flamboyant figure, his russet jerkin and orange sleeves offset by chocolate brown breeches. "You won't meet her," he said. "Duke Bransian's no fool. Ellaine will be sent inland to a safer refuge than Alestron's armed walls can provide." The pause hung for an instant. Then, "It's the volatile paper she carries that's going to fling stones in the wasp's nest."

Again, Rathain's prince would not rise to the bait. "Why not grant the duke the free use of my sword? You have my permission. Deliver it."

Yet this time, the use of barbed insolence misfired. Davien's eyelids swept down, masking an expression *that was not anger*. His form disappeared on an inrush of air that extinguished the wicks and knifed words through the sudden dark. "Then fly blind, my wild falcon. You are making the narrow and dangerous assumption that the sword handed down with your ancestry was ever forged for the purpose of killing."

Arithon started, his inrush of breath spiked through the rustling morass of echoes.

"Oh yes! Now you'll listen." The Sorcerer's sharp laugh held more warning than triumph. "I'm not hazing you with nonsensical riddles. Is your store of trained knowledge deficient, your Grace? Then correct your ignorance! Traithe carries a knife that has never drawn blood."

"I'm not ready for this!" said Arithon, laid open and trapped by a wall of inner reluctance.

But he was alone. The library vestibule was empty. He stood, shivering under a film of chill sweat, with the integrated balance of body and mind undone by the race of his heartbeat.

Too prudent to plunge headlong into deep waters, Arithon spent days immersed in odd books of esoterica. He perused the crabbed scribbles written by hedge talent on flocked sheets of vegetable paper; the smoke-scented parchments of conjurers and ceremonial healers, and the cedar boxes of slate wafers scratched with a stylus, inscribed by the desert tribes' loremen. Of Paravian knowledge on the forging of steel, he found nothing committed to ink. Only the odd reference, amid Ciladis's verse, of craftings done in the Ilitharan forges, then augmented by Riathan and Athlien singers. Such inferences lay past the concrete reach of thought or written words to encompass. Therefore, their access must be sought in mage-sight.

Since his point had been taken, Davien granted Arithon's request to borrow from Kewar's herb stores. Bearing a braided twist of sweetgrass, his own trail-worn wallet with flint and steel striker, and a precious glass phial of rose oil, the Master of Shadow made his way to the armory at last to confront the heirloom sword bestowed on his distant forebear.

The Sorcerer whose riddle had prompted that step kept his meddlesome nature in hand. Rathain's prince was alone as he braved the threshold past the studded door.

The chain-hung oil wicks that streamed from the wall brackets were, thoughtfully, already lit. Ahead of him lay a circular chamber, surrounded by lacquer cabinets. Their abalone inlay gleamed in soft rainbows, patterned in the vine leaf motif favored by Vhalzein's master craftsmen. The breakfront doors were closed, but not locked. A visitor might examine their contents to satisfy curiosity.

Arithon was not tempted. He entered the armory, barefoot, slightly shivering in the chill air. His sword, Alithiel, awaited his pleasure, hung on an upright stand.

The steel had been cleaned. The shining black blade was stripped of the mean sheath he had used through his flight across Daon Ramon Barrens. Quiescent, the inlaid Paravian runes gleamed like opal glass. The exquisite swept hilt and emerald-set pommel gave rise to a quiver of thrill. The exceptional grace that marked centaur artistry must always catch mortal breath in the throat.

Killing weapon, or not, the balance and temper of a sword forged at Isaer could not be equaled, or faulted.

Arithon lit the sweetgrass. Finely trembling, he blew out the flame and fanned air on the crimson embers. Then, decisive, he stepped forward and knelt. With slow passes, he wreathed the standing weapon in smoke, a time-honored ritual of cleansing. For generations beyond living memory, the blade had been carried and used in armed conflict. If Davien's provocative implication held truth, such bloodletting destruction had evoked something worse than an ignorant mistake.

When the grass had burned down, and the air was hazed blue with its lingering fragrance, Arithon closed his eyes and centered himself. He steeled his raw nerves. Then he uncorked the glass phial of rose-oil, and anointed the tips of his fingers.

The rich fragrance enveloped him. He breathed in the scent. Ciladis's writings had taught that the flower's arcane properties touched the mind and entrained the emotions toward healing. Arithon embraced the response through mage-trained intent. Contrite with apology, he sat cross-legged on the stone floor.

Then he lifted the sword and laid the black blade with reverence across his bare knees.

A shudder rocked through him. He curbed his sharp dread. Deferral would save nothing. If this Paravian artifact had been misappraised, he could not make amends, except through the grace of an earnest, unflinching humility.

First step to knowing, he emptied his mind. Blank as clear glass, wideopen to nuance, he murmured a Paravian phrase of apology. Then he used the pure essence of rose to dress the fine steel. His light touch ran the oil into the metal, stroking from pommel to blade tip. As he worked, he could sense the old blood, and the agonized shock of the dying. His own kills, and others, extending back through his father's time; then the reapings enacted by an uncounted sequence of forebears. Arithon stilled further, listened more acutely. Beneath blood and pain, he encountered as whispers, embedded within the same register: the fire in the forges that had first shaped the steel, and the distanced ring of star song retained by the ore, once extracted from sky-fallen metal.

Arithon engaged mage-sight, sounding still deeper. Patience commanded his discipline. He gentled the steel, coaxing its essence to present itself for his inquiring inspection. Such a revelation could not be forced. The elusive qualities he sought to tap would lie octaves above the range of the physical senses. Receptive to impressions beyond the veil, suspending himself in surrender, Arithon waited. He stayed utterly calm. Hands flat on the sword, he slowed his breathing and engaged the fullest extent of his initiate talent.

The encounter began as he least expected. A light thrill brushed over him, testing.

A shiver rocked through him. His skin rippled to gooseflesh. The ice touch of the steel seemed to burn through his body, riffling the ache of an unformed possibility along the pith of his marrow.

"Mercy," he whispered, too well aware: he would find no reprieve, if he faltered. He resisted the primal reflex to stir, kept his mind vised to absolute quiet.

And the touch came again, subliminally distinct. It poised for a moment, more fragile than thought. The slightest disturbance would shear its tenuous thread of connection. As Arithon held, the feeling moved, then swelled, a melting caress that seemed to shower his aura with welcome.

His heart responded before thought. Entrained as he was to his innate compassion, he could not choke his reaction, now. Arithon felt the scald of remorse press tears against his closed eyelids. The tender touch that embraced him did not withdraw. Nor did it disbar him in judgment. Shown grace for his flaws, he shuddered, then broke, then lost separation as the veil he touched suddenly parted. He had no breath to gasp, no time to test impact.

The living spells imparted by the Athlien singers seeped through, then flooded his naked awareness.

No study prepared him. Not when he had expected to find the residual imprint of a forgotten ceremony: a sword blade used as the traditional symbol to mark the east quadrant, for air element.

Instead, his awareness was taken by storm, led into a grand unfolding. He encountered the elements, all four of them, living, imbued in the strength of forged metal. Earth, Fire, and Water embraced him like song, stitched into a tapestry of moving light. Yet of the four, Air stayed predominant: the sword Alithiel had been wrought by Paravians, who had been Ath's living gift to the world to redeem the contention engendered by the drake spawn. They had battled, not to kill, but to hold open the gateway to love and awaken the awareness of healing intelligence.

In the burgeoning hope sustained since the First Age, the old races had forged twelve swords at Isaer, and fashioned their metal with the primal forces to evoke an exalted beginning. Alithiel had been instilled with an aware presence. Her summons called in the essence of Air, a fourfold braiding of virtues that sourced the wellspring of inspiration: responsibility, power, freedom, and transcendence. Her presence incited the breath of new dawn and the innocence of fresh invention.

The blade *was* the contained seed of creative peace. The bearer who wielded her conjured strength could draw the line across time and space that opened the way for forgiveness. Her stroke, handled under initiate awareness, would cut free the constricting, old patterns and unbind the pain of the past. The sword shaped the key to open the mind: *that the flow of water could nourish; fire could burn the residual debris and spark rebirth; and earth element, finally and fully, might bind change into manifest being.*

Arithon bent his dark head and wept, for such a healing beauty abandoned to anguish. The sword on his knees was an instrument of change, razor-sharpened to slice through fear and hate, and blind violence born out of ignorance.

The fact she had ever been misused to draw blood was no less than a tragic desecration.

Embarkation

The rigid fact the s'Brydion men hated women's interference in council posed Captain Feylind of *Evenstar* no deterrent. As set in her way as the duke's wizened grandame, she badgered until she was shown to the door that led to the small barracks wardroom. She was challenged there by two jumpy guards. Without second thought, she blistered their ears, then barged past, ignoring their obstructive arguments.

Once inside, she grinned, flipped her braid over her shoulder, and measured the hammerbeam chamber. Dented war shields adorned the stone walls. The straw floor was sprawled with the duke's fawning entourage of flea-bitten deerhounds and mastiff. Masked by the echoes of racketing voices, Feylind closed a light fist on her cutlass, then approached the trestle, where the soldiers' litter of cards and dice had been thrust aside by the duke's bearish habit of leaning on his outthrust elbows. No one glanced sideward. Head peeled of his mail coif, his whiskered chin bristled, Bransian s'Brydion stayed immersed in his brangle with his vociferous pack of brothers.

"Dharkaron's black bollocks!" Parrien denounced with wild venom. "We've spent all these years like damnfool curs, nosing up the fat rump of Avenor's alliance!" His finger stabbed, incensed, toward the duke's face. "Now you're suggesting we'll skulk in broad daylight, skittish as forestborn drifters?"

Cards fluttered and dice leaped to the bang of Keldmar's mailed fist. "As the Light's affirmed allies, we dare not send less than an escort suited for royalty. Give me the armed strength of a field troop! Let my lancers mow down any sad, sorry force with the bollocks to question our honor."

"Allies?" Mearn coughed back his hoot of deprecation. "After the family just spurned the priest who came knocking with ambassador's flags from Jaelot?"

"We did?" Sheathed knives jingling against his steel byrnie, Keldmar perked out of his slouch.

The debate over Princess Ellaine's due escort suffered a striking break. Eyes widened with dawning, bloodthirsty interest, Parrien also accosted the duke. "An Alliance priest! Showed his chumbling face here?"

Keldmar laughed. "What did you do, brother? Bundle the stripling in his sunwheel banner and use a trebuchet to sling his arse back where he came from?"

"Who needed a weapon?" Bransian's shrug was all chagrined innocence. "Grandame Dawr got in ahead of me. She disdained the bother of using state language and showed the priest emissary and his train a shut gate."

"Well, he would have been naught but a slinking spy," Keldmar allowed in sharkish approval. "Can't have such weasels inside our walls, slipping dispatches back to Raiett Raven. Not until we have Lysaer's wife safely packed off to the care of Ath's Brotherhood."

Mearn snatched that opening to ram home his case. "Which is why I should take our state galley to Spire! We don't need to declare there's a fugitive aboard. If our luck sours, and her presence is noticed, I'll have my fighting strength at the oar, and our ambassador's flags to claim honest support of her station."

"Why sweat our best seamen?" Bransian folded his arms, set his boot on the trestle, and lounged back in his seat in sprawled comfort. "That's a frank waste when we still have the deepwater keel that brought Ellaine sucking up bilge in our harbor."

"I have an offshore rendezvous scheduled!" That pealing, female voice swiveled heads. Pinned under the glare of four sets of gray eyes, Feylind advanced on the trestle. "Not for any fool's errand up Rockbay Harbor will I run the *Evenstar* back to the west."

Duke Bransian bristled; both feet thumped to the floor. "You think your mercantile Innish registry gives you the brass to dictate to me?"

"I don't give jackstraws for the foibles of men, who clash swords over slogans and banners." Feylind reached the trestle and matched the duke's glare, hackled as any hazed lioness. "Just one question matters: are you Arithon's friend, or his enemy?"

Mearn followed the match with keen fascination, fast fingers busied with snatching up cards. A natural gambler who relished high stakes, he shuffled the deck in a slipstream cascade, pitched to see how his brothers would declaw a woman armed with both cutlass and boarding axe.

No fool, Parrien stole his cue from Keldmar, who had brangled with Feylind before, and whose doused cat expression suggested the moment was unsafe to cross her.

Fur was hell-bent to fly: Duke Bransian's clenched jaw and thunderstruck frown forewarned of a hammering argument. "Well, we've kept his made double kenneled and safe. By now, he'll be loaded in *Evenstar*'s hold, dragged aboard by the scruff of his neck. Since my men are relieved to be shut of his misery, why are you not on your brig weighing anchor?"

Feylind braced her fists on the opposite rim of the trestle. "Why won't you say where Prince Arithon's gone? The silence on that score is deafening!"

Mearn's shoulders twitched underneath the bronze studs of his tailored suede jerkin. Since he penned the duke's missives in coded script, he happened to know that Fiark had been informed of the ill-starred foray through Kewar sometime ago. Since none of his brothers would find the right words fast enough to dissemble, he ruffled the cards with a hissing snap. "You'll have to ask the Mad Prophet."

The captain's nailing regard swung his way. "I would," she said crisp, "if I knew where to find the weasel-faced parcel of rat bait."

"That's easy." Mearn smiled, teeth gleaming. A connoisseur at stirring fresh trouble, he jettisoned the cards and snatched up the offered diversion. "I'll take you."

Not fools, his two middle brothers kicked back their chairs. They joined ranks just in time. Bransian's naked relief was eclipsed as, mail gleaming, they padded like wolves, the blond captain shadowed as quarry before their swaggering tread.

"We're going where?" Feylind queried, as her escort tripped the latch.

Mearn flipped open the door with a debonair flourish, kissed her caught wrist, and ushered her through. "The stews by the lower town barracks, of course. No one told you? Dakar has been pie-faced since the moment he got here. Twenty-eight of our greenhorn recruits have been hazed under officer's orders to sober him."

"He came through that undamaged?" Feylind said, amazed.

"Sooner weep for the victims," Keldmar responded. "Not one of the wretches succeeded in keeping the leash on that wastrel for more than five minutes."

Outflanked by rough humor, Feylind was intrigued. "You lot expect to fare any better?"

"We're not recruits," said Parrien with nasty hilarity, and charged into the press on the street.

For Dakar, the secure haven of Alestron's walled citadel afforded the chance to make up for long years of privation. Flat on his back with his spinning head pillowed in the silken lap of a prostitute, the vacuous bliss that parted his lips could have rivaled the cream on a sated cat's whiskers. A dusky-haired doxie was massaging his feet, while another sylph traced an exotic dance on his groin with her gilded nails and a feather.

Sunk into a haze of beatitude and wine fumes, the spellbinder grumbled a slurred retort to the nagging prick of his conscience. "May Dharkaron Avenger threaten me with a gelding if I so much as think to return to serve Arithon Teir's'Ffalenn."

"Best suck in your bollocks, you twice-useless diddler, since wishing on that score won't spare you."

The hussy who spoke was not from the brothel.

Dakar cracked open an offended eyelid as pandemonium arrived and disrupted the peace in his perfumed corner of paradise. The whore at his crotch dropped her feather and fled. Next, the melting, soft hands at his soles were replaced with the punishing bite of male fingers, clad in gauntlets.

Dakar lashed out, too late. The fists on his ankles hauled him like dressed meat from his nest of carnal distraction.

"On your feet!" cracked the harpy who had wrecked his bliss. This time, Dakar placed her memory.

"Feylind!" he howled. "You sexless, cold fish! Keep this up, I'll see you and your dog pack of heavies marooned on a Stormwell iceberg!"

Laughter answered. "Try, my fat ram-dick. That predicament ought to be perishing fun, with you packed along for excitement!" As more sword-hardened fingers clamped on his wrists, the ship's captain finished with relish, "The duke's men aren't sailing, besides."

Fully incensed, and stabbed by the early pangs of a hangover, Dakar hissed a venomous string of obscenities. A slow death by flaying would have seemed kindly, set against the prospect of being dragged on board Feylind's bluewater brig. Riled enough to resist being shanghaied, the Mad Prophet refused to stand up.

A pail of cold water struck him in the face. Roaring with rage, now nakedly dripping, Dakar heaved at his captors. Although he fought like a goaded bull, the s'Brydion brothers contained him. With Keldmar behind, gripping both arms in a lock, and Parrien, unmoved rock, with a belt cinched over his ankles, no drunk had a chance. Not to be idle throughout their rude enterprise, Mearn tore up a sheet for the purpose of binding a gag on him.

"Feylind, just listen once in your born life!" Dakar ducked the fingers that groped for his mouth. "You're making a dreadful mistake."

"Do you think so?" Feylind chuckled with evil delight. "I don't see your ladies shedding a tear or defending your dissolute character."

Stripped to pink skin, and trussed hand and foot, Dakar was hauled from his joy in the pillows and into the open street. There, as captive bait for s'Brydion sport, he was dipped in the public horse trough four times before Mearn drew a dagger and freed his lashed ankles. The reprieve was not done for humane decency. Parrien decided to place bets with some bystanders. The stake rested on how many wobbling steps he could take before measuring his length on the cobbles.

Dakar evaded that humiliation by sitting down, to the ruination of passing traffic. Pebbled with gooseflesh in the scouring wind, he swore incoherently into the muffling sheet, until Keldmar took umbrage, and winched his shivering carcass down to the sea gate, crammed like a bale in the cargo sling.

There, wretchedly chilled and sick from the swamp taste of slobber wicked through by the dripping gag, he was dumped in the bilge of a rolling tender. Four amused deckhands jumped at Feylind's order. They scrambled aboard and threaded their looms to row out to the *Evenstar*'s mooring. While Mearn's busy knife sawed the knot off the painter, Keldmar shouted over the racketing noise crowding the docks at the waterfront. "You can weigh anchor and sail with the tide. Vhan and Talvish are already on board."

Feylind turned her head, fast, her braid whipped in the breeze that ruffled the harbor to whitecaps. "What! Instructions were clear! Those two swordsmen were meant to resume their old posts, and stay in Alestron's service."

"Well, the duke sent them back." Parrien set his boot on the thwart and launched the tender away from the wharf. "Don't argue, woman! You're going to need them. Somebody sharp had better stand guard, or that botched-up work of Koriani witchery will be sticking a dagger into your back."

"The made double?" snapped Feylind, incredulous where she stood, fists braced on hips, and one toe jammed on the stern seat to balance against the jerk as the drifting boat caught the riptide. "Damn your scampish family! What unsavory fact has his lordship kept from me?"

Since Dakar was rendered unable to speak, the reply carried across the widening span of roiled water. "Fionn Areth's determined to help Lysaer's Alliance spit your prince on a sword, then light up the pyre to burn him."

Purple with chill by the time the *Evenstar*'s sailhands had hauled him on board at the end of a halyard, Dakar was dragged, stumbling, into the stern cabin. He dared expect no comforts. The cramped space was furnished with the spare practicality common to seagoing ships. As straightforward in her lack of apology, Feylind unsheathed her cutlass. She snipped off his bonds, then tossed him a blanket and shoved him arse down on a locker.

"Was that the truth?" she demanded, annoyed. "Fionn Areth's a canting sunwheel fanatic?"

Dakar chafed numbed fingers, then caved in to necessity and cradled his pounding head. "How should I know? The poor wretch spent five months locked in Bransian's dungeon, and—"

"No, butty!" Feylind slammed her bared steel back home in the scabbard. "Stow the lamebrained excuses. Your jiggling paunch tells me you kept yourself drunk, and lazed about whoring the whole time." A clipped stride carried her under the hatch grating, where she bellowed for the mate to cast off and set *Evenstar* under way.

"Feylind, no." Dakar had to fight to make himself heard through the raced footfalls of the deck crew and the clanking pawls of the capstan. "I had my sound reasons. You'll just have to trust. We need to exchange some serious talk before you depart from this anchorage."

"And let Alestron's duke heap the pressure back on to haul about and sail west?" Feylind spun, furious. "Not on your life, Dakar! I am not sheltering Lysaer's errant wife back downcoast, or on anyone's roundabout jaunt into Spire!"

Itched by stiff wool after months in silk sheets, and fighting turned senses that would shortly render him prostrate with nausea, Dakar shouted, "This has nothing to do with the safety of Avenor's runaway princess!"

"Damned straight it doesn't!" Feylind stalked to the locker behind the companionway and snatched her oilskins down from their peg. "Are you so certain of s'Brydion loyalty? Kalesh and Adruin fly the sunwheel's standard, did you know that? When we ran the strait to get in here, we all but had to dip flags and declare for the Light. How long can the duke's service to Arithon last, if he can't pass his ships through Lysaer's allies to reach open water?"

"My concern's not for politics," Dakar forced out, hitched short by his roiling belly. "I beg you to stay inside the citadel's defenses for other reasons entirely."

"Huh." Feylind peered down at his green, sweating face. "I'll believe you that far. At sea, you can't drown your wits in a bottle or slink off and hide when I pitch the unpleasant question. Where's the Master of Shadow? Why didn't he stay in your company, beyond Jaelot, and what in the name of Sithaer's fell fires made you miss your scheduled rendezvous last spring?"

Too wretched to shoulder the touchy diplomacy to broach that round of ill news, Dakar shut his eyes and hunched under the blanket. His head spun like sloshed froth. The vertigo seemed much too virulent, despite the swirling kick of the tide that hissed under *Evenstar*'s keel. About to heave, he could do little else but clamp his teeth and look miserable.

"Too skintight to speak?" Feylind slung on her foul weather gear, jerked open the companionway, and stamped out.

Dakar recovered his voice too late, as the door slammed. "Feylind, damn you, come back! I'll explain."

His shout availed nothing. Once on deck, the brig's captain yelled to summon the thug who served as her quartermaster. "Here, straightaway! Haul that drunk to the sail hold. Lock him in with a bucket and leave him. Oh, he'll howl and threaten red murder all right. There he stays, by my order, until he's come sober."

Denied his last chance to lodge urgent protest, Dakar cursed the rough handling that bundled him belowdecks. Worse, his sensible choice to hide Arithon's activity was wasted. The brig's cross-grained captain could not be deferred. She would hear all the rancorous news soon enough from the lips of Fionn Areth.

Evenstar, meantime, would stay under way. Practiced at enduring the disastrous mix of strong drink and the miseries of sailing, Dakar hunkered down with his head in his hands and sought the oblivious solace of sleep.

That respite escaped him. His dream of lush women and soft, scented sheets broke apart as the door to the sail hold scraped open. Dissident voices shouted outside. Then something banged. A struggling, bound body crashed in and landed with bad-tempered curses across him.

Dakar choked, gagging on the fust of mildew puffed out of his nest of spare canvas. Slammed by an elbow, then punched by a knee in the gut, he curled on his side, dumbly retching.

Fionn Areth stopped yelling. Aware he had landed on some wretch's body, he wormed to one side, then said, "Light scorch the black bastards, they've locked me in, too!"

Dakar hugged his griped belly, too ill to swear back. "Just keep on invoking Lysaer's false religion, you'll find yourself chucked off for shark bait."

"The brig's captain's a maniac!" To judge by the random rustles and thumps that jerked through the rumple of sailcloth, the yokel was struggling to loosen the wrists just lashed up by Feylind's deckhands.

"She's Arithon's passionate ally, you dimwit." Since Dakar was too damaged to call up his mage-sight, he settled for shutting his eyes. "What did you expect? I'd have thought, after five wretched months in a dungeon, you'd have more brains than to spew your fanatical opinions in public."

"I didn't speak to her." Fionn Areth lashed an ineffectual kick that billowed more dust from the canvas. "Not one word. The uppity bitch wouldn't grant me the time of day for a hearing."

Feet thumped overhead. Lines squealed through the blocks. Feylind's cried orders were obscured by the whump as more sail was unfurled aloft. Dakar lurched to the kick as the hull slammed the waves, smoking up spray as she gathered way in her trampling run down the estuary.

"What landed you here, then?" he asked point-blank. "We aren't unbrailing topsails for drill on this vessel. Don't claim you didn't spill all the news of Prince Arithon's flight into Kewar."

"I wasn't asked," Fionn Areth said, injured. "The captain was collared and given the worst by Vhandon and Talvish already."

Dakar's bursting laugh was choked short by a wince, as pain lanced his tender head. "No kind reference to vouchsafe your character, I see. Get used to confinement. Feylind's got the mind and long memory of a first-rate offshore navigator, which is a boon, except when it comes to offenders who ruffle her loyalties."

"She holds a mean grudge?"

"Like a jilted shrew," Dakar stated, morose. "Even so, you should hear my advice, and try not to judge her too harshly."

"Why not?" Fionn Areth stopped his useless chafing at bonds that were not going to yield to necessity. "She behaves like a pirate who connives hand in glove with Arithon's marauding clansmen."

"That's part of the problem," Dakar admitted. "How sorely she wishes to run interference on Lysaer's Alliance and their filthy practice of manning their galleys under chained slavery."

As his comment provoked scathing disbelief, the spellbinder turned his head, beaten weary. "Yes, Avenor puts captives for sale at the block. And that last is pure nonsense! *Evenstar*'s registry's kept aboveboard and clean by Arithon's adamant order."

"What for?" snapped Fionn. "His Grace needs the sanctioned front to move his henchmen's lifted trade goods?"

"No!" Dakar sighed, too sore to stay sharp. "Arithon's stood in for Feylind's dead father since she and her brother were children. He's kept *Evenstar* honest for the sake of an oath he once swore to their widowed mother."

"What did he promise?" Fionn Areth shot back, aflame with salacious speculation.

"A binding of honor to hold them both safe from the perils attached to his name. Which is why you'll stop claiming their patron's a criminal. I don't care if you fake a contrite change of heart. You will smile and apologize until Feylind's convinced to unlock the bolt holding us prisoner."

Tackle creaked. The brig hauled her wind, then slammed, bucking against the tidal race in the channel. Dakar gasped, clinched tight as a clam as nausea clawed at his vitals. Every natural instinct insisted that the *Evenstar* should have bided inside of Alestron's snug harbor. While Fionn Areth discovered the horrid discomfort that attended blue-water sailing, Dakar endured, sunk in silence.

He misliked the crawling itch in his bones. With time, the nagging sensation grew worse. Some unseen force seemed at work on the brig, an insidious wrongness he could not pin down in his undone state of distress. Days might pass before he could scry, racked as he was with seasickness and the price of dissolute indulgence.

Late Autumn 5670

Transits

"It's all settled, my dear," said Dame Dawr s'Brydion, teacup laid aside as she arranged disposition for Lysaer's unsettled princess, "the duke's escort will deliver you to Methisle Fortress, into the care of the Fellowship's master spellbinder. From that safe haven, when need permits, a Sorcerer will see you the rest of the way to Ath's hostel in the city of Spire..."

Stinging yet from the cut lately made to reframe his oath by the rite of the Fellowship's auspices, Sulfin Evend arrives in a blaze of raw light at the focus circle in Avenor; and Asandir's swift instructions remain in his mind, as the lane forces fade and release him: "I have business elsewhere, you must fare on alone. Ride straight through to Hanshire, speak to none that you meet, and your face will stay masked by my warding..."

As Asandir refires the lane flux to speed his urgent journey to remedy the damaged grimward in Scarpdale, far east and south, at the hostel in Forthmark, Prime Selidie calls in the attendance of twelve seniors, her purpose to snatch the opportune opening to launch her bid to seize the merchant brig, *Evenstar*...

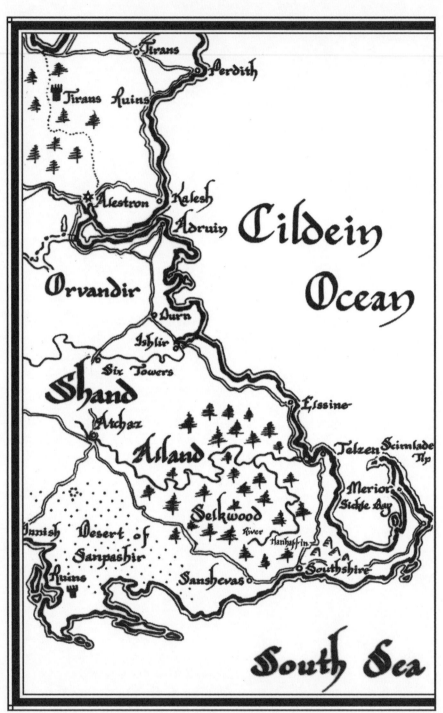

Eastshore and Southcoast of Shand

VI. Counterploy

Chin braced on clasped fingers, Arithon turned the page of an obscure text on the Paravian practice of working masonry without mortar. The hour was late morning. Clad for comfort, he wore an unadorned shirt, and a laced jerkin of black suede. A silver-edged belt clasped his whipcord-lean frame. Though he had not ventured outside of the mountain for nigh onto a year, Davien's quirky habit of issuing challenge had forced him to maintain peak fitness. If he missed the sun, or the frisk of the wind, he showed no fidgeting restlessness.

That discipline was not wasted. A day begun without expectations changed fast as a prickle of energy brushed at the bounds of his aura.

He stood at once, wary. The candles were streaming, a striking departure from form: never before had Davien's arrivals abandoned the high art of subtlety.

He dared a soft inquiry. "We have trouble pending?"

A voice answered out of the ruffled air. "More than you know, Teir's'Ffalenn." Davien's living form assumed substance, his fine-grained skin flushed from the cold. He wore a black mantle edged with silver embroidery. The hood was tossed back, a sign of recent impatience since the salt-and-russet tumble of hair was neatly constrained by a tie of dark leather. "Your associates on *Evenstar* have put to sea," the Sorcerer opened. "They've cleared the narrows from Alestron, bearing southeast, and Koriathain have unleashed a spring trap."

Arithon said without flinching, "I trust I'll have time to gather my sword?"

The Sorcerer laughed. "In fact, you do not." He unfurled the thick cape and extended the weapon as offering. The black steel had been sheathed in a sturdy new scabbard and hung on a bronze-studded baldric.

"You know me too well." Arithon accepted the blade's icy weight. Without pause for argument, he armed himself, not astonished as the tang of the buckle slid into a hole punched for an accurate fit. "Princess Ellaine's no longer aboard?"

"No." For once, the Sorcerer was not inclined to try games. "The brig's captained by Feylind, her mate and crew. For passengers, she carries Dakar, your double, and your clanborn honor guard."

"Vhandon and Talvish stayed on?" Arithon's glance was balefully sharp. "My order released them back to their duke's service. They were instructed to remain ashore!"

"And so you should, also, Teir's'Ffalenn."

"What will I be facing?" Arithon surveyed those stilled, night-dark eyes, and encountered a spark of unease. "Since you didn't ask whether I wanted to go, and unspecified warnings aren't useful, I trust you've a way to transport me?"

Davien raised his eyebrows. "Even your vaunted nerves will require a shielding."

"Permission to stand guard and act in my behalf? You have it." Arithon stepped forward without hesitation. He met and matched the Sorcerer's troubled regard with a trust that was woundingly genuine.

From a stiff, poignant pause, which startled them both, Arithon stated, "Have we not shared guest oath? If you wished me harm, I would be dead. Your nature is not to beg anyone's help. Therefore, I stand, freely offering."

Davien's surprise vanished behind masking reticence. "As you've asked, then don't curse the messenger, Teir's'Ffalenn."

Arithon stood firm, despite that hurled challenge. He did not flinch at the Sorcerer's approach. Nor did he recoil from the touch, when it came, though the contact held nothing physical. Davien's power arose like a well of poised force. Seamless crystal, its silence enclosed him. Sealed inside its ring of forged purpose, mind and awareness were gathered, intact, then whirled upward and out of his body. Enveloped in sudden, devouring darkness, Arithon reemerged through a shower of light.

He sensed air, then wind, then the vault of sky, at one with the flight of an eagle.

Cold rushed across the sleek vanes of his feathers. The ice of high altitude burned pumping lungs. Arithon rode, gloved in the bird's shape, wrapped inside the matrix of Davien's consciousness. All remembrance of his human form was gone, a feat that had happened too blindingly fast to reverse.

Past the threshold of change, the Sorcerer's thought picked up the question left dangling. *'I can't say what you face. Not yet. Prime Selidie has kept her intent tightly guarded. Now that she's launched the close plot she's been hatching, we'll see the design set in play.'*

186

Arithon regrouped his shifted perception, while cloud streamers spun past, and the gusts whistled over the pinions of outstretched, taut wings. Spread below, a crazy-quilt pattern of hills lay seamed by ice-crusted ravines. Such low scrub and briar, snagged with rock at the crests, identified the frost-blasted heath of Daon Ramon. A wing stroke, more clouds, a sensation like dizziness: beneath, now, were snow-dusted vales. Furrowed ledges rose up to white summits that flashed like a crumple of enamel and glass. The bird threaded a tortuous pass through the Skyshiels, a transition that smashed every concept of impossibility. Arithon fought his distracted mind steady. Threat by Koriathain left no option except to pursue the subject at hand. *'You can't guess the extent of Selidie's plan?'*

'Beyond a sigil for tracking set in Evenstar's *keel, no,'* Davien admitted point-blank.

The eagle's head turned. His farsighted gaze scanned the lay of the land, and pinpointed a summit for navigation. A banking arc steered though a slip-stream of air, over the glimmering surge of the fifth lane. Then another vigorous, downsweep of wings. Water now flashed beneath, pocked by a brass sun, amid the indigo ruffles of wavecrests. Eltair Bay; Arithon identified the distinctive shoreline from a vantage heretofore only seen inked on charts.

'The Fellowship can't act, nor can I intervene without seeding a cycle of damaging vindication.' The Sorcerer's shared musing bespoke undertones deeper than balked frustration or open regret. *'The Koriathain ought to be curbed. Prince, you'll have to win through on your merits.'*

Arithon weighed his immediate answer, then probed with the utmost wry delicacy. *'You are not your colleagues' ally, in this?'*

Davien's brittle irony suggested that this time, the nettlesome prick of exposure found him as the unwitting victim. *'You have grown to know me too well, Teir's'Ffalenn.'* He conceded, not hedging, *'I bear the other six Sorcerers no malice. If their choice was to stand, I had to fall. They had committed too much to revoke their position. I expected no more, and no less than the fate their hand dealt me before I chose exile.'*

Another wing beat, and another plunge into the whiteout sheet of a cloud bank. Arithon realized this was no natural mist, formed out of crystallized moisture, but a transverse pass through some unknown frame of conjury that unreeled across dimensional distance. When the eagle broke through, they now soared above the East Halla peninsula, slashed by the mud road that led into Tirans, with the broken walls of the Second Age ruin nestled into the fringes of Atwood, due south. Bound at such a pace, they would cross over the open ocean within a matter of minutes.

The need to curb raw curiosity was painful after months spent in free-wheeling pursuit of all manner of arcane knowledge. Arithon questioned, re-luctant, *'Does Dakar know the ship has trouble pending?'*

'*He can't avoid the awareness much longer.*' Davien dived earthward. The rush of air through his wings became thunder as he used the downdraft over water to plunge from the rarified heights. '*Prime Selidie's engaged the Great Waystone just now, her purpose to waken that sigil. The groundwork she's laid is already entrained.*'

'*No small working,*' Arithon returned in the snatched second before the next uncanny wingstroke.

'*Small or large, her construct is most tightly focused.*' Davien hurtled them through another blind crossing. '*Assumptions at this point will just cloud the facts. Eyes will serve better. We'll survey the territory on our way in.*'

A split second of whiteness, then the sting of salt air, and stiff wind burdened with the moist charge of a squall line; now Davien's eagle form swooped above the jagged, hooked shore that ran south of the inlet to Alestron's deepwater harbor. The long, rolling combers swept in from the east, spouting lace spray on the rocky spurs that guarded the calm inner coves. Here, where the free wilds of Orvandir bordered the ocean, the coast-running galleys took refuge from storms. The sea grass in the shallows showed the scraped gouges of keels where they had anchored in shoaling water.

Near solstice, when the rough weather slowed trade, only the most experienced galleymen put their timbers and crews in harm's way. One oared ship, at most three, might be snugged into shelter in seasons when easterlies threatened; but never inside reach of Ishlir or Durn, and never in bunched-up numbers.

Today, ships were packed in like schooling fish, their decks pebbled with clumps of armed men. The broad-bellied sails were left bent to the yards, with the variegate banners of a half dozen towns flying like tinker's snippets of yarn. Yet the pendant streaming atop every masthead bore the gilt-and-white sunwheel of Lysaer's Alliance.

The Sorcerer broached the uneasy remark on their suspect strength and high numbers. '*Someone's been mustering at Ishlir, assuredly forewarned.*' Every hull rode far too high on the marks to be properly laden with cargo. '*Their position won't be a coincidence.*'

Arithon sorted strategies, speechlessly grim. No natural hazard he could imagine should cause Feylind to alter the *Evenstar*'s offshore course. Fionn Areth's presence on board made any run to the mainland a risk.

The question demanded swift answer: would the Prime's machinations be framed as a goad, or as bait?

'*Seen enough?*' Davien asked, though already his next wingstroke sliced and blurred through the boundaries of time and space. More observation would be useless effort, given the aggressive evidence. The shore of Orvandir had been primed for an ambush. For the brig, any closure would launch a disaster.

The eagle veered due east once again, soaring into the teeth of the gusts, with the Cildein's whipped crests knit cobalt and indigo, patched with the white snags of spindrift. There was a wrongness. Arithon caught the tingle of vigilance that narrowed the Sorcerer's awareness. Through avian senses, he also picked up the ozone that sharpened the breeze. No by-product caused by a natural storm, the scent was too fresh, and much too distinct to be left by a passing cloudburst.

His flicked thought to Davien went beyond warning. '*The brazen bitch wouldn't dare!*'

'*She would. She has,*' Davien confirmed. '*Through the Prime's eyes, this wide world is a game board. She would sacrifice all to snatch victory. Need we tarry? You're going to have less than an hour.*'

Response from the Prince of Rathain was leashed fire. '*Get me aboard* Evenstar. *You already carry my word of forgiveness as the harbinger of bad news.*'

Dark wings swept down. Darkness followed. The form of the eagle dissolved into air, then bled away into memory. Arithon tumbled, bodilessly disoriented. He received the errant impression of a sealed stone chamber. The enclosure was egg-shaped, with polished, dark walls flicked by rainbow flares of moving light, and the echo of trickling water. Then that uncanny awareness unraveled. His consciousness plunged through a whirling, hard spiral, and recondensed back toward the forgotten, firm weight of his flesh...

Midmorning arrived amid stiff, running swells. Still shut in the buffeting dark of the sail hold, though granted loaned clothes from the slop chest, the Mad Prophet stirred. At last, he had sobered enough to try the rudiments of his trained talent. The door remained barred. If Araethurian herders had pig-iron minds, their stomachs were made of no such stern stuff. Mage-sight revealed Fionn Areth, curled prostrate within a nest of mildewed storm tackle. Misery rendered him too limp to moan. The air reeked of sour vomit and urine, with the promise of worse: the bucket secured by bagged sand in the corner sloshed brimful, a hairsbreadth from upset as the brig wallowed and slogged over each trampling wavecrest.

By the working groan of the hull, and the relentless thrum of filled canvas, the *Evenstar* now plowed a rhumbline course through blue water.

Dakar grumbled a thick curse. His tongue felt furred in frog slime, and his bladder was strained full to bursting. He shut gritted eyes. The blackness behind his closed lids fairly sparkled to the white flame of his headache. He groaned, moved, clamped fuddled hands to his brow. Somehow, he must refound the focus to engage his initiate awareness.

Long-suffering patience let him center his mind. Discipline pierced through the muddle of pain, not steady as yet, but sufficient to begin to redress the damage left by his wrecked state of overindulgence. If the battering that accompanied an offshore passage escaped remedy, a blanketing sleep would do nicely to ease the misery of his condition.

Yet his effort to settle his misaligned aura raised a queer, stinging flash that subsided to haze and red static.

Dakar recoiled to a yelp of surprise. No member of *Evenstar*'s crew had been mage-trained. *Nothing* he encountered upon the high seas should provoke a defensive reaction. The cold hunch remained, that this source of disturbance was external, and a part of the brig that now sailed, unprotected, across open ocean with Arithon's made double on board.

That unseen pitfall ripped Dakar to chills.

Eyes closed, racked to dread, he shielded his working, then cast his awareness outward. Sick pain notwithstanding, he combed through the grain of timber and planks with masterfully delicate subtlety. His probe traced the webwork and knots of tarred rigging, then spiraled through cordage, deadeyes and blocks, finding no untoward sign of meddling. He sifted the mineral grain of the ballast rocks. No spellcraft lurked there. Pressed to the edge of his limited resource, now fogged by the turbulent rush of the brine, he tested the sheathing under the waterline. As a barehanded man might grope for a spider, Dakar sounded until he encountered a tingling *snap!* The incursion sourced *here*, an embedded cipher that spiked his headache to redoubled virulence.

Flushed to nausea, the spellbinder hissed through shut teeth. What he laid bare in the humid, thick dark, was a Koriani sigil of tracking.

Dakar collapsed his extended awareness. Racked witless by dread, he pushed straight and slammed headlong against the hatch combing. "Feylind!" he howled through singing pain. "Get down here this second! Your ship is threatened and heading for trouble worse than your most evil nightmare!"

The bar slid back. The plank door yanked open, and a sailhand holding a candle lamp squinted into the redolent gloom. "Shut yer trap, bucko. The captain's asleep."

"Wake her!" On his knees, sweating, Dakar snatched a sail hank and jammed the tight swing of the door. "Move now, you fool! We're disastrously exposed, and primed to fall under an arcane assault by an enemy."

"Now hasn't the whiskey spun you some ill dream! Man, I've told you already. The old lady's knackered. Fought rip currents and a devilish wind through the narrows. No dog with a brain wants to roust her."

"I'll risk that, no question." Dakar rammed the sailhand's obstruction aside and barged shoulder down through the braced doorway. Ignoring Fionn Areth's moaned inquiry behind, the Mad Prophet stumbled the length of the hold toward the gray glimmer of daylight. He mounted the ladder, shivering and sick, and cringed as the salt-laden wind slapped his face. Sea legs, he decided, were a capricious gift that Ath gave to rock-headed masochists. The deficit left him gulping back bile. Dakar reeled his way over careening, wet planks in a rush to bend over the railing.

Dry heaves aside, he required relief. His bladder was nigh onto splitting. Swift footfalls approached. Aware that a pack of deckhands converged with the riled intent to constrain him, Dakar tore at his clothing with hell-bent haste. Let them lay hold of him while he voided. Unless they hauled him away in midstream, his crass tactics would give him a snatched chance to explain. With naught else at hand to forestall their stupidity, Dakar opened his fly. The rush cost him ripped seams, and a button. The deck crew latched hold of his shoulders and arms just as he started to piss. He yelled curses at them, to no avail. The tussle devolved to a brangle, with the wind and the thrashing spray off the swells posing both sides a ruinous handicap.

Sweated fist guarding his beleaguered cock, Dakar snarled, "Listen up, you runt litter of milk-sucking virgins! Your *ship* is packing a Koriani *sigil!* Do you know what vicious trouble that breeds? If you don't, haul your fumble wits out of your bollocks!" The Mad Prophet spoke very fast, after that, while the sailhands pressed in, struck to distrustful silence. Rumpled though he was, and green-faced with misery, the spellbinder mustered the rag ends of dignity, and finished, "This threat is real. Your vessel's been tagged. To track past salt water, you'll have no less than Prime Selidie and twelve ranking seniors, engaged through the force of the Waystone. I can't thwart such power! Not on that scale, and not locked puking sick in the sail hold. Roust out Feylind! Do as I say, or else risk that boy who's set under the word of Prince Arithon's sworn protection."

"What," sniped a man with a seamy, squint eye, "that flea-scratching goatherd who's hell-bent to sell us out to Lysaer's Alliance? Throw him off!"

"Aye," called another. "Feed his tripes to the sharks. He's a nattering nuisance, I say!"

"Rot that!" snapped the cook, burst out of the galley with two fish skewers stuck through his pigtail. "Use his guts as fresh bait for my draglines, I would."

Dakar shivered. "Please, no debate." Hoard the last dribble of piss though he would, his kidneys were already squeezed dry. Resigned to dread, he unlatched icy fingers and endeavored to stuff himself back in his trousers.

That moment, the hag face of luck played him foul: the sigil embedded in *Evenstar's* hull woke and burned, attuned by a circle of *two dozen* ranked seniors channeled as one through the Waystone.

The influx slammed across the lone spellbinder's frail defenses with the thundering force of an avalanche. He yelled, hands convulsed. Though spasmic reflex threatened him with castration, he failed to dodge the connection. Beyond any shadow of doubt, Prime Selidie now knew he and Fionn Areth were aboard Captain Feylind's vessel.

"Ath above!" he gasped, shaken senseless, and bruised in a place that would not let him think. "Now we have trouble!"

"Because you've snagged your wee hairs in your buttons?" The brusque voice was the mate, shoved into the pack to see why his deckhands were slacking. "By Dharkaron's fell Spear, I'll have the lot shaved! Are we a latrineful of dimwit voyeurs, or a two-masted ship trimmed under three courses of sail!"

"Wait," urged the quartermaster, just culled from the wheel for the purpose of handling malcontents. "Look at the man's face. Whatever's upset him is serious!"

Dakar scarcely noticed the crowd parting around him. Pressed to the lee rail as his knees let go under him, he caught only broken snatches of words, flung through the rush of thrown spray. Ripped by the blinding pain of his headache, he grappled to muster his talent. Someone must assay the force of the threat now attached to the hapless brig.

If he was the *Evenstar*'s only trained asset, he was not to have peace for his effort.

Hands grabbed his shoulder and spun him about. "What's happening?" The mate's piercing stare raked him over, now worried. "What's this I hear about meddling Koriathain?"

"They want Fionn Areth," Dakar gasped in distress. "I fear we're too late to forestall them."

"Bloodless bitches," the mate swore, moved to sympathy for the herder. The lad was young for his plight. However he skulked, he could never hide with a face that bore such extreme notoriety. "Trust me, I'd back Feylind and scuttle this hull before we strike flags in surrender. Since we're bound to fight, we'll fare that much better if we know how the Prime Matriarch intends to attack."

"I'll tell you," a stripped, steely voice interjected.

Dakar jerked at the sound, head upturned toward the quarterdeck. Although he had sensed no invasive disturbance, he encountered a lean figure muffled in black, leaning into the wind at the taffrail. The barest glance awoke recognition. A moment that should have brought speechless joy gave rise to explosive remonstrance. "Damn your feckless hide to the nethermost pit! What in Sithaer *possessed* you to come here?"

"My right of free choice," the arrival replied. "No one's pining for a reunion, I see."

The deck crew stared, dumbstruck. This man's angular features might seem, line for line, a stamped replica of the boy Feylind's order had shut in the sail hold. Yet this was not he. The predator's gleam that lit these green eyes had never been bred in the grasslands.

Striding down the companionway to the main deck, the man who *was* the Crown Prince of Rathain took pause. His braced stance was experienced as the brig tossed and slammed on her close-hauled course through the wavecrests. "The occasion's beyond speech?" He glanced aloft, measured the set of the sails, then smiled toward the first mate. "My compliments, fellow. You keep a tight ship." His scouring survey reached Dakar's flushed face. "Not Sithaer," he added with irony. "My presence is actually the gift of Davien."

"Welcome to the massacre," the Mad Prophet said carefully. "We're jammed square in the throat of a Koriani trap. Or didn't the Betrayer bother to tell you?"

"I am fully informed."

That crisp tone revealed nothing. A silver-trimmed cloak, lately worn by a Sorcerer, draped over immaculate shoulders. The trial of the maze and a year in the caverns had accentuated the milk-quartz complexion. Less definable changes carried more force: the adamant clarity of a mage-trained self-awareness had been reforged to a fearfully surgical edge.

Dakar swallowed, despite himself overcome. "Welcome back, Arithon." Foolish tears made him blink. Unprompted, he answered the hanging question. "Fionn Areth is safe, though your friends want to wring his idiot neck on account of his uncertain loyalty."

"He's locked in the sail hold, I already know. Let that problem bide, for the moment." Paused through a rapid, measuring glance, the Master of Shadow searched the faces of *Evenstar*'s astounded deck crew. "Where's Feylind?"

"Resting, your Grace." The mate stirred to go, until Arithon's gesture forestalled his impulse to roust her.

"No titles," said the Master of Shadow. "Bring all hands on deck, *now*. Together, we're going to work them like dogs. If you pray, beg for favor that we can strike sail, drop the yardarms, and unstep the topmasts in less than an hour."

"We're in for a blow?" the mate asked, startled grim.

"A storm like no other." Arithon stripped off the fine cloak. "This vessel's been tagged by a Koriani sigil, and they've meddled. Spellcraft's been engaged that will shortly make us a magnet for fiends."

"*Iyats!*" howled the mate. "We're hard up in a clinch! Such damnable mischief could sink us!" He snatched for the lanyard strung at his neck, shrilled a blast on his whistle, while the crewmen at hand surged up the ratlines without need to be ordered aloft.

Arithon dumped his cloak into Dakar's numbed grasp. "Stow this below." Through the shouted commands as the brig was braced by, and spray scattered in stinging sheets over the bowsprit, the Master of Shadow moved down the list of necessities. "I need you to secure water barrels. Lay them under every strong ward you know to guard against breakage and mischance."

"I can't." Dakar clutched the bunched wool, left utterly wretched. In stripped words he told why his talent was blunted from months of drunken sex and dissipation. "What else could I do? Fionn Areth showed Luhaine an offensive mistrust. We had no opening to claim free permission."

Arithon, rapt, had grasped the sore gist. "Do what you can, then. I have a few theories that could grant a stay from this lash-up. The Prime Matriarch thinks you'll be caught unaware. She doesn't expect to have me aboard, fouling the lay of her plans."

Dakar choked back his self-evident admonition, that Selidie Prime might instead seize her chance to trap both decoy and quarry together. "What will you do now?"

Arithon flung back a madcap grin, then spun toward the galley amidships. "Have words with the cook. Then protect the provisions. After that, if the crew has the sail rig in hand, I'll nip down and release Fionn Areth."

"Not when he's a prisoner on my brig, you won't!" Waked by the commotion, Feylind shot out of the stern cabin. Hair streaming, she whooped through the mate's shouted orders, then pounced and locked her slighter, male target into a choking embrace. "Nor will you escape with no courtesy, this time. You owe me that much, for your absence."

Which had been an inexcusable seventeen years; no glib word could sidestep that issue. Arithon did not try. "My dear, you've surpassed expectations. The fitness of your command is a marvel, but unless you have skills to trap plagues of *iyats*, you'll hear my apologies, swimming." Gently firm, he began to untangle himself.

"Fionn Areth," she snapped. "You'll keep him penned up." Her hold on his wrists did not loosen.

The creature who had walked, alive, out of Kewar suffered the unwanted constraint. The depth of dimension in him was so changed, Dakar lost his breath. Shaken by insight that tingled his skin, only he glimpsed the inscrutable presence behind that unruffled composure.

"Feylind, let go, my judgment is sound." Arithon smiled with no outward sign of admonishment. "The *iyats* will only feed on dissent. Leave the young man locked down, his reckless rage will endanger us. If he's not overjoyed by my company, you'll have to trust me to handle him."

A squealed block, and a clatter aloft divided the captain's attention. "Mind that heel rope, you eavesdropping slackers! That mast takes so much as a scratch, coming down, you'll be varnishing spars in retirement!"

"They need you," said Arithon. His swift peck on her cheek disengaged her taut grip. He moved straightaway to resume his stopped course, but gossip had traveled ahead of him. As he ducked the men stowing the downed topsail yardarm, he all but collided with Talvish.

"It *is* yourself!" The lean swordsman skipped back, already braced to withstand the expected, searing rebuke. "However did you manage—"

Arithon cut him off. "Later!" And, *again*, the stark change clutched the heart: that the smile on his face had no edge, only nakedly genuine pleasure.

As Dakar stood, winded, he saw that familiar, dark-haired form briefly shimmer as though scattered by light. The phenomenon was not strange to him. Ath's adepts, and more rarely, Fellowship Sorcerers, might raise the fire of their being in the discharge of their auric fields. The trial of Kewar's maze had done more than break the guilt that blocked Arithon's mastery. His freed talent had soared to rare heights. A year in retreat would have let him adjust. But thrust into the pressure of intimate company, such fresh power now slipped his restraint: the expanded awareness he carried was probably just barely integrated.

With a fiend storm descending through Selidie's sigil, that stray discharge posed the most dire liability.

Yet even as Dakar measured the threat, the luminous flare brightened, then blinded. The scene burned away in a plunging rush, as the cloak in his arms seemed to swallow his head, and he stumbled into wild prescience. In harsh clarity, he saw: *Arithon's lit form, wreathed in flame and smoke. His hand reached, imploring, to grasp Talvish, who knelt, his thin face a rictus of anguish. About his bent knees, the dead sprawled, strewn and twisted, broken by sword and by arrow. One among them still breathed. She lay, burned and battered, clutched in the clan liegeman's streaked arms with her bloodied, blond head cradled against his mailed shoulder.*

"Dakar!" Hands braced him. Ripped by nausea, he looked up into Feylind's concerned face. "You're seasick, man. Let's get you stowed in a berth."

Too dazed for speech, Dakar shrugged off her support. "Go on. I'll manage."

Through his reeling, sick fear, he grabbed hold of the pinrail. Before him, Arithon was still speaking in lighthearted reproval to Talvish. "Since you wouldn't hear sense and stay with your duke, come along. I'm going to need you."

Cat-quick in recovery, the fair man-at-arms recontained his speechless delight. He padded in stride with Arithon's haste, then ventured his question in warning. "You plan to free that ungrateful yokel? Vhandon won't take that move quietly."

"So, we'll see." Arithon's breathless laughter broke off, as he overheard the mate's order to run a capstan bar aloft to secure the stowed topmast rigging. Hands cupped, he offered an instant correction. "Remove lines and tackle! Strip everything bare! Those *iyats* slip the knots and unravel the stays, anything loose is going to come down and hammer us to perdition."

The Mad Prophet snatched his moment. Thrust between the Prince of Rathain and the sworn liegeman, and crowding the narrow companionway, he demanded, "You can't sing bardic threnodies and dispel them?"

A swift glance, his eyebrows raised in appraisal, the Master of Shadow replied, "For how long, Dakar?"

His point was self-evident: Prime Selidie's attack was impelled through the Waystone. A focus of power sustained through a crystal would outlast the most skilled human voice. A masterbard might sing himself hoarse, then whistle until he dropped prostrate. The displaced *iyats* would still remain, a spell-fed plague that would descend and reap their deferred toll of havoc.

The spellbinder stayed planted in front of the deckhouse, the bundled black cloak clutched too tight, and sweat sliding down his doughy features. "What aren't you telling us? Speak. What else besides fiends lies in ambush?"

"Carry on, Dakar." Arithon's adamant grasp was too firm, and his eyes, starkly haunted, as he edged his way past. "Start safeguarding the water stores. I'll join you as soon as I can."

Talvish had no mind to dismiss the exchange. "You sighted a future?" he murmured low-voiced, as he squeezed through in Arithon's wake.

"Fire. Smoke. Armed attack," Dakar forced out, before the backlashing heave locked his teeth.

Yet the pace of Arithon's orders denied the least chance for appraisal. Talvish found himself left with the cook, strapping down pots, blunting knives, and containing such hazards in lockers. The ship's cooper was fetched, then taught to nail the lids shut in patterns that invoked protection from the cardinal elements.

"No charm is proof against outright disaster," the Master of Shadow instructed. "Which is why, first thing, I will try for delay. That's where the small constructs come in."

"You have a plan?" the ship's steward asked. He was curled in a cranny out of harm's way, pasting small squares of paper to the wood scrap kept dry to kindle the stove.

"I have chaos," Arithon stated in wry admission, and summed up at speed. "When the galley's secured, make rounds of the forecastle. All clothing gets stripped of its buttons and laces. Boot buckles also. Jackknives, and coins— any trove of hard objects—contain them. Nail the men's personal sea chests shut. I don't care who's stashed contraband whiskey. Every bottle goes overboard. No exceptions. Miss out any item that's breakable glass, somebody risks getting blinded." Poised by the threshold, he finished. "When those billets are tagged, take them to the chart desk. Sharpen a fresh quill. If there's a horn inkpot, leave that one."

Belowdecks, the wallow and pitch of the hull made every small movement difficult. The shadows swung to the roll of the lamps, which had yet to be stowed or extinguished. Thumping feet overhead marked the rush of the crewmen, still scrambling to secure yards and topmasts. Arithon made his way to the sail hold. There, one hand braced for stability, he exchanged a wrist clasp greeting with Vhandon.

The staid, gray veteran cracked into a grin of unbridled happiness. "You're a sight I never expected to see! We heard you'd challenged the maze under Kewar. Until now, I never believed you survived. You're going in there?" This last, with a nod tipped toward the locked door. "Well, don't drop your guard. Your double's a kiss-arse toady for Lysaer. Need my dagger? It's best for close quarters."

Arithon slipped the bar, lost into swung shadow as *Evenstar* plowed through a trough. "My blade will suffice, since I don't plan to draw." He wrenched open the door, while the gyrating lamp speared a wedge of light into darkness.

Fionn Areth, on his feet, met his nemesis face-to-face, with no more than the overheard voices as warning. He would have the first word, outraged as he was after cavalier handling and extended months of imprisonment.

A masterbard's diction sliced through like hot steel. "Koriathain have cast spelled designs on this ship. Once again, you are their target. This time, do you think you can keep your sword sheathed till the heat of the crisis is over?"

"I don't swim," said the goatherd, miserably white. "That's the only assurance I'll give, since no bargain you make can be trusted."

"Leave his meddling hands tied," Vhandon bristled. "That way, if we sink, the fool will go down that much faster."

"Dead wood makes no trouble." Arithon reached with blurred speed and drew Vhandon's knife. His shove spun the herder face about. A stroke sliced the fish twine that bound the crossed wrists. "Get above. See the cook. He has my instructions, should you care to help. If you don't like survival, then heave yourself overboard. You're at liberty *under* my sovereign word. If you hinder the crew, or endanger this ship, I'll see you delivered to Jaelot's justiciar, hog-tied and stripped for a burning."

Before Fionn Areth could command his cramped limbs, or turn himself back toward the doorway, Arithon had returned his liegeman's blade and moved off down the passage. Damnably facile aboard a ship, he scaled the deck ladder as quickly.

Tight at his heels, and scarcely less agile, Vhandon shouted his vexed disbelief. "You won't ask me to watch him?"

"Why bother?" Through the work of the hull, and the bangs and thumps of hurried activity, Arithon's contempt carried clearly. "Where will the man go? Poor though it is, my hospitality can't match the speed at which Jaelot's mayor would cut him dead on the scaffold. He'll do his part keeping this vessel afloat. Or dive off the rail, for all that I care, and pray for the Light to come save him."

"Then I stay behind you," Vhandon declared. Emerged into daylight amidships, he backstepped *fast*, as Arithon whirled and refused him.

"A guard at my back will just pose a liability. The cook will show how the deck lamps must be stowed. You'll dull your weapons like everyone else and secure them inside a nailed locker."

"What!" Vhandon barked. "You'd have me disarmed?" Forearms folded like rock across his studded jack, he rebelled. "I'd sooner walk naked among starving wolves, and besides, rampaging *iyats* don't kill."

"This plague storm's not natural," Arithon contradicted. "These fiends have been goaded by Matriarch Selidie's wrought sigils, then primed to cause bloodletting mischief. The perils that threaten the lives on this ship cannot be routed with weapons!"

"You'd blunt Alithiel?" cracked Vhandon, incredulous.

Arithon paused; shut his eyes. For one jagged moment, he fought torn composure. The reeling punch of his prismatic farsight blurred his clear thought, and the exasperation of *any* well-meaning friend would just lure the fiends that much faster. "Vhandon. The Isaervian blades were forged to curb drake spawn. Stop arguing! You're needed. Talvish is locking down knives as we speak. We don't have the time to thrash out better strategy! *Someone* has got to start tearing down lanterns, stowing the oil, and removing the wicks!"

"You die here for an ignorant stripling's mad cause, far more than one ship will be foundered." Yet the grizzled war veteran could not stand his hard ground. That locked glance stripped him naked: the chartless depths within those green eyes outfaced all his worldly experience.

The spirit returned from the trials of the maze was not wont to regard life or death the same way.

Vhandon spun to stalk off, jammed on his course as he all but crashed into Fionn Areth. "What are you about, dolt! Better clear out! Keep your wise distance from our liege's back before someone wrings your damned neck."

As the liegeman's hand snapped to his dagger, Arithon's grip locked his wrist. "Let the fellow go where he will. We've no hands to spare to ride herd on him."

Vhandon backed down. He could do *nothing* else. When the Master of Shadow pushed through to the chart room, the grasslands-bred yokel showed his insolent grin and trailed after.

Arithon ignored every petty dissension. Through the companionway, limned against the stern window, he seated himself at the narrow desk, grasped the readied quill, and uncapped the horn flask of ink. Fionn Areth took position behind him and hovered, wisely not blocking the light. The subject under his dissecting scrutiny spared not a glance, but dipped his nib and began to inscribe patterns of Paravian runes on the paper tags, glued to the billets of kindling. As each was complete, Arithon cupped his palms over the writing. Eyes closed, he sang notes that caused a man's nape hair to lift with a drilling, electrical tingle.

Scowling through his distrust of magecraft, Fionn Areth blurted, "You don't use any blood."

Ringless hands moved, baring a construct that smoked with delicate trailers of light. "Why should I?" The crisp phrase seemed deceptively mild. Not waiting for answer, Arithon leaned forward and blew across the inked symbols.

The air went cold. Sudden darkness fell like a blanket, then blasted away in a starburst of wild light, there and then *gone* at such speed that the eye retained no after-burned image.

Running feet pounded down the quarterdeck stair, the door banged, and Dakar burst in, horrified. "Dharkaron's fell Chariot, *what have you invoked?* Death and chaos, man! You'll bring those fiends down on our necks! What you've made is a blighted *beacon!*"

Unhurried, as he chose his next scrap of wood, Arithon said, "My sealed intent is to draw them."

"What! Are you crazy?" Dakar yanked on his beard. "We ought to be laying down wardings. Ciphers of go-hither, and invisible quiet, set inside a ring of tossed salt to damp down the etheric ripple of our presence."

"That's what you've done to safeguard the casks?" Hands poised, Arithon sang a triplet that shivered the air like a bell. More light blazed forth, then wisped away like spent smoke.

Dakar winced. "What I've done with the casks doesn't bear mention. Not set against the mayhem you'll wake with that working! We're square in the path of a crisis already. How much more explosive are you going to make it?"

"The quicker the tempo, the more frantic the dance," Arithon conceded. "By now Talvish should have my three dozen arrows, with the points cut away, and the fletching soaked in hot paraffin. I'll need them on deck, along with that box of old corks, and the recurve the mate keeps to shoot sharks."

"Why not send Fionn Areth?" the Mad Prophet snapped under his breath. "Murder and mercy, we need to talk, *now*. What I have to say should be kept private."

"He's not going to leave." Through sharp invective, unleashed abovedecks as a sailhand fumbled a lashing, Arithon qualified, serious, "Turn his back for a moment, he's convinced I'll be opening some victim's veins for dark conjury. Therefore, no secrets. The man wears my face. Whatever you say must come to bear on his fate no less than on mine."

"Curse the moment I said I'd help save him!" The ship rolled. Dakar snatched a fast handhold and watched with vindictive eyes.

Sure enough, the green herder was caught off his guard. He staggered, then windmilled backward into the oilskins packed in the hanging locker.

The spellbinder relented, flung out a hand, and hauled him up short of entanglement. Yet his glance as he salvaged the younger man's balance stayed hard with offended contempt. "You're a hovering vulture, discontent not to feast upon carrion."

Jaw clenched, Fionn Areth said nothing. Since he lacked the mature grace to help with the errand, Dakar banged outside. He would personally garner the items requested before he exposed his concerns in front of the herder's pig ignorance.

Left with the soured pause, still immersed at the chart desk, Arithon stifled amusement. "Dakar's that sore because, once, he behaved just like you."

"The feat makes you proud?" As the brig corkscrewed into another swell, Fionn Areth grabbed hold, saving himself from sliding into the lap of his nemesis. "You get your thrills luring lesser minds to corruption?"

Now Arithon laughed outright. "Your logic is boggling, since Dakar's been a Fellowship spellbinder, and therefore corrupt by your posturing Light, for a few centuries more than your avatar's been alive."

A dry wit might have cut back with a stinging reply; Fionn Areth lacked the gift. He clamped frustrated teeth. More than the roll of the ship made him queasy. Whatever occurred under Arithon's hands, the effects made his skin crawl. Those soft, eerie notes sucked the warmth from the air. Daylight itself altered, until colors appeared dimmed, and the gusting wind seemed to comb with less force through the rigging.

"You're draining the elements into that stick!" Fionn Areth blurted out. The discovery appalled him. The brig's movement was settling: he realized the bucking deck under his feet had quieted until he could stand without effort.

"With due permission," Arithon admitted. His fingers poised over the next billet with its fish-glued slip of paper and queer ciphers. "Masks won't keep on shipboard, and I haven't lied. I'm initiate mage-trained, entitled as Masterbard, as well as birth-born to wield shadow. Those skills are now weaving this vessel's defense. Stay as you wish. Measure the evidence in front of your eyes. Just remember, when everything breaks into mayhem, and it will: I never abandoned my comfortable haven in Kewar's caverns for your sake."

Through the unpleasant tension that followed, Fionn Areth might as well have ceased to exist. Arithon pursued his inscrutable business. By the time the steward arrived to inform that the stripped arrows and cork awaited on deck, Arithon's crafted works had shifted the forces of the known world off their accustomed track. *Evenstar* wallowed amid glassy calm. The long, ocean swell had flattened out. Each comment from the helmsman seemed unnaturally distinct. The creak and squeal of the deck boards as crewmen secured the aft hatch sounded magnified in the harsh quiet.

A thunderous splash from the cathead startled the goatherd half out of his wits.

"That will be the starboard anchor, unshackled and cut loose," Arithon stated in swift reassurance. Done with raw conjury, he was now snipping thread: the jet glitter of his onyx buttons were passed off for the steward to secure, followed as fast by his shirt laces.

The mate's barked command filtered down from the bow. "Sway out and cut loose!"

A thump, and a rattle, and more splashes followed. The steward added, for Fionn Areth's sake, "None of the hands are abandoning ship!"

Arithon affirmed this. "I asked for the chain to be jettisoned also. The ballast rock is just as grievous a hazard, but the hull would capsize without it." He arose, shed his rifled jerkin, and bundled his cache of marked sticks. While the servant moved in to dismantle the lamp, and break out the salt-crusted windows, the Prince of Rathain made his way from the chart room. He bounded on deck, met as he emerged by Feylind, anxiously frowning.

If she wished to revile him for freeing Fionn Areth, someone had warned her with adamancy. Her gesture instead framed the ensorcelled waters, sluggish and flat as pooled mercury. "Don't explain how you've done this. I don't care to know. You're making my seamen as jumpy as cats!"

All wind had died also. The air hung like liquid glass. Sounds were now muffled by the oppressive calm. The creak of the ratlines, the groans as the seams worked between deck and bulkhead made the brig seem a ghost vessel, cursed by a haunting.

"Not only your seamen." Arithon took her cold hand, laid her chapped knuckles between his warm palms, and plumbed her concern with unnerving intensity. Vivid and vital, his face had not changed. Beside him, she had matured and grown weathered. The wear of years and a harsh, outdoor lifestyle had stamped crow's-feet in her rough skin.

Despite herself, Feylind was shaken. She endured that scouring, magetrained regard, hard braced for a recoil that never came.

Arithon cupped her cheek the way she remembered, when she had used her fresh tongue as a child. "You are more than I hoped, and beyond what anyone imagined you'd become. I understand you have two children?"

Grown taller than he, every inch the ship's master, Feylind tossed back her blond braid and laughed. "You'd teach them to row, and cozen their loyalty? Well, the fat's been tossed into the fire, headlong. Dakar's warned us the *iyats* are backed by an ambush. First we've got to win free of your enemies."

"Prophets are dastardly pessimists, to a man. '*Come hither, wild sprite with the marigold hair.*'" Still quoting ballads, the bard tugged her aft. His swift step partnered hers with a wildness recalled from the sun-washed sands back in Merior. "Stand up, front and center, and share the first move." He turned his head, shouted. "Dakar! You're needed. Can you invoke the rune that Asandir used to start campfires?"

Response hailed from the quarterdeck, by the stern rail. "Not easily, in this state." A mussed, portly figure broke from a discussion ongoing between Vhandon and Talvish. "Your slings and lead weights are readied, as well, though no one can fathom what madcap purpose you've hatched in your tinkering brain."

Arithon mounted the quarterdeck stair, with Feylind towed breathless behind, and Fionn Areth trailing, still obstinate. Packing a glower that left no one in doubt that his presence was hostile and separate, the herder hung on the fringes. Yet the activity surrounding the Master of Shadow remained too absorbed to take note of him.

"His royal self stated you would not be touched." The unexpected address made Fionn Areth start. Turned, he encountered the *Evenstar*'s mate, broad-shouldered and affable, with blue eyes that were keenly observant. "If you don't understand what that constraint means, then ask Dakar to tell you of Tharrick. The fellow was once a captain at arms for Alestron, before he ran amok and burned down Arithon's shipyard."

As Fionn Areth surged forward, the mate snatched him back with a biting grasp on his shoulder. "You *will* bide your time until things have calmed down. Else I'll break your crown stay of protection myself, and nail your skinned hide to the masthead!"

"You're corrupt as the rest," the goatherd accused. "Entrapped by his charm and fell shadows."

"I am Feylind's," the mate said in acid correction. "Which means I will watch the man closer than you to be certain her interests aren't compromised."

Surprised to encounter a possible ally, Fionn Areth subsided.

The defense of the brig continued, apace. By the stern railing, Arithon hefted the sling, a cork float strung with its streamer and lead pocketed in the mesh. Talvish, head bent, was stringing the bow. Dakar hunkered next to his feet, fiddling with the blunt arrow shafts, while Feylind made comment that lofty excuses were unlikely to forgive his sick penchant for drink.

"Range?" Vhandon answered to someone's pitched question. "He's accurate to one hundred yards, else Duke Bransian would have demoted him."

"That's sufficient." Arithon straightened, his manner turned brisk. "If not, we're beyond all salvage." He whirled the sling. String whistled. His ungainly missile shot aloft in a ranging arc, then tumbled and plunged, dead astern. The strung float of cork tumbled, flailing, behind its tied fish weight, then splashed. Ring ripples spread over the mirror-smooth sea.

Dakar passed off an arrow.

Talvish, not fumbling, strung the nock, drew, and fired in practiced motion. The arrow leaped out in wobbling flight, its tip whittled sharp, and the cut head replaced with one of Arithon's queer kindling constructs.

The shot struck the cork float, and the dipped fletching burst into streamered flame.

Feylind whooped. Arithon whipped the reloaded sling, and the sequence repeated, with the idle crew taking odds with manic abandon.

"We chose them for nerve," the mate said, laconic, then shaded his eyes and surveyed the horizon. "Steady on, boy. Take hold of the ship. No mistake, we're about to get hammered."

There seemed no disturbance. No cloudburst approached. The sun shone on varnish and railings, untrammeled, while the air hung lucent and breathlessly still. Yet the mate's seasoned instinct had not roused in error.

Against the horizon, where ocean met sky, an angry, dark band raced over the water to meet them.

"Deck there!" cried the lookout. "Heads up, we have trouble!"

The mate's shouted order brought the man down from the ratlines, then rousted the crew. "Move now! Dog the hatches!"

Throughout, the paired missiles continued to fly. The sling whistled and released; arrows launched from the bow, until *Evenstar*'s hull drifted inside a matchstick ring of fluttering flame.

Late Autumn 5670

Assault

By the time the battened hatches were nailed shut, Fionn Areth had insinuated himself amid the party on the quarterdeck, close enough to track Arithon's least move, and overhear words pitched too low for the sailhands at large. To judge by Dakar's scowl, the additional fastenings the ship's joiner had set would do little to stop *iyats* from breaching the hold. At best, the deterrent might only forestall airborne objects from straying above deck, there to inflict havoc, or become dispossessed and tossed past hope of salvage into the sea.

No more could be done. The band of riffled waters raced down on the drifting brig. Unsettled murmurs arose from the crew; of sharper interest to Fionn Areth, the tension that flared between the Master of Shadow and the Mad Prophet.

"Why did you leave Kewar?" The scorching intensity of the question was pitched to throw its victim off guard.

Arithon stood, fingers interlaced on the quarterdeck rail. Stripped of his jerkin, he appeared too slight-boned to inspire dread.

Yet *something* caused Dakar to draw a hissed breath. "Your response was ill done," he persisted. Straight courage, or some driving weight of cold fear pressed him further. "You know what must happen. She'll be duty bound, now, to leave her safe place in Ath's hostel. She has no choice but to position herself at your side. Prisoned under her Prime's direct order, what can she bring except heartache, and a wide-open door to disaster?"

Fionn Areth was brushed by an unwonted chill. No name had been mentioned. But the woman implied behind Dakar's rebuke could only be the Koriani enchantress, Elaira. Her entanglement with the Master of Shadow might not be public knowledge; yet in Jaelot, during a healing to restore his lamed knee, the goatherd had witnessed the Masterbard's song, invoked by no more than the spirit of her intangible presence. Even in recall, the incident burned: its stark clarity etched by the strain of doomed love and the agony of enforced separation.

Which cruel provocation turned Arithon's head: his wide-open eyes brightly incensed, he said, "Where did you learn what you know?"

The Mad Prophet flushed. "I partnered Kharadmon through the warding of Rockfell." Arms folded, he held his mulish ground. "The Sorcerer knows of her worth, and her steadfast quality. His concern matches mine. Her love where you are concerned makes too ready a tool for the Prime to enact your destruction."

"*You'll not broach those fears, here!*" Though Arithon spoke for Dakar's ear alone, Fionn Areth shamelessly hovered. Even caught secondhand, the warning bristled. "Your advice is well meant. And henceforward, unwanted. I will not be governed. Not by *her* bravery, and not even once by Prime Selidie's designs, endorsed by your gutless cowardice!"

"The breathing life on this world lies at stake! Against that, the crew on this vessel does not signify!" Ludicrous and fat, eyes bloodshot with drink, Dakar pressed his point, not courageous, but caring. "The Prime covets your capture. To gain that end, every one of us serves as your bait! Had you withstood the pressure to rise to her lure, the Koriani Matriarch would forsake her interest. In time, without provocation from you, we would have all been released."

Arithon bent his head, exquisite hands now clenched on the taffrail until every knuckle gleamed white. "But the teeth in this trap are armed galleys flying the sunwheel banner." Against the savagery of repressed emotion, his last line came wholly mild. "Dhirken died, Dakar."

The riposte scored too hard, after the horror unveiled by today's flash of prescience: the spellbinder lost words, while threat grew, apace.

The voracious fury of Selidie's assault converged across empty water. No storm of fiends ever rivaled the pack descending at speed upon *Evenstar*. The front line plowed in as a breaking wave, rushed by a glassine shimmer of air, fractured to rippling distortion. Yet where a mirage would have settled in silence, the sea heaved, snagged to ominous foam. White spouts trampled skyward. They towered and coiled like whipped smoke, then dispersed as though scattered by whimsy.

"You might still fail." The Mad Prophet dug in, his obstinacy tempered by pity. "Who loses then?"

Softly, Arithon Teir's'Ffalenn gave his answer. "There are many reasons to avoid taking risks. Friendship is not among them."

"You came for Feylind?" At next breath, the fiends would be on them. Too ill to do battle on two fronts at once, Dakar blotted his sweaty palms on his shirt. "Arithon. You are not free to offer yourself as a sacrifice! Your presence here has raised drastic stakes! *Damn* your birth-born compassion to Sithaer! What you call a risk is too likely to stage the horrific potential for massacre."

But response was eclipsed as the oncoming storm trampled into the floating array of lit constructs. If their purpose had been to delay the sprites, enthralling them with the elemental power compacted by Arithon's talent, that hope died. Wood, fire, cork float, and marked runes, the perimeter laid down through arrows and spells became shredded. The papers with their guarding ciphers exploded to matchstick splinters and smoke. Wind and heat, every coiled force contained by skilled talent, ripped wholesale out of constraint.

The fiends fed. They gorged, soaking up the burst energies like the howl of an indrawn breath. Beyond sated, the creatures shed the excess in shearing knots that thrashed up whirling waterspouts. The air itself burned. Sound grazed the ears, too high for natural hearing. The buffeting horde shot off acrid smells and hurtful, sharp flashes of light.

"Merciful mother of invention," swore Dakar. "We can't survive this ferocious an onslaught!"

The first fool who panicked would bring the swarm in.

And yet, no voices raised outcry. Every man present witnessed the force that razed the scrap billets to flotsam. Yet none showed distress. Far from unhinged, Fionn Areth found himself swept by a puzzling bout of deep lassitude. Suspicious, he shared the piquant discovery with Dakar, that the Master of Shadow was not, after all, doing nothing.

Those disingenuous fingers were cupped at the rail, with Arithon, head bent, singing into them. His melody seemed little more than a whisper. Yet that light, keening sound ran into the wood, arousing a tonal vibration. Fionn Areth sensed the low notes through his feet, as the deck planking shuddered to resonance. Phrased in rhythmic song, the bard's spell of calm used the whole brig as its sounding board. Anxious men who should have quaked outright subsided to half-lidded drowsiness.

The spellbinder deduced the primary intent. "A sleep summoning, surrounding Prime Selidie's sigil? That's an ambitious innovation."

For the reactive sprites were not clever. Reeled in by the Matriarch's lure, their interest would hook first on the reckless energies offered by Arithon's smashed constructs. Though powerful spells of attraction bound the *iyats* to the *Evenstar*'s presence, the harmonics of calm now laced through her timbers would offer no sport, by comparison. The swarm might well overlook the hushed ship, or abandon its deadened temptation without contest.

"We won't be invisible," Dakar pointed out, though the bard he addressed stayed engrossed. "The line that you draw is critically fine. How long do you think that you can sustain? There's small chance you can hold your rhythm and pitch without falling prey to distraction."

Even Fionn Areth grasped the frightful extent of the danger: if the brig's crew became too deeply enthralled, or lapsed into an unnatural sleep, they might stagger overboard and drown before they recovered their wits. Yet Arithon's art shaped the sole, fragile stay, sparing *Evenstar* from the trap. Dakar was left to stand guard by default, while the first questing fiends flowed across the ship's decks and explored every object and cranny. All they encountered roused tinkering interest. Their invisible prickle played over the skin, frazzling nerves and striking up gooseflesh. Their invasive tickle poked into men's ears, and their unpleasant, charged warmth flicked the stilled air to whistles and smears of distortion.

Despite the close timing, no loose ends remained to tempt the caprice of the sprites. The pinrails had been stripped. Sail halyards, sheaves, blocks, and running tackle were all stowed out of harm's way. The galley fire was doused. Ship's bell and binnacle were unbolted and wrapped under ward, yet the dearth of fodder did not defer exploration. *Iyats* combed through every spooled rail and bare spar with indefatigable curiosity.

At the helm, one hand lifted to smother a yawn, Feylind watched the compass lose orientation. The needle revolved in erratic circles, with no quiver to suggest true north. The ship's wheel spun next. Though its squealing gyrations plumed smoke from the bearings, no crewman risked breaking a hand in prevention. The mate's astute forethought had seen the rudder pins locked and the steering cables unshackled.

Eyes shut, Arithon stayed unmoved by the diversion. His lyric tones flowed unimpeded, evoking a powerful symmetry that remade all the world as a formless dream. Apprehensive anxiety settled and faded, as thought and senses spun down into blanketing drowsiness.

Time passed without measure. Dulled awareness suspended. Fiercely as Fionn Areth resisted, the melody lulled him until he succumbed. He drifted, lost in a somnolence that lasted until a shadow scythed over his face. The brisk slap of wind that rode in its wake jolted open his drooping lids.

Before him, the startling form of an eagle folded bronze wings on the taffrail.

The bird was not canny. Preternaturally aware, it swiveled its sleek head. A golden brown eye fixed on Rathain's prince. As though called by name, the Master of Shadow fell silent. While the ringing vibrations he had struck through wood dwindled down to a diminished whisper, Arithon matched that intelligent glance. Deep thoughts were shared in communion.

Then the bird peered askance. Fionn Areth found himself raked in turn by a survey of scorching irony before the sorcerous creature took off. The thunderous launch whipped Arithon's hair and moved Dakar to shake an impotent fist at the fan of departing tail feathers.

"Temper, my friend!" the Teir's'Ffalenn warned. "You don't want to risk reckless offense in that quarter, or feed the Prime's crazed visitation."

"*Iyats!*" Dakar slapped his forehead and accosted the prince. "Death's fist on Fate's Wheel, they're the least of the dangers you court!" Perhaps unwisely, since nervous crewmen were listening, he ran on in acid remonstrance. "A madman knows not to consort with Davien! His meddling bargains will tear you apart. Who can guess what terrible price you might pay when the hour comes due for the reckoning?"

"To date, Davien's been the party enacting his dealings with me." Arithon stayed disengaged from his spelled defense, though the running vibrations that thrummed through the brig rapidly passed beyond hearing. "I hope," he said, bland, "that your touch with *iyats* has improved since the last time I saw you."

Dakar's eyes widened. "What do you know? What ill-advised counsel has that feckless Sorcerer whispered into your ear?"

"That Prime Selidie has whistled in fresh reinforcements." Arithon shared that nuance with Feylind and the mate, then pitched his tone for the crewmen at large. "The Koriani Matriarch has raised the stakes and engaged an additional ring of enchantresses. *Their* meddling has hazed in a new pack of *iyats* and dispatched them in pursuit. We won't have an hour. The next wave will strike the ship within minutes, and the unconsumed fuel that's left from my constructs won't be enough to detain them."

"She'll bid for your capture." Distraught, the Mad Prophet jammed his loose shirttails into his buttonless waistband. "We're lame chicks in a maelstrom. What under Ath's sky can you hope to do?"

Arithon raised his eyebrows. "Ever played 'duck, duck, goose, who jumps for the wolf'? What else but give three dozen pullets the headache they richly deserve." While the deck crew pressed close, the better to hear, he grinned with insane provocation. "Listen up, sluggards! We'll need softened wax." His glance toward Feylind begged her indulgent apology, as, speaking fast, he listed necessities. "Plugs of cotton, perhaps torn from the stuffing inside a dry fender, do we have it?"

"We do," said the cook, ham fist stroking his beard. "Is it earplugs you're wanting, mannie?"

"Some of the men might require that protection."

Not waiting for Arithon's clipped affirmation, the ship's cooper already leaped to draw the spelled nails from the hatch. Accosted at once by a loose bar of soap, and a barrage of spools, thread denuded, he cursed, batting objects, and descended.

"You'll have to hang on and ride out the storm," the Master of Shadow explained while the anxious deckhands clustered about him. "It boils down to a brute trial of endurance." With the Koriani sigil set under the waterline, *and* inside the hull's copper sheathing, no hurried remedy could destroy the source. His countermeasure must be diffused through the brig, which meant, as before, the unfiltered effects would also trouble the crew. "I'm going to try dissonance. The backlash may hurt. A few sensitives could suffer headaches, or dizziness. Can we manage to endure a few fiends, and perhaps, a rough spell of dry heaves? Whatever we suffer, I promise, the enchantresses will feel that much worse. The craft they've engaged keeps them linked, in reverse. As long as they test us, they're vulnerable, and while they work to shepherd their spells, they'll be held at my mercy, unshielded."

The mate's boisterous guffaw shattered the tension. "It's a straight game of knockdown with thirty-six ladies!"

As chuckles broke out, Captain Feylind retorted, "Dharkaron's black vengeance, that's scarcely a contest!"

"Oh, aye." The mate elbowed her ribs with good cheer. "Hardly worth spit in the wind, for a wager. Not with a lot that's stone-cold in the twat from a lifetime as tight-lipped virgins!" He glanced at the men, stoked to brazen challenge. "We're agreed? Let the Prince of Rathain serve the mim-faced old sticks their comeuppance!"

Handclaps and cheering broke over the deck. Fionn Areth did not share the coarse round of bravado. Far more than alarmed, he glared at the figure still braced, with his unruffled back to the rail. Arithon's expression showed inquiring diffidence, the deft handling of an appalling dilemma underplayed to the point where his steadfast concern appeared genuine. In fact, he had done little to win peerless loyalty from these rough-cut men, who were strangers.

"They forget they would not be endangered at all if their captain wasn't enthralled by a felon's unsavory company!" Mistakenly, Fionn Areth had grumbled aloud, raising slurred contradiction from the sidelines.

"He leaves them the dignity and freedom to choose." Flushed red, stout arms folded, the Mad Prophet still nursed his sour disapproval. Yet his planted stance—that the Master of Shadow outweighed the game piece of this one brig, and all of the living aboard her—did not extend to supporting a herder caught up past his depth.

"What makes you defend him?" Fionn Areth asked, desolate. "His criminal record of killing inspires no standard of morals. He enacts no grand cause. Nor does he make any offer of betterment, or promise prosperity, or safety."

Dakar sighed, then winced for the daylight that mauled his insufferably sore head. "Stay your tongue for one day, drop your infantile ideals, and you might understand why those exact qualities make an unimpeachable crown prince."

"So does frost kill the grass!" exclaimed Fionn Areth. "I might have been cozened to wear a spelled face, but you people react to *unnatural* straits as though you've been bound in possession!"

The assessment seemed accurate at surface appearance: the helpless brig bobbled like a cast-off cork, bombarded by whizzing fragments of wood, and the random buffet of infested waters. Yet her terrified deckhands still acted in concert. The hatch stayed unsealed. Brave men went below to net the strayed gear and refasten burst lockers. Lookouts ran aloft to check damages. Each one knew he might face death, even drowning, if the hull sprung her planks or lost caulking. Yet Feylind's haranguing steadied them on, and the mate seemed at hand to lend help wherever activity faltered. Such teamwork, deployed amid staring disaster, did indeed bear the stamp of the prince, self-contained where he knelt, hearing out the stammering distress of the ship's lad.

Arithon's patience was more firm than complacent. His words to the boy were not honeyed with false reassurance.

Yet where Fionn Areth misperceived the exchange as a sorcerer's ploy to weave delusion, the Mad Prophet recognized instead the rejection of officious authority. From earliest childhood, Arithon had taught Feylind to know her own strengths, then apply them. He had backed the bold means for her to step forward, and abandoned support, if she shrank. Idolize him though she would, her life in his absence remained self-complete. From the crew she had chosen to man her brig, to the mate who had fathered her children, she had matched the example before her.

"His Grace doesn't pander to weakness," Dakar said. "Until you stop reasoning with other men's thoughts, and start to stand on your own, you won't see. A hollow mind makes you too ready a dupe. You will dance on the puppet strings of his enemies, dumb and blind, for as long as you choose not to think."

"You hated him, once," Fionn Areth retorted.

"I also took the Prime's bespelled arrow in my back to keep him this side of Fate's Wheel." Dakar added, not flinching, "My death at the time would have left no regrets. Had Arithon gone down, a true light would have been lost from the world, with the balance tipped toward disaster."

Unimpressed, Fionn Areth scoffed. "Now who speaks like a hothead fanatic!"

"No, numbskull," Dakar snapped, done with futile argument, "*I speak with the ice-cold eyes of a seer!*"

Fionn Areth was left to himself. Unmoving amid the rush of activity, he stayed fastened on Arithon, now repositioned behind the wheel mount on the quarterdeck. Head tipped askance, the bard appeared to be gathering himself. The flitter of *iyats* tweaked at his hair, plucked his shirt, and lashed at his unstrung cuffs. He paid them no heed. Stark stillness reflected his focus. A moment passed; two. Then he uttered a line in Paravian, whether prayer, or spell, or outright malediction, Fionn Areth could not determine. Yet when the Master of Shadow clapped his palms on the stern rail, the thump seemed to shudder, length and beam, through the brig.

If the frequencies left from his first conjured song had dwindled into subsonics, there was change: the human ear sensed the silence. For an instant, the air hung like crystal. The hustling sailhands ceased movement. The spell-driven fiends also noted the shift. Amid splashing gyrations, they dropped all pursuits as one mind. Wood fragments pattered into the sea and showered the open deck. The ship's timbers creaked, and her tarred ratlines hummed as the swarm reconverged on their drifting target.

Their passage flicked skin, tugged at clothing, and rushed the nerves to alarming sensations. Fionn Areth saw their descent as patchy riffles of distortion. The master initiate's self-aware presence was instantly recognized: Arithon stood erect, his form rippled and hazed as though viewed through a pane of blown glass.

Frightened, but not enough to stand down, Fionn Areth held his post, while the fiends bore in and gadded. Forced to slap down his sleeves, then snatch at his billowing shirttails, the herder huffed curses. His irritation incited the harrying swarm. His hair was tousled, then pulled, and snarled to elf locks. More sprites descended. Reaction did nothing but spur on their mischief. Fionn Areth found himself pinched and prodded, tickled and stung, bedeviled as though plagued by hornets.

If Arithon accomplished aught by the stern rail, his conjury brought no relief. *Iyats* flitted at will through the ship, indulging their penchant for havoc. The cook's shouts arose as they accosted the galley in a swarm of manic fury. Possessed pots clattered and clanked, and whisked airborne, until the jarring clash of repeated collisions made the men wish they had been born deaf. Elsewhere in the forecastle, a sea chest was breached. Loose playing cards kited and fluttered underfoot, and a stray set of dice chased them, rattling.

The mate shouted to the Mad Prophet, "Fiends are fouling the mainstay. Can you do aught to lay down the splice and keep it from coming unraveled?"

"Hungover and sick?" Dakar snarled through his teeth.

Yet the mast could come down, if the troubled rope parted. The spellbinder ground the six of clubs underfoot, wiped his hands, and manfully hauled his fat carcass into the rigging. Battered and poked, then drubbed by hurled water, he clung in the maintop crow's nest. Ill though he was, with raw talents depleted, he did what he could, spinning small wards of binding to prevent the whips on the splices from coming unlaced in the maelstrom.

The *iyats* kept coming. Their relentless invention kinked the lower yard lifts into knots, and rummaged and thumped through the lockers. The objects meticulously battened inside thrashed to burst free, breaking latches. With time, the assault would exhaust the charms of protection set into the nails. No harassed crew could long retain equilibrium amid the unraveling mayhem.

Even a landsman could see that the *Evenstar* was outmatched. Against mounting despair that would shatter morale, Arithon started to sing.

As before, his grasp of trued sound translated itself throughout the brig's timbers. The effect harrowed everyone, a harsh, hurtful dissonance that invoked a stinging range of harmonics. The buzzing frequencies stunned thought and nerve, then trammeled, aching, through bone. The bruising vibration deepened and built. It swelled, relentless, acquired jangling overtones, then drilled into reverberations like mallet-struck iron.

Men winced at each movement. The most sensitive clapped tormented hands to their heads, as their skulls went to war with their eardrums. Others lost balance and tempers. Frayed emotions in turn spurred the sprites to more mischief. Energy-gorged, they scrambled their mad acquisitions on tangents, or plunged them into the sea with vehement spouts of shot spray. Soaked where she knelt, striving to free a man's jammed boot from a scupper, Feylind gasped with breathless laughter.

"Dharkaron's vengeance, if we feel this bad, imagine how wretched those witches must be, linked as they are to a forsaken sigil that's fastened against our ship's timbers."

"Remember, we only have to outlast them!" the mate cried to back her encouragement.

More fiends descended. The assault gained force. Battered and wrung nauseous, Fionn Areth backed against the mizzen mast pinrail. Whirled dizzy, he could scarcely stand up, far less command the concentration a bard must sustain to unreel his bane-song. The effort behind that seamless delivery defied every concept of reckoning. Yet Arithon's stance showed no drastic change. He remained poised with bent head, flattened hands braced on the wheel mount. Around him, the air was pockmarked with ripples. The *iyats* detected his adamant presence. They pestered and pried, testing the least tiny fissure of strain stitched like unseen thread through his aura.

No man could maintain that immutable calm, or withstand the exhaustive drain of the sprites' provocations. One break would touch off a concerted attack. For Arithon, the danger compounded since his trained talent posed him as antagonist. His self-willed composure cried challenge as moment to moment, the pressure increased. The brig bore the brunt. One after the next, her protections unraveled. The chain that had fastened the scuttlebutt mug broke away, hooking fittings and tripping up feet. Shouts erupted up forward: a rolling batch of loose deadeyes skittered over the forecastle, whacking ankles and shins, and knocking a man down, unconscious. Coughs belowdecks bespoke a breached flour barrel, while an unlucky victim, beet-faced and cursing, chased hither and yon to recapture the flapping rags of his trousers.

If *Evenstar*'s crewmen were sore beset, the Koriathain also struggled to hold the wiggling bait in their trap. As Arithon's virulent handling of sound disrupted the Prime circle's control, the odd tempest blasted the face of the ocean. The random explosions at first promised hope, as more *iyats* succumbed to distraction. Tens and dozens soon flaunted their excessive energy, dashing up sheets of wild spray. Other flocks tussled in contrary whirlwinds, or snatched up the played-out scraps of the constructs. Yet the marginal respite was not enough. The hard toll of damages mounted.

No bard, no matter how gifted, could outlast his mortal endurance; limping and crippled, no beleaguered merchant ship could evade the armed might of an Alliance ambush.

No man stepped down, or admitted defeat. But the ongoing pain of their hard-fought resistance crushed morale as each mishap compounded. Inside the stern cabin, the breathless steward batted and pounced on loose bedding. Pillows careened helter-skelter, and ripped apart in midflight. Scattered down loosed a blizzard, while the grim-faced mate made the rounds, collecting reports from below. Arithon shivered, soaked to the skin, while several small fish flopped in stranded panic across the boards under his feet.

On, the squall raged. Length and beam of the brig, the crew was rushed ragged in futile attempt to keep pace. The harder they strove, the more malice unleashed, every freed object made weapon and club, haranguing and slapping them bloody.

Then the mainstay let go with a crack. The mate's timely shout sent a team up the rigging with block and tackle to jury-rig a replacement. *Iyats* coalesced and swooped to interfere. Harsh puffs of breeze and the buffet of torn clothing hampered all movement aloft. Topmen's feet slipped off the shuddering ratlines. Again and again, hard-won progress was reversed, undone by pummeling setbacks. Knots and stout splices came unraveled at cruel whim. Unsecured rope ends became garrotes. Possessed lines bound, squealing, inside unruly blocks, and coils kinked in the sheaves. The sailhands faced lethal frustrations, determined. Uncomplaining, they labored, dependent upon Dakar, who wore himself white, stringing stayspells.

As misfortune mounted, Fionn Areth still hung back, engrossed by his poisonous doubts. Yet as a mess of dropped tackle tried *yet again* to snag a young topman off-balance, and a mate's desperate snatch saved his jostled stance on the footropes, the rigid denial could not be sustained.

Spellcraft and determination were *all* that forestalled the impact of tragic injury. Under siege by a fiend storm, the Alliance doctrine wore thin, that Athera's conclaves of initiate knowledge founded the root of all evil.

Arithon Teir's'Ffalenn and a drunken spellbinder's conjury held the *Evenstar*'s fate by a thread.

Should either one lose his rapt concentration, the plague would breed havoc until the brig lost her fight to stay seaworthy. The Prime and her seniors would not stand down until the brute contest reached closure. Laid hard against the self-evident fact, that *his face had been fashioned as a live gambit to trap the last Prince of Rathain*, Fionn Areth rubbed his aching temples. His righteous dedication to Araethurian good sense began to cramp reason, in hindsight.

That moment, Feylind yelled up from below. The *iyats* were broaching the water stores.

Arithon broke off his resistance at once. "Dakar! Mind the deck! I'll go below!"

For of course, if the casks became wrecked, the brig's crew would be left stripped of options. They must turn for shore and succumb to the ambush, or else waste from thirst one by one.

"Man, you can't!" Up the mainmast, with the jury-rigged stay half-secured, and the mizzenmast ratlines unraveling, Dakar shouted, frantic, "We'll be at the mercy of that sigil, each minute. The Koriathain can't withstand your bane-song. Their tracking hold's loosened. Did you not feel the shift? The web they've cast over us is fraying! Show them one second's respite, they'll rally and slam us all over again."

"I know. Believe me, there's no better choice." Erect, though the *iyats* shimmered and weaved in bilked riffles of wind all about him, Arithon was not calm, or dispassionate as he breasted the storm to the ladder and raced for the main deck.

"Use shadow!" urged Dakar. "You've recovered the natural use of your talent. Damn all to these fiends. We'll stay unharmed if we give in and sail. Turn for shore. The Prime will slack off, once we're bearing the direction she wants to herd us. Surely before we reach landfall, we can raise some form of spellcraft to defang the threat of those galleys!"

"No." The rejection rang, unequivocal.

Fionn Areth glimpsed Arithon's face as he passed, taut with decision that *could come* to cost him his freedom, and worse. His anguish was backed by restless awareness: that if sorcery were invoked, the toll of such reckoning must outweigh even the lives and the friendship of his loyal allies on *Evenstar*. "That fleet is aligned with Lysaer's Alliance! They are innocents, Dakar, bearing arms from blind fear. How many more dedicates will waste their lives if I show their conflict a tangible cause? I will grant no fresh proof that their terrors are real! Not by my hand, and not for self-preservation under my conscious consent!"

Which meant the assault would end here, in victory or hard-fought defeat. *Evenstar* would win free, or go down, with the choice of collateral damage ashore set aside by unflinching adherence to character.

Prodded by impulse, Fionn Areth charged forward and joined the crazed sprint toward the hatch. "I'm coming. You'll need help."

Arithon turned his head. He never broke stride. His rushed glance pierced, for its honesty. "I don't have a solution," he warned point-blank. "If everyone on this ship could sing fiend banes, the Koriathain would still outlast us. But follow along. Grasp at straws, if you wish. For my part, there's naught left but harebrained tricks and invention born out of necessity."

Late Autumn 5670

Fiend Swarm

Belowdecks, enclosed by low beams overhead, the bangs and thumps of the fiend swarm seemed magnified. Fionn Areth trailed Arithon at reckless speed, his heart raced by trapped apprehension. He was grasslands born, accustomed to open sky, with the sun and wind in his face. In this noisome, damp pit, airless dark became nightmare, made worse by the ravaging *iyats*. Possessed objects clattered, hellbent to cause injury. Loose feathers clogged eyesight and breathing. Harried and tripped, he might fall and break bones, even drown, never again to glimpse daylight.

Ahead, the pale glimmer of Arithon's shirt vanished into the gloom. Strewn flour foreclosed any use of a lamp. Never mind the fine dust became volatile tinder, *iyats* would find a live flame irresistible. *Evenstar's* timbers offered too ready a fuel for an explosive conflagration. Fire would doom her crew fastest of all, roasting them in a pitch-fed blaze, or casting them adrift beyond sight of land, crammed into an open boat.

Arithon spared no thought for such matters. As well, a mage with initiate talent would not require a light. He pressed ahead with sped grace in necessity, where Fionn Areth must grope. Stumbling blind through the ship's pitching dark, the herder kept on out of obstinacy.

At the bottom rung of the lower-deck companionway, someone's hands fumbled a grip on his clothing, then steadied his step in descent. "His Grace went that way," said the seaman on guard, breathlessly apprehensive. "The hatch to the hold. He'll go down. You sure he's asked for your company?"

"Somebody ought to stand at his back," the Araethurian said in stout irony.

His grasslands inflection raised instant contempt. "Yourself?" carped the sailhand. "*Watch his Grace's back?* I'd sooner trust him to a circling shark!"

"Let him go," cracked Arithon. "I've already said the goatherd could please himself without hindrance."

The sailhand's clasp reluctantly loosened. "Off you go. That way. Harm comes to him, Feylind will scuttle you like a gaffed dogfish."

Fionn Areth stayed silent. If Arithon fell to mishap, far more likely no man would be left alive on the brig to brandish the punitive knife. The goatherd blundered ahead through the buffet, beset by grisly smells and random barrages of fish guts: the opportunistic fiends had seized on a carcass, then torn it apart in possession. Gagging as he dodged the sting of flung cartilage, the Araethurian held still as his eyesight adjusted to the pinholes of light fallen through the cracks in the main deck.

Arithon knelt by the lower hatch, hazed by rope shreds and sundry whirled flotsam. "Shout topside," he called back to the watchful sailhand. "I'll need a pry bar to draw the last nails."

The man climbed for the main deck, chased by whirled puffs of down and a sleeting glitter of fish scales. He coughed to clear his airway, cracked the overhead hatch, dodged a hurtling shoe, and nipped through in dogged pursuit of his errand.

The brief flare of daylight unveiled the Prince of Rathain, intent gaze locked upon his made double. His stripping search lingered, unswerved by the earsplitting clamor, or the yells of the cook, separately damning his pots. Against such hell-bent noise, a masterbard's diction bit through with razor-sharp clarity. "Why are you down here? I want the truth."

Fionn Areth could scarcely declare that he searched for a reason to hate. The excuse he presented hung, utterly lame. "I don't understand you."

Arithon slapped down the ace of spades that nicked in to gouge at his face. "You can't explain why I have friends, with my history?"

Sweating beneath that unflinching perception, Fionn Areth let fly. "You would let us sink, here. Dishonor the vow you once made to a mother. See everyone you care about lost at sea, all for those others who'd trap you, ashore. Enemies who would just as soon see you burn. Folk with families you never saw. You *dare* the effrontery to act like they matter? *I will not be deceived by such pretense!*"

Their locked stare lasted. Even when the crewman returned and slammed the hatch to, dropping dark like a wall to separate them.

Out of that fiend-festered maelstrom, and through the tread of the sailhand, approaching, Arithon gave his answer. "We're not done. Nowhere near close to losing those casks. This hull hasn't yet sprung a critical leak." Dauntless, he accepted the offered pry bar, then began to draw nails, his exigent haste guided by magesight. "Koriathain know but one way to raise power, *and I am not out of options.*"

A squeak of tight wood saw the hatch cover loosened, and time had run out for discussion. "I'm going down," Prince Arithon said. "If you follow, beware. You'll step into danger. At this point, I have to use fiend banes. The effects cause the *iyats* to disgorge their energies. They'll fight, even turn in attack as they're drained. My banishment cannot act on them cleanly. Not with three diligent circles of Seniors and the Great Waystone actively feeding them."

His rapid statement in fact mapped a war against entities enspelled by coercion. The sailhand took back the pry bar, unasked. "You'll sing interference throughout our ship, the same as you did before?"

"No," Arithon said, then explained. "This pass, I'll have to run the tonal vibrations through air. The Prime's sigil is set into the sheathing and laid against *Evenstar*'s timbers. Opposed in headlong contact through wood, her forces and mine could spark off a conflagration." To the herder he added, "If you come, I can't assure you protection. The swarm is going to center around me. Mishaps in that hold are going to increase. Since a quartz-driven binding won't let the sprites leave, they've no choice but turn viciously violent." To the sailhand, he finished. "Seal the hatch. Keep it closed at all costs. If *Evenstar* burns, or starts taking on water, tell Feylind to abandon the ship. Launch the two boats with all hands and row for your very lives!"

The sailhand's nerve wavered. "Leave you below?"

"And anyone with me," Arithon cracked. "No questions. No argument. Batten the hatch. Post a diligent guard." As a wet crash from below signaled another cask hurled and demolished, he exhorted, "If I need aught else, I'll shout. My voice, do you hear? You'll not answer another."

The seaman nodded, unhappy.

"Good man. Hold the line." Beyond option, out of time, the Master of Shadow yanked open the grate. Airborne water sprayed out, mixed into a gyre of splintered staves. He ducked the macerating onslaught, evaded the scything spin of a barrel hoop, and slipped through.

His agile descent down the ladder was hard followed by Fionn Areth.

The hold was a jet well, alive with the whining, vexed breezes of *iyats* seeking invention. Off to one side, a cask creaked and sloshed. The air smelled of bilge, hot steel, and soaked tarps, stitched by the manic splashing of waterspouts looped up in defiance of gravity. While Fionn Areth stood blind, groping clumsily to reorient, a hardened hand caught his collar and yanked.

He staggered aside, while something bulky whipped past his head and just missed clubbing him unconscious.

"Ballast rock!" Arithon snapped in his ear. "Without mage-sight, you're a helpless target."

Again without asking, the grip steered him on. Fionn Areth was shoved the next stumbling step, then roughly repositioned, close enough to his enemy's back that he felt the man's light, rapid breathing.

"Stay close! The *iyats* must demand all my attention, and no way else can you hope to survive this." Athera's Masterbard gathered himself then, and launched into the threnodies for fiend bane.

The notes were arrhythmic, and difficult. Their tonal balance ached the teeth. Pressed against the singer's vibrating form, Fionn Areth shared a sense of the coiling tension required to create the exacting pitch. Tuned sound pierced his mind like razor-taut wire. Each fluid, transformational run sieved deranging harmonics through the echoing hold of the ship. The flow pierced pandemonium. Its unsubtle, nerve-cringing tempo disrupted the *iyats* and sapped the flux of their energies.

Unable to cross-link their matrix of being into material possession, their hold upon captured objects faltered, then failed. A clatter of noise ripped the dark, as sprung wood staves, whirling barrel hoops and ballast stones, and scooped water sliced out of suspension and crashed. The din was horrific. The brig's timbers rebounded to the bludgeoning impact of who knew what load of dropped wreckage. Without light, the damage could not be assessed. Pelted by spray and oddments of wood, while glued, sweat-soaked, to Arithon's back, Fionn Areth fought blanketing panic as he faced the gravity of his predicament. He knew *nothing* of ships. The fierce slap of liquid over his feet might have been bilge, or a sprung seam that let in the sea. The blanketing dark left him no choice but to suffer the peril of joined battle, tied up by his helpless ignorance.

Beyond such uncertainty, Arithon sang, now pressing for increased volume. Though such harsh triplets *must* strain the voice, and unhinge the most rapt concentration, he struck each piercing pitch without cracking. Throughout the dimmed hold, the *iyats* responded. The freakish swarm shifted, impelled to escape the harmonies that gouged them to entropic destruction.

And there, true to Arithon's horrific forecast, the Prime Matriarch's sigil recontained them.

The hold's contents and casks were no longer an arena for sport, but the field of contention for the energy sprites' basic hold on survival.

Evenstar's stakes were not one whit less. As the trapped fiends recoiled in backlash, their locked contest with Arithon redoubled. Gathered like wraiths, the unseen creatures closed in, lashing up vicious, hot breezes. Small objects and slivers of wood whistled in, stinging flesh and stabbing through clothing. Arithon changed key, raised his frequency, then sounded a drilling overtone through his teeth. The whistle ran chills over Fionn Areth's skin and ripped like sharp pain through his viscera.

Rocked to vertigo, he snatched and caught Arithon's shirt to keep balance.

The soaked flesh beneath was quivering with strain. Shocked by the force of the bard's raw exertion, Fionn Areth almost tripped as a barrel hoop reeled into his feet. As Arithon's fist snatched him short of a fall, then forcibly tugged him a tangential step sideward, the herder realized: the urgent cue pressed him to move with his protector across the beleaguered hold. The Araethurian was forced to keep pace by touch. Smothered in darkness, he could not guess what bent drove the sorcerer's intentions.

But the Master of Shadow engaged no dark powers. Through the bruising collisions, the barked shins, and the stumbling recovery of each misplaced step, Fionn Areth at last discerned the purpose: Arithon labored to shift the imperiled casks farther aft. There, he padded them under a wadding of tarps and ripped netting, scavenged off the baled silk and sundry crates of stacked cargo.

Though clumsy, a talentless partner could help. Fionn Areth hefted barrels and lugged armloads of burlap in shuffled steps through the darkness. If the slippery bilge grating was littered with splinters, broken staves, and flung rocks; if he blundered into the sodden wads of dumped grain bags and snarls of unspun silk, he regrouped, steadied upright by Arithon's shoulder.

Throughout, the bard whistled his tooth-grating threnodies. Marked as their deadly adversary, the fiends whickered and dived, harrying at his person. They hampered his footsteps and snatched at his flesh, and snapped gusts to hinder his vision.

He sang them down. Unremitting, his voice drove their railing jabs back, pealing cascades of triplets that stayed achingly pure. As the casks were restacked and swaddled over in cloth, Arithon spared the astonishing grace to bestow the odd backslap of encouragement.

Fionn Areth blinked stinging sweat from his lashes; spat the bitter taint of splashed brine. He worked himself ragged to distance the thought, that all adamant striving was wasted. How could a man hold those sharp notes without tiring, or keep rhythm with such aching, tight clarity? How long, before Arithon spent his last strength or grew hoarse from extended exertion?

The ordeal reeled on without sign of requital. Against quartz-driven malice, no flesh-and-blood artistry might wrest back the hope to snatch triumph. Then the moment arrived. Arithon faltered. His exhaustion finally racked his critical timing off true.

At the first wavered note, he stopped his fierce keening. Silence clapped down like a shock on the nerves. The restless, enraged pack of fiends came unhinged. Restored to autonomy, they rippled through air, snagging up dropped bits of jetsam. Ballast rocks, loose bits of wood and snarled cloth, the collection stormed down in a battering wave. The volley of viciously animate debris was aimed to pulverize human resistance.

Fionn Areth tucked his head under crossed forearms. The reckoning had come. Coerced to abandon his upright principles, he would die here, entrapped in the feuds of a sorcerer.

"Fainthearted," gasped Arithon on a spent breath. "You don't pray to be saved by the Light?" His manic, phrased mockery masked the movement as he reached, lightning-fast, for his sword.

Blade sheared from scabbard with a metallic chime, ink against jet in the darkness. Amid mobbing fiends, a pallid light gleamed. The Paravian runes woke, blinding, and pealed out a silvery chord as enchanted steel roused to the starspell inlaid at its forging. The clarion cry sang like the ring of struck bronze, expanded through subsonic registers.

Light scattered the dark, and the embattled hold sprang into untrammeled view. Raised bilge wheeled, glistening, through the grinding tumble, as possessed rocks skittered and smashed to fragments. Billows of frayed silk slithered and knotted through the rags of ripped tarps and garroting swatches of burlap. At their backs, their painstakingly piled casks offered no cranny in which to evade the incoming assault.

"We're fordone," Fionn Areth gasped, cringing.

Arithon's fast glance swept the goatherd's tucked rabbit posture and sheltering fists.

"No." The rebuttal raised the hard twist of a smile. "This is where we snatch respite."

Before Fionn Areth expressed his contempt, the Master of Shadow pushed straight. Head bent, grip firm on the humming, live sword, he laid the flat of the upright blade to his brow, and spoke a rapid phrase in Paravian. The actualized syllables maddened the air, and ripped exposed skin into gooseflesh. Arithon shivered. He held to his focus, eyes shut, stripped down to the ruthless poise of a marksman given a life-or-death shot at one target.

Whatever uncanny bidding he framed, the bare steel in his hands interacted. The sword blade hummed louder. Its rune inlay softened, eased back to a glimmer pure as a clear shine of starlight. The fiends crowding in to macerate flesh recoiled just outside that ring of cast radiance. The deflected objects they wielded crashed into collision, snapping off static and bursts of singed cloth in balked fits of frustration.

Saved, half-unmanned by uncertain relief, Fionn Areth unclenched his arms and rubbed clammy palms on his breeches. "You can stand them down with that sword blade? Dharkaron's fell fury! For how long?"

Arithon finished his rapt invocation. Careful movement lowered the weapon. The uncanny steel stayed ablaze with white light, still sounding that bell-toned vibration. Its power surged through skin and bones, and deep viscera, prickling like a wild tonic. Bemused, the Prince of Rathain shook his head. "I don't know. I've forged an active partnership with the craft the Paravian singers laid down for defense. The engagement can be maintained, at small cost. But to hold the conscious lines of intent, I'll have to keep waking awareness."

Fionn Areth clutched himself, shivering, while a ballast rock arced over his head. The thud as the missile slammed into spoiled silk shuddered the keel underfoot. Muffled shouts and the ongoing thumps topside bespoke crewmen still wrestling damages. "If you thought this would work, why not spare us earlier?"

"I didn't know," said Arithon in stark wonder. "We're improvising, remember? I couldn't try out an untested theory. Not while those fiends were rammed full of fresh charge. The bane-song was needful to drain them."

"You call these *drained?*" The smashing crunch of another dropped rock contradicted that sweeping statement.

Arithon shrugged. He had no use for argument. Astute observation would show soon enough: the *iyats were* dropping their possessed grip on the heaviest objects.

Turned back to attend his hoard of stacked casks, Arithon struck the sword point downward through his improvised layers of wadding. The upright weapon shed a ghost ring of radiance, thrumming its uncanny song through the oak staves of the water casks just saved by intervention.

"What now?" asked Fionn Areth, his explosive relief finding outlet in nervous chatter.

"Given we have an established defense? First the lure, then the feint." Arithon hailed to the sailhand still guarding the hatch. "I want wicking string, oil, and the parts to reconstitute a closed lantern."

"Fury and frost!" Fionn Areth exploded. "You're thinking to risk *open flame?*"

Response came from Dakar, just arrived at the hatch, mottled red from the teeth of catastrophe. "Madman! You won't." He shoved down the ladder. Now livid with rage, he arrived with a splash in the rippling flood of the bilge.

The sight of the light-shot sword struck him silent.

"Ath's undying glory!" Still staring, the spellbinder swiped off a frayed length of twine pinched between the doughy folds of his neck. "I've never *seen* Alithiel's power engaged that way. Do you have the first clue what you're *doing?*" He shuddered, and capped with a quote. "'*On the day Mother Dark chose to couple with mercy, Chaos was born of their union.*'"

"The desert tribes' myth of creation? How apt." Arithon's smile held steel, but no warmth. "An unpredictably perilous childbirth. If I'm pressed to experiment, why whimper when we have the option to scream? If you plan to revile me using metaphor, it was Chaos that spat out the seed of the sun."

"Should I have expected that Davien would tame you?" Bloodied and sapped by his lingering headache, the Mad Prophet recouped his shocked poise. "You want a lamp," he repeated. "In case you fall, someone else ought to know just what messy tactic you're trying." His thoughtful gaze locked to Prince Arithon's face, he added, "Do you want my *accurate* spellbinder's opinion on how long you're going to stay standing? No? Then I'm listening."

Words would cost them time. As the sailhand arrived with the requisite items, Arithon opted for demonstration. "Stay here. You'll see."

He accepted the lamp parts and began their assembly at speed.

The sailhand unreeled the wick string, and nipped off the end with his teeth. "Feylind says, hurry. We're taking on water. She needs a team down here to man pumps and sound out the leaks."

"I won't need a minute," Arithon replied. "When you go, tell the mate: he'll be bending on sail. I want this brig on a course due offshore, bearing every last stitch she can carry."

The lamp was prepared, and the reservoir filled. Arithon handed the ring off to Dakar, indulging meanwhile, in wry melodrama from an execrable ballad. "'*Strike a spark, my wilding mage, unleash bold conjury! Swords will speak, and women wail, in ravaged misery.*'"

"They'll be likelier to laugh as you fry us to blisters," Dakar said in sour reference to Selidie's witches. He had never yet encountered the *iyat* that could resist the lure of a fire. Still, he invoked the neat cantrip to spark the lamp, then trimmed the fluttering wick. "You've left those sprites stripped clean out of charge. Starved to mean aggravation, they'll be drawn down like the Ebon Spear from the fist of Dharkaron Avenger—Arithon! Death and mercy, *you can't!*"

Yet the spellbinder's furious screech deterred nothing. The Master of Shadow leaned down and tossed what looked like a tangle of spider silk through the lantern's opened pane. As Dakar foresaw, the seed flame roared up, bright and hot as a solstice bonfire.

Fionn Areth bounded back with a cry, convinced clothing and hair had ignited.

Dakar caught the yokel short before his frazzled panic rallied the *iyats*. "It's a petty conjurer's trick of illusion," he exclaimed in reviling disgust. His soaked beard still dripped, despite the sensation of heat that roared in merry havoc about them. "A display you could buy at a street fair for less than a beggar's penny!"

"Well, the *iyats* seem impressed," Arithon declared. His smile showed no rancor. "Could we drop the high dudgeon? I was hoping you'd take the clown's role and keep the appearances going."

Dakar shut his mouth. As ever outflanked by that arid humor, he stepped through the crackling mimicry and peered into the hold at large.

Lamp flame and pettifogging huckster's trick, the effect on the swarm was profound. The depleted *iyats* were inexorably drawn to assuage their insatiable hunger. They circled the fake bonfire in flitting frustration, pinned flat against the silvery radiance cast by the Paravian sword.

Dakar surveyed the resistance, his trained eye seeking flaws. Something beyond natural appetite seemed to be leashing the sprites' feckless nature. More than snagged in by the lure of the fire, they prowled the ring's edge, pulled as though snared in obsession. Paravian craft did not act in that way.

Dakar grasped the lightning stroke of epiphany and cracked to incredulous glee. "The *sigil?*"

"Dead underneath us," said Arithon, laughing at last. "For as long as Prime Selidie tries her quartz binding, her swarm will stay thralled and flat helpless." While something banged, topside, to unraveling shouts, and a shudder shocked through the brig, he inquired, "Can you keep the lamp trimmed and sustain the illusion?"

"That alone, not the sword!" Dakar amended. "The working you've woven is outside my depth. Ath on earth, I couldn't presume."

"You won't have to." Arithon clapped Dakar's shoulder, prepared to brush past. "There are fiends still needing a bane-ward. I'll be topside, helping until the brig is back under way." Stray *iyats* would still be fouling the gear. His threnodies could be engaged to clear them and dispatch their starved husks to share the spelled circle that knotted the captives, below. "As long as I don't get tossed off the ship, I can hold the intent and keep the blade's warding in active alignment."

Dakar parked his rump on the soaked pile of casks. "I'm sorry," he said, sobered. "Inside safe walls at Alestron, I should have cut back on my drinking."

"I am not your conscience." Wrung hoarse, reduced to a tattered form in dripping, disheveled clothing, Arithon seemed little more than a man in haste to escape the dank chill of the darkness. His soft statement should not have caused a Fellowship spellbinder to turn his face to hide sudden, shamed tears.

Arithon murmured a last word in Paravian, then sloshed on due course for the ladder.

Fionn Areth stirred also, prepared to keep pace.

His nemesis allowed him. "If you plan to come, you'll want to stay close. Those *iyats* are snagged, but not helpless. Only a fool would step outside this circle without ward from a masterbard's threnodies."

Aware of the thump of a yard, abovedecks, and the mate's shouted orders to man halyards, Dakar blotted his cheeks and squeezed in a final question. "You'll draw in the wind and drive us offshore?"

Arithon nodded. "The tactic's worth trying."

The simple offensive meant less could go wrong. More leagues of salt water between *Evenstar* and the coast meant Prime Selidie would need to ride her thralled seniors much harder. The massed fleet of galleys lying in ambush also must spread themselves thinner to compensate. Delay would seed fights between captains. If attrition failed, the plot still could be stymied. A lamed vessel's crew would succumb to the elements before they could limp on a jury-rig back to Orvandir. The farther the hard-pressed quarry could run, the less chance the grueling contest would deliver the prize of a living capture.

"Bluster and guts," the bard said with apology. "We'll lengthen the stakes past the point of futility and wait for the witch to give up."

"If she wants you dead, you'll play into her hand," Dakar cautioned, though the warning in fact was not truthful. He shared an unsettling nuance with the Fellowship Sorcerers that Arithon had never been told: the Prime Matriarch desired Rathain's royal line as hard leverage to destroy the compact.

Yet the rigors of Kewar *had* altered this prince. His moment of fierce, introspective attention crystallized all at once to a flash of balefire annoyance. "We sail, rails awash, fast as wind can take us. She wants me alive, beyond question."

Late Autumn 5670

Dusk to Dawn

By sundown, as *Evenstar* sustains resistance against the invasion of *iyats*, Prime Selidie draws more enchantresses from the Forthmark hospice to reinforce her assault; and privy to secrets, aware that Morriel's spirit actually drives her, Lirenda knows the engagement will not relent for less than full forfeit, and final capture of Arithon Teir's'Ffalenn...

As the Sorcerer Asandir rides his black stallion south and east from the focus circle at old Mainmere, and another cloaked rider masked under his warding fares south from Avenor, alone, a conclave of conspirators casts a shielded scrying, then confers as their select prey boards his sunwheel guard onto galleys at Tideport: "He's coming by way of Hanshire, not good news," then the reply, "Who will he have in defense, beyond the one untrained liegeman? This time, no contest, we take them..."

As day breaks, a disgruntled priest and his sunwheel retinue retrace their journey back to Kalesh; and packeted for dispatch to Cerebeld in the west are the attested facts that will pivot the strategy aimed to fragment the peace: that Princess Ellaine has claimed shelter with the s'Brydion of Alestron, who have also seen fit to employ a shipwright accused of high treason for past acts of sabotage at Riverton...

Western Tysan

VII. Bind

Nightfall on the day following the Koriani spring trap saw the *Evenstar* reaching offshore, the wind on her port quarter. Few of her crew had seen rest, beyond catnaps, and the ship's cooper, not at all. Hammers banged upon chisels, abovedecks, where men labored to fish a broken spar in the bowsprit under the gleam of a wan, gibbous moon. Others wore their hands raw mending chafed lines and tattered sails.

Red-eyed after a sleepless night, Feylind tossed back her ragged braid, chilled fingers tucked under crossed arms. "We look like a tub that got trounced by a gale."

His rawboned hands empty for the first moment since dawn, the mate scraped at the crusted salt that itched his stubbled chin. His hair was in tangles, and his clothing, left fusty from dousings inflicted by *iyats*. No rock in a storm could have owned his staid calm: a solid, dependable shadow, he assessed the soaked crewman hunched at the wheel, then rechecked the set of the stars overtop of the masthead.

For now, the brig's course was aligned by the heavens, the compass being apt to wander in circles at erratic intervals. "I'll say this," the mate answered with slow-spoken care. "Cattrick's proven his worth as a man who knows how to lay a ship's timbers. We still have a keel underneath us."

The crew did not share that unscathed assessment. Cut and bruised, half the hands sprawled prone at their posts, dozing between calls to man braces. These were blue-water sailors paid to ship cargo, and not war-hardened veterans. No merchant brig could carry the numbers to run on shortened watches or withstand a prolonged assault.

"Some of the men must stand down," the mate said, too wise to ignore prudent limits.

Feylind rousted the ship's boy to relieve the lookout. The lad arrived, limping. Tired or sore, he fumbled his clasp on the rigging as he slung himself into the crow's nest.

"Keep a hand for the ship, you!" Feylind barked in warning. To the mate, low-voiced, she shared her distress, "We can't keep this up. Not without risking a fatal mistake."

They had three down, already: two from broken bones, and one with a concussion. *Iyats* were still being lured by the sigil. As *Evenstar*'s charted course led her seaward, the spellbound attractant moved with her. Fiends plying the waves and the winds for raw charge flocked in like flies to a carcass. Under darkness, the sailhands' ragged exhaustion made them easy bait for mishap and malicious sport.

Yet a lamp under canvas posed too dire a risk.

Annoyed to explosion, Feylind clamped her fists. "Dharkaron avenge! I could skewer those witches! We can't even risk using the damned jacklines." Spare rope rigged for safety just posed one more chance to be snapped up for use as a garrote.

The latest effort to ease their dire straits seemed an uncertain prospect at best: again, the chiming tap of a tin bowl with a spoon carried up from the ship's waist. Tucked against the brisk breeze, two black-haired figures attended the brig's stolid cook, who had hauled his store of bashed pots up on deck at the Masterbard's urgent request. The vessels not put to immediate use had been stacked in the scuttlebutt for convenience. The rest were nested in bights of rope to secure them against the tossing heel of the deck. Two kettles were partially filled up with seawater. Bent over a third, a spoon and a ladle in hand, one alike man watched the other, who added water in measured increments, poured from a battered tin cup.

"Strike it again," said Arithon s'Ffalenn to his Araethurian double. A wearied burr husked his tone as he added, "Try the ladle, this time."

The duplicate rapped the pot under scrutiny. Slightly taller, his square-shouldered frame resisted the ship's plunging reach with the matter of fact stance of a post.

By contrast, Arithon knelt with an enviable grace: that indefinably taut self-awareness instilled through a lifetime of training. Head tipped a critical fraction to one side, he assessed the pot's pitch, then added a dollop of water. "Again."

Ladle met tin; the painstaking effort to contrive a mechanical means to sound fiend banes had been ongoing for more than an hour. To Feylind's ear, the latest attempt seemed exactly the same as the last.

Yet Arithon winced, stabbed to visceral impatience. "No harmonic," he snapped. "The slosh acts as a damper. We've got to have clearer tonality."

He shoved erect, snatched the rope-handled bucket with intent to scoop up more seawater. His step toward the rail seemed fluid enough, until like a fray in a fragile silk thread, the mask slipped and exhaustion exposed him. Arithon staggered. He caught himself short on the mainmast pinrail, overcome by a febrile tremor.

Metal flashed, under moonlight. Fionn Areth dumped his ladle and spoon and surged, empty-handed, to extend his help.

Arithon sensed the move at his flank. As though seared, he shot straight in recoil.

Aware what must come, Feylind shoved off the rail. "Sithaer's fires! This can't continue!"

"Let them be!" But the mate's warning grasp missed her sleeve as she left him.

Plunged down the companionway, Feylind thrust past the cook, just in time to catch the impact of Arithon's scalding rebuff. Fionn Areth flinched and yanked back. His awkward weight slammed her breathless. First to recover, she shouldered the herder's stung anger aside.

"You won't do this!" cracked Feylind. "The boy's right, you're a cat's whisker away from measuring your length on my deck!" She caught Arithon's arm, braced his weight, then clasped him.

His eyes met her face without change of expression, wide-open and limpid in moonlight. His gasped oath was savage. Wrenched out of balance, now shaking in spasms, he twisted away from the bulwark of her support.

"Bear up, damn you!" Feylind hissed in his ear. "You can't afford spurning an offer of friendship, no matter how much the pain rankles!"

"Go castrate a bull with your mothering tongue," said Arithon with blistering clarity.

"You don't mean that," Feylind answered. Aware of the sparkle that rose in his eyes, though his adamant, turned face sought the darkness, she sighed. Then she shifted her grip, turned her palm, and cupped his exposed cheek in a desperate effort to shield him.

His fingers convulsed in the cloth of her shirt.

To Fionn Areth, who stared openmouthed, then to the cook, and the riveted deckhands, the captain rebuked, "He won't stand hero worship. Never has. Never will, though such foolish pride drops him prostrate. He can gut you with words. Don't be fooled. He still needs you."

Arithon raked her over with resigned contempt. "Sheathe your harpy's claws, will you? A man likes his pride given back without shreds. I only intended to rest on the pinrail." His effort at boredom *almost* rang true. But the tremors had worsened to shuddering spasms. He could not command the pitch of his voice. Nor could he move: the hot moisture that welled beneath her spread fingers destroyed every effort at pretense.

Aware that his legs would no longer bear weight, Feylind held on through the surge as *Evenstar* plowed through a trough. She had always conceived of this prince as a giant. In fact, he was slight. Lean and finely made as an injured deer, his propped frame required almost no muscle.

"Shredded pride has no place!" she chided him gently. "If you're going to buckle, you can't fall down on Fionn. What if Vhandon or Talvish stepped in? They'd kill first and question appearances later. You'd have a dead Araethurian before either one realized the boy wasn't caught in the act of a cold-blooded murder."

Arithon surrendered resistance and leaned. "Your brother bests all of my arguments, too."

As the gusting wind slammed the ship through the swell, Feylind experienced the taut weight of him: close-knit, compact, nothing like the easy, protective warmth she enjoyed with the mate. *This man was different.* The intimate sense of his aliveness suffused her, an electrical tingle that coursed through her being, and wakened a startling ripple of pleasure. The encounter was sensual, and something far more: a contact that quickened the vault of her mind, then hurled a soundless, ranging cry through the uncharted realm of her spirit.

To that lyrical call, that beckoned beyond silence, she found her own voice as clay, without word or language to answer.

Feylind jerked back her unreeled breath. For good reasons, Arithon kept his touch reserved and shied off from physical contact. Impelled by need, one moment of weakness laid bare what could not be masked: initiate mastery augmented the presence of him, at close quarters. Even unstrung, his reactive sensitivity engaged life with an intricacy that her practical nature could never stretch to encompass.

The grief struck, too poignant: that his aware mind and uncanny affairs lay too far outside her reach. *Evenstar* was endangered, with all her stout company, and for no better reason than the fact that this one, complex spirit had led her first steps past a fisherman's daughter's horizons.

Feylind swallowed, looked up, saw the mate at the fringes. He would read her features as no one else could. This moment of tearing discovery was never going to escape him.

Worse, the rare talent she held in her arms also recognized her tangling turmoil. Caught helpless, Arithon could not respond. Her braid pressed against the raced pulse in her neck by the weight of his head on her shoulder, and with his shuddering balance reliant upon her closed arms, Feylind ached. The binding cruelty spared no one. Two men must share the tremulous wrench as she chose for the life that she led. The one that gave her two inquisitive children, and the more limited challenge as mistress of a blue-water ship.

"Take him, Teive," she said, her throat tight. "Bear him below. Better hope the fat spellbinder knows what to do or can conjure a remedy to ease him."

For the bane of the *iyats* had now devolved to a trial of brutal endurance. *Evenstar*'s resistance could last only as long as Arithon could stave off collapse.

The Master of Shadow was taken from the main deck down to the hold, closely trailed by Fionn Areth. There, the buffeting darkness swarmed with hazed fiends. The air reeked of sulfur and ozone. Confronted by the thrashed wreck of the cargo, Teive paused in his tracks, and swore murder. If the damage to sails and rigging above skirted the grim edge of ruin, the Atchaz silk and the wool bound for Los Mar were rendered a total loss. Wisped lint from the ripped bales whipped by in the crazed eddies, while fragmented wood and odd stones cartwheeled past, picked out of black air by the silvered glow thrown off by the Paravian longsword.

The mate stared aghast through the pause, while Arithon mustered the rags of his resource and engaged his masterbard's gift. A brief, whistled threnody carved them a course through the seething of the fiend pack. As they crossed into the ranging protection cast by the blade's active resonance, the Mad Prophet shoved to his feet and took charge.

"Your liege is played through, no mistake," the mate said, glad enough to relinquish his burden.

Arithon was eased onto the wrapped pile of casks.

"Just overextended," Dakar surmised, his tangled head bent for a cursory examination. "I did warn him. His talent's been pushed far beyond prudent limits. Here, could you help? I need him propped upright."

Blanched as paper, Arithon showed no response, even as the spellbinder shifted the lamp, peeled back a slack eyelid, and measured the sluggish response of the pupil.

"What's to do?" the mate asked. "Has he fainted?"

"No. He's still with us." Dakar shoved up Arithon's unlaced sleeve cuff. The stark lack of protest at such public handling became as much cause for concern as the clammy skin and raced pulse. Even so, the awareness braced up by the mate's solid grasp was anything else but unconscious. Hard-pressed to the edge, Arithon now fought to sustain the concentration that kept the warding sword active.

"He's worn-out, not dying." Amid rolling shadows, through the tumultuous motion and noise as the brig sheared ahead through rough waters, Dakar gave his bitter prognosis. "The best we can do is attend to his comfort, then sit by his side and share vigil."

"I won't lie down. Can't," husked the Masterbard faintly. While the Mad Prophet shifted a blanket for warmth, and the mate eased away his support, the protest sawed on at a whisper. "I'm too likely to drift off to sleep."

"Be still!" Dakar's sideward glare warned off Fionn Areth, who had crowded close, still observing. Then, more gently, "Be still. We're all here. Whatever you need, we'll assist you."

Arithon subsided. Limned in the sword's glare, and the hot spill of the lantern, his features seemed cut into knife-edged angles of strain.

"All right," said the mate. "We'll set watches in shifts. First Vhandon, then Talvish, then me. Dakar stays. We can send down more blankets, dry bread, and small comforts. I'll station a sailhand next to the hatch. He'll run your errands as needed."

"I stay as well." Sea legs still clumsy, Fionn Areth moved in with intent to take charge of the lamp. "One watch should be mine, that a man can be spared."

Evenstar's mate disapproved, his glance caustic. "No." His stiff arm resisted the goatherd's thrust forward. "What you actually want is Rathain's prince, alone. On this ship, you don't ask for a trust that's not warranted."

"Trust, you say!" Rankled, the Araethurian attacked. "Such a creature could see your Feylind destroyed and never look back on the carnage!"

"Watch your tongue." Large, mild-natured, the mate seemed unmoved. "My captain believes the man won't let her down." Yet his taut jaw fairly shouted with warning: he would settle the score with far more than harsh words, if his beloved's impetuous faith should ever come to be broken.

"Let Fionn stay, Teive." Arithon dredged up a brittle smile, couched in recline on the casks. "Like the nettle, and the burr, and the thorn in the rose, his badgering pricks keep me wakeful."

The mate shrugged. "Your risk. I'll send down Vhandon." Brave enough in the pinch of necessity, he regarded the fiends, weaving like ripples through uneven glass outside the sword's sphere of radiance. "That's if you still have an ounce of grit left to get me away through the swarm."

That cynical jab opened Arithon's eyes. He said, stripped earnest, "I could load the small boat with provisions and leave."

The mate paused, raw fists empty. "And your double with you? Would that stop the attack?"

"I don't know." The admission came thin through the groan of the ship's timbers.

Dakar swore at Rathain's prince and pushed straight. "*What are you doing? You swore oath at Athir!*" To the mate, he explained, "A blood binding stands in force, to the Fellowship, that his Grace must use any and every known resource to stay on this side of Fate's Wheel." Turned on Arithon, he said, desperate, "We've gone too far out. Even if you could reach the coast at this season, in an oared boat without shelter, how many would die? You'd still have to deal with that ambush through sorcery! Wrecked galleys won't win you the prize reassurance, that *Evenstar* won't face an impoundment. Her crew might yet suffer a criminal arraignment by town justice as your associates. And Feylind—"

"No, Dakar." Arithon stirred a hand, pleading silence. "Teive's her man. Let him speak."

"*Her* man, you say!" The mate cracked. The festering scab tore away at one stroke and savaged his sturdy complacency. "If you accept that, then why did you come here?"

Arithon met spiking rage without flinching. "The same reason you did. For Feylind."

Teive swallowed. "Then give me one reason why you think you should rightfully stay."

No barrier lay between the two men: one whose steadfast love nurtured the welfare of a woman, and the other, the enticing, mysterious stranger whose entangled affairs had now set her at dreadful risk. The shocked moment stretched. Against thrashing noise, as the brig pitched on her reckless east bearing, and the *iyats* pinned down between sword and sigil strained to feed on the flaring hostility, the question burned, a heartbeat removed from fracturing violence.

Drawn white, Arithon tendered his answer. "Koriathain have bid to claim her, as pawn. But I am the piece they want off the game board. Should they take us with me still aboard, she'll survive. Better yet, my protections may hold. Granted respite, I can destroy that sigil, then salvage this brig's reputation. We all go free. Without prey, the coastal ambush disbands. The Alliance fanatics row home to their wives, without needless fracas and bloodshed."

"Or they'll regroup to fight us another day. You can't keep your grip, not indefinitely." Once started, the mate hurled down the same fears he had worked to allay, in his crewmen. "Your capture is likely to happen right here. This keel could take too much damage and sink. Your enemies won't guard our survival, *your Grace*. Should we resist and go down for your feud? Or waste and die, lost at sea in the tenders?"

"If that happens," said Arithon, "I will be dead. The witches won't have my surrender."

The mate nodded once. His quittance was brisk. "I can ask for no more. Sing me out."

Head bent, his scraped fingers pinched on crossed wrists, Arithon did as requested. While the mate went his way through the packed flock of fiends, Fionn Areth crouched by the lamp and vented his wretched confusion. "How can you risk the lives of such friends? Have so many died that they've become ciphers, dismissed by a callous heart?"

Nervelessly still, his head tipped back to rest, Arithon quashed Dakar's steamed intervention with the barest flick of a glance. Then he said, "Feylind is as close to me as a daughter, and this, her ship's crew, is her family."

"You would kill them all, and yourself as well, just for the well-being of strangers?" Fionn Areth gripped his knees, if only to stay his blazing urge to shatter the self-contained presence before him. "Why spare the Alliance? I don't understand."

Arithon closed his eyes. "Because these people here understand why they fight. Their love and their loyalties are freely given, and based on the truth, however unsavory. Their choice has not been triggered by fear, or embellished by self-righteous vainglory."

When the goatherd's locked fury failed to dispel, the Master of Shadow mustered his overtried patience. "An honest end among friends won't lack meaning. Each will sacrifice what they can for the other in acts that arise out of caring. Their fight is sourced in survival and love. By contrast, those fools on the galleys have sharpened their swords for a lie. Their lives and their faith have been cozened from them. First deluded and set against me by Lysaer, then whipped on by meddling Koriathain, they have been sent blindfold to the slaughter. Like thousands of others cut down by my hand, they would cross Fate's Wheel for reasonless hate, and their deaths would serve nothing but ruin."

Left silent with thought, Fionn Areth lost wind, while Dakar allowed his claimed place by the lamp in a storm cloud of stifled censure.

A taut interval passed. Amid grinding noise and pervasive, dank chill, the gyrating corkscrews of each breasted swell framed a trial of bruising endurance. To lie down was to suffer bone-rattling discomfort. For any man tested by sleepless exhaustion, the jostling effort to sit by itself became a draining exertion. Hour upon hour, Arithon's taxed face showed the focus required to hold mage-sourced intention in wakeful alignment.

If Fionn Areth regretted his choice, his obstinate need to plumb truth from falsehood kept him tenaciously rooted.

Then Vhandon arrived, brisk-tempered and swordless. His grizzled frown and his veteran's strength seemed displaced, clutching a bundle of blankets. If the shrilling tones of Arithon's whistle brought him unscathed through the rampaging *iyats*, he emerged, no less discomposed. "This is havoc!"

His baleful glance raked the assemblage of stacked casks, marked out which of the dark-haired doubles to guard, then fastened on Dakar, who now looked more rumpled and dissolute than he had on the hour he woke from his bingeing. "He's ailing, you say?"

The clipped line referred to the Master of Shadow, arranged with his slackened hands in his lap, and his head lolled back with closed eyes.

"Mage-trance," said Dakar. "Best not to disturb him."

"Sithaer, don't worry." The intrepid liegeman unloaded his burden. "I'd just wring his royal neck for the folly of sticking his head in the noose."

"You'd rather he should break his oathsworn promise?" Fionn Areth inquired from his perch next to Arithon's feet.

"Should I answer?" Vhandon's lip curled. "You're dangerous as ice on a hot spring, young fool. Nobody knows which damned way you'll erupt. Were I the man who trained you for the sword, you'd be digging latrines and nowhere near handling weapons!"

Fionn Areth's sparked temper crashed against Dakar, who shoved a placating arm in between. "Vhan, let him be. Of course he can't think! His peers had no further use for edged steel beyond shearing and slaughtering livestock."

Vhandon shrugged, his blunt manner unraveled by an irrepressible chuckle. "All right, whelp. Hear the truth. His Grace's stickling way with a promise is why he needs such as me to protect him. By my call, you'd have died on the scaffold, and bad cess to Jaelot's warped justice. Therefore, *you will mind your tongue.* My fist at your throat, if you try my patience. I won't waste my breath on a warning."

As the pigheaded herder subsided, the liegeman turned his stolid back. "Grudges just feed the *iyats*, besides."

While Dakar rearranged the blankets for warmth, Vhandon surveyed the rest of the hold. His vigilant eye tracked the ripped tufts of silk, then the flotsam of spoiled cargo: the smashed barrels and cracked rock, with the wink of a game card, flitting an aimless, fiend-driven course through the gloom outside of the ward ring. "Until now, I never appreciated the old centaur magics laid through the stones of Alestron's walls." His icy regard fixed back on Dakar. "What's to do?"

"Watch. Wait. Keep your liege wakeful." Hunkered under a cowl of blankets, the Mad Prophet sank his bearded chin on propped fists. "If aught else can be done, I'll instruct you."

Too upright to shirk while standing on watch, Vhandon raked an irascible hand through gray hair and finally measured his stricken prince. "How long can he last, so?"

Dakar sighed. "Five days, supported by mage-trained faculties, if he wasn't sustaining a siege. Under present conditions, he'll have bested fate if he can hold out beyond morning."

Rocked back on his heels, the scarred liegeman absorbed this. His silence thereafter spoke volumes, while the nerve-racking hours of vigil began, that unbearably stretched each passing minute, and magnified minor discomforts. The sloshing pound of water on wood, the watch orders called abovedecks, and the stirring pressure of caged *iyats* played on, a repetitive cycle of unreal dream, cast outside the sword's silvered radiance.

Inside, there was nothing to tend but the lamp. Worse, on occasions when movement was needful, and circumstance called upon Arithon's skills to sound the precise tones for fiend bane: to let a man come or go through the lines, in order to eat or relieve himself. Between times, sunk into his fathomless trance, the Teir's'Ffalenn huddled without moving. Awareness pared down to a pinpoint spark, he maintained the fragile strand of intent that upheld the warding spun over the sigil.

As additional *iyats* converged on the brig, he dared not expend further effort to rout them. The crew must carry on as they could, standing down fresh bedevilment through emotionless boredom. Starved out of reaction, denied prodding sport, the sprites would flit and possess things at random until the forced draw of the sigil eventually winnowed them into containment.

Fionn Areth stayed complacent. Between catnaps, or loose conversation with Dakar, he reset the wick of the lamp and refilled the depleted reservoir.

Toward midnight, Vhandon relented enough to try him at arm wrestling. No weakling, the younger man learned from mistakes. Beneath thin-skinned nerves and volatile temperament, his innate perseverance lent him a natural prowess.

Daybreak arrived. The bosun shouted the change in the watch. Clad in unlaced jerkin and shirt, Talvish appeared at the lower deck hatch. "Relief," he called down. "I've brought cheese and biscuit and a hide flask of rum. That's if the *iyats* don't savage them, first."

His voice, or his agile step on the ladder, roused Arithon out of reverie. He whistled the piercing notes of the threnodies, eyes pinched shut, while Vhandon let down his rolled-up sleeves and relinquished his post to his fellow man-at-arms. Given a parting clap on the back, Fionn Areth was left with the cheerless last wish for survivor's luck on the battle line.

"Perish the luck, he has my strong arm," Talvish cracked in astringent humor. Arrived, intact, through the dense swarm of fiends, he assessed the disparate company. "What were you lot doing all night? Vhan, you look thrashed. Glassy-eyed and useless as a hooked fish someone left too long in the creel."

"Later," said Vhandon, "I'll best you at knives. Sixty yards at a flying target." He crossed through the ward, urgent with need to spare Arithon's dwindling strength.

Affronted by Talvish's quicksilver tongue, Fionn Areth regretted to see the older campaigner depart. As the bard's notes of fiend bane echoed and died, the herder waited for Dakar to stop the barrage of vexation.

Instead, Talvish was greeted with naked relief. "He's losing ground, quickly."

Eyebrows raised, fair hair gleaming under the glow of the ward light, Talvish peered downward at his prostrate prince. "Are you comatose, or just sleeping?"

However ragged, the faint smile from Arithon showed welcome.

The swordsman grinned back. "My wee man, it's tomorrow." Rejecting every fraught sign of depletion, he shot out a lean hand, snatched the nearest slack wrist, and hauled his unsteady liege to his feet. "Bear up. You've got enemies counting on you to maintain your half of the contest."

"Talvish," husked Arithon. "You rival the night-stalking weasel, my friend, for your hair-raising cures to clear drowsiness. I'd better pace. Less risk, I think, to fall on my face than lie down for your throat-nipping slaughter."

"Aye, very well. The cockerels upstairs were glad to be rid of me, too." Talvish adjusted his taller frame to assist his liege's uncertain balance.

One glance at the other's stripped face, and he added, "Did you know the cook's fashed because his best pots got swooped by *iyats* and chucked themselves overboard?"

"I thought things had gotten a little too quiet." Arithon paused for strained laughter. "I'll have a set cast, when we get back to shore. Ones endowed with the bell tones for fiend bane as part of the foundry's bargain."

The exchange touched Fionn Areth to mollified silence. He had known Talvish as jailor, for months. The man had always struck him as cold, each thought, word, and movement precise as though drilled to impervious perfection. As a killer, the creature knew his job too well. Yet here, that rigid perception broke down. Beyond all regard for stripped pride, Talvish laid his heart bare. No ice remained in those eyes, only grief. An observer could not miss the caring concern as this liegeman attended his prince.

The apparently casual touch; the irreverent reproof: all were enacted with tacit design to lift Arithon's flagging spirits.

"Well, I feel like the post propped up by the gate," the Master of Shadow replied to the latest prodding remark.

Talvish grinned. "If your joints moaned that much, we would grease them." Braced against the plunge of the brig, he held on as his weaving charge faltered. "Fits and staggers aside, you're not going to sit down."

They walked to keep Arithon wakeful. Tortuous slow-motion, wobbling circles, around and around the stacked casks. Talvish withstood the tireless course. If the mask sometimes slipped, and his smiles were forced, his agile hands kept their gentleness. At intervals, Dakar broke from his naps and made conversation to revive the bard's slipping focus.

Fionn Areth overheard disparate fragments, between his moments of blackout sleep.

"...centaur forges." A next scraping step, and Arithon's tentative question, "Did you know? About the awareness instilled by the Paravian craftsmen when they forged my Isaervian sword?"

"No." Dakar shifted his haunches, uneasy, or else tiredly reluctant.

A pause, while the lamp flame flared in the draft. Then Arithon said, "Why did Asandir never tell me she carried mystical properties not meant to be sullied with bloodshed?"

"I didn't know!" the Mad Prophet repeated. "Between us, you were the initiate master. No Sorcerer will offer advanced knowledge unasked. Even if that stricture had not been kept, were you ready to hear, Teir's'Ffalenn?"

The glimmering radiance from the dark blade bared Arithon's unshielded expression: guilt, and black fear, and the suffocating weight imposed by yet another charge of immeasureable responsibility. "In truth, no," he admitted. "Little has changed. I would still refute the entrapment of my crown ancestry."

The ship rolled. Talvish compensated. Abovedecks, Feylind's call to the quartermaster demanded another point on the wind.

Propped upright, brow knit, the Master of Shadow chased the difficult bent of his thought through his fogging exhaustion. "Kamridian must have been an extraordinary king to have had such a gift bestowed on him. If I had to guess, I would have supposed the potential instilled in this blade was never meant to be borne by a mortal."

"You can't know that, my friend," Dakar stated quietly. "Kamridian challenged Kewar's maze and met his destruction. In his footsteps, you have passed through and survived."

Arithon winced. "If my life was foretold by aught else but your prophecy, grant me the kindness. Don't say so." Yet the shifting prism of his altered awareness threw back the cut-crystal memory: of a centaur guardian's words in the maze, spoken in tender remonstrance. *'Fate's forger, you were Named. There lies your destiny, ripe for the hour when you finally embrace the full reach and strength of your power.'*

A slow hour passed. The next followed, arduous, as Arithon's stumbling progress became too harsh a demand to sustain. When the mate returned to give Talvish relief, the whistle for fiend bane was almost too faint to stand down the horde clumped against the lit circle.

"You should stay outside, Teive," Arithon grated. He crouched beside the mound of stacked casks, half-unmoored where his liegeman had left him. "I can't last much longer. Feylind ought to have you at her side if the time comes to launch off the boats."

The mate's silenced gesture released Talvish, who had paused in torn question halfway up the ladder. To Arithon, Teive listed crisp facts. "It's midday already. We're past a hundred leagues off the coast with a following wind, and a bank of high cirrus for warning. We've got heavy weather bearing in from the north. Try the boats, we'll be dead in a day, either from storm, or exposure."

Arithon lifted his head, green eyes tortured. "Then we've won by stalemate. The Prime Matriarch *has to know this.*"

Teive clamped his jaw, silent, while Dakar, from the casks, gave a negative shake of his head. Mage-sense informed him: the sigil embedded in *Evenstar's* sheathing still emitted its dissonant spellcraft. Hours had passed without any changes. The relentless flux of quartz-driven assault showed no sign of a wavering break.

Aware of the bane as a continuous ache, drilling each separate bone, the Master of Shadow shared the agonizing assessment. Alone, beaten white, he sustained the blunt weight of the mate's speechless accusation.

Unable to bear the inimical silence, Dakar reminded, "His Grace is oathsworn, since Athir. The Fellowship Sorcerers hold his bond in blood. He can't surrender. Not while he still has access to resource, and not for as long as he lives."

Spoken words, and the sting of a knife cut: by such small acts, a sealed thread of intent, that now spun whole cloth into tragedy.

Yet it was Arithon's whispered reply that seized the heartstrings and cruelly twisted. "Just keep me awake," he implored the mate. "By my witnessed permission, *freely use whatever method that takes.*"

"Then, at your word, we'll proceed as you wish." Teive shouldered the watch. The choice was not willing. The dangerous spark of his latent hostility set even Fionn Areth on edge.

For as Dakar had forecast, Arithon had worn himself down beyond gentle means to redress. Tranced calm could not restore his taxed resource. Beyond walking, past ability to track an intelligent conversation, he would drift when his shoulder was shaken. Cold water came next, until he started to shiver. Dakar called a halt, then kicked the emptied bucket away as the mate bent to scoop from the bilge.

"No, Teive, no more." Knelt in the puddle at Arithon's side, the Mad Prophet gentled the icy, racked flesh. "We can't. More such mistreatment will just drive him down." Extreme chill now would only hasten unconsciousness. "Help me bundle him into dry blankets."

The abusive measures they had to use next choked Fionn Areth to tears. Snapped back, time after time, from the sliding fall toward oblivion, Arithon set his teeth. He did not complain. Scarred by past horrors he would not repeat, he endured the crude methods, beyond dignity. Too spent to stifle his reflexive cries, he surfaced, again and again, until his body shuddered and shrank, and flinched at the touch of hands on him.

When the mate finally balked, the Master of Shadow gasped Feylind's name. For an interval more, that incentive forced shrinking nerves to sustain.

Then Dakar recoiled. Arithon railed at him through clenched teeth and reviled the weakness of pity. "I have survived Kewar. Can you imagine this feels any worse? Then let me correct your tender presumption. Against loss of this brig, and any life on her, your tormenting jabs are a pittance."

Yet his jagged appeal could not lift distress. Defeat lay at hand. A bard racked by such tremors could not hope to whistle the critical pitch for a fiend bane.

"You will *not* risk her life," Arithon insisted, his fury brought to a scraped whisper.

Propped by the barrels with his head on his knees, he had roused, barely in time. The ward flickered and dimmed, pale as spun smoke. The ravenous fiends sensed that instant of weakness. Closed in, voracious, they darted and circled, testing the integrity of the barrier.

Soaked in sweat, Arithon marshaled his fragmented will. He reforged the frayed thread of connection. By arduous increments, the sword's song leveled out, then burned to full strength, and continued. Dakar offered water. Arithon averted his face. His lips moved without sound, in refusal. The lamp touched his sweat-glazed features like varnish. His eyes were black wells, from the pain. Such extreme pallor might have been bloodless, except for the flushed patches where the nerves ran under the skin. The light taps to cause hurt had been done without marking him, a bitter mercy that served to prolong his wretched state of extremity.

And already, before the next breath, his lifted chin started to droop.

"As I love the captain, I wasn't made for this," Teive objected, wrung sick.

"I'll say not," whispered Arithon, rammed against the stacked casks. His hands rested limp on the boards where he curled, knees to chest in a trembling knot. "Feylind would choose a man with high heart, and not an ounce of viciousness in him. Give Dakar a turn. If he can't, call on Fionn Areth."

Yet the drastic hour had come. Further torment could not drive back the abyss or stave off the numbed surge of exhaustion.

As the damp, black head dipped, and finally nodded, Dakar arose. He scrounged a scrap of silk, wrapped his grip, and reached to take up the Paravian sword from its upright position in the soaked tarps.

"Mercy, no," Fionn Areth cried protest. "He's helpless! You can't draw his blood."

Reviled past words, the mate surged erect and restrained the Mad Prophet's wrist. "Enough. No more! Any longer will just break his mind."

"I know." Dakar swallowed. "Trust me this far, I can't continue this, either." As the mate's grasp stayed adamant, he worked his arm free. "I'm only going to do as Arithon asked, and lay the sword into his hand."

Touch masked by the silk, the spellbinder freed the jammed blade. Each juddering movement came scored in light. The steel spun its radiant mystery, unchecked. Starred rays pierced the darkness like opaline glass, and grace sang beyond hearing, alive with a purity that scoured the hidden depths of the heart. Dakar placed the pommel between Arithon's slack palms and rested the flat of the blade upright against his slumped shoulder.

Naught remained to be done.

Helpless, the three standing vigil confronted the uttermost face of defeat. The Mad Prophet knelt. He gathered Arithon's hands and closed slackened fingers over the sword's grip. As he offered the warmth of his presence to ease the slide into unconscious surrender, the mate fetched a blanket. He covered Arithon's contorted body out of unself-conscious respect.

"You are worth her love," he admitted, though the ear that received his tortured tribute had all but passed beyond hearing. "Ath grant you peace, I wish I had known that in all other ways, except this."

The lamp wavered. Fionn Areth seized on the coward's excuse to adjust the failing wick. He could not stop listening. Nor force back the wretched, salt burn of his tears, while Arithon dragged in a ratcheting breath, then another, and another one after that. As the soft, silvered glow of the sword flickered also, the Master of Shadow recoiled. He battled in desperate, painstaking stages, until the ward was snatched stable again.

"Don't fail me," he pleaded. "One minute more. Prime Selidie could give way and free us."

Yet reprieve did not happen. The terrible, wrenching shudders slowed down and subsided. Bruised eyelids fluttered and closed. Crushed under by tiredness, Arithon succumbed, spun down into oblivious sleep.

First the hazed glow from the sword flickered out. Then the faint, sustained thread of unearthly music faded under the threshold of hearing. The instant before silence let in the fiends, Dakar straightened.

"Douse the lamp!" he cracked, urgent.

Clumsy with cold, Fionn Areth was caught unprepared. He fumbled to unlatch the hot casing.

The mate surged to help. Spurred to panic, aware of the horrific calamity posed by a fire at sea, he tangled his foot in the blanket. His trip pitched him sprawling across Arithon's lap, just as the wave of starved fiends arrowed in. Their ravenous plunge sucked the flame to an ember as they absorbed light and heat for replenishment.

Dakar's cry for retreat arose over the tumult.

Then the last, static flux of the ward crumbled down, and more *iyats* swooped in like fell vengeance. The hostile pack punched in from all sides with the howling force of a hurricane.

The lamp toppled over. Flame and spilled oil soaked the rucked blankets. Dry cloth served as a wick. A whoosh of raised fire curtained the air. On a buffeting, hot breath, the conflagration seared and spread, lashed into an unnatural, crackling scourge by the horde of rampaging fiends.

Dakar's cursed exhortations drowned under raw noise, then a pealing yelp, as Fionn Areth jerked back, cut off by a burgeoning wall of inferno as he snatched to retrieve the dropped bucket.

"All hands!" yelled the mate, choked by roiling smoke. But the crisis had passed all containment. No frantic salvage by *Evenstar*'s crew could avert the cascade into ruin.

Except, at next second, the fire snapped out.

Darkness plunged down. Dense as thrown ink, shadow sliced like a blade through the carnage. Dakar sensed the slamming descent as a blow, as Arithon, wakened, engaged the birth gift of his mastery.

Night slapped through the raging wildfire like the dread stuff of chaos, unleashed. No mere barrier to quench light or heat, or subdue the maelstrom of roaring air, this conjury hammered with walloping force. Dakar felt his mage-sight go cold, clapped down, then snuffed as though strangled.

"Arithon!" he shouted. "Desist! The raw might of such power could kill us!"

The spellbinder had endured through hard bursts of elemental shadow before. He had stood on Kieling Tower, when Desh-thiere was imprisoned. Much later, he had suffered a hostile assault, when cursed insanity had claimed Arithon, at Riverton. This bout was different; utterly changed.

The darkness that howled through *Evenstar*'s hold held a virulent edge that was frightening.

The range of Arithon's core talent had strengthened. Exhaustion erased stays and limits. No man had witnessed the scope wielded now, a wave of jet ice that sheared through skin and viscera, and reduced the prime reflex of life. The blast did not pass, but set in like dropped lead, a blind scourge unleashed to annihilate.

"Arithon!" Dakar urged. "Let go!" A barrel hoop sprung, to a scream of stressed wood. "Ath save us, man! The freeze is going to burst all the casks!"

Out of the howling maw of let dark, over the ship's groaning timbers, Arithon's protest ground through like rasped glass. "The fiends. They've backed off? Has the fire gone out?"

And there, in stunned shock, the unlooked-for reprieve broke into awe-struck epiphany: Dakar realized the marauding whirlwind of *iyats* had vanished. Nothing stirred in the hold. Only the lap of the bilge, and the white rush of spray cleaved by no more than the power of sail and the surge of seagoing timbers.

"Dharkaron's Five Horses and Chariot!" The mate coughed inhaled grit from his sanded throat. "By glory, sorcerer! We're snatched from the brink. Have you any clue what you've done?"

The reply returned through the glassine black air came equally mangled by wonder. "Shadowed the fiend storm, apparently."

Steel chimed against wood. Frozen cloth crackled as Arithon stirred. The ice and the darkness relented, a fraction. With the lamp doused, and the sword's spells quiescent, the closed hold should have been lightless as pitch.

Yet everywhere, scattered across the shocked dark, pale flecks of marshlight were drifting.

They hung like small stars, a sequin glimmer in fine shades of blue, tinsel silver, and even a glimmering, delicate violet that strained the far boundary of vision.

Dakar lifted a trembling hand. He touched one. A prickling snap snicked his palm, not unlike a brisk discharge of static. In fact, he could rake the quiescent wisps up, like so many dry autumn leaves.

Eyesight adjusted to the pallid light: showed the mate on his knees, blistered hands pressed against his streaked face. Fionn Areth cradled seared knuckles. Next to the enamel gleam of the sword, a limp wrack of flesh lay curled in on itself beneath the bulked loom of the water casks.

Left stunned to awe that the brig had been salvaged, Dakar clambered over the ice-coated tarps. He plowed away oil-soaked blankets. Clumsy with chill and overstrained nerves, he rescued the Paravian sword and laid it aside, somehow without slicing his fingers. On his knees, choking back strong emotion, he laid his bruised hands upon Arithon's shoulders.

"How long?" croaked the mate from the darkness behind. "Your Grace, if the fiend storm is bound, will you be able to hold them?"

When the desperate query dangled, unanswered, Dakar shoved back his hysterical tears. "We are saved, and indefinitely. Arithon's gift is an inborn force, a direct access link to the elements. I've seen him sustain glamours wrought from shadow for days. At need, the act becomes reflex."

Erect now, a scarecrow swathed in singed clothes, the mate recovered his dignity. "Your liege is asleep?"

"I think so." At least, the breaths rose and fell in a regular pattern under the Mad Prophet's explorative touch. "We should make him more comfortable."

Yet that cursory assessment proved premature. A jarring tremor combed through Arithon's stilled frame. His fingers plucked at Dakar's sleeve cuff.

"Be still," soothed the spellbinder. "Mercy on you, be still. I'll divine what you want without speaking."

The instructions were scarcely a trial to fulfill. Arithon wished the Paravian sword left unsheathed and set near to hand. The drifting *iyats* were to be netted up, then contained and placed at his side.

"You'll have help." The mate crunched over debris toward the ladder, where his deck watch relayed swift orders.

Using silk, and the labor of three steady men, the tight, pinprick flakes of raw light were recaptured, and clapped into the cook's last available pot.

When the lidded vessel was laid at his feet, Arithon roused back to awareness. He sealed the trapped fiends inside with his gift. Then he adjusted his conjury and bound the brig from stempost to stern under an unnatural twilight.

Dakar rose to ascertain the strength of his handiwork. "Rest," he urged. "Your ward's stable and sound. No sprite should cross your spun shadow. The blanketing filter of force you've laid down ought to keep us in shielded protection."

At last, replete, the Master of Shadow accepted the pillow that Feylind tucked under his head.

Vhandon and Talvish arrived in hushed quiet. They stripped Arithon's soaked clothes, then strung up the hammock the sailhands sent down to ease him. Swathed in dry blankets, Rathain's prince had no choice but recuperate where he lay.

Topside, for the first time, the deck lanterns burned. Compass restored, *Evenstar* plied her warded course to the east. Until the sigil could be stripped from her hull, she could not sail undefended. A man at the hatch guarded Arithon's peace, with Fionn Areth set on his obdurate choice to remain in the hold through the aftermath.

"You'll do him no good here," Dakar said, unstrung by impatient exhaustion. "Let go. Leave him be."

The Araethurian stayed planted, even as Alestron's gruff liegeman prepared to drag him away. "Is the Master of Shadow injured, or sick?"

"May Daelion's Wheel turn quick for a fool!" Dakar snapped in exasperation. "He's stood down a frontal assault through a sigil, and reduced a storm of *iyats three hundred strong*. His Grace is blessed worn-out!" As reason failed, Dakar warned Vhandon off, and tossed up his hands in disgust. "What earthly use do you hope to serve, Fionn?"

A faint voice emerged from the shrouded form in the hammock. "He's burning to ask me a question."

Arithon Teir's'Ffalenn had opened his eyes, their febrile gleam far too bright in the flood of the lamp slung under the deck beam. He surveyed his recalcitrant double. "I cheated you out of your fair match, with swords. Therefore, by forfeit, you have the right. Ask."

Before anyone moved, or forced him to silence, Fionn Areth let fly. "Why did you let children die in your name when Etarra marched on Tal Quorin?"

The Mad Prophet sucked a shocked breath and blocked Talvish's incensed rejection. "Wait. Can't you see? As a crown prince, *he has to answer.*"

And the wearied words came. But not with the self-poisoned, tearing remorse that close friends had braced themselves to deflect.

"Because all I was then, every wise skill I knew, could not keep them safe and living." A taut moment passed. Then, since his answer did not seem profound, or satisfy his inquisitor, Arithon delivered his compassionate promise. "There are survivors. Stay, and I will provide you the chance to question them in your own right."

Early Winter 5671

Rift

On a mild spring night seventeen years ago, a brash, young captain at arms had pounded from Hanshire's gates at the head of a column of riders, his assignment to escort three Koriani Seniors on urgent business to Korias. His hand had been a white fist on the rein, and his face, flushed with fury from a savage fight with the Lord Mayor, his father.

Youth and hot rage had claimed their bitter toll. For the sake of political rank, and his safety, his light horsemen had delivered their Koriani charges, then followed his impulsive orders. Their elite skills had been offered to Riverton's town guard to spearhead an urgent search for the Master of Shadow.

The chase had led them through the bounds of a grimward, and not a fighting man had returned.

Since that day, the surviving prodigal son had viewed the tall towers of Hanshire just once, from the deck of a seagoing galley. His momentary stop on the wharf had spurned every overture toward a contrite reconciliation. His uncle Raiett had boarded the ship with the intent to cozen him home. Instead, the family's most powerful statesman found himself bedazzled in turn, swept into foreign service, and granted the post of the Light's High Chancellor at Etarra. The estranged heir kept his officer's post at Lysaer s'Ilessid's right hand; and Lord Mayor Garde was deprived at a stroke of the brother whose shrewd brilliance guided his council.

Now, under the stars of a fierce winter's freeze, the commander of the Alliance armed force reined his lathered horse from the covering scrub. Its lagging stride rang down the cobblestone thoroughfare that led to the torchlit main gate. He rode alone. At the vigorous height of maturity, under challenge by dangers beyond precedent, Sulfin Evend returned: to face his aged parents and the final destruction of his family's expectations. To a reunion that must scour the scars of old pain, he bore the knife-cut sting of an oath sworn in blood to a Fellowship Sorcerer: a vow of life service that no mortal power under Athera's wide sky might revoke.

Sulfin Evend shoved back his rough hood. A useless ploy, now, to keep his face hidden. Even mounted on a nondescript post-horse, and wearing no sunwheel blazon, his covert approach from the northern wilds was bound to be marked in advance. The Koriani scryer employed by Hanshire's council watched over the town's interests like a vigilant hawk.

The Sorcerer's parting words had not promised immunity from the family's store of pent rage. Nor might a steadfast resolve to fight necromancy forgive the unresolved impact of past scores. '*Sethvir has given his sage reassurance. You will reach Hanshire on the hour when you are most sorely needed. Once there, your oath to the land must come first.* Caith'd'ein, *you are bound before ties of heritage. You stand outside of sovereign allegiances. By choice, you must tread the razor's edge. Lose your focus, or waver one step, and you will reap the hideous consequence.*'

Sulfin Evend drew rein before the stone gate keeps that flanked the land entry to Hanshire. Deep shadow layered its cut arch of black basalt, shadowed under the streaming torches that illuminated the gaudy panoply of draped banners. Yet no sunwheel standard hung from the wall. Dazzled after hours of star-studded darkness, Sulfin Evend resisted the need to wheel his mount and retreat. At his back, the harrowing cross-country ride through the wilds, plagued by Second Age haunts and the unquiet sorrows left imprinted by bloodshed; before him, a living trial by fire: never in his bleakest hour of doubt had he thought to reach journey's end and not find the Alliance army encamped at full strength by the gate.

Yet no tents were in evidence; no pavilions. No party of loyal officers awaited to give updated reports or provide him with the impervious shield of Avenor's state backing. Alone in soiled clothes, Sulfin Evend dismounted. If the guard at the sallyport did not know his face, he was going to suffer no end of snide ridicule.

Yet challenge did not arise from the sentries. The main gate was unbarred by a captain in formal parade arms. He strode forth, no less than the officer who had once commanded the misfortunate company lost in Korias. Two mounted lancers rode at his heels, trailed by a liveried groom who led a fresh horse, saddled with a cloth bearing Lord Mayor Garde's gold ribbons and family blazon.

Chin up, eyes like ice, Sulfin Evend voiced no greeting. He foisted the reins of his hack on the groom, then held out his gloved hand for the remount.

"You have the nerve in you!" The guard captain spat with revilement. "Seventeen years! Thirty-nine dead who were my finest, and now you. Alive, thrice-entitled, and still with no word!"

Sulfin Evend knew how to mask gouging grief; one learned, under Lysaer s'Ilessid. He mounted the horse. Under the merciless flood of the torches, he stared downward until his accuser flushed red.

More worn, looking suddenly old in his gleaming appointments, the captain struggled not to be first to break under his own round of punishment.

His discomfort bought pain, before triumph. "You sent your finest," Sulfin Evend allowed, finally. "They faced horrors your troops here could never imagine. Nor can you measure the cost I have paid to be crossing this gate, still alive." He wheeled the horse. As the waiting escort scrambled to respond, he spurned them without a glance back. "I know the way to my father's palace."

The captain cracked. "Damn you to Sithaer! You *ungrateful* craven!" Hard-clenched to stay his hand from his sword, he signaled his bewildered outriders. "Orders. See him through!"

"Sir." The men spurred ahead, angry. Their charge did not rein in, which forced the spokesman to shout like a yokel to make himself heard. "Lord Mayor Garde is in council. He demands your presence for audience straightaway!"

Hanshire's hall of state lay between the town's central guard keeps, overlooking the steep fall of the bluffs. The stone terrace, with its slate-capped battlements, still bore the weathered triaxial knots carved by the ancient Paravians. In Third Age Year Ten, rule had been passed to a clan family appointed by Tysan's High King, Halduin s'Ilessid. Times changed, since the mists. The ancestral descendants now skulked as drifters on the wind-raked downlands, tolerated for the bloodstock they raised and sold at the West End fair every autumn.

Blood-tainted by an outbred clan lineage he rigidly wished to disown, the current Lord Mayor enforced the ascendancy of town law with an iron fist. The Divine Prince of the Light was his ally in name, but no friend; not with Avenor's crown might tied to interests aligned for a unified conquest.

Coldly received for his title alone, the Alliance Lord Commander left his mount with the sentries who guarded the arch. He strode ahead, still unspeaking. His step echoed off slate flagstones and battle-scarred revetments, glistening with the odd patch of slag left seared by the balefires of dragons. Where the veteran captain who trained him had aged, centuries-old stonework endured without change.

Seventeen years could have passed in a day. Sweating despite winter's chill on the air, Sulfin Evend disregarded the expectancy that would have rushed him through the hall doors. He took pause instead and gazed over the battlements.

From that eyrie vantage, the lower town spread in a jumble of roofs, rammed tight to the flank of the coast. The damp wore the taint of wet thatch, peat smoke, and kelp from the apothecary's shacks. Below, the cove harbor lapped the darkened headland, fringed by torchlight where the waterfront wharves met the teeming balconies of the brothels.

The distant lamps of the anchored ships rode like spangles across silken water, except one: ablaze in state trappings, the vessel that flew Lysaer's sunwheel banners stood out like a beacon.

Sulfin Evend could have shouted aloud with relief.

"My Lord Commander, if you would?" The liveried lackey sent out to collect him bowed with unsettled urgency. "Lord Mayor Garde and the council are already seated in session."

"You may send word ahead." Since a state delegation could not wait on raw nerves, Sulfin Evend turned back and entered the doubled doors. As the lackey's rushed footsteps cast their whispered echoes ahead, the absentee son revisited his privileged origins: a melange of patchouli, citrus polish, and ink, and smart servants receiving his mantle and gloves. The one who brushed down his plain, mud-stained leathers met his duty with lofty disdain.

Only the white-headed fellow who knelt to wipe his grimed spurs slapped his calf with familiar affection. "Young master, you are returned none too soon. Off you go. Your people expect you."

"Freyard," murmured Sulfin Evend, surprised. He had not expected a welcome.

The old lackey grinned, ancient now, missing teeth. "Your gear looks to be overdue for a polish. I'll do that myself. Here's your escort."

The steward's officious reserve suggested that no travel-worn swordsman should receive state admittance, far less any officer bearing authority bestowed by crown rank at Avenor.

Piqued by a flare of perverse enjoyment, Sulfin Evend strode on, while the council hall doors of Vhalzein lacquer were whisked open with dispatch before him.

Beyond, the vaulted chamber lay deserted. The vast silence from the galleries was crushing. The dais of carven, serpentine jade left by the ancient Paravians gleamed under the crystal chandeliers. In place of Mayor Garde and his rapacious advisors, Sulfin Evend confronted no worse than a grandiose row of tasseled covers on the state chairs.

"They're gathered in the privy chamber," the steward said, tart. "This way, if you please."

Sulfin Evend sidestepped the mores of officious ceremony. "I'll go on my own, without fanfare." Pushed past, he cut through the warren of clerks' desks and ducked through the alcove door.

Inside, the air was a stifling blanket, overburdened with perfume and fraught tension. The floor seats were crammed full, and the high dais as well, installed with the full complement of Hanshire's advisory council and graybeard heads of state.

First sweep, Sulfin Evend surveyed his estranged father: the meaty strength of the face now sagged with pinched discontent. Grizzled as a bony, aged wolf, Lord

Mayor Garde leaned back in stiff clothes, in command with laced hands and crossed ankles. Behind his chair stood four Koriathain wearing floor-length purple robes. All wore the red-banded sleeves of ranked seniors. One showed five stripes, an authoritative presence that plucked Sulfin Evend to resharpened wariness.

At right hand, also standing, the weathered Champion of the Guard wore his ceremonial breastplate; seated left, the hawkish High Minister of Trade lounged in boredom and crusted jewelery. Beside him, the corpulent town justiciar was speaking with stinging disparagement. "You can't imagine you'll accomplish that feat without forging a Koriani alliance!"

The voice that replied wore frost like white diamond. "I will do all I say, with or without any ties to the order's practice of obligation."

Lysaer, past the jammed ranks of the dignitaries, the gold-etched figure was on his feet, reduced to the station of common petitioner in front of the mayor's dais. That shaming slight smashed the last pretense of protocol, and prompted Sulfin Evend to intervene.

"Just what bargain would the Prime Matriarch demand? Access to the gifts that lie latent in Dari s'Ahelas's old lineage, perhaps?"

Met by the sharp turn of Lysaer's head, Sulfin Evend shoved toward the front of the chamber.

"Oh, yes," he assured, as he pressed his way through, disarranging rare furs and trimmed velvets. He made no apology for his disgruntled wake. His concern only measured the whipped start of surprise from the Blessed Prince who, at Erdane, would have discovered *just what* such a line of descent might entail. Sulfin Evend locked eyes with his liege. Then, barefaced before his disowned family, he savaged the tissue of long-standing scars. "Koriathain do occasionally breed children. In the cloistered, dim corners of their sisterhouses where outsiders aren't invited to look."

Mayor Garde's incensed shout burst decorum. "That's enough! Are you mad? Your impertinent remarks serve no purpose but mayhem!"

"Truth!" cracked Sulfin Evend, arrived front and center before the candlelit dais. "I notice your fifth-rank senior dares to say nothing at all."

Purple silk rustled through the cooler voice of denouncement. "What should be said of a son who forsakes his family obligation? Your return, you'll insist, was arranged for a loyalty you claim to have made in free choice." The enchantress bearing the red bands of accolade gave a small shrug, then attacked. "By all means, let's hear honesty. Have the man you name master ask what you were doing in conference with Sorcerers at Althain Tower."

The jerked flash of gold exposed Lysaer's swift breath. Though the blue eyes remained steady, their depths had now darkened with clouding distrust. "Were you in fact?"

Sulfin Evend stared back, level. So soon, his fresh oath must be put to the test: a trial exposed before bitterest censure. He withstood his father's towering

---
JANNY WURTS

rage, and, more cutting, his coquettish mother, whose agonized frailty stripped his skin like sandpaper and glass; then the Koriani Seniors, smug and still in their silence. Most of the packed ministers present recalled his rebellious childhood. Worst of all these was his prince, recovered and wearing the terrible mantle of his inborn self-command.

"I will answer your Blessed Grace, and in full. But the matter ought to be private." Though his life might ride on the issue laid bare, Sulfin Evend placed duty foremost. "I am ever your man, sworn to serve the Alliance. For the sisterhood's proposed offer of service to you, I ask leave to know: what is the order demanding?"

"Partnership," said Lysaer, "in exchange for defenses. They want the Spinner of Darkness cut down, and I need a trained shield against practicing necromancers. Too much has gone sour at Avenor, out of sight behind someone's closed doors. I won't have secrets." Brows raised in inquiry, not overtly distressed, he added, "I presume you went to the Fellowship to dispose of an unclean sacrificial knife?"

Gifted that firm affirmation of trust, Sulfin Evend returned the hint of a smile. "The appeal was met, and without laying claim to your Blessed Grace's autonomy. If I might presume? Then rest assured, I've already brought back your protection."

The Koriani Senior hissed through her teeth. "A clever half-truth! My lord Prince, listen now and avoid a betrayal! Your commander at arms is no longer yours. His loyalty is compromised, and now he plays an insidious game of deception. Ask why he wears a fresh cut on his wrist. Protection, he claims! What bargain was struck? What binding was sealed by his own let blood, in formal oath to a Fellowship Sorcerer?"

"Forgive me," whispered Sulfin Evend, flushed before the sharp startlement that hardened Lysaer's straight regard. "This is no equable hearing, Blessed Grace, but a fight over spoils involved in a feud that divided me from my family long years ago. By your leave, I ask to defend myself."

Lysaer s'Ilessid inclined his head. Fairness commanded him. His deliverance at Erdane demanded that much, whether or not there was privacy.

Sulfin Evend confronted his grim row of accusers: a father, whose hardset expression suggested no tactic was too cruel to compel a son's shirked obligation. His mother, a poised doll in her high-wire headdress, whose tight-laced hands masked a rapidly breaking composure. Lastly, by far the most ruthless of all, the unified row of Koriani enchantresses, whose grasping subterfuge had no limit. No cost was too high, and no ploy too low, in their bid to depose the constraint of the Fellowship Sorcerers.

Committed beyond risk for his personal integrity, Sulfin Evend shattered the last, fragile hope he might reconcile with his past and come home. "The oath I accepted binds no one but me. Its terms were not made in demand by

250

the Fellowship, but fulfilled as a promise to a blind seeress whose help I required in Erdane. My service is given beyond power to revoke, to this land and the weal of its people. As Regent of Tysan, and Divine Prince, Lysaer's interests are one and the same. Therefore, I stand steadfast at his right hand. Compromise him at your peril."

From Lysaer, no word; from his father, checked fury; from his mother, a flood of silenced tears for a grief grown too harsh to bear. For that, Sulfin Evend swore he would have blood, provided the vicious reckoning ahead did not come to destroy him.

For the deadliest enemy would not back down. The fifth-rank enchantress stepped forward, incensed. An upstart male had obstructed her order's interests, and she would spare nothing to see him cut down.

"Your s'Ilessid has compromised himself well and fully without any move on the part of our sisterhood. Since your sword can't defend against vile assault by the cabal that's choking Avenor, what have you sold in exchange for a covert Fellowship backing?"

"There is no such backing," Sulfin Evend insisted. "I asked for a Sorcerer's stay of protection *for myself alone*. That risk, I bore for the sake of necessity, in line with my duty as liegeman. The Light of his Grace is in no way affected."

"Then stand back, little man." Beyond scornful, the rankled senior's dismissal gouged for a deeper reckoning. "Leave your birth obligation and Hanshire's interests forsworn! You may have balked the will of your father, but not ours. Your Blessed Prince must seal his own fate. Leave his safety to us. Or dare you lead him naked into Avenor, a blindfold lamb to the slaughter?"

"How you ladies hate to admit that Athera holds living powers other than yours." Sulfin Evend reached into his jerkin and removed the deerskin-wrapped knife from its thong. "Here is Lysaer's protection. My charge to stand watch and guard for his safety comes to him without any strings."

A stir whispered through the packed seats at his back. The council would not recognize a Biedar knife; nor did his father, whose beet fists and clamped jaw still displayed overt irritation. But the Koriani witches must acknowledge defeat. Their fifth-rank senior could probably name the seeress whose wise counsel had arranged for Lysaer's deliverance.

"I have no more to say, here!" Sulfin Evend pronounced. "My loyalty and my close affairs are not yours to question at whim. The birth ties I once owed to Hanshire were stripped on the hour I gave my blood oath to the realm. I rest my case. The matter of my integrity must lie between me and the prince who carries my grant of feal service."

Caithdeinen offered their lives to test princes. Sulfin Evend withstood the rank pressure of fear. He did not give way to his mother's heartbreak, or apologize for his father's overpowering rage. His case must stand or fall in the end on the strength of s'Ilessid justice: a virtue warped by the Mistwraith's curse, that could foul the most stringent perception.

Lysaer said nothing. The quiet spun out. Sulfin Evend endured through the hard-breathing rustle of finery from the rows of town officers ranked at his back. As ruthlessly public, his mother's bowed head received no grace of reprieve amid cracking tension. The Koriathain maintained their adamant discipline. They would justify him with no saving word, that the flint knife was a genuine talisman. All ears strained to hear how the Blessed Prince would choose to call his ruler's power of judgment.

Sulfin Evend *would not* turn his head in appeal. He knew, *too well*, the fierce majesty that cloaked Lysaer's form through those times when the law called for a harsh consequence. From brushed gold hair, to dazzling jewels, to the fall of immaculate clothing, his Grace was the blinding epitome of authority and attentive poise. Beside that dizzying, unearthly charisma, the traveler rough from his overland journey could not seem other than discredited: an unshaven ruffian in his muddied leathers, with a primitive knife offered up by a beggar's hand.

As the silence extended, he swayed on his feet. He had ridden without a snatched moment for rest; twenty-five leagues through the haunted wilds, on post-horses bartered from drifters. The great oath just sworn at Althain Tower had reforged the core of his being, perhaps to die here as a branded traitor, under the eyes of his heirless parents.

Pride ruled him, at last. He had not broken loyalty. Sulfin Evend sustained accusation, the flint blade his naked, last testament.

Cloth stirred at length, then a whispered breath, drawn against the glass-etched stillness. "They wanted your child?" Lysaer asked, too quiet.

Sulfin Evend swallowed. "In exchange for arcane service to my family. Yes."

The blunt question followed. "By your Lord Mayor's knowledge, the Koriani Order has placed demands such as this one before?"

Stiff under the weight of his father's shame, Sulfin Evend spoke out. "The sealed bargain with Hanshire's ruling council is renewed with each generation. Before the obligation demanded of me, the sisterhood has asked no more than buildings, or land, or sometimes a tithing of labor. The obligation began in the years of the uprising, when our mayors asked service, and provided a safe haven for enchantresses who were in flight, or left homeless at large on the countryside."

Diamonds flared like white ice; the Blessed Prince had stepped forward. "Liegeman, your life is bound under regency law. Give me the knife."

Sulfin Evend did not recoil from the touch as the weapon left his willing hand. Sworn man to master, he held still for the sentence: exoneration or execution of a summary justice. One thrust might finish his life in a second. Sulfin Evend clamped down on his shuddering nerves. Somehow, he kept himself standing.

From his side came the verdict, glacial in delivery. "I will take my protection from those I can trust. Not from factions who think to play me for a game piece. Once, on Corith, I gave the Koriani Order my warning. I will not have my Alliance suborned! *The needs of my people are not put to usage for gain.* Ladies, consider this audience closed! Meddle outside your soft nest here at Hanshire, force any man for his seed in duress, and I promise, such dealing will see you arraigned! I will tear down your sisterhouses, stone from stone, and put your ranked seniors to fire and sword for criminal oppression and acts of dark practice!"

Stunned himself by the resounding force of that closure, Sulfin Evend startled to the incongruous, warm touch as his prince placed a steadying hand on his shoulder. "Come away, Lord Commander. You'll retire to my galley. There, be assured, you'll receive your due rest and the courteous welcome that this town of Hanshire and your own blood kin have denied you."

Early Winter 5671

Reversal

Two days after their Matriarch's failed effort to capture the Prince of Rathain, Forthmark hospice's high-ranking senior enchantresses remained exhausted and beaten limp. Stiff with the bone-deep ache of defeat, the Prime Circle lately called back into session kept to the comfort of their cushioned chairs. They might yearn for the sleep today's duty denied them. Yet the tradition surrounding a novice's oath taking required their presence as witness.

Before their worn faces and critical eyes, Lirenda did not share the suffocating panoply of their formal red-banded robes, or a weighty mantle of purple and silver. Demoted to the gray shift of low service, she shouldered the brute work of screening the young girls gathered for their induction into the sisterhood. Five had been presented for today's review.

The paltry number displeased the Prime. Enthroned on her couch, flushed under draped silk and the jewel-strung net confining her jonquil hair, Selidie confronted the last of the untested candidates with slitted, lynx eyes. Her blame for the shortfall wore an enemy's name: Arithon Teir's'Ffalenn had instilled the changes that reshaped the surrounding territory. The Vastmark tribes that once had backed him in war were no longer severely impoverished. Ships now moved the wool trade, disbanding the network of brokers. In the hard years, when misfortune and shale slides reduced the flocks, shepherd parents no longer sent daughters to Forthmark to spare them from wasting starvation.

Today's applicants ranged in age from four years to ten, lined up in a shivering row in the hospice atrium. Streaming light from the windows struck their brushed hair and scrubbed skin, and hazed the coarse nap on their clothing. They stared at their feet, or fidgeted, faces pale with a justifiable nervousness.

Amid silence that tagged the least movement with echoes, a creeping chill pressed the air: the Great Waystone itself lay unveiled to record their novice's oath. Since the induction process could not be rushed, the jewel's raised focus would not be released for some while yet to come. Through the lengthy pauses, the day's petitioners to the Prime came and went, their low talk a droning backdrop.

Lirenda endured the unbearable tedium. Attached to wealth, and fine clothes, and the cosseting of high position, she detested the depth of the probes required to determine each candidate's fitness. The intimate sounding of a girl's inner faculties felt like the pinch of tight shoes, replete with the mental suffocation left from their disadvantaged backgrounds and former experience.

The two cherubs gone first had been guttersnipe orphans, charity cases taken in from the dockside stews of the southcoast. Their minds had been dim, cluttered with memories of hunger and sores, and summer rains spent huddled under piles of fish-rancid packing crates. Neither child showed a glimmer of curious thought. Life's hardships had already crushed them. Oppressive fears wounded their brilliance of spirit; malnourishment stunted their hope.

Lirenda told over the timeworn, sad patterns. Here again, the imaginative sensitivity that forepromised arcane potential had been ground too far down to break out of stoic resistance.

Now finished with the third child in line, the disgruntled enchantress aroused from her disciplined trance. She wrapped the paired quartz spheres that held the child's imprint and passed the bundle across to the waiting peeress. Then, slaved under the Prime's directive, she declared the candidate's fitness. "A gray robe, and no schooling for rank. Her destiny lies with the hostels."

The girl curtseyed, trembling, as the peeress's touch guided her on to Prime Selidie's chair. At eight years of age, she knelt to swear oath: to grow up and shoulder the menial tasks of laundry, or cooking and childcare, or to fill some minor niche of secretarial work. If she developed gentle hands and a kind nature, she might progress to assume convalescent care of the infirm.

"Next, please step forward," Lirenda intoned.

The skinny, older candidate presented herself. Her hair hung dull brown, and her chilblained hands were a crafts child's. She could have been expelled from apprenticeship for laziness; or her parents might have offered her up in exchange, to fulfill a past oath of debt. The rare applicant, these days, would be a volunteer, encouraged to serve by her family.

Moved to yawning distaste, Lirenda selected two more quartz spheres cleared to a state of blank dormancy. Careful to keep her touch shielded in cloth, she said, "Give me your hands, child."

The paired crystals were placed into the offered, chapped palms. "Hold these, place your thumbs on their surface, and wait. When I ask, give them back over to me."

Those basic instructions might last for minutes, or extend as long as an hour if a child's grasp lacked the vigor to imprint the stone's matrix. Throughout, Lirenda endured her cramped perch, forced to wait in subservient boredom. To her right, the frightened girl child now taking oath knelt and laid her palms against the faceted Great Waystone. Standing opposite, the house peeress gloved her hands in white silk, then touched the imprinted spheres to each side of the unshielded amethyst.

Then, prompted carefully, the lisping orphan recited her lines. *"I, Nayla, declare myself free to bind oath to the Koriani Order. From this breath, this moment, and this word, until death, I exist to serve, this I vow. My hands, my mind, and my body, are hereby given to enact the will of the Prime Matriarch, whose whole cause is the greater good of humanity, this I vow. All states of fleshly desire to renounce, this I vow. All ties of heart, of family, of husband and lover to put aside, this I vow..."*

The raw power of words, spoken over by thousands across a history that bridged generations, unleashed the energy of a living force. The ancient crystal remembered: each named initiate, and each former prime, extending back to the dawn of the order, before cataclysmic war had sent a destitute enclave of mankind to beg for settlement on Athera. The amethyst focus that had recorded the order's past origins retained each initiate sister's embedded imprint. The young, open heart and the vulnerable mind could not be less than swept away by the torrent.

Lirenda recalled that branding, first thrill. The answer to every stark longing had seemed within reach on the moment when she sealed her oath. Declared as a candidate for the prime succession, she had never foreseen the shaming failure that would cast her down and deny her the ultimate glory of accession to supreme rank.

Nor would today's girl child glance aside from her rapture. Enveloped in bliss, she would not yet comprehend the binding scope of her promise, or fully grasp that a single, willed word from the Matriarch could deprive her of life, or limb, or intelligence.

The formal investiture wound onward toward closure: *"...And should I weaken or falter and come to forswear my commitment, all that I am shall be forfeit, body and mind. This I vow, no witness beyond the Prime Circle, no arbiter beyond the crystal matrix into which I surrender my Name and my imprint as surety through all my living days."*

As sworn novice, the young girl arose and received the Prime's kiss on both her flushed cheeks. Her smile shone radiant, as Selidie intoned the timeworn phrases of closure. "Nayla, may you serve peace and charity with dedicate grace. Wear the order's mantle with pride."

The hospice peeress released the imprinted spheres into a basin of salt water for clearing, then bestowed a white ribbon, to be sewn on the sleeves of the gray robe today's young initiate would wear until death. The child bent her knee in a dutiful curtsey and received her due leave to depart.

Lirenda looked on, wrung to ferocious envy for that talentless chit's simple freedom. She suffered the prolonged wait, while the next, rawboned candidate completed her crystal imprinting. Once the energies in the paired spheres became gravid, Lirenda gathered them back in hand. The girl candidate watched, anxious, as the adult who would determine her future closed the stones in her grasp and engaged trance, then fused her awareness with the replicate pattern imbued within the reactive matrixes that now mapped the flow of polarity between the candidate's rightside and leftside balance.

For Lirenda, as always, the moment of full immersion felt as invasively horrid as drowning...

...vision turned dim. As her senses became felted under a muddle of random thought and jagged, disordered emotion, she thrashed to escape the suffocating contraction as her state of trained clarity compressed downward into tight space and muffling darkness. Imprisoned, Lirenda felt her private self strip away, until her eighth-rank awareness squeezed into a mold that was abhorrently other: she knew abuse and cold; the memory of filthy hands, scratching fleas, and smells that revolted the senses. Sunk into a morass of self-pity and need, she lost even the hardened spark of her rage. Defeat became helplessness that numbed, then putrefied, leaving knots dense and solid as brick. Beliefs became walls. Despair framed a cage. Under the murk, just barely smoldering, she encountered one stubborn ember that survived the strangling defeat of adversity. She touched on that point. All but deaf and blinded, she blew the breath of expanded knowledge against that pinched glimmer of hope.

True talent responded. The small spark became flame. Into that flickering promise of light, reflected in faithful, quartz imprint, Lirenda applied the meticulous discipline of her developed awareness. From raw potential, she mapped the latent channels that opened, then traced where they might be coaxed to expand.

Yet the narrow vessel reached its capacity too soon. The influx of forces jammed still and backed up. Lirenda suffered the wretched constriction, forced to remain in rapport until she had assayed every sigil of testing, one exhaustive level at a time...

In due course, Lirenda recovered herself. The unfettered range of her power resurged like circulation restored through a cramped limb. Breathless and damp, she pronounced the result.

"She is for the sisterhouse." Shown the peeress's smiling pride, Lirenda added the rest. "A first-rank talent, confirmed, with potential for third, if she masters her fear and responds to the training to release her conditioned resentment."

Yet the candidate was not ushered away to declare her obedience over the Waystone. The morning's proceedings had been interrupted when the seeress who minded the lane watch arrived, bearing an urgent report.

Her hushed phrases threw a scatter of echoes through the vaulted stone chamber, "...inbound message from the fifth-ranked, stationed at

Hanshire…Morriel's past hope is ended…now lost our option to secure a possible candidate for prime succession off the branch line of s'Gannley. We are desolate, Matriarch. The effort has failed, in no small part due to a new interference engaged by the Fellowship Sorcerers."

The setback exposed an ongoing sore point: that no talent with ninth-rank potential now trained under oath to the Koriani Order. That shortfall had posed a critical problem for the last prime, caught facing the dissolution of extreme old age. Morriel's straits had been desperate enough to risk forcing the birth of an infant candidate, conceived through an oath of debt. The strategy had been set to cover the deficit, should Lirenda's initiate passage to ninth rank fail: a critical safeguard, made meaningless after the usurpation of Selidie's life span. Young again, Morriel had snatched the victory from death and bought herself a twisted reprieve.

Since her heinous crime had gone undetected, the eldest senior delivered her placid opinion. "The random induction of orphans eventually should provide us with the requisite gifted talent. Let the wretched idea of planned breeding be dropped. The risks outweigh the benefits. That branch lineage derives from a *caithdein*'s legacy, and would tend toward offspring with headstrong will and ungovernable independence."

Lirenda wrapped and passed off the imprinted quartz, desperately straining to track the course of the ongoing debate. Last chance of reprieve, she raged against ebbing hope, that the proven asset of her eighth-rank talent might see her released from her insupportable punishment.

Selidie leaned back in her carved ivory chair, bored composure suggesting the setback at Hanshire posed no more than a trivial inconvenience. "Wait or not, we have set a better alternative in motion already." She gestured her bandaged hand to cut off the tiresome discussion. "As prize, or as forfeit, we shall shortly know if the inducement set forth is sufficient. Given development, I fully expect that our sisterhood's shortfall will be most handsomely met."

Chafed frantic, Lirenda burned to hear more. But the seeress was dismissed to resume her post. Scheduled business would continue: the screened candidate awaited her oath of investiture, and the last child in line had yet to undergo testing.

Yet the snap of Selidie's spoken command halted the ceremony forthwith. "All are excused! I require Lirenda. The oath and the last screening shall wait."

The will of the Prime was held above question. The Senior Circle arose, gave obeisance, and filed out, while the sisterhouse peeress hustled to gather her bewildered charges. "Here, child!" she whispered. "My dear, ask me later." Her admonishment silenced the girl's disappointment. "Our simple task is to obey."

Once the chamber had cleared, Lirenda was summoned, her powers to be used as the vessel to extend the Prime's eyes and ears. The demand would be arduous, no sharp surprise. By the terms of imposed sentence, Selidie could expend her schooled talent like riches poured out of a jar. "You will engage in trance while I align the Great Waystone to cast a scrying over salt water."

Lirenda knelt as bidden. Puppet to the Prime's least command, she laid her hands on the stinging chill of the amethyst. Contact wrapped her senses in harrowing cold, a brief agony. The Prime's master sigil reached through with clamping force and claimed her receptive contact. Insatiably demanding, it grappled her being and jerked forth a quickened thread. The unraveling plunge dropped her through spinning darkness. Her being became a spun line that hurled through a portal of purple fire. Now nameless and faceless, poised over what felt like the eye of the world, Lirenda received the Prime Matriarch's directive: '*Find Arithon Teir's'Ffalenn. Watch and listen for as long as it takes! I would have the name of the place where he plans to make his next landfall.'*

A command sigil blazed red as a signpost. Aimed arrow of purpose, the bound spirit dropped through the gateway framed at its heart. Now tempered as a tool, her consciousness broke through and emerged into the scald of bright sunshine, and ocean-fresh air, spiked with the pitch tang of oakum…

"…how aware are they?" Dakar the Mad Prophet was saying. Seated cross-legged on the warmed planks of a ship's deck, he resembled a dollop of suet rolled up in a knot of old rags.

"I don't actually know," mused the Prince of Rathain, poised intent by the pinrail above him.

Something banged in the hollow space belowdecks.

Arithon paused. Equally rumpled in torn breeches and soiled shirt, he raised dark eyebrows at the shouts that erupted from the depths of the *Evenstar*'s hold. To judge by the cursing, her sailhands encountered some fouling nuisance involving pinched fingers and ballast rocks. Though the brig where he lounged was left becalmed in the aftermath of a seasonal storm, the cant of the timbers beneath his braced feet bore a distinct list to starboard.

Planking shuddered to another booming report of a large stone being shifted to port.

Dakar winced with his eyes shut. "If the crew keeps on fumbling boulders like that, we'll spring all the dastardly seams in this tub long before the keel's sitting level."

Arithon grinned. "You happen to be sitting on Cattrick's best work. If he ever hears of your slanging remark, you'll become dropped meat underneath his bludgeoning fist."

"We have to reach shore, first." Dakar's jaundiced attention shifted and measured the vital figure above him. "Who needs Cattrick's rough temper? *That* look on *your* face spells trouble, right here."

Impervious to rancor, Arithon pursued the lapsed thread of his earlier reasoning. "Fiends don't appear to originate thought."

Dakar's horrified flinch also failed to swerve him off topic.

"...or emotion. At least, when I ply them with musical tones, they don't respond, except by reflection. They experience by imprint, without innovation. Complex patterns will draw them with insatiable greed. That's probably why they fixate upon our intense feelings and delight in our rage and frustration. The innate creativity of conscious awareness lies outside their range of experience."

"They are drake spawn." Dakar's emphatic shrug dismissed a conundrum far better dropped *now*, without further tinkering speculation.

"Fragments of awareness," Arithon plowed on. His gaze surveyed the sail crew at work on the masthead, then the drifting, puffed clouds overhead; ignored outright, the Mad Prophet's furious, mouthed cue to *be still at once* and stop speaking.

Dakar signaled again, his chopped gesture disregarded: as ever, such galling perversity seemed ingrained in the fabric of Arithon's character.

"...beings conceived from an experimental idea that was never balanced into completion." Through yet another shuddering crash, and Feylind's yell of admonishment, the Master of Shadow reconsidered the shapeless sack by his feet. His mood of suspect mildness remained throughout his bout of oblivious monologue. "Davien's notes were explicit. He explained *iyats* as raw energy granted the willful drive to exist. They sustain as parasites, feeding off borrowed charge, but lacking the self-aware memory of an entity able to grow and evolve. That explains how a sigil was fashioned to hold them. And yet, I imagine coercion through force may have been a bullying waste."

Dakar stared, aghast. "No," he blurted. "You couldn't. Dharkaron's Spear drop you for taking mad risks, *you can't try such a damnfool ploy, now!*"

"*Iyats* crave complex patterns," Arithon repeated. Eyes level, hard as the glint off chipped emerald, he finished his razor-edged point. "They might, therefore, respond, led on out of straight fascination."

"Arithon! Be quiet!" Harried past subtlety, Dakar ripped at his beard. "The Koriathain are onto your game board, again. Their forsaken sigil's turned active."

"Some minutes ago, yes. The dissonance stings. But I have no intent, now or at any time, to grant their meddling wiles even one step off my chosen course." The Master of Shadow turned his head aft. "Feylind! The men aloft, have they restrung the topsail halyard?"

"Almost," the captain's reply floated forward. "The cracked sheave's repaired. The boy's catching his breath before shinnying back up to the masthead."

Arithon's manic interest flashed into a grin. "Let's whip up a little experiment, shall we? Could Teive perhaps pass me a suitable line? Then call the hands down from the crow's nest."

Dakar loosed a martyred breath through his teeth, then clambered aside to make way for the crewmen descending the ratlines. "Are you dead certain you ought to try this?"

Arithon laughed. "Sure as the scryer's eye tracking my back!"

He received the coiled line, then bent and untied the knotted strings securing the sack. A lightning-fast reach, and his fingers emerged, grasping a glint of rarefied light. Two days of experimentation had let him define the precise frequency required to shadow a fiend. Tuned in to the range of their volatile energies, the sliver of effort required to stay them had been reduced to an artful subtlety.

Trapped *iyat* in hand, Arithon engaged mastery and tightened his intent into crystalline focus. His etched purpose defined the sequence required to raise and rethread the lift for the topsail halyard. Then, ordered thought framed as template, he let the *iyat* soak up the imprint.

"Stand clear," he cautioned. He placed the flaked rope, then loosed the charged fiend from his grasp.

The *iyat* dispersed to a wisped shred of light and faded from view altogether. A drawn second passed. The sailhands watched, riveted. Another moment, while the grousing quips from the hold rang on the windless air. Then the rope twitched. Snakelike, its hemp coils stirred in possession. Sprung out of its coil, it unreeled in a vertical rush, aimed for the topmast crow's nest. The end threaded through the appropriate block, swooped back down, then veered awry in a gleeful dive toward the wallowing swell of the Cildein.

Arithon, laughing, snapped off a fresh shadow. His timely move stripped the fiend from the rope, while Teive's thrifty reflex captured the flailing end before valued cordage lost itself overboard.

"Feckless creature," chided Arithon, thoughtful. Mage-sight let him track the creased bolt of distortion left by the fiend's streaking departure. "We'll just have to try the maneuver again."

"You shouldn't," Dakar grumbled. "You're likely to find the rope turned as a whip, if not hanging you up by the throat."

"Free will, my Prophet, in law and with strictures." The Master of Shadow delved back into his warded sack with enthusiastic delight. "No starved creature bites the hand bearing gifts. I only have to toy with the mix. You don't think my demand can be tailored to taste? Shall we find out which frequency dazzles a fiend and which drives it to intoxication?"

The ongoing trial required three attempts. The deckhands observed with opened mouths, then played the stakes, taking bets. They slapped their knees and yelled ribald encouragement, while the fiends that had ripped them to shambles and shreds were cajoled into rerigging the topmast tackle. Arithon plied his mastery and refined his touch. His subsequent pranks grew flamboyant. When he set an even dozen to stitching a rent sail, Feylind whooped and

261

cried tears, doubled over in gales of mirth. If a needle was lost, and three fiends defected, the nine that stayed on did a passable job.

None complained of the uneven stitching.

Which dalliance did nothing for Dakar's nipped frown. "We still have a scryer riding that sigil," he reminded with acid remonstrance.

"Trust me, I know." Arithon caught his breath. A snared fiend in hand, he nodded in deference toward Teive. "We're fit to bear sail?"

"Oh, aye," the mate said, easy candor restored. "The boys just sent word. Our ballast's restacked. Give us a fresh breeze, we've just got to bend on the canvas."

In fact, the brig's keel rode trim again. Her hull settled tight in the water as ever, except for a stripped patch of sheathing.

"Welcome back, ladies," said Arithon s'Ffalenn. He glanced briefly downward, as though something pained him: and the eye of the scryer, far distant in Forthmark, spied the green edge of metal, pinned underneath his placed foot.

All the while, the active sigil of tracking had been removed from its original fastening. Under the opportune gift of a calm, shifting the brig's ballast had raised the watermark high enough to let a swimmer down on a rope. Short work, from there, to spring the fastening nails and pry off the thin sheet of copper. The inscription had not been disrupted, or destroyed. Pressed flat to the decking, unremarked until now, the aggressive sigil now covered a second inert inscription fashioned from charcoal.

Bound into live scrying, the Koriani observer had barely that moment to ponder the cipher's significance. The mark bore no trace of resonant power. Masked out of view, obscured by the Prime's sigil, its form became vexingly hard to discern. Since the figure was copied, it *might* be recognized as Selidie's own construct, lately used to incite a rank plague of fiends. The slight caveat distinguished: *that this configuration had been reversed, line for line executed in mirror image.*

Arithon, meanwhile, had not paused to laugh. He now sang a lyrical phrase in Paravian. Two days in recovery, his clear tones struck the air and revived the remembrance of flame: and a coal, once reduced from a living tree's heartwood, refired to the call of the element. The charcoal mark quickened. Held in passive contact, pressed overtop, the copper-scribed sigil captured the pattern in resonant sympathy.

The Master of Shadow seized the moment and flipped the bright fleck in his hand. "Well, ladies, you've had more than plenty of warning to let go and back off your damned spying!"

He flattened his palm. This time without pause to temper his thought, he tore off his stayspell of shadow. The *iyat* he held unfurled and reclaimed its lost freedom. Gifted the limitless bait of live charge, it darted *straight down*, drawn first by the brightened promise of fire, then hooked by the vortex of the active sigil, still linked through the Waystone's roused focus...

* * *

Lirenda possessed no resource to break off the scrying's engaged connection. Denied personal autonomy, she could not frame a banishment or disengage the great amethyst. No critical step in evasion was possible without orders, made on the Prime Matriarch's initiative.

Then the moment flashed past. The *iyat* crashed in like a vengeful, shot arrow, consuming the energies of every last stay laid down for guarding protection. Unable to warn, Lirenda suffered the burn of wild forces as the fiend snagged the raised field of the Waystone. Chaos erupted. Sucked down, whirled under, then punched blind and witless, Lirenda lacked voice for her agony. She could not breathe, could not think, could not feel her own heartbeat. A whisker from death, she raged, helpless.

Then the Prime's shriek of fury shattered the dark. "*Alt!*"

Lirenda snapped free. Dropped limp on the carpet, wrenched dizzy and heaving, she regained a grip on her upended senses. Prime Selidie stood above her, wrestling to quell the raging might of the Waystone. Her mastery was contested with virulent force. The loose fiend inside had no mind to relinquish a feast of near-limitless power.

Its fight was not scatheless. As energetic contention flared and whirled through the jewel and torqued the spin of its axis, a sawed note of vibration ripped through structured quartz, chopped short by a spang like snapped wire. A crack sheared one side of the great jewel's matrix, spreading a crackle of craze marks that threatened to shatter the sphere.

"*Alt*, damn you, *Alt!*" the Matriarch howled, desperate. Splashed by filth as Lirenda spewed on the floor, she rammed through the last sequence of ciphers.

The stone's power doused. Just shy of disaster, its aligned focus slammed shut. The invasive fiend stayed locked inside, trapped as a fly caught in amber.

"Damn the man, *damn him!*" Prime Selidie gasped. Shaking, drained white, she dropped in a limp huddle onto her chair. Her shocked eyes regarded the gossamer smoke that dispersed off the stress-heated crystal. "Cursed seed of wild talent, what *have* you done?"

For the massive amethyst had been pressured too far. Not only flawed, not only polluted by an embedded fiend, its clear purple heart was streaked through: intense heat had feathered a raw streak of citrine across the jewel's dark center. The irrevocable change would alter the quartz matrix and shift the sphere's frequency and alignment.

Struck dumb by the penalty of her morning's work, unable to measure the damage done to the order's most irreplaceable resource, Prime Selidie pounded the scarred stubs of her hands in wordless, ferocious frustration. While her spoiled slippers and soaked hems chilled her feet, her tears forepromised a vengeance beyond words upon Arithon Teir's'Ffalenn.

Late Winter 5671

Interludes

By the lamplit glow of *Evenstar*'s chart desk, Arithon prepares a packet of dispatches for Feylind to sail on to Southshire; and to her sharp protest, he answers, unswerved, "Your delay will be passed off as damages caused by a natural storm. I shall be gone, with the four in my party well away aboard *Khetienn*. A snared fiend can be dispatched to summon her north and arrange for an offshore rendezvous..."

With Lysaer s'Ilessid bound upcoast by galley, along with his remnant war host, High Priest Cerebeld meets with Avenor's high council, elated by news just arrived from Raiett Raven's suborned spy ring: "*A colossal mistake has just turned in our favor!* Once the Divine Prince receives King Eldir's sealed dispatch, the hard proof that set his princess to flight will lay the ground for our opening to break him..."

Immersed in the earth link, the Warden of Althain dreams a thread of interlinked possibilities: of an enchantress at Ath's hostel, now fated to shoulder a perilous journey; of a flawed amethyst and a Prime Matriarch hobbled; an eagle whose mettlesome impulse has seeded a whirlwind whose harvest will reap bitter fruit, followed hard by the telling, first link that forges the chain into ill-starred event: a vivacious, laughing carrot-haired bride is promised a bolt of scarlet silk for her wedding...

Sunwheel Square at Avenor

VIII. Avenor

Sulfin Evend had never been dazzled, firsthand, by Avenor's former princess from Etarra. Her fabled beauty and her fiery wit were volatile subjects, wisely avoided in his liege's presence. Since her death had occurred before his appointment to rank, the repercussive response caught him off guard when the dispatch set under King Eldir's seal reached the hand of the Blessed Prince. The packet exposed an intractable truth, backed up by names and hard proof. Talith's murder, concealed by a conspiracy as suicide, sparked off an explosion that smashed the restraint of eight months of sensible planning.

Every painstaking, laid strategy became swept aside.

The insane speed at which Lysaer put his galley to sea and on scorching course for Avenor pitched his Lord Commander at Arms to a state of stripped nerves without precedent.

"You are taking an unmentionable risk, and for what? A woman whose demise happened years ago! Another month, and you'll have our new recruits behind you. Go forward with less than five companies at your back, and you won't have enough strength to cordon your gates. Who knows what evil might slip through the breach? This rush to move now is stark madness!"

Lysaer s'Ilessid chose not to reply. His stance on the deck was as steel, utterly set against reason.

Sulfin Evend had known he might face his own death; peril in war was his venue. Yet at the end of the galley's drenching run north, tied up at the dock at Avenor, the dread that reamed chipped ice through his veins outstripped every concept of fear. He had argued himself raw, held his ground like scraped flint, that Fellowship counsel gave short shrift to the folly of standing untrained against necromancy.

No adamant word changed the outcome. The party of picked officers gathered on deck, resplendent in parade arms, and glittering braid, and immaculate sunwheel surcoats. Sulfin Evend shut his eyes against the stabbing glare, while the clammy sweat trickled under his mail coat and gambeson.

"You are the right hand of justice," addressed a taut voice at his side. "More than Tysan's people rely on the justice we march to enact here, today."

"I would be elsewhere," Sulfin Evend replied. A kind hand clasped his shoulder, provoking recoil. He opened his eyes before thought.

The vision that met him was substance: Lysaer s'Ilessid regarded him, clad in white silk clasped with abalone shell buttons, and without other jewel or ornament. The only gold accent was his bright hair, feathered in the light riffle of sea breeze; the only intense color, his glacial blue eyes, which matched worry with magisterial candor. "If I had anyone else, on my word, your desire would be made true. Is this so very bad for you?"

No reply served. Sulfin Evend did not wish to speak of the spirits, swirling like silver and gossamer foil on the surrounding air. His recent, night ride through the free wilds to reach Hanshire had shown him enough of such things to unsettle his peace for a lifetime.

'*The seers of s'Gannley do not view the course of the future,*' Asandir had explained on the hour Sulfin Evend had honored his full commitment to Enithen Tuer. '*Their gifted talent encompasses truth and reopens the gateway to what has passed. If you take oath for the land under Fellowship auspices, I must warn: the ritual will awaken that latent cognition. I cannot make the process selective or reseal your eyes should you live to regret. Nor would I, if the choice left the option. Every resource you have will be needful.*'

Too late now, to revoke the binding done in the King's Chamber at Althain Tower. Too late as well, to curb Lysaer's impatience. Outside, the deafening noise at the waterfront revealed a populace gathered to witness their idol's return. That such an effusive celebration should turn out to greet an unscheduled arrival boded no earthly good.

Sulfin Evend regarded the white-clad figure before him, solid and warm; too hurtfully vibrant against the wisped ghosts of the sorrows left imprinted upon the site of Tysan's crown capital. Gray-eyed and mortal, he granted his liege his scorchingly brutal response. "Sight or not, I am no trained talent. Being able to see beyond time is not the same thing as a guarantee of protection."

Lysaer lashed him back with incensed conviction: "*I will not suffer the murder of innocents!*"

"You feel that your victimized subjects are due your sovereign protection," Sulfin Evend restated. "Then for their safety alone, I should force you to run!" Against jingling noise as the armed escort prepared to form ranks, he added, "Since you can't embrace reason, you won't leave this ship, that I do not stand at your shoulder. You're wearing a mail shirt and the Biedar knife?"

"Here." The Divine Prince tapped the breast of his doublet, a quilted garment of satin-stitched silk that shimmered like mother-of-pearl. "I'm determined, not foolish."

A rumble signaled the gangway, run down, then the milling tramp as the men-at-arms debarked to assemble on the cleared dock. The standard-bearers fell in at the fore. White-and-gilt icons, they unfurled the state banners to stream in the wind: the Alliance sunwheel, opposed by the crown-and-star blazon of Tysan agleam on its field of deep blue. Arrayed five abreast in two parallel squares, fifty of the elite royal guard stood for their field captain's inspection. Their spired helms gleamed, and their war-sharpened weaponry hung parade-ground precise. Today, with no spare attention for oversight, Sulfin Evend was compelled to turn out his most reliable veterans. After Daon Ramon, the necessity galled him: against irrational odds, he knew that he risked the most steadfast core of his troop.

"I will not cower," Lysaer insisted, stonewalled by his Lord Commander's resistant silence.

No option remained, except to bear up and issue the order to march. "Positions!"

The troop captain took his place at the avatar's back, along with the muscled bursar and two petty officers. Whichever men carried the forged silver shackles, the fine cuffs and thin chains were well muffled and hidden. The Divine Prince's party assumed their place with the escort, whose smart columns wheeled and faced straight ahead. Sulfin Evend covered his liege's left flank. His finest point men strode at right and left, bearing the fringed royal banners. The finials on the standards had forge-sharpened points. Steel chimed to each step: the advance herald's tabard concealed enough weaponry to stand down an assault at close quarters.

Against arrows, or crossbows, Lysaer wore only mail, and the birth-born power of elemental light. "This is as it must be." His quick glance showed confidence to scald the raced heart. "I am in the best hands. Carry forward."

"On my mark!" shouted the troop captain.

The baton fell, and the ranked squares marched shoreward, with the world's divine savior a white diamond clenched in their armored midst.

A wall of sound met them. Although the s'Ilessid regent had not entered Avenor for over a year, his magnanimous presence had made itself felt on the heels of defeat in Daon Ramon. Through summer's famine, his tireless work on the coast had seen laden galleys and supplies routed north. His draft teams had braved the clogged roads, and his war host had stooped to guard caravans. Beset by the torrential lash of the rains, their trained strength had battled the flood, slogging the relief carts through cresting rivers and sucking mud that wore the hearts out of men and horseflesh. No village had starved. Packed against the breakwater and along the warehouse sheds at the harbor front, Avenor's populace shook earth and sky with their cheering.

Sulfin Evend moved into that welter of noise, nerves keyed to unbearable tension. Lysaer's step beside him stayed measured. The caparisoned horse sent from the palace to bear him was refused with lordly disdain. Whether that shocking departure from form had been done for courage, or arrogance, or spurious whim, the act already lay beyond salvage. The avatar's will was no man's to question.

Past the rebuffed consternation of the grooms, and the prance of retreating horseflesh, Sulfin Evend pressed the company ahead through the clouding swirl of the spirit imprints. Unseen by his men, they hovered and danced, ethereal as dusted silver wherever the land held a confluence of lane force. Avenor had once been a Second Age stronghold built by Paravian founders, each of its laid stones aligned into harmony with the tidal flow of the mysteries. The earliest structure had not been ornate. A narrow, walled keep had once crowned the rise, overlooking a coastline left wild.

Lysaer's restored rule had dismantled that ruin in defiance of ancient history. Now, square brick towers supplanted the tumbled remnants of the foundations. Warehouses and wharves jumbled over a shoreline opened to bustle and commerce. The slab that remained of the Paravian landing had been smashed, its mossy, whorled carvings and rusted spikes for ring moorings reduced to sunk rubble in the green surge of the tide. Yet if the granite that had received the law-bound step of past high kings lay fallen, the magics instilled by the centaur guardians were not wont to yield their reach lightly. Power yet flickered like undying light, spun off as the lane flux caressed the crushed shards that retained a tenaciously living awareness. Where currents snagged through those caught bits of held memory, sorrow still spoke with a subtle dissonance. The burning flow of subliminal forces, snapped and snarled off course, refired the forgotten past. Sunchildren sang, their heads crowned with garlands, while wraith-frail boats carved into bird forms and fish crowded to launch for the seasonal water festival. Echoes once sounded by crystalline flutes plucked the heartstrings and closed the throat.

Overwhelmed from the moment he stepped on dry land, Sulfin Evend lost his footing and stumbled.

An anchoring clasp closed over his wrist. "You look like a man on a march to the scaffold. Is this regret?"

The Alliance commander turned his spinning head and regarded the grave countenance of the man he had sworn an irrevocable oath to defend. "At Hanshire, my life was never my own. This at least is a path I have chosen."

Lysaer's answering smile both dazzled and blinded. "You have not let me down even once under fire."

The flame of s'Ilessid regard stole the breath, raised a swell of fresh pride to lull caution and flatten resistance. One might live for such favor. One might die to answer the unearthly craving instilled by this prince's affections.

Before the wreck of the campaign in Daon Ramon, Sulfin Evend would have gone forward to bask in that addictive radiance. Afterward, he had braved Althain Tower to prevent the same brilliance from falling enslaved. A knife's edge had severed that piece of himself, which could have gone forward, self-blinded. His pledge to a Sorcerer had, now and forever, torn off the glittering veil.

Today, he held firm to keep such rampant charisma from carving the less-ordered world into chaos. Seen beside the exalted, clean grace of the spirit forms, or the spun dream of a sunchild's flute, Lysaer's grace was exposed as gilt over clay: all promise, without truth as substance.

"My trust is unshaken," Avenor's regent insisted. "Who else but you could walk steadfast beside me?"

"Better me than another," Sulfin Evend replied, surprised to be galled by that irony.

Lysaer's friendly touch fell away, scalding far less than the afflicting, sorrowful silence left by the Paravian ghosts. Sulfin Evend pressed on, rocked to reeling grief. Over the site of the Second Age wall, the unquiet onslaught intensified. Awake at the threshold that opened the gateway to perceive Athera's live mystery, he walked the duality behind Asandir's warning fully and finally at firsthand.

Attack, if it came, would not find him prepared. The fell workings of necromancy unraveled the shining law that had once given these spirit forms breathing substance. The core harmony sustained by Athera herself shrank before the wounding blight of cult practice, that ensnared the living, then parasitically fed on trapped agony to crystallize flesh into an unnatural state of longevity.

Against dire threat, Sulfin Evend walked naked. Steel could not defeat a warped creature whose ways had defied the Wheel's crossing. Muscle and brute force held no power to vanquish the forces that moved past the veil: only conscious awareness, raised beyond the bounds of the physical senses and trained by the ways known to mages.

Creeping doubt seeded dread. Sulfin Evend battled the ebb of his courage, all too keenly aware the commitment he shouldered would not forgive ignorant failure. While the silenced light of reanimate grace seized his raked heartstrings and twisted, the roaring voice of surrounding humanity hammered into the morning air. The rising ground from the harbor led his company into the shade of the sand-brick towers of the inner citadel. Changed Sight showed no glory of human architecture flying the realm's snapping standards, but a planted impediment that shaved the dance of the mysteries into shuddering disharmony. If clanbred barbarians discerned with such eyes, small wonder they hated the towns! Sulfin Evend reined in the strayed bent of his thought. His duty demanded strict vigilance.

'You must safeguard against the ritual knife blade, and other things far more difficult,' Asandir had forewarned. *'Where the rites of necromancy might be at play, a small wound can pose lethal danger. A pin in the hand of a suborned servant, or a sharp edge on a ring might break the skin during casual contact. Because Lysaer has succumbed to a binding before, he will be doubly vulnerable. If a man set under the sway of cult influence sheds the least drop of his blood, you don't have the skilled grounding to offer a remedy.'*

Battered numb by the deafening adulation, with his vision awash in the glittering static of flux, Sulfin Evend could scarcely walk upright, far less absorb threatening details. Whether or not he harbored regrets, Lysaer was not going to turn back.

The thoroughfare narrowed past the customs office. Forced into close quarters, his armed columns re-formed and dressed ranks. Pressed on both sides by cheering fanatics and hailed from the dormers above, the Blessed Prince and his retinue crept toward the main gate. Amid the smart polish of his men-at-arms, Lysaer wore no gleam of metal. Stark as a snowdrift, his form drew the eye, an exposure no less than frightening: from overhead, and in frontal assault, he was guardless and desperately vulnerable.

Sulfin Evend choked down his driven need to signal an instant retreat. A dried posy shied down. Torn leaves and trailing ribbons brushed across Lysaer's shoulder. He never flinched. His gracious nod acknowledged the young woman, whose wedding circlet dropped at his feet. Patchouli and rose, lavender and citrus, the scents swirled on the breeze as more favors rained down, blithe as a blizzard upon him.

"You would have more security," Lysaer observed, not oblivious. "We haven't much farther. The archway's just ahead."

"One crossbolt would kill you," Sulfin Evend said, curt. Eyes fixed forward, he *stared through* the gossamer form of a high king clad in unadorned deerhide. That royal, also, had walked without arms. In an antique serenity lost with the rebellion, the pellucid imprint of a young woman awaited that forgotten, past homecoming. The young king enfolded her in his embrace. Her loose hair streamed over his shapely, taut hands; words or laughter, their reunion stayed silent.

At next step, their twined forms flickered, then vanished. The trammeled air cleared. Dropped out of tranced vision, hit by deafening noise, Sulfin Evend swore and recovered himself. His foot columns now crossed over the old city gate, where Avenor's past keep underlay the new paving. The cavernous new portal of brick just ahead obscured his critical view of the square, foreclosing his chance for advance preparation. Since an ambush might easily lurk behind the effusive welcome, Lysaer s'Ilessid saw reason enough to awaken the light of his gift. Illumination bloomed overhead as the column marched into the passage spanning the four outer keeps.

Despite flooding brilliance, Sulfin Evend felt cold as his tight-knit company tramped under the embrasured defenses. The mounted, caparisoned ranks of Avenor's royal guard met them on the far side. The moment stung, for the fact there was no princess waiting, and no red-haired crown heir standing tall to greet his father's return.

Like a blow, one recalled that Kevor s'Ilessid had been killed by Khadrim fire on a past winter foray through Westwood.

How Lysaer s'Ilessid managed his grief, no man knew. His beautiful features were forge-hammered iron as the spires of the state palace fell behind, then the pennoned cornices of Avenor's guild houses and garrison armory. Beyond the inner gate and the citadel bastion, the roadway disgorged into the open plaza, its paved sunwheel a dazzling glory of gold-and-white brick, and its central, railed dais with its gilded cupola, shimmering under full sun.

No more spirit forms lurked. Instead, the cold air abraded the skin with something more than winter's ice clarity. Here, where a Second Age focus circle underlay the Alliance renovation, the converging flux of the first lane's current scoured off the wisped cry of past history. On the hour Asandir had arranged the arcane transfer from Althain Tower to this place, Sulfin Evend had encountered no Sighted visions. Only the surging pulse of Athera flowed here, an ephemeral sense of the magnetic forces that shimmered past range of perception.

By night, stars had burned with unnatural brilliance. Under daylight, without any Fellowship escort, the plaza heaved with movement and noise. A packed mass of pink faces and wealth, Avenor's court displayed its full plumage to greet the return of the Blessed Prince. The celebration seemed a sure sign that the high council had touted the stalemate at Kewar as a victory for the Light. Effusive citizens stamped and teemed, bearing lit candles or flourishing streamers. At the first dazzling glimpse of the avatar, the barrage of raw sound became shattering.

Aware, through the tumult, of Sulfin Evend's locked frown, Lysaer said, "What did you expect? No matter how sudden my homecoming, the masses thrive upon spectacle and formal ceremony."

"I don't have to like it," Sulfin Evend snapped back.

Hand closed on the cross-wrapped grip of his sword, he glanced forward to measure the welcome turned out on the central dais. And there, underneath the domed roof and draped banners, the uncanny danger he feared lurked in state finery to meet them.

Shade itself seemed to darken in that one place. Unlike the Sighted shimmer of spirit forms, this horrific, smoky roil of trapped shades seemed the dance of the damned out of Sithaer. Their shrouding presence spindled the air like black snags of raw silk, naked forms wound and pulled to distortion. The horror he viewed was no trivial handful of violations enacted on innocent victims. In cold fact, the aberrant corruption of the realm's ranking peers was entrenched, the work of a cult fed to saturation by long-standing practice of vice. The glittering party arrayed on the dais wore its unseen miasma, thick as the clogged scum on a pond.

"Mercy on us, they're riddled!" Sulfin Evend gasped, appalled. "Strike them from a distance, I can't promise they'll drop."

"Then we shall close in and trust to surprise," Lysaer answered. "I refuse to retreat. The fifty we have must rise to the challenge. You handpicked each one for his courage."

Yet a fearless advance could not abrogate danger. "You face power enough to make dead flesh walk!"

The nightmarish warning posed no deterrent. Lysaer held to his steady advance, where even a madman should falter.

Sulfin Evend swore desperately under his breath. Cult minions relished murder as a hunting sport. They would have their eye fixed on one standing target, where, from a distance, his men-at-arms had no means to differentiate the blameless bystanders from the afflicted.

His sharp guard of veterans would be utterly hobbled. Puppet shells ruled by necromancy wore their haze of infection beyond range of unSighted vision. No abnormal behavior marked them apart. They awaited Lysaer's approach in cold ambush, *knowing* he had slipped through their cult's fingers at Erdane, and now lurking shoulder to shoulder with innocents, secure in their mantles of high office.

Sulfin Evend battled an uprush of nausea. To a seer whose gifted talent was truth, the dais ahead was murky and *crawling*: a rippling, tormented fabric of shades whose slavery transcended mortality. Smeared faces reflected their ghastly torment, gibbering in silenced agony. Elongated hands snatched and plucked and implored, each pitiful gesture a mute cry for mercy. Women, children, babes, and old men, the necromancers' captive prey drifted as smoke suspended in swirling oil.

And through them, a thousand dire sources of threat: the jeweled pins, the ceremonial knives, the gentlemen's spiked canes, and parade arms—*any one of which might be turned to draw Lysaer's blood*. Sulfin Evend wondered in harrowed distress if his sole option would be to throw himself bodily in front of his heedless prince.

Worse, the palace guard stood at the fore. Well trained, fully armed, their front ranks were equipped with crossbows. Sulfin Evend saw, horrified, that he could not be sure the elite captain appointed to their command was untouched by the deadly taint.

"Lysaer, your light!" he exhorted. "You have to dazzle them, *now!*"

"…seems excessive to stage an intense display," Lysaer s'Ilessid demurred through the welter of noise.

"Do it, no argument!" The Lord Commander's shout was imperative. "Fires of Sithaer, this is a staged trap! Your regency ministers are not just suborned, but *replaced* by cultists who practice enslavement. Fail me once, and you won't leave this plaza unscathed, nor will one man among the picked company I've brought to stand at your back."

"My high council's turned? *All of them?*" Lysaer's shock was shrill. Targeted by worse than invasive conspiracy, he did what was asked: augmented the halo cast by his gift. The blast cracked the surrounding air to white fire and unleashed a harsh backlash of heat. "Names," he insisted, his face a stamped mask. "Give me names! I'll serve every one who's transgressed by black arts under the arm of crown justice!"

The roar of the awestruck crowd redoubled and slammed like a living wave through the square. Sulfin Evend walked battered and blinded. "I would give you corpses, run through with cold steel," he snarled, though grisly truth made that promise a mockery. Brute force could not grant his liege a defense, or win his best company their deliverance. Not against a worked evil that fouled the natural turn of Fate's Wheel.

Fear numbed the mind, that the horror ahead outstripped every mortal protection. Sulfin Evend was seized by the anguished *need* for a greater wisdom to stand alongside him. His scalding appeal expected no answer. Yet he walked inside a Paravian focus ring, bound by a *caithdein*'s blood pledge. An arcane confluence of energy aligned. His acute, inner cry burned into the flux as it peaked toward crest at high noon.

Forces inherent in the land itself captured that crystalline thought, and one man's piercing desire for balance engaged the heartcore of the mysteries.

Sulfin Evend felt a fist of pure energy punch through the wall of his chest. His breached heart opened up. Ripped through by a thundering wind from the void, he reeled, all but unmoored. The bone-rattling din of the mob fell away. Firm boundaries dissolved into distance. Between one step and the next, he was *here* and *also* there, hurled back to the moment at Althain Tower *as he spoke a vow to serve Tysan, and a knife in the hand of a Fellowship Sorcerer touched his wrist and cracked open the vault of his inner awareness.*

Then and now, Sulfin Evend's perception arced upward. A force outside comprehension embraced him: fluid as light, gentle as breeze, and as joyously silent as dew on a leaf under starlight. The moment here, *now*, and there, *then*, became as unknowably vast as eternity: but the Sorcerer who cradled his being was not any longer Asandir.

Instead, Sulfin Evend *knew* the Warden of Althain. Sethvir appeared first in his robes of maroon velvet; then as a presence half-seen, bundled into an astonishing weave of soft light; then as a withered old man, pillowed uncon-scious in the flood of a candleflame...

"I don't understand," Sulfin Evend gasped, startled. His words echoed. Their form was both spoken and not: *he existed in twofold awareness.* Both in *and not in* the King's Chamber at Althain Tower; and also, amid the winter chill plaza in Tysan's capital of Avenor.

Sethvir's response reflected grave calm. "Don't try. Stop thinking. Just lis-ten. Accept the gift of my experience."

Sulfin Evend still heard the din of the throng, registered the passing im-pression that Lysaer s'Ilessid was speaking. Yet the core of his mind that ex-isted at Althain enfolded him in pristine silence. All else lost meaning. *Here*, the cold air glued his skin into space. From *there*, his earthbound form sheared to gauze, while his unfettered mind spiraled free.

As well, the dazzle of Lysaer's gift seemed reduced to translucent glass. Where the cupola loomed, packed to crowding with state figures clothed in gaudy panoply, Sulfin Evend saw outside the shocked shell of his intellect. His greater Sight unveiled *all of the names.* The creatures entrapped by the cult's twisted influence stood exposed, their corrosive threat vivid as blight.

'How can I contain this?' Sulfin Evend quailed, winnowed helpless before the depth of a horror that held force and darkness to swallow the spark of his fragile mortality. *'Such knowledge lies past me.'*

'Knowledge is of the moment,' Sethvir stated in gentle correction. *'Caithdein, Sulfin Evend, your claim to serve balance has been witnessed and heard. Your oath as permission: my wisdom is freed to stand upon yours. Go forward, self-determined, and place trust in that truth. Let my actions speak through you. Or fail. You act on your merits, both ways.'*

Sulfin Evend knew terror. The withering sense of his personal inadequacy crushed him down. Against cringing retreat, he held one silken thread: a touch sustained in ephemeral connection through the heart of Athera's grand mys-tery. Faced by the unknown *on both fronts*, he chose.

He answered the force that addressed him with tenderness and supported his shortfalls with caring.

Sulfin Evend advanced, still subsumed by the paradox. The slipstream of time flowed around him *and through* the pinpoint moment that sealed his blood oath. *Caithdein*, he had been forged by a Fellowship ritual that made him as vessel and conduit. Amid his drilled column of steadfast, armed men, he heard himself call for a cordon. "You'll surround the state figures installed on the dais!" His following instructions were fast and explicit: the deployment must happen without fuss or fanfare, an apparent precaution to curb the flash point excitement showed by the crowd.

As his armed column closed in on the cupola, Sulfin Evend capped his hurried instructions with specifics for his bursar and both petty officers. "By the laws of crown justice, we have thirteen conspirators to arrest before the hour of noon. They will be charged here. You will not touch their flesh! Leave me to set them in shackles. If they resist, or try to flee, by my orders the men will drop them point-blank, using the iron-tipped crossbolts."

Netted in Lysaer's light, enveloped amid the transcendent shimmer of lane flux, Sulfin Evend charged his acting captain to make ready with the silver manacles.

Then he delivered the list of the conspirators to Lysaer s'Ilessid, beside him. "High Priest Cerebeld, and his four senior acolytes. Lord Chancellor Quinold, Lord Secretary of the Treasury Eilish, Gace Steward, the Lord Keeper of the Gates, Erdane's Guild Ambassador Koshlin, the Lord High Justiciar Varrun, Avenor's Guild Ministers Odrey and Tellesec. My prince, no heroics! For self-preservation, you will stand out of reach as you denounce each offender for treason."

Then the cupola loomed through the fireburst of light. The archers deployed. With the standard-bearers positioned at either flank, Sulfin Evend advanced up the dais stair at the side of the Blessed Prince. Split perception showed him the high council officials in their welcoming row, clad in scintillant finery and squinting into the dazzle of Lysaer's explosive display. Though he moved, his frame of perception seemed arrested: the twined confluence of lane flux and awareness reduced the flap of the banners to slow-motion ripples; at Althain, the knife cut still flicked his bared wrist. Framed through sundered senses, Sulfin Evend heard Lysaer's voice, pronouncing the accusations. Each syllable seemed unnaturally stretched out, sound suspended over the infinite well of a cognizance hurled past the veil.

In simultaneous presence, the Fellowship Sorcerer linked through his being spoke also: *there and now and forever*, Sethvir's phrases in actualized Paravian struck the air like bronze chimes and rippled a wave through the cloth of existence.

Awareness transfixed, Sulfin Evend shuddered with gooseflesh: for the Sorcerer's greater knowing arced *through* him. Eternity held the strung pause between words. Self-doubt burned away in the fire of willed choice. The required authority to secure the land arose from the core of his being. His consent shaped desire to partner the grand dance and see discord reworked into harmony. As Sethvir's masterful guidance touched through, Sulfin Evend let go in release; and mystery answered, *unstoppable*.

"...for the crime of conspiracy, murder, and dark practice," the Blessed Prince was pronouncing; while *through a man who stood, blood and bone, as* caithdein, Althain's Warden's words wound and braided, in and between time and space. '...*for transgression of the sacrosanct freedoms held by the compact, your rights are called forfeit...*'

Dizzied by the multiplied stream of sensation, awash in the uncanny blaze of the lane flux, Sulfin Evend reached the stair head. He accepted the first set of shackles. Then he advanced on the creature before him. What had *once* been human wore gold-edged robes and fair skin. The being that bore the semblance of smiling form was not at one with life, but stitched with dark lines in a scatter of ring-rippled patterns. It moved and breathed, but *did neither*. Its presence cried wrongness, until the very air drawn into its lungs recoiled from the aberrant state of warped flesh.

Sulfin Evend met that one's eyes, saw them narrow with sharp recognition. Braced by the powers of a Fellowship Sorcerer, he moved, against horror, into an aura poisoned by the trapped shades of three women and a girl child. Wisps though they were, their piteous cries shredded the world, without sound. "High Priest Cerebeld!"

Against his bold denouncement of the accused, Sulfin Evend heard, far distant, from Althain, Sethvir's voice Name the ghosts of the women, then tenderly claim the small child. Their tears fell and fell, in yet another place; while the lane forces crested in the plaza at Avenor, crackling the winter air into bands of blue-and-violet lightning.

"You!" gasped the High Priest. His address was directed to something beyond sight, and his outraged stance seemed struck torpid. Sulfin Evend matched the cult puppet's scorching glare, *unafraid*: for another presence at Althain Tower also looked out of his eyes.

"You are doomed," he felt himself prompted to say. "The blameless spirits your masters have bound are set free, and the law of the compact declares the vessel that used them as forfeit!"

Sulfin Evend lifted the silver shackles to take charge. *Other hands moved, as though covering his own.* The Alliance Lord Commander had no chance for wonder. He was kneeling at Althain, *and* standing at Avenor: one being whose greater existence had burned into form, split by a lens of simultaneity. His fingers *and Sethvir's* seemed gloved in white light. In shared volition, Sulfin Evend reached out and bundled the High Priest's arms behind his back. When he snapped the locks shut over the prisoner's wrists, runes drawn by the trained might of a Sorcerer flared and sank into the metal. A brief chill swept his senses. The tormented shades dissolved out of bondage, whisked away by a shimmer of opalescent flame.

Sulfin Evend breasted the scour of lane flux. Each word and step guided, he shackled the next man in line, then the next. As the corrupt accused were bound into custody, he heard the distanced echo, as Althain's Warden pronounced other names: and the spirits enslaved by the dark arts of necromancy received the mercy of their release.

Seconds lagged in suspension. Each figure set in manacles seemed a slow-moving wax doll, frozen between breath and motion. Voice spoken in Avenor and *voice* heard at Althain seemed two dreaming threads spun into a single twined strand. Sethvir's phrases razed a bell tone through muscle and bone, while ephemeral light scoured, and the lane flux sleeted bands of harmonics through the matrix between body and spirit.

The twelfth pair of shackles had been set in place when the noon lane tide's crest waned and subsided. The confluence of the grand mysteries receded. Streaming sweat, Sulfin Evend folded back into himself. Alone as a man, he found himself mortal, and locked eye to eye with the trapped fury of a dozen crown traitors arrested for dealings with necromancy.

"This won't end here, I promise!" snapped Ambassador Koshlin with dipped venom. His acid glance shifted to High Priest Cerebeld, and a silent thought crossed between them. Sighted vision caught the split-second exchange, like the clash of sword steel and lightning.

"But it will end here!" Lysaer s'Ilessid stood at the dais stair, his stainless splendor hard as cut diamond as he regarded the fettered knot of conspirators. "With a sword through the heart, and a cleansing by fire, as I stand upon the realm's justice before you. Take these murderers away! The sight of them is an offense against nature and an affront to the people of Tysan!"

The thirteenth conspirator escaped the armed cordon. No man knew how. He had been High Priest Cerebeld's least notable acolyte, and his flight went unnoticed as he slipped from the dais through the watchful ranks of the stationed guardsmen.

Left short of temper, Sulfin Evend could not wrest himself clear to give chase. Nor could he delegate. As the only man bearing a Fellowship warding against the fell workings of necromancy, he dared not send his eager, but unshielded, officers into jeopardy to run down the fugitive. Nor could he assign them to watch the chained captives already in hand. Although the creatures were stripped of the enslaved spirits that sourced their dark powers of influence, each had been suborned as a powerful tool, still linked to a practicing cult master. If silver chains bound them, they were not rendered harmless. Mind and flesh, they were subsumed by dark forces that fed upon life.

Against every sane argument, their immediate execution had been rejected by Lysaer s'Ilessid.

"No man dies under my rule without trial!" Backed against principle, the Blessed Prince stayed insistent, no matter how urgently he was pressed. "Justice under my hand is not revocable! The accused have firm rights, first among them that human dignity in this realm cannot be waived for convenience. No. Guilt will be established by means of due process, regardless of whether my tribunal holds their inquiry as a formality. I will not be denied in this matter. We shall not put down sorcery by means of dishonor, or what do you think we become?"

"Survivors with our free autonomy intact," Sulfin Evend cracked back, and found himself excused from the royal presence forthwith.

By late afternoon, he paced like a surly, caged cat, up and down the cramped floor of Avenor's dungeon wardroom. The frustration that gnawed him had no other outlet. While the relief watch he turned away out of hand whispered that he was overwrought, the prisoners locked in detention appeared passive. Restive senior officers delivered their reports and chafed at his insistent restraint, until their irritation bordered upon insolence.

Sulfin Evend barked back and hardened his will. The men were sent packing, although the deceptive ease of the day's public capture had sapped every warning of credibility.

The captives who importuned using civilized words, or who slumped in their spelled chains, posing the shocked stupor of innocents, were perilous beyond all imagining. Any guard in their presence would be nakedly vulnerable, once the master who ruled them sought contact. As he must: the secretive cults defended their own. The danger would intensify after dark, since the aberrant nature of necromancy shunned the balance endowed by the light.

The shells of the men taken captive, meantime, could not be left unattended. Of them all, High Priest Cerebeld appeared most unresponsive. Unnaturally listless for a powerful man who had been the Light's voice in Avenor, he stayed sunk in a glassy-eyed stupor. The persistent whining arose from Gace Steward, still onerously protesting his innocence.

Sulfin Evend watched, cold. As often as he had seen stress and battle crumble men's dignity, this queer shift in roles between a ranking superior and an underling disturbed his commander's instinct.

As sundown neared, and the sensible order to hasten the trial did not move the wheels of state, the Lord Commander became pitched to increasing unease. The affray in the square had left him light-headed. Not helped by the fact that he worked on short sleep, he stayed on his feet in a frazzled effort to keep overstressed senses alert.

While the ferrety palace steward launched into another bristling complaint that Talith's murder was none of his doing, Sulfin Evend flung back an acid correction.

"You are all answerable! Lives are not taken to tidy the realm's image! Talith's death was not under the high council's purview, nor any courtier's duty to carry out, ahead of state trial and crown sentence."

With his sallow, pocked features pressed against the barred grille, the palace official blinked rat-shifty eyes. "But I did not kill the realm's former princess. No man here caused her fall. She was alone. Her plunge from that tower was a sorry act, no more and no less than a suicide."

"No one pushed her." Agreeable as a viper too chilled to strike, Sulfin Evend took pause. He measured the steward through Sighted eyes, but perceived nothing more than an oily coward, afraid for his miserable life. His strung nerves did not settle. Each time he surveyed the group in the cell, his very skin crawled with revulsion. He added, "Talith fell during an attempt to escape, but a crossbow bolt sheared through the rope that supported her. We have found your marksman. The payment that bought his skilled shot is already attested under a crown bailiff's signature."

"Forgeries!" snapped Gace. "You have been duped by the disaffected in league with the Master of Shadow."

"Not the case. Your crossbowman was seized by my men just past noon. His confession has matched what we have seen on paper. That seals your arraignment, and if I could choose, your execution would take place this moment."

No flicker of reaction arose from High Priest Cerebeld; such lackluster response seemed unnatural. Sulfin Evend rubbed his neck until the bones cracked. He could not shake off the nagging suspicion that an unseen current was still at play. A hidden blade that might turn in the hand, or some sly trap, perhaps set by the thirteenth conspirator. Caged here while the regent stalled for *no reason*, a man could do nothing but probe with lame words, hoping to jab a soft nerve. "That escaped acolyte will be pursued. If any should shelter him, they'll be put to death along with your other collaborators."

The upstairs door groaned. Inbound footsteps pattered over the threshold, and mingled voices rebounded downward. Yet one man's tone stood out.

Sulfin Evend froze. Shocked aware as though doused by a pail of shaved ice, he realized that Lysaer s'Ilessid was amid that company of unscheduled arrivals.

Fast as a man moved, loud as a shouted order could peal up the stairwell, the effort to salvage the lapse came too late. Sulfin Evend watched, horrified, as three prisoners in the cell slumped into collapse, then dropped in an unbreathing heap. Gace Steward snapped his jaw shut between words. Wrist chains chinking, he scrambled clear of the barred door, making way as Cerebeld stood up. Now, the High Priest's eyes were wide-open, glinting with unshielded malice. Sighted talent unveiled the hideous moment as his aura streamed unclean. This time, the leaden shadows had faces: the creature wearing Cerebeld's form had subsumed the trapped shades of *three* of his prostrate colleagues. Their corpses had been drained *that fast*, with no sign of the vile spell that enslaved them.

Sulfin Evend snatched up the crossbow kept loaded and ready. The quarrels were tipped with cold iron. His fast shot snapped through the sunwheel emblem on the breast of the High Priest's mantle. Heart's blood flowered and spurted. Dead, but still animate, the creature came on, teeth bared in a feral grimace.

"Sundown," stated Cerebeld, haughty with triumph. "My master rules now."

Then he wobbled, lurched forward, and measured his length, fettered wrists still linked at his back. His robes pooled on the floor, a muddle of stained white. The air around his twitching corpse seethed with ephemeral movement as a boiling rush of dull silver bled out of his dying flesh. The taint streaked from the aura, no longer bound. The rooted stream of corruption expired from emptied lungs and poured out of nose and slack lips. Like a haze of fine mercury, the reanimate forces coalesced within the locked cell.

Sulfin Evend stared, horrified, as the amalgamate shades of the corrupted dead moved on and poured into the open mouth of Gace Steward, who howled in shock from the sidelines.

Measured and marked, already prepared as the vessel of a practicing necromancer, Gace's human instinct to scream became choked. His eyes strained wide open, then bulged as he gagged. The reflex retained no intelligent will: only the animal urge of warm flesh to cling to instinctive survival. The struggle lasted no more than an instant before the assaulted body gave way. Gace's lungs filled. His auric field bloomed like sludge with the haze of its unclean possession, *that fast*.

Sulfin Evend saw, sickened. Harrowed urgency drove him. He wrestled to span the discharged crossbow, while the shuddering frame of the palace official completed its grisly transition and became the empowered receptacle. Slack-lidded, replete, it surrendered to the addictive yoke of the master.

Gace Steward straightened to the chime of spelled chains. Infused with the presence of undead magics, he leaned on the barred door. His foam-flecked lips bowed into a smile.

"Sundown has arrived!" The evil he bore was a palpable force. "Kill us, sweet fool. Did you realize you had left my master's minion in charge of a prearranged stable of surrogates? I have seven other gibbering shells that your heroic work has sucked vacant!" Glittering, dark eyes raked over his adversary. "Can't you see, bantling? Althain's Warden has failed you. He's left them unsealed and well bridled for riding! We'll just mount another. For each one you drop, our strength will increase! Kill the last, and we'll jump. What can you do? We'll just seize the next whole man we encounter and crush him to serve by strangling his will by main force!"

Less than a second had passed since first contact. Repossession happened that quickly. Sulfin Evend rushed his hands, fumbling the last crank of the windlass in his need to engage the trigger latch. He slotted a fresh bolt. Clammy with sweat, he already saw that his striving was useless. The spells that Sethvir had set into the chains secured no more than the body, with the opportune ending by fire and sword thrown away with the advent of night.

Why had Lysaer s'Ilessid deliberated? Worse yet, why had he broken orders and come, against every adamant warning? For his sovereign step still descended the stair, straight into a morass of danger.

Winter 5671

Gambit

Sulfin Evend gave a frantic shout up the stairwell for the Blessed Prince to stand clear. Then he slammed the wardroom door in between. He could not drop the bar. The panel was designed to bolster security, and never fashioned to lock from within. Shoulder braced to that insecure barrier, loaded crossbow in hand, he faced the warped creature shut inside the cell, along with four corpses and the shells that seemed as men, but were no less than a deadly, suborned pack of surrogates. The wrists of each one remained cuffed in silver. Their hands would stay shackled. Stout locks were tongued through the reinforced slot in the barrier that restrained them. Unless this fell cult could walk its possessed through forged steel, the corrupted could not break out of physical containment.

"Give this up," the Lord Commander said, steady. "To have Lysaer, you must first go through me. Nor will I let his Blessed Grace cross this threshold while I have one resource to stop him. Posture on, you stick puppet! Rant all you like. That won't change the fact you can't touch me."

Brave words, or more likely, the stance of a fool. Cult spells, or loosed wraiths might slip through such barriers at whim. Yet a defender with his back to a door, and no options could but hope Asandir's given word backed the truth: that free will held aligned by a Fellowship warding could not be displaced or fall to the crippling coercion of necromancy. For the stakes at play now risked far worse than his life. Should he die under rites, no matter how foul, Sulfin Evend stood his ground on a Sorcerer's promise that his self-aware spirit could not be denied a natural passage across the Wheel's turning.

Behind the barred grille, the reanimate flesh that had once been Gace Steward proffered an oily challenge. "Guard your prince if you can. Though how can you react? He has not paid heed to your warning."

The threat was not empty. Outside, the filtered sound of raised voices moved nearer. Descending footsteps came on, undeterred in their disastrous approach down the stairwell. Then Lysaer's called inquiry affirmed that restraint had been thrown to the four winds and jeopardy. Or, *perhaps not*: the invidious smirk on the face of the captive suggested some form of a lure.

"What have you done?" Sulfin Evend cried, shocked. He had no mage training, could not guess what vicious mischief might have been tried to turn Lysaer's sensibilities.

A desperate, split second remained to respond. This time, Sulfin Evend must act alone, without the mystical powers of a Paravian focus at lane crest, and with none of Sethvir's strength to back him.

He spun, shoved open the door, and plunged into the gloom of the stairwell. A kick slammed the iron-strapped panel behind him. No moment to spare, to engage bar or lock, or snatch the lit torch from the wall sconce. Ahead, through the welter of uncertain light, four men approached unaware. Only one might be saved. Sulfin Evend's live body must become Lysaer's shield. Without time for outcry, past reach of sane action, the Alliance commander slapped the spanned crossbow into his left hand. He drew his knife in the course of his pelting dash upward.

Between the slapped echoes of his own raced strides, he heard his most competent captain call downward in concerned inquiry.

Sulfin Evend ran silent. He had no breath for grief. Reason and words would be *far* too slow to deflect the oncoming disaster. He could do *nothing*. Just hurl himself, sprinting, up the turnpike stair, driving muscles that screamed from exertion. He kept on. Watched the curve of the walls unveil course after course of blank risers. More torches passed. His wake set them fluttering. Warped shadows capered around him. A man who prayed might have beseeched fate. Sulfin Evend drove forward, panting. Let the distance from the closed cell be enough. He needed no less than sixty feet, with an additional margin for safety. He counted each pace, three stairs to the yard. Seventeen, eighteen, with his winded chest tight unto bursting.

Then at last, a clear view: Lysaer s'Ilessid in shining white, his bare head raw gold in the flame light. By strict orders, three trusted, armed officers accompanied him.

Frustrated agony found no release. Their Lord Commander saw his dread realized. The royal party had already drawn too close, with the tactical blunder past help to reconcile. Asandir had been ruthlessly explicit: under darkness, a cult working could encompass the energy field raised by its operant source. *There lies the range of an enabled necromancer, and by extension, any thralled subject who has been suborned under his power.*

The abomination in the cell had attached three subordinate entities whose drained corpses had dropped without fight. Cerebeld's death yielded four, then Gace Steward, five; attack, if it came, would be fiercely potent. Conquest might come without warning. Climbing, sides splitting, Sulfin Evend dared not gasp even a last-minute plea. He could only act to ensure Lysaer's safety by the only crude measure at hand.

He leveled the crossbow. Aimed and squeezed the trigger. Cable spanged in release. The shot bolt hissed upward and slapped the lead officer in the pit of his throat. His choked, surprised corpse and the discharged weapon fell and struck the stair simultaneously. As the tumbling body and discarded weapon crashed downward, Sulfin Evend threw his small knife. The missile took the man just behind Lysaer, the blade struck stark through the eye. The kill fell, gouting blood. The dying man's weight jostled the Blessed Prince, just stiffened in shock, and now staggered forward into the last man-at-arms, who led a purposeful half pace ahead.

While the soldier's rocked frame swayed to recover balance, Sulfin Evend leaped the threshing tumble of dead limbs as his shot officer caromed down the stairwell. Gagging on bile, he charged upward, sword drawn, and cut down Lysaer's last standing guard: *his most trustworthy field veteran.* The hard, upward sword thrust rammed between ribs and pierced a true man through the heart.

Sulfin Evend met his victim's betrayed glance, eye to eye. The stabbed carcass jerked, cramped to spasms of agony. His sunk blade wrenched away as he hurled the body aside. Strangling down nausea, the Alliance commander bore on. He knocked into Lysaer, slammed the white-clad form backward and tripped his legs at the ankle. They fell, locked together. For cruel expediency, Sulfin Evend pinned his liege flat amid the splashed filth and blood that befouled the risers.

"Burn the dead!" he snapped, tortured. Though a slaughtered man voided and drummed heels at his elbow, and two others thudded in a downward plunge toward the shut door of the wardroom, he slapped down Lysaer's outrage. "Torch them! Now! Trust me, trust my Sight! I am not possessed."

Vivid with fury, Lysaer snarled, "Are you not? Then why did you send for my presence?" His wrestler's response replaced accusation. He thrashed to hurl what must seem a rogue murderer over backward down the stone stair.

Pressed to dirty tactics, Sulfin Evend snapped a knee into his liege's groin. Lysaer's resistance broke instantly. His gasping surrender could not last a moment. Even in agony, eyes pinched against tears, he shuddered and clawed to retaliate.

"Damn you, *listen!*" His relentless strength pinned hard overtop, Sulfin Evend snatched a fist in splashed silk. "I never sent, do you hear me?" He ripped the Divine Prince's collar. Rich fastenings scattered. The rebounding clatter of flung pearls echoed downward, each pinpoint impact struck like tapped glass through the shuddering throes of the dying.

"Burn my fallen!" Hands still moving, Sulfin Evend spoke fast. "For the Light's sake! You must do as I say."

Lysaer bucked, enraged. "You are not yourself! Or why would you slaughter your best officers!"

His Lord Commander hardened his fists. Stressed silk tore asunder. "Damn you, liege! *Be still.* Your life, or theirs, I had to choose!"

Wasted entreaty; Lysaer freed his arm. His punch slammed into Sulfin Evend's left side, hard enough to damage a kidney had the impact not clashed into mail. The Lord Commander hammered in with his knee: again felt abused flesh recoil. This time, beyond mercy, he followed up, ground an elbow into the hollow of Lysaer's shoulder with a pitiless force that would paralyze.

No more pleading leave, he grappled through the ripped tunic. His bracer gouged scrapes into fine-grained skin. Heedless, he burrowed beneath snagging silk, seeking a hide thong and slung knife sheath. Lysaer's ragged gasps were obscured by the scream of rent fabric. Sulfin Evend bared the Biedar knife at long last and closed his desperate grip on the handle.

Already, wisps of dull shadow moved at the corner of his eye. *Something* unleashed by the necromancer's craft encroached on his peripheral vision. Lysaer jerked. Perhaps aware that an uncanny invasion nipped through his aura to claim him, he tried a mad wrench to break free.

"Damn you, hold!" Sulfin Evend snagged the desert-worked knife from the sheath. While his instincts cried scintillant warning of danger, he laid the flint weapon crosswise against Lysaer's throat.

Barely in time! The creeping invasion of uncanny forces coiled above the unwarded victim's nose and mouth. Past reach of finesse, Sulfin Evend bore down. He sliced a shallow nick through fair skin.

Lysaer recoiled.

Desperate to keep contact, and not cause lethal harm, Sulfin Evend pressed the warded flint against the seeping edge of the wound. "Hold still!" he pleaded. "You are under attack, and this blade frames your only protection!"

Lysaer shut his eyes, then grated, choked short, "If you're not turned by the enemy, what do you See?"

"A spirit or vile sending of some sort. I'm no sorcerer! Damned if I *know* what ugly powers have stirred, or what creepish force has come stalking. Don't move!" Still winded, Sulfin Evend fought each word through agonized, galling bitterness. "Breathe the thing in, it will taint your blood. Your heart might be touched. This blade is your warding. Contact is binding your fragile protection, so sting and be grateful, your Grace. *Why didn't you trust me?* Under no circumstances were you to come down, far less seek this place after sunset."

His anguish towered: three brave men were dead.

Now the horror that might yet enact a possession was arrested *just barely* from flooding its victim. It poised in midair, a sinuous veil, arrested by *unknown* eldritch powers worked into a tribal dagger.

"A page brought your summons," Lysaer said at strained length.

"His name?" snapped Sulfin Evend. "One of ours, or from the palace?"

"Does that matter?" Lysaer ground out. Dispassionate ice-blue eyes raked back. "How do I know that you're not corrupted?"

"Sithaer's damned! Have you heard me? My best men were killed *because I had no means to defend them!*" No protection existed within this bleak place that could spare them from becoming taken in thrall to a necromancer. "You have just one knife," the commander appealed in snatched grief. "I had to choose which life should be saved. Now burn my casualties! I won't see them rise! You owe them that much, for their sacrifice."

Lysaer coughed, his tangled head jammed against the stone stair, sullied gold in the glimmer of flame light. Whether he sensed the threatened invasion, or whether the harsh knockdown had dazed his wits could not be determined.

"You must raise your light!" Sulfin Evend insisted. "Tysan's safety *right now* depends on your gift. Or your hope to rout out this corruption is ashes!"

"You have lost hope, regardless," declared an intrusive voice *from below*.

Sulfin Evend froze. Through his strained breathing, he heard furtive movement, then an uncanny shuffle. One of the freshly killed corpses had stirred. Puppet to the black will of a necromancer, it would mount the stair and wreak every form of fell horror.

"*Burn them!*" he gasped. "Lysaer, do it now!"

Whether or not his liege meant to comply, the reanimate body kept speaking. "I have news of the Master of Shadow, Blessed Prince! Arithon the bastard has flung you a challenge!"

Which statement changed *everything*. A repeat of the horrific event in Daon Ramon, Sulfin Evend watched a terrible, sweeping change eclipse the reason in Lysaer's eyes. Asandir had declared the effect was a curse, laid on by the Mistwraith's malice. Cast geas, or mad principle, the effect was the same: ruling power tossed like straws on a game board set for unbridled disaster.

"*Lysaer!*" Frantic, Sulfin Evend bore down until the flint blade razed into raw skin. "You are being played for strategic diversion. Tell yourself the truth! Fight back, man. Hold your rage. Don't rise to the bait of an enemy!"

The plea fell on deaf ears. Lysaer's features contorted to a rictus of fury, while down the stairwell, an obscene aberration with a hole in its heart staggered erect and continued in monologue, "Did you know you are betrayed? Arithon s'Ffalenn has suborned the s'Brydion of Alestron. They have sheltered your renegade shipwright, Cattrick, and more. Your wife, in their hands, is now being dispatched to a hostel of Ath's adepts. The master I serve could hand you the victory. The death of the byblow who has shamed your name could be delivered into your grasp."

"Lies!" cracked Sulfin Evend. "Burn the dead, or we're lost!"

Lysaer heaved. An animal whipped to an insane pitch of fury, he battered to dislodge the stone knife from his throat. Sulfin Evend wrestled the slighter prince down. His ruthless fist hardened against Lysaer's neck, now become as much a deadly liability as an indispensable stay of protection. "Hold, liege! You must! You're being reeled in like a fish!"

"Let go." Implacable, Lysaer clawed to throw off restraint. "Stand down. Or burn! I will not be thwarted."

"I will not see you make an alliance with havoc!" Sulfin Evend used his studded bracer as a club and tried to stun his liege unconscious. The effort fell short. The knife gouged and slipped. Blood pooled in the hollow of Lysaer's throat, while the unmanageable grip of Desh-thiere's curse trampled down ethics and reason.

The crux wrung the loyal heart beyond bearing: to burn alive in Lysaer's crazed assault, or to drive home the knife like a butcher. *Yet even the choice to serve death had not spared the other three officers trapped in the breach.* Black spellcraft had claimed them in ruinous usage, a fate now poised to overtake the most powerful ruler in the five kingdoms. The weal of the Alliance, and who knew how many innocent lives, hung in the horrific balance.

"Lysaer!" Sulfin Evend shouted to break concentration, *any* effort to redirect the burgeoning riptide of light. "Fight your war! But not this way! Don't join hands with the dark cabal whose twisted acts drove your wife and your son into danger!"

Slammed into a riser, battered half-dizzy, the s'Ilessid prince sucked a racked breath. "They were pawns. Stand aside! Don't think to obstruct me."

Out of the cold dark, the spelled voice kept taunting. "But your son's name is not on the rolls of the dead. This I vow! The master I serve could tell you what forces have laid claim to Prince Kevor's destiny."

Sulfin Evend felt the hardening under his hands. "No!" His scream shattered the welded tension with echoes, while his liege's mad fury unleashed. Lost beyond hope, the lord commander cried out, "Lysaer! Destroy the conspiracy that murdered Princess Talith! Then handle the Spinner of Darkness in a conflict at arms, untainted by black ties of necromancy!"

Success or failure, the shocked air burned white. Dazzled blind, scoured by heat, Sulfin Evend hung on, as hammer to anvil, the percussive clash of Lysaer's raised light smashed down. He heard ragged speech; realized his liege was weeping the name of his departed beloved. For *Talith*, the force of Lysaer's outraged assault turned upon the worked tool of the gray cult below him.

The strike roared through the keep like the fires of Sithaer. Flash-point heat glazed the lower cellar to slag. Both wardroom and dungeon were scoured.

Doors, walls, and steel glistened red, then ignited. The unnatural fires belched up a curtain of black smoke, as razed masonry bloomed orange and ran molten. The stairwell above became a chimney, blasted by the winds of inferno. Clothing smoked. Skin blistered. Whipped hair singed in the blast. On the landing below, the downed guardsmen sizzled, flesh and bone seared away, while the stink of the fumes ripped the guts of the living into paroxysms of nausea.

Retching, flash-blinded, Sulfin Evend slammed his liege into the stone step with stunning force. Then, scoured fingers still gripped to the knife, he locked his left arm and dragged his unconscious charge in a stumbling rush up the stairwell. He reeled ahead, hauling Lysaer along with him. Hot air seized his throat. Swirling fumes turned his senses. Sulfin Evend could not see, only grope his way upward. If the mercury shadow of spellcraft still stalked, his gifted talent was blinded. He could but hope the uncanny assault had been thwarted when the necromancer's string-puppet cabal had been consumed.

Fire raged, beyond salvage. Bricks shattered, red-hot. The dungeon was blasted to ruin.

Coughing, stung bloody as the blast fragments raked him, Sulfin Evend rounded the bend. He saw torchlight, then the pallid square of the upper postern, stamped amid the morass of churned smoke. Cradled in his locked grasp, his liege lay rag-doll limp, a wound running red at his throat. Ahead, faint shapes against the trammeled twilight, he saw his posted guardsmen, responding. Their distressed shouts seemed far off. Sulfin Evend had no voice left to cry warning. He was fordone. If wisps of vile spellcraft streamed through the murk, no recourse remained. He could not enact further remedy.

Above, the grand hall of state was in flames, gone up like a torch to the roof towers. The foundations already crumpled, below. In moments, the whole lower stairwell would give way and collapse into crumbling ruin. Sulfin Evend could not do any more than continue his harried flight upward.

The men reached him. Hands fumbled and grabbed. Their touch woke his seared skin to agony. Sulfin Evend cried out, even as saving strength hauled him up, then dragged him along with his unconscious burden in a careening rush toward the doorway.

"That's the Blessed Prince himself!" someone cried. "Mercy on us, he's bloodied! What ill force attacked him?"

"Get him out!" Sulfin Evend managed to gasp. He could scarcely see, barely hear, while the wheeling roof seemed to plunge in a downward spiral upon him. Before faintness claimed him, he croaked, "Chain my liege in bed. Strap this knife to his skin. My orders, on pain of treason! No man is to take me away from his Grace's presence!"

Aftermath left the harsh, appalled silence that followed an earthshaking thunderclap. The blackened, raw scar of the grand hall of state still belched sullen fumaroles of black smoke. Ash sifted over Avenor's smudged rooftops, while the smoldering talk in the streets placed the blame on the Spinner of Darkness.

There would be war.

Clad in stark white with a discreet, buttoned collar masking his bandaged throat, Lysaer s'Ilessid confronted his Lord Commander, who lay swathed in dressings soaked with medicinal unguents to cool the raging sting of his burns.

"I will not deflect the course of this outrage," Lysaer declared with crisp sovereignty. "This nest of conspiracy at Avenor is cleaned, but connections remain under question. If corruption did not work hand in glove with the Spinner of Darkness, ties existed. Find my wife, or my son, and I'll prove them."

Prostrate on pillows, and sweating in discomfort, Sulfin Evend glared back. Hoarse, he still argued. "Etarra, first, liege. More trouble lurks there. If the corruption we just defeated has tapped into Raiett's massive network of spies, the connection you attribute to Shadow is falsehood." He held firm on that point. His harrowing acts in the stairwell granted his claim to that license. Yet the privilege did nothing to lessen the force of his liege's imperious displeasure.

Sulfin Evend did not waver. If his eyes were raw red, his wits stayed ice-cold.

A populace convinced that the heart of their regency had suffered an assaulting strike by raised sorcery might be blindly convinced to lay blame on a culprit. Frightened guilds would bring outlays of funds for fresh troops; a unified council would speed restoration. But here, in this sun-washed, taut chamber, alone, the Alliance commander would not play shell games with the truth. The palace page who had carried the false message was missing, with the thirteenth fugitive still somewhere at large.

"Your interests are being played against sorcery," Sulfin Evend insisted. "You must realize that, liege. A clan war and a siege of Alestron will undermine the Fellowship Sorcerers, then whittle away at the talent that safeguards the open countryside. Distrust of Ath's adepts will only serve the cult factions that just tried to lay claim to your talent for their use as a private weapon."

"Light has triumphed." The statement was too polished. Jewels threw off scintillant glints in the daylight, while the icy draft through the casement still wafted the flint reek of char. "Today, the streets of Avenor are safe." Lysaer moved, found a chair, and sat by the bedside. His pale grace caught the breath, for the spark of conviction that fuelled what seemed bedrock earnestness. "The plot to destroy my regency is disarmed, and your loyal defense will not be disowned or disparaged."

That lost love for a woman had been the stay that spared the staunch hero from immolation had gone unspoken. Yet Sulfin Evend's taut stillness spoke volumes.

"No disgrace will arise for our difference," said Lysaer. "A discharge with honor is yours, at a word."

Sulfin Evend held to his stark silence. He dared not state his view: that war against Fellowship interests, and clan presence, may have been the main thrust of the treasonous cabal's agenda. If so, then the cause of the Kralovir necromancers had been brilliantly served. When the Light of the Blessed raised arms against Shadow, an untold evil might bid for free rein to slip through the ragged breach.

"I will fight alone as need be," Lysaer promised. Such regal poise would never beg, even at risk of dismissing the sole, selfless friendship that touched his humanity. "You need not retain your Alliance rank if my service wears too heavily upon you."

While Sulfin Evend refused speech, those piercing blue eyes dared not waver. Lysaer pressed on. But his immaculate hands now had locked in his lap, while the trembling flicker of gold braid at his cuffs exposed the pent force of his feelings. "This much of your counsel I will take to heart. I promise to test my convictions. Once the hard evidence has been disclosed, woe betide Duke Bransian if his family has worked a covert betrayal against me. For Alestron's fortified strength is too powerful a resource to align with the powers of Darkness."

"I shall keep the command," Sulfin Evend rasped back. He had little choice. What he could not blunt, he must now strive to temper.

His oath to a Sorcerer married him to the land. With eyesight unsealed, he had glimpsed the deep mysteries preserved by the Fellowship's compact. Too late, he perceived the raw conflict: that the blinding effects of the curse that drove Lysaer could never be leashed in restraint. The Alliance ideology would not be laid to rest before the bastard half brother's blood stained the field. As a weapon, the geas of Desh-thiere offered a tool without parallel. The inflammatory words just unleashed by the Kralovir's machinations surely seeded a deadly design: for a wife in the custody of Ath's adepts, and a clan ally turned, and a son kept alive by no less than mystical sorcery, swords would be raised for the cause of the Light. With Arithon Teir's'Ffalenn as the dangled prize, Lysaer's flawed will would forge a new war host to launch another assault against Shadow.

Strapped by a blood oath and conflicted honor, the one man at the right hand of the avatar foresaw the tragic crux. The invidious play was poised to destroy Athera's bright powers of initiate mastery. For dark ends, the black cults wanted the world's greater mysteries torn asunder and broken.

"I should weep to take up the challenge," Sulfin Evend grated at length.

The words raised his liege's most dazzling smile. The gift of such trust was undeserved. Shamed to the quick, he ached for grief, that an upright man's justice should have been suborned to spearhead annihilation. Against curse-flawed charisma, and the risen star of a self-proclaimed avatar, Sulfin Evend became the last voice of sanity, wedged in the bleeding breach.

Late Winter 5671

Signatures

Midwinter to spring, when the passes were closed, all items crossing the continent followed the shipping that plied the prosperous, southern sea routes. As terminus for the silk caravans from Atchaz, whose raw bales were in prime demand, the port of Innish on the coast of Shand became the stewpot for breaking news. Dispatches moved with the commerce of trade. The factors who handled the lading of ships also passed the brisk traffic of state correspondence.

Though Fiark's obtuse network might be the least recognized, his unerring eye for profitable cargoes suggested the unusual depth and diversity of his contacts. Close-mouthed and quiet, his discretion was legend. He met with his hired captains in public and kept the family interests carried out by his sister the carefully guarded exception.

"Did you know," Feylind groused, "that they call you 'the clam?'" Sun-burned and raffish, and wearing a man's jerkin redolent of ship's tar and fish oil, she grinned, then perched herself with flagrant abandon upon the most comfortable brocade chair. "You owe me, for patience," she declared without fuss as her brother winced for his cushions. "I'll buy you two beers, *with* the fact, I didn't kick any nitpicking customs men off my decks into the harbor."

"That's because Teive kept your temper in hand," Fiark denounced, though not without sympathy. Since the Innish port officers had noses like weasels and a rabid aversion to contraband, the *Evenstar*'s logged movements were dealt a devouring scrutiny each time she hove into home port.

Feylind shrugged. "You'd think the damned vultures would tire of picking for carrion on a clean slate."

No thanks to her brother, for the obdurate fact that her registry stayed aboveboard. Her late trials had been no whit less, for that honesty. Long delay, a spoiled cargo, and an unscheduled holdover to refit storm damage at Southshire had ruffled the hair of the clerks. The customs keeper's grilling had been worse than cantankerous.

Fiark's wry delight stayed undimmed behind the privacy of shuttered windows. "They didn't much like the fact you switched shipyards?"

"Not!" Feylind snapped. The tapping search for hidden compartments had lasted two nerve-racking days. "The old outfitter's peeved that we took business elsewhere. And Southshire's so dazzled by sunwheel banners, I daren't explain that some Innish port rat with a grievance sold us out for a Koriani sigil meant to entrap the Master of Shadow."

"They wanted Fionn Areth," Fiark corrected, as always averse to high drama. "So you swore them to prostration and headaches instead?" His timely snatch saved his stacked papers, as his sister lounged back with intent to plant her sea-booted feet on his desk. "I know better than to think a few reddened ears might civilize your randy tongue."

"If oaths could snip bollocks, I'd have gelded the lot," Feylind agreed with bad humor. She delved into the satchel strapped at her waist. "So what have you done in redress?"

"Sent an inquiry." Fiark neatly fielded the catch as a sealed packet was tossed his way, granting discharge on the *Evenstar*'s bill of inspection. "I have a man, a desert tribe half-breed, who works an orange press at the docks. He'll track down your spy. Although I suspect he will find nothing worse than a shamefaced laborer caught up in a sworn oath of debt."

"I'd spit him, regardless. You'd better check out the excisemen here, too. One of them wouldn't look me in the eye the last time we got laced by a round of impounded inspection." Feylind trained her farsighted squint on the disarranged letters on Fiark's desk. "That's King Eldir's seal? Did he sign you a trade grant? He should, for the service you gave through the famine."

"You're digging for news?" Fiark raised his eyebrows. "Don't say! The Southshire yards were *that* starved for new gossip?"

His sister tossed back her wisped rope of hair, her shore manners in place: at sea, she would have spat over the rail in excoriating contempt. "That port has the Light in its eyes to the point where the adult population couldn't whack the butt end of itself with a stick! Teive's with the children so I could come here and badger you for the truth."

Fiark flicked the ship's papers. "Insurance, first," he stated point-blank. "Your happy rendezvous on the high seas happens to have lost me a cargo."

Feylind stretched forward and snatched up a pen. "I'll sign three blank sheets. You can copy the rest. The manifest's been inventoried five times at least, by the customs keeper's zealot accountants."

"They would inflate the values," Fiark said, douce. "I'd much rather settle this quietly."

Which careful comment made Feylind glance up. "You talk like a merchant expecting a war."

Fiark blinked. The uncanny way that his twin shared his mind was not always a comfort. While his sister uncapped the ink and scrawled signatures in her emphatic capitals, he recited the gist of the scandal that had all of the north taking pause—a blistering purge of Avenor's high council from a covert incursion of necromancy. Lysaer's summons in appeal to rectify damages had followed the shock to his dependent allies. Representatives were sent by Alliance-sworn mayors to help draft astringent new laws. These returned to their towns, clad in white robes and gold sashes, and quoting policy with assured serenity; of young talent recruited to speak for the Light, and a new order of priesthood expressly dedicated to expose the secretive workings of sorcery.

"This batch has arcane awareness guarding its works, fledgling seers declared for the Light. Far from shaken in faith, we're seeing complacent delusion. Lysaer's distrust of sorcery is fast becoming a rigid doctrine," Fiark finished, saddened. "After such a betrayal, which threatened a black nightmare, we are now promised that any man taking arms against Shadow will receive the reward of death without Darkness. Avenor's sent out a starry-eyed flock of recruiters—"

Feylind broke in, "Those fanatics who pitch sunwheel tents in the fields and hold meetings? Folk wander in out of friendly curiosity, and leave euphoric with strong wine and slogans."

"You heard about those?" Fiark said, surprised. "But that trend is recent!"

His sister chuckled. "Word's carried, and fast. The waterfront landlords are loudly displeased. Free drink dents their profits. The brothels haven't loved Lysaer for years. Not with the herb witches hounded from practice. The simples business has gone over to Koriathain, which change has raised venomous catfights. The order's always been greedy for girl children. Any tincture they brew to stay pregnancy goes at an extortionate rate." Paused for assessment, Feylind shook her head, serious. "What does King Eldir say? Is he worried that s'Ilessid evangelists are foaming too much at the mouth?"

"Not words. A crown warning." Fiark ticked the sealed paper. "Lysaer's priesthood's not welcome in Havish. Their ruling on sorcery threatens the compact, and their blithe stance on cult practice is dangerous."

Feylind moved, straightened, then lifted her crossed ankles and assumed the first sober posture her brother could remember, away from command on a ship's deck. "The High King would dare close the ports to this threat?"

Fiark winced. "It must lead to a royal edict eventually, but you're right. For now, the subject's too volatile. Lysaer himself does not preach violence.

Nevertheless, the view is widespread: the guild merchant who shares his wealth with the Blessed gets an armed pack of sunwheel dedicates to defend his interests from clan predation." He shot his neat cuffs, then searched out a sheet and read in direct quotation, *"'Teach them kindness, that the masses will learn to despise evil. Attach them to beauty, security, and allegiance, and they will grow to resent the least hint of a threatened intrusion. Let the Master of Shadow assume his due blame for all discord. Outrage will set the more deeply and grant us the strength of a fear-based response.'"*

"Whose lines?" Feylind gasped. "Ath on earth! What a bundle of cock-and-bull rhetoric!"

"Etarra's new Minister of the Peace at his finest." Fiark sighed. "A misnomer, truly. War's brewing. Not quickly. The Alliance of Light has to rebuild its troops. My contacts assure that Lysaer will move first to secure his runaway wife. He's launched stringent inquiries concerning a rumor that questions the fate of his son. Deeper intrigues are moving. I have inside word that the s'Brydion at Alestron may have been exposed. Their transgressions will be probed through diplomacy to mark time as the Light's new war host is mustered. If there won't be armed bloodshed next season, the tone at large is brewing toward resonant hatred. Is Prince Arithon warned of the danger that's rising against him?"

"Oh, he knows." Feylind frowned, conflicted by difficulty. How to explain the change in the man who had emerged from Kewar's trials alive? Liaison with an eagle who shapechanged to a Sorcerer kept Arithon tightly apprised. Yet against the shifting tangle of politics, even Davien dared not presume to foretell the Master of Shadow's response. "Who can guess what his Grace will do next? Let me tell you, Dakar squirmed like a moth in hot wax each time the subject was mentioned."

"Well, the question's not dangling," Fiark said, drained. He tossed the damning copy of Etarra's state document onto his disarranged desk. "The Prince of Rathain is coming ashore; I received his royal word yesterday. I've pleaded with him to stay at sea with the *Khetienn*, again and again, to no use. When his Grace decides he has unfinished business, no one alive can gainsay him."

"Not now, they couldn't. Nor Dharkaron himself, with his damnable Chariot and Horses." Feylind met her twin's splintering stare. Then she locked shaking hands, sucked a deep breath, and came to an inward decision. "You've got a cargo outbound for Havish? Then I beg you, send *Evenstar* west."

Fiark considered this, quiet. On matters that counted, he could become the very soul of considerate tact. "Teive doesn't like Arithon?"

A desperate, fast headshake came back in reply. For drawn moments, Feylind managed no speech at all, while the razor-thin mote that glanced through the cracked shutter splintered against the seal of the High King's distressed correspondence.

Feylind masked the sight behind her taut hands, then admitted, aggrieved, "Teive likes our difficult friend all too well. Honest as pig iron about it, forbye!" Defeat, when it came, was all bitterness, tempered by an ineffable sorrow. "So I'll choose life, for both of us. I don't want my mate pulped, or my children left parentless. Not for one of us speaking our mind in the breach to these packs of Light-blinded fanatics!"

Late Winter 5671

Movements

In the dark of the moon, cowled figures crouch over a fire, savoring the flesh of a slaughtered page, while the fifth, starved lean from an overland flight, speaks of colleagues, whose covert roles as priests of the Light in Rathain must shortly fall into jeopardy: "Two are gambits, planted as an intentional sacrifice to Fellowship intervention. The other insinuates his cabal behind Etarra's new-warded walls. In Asandir's absence, he'll be forewarned should Sethvir dispatch a discorporate colleague to disturb him beforetime..."

As sun glares off the icy mire at Mirthlvain, and streaming mists mantle the lake, the master spellbinder, Verrain, presents his regrets to the guests who have wintered with him at the fortress: the last leg of Princess Ellaine's journey to Spire must be delayed since the Sorcerer, Traithe, expected as escort, is deferred by a more urgent errand to Atwood...

On the same day a small pleasure sloop casts her towline and charts a course toward the southcoast mainland, a caravan bearing a guild shipment of woven silk leaves Sanshevas for export at Southshire, at the last minute reinforced by the mayor's train, bearing the tribute gold gathered to bolster the cause of the Light...

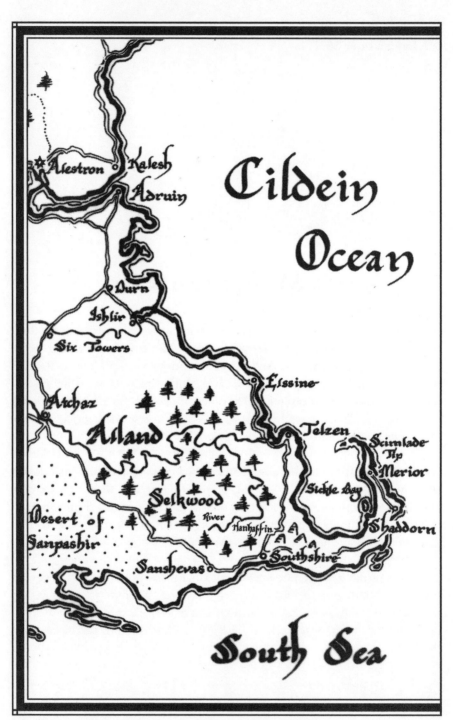

Alland and Southcoast of Shand

IX. Alland

The small sloop made her landfall just before dawn, disembarked her five passengers, then put back to sea, still under cover of darkness. The party delivered to Shand's southern shore slipped unnoticed down a small estuary. To avoid leaving tracks, they bypassed the dunes and breasted the reed beds, plowing through clouds of bloodsucking insects as they waded the lead pools of the salt marsh. Dripping, they crossed the packed earth of the trade road, unseen by the galloping couriers bearing dispatches west through the gloom. Daybreak found them under the shadowed black pines that marked the free wilds of Alland. There, no matter how quiet their step, their presence came under the piercing review of the clan scouts who guarded Selkwood.

Perhaps warned by the change in the chorus of birdsong, loud under the dappled sunrise, the cloaked figure leading them signaled a halt. "Let me handle this," he murmured to the paired men-at-arms who hovered in step at his back. To another muffled companion behind, he repeated his earlier warning. "Whatever occurs, keep your hands off your swords. The archers here are stealthy as cats. Depend on the fact we're surrounded."

While the fat, huffing laggard scratched his welted arms, the speaker stepped away from his fellows, alone. His trilling whistle signaled the cordon of scouts, concealed in the windless forest. Then he cast off his hood. Brazen, he stood in the burgeoning daylight, though his black hair and sharp, angled features were hunted the breadth of the continent.

Unconcerned for the bounty promised in gold for his body, living or dead, he announced, "Lord Erlien was told to expect me."

"Your Grace of Rathain?" someone ventured in cautious response from a nearby screening of pine boughs.

"None other." Poised, yet not smiling, Arithon dropped his cloak. Clad in hose, wet suede boots, and a nondescript jerkin, he was not armed. Though the Paravian blade would have affirmed his identity, his sheathed weapon and baldric had been left in the hands of his flaxen-haired liegeman.

The signal was silent. But twenty archers in plain leathers emerged from the wood with scarcely a rustle of evergreen. Mostly men, but not all; in clan fashion, some of the young women bore arms. Their bows were nocked with plain arrows and primed to be drawn at fast notice. Bristled with swords, long knives, and packed quivers, the party was winter lean and fit as a wolf pack gathered to hunt down rough quarry.

"I've seen headhunters carry less bloodthirsty steel," said Arithon in tacit greeting. Apparently careless, he hooked up his mantle and shook out the chaff of caught pine needles.

His nonchalant manner did not ease strained diplomacy. The bearded scout who stepped to the fore raked his person with tigerish appraisal. He noted the presence of the made double. His wary glance jumped as Dakar stirred behind. But the fat prophet only raised placating hands and parked his panting bulk on a deadfall.

Mindful of a past hot reception dealt him by the High Earl of Alland, Arithon draped the cloak back over his frame and offered his upturned wrist. "What must I do to convince you I'm honest, or is Erlien lining his treasury for bounty gold?"

The circle of archers remained at the ready, while their spokesman accepted the courtesy. "Nothing so shady as double cross, your Grace, though the price on your head defies reason." The exchanged clasp of amity was brisk. "This foray's been pulled off of an ambush gone bad. We're moving north, and in a smart hurry. The road will be crawling with townsmen by noon. Jumpy as walleyed ponies, the lot. They're wont to shoot crossbolts at bushes through each twitching change in the breeze."

Arithon raised his eyebrows. "The bullion train out of Atchaz, I hope? Or else, Ath on earth, I should worry in fact? It's Erlien's avarice after all?"

The scout loosened to wry laughter. "Damn the Light's tribute. We were sent to snatch silk. Would've gotten it, too! Except the forsaken guild caravan chose to join up with the mayor's guard at Sanshevas. We still could have raided. Mind you, the goods would have gained a few bloodstains. We're not squeamish, your Grace. But the cloth's for a wedding. Lord Erlien wanted it clean."

"No titles," said Arithon. "The formality's tiresome, and Dakar's too hot to stay thirsting for beer on a pine log."

Vhandon and Talvish were beckoned forward and introduced. Throughout, the taut scouts held their stance with raised bows. If they marveled, wide-eyed, at

Fionn Areth's resemblance, their predator's vigilance kept Arithon's paired liegemen drawn to the edge of snapped nerves. Caught in between, the Mad Prophet strove to disarm the cranked mood of hostility. "Who's marrying? Not Erlien."

While the female scouts masked their reproving grins, the touchy clan spokesman affirmed, "Not Erlien." His following gesture relaxed the scouts. Through the rustle as nocked arrows were slipped from gut strings, he expounded, "Our High Earl's got mistresses who'd have his head if he favored one woman over the rest. They've all borne him children. It's his youngest son, Kyrialt, whose saucy wench has demanded a bride-gift of silk."

From the sidelines, another scout snipped, "The High Earl's sprig is a feisty stud, to think he'll hobble that vixen's feckless temperament!"

"She's a gamine?" asked Arithon, rapt as he sized up the company Shand's High Earl had dispatched to meet him. "You'd think a few bloodstains would heighten the sport."

The onlooking clanborn turned their heads, fast.

"Sport, is it?" Lithe and dark, and hackled to peppery pride, their spokesman narrowed his nailing regard. He had piercing eyes. Gray as pressed ice, they fixed on the prince. "With a round hundred lancers in the vanguard alone? Sixty-four foot, the best half packing crossbows. That's without counting the outriders consigned with the caravan guard. Their trackers wear headhunter's badges from Ganish. They go nowhere without four dozen diligent fellows scouring the brush on the flanks at the front and rear. Erlien mentioned that you could be difficult. But how many dead would a visiting prince care to bring to the feast on the eve of his lordship's son's wedding?"

Dakar remarked from the sidelines, "Even for bullion, that many men seems an excessive protection." A fresh tear in his breeches had made him reappraise the wisdom of sitting on deadfalls. Sidled in closer, he overheard the exchange with ever-increasing suspicion. He knew that bear-baiting style too well; had observed too many men being expertly tuned for who knew what guileful purpose.

"Try amethysts," said Arithon, stripped of smiling charm. "Mined from the Tiriacs by a rogue prospector who neglected to honor the principles of land rights. Difficult, surely? And Lord Erlien's charge, since the offender has crossed his ill-gotten gains into Shand."

"By Ath! How'd you know this?" Flustered to shock, the scout spokesman reddened.

The seething mutters exchanged by his company gave rise to a dissident voice. "There's a crook in the road not two leagues distant that we could have primed with an ambush. Looted minerals, you say? For this, we'd have dug a pit trap with stakes, scalpers with crossbows or not!"

"Leash that! We're too sorely outnumbered." To the prince's gadding comment, the scout spokesman explained, "Our crowd of crack bowmen was sent back to camp. We could thwart the horsemen through a covert strike from the bluff. But without heavy cover and dense flights of arrows in support, we'd be dead meat the moment we moved onto the roadway to rifle the carts."

The affable interest on Arithon's features chased a grue through Dakar's bones. Talvish and Vhandon stirred, touched uneasy, which in turn cued Fionn Areth.

"These guards," pressed the Master of Shadow, conversational. "Do they travel in state?"

To his left, a wiry scout bowman spat. "With the tribute chests for the Light, bound to Southshire? You're kidding. They're flagged and tasseled and prinked for the ballroom, except the damned weapons are lethal."

The threatened smile gave rise to a chuckle that caught the clan reivers aback. "I'd hand you that silk," said Rathain's brash prince. "And the looted stones, too, without anyone pricking a finger. Are you up to the challenge?"

The lead scout stared back, breathless. "The bride's name is Glendien, and she'll hack your bollocks to mincemeat for sure." He eyed the slight frame of the royal before him, still trying to measure the fitness beneath the unassuming, loose shirt. "That's if Kyrialt doesn't dismember you first, for starting a war on his wedding day."

"No deaths," promised Arithon. "Every townsman who marched from Sanshevas this morning will be left hale enough to salve his disgrace in the arms of the harlots at Southshire."

The clan spokesman shifted his piercing regard. To Vhandon, whose graying hair and old scars suggested more sober experience, he questioned, "Your liege is delirious?"

"Moonstruck? Not in this case." The veteran swordsman nodded toward Talvish, whose long fingers were tapping a fretful tattoo on the held scabbard of Arithon's sword. "We were Duke Bransian's, before we swore oath to Rathain. Though we serve here by choice, the Sorcerer Luhaine was the one who passed us the appeal for the violation done in the Tiriacs. Our liege plans to answer. If you don't come along, I can assure you, he's committed enough to finish the errand alone."

Talvish broke in, offhandedly mocking. "As you see, he's born reckless, and mettlesome, besides. Why leave him to claim all the glory?"

Which vaunted dare, no young creature from Alland could pass off. Not in front of five cheeky foreigners whose pressuring taunts tossed them the rank provocation. The clan spokesman returned a caustic grin. "West," he said briskly. "Better not regret. If the fat prophet lags, we'll have no choice but to leave him."

The company of scouts coalesced and moved out, swift as wraiths through the resinous shade of the forest. Fionn Areth earned their jeering comment as his footfalls snapped twigs, with Talvish's tirades in his defense giving even their raffish tongues pause. Arithon's tread made no sound on the matted needles, and his eyes, like sheared emerald, watched everything.

"Why are you conniving?" Dakar pressured point-blank. A low branch hooked his beard. He clawed the sprig off, puffing at a short-strided trot in his effort to stay abreast.

The Prince of Rathain flashed him a fathomless glance. The quiet in him was a fearsome force since his return from the maze under Kewar. Deepened into a secretive well, his presence seemed immutable as the patriarch pines, whose moss hoary trunks wore a silence to outlast the snags of mortality. "A bride-gift," was Arithon's simplistic reply. But from him, such self-honesty always raised far more goading questions than answers.

If the rushed pace was meant to defuse the madcap thrust of the enterprise, the tactic fell short. The prince's two liegemen proved as fit as steel nails, and his young double, too pridefully game to give way. Dakar stayed the course from tenacious concern for the havoc he hoped to subdue. Arithon himself kept his jocular spirits. The scurrilous tales he shared with the clan archers provoked groans, which devolved into breathless, choked laughter.

"A damned masterbard's memory," Dakar groused, sorely tried, his arms crossed to clamp down a chuckle. Even to his jaundiced ear, the collection of gossip was dazzling.

Wiser than before, Fionn Areth said nothing. Padding at heel behind Vhandon and Talvish, he watched the slight man who wore his mirrored face use bold humor to refigure the archers' distrust. The method held a certain deft familiarity. With engaging skill, Arithon tried the Shandian scouts, sparking their differences of character and temperament much as he had done with the *Evenstar*'s sail crew. His teasing barbs, in fact, were not playful. Inside an hour, he must weave this band's loyalty into a force that would risk life and limb at a word.

For the smallest misjudgment must surely tempt fate; the mistake enacted by one hesitation would bring down the hornet's nest on them. Cold sober amid the snatched bursts of hilarity, Vhandon admitted the odds of assaulting the caravan were tantamount to a suicide. He did not appear unduly concerned, which drew tacit inquiry from one of the female archers.

"This isn't about killing," Talvish agreed. "Yon prince has his ways. He'll shred your nerves, easily, six times in a day. But he doesn't go back on his promises."

They reached the sand bluffs with an hour to spare, a reckoning that would be reliable. Selkwood's clansmen knew the habits of every road master plying the coast road from Sanshevas to Southshire. Sprawled in the shaded brush at the crest, and avid as weasels awaiting their moment to fall on the boastful fox, they watched Arithon s'Ffalenn size up the terrain. They noted the fact he took nothing for granted, but tested the dry, crumbled slope for assurance the footing would be a hindrance to horseflesh. His prowling assessed the sun angle and vantage, then measured the curve of the roadbed below. Immersed in their bristling, insular silence, the scouts approved: his activity did not hush the scrape of the crickets. His soft step left the weeds undisturbed.

The clan spokesman dispatched a fleet messenger and another hidden observer, with instructions to keep watch past the western rise. Then he hooked a brown, callused thumb through his belt, obstructively primed to thrash every detail of the prince's forthcoming deployment.

Contrariwise, Arithon suggested the interim amusement of a high-stakes contest of darts.

The archers were thunderstruck. Arrived on location, they expected the tight planning that trademarked a successful foray. Shown this dismissive, frivolous attitude, their morale devolved to disgust. The Master of Shadow, oblivious, began naming tree knots for targets. Head bare, cloak discarded, he paced out distances and set the lines. Talvish looked on with impervious jade eyes. Of Vhandon, standing with folded arms, somebody asked, breathless, if his Grace was light-witted, or drunk.

A splutter of laughter greeted the jibe.

Arithon gave back his effusive amusement. "A splendid idea, if we had any beer. Perhaps we should start? Or we won't have the time to settle our bets on the champion." From inside his jerkin, he produced a wrapped bundle, which, unrolled, contained twelve feathered darts. He passed three to Fionn Areth. "First round at ten yards. Show these infants what fiber you're made of?"

His double flushed with surprise and accepted. Fionn's style turned out to be enviously precise. Shown a calm disregard for their festering contempt, and left with a score that would tax the steadiest eye of their favorite, the scouts joined the match out of devilment. Their first man threw well, and their second, still better. Pitched to simmering curiosity, their spokesman held back. He would wait to see how this prince caught their backlash when the caravan appeared with its escort of three hundred strong.

Fionn Areth lost at darts when the winded lookout arrived to announce the approach of the cavalcade, and a negligent throw by Rathain's prince as he turned, capped the Araethurian's score by a point. The nettled clansmen closed in a tight ring, as the quarry's deployment was mapped in detail. Arithon heard. His dark head stayed bent, his downturned gaze fixed on the ground without focus. Dakar, who owned mage-sight, saw past daft distraction and noted a man who listened with more than his five mortal senses.

"Watch out for the lancers. They're hot, but not drowsy," the impertinent runner summed up. "Their mounts still act fresh. The stinging flies will be keeping them restive, never mind that the league out of Ganish won't hire themselves out to nursemaid a trained pack of fools."

Arithon stirred. "Ten to the cartload with a round fifty, slogging at head and tail. The league scouts are the problem. Dakar, you'll divert them? Something petty that sends them astray. Sun in the eyes? A snakes' den in the rocks? I won't need even ten minutes."

If mirth still threatened the ghost of a smile, the crisp phrasing redressed the earlier lack of authority. Nor had the contest at darts, after all, been a gambit launched out of whimsy. The six clansmen ranked behind Fionn Areth found themselves called out in succession. Each was issued two darts and told to seek a concealed position at spaced intervals above the highway. There, they would wait upon Arithon's signal.

"Pink the mules where your missiles will cause the least harm. Your task is to incite pandemonium, then to pull back. Under no circumstance will you risk being seen," Arithon finished off, firm. "If one of the lancers throws straight with a knife, I won't drag a carcass where a strong back could have been better used to haul booty."

Released to their posts, the dartmen slipped away through the scrub fringing the rim of the bluff.

The Prince of Rathain made his last dispositions. "Fionn, your sword will guard Dakar's back. Will someone loan Vhandon and Talvish a bow? They'll shoot to wound on the odd chance any headhunters blunder through the Mad Prophet's spelled screen of diversion."

The assigned parties moved out, which sensible bent began to appease the scout spokesman's outraged sensibilities. Rathain's sworn liegemen could be trusted to defend their own. In positions that carried the most critical risks, this prince had not placed his casual reliance upon strangers sized up through banter. The avid pause hung. Wolves on a scent, the rest of Alland's clan company awaited the follow-up plan for the raid.

Yet the Prince of Rathain bestowed no more orders.

The scouts shifted, impatient. They exchanged pointed glances. A few fingered their knives as no further development happened. Arithon stepped to the edge of the bluff without another word spoken. There, he settled, his weathered jerkin melding his form into the patched shade of a thicket.

Left at a loss, the clan spokesman closed in and pushed the exasperated question of tactics. "A dozen target darts in some mules will leave us the prey of three hundred enraged men-at-arms." As his pique raised no impact, he flushed slowly scarlet. "If you've evolved a supporting plan, we're waiting to hear before the damned vanguard's on top of us!"

"Catch the spoils," said Arithon. Unswerving, his gaze remained on the road. "You'll need your hands free. The method at hand being an untried experiment, the silk you've promised to Kyrialt's bride might wind up wedged in the treetops."

"Dharkaron's black vengeance!" the clan spokesman ranted. "For *this* I've left my best bowmen to risk a fatal encounter with scalpers?"

"Risk?" Arithon faced around and encompassed the scouts, now formed into a mutinous cordon. Slightly made, drawn erect, his hands loose at his sides, he displayed unconcern that verged upon lethal insult. "Your initial objection was bloodshed, I thought? My word as given, those terms won't be compromised."

Fenced in by stiff silence, the Master of Shadow raised his eyebrows. "Mounted lancers and men-at-arms traveling in state will not scale a sand scarp for the sake of a few jabbed draft teams. Your companions were told to stay outside harm's way. Do you fear they might compromise orders?"

"What does such a prank have to do with lifting secured goods from the hands of an armed division?" The clan spokesman forestalled several hotheaded scouts, who shoved in a murderous thrust forward. Just as openly cross, he let fly in contempt. "Your Grace. You cannot expect our score of bowmen to hold open the bleeding breach."

"I don't." Arithon's brazen calm was raw flame, to raise hackles and spark conflagration. "Unless you wish yourselves martyred for no reason at all, you will leave the armed townsmen to me."

"Arrogant upstart!" The incensed spokesman would end the charade. Prepared to allow his chafed company to draw steel, he issued his final warning. "You are dangerous, prince! I swear by the forebears who hallowed my lineage, royal bastard or not, the protection you offer is folly. Call off the raid. Stand down and disarm. Or I will cut you off at the knees as a creature who's lost to insanity!"

"Do that!" cracked Arithon. "For I need to know *now* whether Erlien's finest have the nerve I will need to curb a false religion without starting a massacre. How long do you think your clans can survive the unified onslaught of Lysaer's new breed of fanatics? Today, I admit, we're redeeming poached crystals. Tomorrow, next week, the stakes are no less than the blood heritage of your families. We are talking the future fate of the free wilds that uphold the compact in Shand."

The clan spokesman gaped, while his crowding companions looked on in dazed shock.

"Please do as I say?" No longer smiling, or harmless; not anything less than an initiate master clothed in the force of his self-aware presence, Rathain's prince dropped his disarming pretense. "Leave me to my work. Or your dartmen will be unsupported *in fact*. Let that happen, my word as my life, I will call in my friends, turn my back on your High Earl, and forget this place ever existed."

*   *   *

Unaware that one man was their self-proclaimed equal, the sunwheel lancers and the company of foot hired as escort to Southshire led the caravan around the bend. The risen sun cut the humid air like ruled brass. Hot in their state finery, and bedeviled by flies, the mounted troop tussled with sidling mounts. If their lance pennons frayed in the stiffening sea breeze, the tips wore a razor-edged polish. Ganish league's trackers prowled, hungry for scalps. Since their pay shares were kept deliberately lean, the dearth of earned bounties made their patrol of the thicketed verges dead keen.

With the last fifteen leagues and a straight road before them, the hardened men guarding the Light's gathered tribute breathed the flat tang of stirred dust. They spoke softly and stayed sharp. A veteran riding the wilds by Selkwood well knew not to slacken his reins. Because of the bullion, the drays were mule-drawn. The loads were kept light to hasten the pace, an advantage not shared by an ox train.

"Move on," the road master exhorted the drivers. "Push those teams. Keep them going!"

The lancers held to their nervous formation, given the inauspicious lay of the land. Low sun cast a scintillant glare through the brush at the rim of a sandy bluff. The dazzle shone from buffed helms and gold braid, with the panoply of crested saddlecloths and surcoats a gaudy welter that muddled the eyes.

A jay called in the scrub. A louder one answered. The chief tracker from Ganish had reported no sign of clan presence, which only whetted the road master's jumpy unease. Ruffled by the same wary instinct, the lance captain raised his voice and reordered his mounted lines. The wagons were pinched inside his bristling defense when the first of the mules flung up its head, brayed, and bolted pell-mell down the highway.

The guard riding nearest did not see the dart embedded in its left haunch. He was yelling, doused under his flapping surcoat, which had jerked itself free of his belt, and blanketed his face and head. The spire on his helm had poked through, with the fabric pinned like a tent. His shrieks emerged, muffled. As he clawed at crazed clothing, his mount shied hard sideward, and crashed through the ranks of his fellows. The formation collapsed to a clattered snarl of lances. The cloth-bundled victim fell off.

"Mind your damned lines!" the troop captain screamed. His mount backed and sidled, and snorted with nerves. While fighting the reins, he had time to notice that, length and breadth of his column, the upset was disastrously spreading.

Every third man seemed beset by his clothing, and every horse snapped and kicked as though air itself turned and badgered its sweated flanks. Then his seasoned mare bucked. He was rammed from behind by a four-in-hand team, rampaging in stampede. The wagon dragged after them, shorn of its wheels. Its bashed undercarriage furrowed the road like a plow, and its sprung planks belched trade goods helter-skelter. The ruckus proved too much for his horse, which skittered, then bolted in panic. Tossed in an ignominious heap, then forced to roll into a thorn brake to escape being trampled, the troop captain reached for his horn with intent to rally his dismembered troop. The drill call was a loss. The brass instrument had been flattened beneath his mailed hip, and the mouthpiece was jammed full of gravel.

Standing again, he bellowed, in vain. A choking dust spiraled up on the breeze. Pandemonium milled all about him. Men's voices unraveled to yelps and shrieked curses. Chaos worsened from moment to moment. The lance captain craned his neck, seeking one mounted rider, or the capture of a loose horse. He was met instead by three staggering cart wheels bearing down on a collision course.

"Damn things are possessed!" his lieutenant's cry warned him.

Past recourse, the captain dived flat in the ditch to escape becoming mown down.

"Fiends!" the beleaguered road master howled. "The talisman's failed! Lost its charge, or went wrong. Now we're plague struck!"

Around him, beset drivers yanked in vain on their reins. Their veering mule teams locked iron mouths. Eyes rolling, the beasts entangled themselves and kicked up their heels, snapping traces. Some snarled in knots and jostled their way off the road. Drays slammed into trees. Others were gutted, hung up on bushes and rocks. One after another, more vehicles wrecked. With disconcerting intelligence, the nimble sprites were still jerking the linchpins from revolving wheel hubs. Wagon beds tilted. Dropped axles gouged earth. The hard slew of the impacts sprung the pegged boards and broke the fastenings holding the tailgates. Tarpaulins tore, and stacked bolts tumbled out, burst their ties, and disgorged a rainbow cascade of fine silk.

Bedlam reigned. Length and breadth of the roadway, the caravan unraveled as fast as a snag in knit wool. Unshackled wheels bowled over the foot troops. Surcoats wrapped wrists and fouled weapons. Blinded men snarled and cursed. Snared beyond remedy, they drew their edged weapons, hacking until their fiend-possessed finery subsided in twitching shreds. Those naked few who stripped to win free raced to catch the crazed mules. One step, or three, they soon toppled over, tripped up by the unreeled fabric. The dumped tribute chests had smashed into splinters and kindling. Coin sacks untied, and the air clinked and flashed as the *iyats* snatched up their contents. The liberated bullion spun into a glittering swarm and scattered into the scrub.

Ballroom sarcenets flapped like flags and festooned the verges. Pink, pastel, and puce, draped animals bucked, while their gadded handlers punched and spat irate oaths through brocades. Batting tucks and pinched ruffles, or leaping ripped harness straps, the entire troop of veteran guards were thrashed helpless.

No one noticed as some of the cloth bolts sailed upward, still neatly bound in their ties. Like the departed coin, the goods crested the sand bluff and vanished from sight, followed, spinning, by the strongbox holding the Tiriac amethysts.

Above, scarcely able to stifle whooped laughter, the clan scouts from Alland raced to and fro, their shirts stripped off to bag bullion. Others pounced to capture the errant rolls of white silk wheeling airborne over their heads.

At Arithon's side, their jubilant spokesman surveyed the mussed snarl left of the caravan, whose beasts and men, provender and haulage, lay scattered amid a whirlwind morass of ripped shreds. "They'll surely regret they were traveling in state," he gasped, choking back his amusement. "Why take the white silk adorned with gold tinsel? Do you have a source with a use for it?"

"Another day's plan," Rathain's prince admitted, engrossed where he knelt, hand thrust in a sack placed before him. By now adept at imprinting his will, he blew on his knuckles. "You're not tired of the fun?" He released another handful of *iyats* to disorient a party of crossbowmen who had somehow kept charge of their weapons. "Did I hear mention that Kyrialt's bride wished to be married in scarlet?"

The clan spokesman shrugged. "She's said her man gets no welcome in bed if he can't keep pace with her passion. The red cloth seemed a fitting retort. Those fiends are still taking your detailed instructions?"

"Most of the time. Like the odd ninth wave, they sometimes defect." Peering askance through the sheltering thicket, Arithon located an intact bolt the appropriate shade of vermilion. He dispatched another fiend to go fetch. It did not turn errant. His chosen prize arose from the ground, swooped a circle, then zigzagged, and finally lofted over his head.

While the scouts behind scrambled to catch the bride's gift, the Master of Shadow tipped a nod toward his feet. "These were more difficult. Would you care to collect them? The winners deserve a keepsake for their efforts, which I'd say were no less than splendid."

The clan spokesman glanced down and saw the impossible: twelve bloodied darts lately retrieved from the hurtling flanks of the mules. "By Ath, you'll have pulled off this raid, and left not a telltale trace of hard evidence!"

"I scarcely expect the silk will be missed until someone sits up and takes inventory," Arithon admitted, nonplussed. Deprecation at odds with his piercing glance, he secured his odd sack with its volatile contents. "I think we should leave, fast as scuttling rats."

This time, the clan spokesman's smile was genuine. "You're expecting they'll notice the tribute is gone the moment they start to regroup? No one's dead. They can quarter the forest for *iyats* all night, with nary a wee coin to show for it."

Wormed out of the brush in time to meet Dakar, just returned, with Fionn Areth trailing behind, Arithon swiped a runner of briar from his sleeve. "All accounted?" he asked, quiet. "No bagged scalps for Ganish?"

The Mad Prophet mopped his soaked face, and huffed, "There could be, if we don't pull out quick with no tracks."

Fionn Areth, cheeks glowing, seemed more effusive. "Vhandon and Talvish had bets with the scouts. We'd better camp in a secure clearing, they said, so they can get drunk and collect on their winnings."

The clan spokesman stared, rendered owlishly speechless until the mismatched pair of liegemen strode in. Though hemmed by the pack of disgruntled dartmen, Talvish's inquisitive jade eyes stayed half-lidded. The more stolid Vhandon looked deadpan.

Behind the grasslander's innocent words, the *caithdein*'s picked emissary understood that his forestborn scouts were being exquisitely mocked. Beyond doubt, their skilled prowess had been upstaged by unmerciful cunning and sorcery.

In an atmosphere grown too corrosively smug, the royal who held the two liegemen's loyalty spoke first. "I'd sell that pair out, if we weren't overburdened with fripperies. Who's left to handle a knife in defense?"

The clan spokesman retorted without humor as the two swordsmen stepped close, a faultless guard at their prince's shoulders. "You want to escape with your carefree necks? Who else do you have to haul your wealth out of here, unless my men act as your pack mules?"

"But I do need your men." The Prince of Rathain succumbed to a hitched breath that stifled indecorous laughter. "Relax," he gasped. "My brief foray is finished. You don't think there's bound to be murder to pay?"

The clan spokesman paused. Then he folded in half, wrecked to tears by the prince's double entendre. Empty-handed at Southshire, a crack troop of lancers and their company of foot would be forced to explain how they had misplaced the Light's tribute.

"A plague of rogue *iyats*?" The young clansman wheezed, helpless. "Ath save the poor fools from an undying shame. They'll face jail and certain dishonor. Ganish league's like to gut them for smearing their upstanding character. Fatemaster's pity! In that captain's shoes, I'd be quartering these forsaken bluffs until I was half-starved and ragged!"

"Surely." Arithon grinned. "On top of the fact they'll be questioned as thieves, they've got to weather their public arrival exposed in a wretched state of undress." He flung out an arm, helped the shattered clan spokesman erect and on stumbling course toward the forest. "By all means, have your scouts guide us safely through Selkwood. In friendship, we'll drink to white silk and gold, and the glory of discord sown through the ranks of the Light."

* * *

Lord Erlien s'Taleyn, High Earl of Alland and oathsworn *caithdein* of Shand, was a strapping bear of a man who lived for combative aggression. Within the close grotto used for winter quarters, he could barely stand without bending his neck. The hair Rathain's prince would remember as dark, licked with silver, now gleamed snowy white in the rush-lit gloom.

Turquoise eyes that bit like clear sky, the passage of years had not changed. Still fit in trim clothes, just as keen to provoke, the chieftain whose rule enforced old law in Selkwood searched the party of guests just delivered by the picked spokesman he had dispatched with his escort of scouts. That young man's rankled frown was expected; the other, a masterpiece untouched by time, walked in and stared at his host.

Mouth hung open, he looked like a creature out of sorts with his natural skin.

Less nervy, perhaps stockier, he peered upward. The top of his seal head just barely reached the black pearl strung on the thong at Lord Erlien's collarbone.

Thrilled by the instinct that tagged easy prey, the High Earl of Alland hiked a booted leg over the tabletop, perched, and extended his hand. The fingers he offered were sword-callused horn. The force of his grip strangled dignity.

The creature he tried masked a desperate wince, then stood nursing his savaged forearm.

"Nary the same welcome you've brought back to Alland," the High Earl announced with contempt. His prowling glance already dismissive, he watched the rest of the royal party squeeze in through the grotto's entry. Two men-at-arms, the fat, puffing prophet once trained by Asandir, and another, whose face was alike to the one he had just abrasively greeted.

Except this man's carriage was quicksilver and light, unchanged, after all, from the searing encounter over crossed sword blades twenty-six years ago. Lord Erlien beheld the same vision: a grace that could murder packed into a diminutive frame that stood four fingers shorter than the replica standing before him.

"By Ath!" The earl's beard cracked to a carnivore's grin. "For a second I thought I could not tell the imposter. Does your half brother know there are *two* of you? He'll split himself once he hears. No doubt that's precisely what you intend?"

Arithon Teir's'Ffalenn smiled in the same feral vein. He paused beyond reach of that badgering wrist shake, though this pass, he was not cut and bleeding. "The work isn't mine. The Koriathain wrought plans with my capture in mind, and the effect is unfortunately permanent." He went on to introduce the stunned grasslands herder to the most powerful authority in Shand.

"The High Earl bites with all of his teeth. The best tactic you have is to smile, then guard your back like the sting on the hornet."

"Runt insolence," the High Earl declared, never laughing. Firsthand impact of Arithon's longevity scarcely hazed his tough nerves. The eyes of the man, *so different*, were what vexed. Here walked a contained self-awareness to freeze heat, or stun silence from kindled aggression. "Don't claim you've come back to grace my son's wedding."

"He would spurn my lyranthe?" Arithon's regard stayed wide-lashed and open. "Then I've brought him red silk as a poor consolation."

"Sopped in how much blood?" Erlien shoved bolt upright and towered. "You high-handed meddler! I called that raid off! For scratching the varnish on one of those tribute chests, you're asking to get my outlying camps run down and slaughtered for scalps."

That moment, an upsurge of commotion from behind, several jubilant scouts from the company shoved through. They all talked at once. The spokes-man elbowed his randy fellows aside, also shouting to make himself heard through their clamor. The wild tale of the plunder on the Southshire road emerged in a cacophony of entangled phrases.

Lord Erlien banged his fist and demanded the tale twice. Assured that no scout took a wound, and no headhunters chased in hot vengeance, he bent his rampant displeasure aside and dissected the Master of Shadow. "*Iyats.*" He coughed back an incredulous chuckle. "That's novel. Ath above, you'll need worse. I presume you're informed of the grandiose scheme Avenor is raising against you?"

"Every dazzling detail?" Arithon back-stepped, and reclaimed his sword from the custody of his blond liegeman. Head bent as his fingers rebuckled his baldric, he said, tired, "I'm amazed there's a man or a woman alive who was born with the blind wits to swallow it."

Erlien grunted. His wrestler's arm reached the shelf where his papers were stored, fished through a sheaf of guild inventory lists, then drew out a state missive with ostentatious gilt ribbons. He passed over the document, silent.

Arithon's features stayed blank as he read. The trapped light in the emerald set into his sword hilt burned a baleful green, never trembling. He absorbed the last line, skipped to the flourished signature, then flipped the leaf over and perused the wax seals.

"I should be impressed?" he commented finally. "World renowned for foul works and mayhem, whether I practice such doctrine, or not? A shame. Shown such vulgar taste, what man with a mind would scarcely wallow to seek further clarity? Sweet faith, bliss, and bathos, it's an execrable drama. Never mind that the theological concepts are glorified platitudes sprung out of lies."

"Why have you returned?" Locked in moist rock and gloom, that pe-remptory inquiry called due a past debt, left as a torn thread of iniquity: once before, Rathain's prince had asked the grace of an audience. That time, with no courtesy and no thanks for the law-bound gift of support, or the backing of Shand's steadfast clans, he had been uncivil, and slipped off like a felon to fight his campaign in the barrens of Vastmark.

Caithdein to a realm whose best strength had been spurned, the High Earl's demand brooked no apology. "What will you do?"

"About this religion designed for my downfall?" Arithon cast the creased parchment aside. The froth of sarcasm melted away. Bone and flesh, what stood poised was an initiate master, whose grasp of the mysteries was no figment at all, but the *living* grace of what lay at the core of clan destiny, and the very marrow of the Fellowship Sorcerers' guardianship. "I intend to oppose this false god with every resource set into my hands. Survive or not, fail or fall short, I will stop this grand edifice of the Light and its splintering disillusionment. If I can."

Lord Erlien weighed that claim through a harsh, settled stillness. Then he glanced from the prince pinned before his review and addressed the young clan scout dispatched as his primary spokesman. "Kyrialt, would you follow this man's lead?"

The vivid person revealed as the High Earl's blood son returned a spirited shrug. "Father, the issue's a moot point. Because with polite disregard for your orders, in fact, we already have."

Arithon's gaze wavered. As though brushed by a fleeting instant of dizziness, he braced an arm to the wall in support.

That moment, while some internal landscape threatened to shatter him like hollow glass, the High Earl of Alland made up his mind. "Your Grace, I shall grant you the chance to address my clan chieftains. Let them hear you after the wedding. You won't find Orvandir's council complacent. They've had my consent to place ears in the towns. By my orders, last month, every courier bearing the sunwheel blazon has been stopped, regardless of cost."

For one fleeting, racked second, Arithon's regret showed. Then his piercing stare dropped. He knew, none better, since a red dawn in Riverton: however careful the covering disguise, a clansman caught inside a walled settlement would not receive trial; only the horror of a public maiming, followed by execution. The document tossed aside on the trestle framed its own desolate statement: Shand's *caithdein* had been more than generous with the lives placed at his command. Already his people risked life and limb for a cause that was none of their making.

Arithon swallowed, glanced up, then offered his wrist with the unmasked pain of his sincerity. "I'm grateful you've spared me the indignity of asking." He did not wince at the crushing grip that sealed pact of honor with the chieftain who had once tested him to death's edge, at sword point. The distress that rang through as he closed was profound. "This time, to my sorrow, I believe that the stakes on the outcome are greater than all of us."

Spring 5671

Vixen

Far from the sun-slashed greenwood of Shand, the brisk northern winds howled over the clouded peaks beyond Eastwall. Snow whirled down in glass-tipped flakes. Their icy tap rattled into the panes of the casement window seat where Elaira curled with a mug of hot tea, a quartz sphere tucked in her lap. Another storm smothered the passes in drifts, again delaying her departure.

Where once she would have chafed with impatience, this afternoon's calm retreat reflected the change undergone through her months of reclusive study.

Five seasons in the company of Ath's adepts had shifted the range of her knowledge. Now awakened to the inherent design of natural flux and wild forces, she could sense the living coil of energies that presaged the shift in the season. In the deep of the earth, through the whine of the gale, between the restless cycle as frozen water melted to the blazing light of the sun, she heard language.

The thaws would come, soon. The snowpack would retreat and reopen the road, and the respite she had snatched in the quiet of Ath's sanctuary would draw to an end. Her decision to leave was not challenged. The adepts' code of silence honored free will. If she asked their wise counsel, they answered her need with simple, but searching questions.

'How do you feel? What do you believe? Where does your heart's whisper lead you?'

Her careful reflection converged to one thread. She cherished Rathain's prince and trusted his strength without reservation. Kewar's maze had affirmed his true quality. As an oathsworn enchantress, Elaira believed—no, she *knew*—that the sisterhood named her beloved as their inveterate enemy. The Matriarch's resolve to chase him down would wait only so long, before Elaira's lapsed charge would be handed off to another, or worse: rechanneled into a fresh avenue of pursuit more insidious than her given assignment. Against certain distrust of the Prime Circle's intent, Elaira's self-honest, caring involvement offered Arithon a tenuous stay of protection.

At least if she failed, and he fell prey to the Koriani design for his capture, she could be present to temper the end game. Determined, she could try to ensure that he would not be violated in ways that might destroy his inner integrity.

Her heart's whisper led her, courageous, to take the steadfast course of firm character. To stay by his side, and not to run, though the razor's edge her decision must tread threatened to tear her asunder.

If love were to rule Prince Arithon's fate, and not hatred, Elaira would leave Whitehaven hostel at thaws. She chose that road with concern and raw dread, but not with self-questioning uncertainty. Attuned with the living pulse of Athera, now trained to partner the awareness of crystals, she had learned to access the mysteries without use of blind force or coercion. Opened to new resource, she sought the midafternoon quiet to measure the storm. Amid the untamed voice of the elements, she listened for the subliminal whisper that spoke of rebirth into spring.

For Arithon Teir's'Ffalenn was finally in Shand.

The burst of excitement raised a tingle of nerves. His landfall that dawn at last opened the way to take charge of the burden that bonded her love to his fate. Selidie Prime's orders had been known to him since his passage through Kewar's maze. He had awarded Elaira his firm promise then to share the responsible course of that destiny.

The enchantress raked back her unruly bronze hair. Pulse racing, she lifted the quartz sphere between her cupped hands.

"Arithon, beloved," she whispered. Her mind framed his memory. The sweet wave of longing that swept her, bone deep, became the piercing focus to anchor her line of intent. Permission to stone was asked, and received. The crystal sphere in her clasp warmed and wakened. Long since tuned in concert with her affection, its conscious presence embraced her patterned awareness and amplified her request. Since her tie to Arithon was a sealed conduit, forged through the gate of the heart, the whiteout snowfall over the mountains cast no veil of interference. The thread of his life-stream entwined through her being expanded to intimate focus...

He was standing alone, as often occurred when her desire reached out for close contact. By who knew what alchemy, or what gift of mage-sight, his spirit was waiting, aligned to receive her.

Arithon had chosen the site to frame the connection, a tender forethought made in design to expand upon her delight. His surrounds were the afternoon shade of a pinewood, warmed by sunlit air, and the velvet fragrance of ever-green needles and earth. The natural element founding her craft enhanced the quartz-driven connection. Water flowed near him, a streamlet that fed into the south branch of the River Hanhaffin. The slide of tranquil current through moss-capped rocks played through the hush and made sacred the melding between them.

Elaira felt his smile of welcome, as her inward awareness embraced him. He did not respond with the disturbance of thought. His mind, gently open, welcomed her in. A fish in a deep pool, she immersed in his presence, sharing the moment's intimate force, then the fierce, wild thrill that rippled his skin, as her spirit-touch fingered over and through him.

Mage-schooled, his poise displayed no other sign. The hands loosely clasped at his back stayed relaxed. His breathing remained light and even. His greeting alive in the core of her heart, he framed her name, couched in a golden shower of music. *'Elaira, beloved.'*

The timing for an outside interruption could scarcely be less opportune.

Yet the relentless perception of initiate mastery brushed Arithon with warn-ing that someone had broken his chosen moment of solitude. As the intrusion crossed the fringe of his subtle awareness, Elaira felt him assess the electrical eddy that rippled across his stilled thought. The arrival would soon break his guarded privacy. No rustle of footsteps raised a disturbance. Whoever came would be clanborn. Vhandon and Talvish still stood as his sentries; since they were not wont to relax while on guard, Arithon chose not to move, or ac-knowledge. The approaching party would not bear arms, if his liegemen had not issued challenge.

That measured fact did not mean the coming encounter would not prove to be dangerous.

Far distant, at Whitehaven hostel, Elaira gathered herself to withdraw from Arithon's inner mind.

'Please stay,' he bade her, a purely reflexive cry for the untoward theft of his pleasure. The tenderness that cradled her being, within his, was a clasp that held love beyond measure: a tie that cherished but did not contain.

Since natural preference quashed her better sense, Elaira did not retreat.

Therefore, she was most keenly present when the clanborn woman strode up from behind, and with a brazen, self-possessed passion, closed her hands over Arithon's wrists.

Initiate master, his furious recoil was trained entirely *inward*. His physical nerves displayed no reaction; loose fingers betrayed no jerk of startlement. Only the naked weave of his shared awareness exposed the hair-trigger leap of his thought. Elaira felt his touch at her heart's center, *first*, steady and sure and unbroken.

'I don't recognize her, best beloved.'

The price of that signal honesty cost him. The woman pressed closer. As though she owned him, flesh and blood, the silky tumble of her unbound hair trailed down his back. Her breath brushed his ear. Then her lips pressed a kiss on the side of his neck that could have boiled rock into lava.

Arithon wrenched down his savage distaste. Physically contained, ruled still by the ironclad core of his will, his instant thought was Elaira's: *'Whoever she is, there's no profit in stealth. I don't need to look to know I've been insulted by a hussy with ulterior motives. Stay, or leave as you wish. Had I known in advance, I'd have spared you the rank irritation.'*

He sucked a breath, scalded to fury, as the violation of those sensuous fingers tried the tight cuffs of his shirt, intent on unbinding the laces. Sensitive, there, because of his scars, Arithon firmed his forearms in warning. His exasperated move detached her hot grasp, and his fast, forward step parted her openmouthed kiss, that already had purpled a throbbing bruise on the fine grain of his skin.

Spun around, he looked into a ravishing face, lightly freckled, with golden eyes speckled and brilliant as a flawed topaz.

"I heard that I owed you thanks for a bride gift," she said, her deep voice as warm as spring earth.

Arithon measured her, tousled head to bare feet. She appeared to be just come of age, not ripe, but lean, with pert breasts under a sheer linen shirt that caught on her hardened nipples. The cascading fall of her carrot red hair framed a beauty to wreck a man's peace.

"I should apologize for the flagrant dye in the cloth?" Arithon answered her, cool. The scarlet that her bridegroom had asked for was going to wreak damage, when matched with her coloring.

Small white teeth, parted lips, a seductress's smile; since Elaira could not fail to miss his reflexive male surge in response, she received the pure echo of Prince Arithon's sent assurance. The vixen's wiles had not tempted. Even had the woman not been Kyrialt's handfasted bride, the prince whose affection clasped her distant thought burned as steadfast as a fixed beacon.

Since he seemed a Masterbard at loss for words, the enchantress smothered a laugh and extended her humor to rescue him. *'Dare I ask? What under Ath's sky did you do to her man?'*

'Tested him. Sorely.' Arithon lost to his spontaneous joy, for the idiot crux of the challenge.

'Well, she's doing the same.' Amusement spiked through, as his fight to command his animal senses burned a redoubled ripple of sensuous awareness between them. Elaira sent rueful, *'Your nerves can withstand her? She's ill prepared. I see that her style of frontal assault means she's used to creating an impact.'*

Arithon forcibly curbed a sharp gasp. *'Mercy, beloved! You're going to destroy me. If I should break down and laugh in her face, pride will drive her to claw for my vitals! Please leave the delicate recoil to me. I've experience enough from the taverns.'*

'Well she's not a bar wench!' retorted Elaira. *'For what reason did you try Kyrialt?'*

Whatever controlled answer Arithon intended, the raw storm the question awoke was too much. Set on top of a flagrant distraction, his talent for farsight burst free. Knocked reeling, he backstepped, thumped into a pine trunk, and salvaged his balance by leaning. As the onslaught of future images welled up and slammed the shut gates of his mind, he lost himself, forced to fight for their recontainment. That moment cost also. Glendien came on, pressed her lush body against him full length. and kissed him hard on the mouth.

Since he could not disengage her assault without violence, he closed his eyes, doused the sensory scald of his flesh, and shielded the core of his mind. There, with Elaira fixed as his sole focus, he told over the truth like a litany. *'Beloved, she glitters, while you are the substance that binds the marrow inside the bone of me. I shall come north to meet you as soon as may be. Are the west passes clear yet?'* Her pang of impatience informed him at once; shared the snapped imprint of snowfall, bleak as ice through her desolate eyes. His response was the warm, summer sun on her heart, and his salve, the firm promise to ease the ache of their long separation. *'Seek me in Halwythwood. Guest with Feithan, the widow of Jieret s'Valerient. Let her lodge shelter us when I bestow rightful place at my side in your hand.'*

'Well, you've got to survive today's escapade, first.' Her laughter held more than gratitude, more than joy, more than the mind's touch could capture. *'Don't savage her feelings,'* Elaira sent back, *'since I've gathered you will need the support of Kyrialt s'Taleyn's fixed loyalty.'*

His startled flinch told her she had read far too much through his muddled explosion of prescience. Which forced the need to take charge; Arithon collected himself, as he must. *'You only, beloved.'*

And then he was gone, to manage the awkwardness shoved into his arms, in the pine glen far distant in Alland.

Prisoned by weather behind gray panes of glass, Elaira lifted the quartz sphere from her lap. She thanked its bright service, smoothed its raised field of resonance, and laid it aside on the window seat. Then, eyes brimming, she laced her arms to her ribs and collapsed into helpless laughter. "Oh beloved!" she gasped, when next she could speak. "Halwythwood's not going to be soon enough!"

Yet anxiously as she yearned for the moment she would feel the touch of his hands and set free the raw need for completion, the gift must come to her burdened with dread.

On the hour Elaira left Whitehaven hostel, she must shoulder the paradox that might poison the unwritten future. Inevitably, her newly refigured perception must clash with the precepts of her order's oath. Ath's adepts had well warned her: the clear grace of the mysteries *must* inflict a bind of incompatible conflicts. The Koriani practice of weaving sigils of applied force was now revealed as a needless misuse of the balance of Ath's creation.

In the pine glen, his blood raging, and his heart torn for the rape of his cherished privacy, Arithon snapped his face to one side. "My dear," he addressed Glendien, "you're a gift to leave a man breathless and begging, except..."

Her fingers, nails extended, locked his temples and cheek. That grip was dead serious. Should he resist, his flesh would be crudely laid open. Twisted to face her, enwrapped in her scent, her mouth on him like scalding vengeance, Arithon stiffened.

She bit his lip.

He tore free, anyway, bleeding, now angry, "...except I can't recall..." Arithon dodged her riposte, snatched her rippling hair at the nape, and using main strength, pulled her demanding kiss from his mouth, "...asking for an assignation."

"Sithaer! You're a gelding," she said to his teeth.

Arithon laughed. "Not yet. Though I'm wary if you keep this up, your husband will finish the question."

"I'm handfasted, not married." Glendien eyed his disheveled hair and flushed skin, moved a sultry hip, and backed off him. "Until tomorrow. Then I'll be wed. You could be left with a lifetime's regret. Why sweat in your dreams for the missed opportunity?"

"Regret?" Arithon blotted his torn lip, saw with distaste that his cuffs were untied, and leaned back upon his tucked forearms. "That's an interesting word. Let's see which of the pair of us wears it."

He looked at her, then. Masterbard, sorcerer, his prolonged survey was no less than a flaying experience. He said presently, "Why do you want Kyrialt's blade at my throat?"

She raked him with her brilliant, topaz eyes. "Where did you get your scars? If you want a look at my heart, you must pay. One for one, we'll trade knifing answers."

If her quick stab had cut him, he would not let that show. As fiercely as she could rope men to heel, Glendien must realize there would be no governing this one. His quiet would not release, would not dismiss, but could only shatter the pain she held at the vibrating core of her.

Then he spoke. "Very well. I'll disarm yours first. You are jealous; no, afraid."

Not cruel at all, that insight tore through every tight shield and presumption. "Terrified, in fact," said Arithon s'Ffalenn, "that your bridegroom might choose to support me."

"Not might." Glendien flung back her wild banner of hair, too proud to hide her contempt. "Your sort of service will see him cut dead. Prince of

Bones. Master of Carrion. No price I could pay is worth risking the father I've chosen to sire my children."

Arithon moved. Wind stirred his dark hair as he pushed straight, his awareness still locked upon her. "You had a parent who died in Vastmark? A father, perhaps?" The truth of his guess caught her breath. As though he might strike, she flinched from him.

"I'm sorry," Arithon Teir's'Ffalenn said. The words were sincere. If she wanted to hate, he reft even that poison from her. "My lady, I once spurned Erlien's goodwill and his ruler's just pride in a badly failed effort to spare Shand its toll of clan losses."

Glendien spun away, her flame hair a curtain to hide the taut fingers pressed to her face. When her shoulders shook, Rathain's prince made no move to console. He would not step forward, or touch her.

The harsh moment passed. When she stirred again, her natural grace was a passionate wine, self-contained now, and no harlot's. "Spare me my husband," she begged.

Arithon studied her. Washed in the softened shade of the pines, the blood on his face a violation, he seemed woven into the natural setting, a presence both touched and untouchable.

"Very well." He presented his back, quick fingers busy restoring his rifled cuff ties. "My lady, return to the camp."

"Go now!" Glendien's fury resurged. "What is left settled between us? Kyrialt's honor will not let him back down! He will fight and die for this wretched incursion your enemies are raising to exterminate our old bloodlines!"

He was patient. "Then make your cause stronger. Take your chance. Rip your shirtfront. Since seduction won't work, you might change your story. Insist that you pushed off *my* assault, and I can swear not to gainsay that. Play my pride for your ends, I've none left to save. But realize, Glendien. When your man Kyrialt calls me to fight, I will not draw my steel against him."

Minute to minute, poised between choice, she stood trapped by her rooted uncertainty. He listened. The earth turned, and the pines rustled to the humid play of the sea breeze. At last, wrapped amid the deep web of his magesense, Arithon heard Glendien move.

The slide of fabric against her young skin burned his heart, then the following sound, of tearing cloth, cut him to shivering anguish. He held himself still, but for the unfinished, small moves, as he tied up his last, unstrung laces. He stayed faced away as she walked to the streambank, doused her hands, and perhaps, washed her face. Her tears still fell, anyway. Those fine, topaz eyes were now red-rimmed with grief.

Arithon waited. Her step on the fallen carpet of needles made almost no sound as she closed on him. Her fingers reached out, touched his, cold and dripping. Into his hand, she pressed the shorn swatch from her shirt, soaked in the brook as a compress.

"For your cuts," murmured Glendien, a wretched apology. "I was wrong. You are a prince more than worthy of Kyrialt's loyalty." There, she paused.

Arithon remained suspended between thought. His slight frame was weaponless, unguarded, alone. The patriarch pine trees soared upward, and dwarfed him. His calm held no peace, but seemed strung on a wire, grimly held from one breath to the next. He wished her gone, while the heat hammered down, weighting the resinous air to pressed glass.

"Please go," he said presently. "Too long a delay would be dangerously unwise."

Clan law in his case would be swift and merciless, if in fact, he appeared to have forced her.

Glendien stayed frozen. The saving course she had cold-bloodedly plotted had turned viciously in the hand. A man she did not know, had seen as a pitiless, warmongering threat, had just offered his priceless integrity to underwrite Kyrialt's safety. Not without care, never without scruple: the misery she experienced was not mirrored, but drowned behind his meticulous silence.

Faced away, the stillness in him as deep as the pines he now used as his anchor against a most vicious onslaught of forerunning prescience, Arithon sheltered behind his hard-leashed quiet. He would not augment pain; not have the young woman who battled to escape a harsh fate understand the scope of his initiate perception.

That future upon future, the range of probabilities cast themselves outward like ripples upon windless water. *For in fact, her desperation held real foundation.* Kyrialt was as a living flame, struck from his sire's belligerent honesty. Drawn into the snarl of an idealistic conflict, he was unlikely to raise the family this young wife appealed to preserve. Cast clear, he might live, might stay on this side of Fate's Wheel long enough to conceive a successor.

Such brazen courage as this woman possessed deserved the accolade of a calm acceptance. Each moment she lingered, Arithon must endure every tear that welled and spilled down the spirited curve of her cheek. He would not have her see what that cost him. Such carefree beauty torn to sorrow could rend the very marrow out of his heart.

"Go, Glendien," he urged. "Don't think. What worth do you think I attach to my name? Should Kyrialt's survival mean less to me?"

"Daelion show us both mercy, your Grace! I can't risk him, or act without selfishness." Glendien fled, already knowing that the Prince of Rathain had absolved her. The gift stung no less as she regrouped her smashed pride and drove on to spare her man from the throes of a fatal alliance.

Spring 5671

Wedding

Arithon lingered on in the sheltered glen, delay on his part a prudent necessity given the indelicacy of his position. Though he chose not to flaunt his laid-open face through the first storm of reaction, his snatched moment of peace must be short. Young Kyrialt's enmity, and the High Earl of Alland's murderous temperament now spun him a thorny entanglement.

Here, the play of the breeze through the trees only whispered of spring, and the mysteries of renewal. Yet the haven first chosen to delight Elaira had lost every power to soothe. Plagued by the lingering sting of his weals and the throb of his savaged mouth, Arithon set his back to the patriarch pine whose whorled cones had seeded the grove. Eyes closed, he let go, while the shifting template of prescient reflection unreeled the posited future. No other choice opened.

He required a solid alliance with Shand. No bloodless plan to defuse the sunwheel fanatics could succeed without clan-based support in the south.

Time slipped through his fingers. West slanting rays nicked the wings of the sparrows that foraged in wheeling flocks through the shade. His solitude fled as his earned loyalties betrayed him: Vhandon and Talvish inevitably assumed the grim task of coming to fetch him. Of the slashed temple and cheek, the bitten lip, they said nothing. But their stopped stance before him stayed stiff and implacable, with the tenor of their silence hard-braced against oaths for his idiot timing.

"There will be rage," Arithon admitted. "Above anything, you're not to draw steel on them."

"May Dharkaron's Five Horses have trampled me first, that I should be confronting the prospect!" Vhandon exploded in anguish.

Touched off by the older officer's shame, Talvish's salvo came next. "If you needed a woman as badly as this, why under the score of Daelion's judgment did you have to meddle with that one? You say, don't draw steel! You foreign-born fool! You claim a masterbard's knowledge of law. Don't you realize how you've offended? "

"For rape of a clan woman, she keeps the child," mocked Arithon with scathing impatience. Shoved off from the tree, unflinching as ice, he trampled the last shred of decency. "Except, angry man, things did not go so far. The bitch used her claws like a wildcat."

"Not use steel?" Vhandon echoed. Beneath tan and scars, his hard-bitten face had drained white. "Not defend?" Incredulous, he rushed on, "This is a *caithdein*'s handfasted kin you have violated! Fires of undying Sithaer, your Grace! I should call you to draw for that insult first, to spare myself from the slur of demeaning an oath of crown service."

Swiftly as Arithon could rise in retort, Talvish's reflex was faster. His viper's grasp caught the older campaigner's taut wrist and locked sliding steel in the scabbard. "Stop this! Now. Can't you see? When his Grace hurts, how he strikes to provoke? Don't do as he wants! He would turn us off. Has tried to, and with wretched persistence, since the hour he left us for Jaelot."

Wrenched back to reason, Vhandon stood down. "If that was your purpose, Arithon Teir's'Ffalenn, there are limits! Should I listen to orders from a schemer whose wiles don't cavil at playing a young girl's flesh as a game piece?"

"He's right," Talvish added, eyes stony. "If you wished us gone, that was a low ploy. Nor can we go, now. Leave your side, we'd be branded for slinking desertion and cowardice, since son and father will be honor bound to hack you in shreds for this infamy. Your assault on clan lineage enacts charter law, not to mention your flagrant abuse of this realm's good faith hospitality."

"Even so," stated Arithon. "I will stay alive. But not if you don't let me handle them!"

"Oh Ath, get this over with," Vhandon snapped, sick. Grudging, his crisp step made way for his unarmed liege to accept the defended position.

Placed at right and left hand, the paired men-at-arms escorted their prince from the greenwood. Their brisk pace and stark censure rammed against searing silence as they approached the rock caves that concealed the chieftain's main encampment. Their liege awarded their staunch duty no graceful apology. Their oath-given support was as a branding wound, and their guilt, that their wry choice to allow Glendien past as an afternoon's sport, played in trust against Arithon's character, had brought such an ill-starred betrayal against them.

Crown prince and reluctant escort were met at the head of the vale. Against lush, southern greenery, and west-slanting sunlight, the distanced glint of dyed finery flashed through the trees like an intrusive shout of alarm.

"Oh, this is not good," Talvish said in fierce dismay.

Caithdein of the realm, Erlien s'Taleyn awaited, a gold fillet bound over his white clan braid. Mantled for high office in the absence of a sanctioned sovereign, he bore arms. The great sword once drawn to fight Arithon to a standstill was slung over the rich weight of the tabard, loomed with the purple-and-gold chevrons that for five millennia had denoted the adjunct territories comprising the Kingdom of Shand.

He was not alone.

His youngest son, Kyrialt, stood arrow straight beside his sire's vested authority. Sword, paired daggers, and lacquered recurve bow, and with his ice chip eyes unsmiling, he bore the more ancient device of a crescent moon and black falcon upon the spiked targe strapped to his wrist.

Vhandon met the sight of state panoply with a locked jaw and steel resignation.

"What did you expect?" Talvish snapped, just as clipped. "A vaunted public ceremony? At least the charge will be formal and quick. We'll finish the inquest without risk of a mobbing, though by *Ath*, this affray sticks in my retching craw, sideways."

"We aren't leaving Shand," cracked Arithon in rebuttal. "No matter what unpleasantness happens, my plan for these people goes forward."

Thrown a censuring glare from his liegemen, the Master of Shadow insisted, "This rising whipped up by misled town fanatics will destroy the breathing heart of Athera's sacrosanct mysteries. You both know this!"

Silence, marred through by leashed breath and checked temper.

"You might have thought of that, liege," Talvish said. "It's a steep price to pay, there's no question."

No longer impervious, his marked features drained white, Arithon remained adamant, refusing their plea for retreat. "If these forest clansmen hope to stay free to preserve their ancient tradition, they'll have to deal. Charges or not, they have no choice. They need my support to survive."

"Brazen harlot!" Vhandon flushed to the roots of his iron gray hair. "I don't know how you summon the dung-licking nerve! Don't expect us to stomach the slur on your character. Survive the day, and our oath is discharged. Be sure Duke Bransian will hear from my lips what low sort of ally he's brought to lean on the strength of his family name!"

"Vhan!" cautioned Talvish. For in fact, their advance had brought them within earshot.

Yet in shattering departure from his stern form, Vhandon refused to be placated. "If Shand covers this up under law by a decree of forced marriage, Teir's'Ffalenn, I'll break your randy, insolent neck with naught else but my own two hands."

Arithon wrenched to a stop and let fly with a venom rare even for his savage tongue. "I suffer the penalty for one stolen kiss! You are disgraced, and dead by my hand, if you *ever* dare imply past that."

Talvish's lightning shove to disarm the combatants was struck short: a surge of rage burst through Arithon's presence, palpable as a pressed wave. Such power, forced in check, might have stopped time, or scorched the free-falling rain into cinders.

"I will answer the charges," Prince Arithon said. He sidestepped, and resumed his resolute course. The two liegemen recovered their stride and moved with him, stunned to an uneasy quiet. Three abreast, they broke through the last stand of trees, into sunlight that stabbed down like a blade.

Lit without mercy, they halted. Unabashed, the sanctioned Crown Prince of Rathain presented his welted face to Lord Erlien, High Earl of Alland, and the son, whose handfasted woman had used nails and teeth beyond all excuse to beg pardon.

Only Arithon had the courage to meet Kyrialt's eyes, gray as pressed ice, upon him. He held his ground, wordless. Before his straight stance, the spiked targe and the sword: beside him, two liegemen stamped rigid with shame, oathsworn to shed blood to protect him.

The moment ached, for its motionless dread.

The Shandian clan heir was taller, and broader, a muscled lion poised over prey. "By Ath," he remarked through the pregnant pause, "she's marked you up and down like a scratching post. Poor wee man. What did you do to receive the scourge of my lady's disfavor?"

Light wind through the glen riffled Arithon's hair. Black strands, glued with blood, stuck to the scabbed gashes furrowed at his left temple and full length down his opposite cheek. Hands clasped at his back, he never quailed. His adamant stillness stretched, then extended, and his silence admitted to nothing.

His oathsworn liegemen held out with stopped breath. Vhandon's bearing stayed rigid. In wary form, Talvish kept his trained eyes on the clansmen, who, by affronted insult, now must be adversaries.

Yet no spoken reproof or overt hostility shattered their anxious suspension. No accusation was issued. Erlien s'Taleyn, High Earl of Alland stood at his full height, gaze frosty as midwinter sky. Then he reached over, drew his son's sword, and knelt in the tough stand of grass. He drove the bared steel upright in the earth. With his wrists crossed in salute at his chest, he bent his proud head in submission. "Your Grace, for the life of my son, what will happen next has my sanction."

Taken aback, Talvish gasped out, incensed, "My lord, you will not kneel to this man! For such as he's done, he'll be stripped of crown title. Once formal word reaches the Teiren's'Valerient in Halwythwood, his Fellowship sanction will be revoked by the terms of Rathain's royal charter!"

Yet Shand's *caithdein* failed to arise.

When Vhandon shoved forward, the hard thrust of Kyrialt's shield arm checked the move to haul his father back onto his feet. "His Grace has told you he tried to force Glendien?"

Still down on one knee, Lord Erlien broke in with the bite of a ruler's authority. "Liegeman! Take care how you answer! The credibility of my daughter-in-law's word will come to rest on your testimony, not to mention the character of Rathain's oathbound crown prince."

"What character?" Vhandon spat in contempt. His flustered glance sideward smoked with disgust. "I've got eyes, more's the pity. I've seen such evidence as I shall take to my pyre with cringing embarrassment! Will you look, there? Yon gutsy savage has got a dog's nerve, to breathe the clean air in our presence!"

Throughout, reviled as though he was deaf, Arithon Teir's'Ffalenn stood detached. With Glendien's handling stark on his face, and the bruise on his neck livid purple, his stillness itself framed a damning refrain to his liegeman's ruthless refutement. Talvish broke custom and averted his glance before suffering the humiliation.

"What *exactly* did his Grace say?" inquired Kyrialt with razor-edged delicacy.

"He won't speak, himself," Vhandon evaded, distressed. At the crux, his innate distaste ran too deep. He could not, after all, say the requisite words to condemn a man he held liege-sworn.

No less revolted, Talvish just wanted the harrowing inquiry over with. "Precisely?" His sigh sawed across the strained pause. "The tongue in his Grace's head was right churlish. He allowed he was guilty of one stolen kiss."

The bridegroom, who should have exploded with rage, instead fought a choked snort of laughter. "Not from Glendien, then. She's too brazen to run. No matter how damning the evidence, I've seen her provocative manners when pushed. A man keeps his distance, if she's displeased. As my rakish friends have discovered, that she-wolf stands her ground when she's cornered."

"You don't believe her?" cracked Vhandon, incensed. And again, his blond comrade's snatched grasp restrained him.

"Stand down!" Lord Erlien arose to his towering height, discomposed, and finally offended. "You don't see her knife in his ribs, foolish man?" As the prince's paired liegemen looked on, one gaping, and the other stunned into guarded suspicion, the High Earl of Alland completed his statement. "Then Glendien has told us no less than the truth. The assault that occurred was not caused by your prince."

Erlien's keen regard fastened back upon Arithon, who had not moved a muscle throughout. "There's my son's sword, upright at your feet. A woman handfasted to my household has entangled you in a wrongful effort to shelter her bridegroom. Your Grace, here's my lawful settlement. S'Taleyn would have you kneel to swear oath, since Kyrialt would grant you his fealty."

Arithon shivered. "I can't take this charge," he insisted, steadfast. "Whatever Lady Glendien has told you, no grounds exist for such gratitude. Not to receive grant of a crown obligation from Shand, or to bear a loyalty as deep as this one."

The High Earl of Alland met and locked with those fathomless eyes, that perceived with the chill of a sorcerer. He did not back down, or shrink, though a fine sweat sprang up and beaded the lines of hard living scored into his features. "Then, Arithon Teir's'Ffalenn, swear by the promise of Dharkaron's vengeance! Claim that my son's handfasted woman has lied. Then draw your steel. For you'll have to fight me to defeat again, if you think to enforce your will over the attested word of a kinswoman."

Of them all, the fair swordsman correctly interpreted the instant of searing tension. He alone saw the shift as his liege marked the challenge, and for the first time, drew breath to answer his case.

"No!" Talvish cried. "Hold your weapons! My lord Erlien, can't you see? His Grace will snatch his chance, and all of this country will bleed for it." His horrified eyes fixed on the Prince of Rathain through a dawning rush of epiphany, he snapped, *"You were sparing that boy, and perhaps us as your liegemen! If so, I am having no part of this!"*

Then Kyrialt broke in, sharp and fast in support. "Deny that statement as truth, Teir's'Ffalenn! Refute Glendien's confession, as well. Swear that for my life's sake, you never offered to shoulder the blame for a crime that our clan tradition holds outside of any forgiveness." Smiling, the youngest blood son of s'Taleyn bent his knee. He laced his hard fingers over the hilt of the weapon his father's own hand had struck upright. "Your Grace of Rathain, I will bind myself first. Unless you can give me a single sound reason? Why under Ath's sky should I not serve a prince who counts a stranger's life as more precious than his royal dignity?"

"Debt of blood," Arithon admitted, his sorrow laid bare. "Your Glendien lost a parent at Vastmark."

His glance shifted, raised to bridge the disparity between his slighter stature, and Erlien's winter-clear eyes. "Her sire was Tanuin? If so, he fell while guarding a notch. The ending was cruel. He held his ground against twenty bowmen while a tribal grandmother and five children were being assisted to safety." Arithon loosed a shuddering breath, as though feeling the stab of barbed steel through his viscera; as, within Kewar's maze, he surely had: the resurgent bite of remembered pain was that desolate. "My lord, *caithdein,* keep your son at your side. I was wrong, beyond question. I should never have failed to acknowledge the courage and strength of your clansmen's sacrifice. But I could not thank you for sending those scouts. Too few of them lived to come home to you."

"Each one fought for Shand," the High Earl corrected. "They had a prince under Fellowship sanction on the battle line at their shoulder. The grace of that presence but honors the soil of the free wilds they died to hold sacred. Now accept my son's blade. Swear your royal oath! Or by Ath's very grace, I will have the act done inside an armed circle of archers."

As Arithon rallied his shocked nerves to protest, Talvish cleared his own weapon. "I'll stand sword's honor for the formal oathtaking," he volunteered with expedient grace. "Arithon, kneel! You've earned the award of this man's redress. Such heart as you've shown must accept defeat kindly. Or Vhandon will just have to break your damned legs. Don't think he won't. He's my senior officer by more than ten years. One day soon, he wants to retire."

"A stand-down?" said Arithon, taken aback.

"On your knees, prince," Alland's High Earl insisted. "I swear by my pride as a father, you *will* bend your miserable, stiff neck here and now, else I'll run you out of the kingdom!"

Returned to the clan encampment on the heels of the unplanned oathswearing, Arithon Teir's'Ffalenn appeared more than harried. Inflamed scabs and raw swelling did not fully explain the haunted look in his eyes. Against the whipped-dog contrition of his two liegemen, his somber quiet posed a striking contrast to young Kyrialt's euphoric enthusiasm.

No bristled word of dismissal sufficed. A flagrant, trim figure in his trappings of state, the young man determined that Glendien's outrageous behavior deserved abject care. The insistent choice followed, to escort Rathain's abused crown prince back to the comfort of guest quarters in person. Arrived at the shaded entry to the grottoes carved out by the flood of the Hanhaffin, the royal party ran headlong into Dakar's blistering censure.

"The fool tangles you spin!" the Mad Prophet accosted, as the miscreant prince darkened the cranny appointed to shelter Rathain's delegation. "You could have lost everything for the sake of one life! Not to mention the fact that the Teir's'Taleyn could have finished off his past effort to butcher you!"

"Worry instead that I might gut the High Earl," snapped Arithon in brittle annoyance. "More's the pity, I can't let go and try. Or break his arrogant head on a rock. I need his scouts, and he needs my help. Which sterling *fact* is the only weak thread holding a stay on the peace."

"Dakar. Don't press him," Vhandon urged, breathless. "Not if you don't want your skin peeled."

"Would I so!" the furious spellbinder cried. "And how much of everyone's skin should be risked because our prince can't contain his bleeding-heart gift of compassion? Was one woman's tears worth what he just staked? Is any man's life price enough to endanger the stability of the realm?"

Spun on his heel to stalk off, the Mad Prophet found himself nose to chest with Kyrialt's virile bulk, the spiked targe with the ancient device of Shand a gleam of cold steel at his breast. "One party agreed that the action had merit." Vivid and brown, the young man amended, "It's my life you're tossing like straws on your tongue. I've sworn my feal oath. Does the act not demonstrate my proper gratitude, or the sincerity of my family's honor?"

"You admire the order his Grace keeps with sharp words?" Dakar raised pudgy fists and yanked at his hair in a fit of hobbled frustration. "Well, I doubt that sits well when you're the next target. Don't think that won't happen. Arithon's nerveless. The more so whenever the rest of us fail to keep pace with his fiendish conniving. Look at Vhandon's face! Or Talvish. Ath's living tears! Both of them were blindsided today, and they've served Rathain's crown prince for years. Ask them, if you don't believe me."

Kyrialt shrugged, compressed to acid pride. "I'd be a sight less comfortable on my knees in white silk, swilling the spout of lying divinity. Give me Sithaer with its nine levels of hell, before I go blind and seek paradise under s'Ilessid."

"Arithon could have lost you the free wilds of Shand!" the stalwart spellbinder exploded.

Kyrialt showed teeth like the grin on a snake. "Could, is it?" He seized Dakar's collar, and muscled the recalcitrant prophet like a fat puppy to the rim of the ledge. There, above the sweep of the hollow that led to the river's edge, he snagged his targe against the hide flap strung across the open-air entry. "See what's happened. Perhaps you're actually jealous?"

His gesture tore off the curtain.

A gathering met them. Bearing sheathed steel, and strung bows, and the badges of house lineage, the clan chieftains of Alland were packed outside to pledge their support without the formality of a hearing. Kyrialt spoke over their raucous acclaim. "My father still talks of your prince's skill with a sword. Here's twice we've had to acknowledge his mettle." He brandished his fist, while the boisterous cheers rocked against the steep face of the cliff. "Lysaer's new troops had best tremble. For your Teir's'Ffalenn will now be the voice directing our raiding war bands."

"Well, on that score, you're certain to face disappointment." Dakar tugged himself free. His offended shrug yanked his skewed tunic straight, and his cinnamon eyes remained hostile. "Argue or threaten, his Grace won't listen. Your war bands might as well toss their drawn blades in the Hanhaffin. You think I'm mad? Then stay and find out. I already know that Arithon's plans will never launch the stupidity of a pitched fight."

The presence of the Masterbard at her bridal feast scarcely dampened the scorching fire of Glendien's nature. Clad in fine deerhide with sandy embroidery, and flaunting an outrageous shawl cut from the raided silk, she was a sight to brand memory and eyesight as she weaved her determined way across the torchlit festivities. Warnings failed to deflect her picked course; the thorny thicket of legend that surrounded the Teir's'Ffalenn's past posed no obstacle. She raised her beautiful, willful chin and sailed straight ahead, trailing scarlet fringes and wide-eyed young men in her wake like an errant comet.

"Just stop me," she challenged, as Kyrialt blocked her.

"You don't think you've degraded his Grace enough in the course of a single day? As you wish. Naturally." Her frowning bridegroom shrugged and gave way.

Glendien girded herself with a challenging smile. Then she barged into Arithon's presence and asked questions that caused Vhandon and Talvish to flinch, and Dakar to choke with his face half-immersed in his beer jack.

Even Lord Erlien paused, transfixed, to observe the offended reaction.

Arithon deflected her sallies with smoking ridicule. His ripostes lost no whetted edge to persistence, until Kyrialt silenced his woman's mouth with a kiss that raised ribald whistles and laughter.

Glendien ripped free of him, flushed, her topaz eyes unabashed. "Love, I don't cow in the face of seduction." She ducked past her protector. Leaned over the trestle where the prince sat, graciously winding new strings for the lyranthe loaned out of somebody's lodge tent, she announced, "I'm sorry."

Arithon did not look up.

She raised a bold hand, would have traced the welted scabs on his cheek.

His stinging, swift parry arrested the touch.

Her verbal dart followed, undaunted. "Your Grace, I lost the guts to see through the end game. Don't tell me you're sorry as well?"

"Woman!" snapped Vhandon, on guard to one side, his weathered stance stiff with embarrassment, "Your wiles have made things all that much worse. Your madman of a husband bent his knee, drew his steel, and accepted crown oath to Rathain. That act means your future children will become his Grace's feal subjects!"

"This prince?" Glendien's mirth pealed out like bronze bells. "Who else could I trust to keep such as Kyrialt alive long enough to be raising them?"

"Trust Dharkaron himself, *ei'an ist'thalient*." Done with twisting silver, Arithon arose, flipped the loop over the drone peg, and rested the lyranthe across his knee to raise the new string to pitched tension. The fall of the torch-light threw his tipped face in shadow, masking the hard spark of irony that might have exposed his true thought. A minute passed, hanging, while Glendien waited with bated breath for his translation.

"You know your Paravian quite well enough," Kyrialt chided her presently.

Arithon said nothing. His fine hands nursed the tuning pegs. At due length he cradled the instrument and caressed the first notes from taut strings. A harmonic triplet speared through, arresting the bursts of coarse comment from the sidelines. As the onlookers quieted, Athera's titled Masterbard tilted his torn face to one side. A snapped sparkle of notes winged from his trained touch. Satisfied with the instrument's quality, he straightened, bowed, and ex-cused himself with soft irony. "Breed up your impudent clutch as you can, little bride. Tonight, for my part, you'll be merry. Tomorrow, be warned. For I am quite done being burned by your cutting, mettlesome fingers."

Before Glendien could retort, or Kyrialt move with redoubled intent to restrain her, those skilled hands moved, and launched into sheer captivation.

The rollicking measures of a fast-paced jig ripped the feast into giddy celebration. Arithon played. He danced the clans of Selkwood to shouting, exuberant exhaustion, and this time, accepted their offer to get reeling drunk in their company.

Dakar abetted the choice. Shoved into the press, he volunteered to broach the bung on a tun of fine claret. That the branded staves wore the house seal of the Mayor of Telzen only heightened the mood of piquant enjoyment. Arithon folded himself into the thick of the revels, his presence met by slaps on the shoulder and the inevitable ribald good cheer. The quips he gave back tied knots in loose tongues. Challenge and match, the serious drinking devolved to a contest with bows. Arithon shot drunken, as Dakar had not seen him since a long-past winter, spent with tribal shepherds in Vastmark.

While the whining, sped shafts ripped the targets to stuffing, Fionn Areth delivered his stiff-lipped opinion, that such careless abandon was a disgrace. "Those arrows pack broadheads, not target points. A man with a bow who can't walk a straight line is begging to cause someone an injury."

"Leave him be," Dakar murmured. Determined to savor his evening of peace, he stowed himself at the trestle where the borrowed lyranthe lay, abandoned. He deserved the escape. Alestron's paired liegemen could be trusted to keep their vigilant eye on the dark head ensconced amid Alland's rough pack of roisterers.

"Your liege has not known a true moment of ease for over a year," the Mad Prophet admitted. "Certainly not since the hour he used Sanpashir's focus to launch his crazed foray to rescue you."

"What?" the Araethurian retorted. "Fourteen months in the caverns of Kewar were not enough for his restful amusement?"

Pudgy fists clamped to his jack of fine spirits, Dakar shook his tousled head. The mad leap of the shadows thrown off the pitch torches made his features look old, with the silver thread through his chestnut beard grown pronounced since his trials at Rockfell. Eyes owlish, he kept his secret thoughts to himself, that Arithon's release was more likely an ominous sign of the storms the near future might presage. "Davien gave the prince shelter," he admitted at length. "But it's the rash fool in that Sorcerer's company who would let down his guard for one second."

Another shaft ripped into the mark, to a fresh round of whistles and clapping.

"Arithon will get whipped," Fionn Areth insisted through the groans of the vanquished bemoaning the score. "Watch me. I'll cheer when that happens."

Talvish turned his flax head. "That's just because you can't beat him, cold sober," he remarked without rancor. "Take your sour tongue off. If you're wanting a shoulder to cry on, go mope in feminine company."

Fionn Areth fixed disgruntled green eyes on the swordsman, who took his ease like a lounging lynx with an insolent hip braced on the trestle. "As if I could treat a clan woman like a bawd, and not lose my head to her kinfolk!"

This time, Vhandon's muscle jerked Talvish short. "Let the grasslander go. He's confused enough. How will he ever learn who he is? With that face, he'll probably never find means to stand clear of the royal shadow."

The arrow shoot lasted until the sore losers decided that Arithon was safest pried loose from the bow and tucked back amid their musicians. There, Rathain's prince chose to entertain himself further by trying their wind instruments one at a time. For each slipped mistake, he downed a neat draught of claret. Vhandon refused to place silver with Talvish, that his Grace would become last man standing.

To their novel astonishment, the musician's quick fingers tripped less, as the effects of hard drinking undid him. If his eyes brightened, and his speech blurred, his wit remained stinging, and his music retained the ache of its vibrant clarity. Swaying, abstracted, a carved flute in hand, Arithon wove melody with the crystalline tang of frost on the grasses of autumn.

He refused the lyranthe until the last. Just after the traditional wedding at dawn, he retuned the silver-wound strings and delivered a performance that surpassed the predecessor who had taught him. The net of matchless harmony spun through the mist silenced even the most raucous reveler.

Dakar lay snoring, his cheek mashed on the trestle; Vhandon and Talvish stared at their fixed hands. Glendien turned her face into her husband's braced shoulder, and Lord Erlien openly wept.

No one, grown man, woman, or child, escaped the tug of the melody's lyrical passion. No eyes looked up, or noticed the eagle perched amid the stilled pines overhead. None moved or spoke, through the seamless delivery, and none sighed, till the final note faded.

When Arithon finished, those who knew him best realized he was not sober. He still slipped his admirers with casual ease. His leave-taking granted their stamping cry for an encore no shred of satisfaction. While daybreak speared through the crowns of the trees, and the torches smoked, spent to cinders, Vhandon and Talvish arose together and saw their sworn liege off to bed.

Lord Erlien, watching, was shocked to discover his stiff beard was dampened with tears. To Kyriat at his side, and the scarlet-wrapped bride, the High Earl observed with scraped grief, "It's a straight violation of Ath's grace to set such a talent at risk for a war. That man should never have touched killing steel!"

Kyrialt shut his eyes against more than the night's chill. His clasped arms tightened over his shivering wife while, in the gray flood of light, he returned a low snarl of rage. "If that accursed s'Ilessid pretender succeeds, and his upstart religion takes root, we'll see that rare gift forced to battle for nothing else but survival."

Erlien responded, cold as the fog that purled like ghost shades through the forest. "Then by Dharkaron Avenger's Black Chariot, we had better fight to make certain the false doctrine withers."

Overhead, still unnoticed, the perched eagle unfurled broad wings. Its pinions hissed down as it launched and soared, then vanished amid a pale shower of sparks that could not be seen, but by mage-sight.

Spring 5671

Entanglements

Cold drizzle falls on the morning that Arithon leaves Selkwood for Telzen; behind, he leaves Kyrialt s'Taleyn with a penned sheaf of orders, eighteen bolts of white silk, and the tribute gold taken to sow conflagration amid the new legions of Light; with him go his double, the Mad Prophet, and two liegemen, bearing between them a borrowed lyranthe and a chest of poached amethysts to be restored to the reigning *caithdein* of Melhalla…

Past the waning fury of the equinox storms, as a trade galley leaves the shelter of Eltair Bay to ply southward, an initiate courier bears a wrapped packet containing Elaira's personal quartz crystal to Ithish port, where it will see transfer to another enchantress bound overland to the Forthmark sisterhouse, and final delivery to Selidie Prime…

At the edge of the windswept wastes of Atainia, the Warden of Althain dreams: of a sinister figure riding the Camris road, and black webs of horror spinning cold shadows in Jaelot, Darkling, and Etarra; and the clean, searing line of his summons arcs out, touching a distant shade, a raven, and in tenuous plea, an eagle that soars on the icy winds of high altitude…

Fortress at Methisle

X. Appeal

Two nights after the wedding in Selkwood, the ice point blaze of the spring constellations glinted on jet above the slate peak of Althain Tower. Their silver light fell as a gossamer whisper through the opened east casement, where the Warden reclined, head propped on a padded chair, awaiting the late rise of the moon. A blanket the color of wine warmed his limbs from the breezes that fluttered the candles. The frail lids of his eyes remained closed, while a dark-skinned adept trimmed his unkempt hair using the knife he kept sharp to cut wild goose quills for pen nibs.

'*You know your best asset is northbound toward Telzen?*' The whisper threaded the empty air, not a handspan from Sethvir's left ear.

'*Was,*' the Fellowship Sorcerer responded in silent reply to the unseen arrival. One whose presence escaped an adept's tuned awareness, a feat of unrivaled astonishment.

But then, only one busy mind on Athera pried into the mysteries with such startling invention. To the shade, whose stealth wore the fierce tang of the magics imbued by the drakes, Althain's Warden proffered the image of Arithon s'Ffalenn, his cloaked figure in the company of the Mad Prophet, disguised as a button seller. The errant pair made their way westward on foot, down the Southshire trade road. Sethvir added, '*Did you think me behind on current events? The ruckus at dawn could have called up the dead, never mind the display that stamped warding patterns into the lane flux.*'

Fionn Areth, Talvish, and Vhandon had fallen asleep to the memory of Arithon tuning the lyranthe bestowed as a parting gift by the clansmen. After their night of oblivious sleep, they awakened to the stunning discovery that prince and prophet had gone. A note was left tucked with the strongbox of amethysts. Arithon's script directed them northward to keep the planned rendezvous in Atwood. Fionn Areth was placed under Rathain's crown protection, the bold lines of writing assured; Koriani interference should pose them no difficulty. Sethvir's earth-sense had captured the binding involved when Arithon invoked his initiate awareness and sealed the penned note with his Name.

Since Vhandon and Talvish knew charter law well enough to grasp the full implications, Althain's Warden finished his thought with disingenuous calm. *'The young double ought to be safe for the nonce.'* Prime Selidie dared not try the Waystone before she reconfigured her sigils to match the crystal's changed resonance; and Arithon's signature enabled a crown obligation, leaving the clearcut grounds to allow a Fellowship intervention.

'Flawed logic,' the subtle intruder responded, a flow of consciousness slipped through the sussurrant snip, as fine steel sliced through hanks of white hair. *'Without Selidie's impairment, whom could you send?'*

Sethvir was too enervated to argue. Particularly since the Fellowship's shorthanded state had invited the mocking exchange in the first place.

Aloud, he said, "Welcome to Althain Tower, Davien."

The startled adept flinched. The knife flashed, and a cut fleece of hair drifted down and strewed the wax shine of the floorboards. "Your colleague is *here?*"

"As he wishes, he could be." The Warden's mouth turned in tacit acknowledgment of the adept's contrite touch, lamenting the gap just razed through his beard. "My dear, no apology. My roof sparrows will use the spare wool for their nesting, and my vanity shall mend, over time."

The adept set down the knife. Her other palm pressed the Warden's frail shoulder, the brief contact a warning to guard his racked strength. "Call as you have need." Her passing shadow darkened the lacquer-worked clothes chest as she departed and latched the door shut at her heels. Left to resume his discussion in privacy, Sethvir opened forthwith, "I sent because I would ask for your help."

Behind closed eyes, he unreeled a string of images winnowed from the ongoing stream of his earth-sense: *of Raiett Raven, at Etarra, lying in wakeful dread of the coercive voices that riddled his sleep; of the subtle ties, spun like lead foil and shadow, that streamed from his tainted aura and afflicted others of his acquaintance. Of a spy network, compromised by insidious forces, and of officials in three of Rathain's northern towns, slowly bent to embrace an inexorable dance with corruption invited by their blinkered prejudice. Vision revealed the first cobweb strands of the ties that might one day solidify into a network that fed upon torture and death. Althain's warden foresaw the thousands of afflicted spirits burning in their torment. The auric force woven from their captivity flickered at nightfall like candleflames and cast a shadow deep as the abyss.*

Reeling through that horrific future, where the practice of necromancy spread like a plague on the false sacrament of the Light, Sethvir resumed his strained plea. "I can send a discorporate to clear the corruption in Jaelot and Darkling."

Davien leaped ahead and captured the gist. *'Etarra requires an incarnate presence. How inconvenient, with you and Asandir caught busy as jugglers, with your hands full of imbalanced grimwards.'*

Sethvir added nothing. The conclusion was obvious. If the cult incursion stayed unresolved beyond the next winter's solstice, its extended roots would establish tight bolt-holes, and finally become entrenched. "That city already traffics in child conscripts," he rasped. "Before those unfortunates are ritually bound and put to use for abomination, the compact demands our response."

No Fellowship awareness could evade that glaring truth. Such horrific rites, done in that trammeled pass, must disrupt the resonance of the fifth lane and finally unbalance the seat of grand confluence that anchored through Ithamon itself. The sharp shift in frequency would wreak permanent change; the heart of Athera's greater mysteries could not do other than falter beyond recovery.

"You have not abandoned your care," Sethvir added. "Or why else did you break your sealed silence in Kewar? Why, on the very moment that Lysaer s'Ilessid first let his blood with a tainted bone knife?"

That perceptive statement caused the tight-knit thread of contact to resolve into a standing figure. One with flame-and-salt hair tumbled over proud shoulders, and clad in a tunic of russet, accented with sable embroidery. Davien's long stride brought him up to the colleague who sat tucked as an invalid in the stuffed chair.

"Your words are too generous," the renegade Sorcerer said. Flesh and blood, breathing, he stood his cold ground with authority, but not repentance. "Who could defy the charge that we seven stand guard for?"

Eyes still closed, although the live flame of his visitor's aura beat against his exposed skin, Sethvir smiled. "You cared too much, rather." A raw effort of will, he turned a rested hand palm upward: no reconciliation, but a gesture of bare supplication. "In fact, what has changed? The Kralovir hope to root a cult branch at Etarra. Their dedicate cause to eradicate clanborn will move forward under the sunwheel banner. One might hope your concern will prompt you to assist. Or else why respond to my summons?"

Davien stared downward, eyes hard as lacquered walnut. "I left you a capable weapon to address this. You do have the means to respond."

"Arithon!" Sethvir's lids flicked open. He stared back, incensed. His failing frame might be swathed in a blanket, yet that burning gaze masked the power of nova and cataclysm, leashed quiescent by an endurance that ran beyond time. "Ath's grace on earth! Will you never stop your invidious scheming?"

"A double jeopardy throw," pronounced Davien. "Let's see which priority rules your choice this time. Our binding made under the will of the dragons to preserve the mysteries for Paravian survival, or else the bleeding-heart clemency that gave rise to the threat allowed in by the compact."

Ingrained beyond words, the contention that had chafed to unreconciled argument, then the wounding fracture that had rocked the world to the brink of disaster. The silence cut, while the far-distant stars spun their undying splendor across the black arc of the deep.

"We both care," admitted the renegade Sorcerer, first to snap off that locked stare. "But we do not agree." Restless as a wind-driven leaf that crossed and recrossed the smooth floor, Davien paced. "Not over the risk of a human presence kept within bounds through your vaunted charters. We've been through this before. Shall I try again? Your system of clan intercession, based in a law administered by the high kingships, is unstable. I have no desire to labor for ages, with failure the axe blade poised over my neck."

Sethvir sighed. "Are you angling to shatter our ties with Athera? If so, at what price? Beneath all the layers of gimmick and subterfuge, do you actually wish to be finished, or are you just yearning to snap the drakes' hold on our hearts and go free?" Althain's Warden stirred, closed his fingers until the knuckles gleamed bloodless as ivory against scarlet wool. "Would you abandon the grace of the mystery that gave us our release and redemption?"

"Would? Or could?" The glance that Davien shot over his shoulder revealed peaked eyebrows and a piquant irony. "The question beckons, Sethvir, does it not? Can you say in the depths of your tormented dreams you have not pursued the temptation? To just walk away? Cross Fate's Wheel and be done? Leave Athera's fate to fall or to languish—why not let the flow of the mysteries fail? Death is the mask that drives the illusion. Why not let the darkness unveil its own light, and resurrect its next hope of salvation?"

"Ciladis could not," Sethvir whispered. Anemone pale in the thin flood of starlight, he kept up his labored speech. "After one armageddon and its cost of deliverance in slaughter, I believe he would finally go mad." Older than the drakes dream of summoning, the Seven's ties of sworn fellowship: *not to risk another division of forces or a parting of common agreement.* One such failure had brought downfall to a mighty civilization, strung between far-flung worlds. "Would you finally tear us asunder, Davien, and seal this planet's entropic destruction?"

"Ah, that's too weighty an anguish, my friend. No grandiose causes, please. We're past dealing." Stopped short with his artisan's fingers flattened against the stone windowsill, Davien finished his thought. "Let in the bad cards, I always argued we'd lose the first hand. Scrub the second, then the third, perhaps sweat through a fourth, a protracted game makes no difference. We'll *still* wind up forced to destroy the ragtag remnant of humanity, instead."

"We are not discussing the fate of mankind," Althain's Warden reminded. "The matter is necromancy and our destined charge of attending Paravian survival."

Davien spun on his heel, cat fast, now offended. "For that, you have Arithon Teir's'Ffalenn, trained and fit." His citrine setting flared as he capped his flourish with the low parody of a performer's bow. "A transcendent initiation in the maze under Kewar, and a year of erudite knowledge have prepared him. Have I not answered? Your crown prince has been formidably well groomed to take up your thrown gauntlet at Etarra."

Sethvir's sorrow filled all the room, which tonight might as well have stayed empty. "You are no friend to his Grace, if that's your best answer. One last time, I will ask. Why not make the choice to assist us?"

But Davien shoved away from the casement, his mercuric rejection recalcitrant to the bone. "Why now? Give me one sterling reason!"

With this colleague, Sethvir was wiser than to tender his argument straight on. "Of us all, Asandir has the most cause for resentment. Now his life's in jeopardy once more. He's had to restabilize four grimwards without any thought of rhetorical hesitation."

"Spare me your line, that he just soldiers on! You've leaned on our knowledge for your ends before." From the far wall, turned on his heel once again, Davien cracked from behind, "Why should I change principle and come back to heel now?"

Althain's Warden regarded his ringless, thin hands. "To spare Arithon."

"For what?" Davien's stinging mockery came back, untamed. "Pray tell, Calum Kincaid, *for what?* A future that brings us mankind's execution? Armageddon, *again*, because the drakes chose us for the staggering task of lifting their legacy of remorse?"

Turquoise eyes slipped into farsighted distance, until snow-white lashes swept down and veiled them. Images unreeled behind Sethvir's closed lids. The dizzying array of mapped possibility revealed the structured course of the war host now re-forming under the sunwheel banner. The Sorcerer's awareness discerned the raising of two armed forces. One inspired by the fervor of false faith, arising out of the west, and another, more sinister, about to be birthed through the pull of cult influence, that would sow the whirlwind by storm in the east.

Etarra, not Avenor, would shape the policy that sharpened the lethal edge on the axe.

The sole path to disarmament lay in Arithon's guile: and the intricate, visionary plan he had forged to defuse fanatical conflict. *A course one man could never hope to accomplish without the full backing of a Fellowship intervention.* A Sorcerer's hand would be required to clear the Kralovir from Etarra.

"The Teir's'Ffalenn must not be asked to exert his trained strength in the open," Sethvir finished in toneless exhaustion. "Such a move, even made for expedience, would destroy his intent for a bloodless denouncement. Ask him to strip the mask off the Kralovir, and all of the north will be driven to recoil! Misguided terror will only spark a more vicious persecution."

Sethvir foresaw the site where the hammer would impact the anvil: where the fury and blind fervor would ignite into flame and strike against the immovable pride of Arithon's staunchest supporters. Afraid for Alestron, the Warden's final line of appeal remained his implacable silence.

"You'll have to choose, won't you?" Davien closed at length. "Which structure to spare: Rathain's monarchy or the compact?" No ripple of air marked the shift as the renegade Sorcerer dissolved his bodily form for departure. His last word impressed the stillness with cruel clarity. *'Don't wait too long. The more you waver before you decide, the more perilous the stake on the outcome.'*

At Althain Tower, the rise of the moon brightened the sands of the Bittern Desert: where once, in a past that predated history, two dragons had fought and scorched hills and glades with their wasting breath. Where later, Paravians had bled and died in failed sacrifice for redemption. Here, the murmur of wind bespoke an undying cry of lament.

Tonight's sorrow was no less bitterly fierce. In the space where a centaur warden had once stood, facing the same bleak hills with their grievous burden of bones, the whisper of light fell as kindly over Sethvir's crinkled face. The rays silver-lit the slow well of tears that slid through the hacked gap in his beard.

After dark on the roadway bound from Sanshevas, a bonfire threw a torrid glow over the wind-raked stand of the broom. Sultry flares cast the shadows of irritable men and lit the stirred backs of disgruntled beasts. Wrapped in the smoke-tainted breath of close heat, echoing across the tangle of mussed goods and racked wagons, raised voices marked the seething frustration of the guarded caravan, whose journey to Southshire had come to disaster. Dissent raged over whether to build up the blaze or douse the last embers outright. Half the armed men feared attracting more *iyats*, while the road master swore by the gray in his beard that a darkened camp would invite stealth and murder by Selkwood's marauding barbarians.

Factions splintered the argument: the tradesmen and drivers wished to turn tail and limp all the way back to Atchaz.

"Torn silk can be sold for cost to the quiltmakers," the road master insisted, morose. "Get into Sanshevas ahead of the rains, we'd at least avoid mildew beneath those ripped tarps. Catch bad weather, and we'll be left stirring pots for the ragmen who bleach out the dyes to make paper."

"You can't sell for salvage," snapped a headhunter tracker, hunkered down to sharpen his knives. "Damn you man, think ahead. What's left but wreckage to save our good name? We don't show something to prove we were fiend-plagued, we'll have no evidence to escape a criminal case with the magistrates."

The troop of lancers now answerable for the Light's vanished tribute supported Ganish league's adamant stance. Shouting, they insisted the hard luck party should remain intact to corroborate their bizarre mishap. "Stay the course of Southshire's grueling inquest. If we don't stay together to back up the truth, we'll all be charged as collaborators."

Into the tempest, by no chance at all, strode the itinerant bard and the button seller. They were blameless wayfarers bound downcoast for Sanshevas, they explained, while the headhunter skirmishers prodded them in, and several lancers pinned them at weapon point.

"Just let us lay our bedrolls down for the night. We could share our goat cheese and raisins," the stout button seller offered hopefully. "Your campfire's what kept us walking since dark. We thought we'd be safer in company." When the lance points stayed fixed, he shrugged with fidgety apprehension. "Less chance we'd be stalked by barbarians, though I'm sorry to see we've misjudged. Clan brigands might sneak in and pilfer tin buttons. But chop no green wood, they don't cut your throat. You fellows here seem worse-tempered."

As one lancer bristled, the minstrel laid a restraining finger on the crowding tip of the weapon. "My friend means no harm." A slender, cloaked figure, he engaged a smile and flicked the canvas strap hanging his lyranthe. "I could offer my touch on the strings for a tune." As the caravan's road master shoved to the fore, he added, "You've suffered a mishap? Those wagons look wrecked. You actually do seem in need of an hour of light entertainment."

"That might keep your mad Ganishmen from drubbing my drivers!" the grizzled professional felt moved to point out. "Since you rock-heads won't back down and let us cut losses, why not pass the evening with music?"

The sunwheel guard relented and lowered their steel, if only to seize on the chance to escape the debate on their festering predicament.

Button seller and free singer soon sat by the fire. They ate their rough meal, while listening through the recounted plague of rogue *iyats* that had spoiled the townsmen's caravan.

"It's not canny, what happened," confided a field archer in dismal distress. "Who's going to believe we didn't spin the wild tale to cover a robbery? By all that's true! Who but a Shadow-blind fool would make off with the tribute gold bound for Avenor?"

The singer twisted the grass stem just plucked to clean out his teeth. "I don't know," he mused. "A troublesome *iyat*'s more reasonable, surely, than a pack of grown men who've worked themselves dizzy running in fear of the dark."

A stunned pause ensued. Through the gasp of more than one intaken breath, the lance captain rapped off a question. "You have no faith in the cause of the Light?"

"And why should I?" The singer stared back, eyes of an indeterminate hazel turned suddenly vivid with mirth. "Is this avatar so almighty powerful? If he hates the idea of darkness that much, why not birth the miracle of a new sun? That way he could rid himself of the night. You lot could work double shift, chasing heretics. Or, perhaps not. That might cost his holiness too pinching much, since each man would be owed twice the pay share."

Outrage, shock, then the cracking pressure of long days spent chasing lost coin on a fruitless search through the brush: the weight proved too much. A muffled snigger disturbed the quiet. Then the lance captain broke and guffawed.

"Oh, please!" the raffish minstrel objected. "This issue is *serious*. Some flattering daisy's named himself divine. What does that mean? Should rats in the sewers pay him respects? Will they sell off his night soil for perfume, do you think, or does immortal virtue *in fact* grunt and void straining bowels like the rest of us?"

"Watch your tongue, friend," the button seller warned. "You might cause offense. After all, if the rag on yon captain was a sunwheel surcoat, the dedicate soldier beside you is probably one of those life-sworn."

"How pious." The free singer leaned back, stretched an arm, and tugged the cover off his lyranthe. "To me, the whole bunch look like worried men. Next week, they could face a branding as criminals in front of a Southshire magistrate. Can't a god sent immortal distinguish a truthful man from a sneaking thief and a liar? Seems plain to me, actually. This idea of tribute smells a bit suspect. If heaven's minion needed to traffic in gold, should he not clap his hands and call down a shower of bullion from his supreme connections on high?"

"His Divine Grace hates clansmen," a hatchet-faced headhunter commented. "That's good enough cause to suit me."

The minstrel smiled. "Very good." His fingers stabbed a spray of notes from the strings he began tuning by absent habit. "But why should his exaltedness keep paying your bounties, when the whole countryside's turning out elite troops to slaughter old bloodlines for nothing?"

Shot erect, now outraged, the lance captain puffed up to take issue.

Before he spoke, the insolent singer dug an elbow into the button seller beside him. "Friend, these grunts are too glum. You've still got those brandy crocks tucked in your pack? Pop the corks. Why not share? If something's not done to lift this sour mood, every last errant fiend will come back. You might not value your shriveled equipment. But I'm tender and young. Not a bit ready to ruin my sport in the blankets! Or didn't you *look?* These poor wretches are scratching themselves raw through ripped clothing. Makes me wince, just to think of risking the breeks that keep gnat bites from welting my bollocks!"

The brandy, exhumed, was exceptionally sweet. Perhaps even suspiciously potent. The jugs passed hand to hand, while the minstrel's satire kept its keen edge, catchy enough to invite uproarious laughter and knee-slapping rounds of shared choruses. The lyrics maligning the Light became insidiously infectious. Although singer and button seller moved on at dawn, they left every man from the disarrayed caravan singing into the morning.

Beyond any doubt, the minstrel's bold repertoire would survive and spread through the port brothels of Southshire. In the mouths of the headhunters and drivers, the scurrilous verses would travel on and take the stews of Sanshevas by storm.

"You're evil incarnate," Dakar accused, well away and sweating his hangover through a waist-deep slog across a tidal marsh. They had left the road under the cover of mist to make rendezvous with a fishing smack. "My brash singer, do you realize how near you came to earning a lancer's steel through your guts?"

"As close as the salvation in your spelled flasks of brandy." The bard's teeth flashed beneath the lyranthe he balanced on top of his sable head. "I'm not dead. Nor was the binding of Davien's longevity put to the test on a goring. We're ahead of the game, actually. I'd hazard the guess: a few sunwheel dedicates will defect rather than cling to an idiot's honor and molder in irons at Southshire. Aren't you eager to tackle the morass we'll find down the coast at Shaddorn?"

"Not if you're stoned out of town by a mob," Dakar puffed, flailing to haze off humming insects and the chaff sifting down from the bulrushes.

"What a fine lack of faith you place in the ridiculous," stated Arithon Teir's'Ffalenn. He strode forward, nonplussed; perversely still merry since he had been too busy with playing to sample Dakar's doctored drink. "I thought the objective was to turn the mob with the stones on the tents of the sunwheel recruiters?"

"No more swamps," Dakar grumbled. "Or I swear on my blood, I'll hoard the drink for myself and join ranks with the pious offenders."

The fishing smack hired to board two soggy passengers breasted a brisk chop and made rendezvous with a merchant brig, hanging offshore just past the horizon. The boat grappled her lines long enough to relinquish the contents of her hold, which consisted of contraband goods wrapped in tarpaulin and concealed beneath the glistening shine of the night's catch of mullet. For two extra silvers, her skipper was also persuaded to part with his small barrels of spoiled mackerel, stewed to reeking as bait for the crab trappers whose skiffs worked the shallows inside the reefs.

The brown-haired, agile passenger who had given no name helped his stout companion aboard, then waved the fishing smack off with good cheer. The brig's sun-darkened crewmen cast off her lines, while the grizzled, blue-water captain looked on with a dubious squint.

Lips pursed, he measured the sealed barrels and heaped fish, shoveled in an oozing, silvery heap that drew clouds of flies on his foredeck. "Man, in this heat, we'll be wearing a weeping, ripe stink, since I notice you didn't pack any salt. I swear by Dharkaron's cast Spear, you'd better know what in Sithaer you're doing. Or I'll chuck the lot overboard, and your carcass, too. In these waters, believe me, the sharks never pause. You'll be torn to shreds in a heartbeat."

The scoundrel brought aboard at Fiark's behest smiled back with errant delight. "You've brought the empty wine tuns I wanted from Innish? Very good. Let's bring them topside at once."

Comprehension sharpened the captain's astute face. "Oh, man! You're not going to—"

"Oh, yes. Just watch me," the visitor promised, then proceeded to fill the twoscore emptied hogsheads bearing the sunwheel brand with his load of puddled, dead fish. He seasoned the mix with the brew in the bait casks, then had the ship's coopers seal in the bungs, while the southern sun beat down like a torch and rotted the contents to sloshing jelly.

While the sailhands set the brig on her eastbound course, and the fat land-lubber napped in the shade, the nameless man shared peppered sausage and bread in the aft cabin with the squint-eyed captain. Behind a closed door, the probing questions continued, each sally aimed to sate an unsettled curiosity.

Deflected by his visitor's suave tongue, the captain at last tried a frontal assault, his massive hands clamped to a jack of black rum, brewed from Sanshevas molasses. "You know you can't just sashay up to the docks, then switch out your barrels for a prized shipment of Orvandir red. Not under the noses of the Light's armed guard. Nor will you evade the devilsome eyes of the customs keepers' wolf pack of excisemen."

"I agree." The strange young man seemed roguish enough, except for the fact he refused any drink, and his stare seemed to pierce a man's silences. "That's why you'll lend me grade paper and ink."

"A forged requisition?" The brig's master chuckled, dismissive. "That rum you're too proud to sample today will taste like pure joy, at your hanging."

The visitor grinned. "You're right. Shall we wager?" He leaned down, delved into the canvas lately drawn from the heap of dead fish, and produced an intact seal in gold wax, affixed with a pristine white ribbon.

The captain's eyes widened. "Damn me! That's genuine!"

"Nothing less." Clever fingers accepted the pen from the chart desk, then paper, and in professional script, proceeded to fabricate a bundle of documents of lading addressed to the customs office at Southshire. One commanded the Light's resource to hire a team of longshoremen to debark a wine shipment for the sunwheel recruitment tents. The other, less complex, enjoined the port authorities to release a like number of hogsheads, stacked and lying empty, to be onloaded for transport to the wineries' guild agent at Durn.

"You will then burn the new list you receive at Southshire and finish your run on the original papers Fiark dispatched from Innish. The delivery you leave will be the ones I've just borrowed, that now keep my haul of prime baitfish."

"But yon barrels at wharfside are going to be full!" objected the brig captain with pigheaded logic. "No longshoreman's going to miss that sore fact! Not as he rolls your suspect replacements under the eyes of the clerks at the docks."

That glaring concern left the swindler unruffled. "This will be handled. Leave the details to me. You need do nothing but dally tonight. Stay hove-to with your lamps dark, at sea. Arrange to reach anchorage at Southshire by the dawn tide. Present your papers to the port authorities as usual. Then take my advice and slip your cable again before the full ebb at noon. Now, if I could be so bold as to charter your pinnace? For what fee? Not too dearly, mind! You're free to collect her again in three days. I plan to leave her legally trim. You'll find her tied up and waiting in a paid berth on your next upcoast run through Shaddorn."

"You know how to sail?" the captain asked, doubtful. His mesmerized gaze watched the sum in bright gold, just now being stacked by his rum flask.

"As well as I write," the odd guest insisted. He lifted the sconce off the candle, then dripped off the wax to affix the seal of the Light's priesthood over his falsified documents. "Are you asking for surety?"

The brig captain selected a coin and tried the edge with his teeth. His blunt smile returned. "Since you didn't foist off your payment in tin, naturally, your bonded signature will suffice." More gold chinked and glinted. His expansive mood brightened. "In fact, a simple handshake will do, and I frankly won't care if you wreck her."

The pinnace was unlashed and swung out, forthwith. Her mast was stepped, and her gear smartly rigged. She launched inside of an hour. By the handy way the departing visitor threaded the mainsheet blocks, he well knew his handling of boats. His torpid comrade was kicked awake, and stowed, complaining, amidships. The lines were cast clear. As the craft clawed away on the stiff, off-shore breeze, breasting the indigo swell, the captain regarded the stacked tuns left behind, contents cooking to noisome sludge under the scouring sunlight.

The mate paused at his side, a sharp-witted man as mean as old rope who still tracked the tender's expert retreat toward the landward horizon. "Who was that man, and why do I sense in my bones that he's up to no good?"

The brig's master shrugged. "He's left us a round fifty royals and no name. Yet Fiark's instructions on that score were plain. If a whisper of scandal sticks on us at Southshire, we're to claim our pinnace was stolen at sword's point by sea-roving clansmen. Then we're to leave an accurate description on record that fingers yon shady brigand as the thief."

By afternoon, the brig's pinnace nosed across turquoise shallows, parallel to the white thrash of spray on the coastal reefs. Sweating and red, Dakar nursed the tiller. Arithon stood in the wind on the foredeck, singing a passionate ballad that wrung the flux currents into high turmoil. To mage-sighted eyes, the rampant emotion unleashed a tempest of charge: prime target for the *iyats* that soaked up the energy churned up by the breaking surf.

As the sprites arrowed in to make sport with the pinnace, Arithon wove shadow and locked them captive. He had gained in finesse. His reaped salvage of drake spawn was soon wound, bright as jewelery, onto his little finger. When his gleanings flashed silver, indigo, and deep purple up to his knuckle, he footed his way aft and reclaimed the rudder from Dakar's white-fisted grasp.

"We are owed a night's drinking in Southshire, I think. Your boots aren't dry yet?" Seated, his white shirt riffled in the afternoon breeze, and his hair like flicked ink in his eyes, the Prince of Rathain propped a bare foot on the thwart. "Well, cheer up. Come the morning, there won't be another hike through a swamp."

"We'll be sailing," groused Dakar, not one whit appeased as he shifted in vain effort to ease his back against the stay that anchored the mast. "My tender stomach will scarcely pause to sort out the unpleasant difference."

"Then don't be hungover," Arithon said, altogether too vibrant when any natural creature should languish in the perishing afternoon heat. "I'm not going to task very much of your resource."

"It's the worry," the Mad Prophet admitted, eyes shut. Pink hands laced on his belly, he settled to doze in the shade of the thrumming mainsail. "Don't wake me until we're at rest in the harbor. That way I might slip the burden of fate, and reach shore without getting seasick."

On schedule, the pinnace hove into Southshire. There, the prankish gusts lifted the wings of the gulls and sent them flocking over the rooftops. The dockside hung thick with the pitch tang of oakum, and the dust devils danced, whirling sawdust. The shipworks were winding down for the day. Banging mallets dwindled and died, and the doused coals smoked under the steam boxes. Sundown painted a pastel sky when Arithon flagged a lighterman to row him ashore.

Now red-haired and brown-eyed, he looked comfortably plump in the stuffed cloth of Dakar's spare tunic. He carried his lyranthe for carefree entertainment, to be back, he assured, before daybreak.

As good as his word, he amused the off-duty watchmen, and the packs of dice-throwing sailhands crowding the waterfront taverns. He ate dinner, listening to idle talk, then tuned up and composed a bright satire. Swept off with a rowdy smith and a chandler, he went to taste the free wine doled out by the sunwheel recruiters. For an hour, he sat on a bench with laced hands in the shadowy dusk of the tent. Since he never moved, no one blamed him for the fact that, thereafter, every cask the priest broached appeared to have soured to vinegar. He took polite leave of his casual acquaintances and returned to the dives along Harbor Street.

There, the snake venom sellers were just hitting stride. A juggler with torches was swallowing fire. Skin flasks of rum could be bought for a copper, and a cocker was setting his boards in the street, contenders and bettors crowding his crates to size up the hackled combatants. The bard skirted the crowd, whistling, and chose a snug berth between wineshops, where he played ditties for coin and sweet serenades for the young lovers. Dakar saw him, still there, when he reached shore at midnight, parched for a drink at the Fishnet. When the Mad Prophet emerged from the tavern, replete, the bard was down by the waterfront sheds, cracking jokes with the sunwheel guardsmen. Two of the customs keeper's watchmen were with them, bent over in howling stitches.

Dakar parked against the signpost of a trinket shop and wheedled for favors from three painted doxies. Their simpering drew whistles from a muscular galleyman, who flashed coin, and left the deserted spellbinder brooding. The sunwheel guards on the dock poked fun at his stiff state of misery as they moved off to pick up their beat. The carrot head bard was nowhere in evidence when the three of them paused by the customs' shack, and unaccountably, snoozed at their posts.

Only Dakar noticed the *iyats* steal in. He watched through slit eyes as they pried all the bungs from the wine tuns stacked under their cover of tarps on the wharf. The excisemen's seals gleamed under the rise of the moon, undisturbed by a pilfering hand as twenty-eight barrels of Orvandir's best spirits gurgled until they were emptied. Their contents trickled through the cracked boards and into the black slosh of the tide with no official at Southshire the wiser.

Crimson dawn saw the pinnace away. The change of the tide brought the inbound brig, complete with her forged bills of lading. Just past the morning change of the guard, the drained barrels on the wharf were replaced by a paid crew of sweating longshoremen. They onloaded the dry barrels, then unladed the brig with their equal number of filled replacements.

The wagoner who served the recruiting tents arrived later. He collected his load and delivered his haulage for pay, all unaware he had replenished last night's soured stores with twenty-eight tuns of rank fish bait.

By then, bard and prophet were well gone, sails spread to catch the spanking breeze that chivvied them on toward Shaddorn. They made port in two days, left the pinnace sedately tied, and sought a performer's lodging in one of the tile-roofed, dockside taverns.

The landlord wiped wet hands on his apron and surveyed the odd pair on his doorstep, lukewarm. "A free singer, eh? You'll pay for your bed. If the company appreciates your balladry, they'll leave a coin or two in your cap. If they don't, you'll not hear your own notes for the noise. If you want yesterday's bread and the fish stew on the hob, you'll have dinner at the sailhands' cost of two pence."

"That's fair," said the minstrel, his blithe nature unruffled. Now sporting a tangle of pallid blond hair, he entered the salt-musty common room, while the stout companion who tagged at his heels grumbled that the inns on the Tip were unfit for the manners of stable flies. "It's pinching indecent not to give a free singer bed and board, never mind an allotment of beer."

The minstrel took a room. Not withstanding, he paid, and slept undisturbed until dusk. Returned to the taproom, clad in garish motley, he straddled a bench and tuned up his lyranthe. The tables were bustling when the fast courier rode in, bearing word of the riots at Southshire.

"Fair tore those sunwheel tents into shreds, will you know! The fracas started when the priests ran out of wine and tried to serve up the Light's supplicants with rotten mullet." Paused for a drink, the parched messenger slapped settled dust from his leathers and broke into braying laughter. "When the daisies in their sunwheels accosted the stevedores for restitution, let me tell you, the fisticuffs started in earnest. They say you'll know the Light's minions by their black eyes, and the longshoremen's guild, by the overripe stink o' thrown fish!"

To no one's surprise, the resident bard composed a satire in commemoration. The packed crowd stamped and clapped, begging for the same ballad again, and crying themselves prostrate with mirth.

The delighted landlord refunded the minstrel's lodging and generously forgave the stout companion for his mean-spirited comments. "Stay the week," the inn's red-cheeked matron entreated. "A month, even."

The fair-haired bard smiled, and firmly declined. "I'm bound north, for Etarra." Since his performance had captured the bystanders' interest, his explanation cut through conversation. "Folk say that the troops who are billeted there have so many gold buttons they're wont to stake their spare clothing at cards."

A startled guffaw cracked the ambient quiet.

The minstrel winked, snapped a rollicking arpeggio, and gushed on, "And I've heard! The white avatar who pays them to die cannot sleep without candles alight at his bedside. If that's the truth, then he's no god at all. Any wretch who hates darkness needs no divine Light! Give me a sweet lay and a halfpenny wick for my prayer to bring in a safe morning!"

The Southshire courier roared with delight. Half of the inn's replete patrons joined in. Badgered by threats of shadow and war, and pinched by taxes to fund sunwheel troops, they met the free singer's bold, shafting comments with stamping appreciation. Before their mood shifted, he flipped back pale hair and launched into a medley of reels. Each break between tunes, he added a new verse to the infamous saga that described the demise of the righteous to barrels of fish bait at Southshire.

Midnight drew nigh. The taproom was crammed beyond bursting. The pot washer ran to a neighboring tavern to roll in a fresh hogshead of beer. The landlord scarcely had cause to complain that the price asked for the brew was extortionate. Both of his cash chests were jammed at the hinges. The customers who were too tipsy to stand overflowed and fell down in the street. The door banged, admitting a stream of newcomers, drawn in to hear the uproarious comedy. Their shouted choruses threatened to raise the wooden pegs from the floorboards.

The raucous celebration ran unabated until the last keg in Shaddorn was sucked dry.

"Man, we've not had a night to match this!" the landlord enthused.

He surveyed his taproom and addressed the need for fresh sawdust to sweeten the privy. The teeming moil of bodies thinned, finally, until only the prostrate remained, draped over trestles and benches. Others lay snoring in heaps like dropped rags, under the guttering prickets.

Gray dawn seeped through the seaside casements when the bard finally laid down his instrument. A shuffling barmaid brought him juice and a sweetcake, then sat down to ease her sore feet.

"You scarcely seem tired," she observed, peering sidelong and smiling with invitation.

"Oh, I'll sleep," the singer assured her, "and alone, once the fiends in your hops quit their hammering on the tender insides of my noggin."

Slumped over the trestle nearby, the fat tinker opened one eye. "Swilled the lion's share, did you? A sore head's your just penance. Unless you wish to engage a rough passage round the Scimlade on some fisherman's reeking lugger, we've a hot, weary tramp through the hills. Or have you in fact decided to stay and try your luck reaping the whirlwind?"

"Our playbill's too volatile?" the minstrel quipped back. "You don't think the free singer's code will stay the wrath of the priesthood we've slandered at Southshire?" He laughed, his sly features veiled in the gloom as the innkeeper's wife snuffed the tallow dips. "By all means, then, the safe route is by sea. If I opt for the lugger, you'll knife me instead?"

Whatever the tinker meant to reply, the inn door slammed open. Stabbing daylight speared in, chased by a young woman's vituperative scolding.

"Husband's in his cups and didn't come home." The barmaid shoved erect with a sigh, scanned the heaped floorboards, and pointed. "That's him, there, madam. He won't hear a word. You might spare us some peace, and pipe down."

The skirted silhouette left the doorway. Not in concern for her errant wastrel, but vengeance bent for the bard eating breakfast at the inn's table.

"You!" Her contemptuous glance raked him, from his tousled blond curls to his unlaced shirtfront, and his disheveled jacket of motley. "You are a breed of dog that rends families. What have I to show for your night's ill work? At home, I have six children to feed, and here's a week's silver drunk down by my man in another night's foolish bingeing!"

The minstrel dug into his scrip and skidded a half-royal across the beer-streaked boards of the trestle. "If your weans are crying, by all means visit the market, then go home and feed them."

"That can't salvage dignity," the woman bit back. "Your insolent charity can't mend slack morals, or forgive the temptation you place upon lack-witted fathers!"

"Perish the thought," the free singer said, amiable. "If the rose has such thorns, no wonder the poor, tongue-lashed creatures are drawn to embrace the joy of the tankard. They'll suffer aplenty, once they wake up. I'll tell you now, this inn's brew packs a punch that makes a thrown brick feel like swan's down. Take your coin, madam, and your shrill abuse some other place on this fine morning."

"She won't," the barmaid confided, low-voiced. "This rabid hussy stays on and shouts. The last time, we got bullish and paid for a longshoreman to roll her sot home in a barrel."

"Did you, indeed?" The bard raised an eyebrow, reached for his lyranthe, and launched into the "Tinsmith's Implacable Wife."

Worn as he was, with his voice husked from the pipe smoke, he had not lost his immaculate timing. Line for brilliant, scouring line, he performed the ballad with infectious delight, providing strategic pauses for the matron's rife tongue to add her part to the performance. Several casualties in the taproom sat up. Sides gripped, sore heads cradled, they shook with laughter.

The bard reached his last stanza and closed. He stood up and bowed to the glaring female, now planted in pinched fury before him. Before the rolling gales of mirth died, or the enraged wife found a rejoinder, a bystanding galleyman granted the singer the mercy of his appreciation.

The fat tinker accepted the offer at once, of swift passage by sea up to Telzen.

Late Spring 5671

Escort

Morning sunlight sliced through the mist over Mirthlvain, a blaze as distinct as an edge of hot metal scraped against exposed skin. The flat-bottomed skiff razed through the reeking shallows, bearing its three mismatched occupants. Bent reeds scraped the thwarts. Scum slid under the keel. Poised upon wide-set legs in the stern, Ianfar s'Gannley flipped his blond braid off his neck and poled the vessel ahead to the explosive clap of wings as a wading heron burst into ungainly flight.

The master spellbinder who knelt by the thwart tracked the bird's wheeling circle. "*Dediari*," Verrain murmured, the word a bright cadence in Paravian. "Forgive." He frowned as the creature's skimming descent looped back and resettled to resume its slow stalking.

"Take heed, my winged sister," Mirthlvain's guardian warned. "The fish here keep vile company." Soaked sleeves pushed up to his elbows, both wrists and each finger scarred, he clapped his tarred bucket under the surface and gouged up another dollop of bog slime.

The Princess of Avenor stirred from her perch in the bow. Lean and brown from her months spent at Methisle Fortress, and clad like a waif in men's clothing, she and the s'Gannley clansman who tasked himself as her escort ignored their host's habit of thinking aloud. Ellaine offered the empty bucket she held, in trade for the guardian's filled one.

"Gloves first!" Verrain chided. The melting concern within his brown eyes had once conquered the court ballrooms of Shand, before the rebellion had torn them to ruin.

A court lady no less irresistibly charmed, Ellaine returned her shy smile and retrieved the reinforced gauntlet.

"Don't slosh that, mind!" Verrain resettled himself, poised to make a fresh capture.

Sunlight lanced through the thick air like ruled gauze as Ianfar poled the skiff across the next reed bed.

As the princess dug wrist deep through the noisome muck, a shelled creature with needle-sharp teeth fastened over her leather-clad finger. "Another!" she announced with cheerful good grace.

Ianfar hissed an oath and clapped a fist to his belt knife.

A needless defense; Verrain's recoiling move reached the lady's side as her bloodthirsty catch broke the surface.

A leopard snail studded with black-and-red pincers labored to gnaw its way through the soaked glove.

Verrain's barehanded grip pried off the disgruntled creature. "Here, you. Let's see." The lilted phrase was more sorrowful than disgusted, a disarming gentleness that had cozened his guests to lend help with the exhaustive task of spring inventory.

Humidity beading her hair and a smutch of slime on one cheek, the retiring princess leaned close as Mirthlvain's guardian mused, "If you wade in here barefoot, this strain of methspawn would snip your flesh to the bone. See the mouth structure? No fangs should mean this fellow's not venomous. Still, let's be sure."

He pinned the snapping mandibles and peered past the prod of the mollusk's serrated tongue. "Harmless. Some others with brindle markings are not. Even worse, some have tail spikes. I've seen strains like that pack a walloping poison."

Ianfar reset his pole. The craft bobbled forward, while Verrain released the distraught mollusk into the sable silk sheen of the water.

"Oars!" he announced. "We're going back."

Again, Ianfar slapped a taut hand to his knife. "Trouble?"

"Mercy, no. At least, not from the mire." Verrain tilted his chin in salute to the lady, inelegantly perched with sunburned shins in a rolled up pair of old breeches. "Princess, word's just been dispatched here from Althain's Warden. Your overdue escort is soon to arrive. That means I shall have expert help with my snails, and you might prefer the chance to retire, at least for a change of clothing. In barely an hour, you're to be given a Fellowship Sorcerer's reception."

The drafty fortress at Methisle kept no servants. Its Second Age sprawl of masonry towers had been raised first to house detailed records: exhaustive genealogies compiled when Paravian lore masters and Fellowship Sorcerers labored to cleanse the dark mire of its parasitic intelligence. At the change in rule, when mankind took refuge, the aberrant wraiths called *methurien* had been banished from Athera for six millennia. Yet the lichen-stained citadel on its tufted knoll was still maintained in solid repair. Night and day through the turn of the seasons, Mirthlvain's watch keeper worked the age-old bindings, his charge to confine the savage array of warped creatures that, even now, inter-bred and gave birth to malevolent offspring.

Lady Ellaine did not feel at ease with the screeling wails, the chitterings, and the bone-chilling night whistles of the amphibians the locked gates and tight wardings restrained. If a season in Verrain's unperturbed company had shown her the misted beauty that enfolded the cypress groves and the eerie delight of the marsh lights that drifted like tufted silk through the reeds, today, her hoydenish freedom would end. Flight from Avenor had brought her to face the power of a Fellowship Sorcerer.

She felt no regret, as she set the garnet pins from Dame Dawr to tuck the tight coil of her hair. Her return to clean petticoats and elaborate skirts did not constrict her in spirit. On the contrary: raised to the demure propriety of the westlands, Lady Ellaine took comfort, if not consolation, in the boundaries drawn by court manners.

She arose, smoothed the lace on her satin sleeves, then used a two-handed grasp to lift the massive latch that fastened her chamber door. Cats scattered before her as she gathered layered hems and descended the worn stone stair-well. Her step stayed firm, despite trepidation. If she must, she would move to the next place of sanctuary. Not for man, or avatar, or sorcerer, would she cede her determined ground. Not until her royal husband came forward to answer for two prearranged acts of murder.

Ellaine raised her chin and swept on through the carved doubled doors that let into the upper-floor gallery. Verrain sat below, furled in a fresh robe of peat brown. Broad-shouldered and poised, Ianfar s'Gannley stood beside him in clan braid and leathers, bearing his sword, with his fingers clasped at his back. He heard the silken swish of Ellaine's entry. Faultlessly courteous, he strode to the landing, prepared to usher her to a seat.

The board trestle was empty. The stuffed chairs supported nothing but cats, watching the shadows in the deep corners with haughty, emerald eyes. Of the Fellowship escort, forepromised for months, no trace as yet seemed in evidence. Ellaine shivered. Despite the full sunlight that streamed through the row of open-air casements, her skin felt brushed over by a wintry draft that appeared to have sprung out of nowhere.

"Where is the Sorcerer?" she inquired.

Ianfar drew out a carved chair, winced, and scuffed a felting of hair off the faded upholstery. "Just arrived," he admitted. The sparse glance flashed in Verrain's direction disclosed an unusual uncertainty. "Traithe could not come. My lady Ellaine, you must be aware? About Fellowship Sorcerers, that some of them aren't quite—"

"Behind you!" a voice broke through with clipped pique. "A split second sooner, and a span to your left, and you would have trodden straight through me."

Ellaine turned her head, startled, and found herself facing the apparition headlong.

Shade or not, the Sorcerer's presence pinned the nerves like a whetted-steel needle. He was tall, and rakishly slender in pearl-studded cuffs and dapper, green velvets. A short-cropped beard sported a badger's streaked white, and his roguish attention showed merriment. "Forgive the discourtesy, but we've no time to dawdle explaining the fact I'm not corporate."

Gallant gesture abandoned, Ianfar s'Gannley left off dusting the chair and raised his fist to his heart in a formal salute. "Kharadmon," he addressed, "As *caithdein*'s heir, how may I best serve the land?"

"At home!" The Sorcerer's impatience rejected the bother of court introductions. "Your cousin, Lord Maenol, must act at once on a message that carries an urgency. Your charge will be to deliver swift word. A horse to bear you at speed to the Thaldeins awaits you at Isaer's Great Circle."

"But that site lies on the far side of the continent!" Lady Ellaine burst out, then bit her lip in crimson dismay as Kharadmon's disconcerting regard settled back upon her.

"Your steadfast clan escort will not need to fly," the shade reassured with asperity. "Though the prospect would shock the mortal wits from him, the logistics involved are too clumsy. He will be sent on the winds of the flux raised by Athera's magnetics. A three-lane transition across longitude might wreck his digestion, but not to the point where he will be left unfit to stand up and ride."

Battened behind her mask of state poise, Ellaine fought to calm her quickened pulse. Deportment availed nothing: Kharadmon's intent interest reached past masking pretense and fingered the hidden fear in her heart.

"My lady, you shall not be forced back to Avenor. Ianfar's journey is asked for the realm, but I would not risk his life in a town, any more than you should be exposed to the mysteries at large within the free wilds. You cannot be sent along with this man or take shelter with the clan outpost in the Pass of Orlan."

"Our people's bitterness can't be laid to rest," Ianfar made haste to apologize. "My lady, your husband's execution of Maenalle s'Gannley was deemed an infamous act. She is the only *caithdein* in history to have been dealt a criminal's death on a scaffold."

Ellaine locked her trembling fingers. "If Lysaer is the killer your people have named him, I would tender your clans my apology." Her bravery nonetheless was sufficient to challenge a Fellowship Sorcerer. "Don't expect I'll return to a political marriage that excuses the sacrifice of a son."

"Lysaer was innocent of what befell Kevor," Kharadmon stated point-blank. "Nor was your husband involved, or aware of the traitorous plot that killed Talith." His turbulent brevity did not rest there, or disregard all tactful kindness. "How strictly would you have me interpret the law?"

Fragile in that moment as kiln-fired porcelain, Ellaine stated, "With honesty."

Ianfar went still, aware of what must come, while at the table, Verrain's taut quiet held braced with compassionate pity.

Kharadmon scarcely hesitated. "The crown regency of Tysan has never been recognized."

Through the brief, warning pause, the s'Gannley clan heir pressed a hand to his face. While the sunlight poured down with harrowing clarity, he was, after all, unable to witness a brave woman's desperate poise crumbling.

Inexorably harsh, the sentence must fall, as a Sorcerer called to deliver the truth was compelled by bound service to qualify. "Therefore, all right to raise arms and each separate claim to serve royal justice must be declared false authority. By kingdom charter, this counts as misrule. Every life lost, and every last drop of blood spilled under Lysaer's cause, no matter to which side the dead or the injured claimed to have rendered their loyalty, must be accounted as a willfully negative impact."

Ellaine's tears welled and spilled. Straight and pale, she held on, as Kharadmon's level voice gave the verdict. "Straitly set, that means murder, by wrongful injury. Lysaer is descended from s'Ilessid, and of Halduin's direct lineage. But the accident of birth has never in history implied any claim to high kingship. Nor, under the law that upholds the compact, is any mortal man god sent, or due any right to impose his held principles over the lives of his fellows."

At the end, Ellaine crumpled, while Ianfar's grasp, strong and warm, supported her shoulder. "She cannot return," he told Kharadmon. "At Avenor, she will become shut away, wrapped in silk, and imprisoned in silence."

Head held high, her sienna hair threaded with gray where the ringlets sprang from her temples, Ellaine rallied her shaken poise and bore up. "My husband is right to cower in fear of your Fellowship's sentence and punishment."

By her side, Verrain started. Ianfar's shocked fingers tightened.

"Fear us?" Kharadmon's semblance of form momentarily shimmered with sparkling light. "We are not Lysaer s'Ilessid's accusers! Nor does the hand of our Fellowship mete out any torment in retribution!"

Ianfar recovered in time to redress Ellaine's frowning bafflement. "Mankind was permitted to settle Athera beneath the mantle of the Fellowship's promise of surety. Since Lysaer s'Ilessid has declared himself above the Sorcerer's grant of protection, his witnessed refusal to answer to them means that responsibility for his injuries cannot be deferred. Nor can any power on

Athera's soil offer him an intercession. He stands outside the compact, by his willed choice."

"Then whose law will answer?" Ellaine asked, courageous.

Since Kharadmon looked tried to knife-edged impatience, Verrain's steadfast calm claimed the burden. "No law, but the authority of free will. Athera's mysteries are her own defense. Lysaer must stand before the Paravians and speak his case in their unshielded presence."

Ellaine swallowed. "He survived what occurred in Daon Ramon Barrens." At least, rumor held that a centaur had appeared on the field to oppose the trespass of his war host.

Kharadmon shook his head, charged by obligation to cut down even that misperception. "What Lysaer faced was an incomplete presence. The Ilitharis may have seemed solid enough to the mortal troops on the field. Yet the majesty of a guardian's will can cross time as a parallel projection. This one's living thought form did not leave tracks."

Yet a precise understanding of Athera's greater mysteries lay too far beyond Princess Ellaine's sheltered experience. She could not question further, even to know what fate might shape Lysaer's future. "Where is the hope?" Silk rustled as she raised her hands to catch the sparkling fall of her tears. "The son who might have salvaged the peace has been lost to us both."

Silent as only a shade could become, Kharadmon could not offer her the least human touch to lend comfort. "The lady must decide the course of her own fate," he pronounced at due length. "I am here to serve the mother of a s'Ilessid son and deliver her where she wills. Either back to mend her torn marriage in Tysan, or else to accept the inviolate sanctuary within the hostels of Ath's adepts. Nowhere else in the land would be safe. Ianfar's clans cannot extend shelter without drawing the vengeful assault of Lysaer's reorganized war host."

"What if I wished to stay on at Methisle?" Ellaine managed a watery smile for Verrain, grateful for the antique gallantry that had supported her without stint.

"Lady, I'm charmed." The spellbinder stirred like a moldered leaf. His absent, scarred hand stroked a tortoiseshell cat, leaped up to parade on the trestle. "But I can't recommend this. You already know the long winters are miserable. Hot weather brings the high season for spawning. Dangers move abroad in the summer from which I've no adequate means to protect you."

Lady Ellaine bowed to the inevitable. Her parting words and her curtsey to Verrain showed the instinctive grace that should have shared a ruler's throne without shame. The chaste kiss she bestowed on Ianfar's rough cheek was impeccable for its sincerity.

At last she confronted the discorporate Sorcerer. Escaped from Tysan in a slop taker's cart, she stood with empty hands and the naked cloth of her dignity. "Let me go on to the hostel at Spire," she concluded with strained trepidation.

Kharadmon gave her wounded heart a smile like an unveiled diamond. "My lady, let me say I'm impressed. As a jewel too rare for the hand of your husband, you are not renouncing Tysan's captivity for another term of confinement. The adepts by their nature must honor free will. They will bid you welcome and respect you with kindness for as long as you care to stay."

Scarcely prepared for the speed of event, Lady Ellaine found herself deep in Methisle Fortress's cellar, with her hand gripped to Verrain's lean wrist. The chamber had barren brick walls, and an oddly concave floor inset with mystical patterns. Her edged nerves had no chance to settle. As the Fellowship presence commanded the raw flow of Athera's lane flux, the pale inlay of the old Paravian focus circle flared into an incandescent burst of white light. She was blinded, not burned. The dire forces scoured out vision, there and gone in an instant. The after-flash took several seconds to fade.

Restored to dank dimness, awash in the flickering glare of the spill left burning at the base of the stairwell, Ellaine shuddered. Where Ianfar s'Gannley had stood: *nothing*. A long exile had ended. Kharadmon's ineffable, sorcerous working had dispatched the young man on his way to his kin in the wilds of northern Tysan.

Through the ringing of tone that was *not sound*, but the aftershock of harmonics strung like cobweb through the charged air, Ellaine realized Verrain was speaking.

"…won't suffer that sense of spinning disorientation." Lined features and wide-lashed brown eyes reflected the spellbinder's tender concern. "Your traverse will take you through by way of the adepts' sacred grove. As you wish, you can make the crossing in sleep. You'd rest in my arms and feel nothing."

Ellaine shivered. While the focus lines flared from blue to deep indigo, then subsided to pearlescent violet, she grappled with her rattled dignity, then set her spine straight and responded. "Thank you, but no. If I am to walk through the heart of the mysteries, I'd rather hold on to awareness."

"Brave one, go in grace. No traveler who enters a mystical grove leaves with the spirit untouched." Verrain bowed, then steadied her elbow in the grasp of his dauntless, scarred hand. "I bid you farewell. May Ath's lasting peace shape the change that attends you."

Gone, the chance to renounce that decision: Kharadmon's summons flared out of the flux, and Verrain steered her uncertain step onto the focus.

Ellaine crossed the scribed circles of runes, undisturbed by uncanny sensation. Only her loose strands of hair snapped with static as she passed over the grand cross at the central axis. There, Verrain's kiss on her hand bade farewell and framed Methisle's final remembrance.

Light sheeted over her senses and form, a white fire that swallowed awareness. Ellaine plunged through a blanket of azure, then indigo, then lost herself into the deepest black-violet, which faded into full dark. A cry like song rushed through the unraveled knit of her form, then consumed her familiar senses. She tumbled, without voice, and for time beyond measure, danced to the mad gyre of a whirlwind.

Force that *was* naked power itself cradled her fragmented self. A fleeting recognition informed her that the touch was Kharadmon's personal signature: a taste like storm lightning, and mercuric space, stitched through by fiercely barbed humor.

Then awareness of her lost body returned. Ellaine felt her stomach turn over. Pressed downward, too heavy, she heard running water. Restored to her feet, she found herself standing once more upon firm ground. A streamlet burbled over a bed of white stones, under an ambient twilight. Stately trees twined a leafy roof overhead. Their crowns soared upward, enfolding a nightingale's song, while a horned owl preened on a branch, yellow eyes wide in the half-light. A deer grazed on the dew-drenched carpet of grasses, while a fluttering snow storm of tiny white moths dipped over the cups of pale flowers. Ellaine stared in wonderment. Her very skin appeared remade from silk, ablaze with the ghost gleam of spangles.

"Where am I?" she gasped, amazed. Her tissue of clothing seemed stuff spun from dream, shot through the mist of a milk-warm, midsummer evening.

Kharadmon's presence still remained at her back. Here, the vortex that defined his being was not cold but fierce as a fire upon her.

"You are in the grove of the hostels, a place never found on a mapmaker's chart." The Sorcerer's words seemed to strike the taut air, percussive as a hawk's feathered wing beats. "One will come to guide you the rest of the way. He will be the spirit who answers your soul. Be patient. Stay still. Let him hear you."

She did not see him enter.

Whether he had emerged through the leaf-filtered quiet, or if he arrived through a gateway punched out of the void, the princess heard no whisper of footsteps. Only the voice that murmured her name and shattered the locked vault of her memory.

"No!" Ellaine's pulse all but stopped. Breath unreeled and froze. Disbelief tore past numbness. Then resurgent grief ripped her open and bared the deep pain that had wounded her life beyond healing. "Spare my mind, I can't bear this!"

But the young man's warm fingers laced into hers, alive and exquisitely tender. "Ellaine, my mother, be welcome."

"Ath, oh Ath, Kevor!" Tear-blinded, she stumbled to meet him.

His strength caught her close. Standing whole, without blemish, her lost son embraced her. The uncanny shimmer of what he had become soothed the last of her wrenching distress.

Joy followed. Ellaine buried her face into his white-clad shoulder and wept out the crest of the storm. Unseated, unstrung, she ached for her answered longing, and also for love that could not be assuaged. Her tears unchained torrents of silenced rage, instilled by the imprisoning years of her marriage. Lysaer's chill indifference, and two brutal nights given over to his harsh handling had left scars. The ache of mute hurt and stark isolation burst every wall of restraint. Ellaine acknowledged the self she had discarded with an inward honesty that stripped to the bone.

She stayed unaware, though her adept son marked the moment that her Fellowship escort departed.

Kevor wrapped her in patience more steadfast than time, until her racked anguish ran dry. She remained, no more separate. Rejoined to herself, surrounded in calm, she refounded her being in the trickle of water, singing over white stones. As pure were the robes of Ath's adept: the son who clasped her in reunion.

Unafraid now, assured that he was real, Ellaine finally dared raise her eyes. His face was so changed! Her pulse missed a beat. Happiness rekindled. She indulged her pleased urge to examine him.

Kevor still wore the mantle of youth. Yet there, all trace of the boy he had been fell away, strained like dross from a crucible. He stood and breathed with an unearthly peace, bone and muscle and flesh realigned, a sculpture refigured to manifest beauty that scalded the senses to witness.

The unmarked blue eyes did not see as a man, but as a creature lifted beyond earthly clay to a vantage that conquered mortality.

"You will not return," Ellaine ventured at last.

Kevor's smile moved her to wonder like a touch made direct to the heart. "Stay, instead," he invited, and raised her chilled palm to a cheek that was golden, and bearded.

The rightness of that choice at last eased her being. The mystical quiet in the grove heard her need and moved something sacred inside her. Whole in herself for the first moment since she had wept in the trammeled sheets of her marriage bed, Ellaine passed beyond pain. She laughed and stood tall, though she knew not where the unknown future might lead her.

Late Spring 5671

Infamy at Innish

The plan would have proceeded with no hitch at all, had the driver who pro-vided the teams not yoked them with several bull oxen. Surly at best during this time of year, the creatures still had the spring rut in their blood. Rivalry lit their rolling, dark eyes. Sullen temperament made them paw dust. They bumped fractious shoulders and swiped their capped horns to gore the least hint of movement about them.

The slight-boned filthy boy sent to handle their nose rings was of desert stock, and a mute. At each jostling challenge, the rank creatures all but lifted him off his bare feet. Outfaced, he wrestled to stem the libido that threatened to wreak a disaster.

Alerted to the draft beasts' wrangling pull by each straining grunt from the boy, Kyrialt rapidly knotted the lines to secure the filled barrels stacked in the adjacent dray. The maneuvering animals forced him, again, to snap his toe clear of a wheel rim.

"Dharkaron geld those damned bullocks!" he swore, then turned a peevish glance through the gloom that foreran the hour of dawn. A blurred form in gray mist, the boy glowered back through his veil. The dust-faded cloth worn by Sanpashir's tribes masked his hair and obscured his features. Kyrialt's glare en-countered dark eye slits. "You sure you've the muscle to manage those beasts?"

The grunt, this time, scaled into a shriek of soprano frustration. "No!"

Slim hands loosed the straps of the lead team's nose rings, then clawed the headgear away from lips that were shapely and full, and no mute's. "No! Damn their ornery hides straight to Sithaer!"

Kyrialt turned his head, dropped his jaw, and stopped breathing.

"No," repeated his wife, looking hot. She seized back the straps, tugged in tardy response as the left-facing bull lashed its head and tore through the hem of her tunic. "Piss on your mother!" she shrilled into its ear. "Try that again, I'll rip off your bollocks if I have to use my damned teeth!"

"*Glendien!*" Kyrialt gasped, all but strangled.

He jettisoned the trailing ends of his rope, sprinted eight steps, and jerked the harness straps out of his wife's inept hand. His heave bent the offending bullock's neck and brought his eyes level with its foamed muzzle and heaving nostrils. "What on the soil of Ath's earth possessed you!" he shouted in savage astonishment.

"That cow, in the wheel trace," Glendien stated. "She's in squirting heat." Nonplussed, red hair uncrimped in damp waves down her back, she rubbed her raw palm on her breeches. Her two-fisted chop on the second bull's strap dealt its nose a clouting shove sideward. "None of that, randy boy! Your sweetheart's off-limits as long as you're shackled in harness."

Kyrialt swiped off a stringer of slobber. Struck at once by the jiggle of breasts pressed under his wife's noisome tunic: *how* had he missed that? And those curved hips—even in the near darkness, clad in boy's clothing, the woman could fire his blood. "Glendien! Damn your brass! *What are you doing here?*"

Finished maligning the amorous bull, his bride of two months glanced sidelong through her tumble of hair. "Picking posies, of course." She smiled. "Where's the fun, staying home? I'm not sick or pregnant."

If not for the need to restrain the crazed beast bawling into his eardrum, Kyrialt might well have thrashed her. "You can't go to Innish!"

A flounce of scarlet locks, then, "Why not? Two wagons, two teams, each one yoked with bullocks. You'll drive both wains? Or no. I see! Which can you leave? This one with the gin, or that, with the white silk? Your liege's plot fails, one without the other." Warned by Kyrialt's thunderous pause, Glendien stood straight, the bull's strap tapping her buskins. "I wanted to meet Fiark," she admitted point-blank.

Kyrialt forcibly reined in his temper. "As Arithon's town factor? You'll go nowhere near him!" He knew his wife; loved her spirit, none better. He also understood the futility of wasting his breath with any attempt to upbraid her. Whatever had happened that day in the glen, Glendien's private audience with the Prince of Rathain had stoked her insatiable curiosity. Such whims always drove her with juggernaut force. A man learned to bend, if he hoped to harness the surge of the tides, or the weather.

"Pass me that strap," Kyrialt snapped, resigned. Ahead, he foresaw the need for fast talk and a feckless turn of invention. No way else could he hope to coerce the hired men to let him stay through the last phase of Arithon's tightly planned strategy. Which meant, damn the wife! he must undertake the foolhardy risk of entering town with the wagons.

His exasperation bordered on fury as he snatched up the tossed rag from the trampled ground. "Here, minx. Stuff your insolent face in this headcloth before I tumble you here for a kiss."

Glendien flashed him a grin, doused at once beneath crumpled fabric. "Later, rude man," she declared, "the ginger-coat cow won't say no."

Kyrialt seized the reins of the recalcitrant bulls, moved to irrepressible laughter. Like his father, he reveled in dangerous byplay, and women with claws and hot temperament. In fact, he looked forward to winning the match, for the only way to swerve Glendien's interest was to accompany the madcap venture to Innish and keep her too busy to bid for the endgame.

An hour past sunrise, the two drays trundled into the thick stream of traffic jammed under the wall by the trade gate. Steaming under the mist where the Ippash delta met the southern sea, the port town of Innish already teemed. Past the slack season that followed the thaws, the galley trade surged through the brief months of calm that preceded the squall lines of summer. Dust raised by caravans curtained the air. Short-tempered carters hastened to finish their commerce before the heat baked the wharves to a sultry inferno.

By now, the paired ox drays crept with the press, steered by two competent drivers. Despite virulent objections, they still bore their intrusive pair of clan passengers: a slender, boy mute and a strapping young man whose taut build and fierce eyes were no tradesman's. The unrest in Shand's wilds had tightened the checkpoints. Both carters stewed in their uneasy sweat, while the mute was passed by, and official scrutiny measured the swordsman's build of his fellow. Folded into a tattered tarp, the barbarian sneezed in the face of the guards, then croaked his answers through the faked onset of a perishing sore throat.

Relieved to be hustled ahead through the arch, the nervous lead driver let fly. "Catch yourselves short on this idiot escapade, my back will get flensed on the gibbet. Did you know," he ran on, incensed, as he steered through the jam packing the turn toward the harbor, "the sharp dirk you wear at your hip is no use? Not here, within walls, while there's piracy rampant. I'd cry you down for the bounty myself, except that my cousin was burned by examiners. I found that I hated sunwheels worse than all of you slinking clan animals."

Kyrialt coughed, forced helplessly silent as a belled trollop swayed past, suggestively teasing the tarp that covered his ankle. While Glendien grinned behind her sour facecloth, the drays trundled into the ramshackle maze of bylanes lining the waterfront. There, the larger one bearing the barrels split off to park in the shade in a dead end, under a gallery. Its driver lounged next to the laundry-house well, to all appearance a man with the itch to bed with a two-silver whore.

The yoked team with the cow lumbered ahead to the docks. In snorting, minced steps, the oxen were goaded to back the wagon down to the quayside.

By then, the early mist had burned off. Across the scintillant dazzle of water, surf creamed on the reefs at the mouth of the cove and jetted the decks of an outbound galley, skimming away with the tide. Tattooed longshoremen lounged by her discharged cargo of packing crates stacked on the dock. They teased the boy and chaffed at Kyrialt's silence, each tense minute the haulage was loaded. A hawker sold lemons in the open street. While idle deckhands strolled past, hooting catcalls at strutting harlots, the hustling factors of Innish pursued what began as a normal day.

The last crate was hefted, the tailgate chained up, and the dock crew paid off for their labor. The carter slapped his oxen awake. While the yoked team lumbered on its unhurried way past the sagging eaves of the tenements, Kyrialt shot a hard glance toward his wife's insouciant headcloth. "Dharkaron avenge! I was moonstruck. Far better we both had not come here."

"Did I wed to be left stretching hides back in camp?" Glendien flipped him an insolent gesture between the knees of her soiled trousers. "Sneeze. You're being sized up by a doxie, and the man wasn't born who could cage me."

They trundled past the blind alley. The parked dray's attendant was absent, apparently strayed to indulge himself in the sheets. The amorous bullock still pawed in the yoke. Winding the pungent scent of the cow, it lowed with frustration, then shouldered its teammates into the lane, hell-bent to challenge its rival.

The dray rolled, unobstructed, its negligent driver having forgotten to set the brake on the wheels.

Unaware of the bovine trouble that ambled behind, the leading dray with its boxes and silk pressed on with its scheduled errands. The brand-marked crates were left as a gift to the woman renowned as the queen of the Innish brothels. Wrapped in beads and feathers, she looked askance at the boxes piled on her dyed carpet, then beckoned for muscled assistance. The shave-headed brute who ejected rough clients shortly pried off the lids. A single glance at the tissue-wrapped contents raised a cackle of evil delight.

"Ladies!" The madam shouted upstairs, "Come down! The hand of fate has dealt us the trump to enact Dharkaron's sweet vengeance!"

Outside, in accord with Arithon's scripted plan, the driverless wain with the lust-driven bull and the barrels now careened through the sea-quarter market. Traffic suffered. The town watchmen, absorbed in their dice, dropped their game as two oncoming wagons swerved into collision. The crash and the shouting compounded the trouble. The loose team of oxen panicked. Tails curled, they charged, pounding through the rowed stalls with the leveling force of a battering ram. Baskets flew airborne. Fruit and wares crashed and burst. Cries of outrage followed the beasts' zigzagged course, then outbreaks of curse-ridden screaming. A wealthy merchant's carriage was wrecked. Trailing peacock fans and strings of glass beads, the yoked oxen galloped amok. Citrus crates squashed. Poultry flew squawking. Iron-rimmed wheels smashed crockery. More stalls were swiped flat. A livestock man's string of young horses tore loose, and the tumult gained force like the tumbling thrash of an avalanche.

By the time the rampaging team was waylaid, the authorities yelled to make themselves heard through the irate howls of the vendors. Footmen from the splintered carriage pushed in to fight for their master's claim to charge damages. No teamster appeared to collect his marauding beasts or set right the offending wagon. Which faced the Innish town guard with a choice: they could draw steel, or assess the dray's contents before the brangle devolved into fisticuffs and knifing bloodshed.

One gin barrel was broached to cool ragged tempers. Since no one seemed interested in resuming business over their torn tarps and splinters, a second cask was opened as consolation, then a third, for sheer joy and devilment. An impromptu holiday bloomed on the spot, as the crowd in the market immersed itself in jocular commiseration.

The celebration was just reaching stride when the unloaded dray with its two unscheduled passengers ground away from the Bower of Bliss. Turned downhill again, it creaked through the sea-quarter tenements and briefly stopped in another bylane. There, the errant driver made rendezvous. He climbed aboard, emerged from the arms of his trollop with cleaned hair and fresh clothes, and equipped with a satchel bearing the respectable tools of a tailor.

"We need to visit the shoreside warehouse," he announced to his disgruntled henchman.

"That stop's not in the plan," Kyrialt hissed. "My knife says you stay with your orders."

"Well, who put the snag in the schedule, first?" the grizzled head driver protested. "Carve me up, you'll be dead on the scaffold by noon. Stay quiet, or walk, since I don't take guff from savages riding as contraband."

The wain trundled under an overhead footbridge, as Kyrialt reached for his dirk. Cat-fast as his forest-bred instinct reacted, the sheltering tarp foiled his reflexes. The lead-weighted fishnet dropped from above snagged and bound over his head. Aware, far too late, of more racing footsteps, he struggled to cut himself free. Glendien's frantic scuffles beside him only tightened the mesh on his shoulders. He managed to kick off someone's gauntleted grasp. Then another thug with a fist like a truncheon cuffed the back of his neck. Kyrialt slumped into wheeling dizziness, fast followed by starless oblivion.

The ache as he woke all but shattered his skull. His outcry jammed against the tight cloth of a gag. Queasy with sickness, Kyrialt peered through cracked lids at the dim, moldered boards of a warehouse. Crates and boxed stores hemmed him in on all sides, and the light in his face was a reeking flame cast by a fish-oil wick. The smell turned his stomach. He moaned, discovered his bound wrists and ankles, then shut his eyes in racked misery.

Someone's hand pressed a cold compress at his nape, and Glendien's voice said, "He's rousing."

"None too soon, the damned fool," snapped a deep, gravel voice bearing an East Halla inflection. "Lucky he's alive to feel queasy, and not staring at his own unwound tripes in the hands of the mayor's executioner."

Someone's biting grip closed over his shoulder. The chill blade of a sword sliced the gag, after which the rough benefactor wearing a steel-studded bracer hoisted him like a limp kitten.

Kyrialt swore. His revolted stomach barely under command, he was shoved back with his shoulders braced against the splintery slats of the packing crates. His legs were spilled jelly, extended before him. Sea-humid air jammed his throat like hot glue and threatened to black out his senses.

"Who are you?" he slurred through his unruly tongue, while Glendien's touch nursed a bruise on his jaw he did not remember receiving.

"Friends," said an accentless, baritone voice, "though at the moment, you might not think so."

Through swimming vision, Kyrialt picked out two forms: an armed, gray-haired man with the build of a mercenary whose sleeve bore a factor's insignia, and a slight, refined blond, who filled his lace and prime velvet with the poise of a merchant who knew the price of the dye in each elegant thread.

Brows raised, the townbred pronounced with freezing asperity, "The man would not be here, who thought today's plan could succeed in the face of a fool's interference. Did nobody warn you? Lysaer's new acolytes are hand-picked for keen talent. The wise of your kind would steer clear of them."

Flushed anger burned through Kyrialt's clogged senses, that his wife had snatched her ill-gotten triumph. The band that had netted them out of the street had been dispatched by no less than Prince Arithon's shoreside factor. The warehouse guard would be the man's stepfather, Tharrick, a former captain at arms who had trained for the sword at Duke Bransian's citadel. The towhead had to be Fiark himself, a rank embarrassment, since Glendien would spit nails before she confessed that her wiles had landed him here in the first place.

Nor was her rampant curiosity abashed. "Talent? Do you say these new zealots are clairvoyant?"

Fiark sighed, sparking light through his sapphire earring. "Past doubt. They'd have noticed the taint of your ancestral lineage and seen you skewered on faggots by sundown. If you crashed the gates as a prank, let me tell you, the byplay is serious." His chill frown scarcely thawed, he watched Kyrialt's wince. "Do you ache? I hope so! That's no less than your folly deserves."

"Well, your thugs might have spoken before they attacked." Kyrialt pushed to rise, grimaced, then fell back as the move spun him dizzy.

"Should I take such a chance?" Fiark looked outraged. "Tharrick's men are not thugs, and I dare not allow my affairs in this town to be compromised. Too many innocents stand to be hurt if the wrong faction suspects my loyalty. May I ask what mad impulse possessed you?"

Kyrialt shot a venomous look toward his wife. "Curiosity was the mistake that got the cat skinned."

Fiark's quick perception caught the exchange. Insight shattered his mood to an outburst of laugher. "My dear man," he said, all at once gently cordial, "Let's make sure your woman never meets my twin sister, who is thankfully not in home port."

That moment, yanked from their slow toil uphill, the yoked oxen dragging the remaining wagon were seized by a uniformed guard and two fellows bearing halberds. "No drays pass uptown."

The cheeky, fat driver reshuffled his reins. "We're turning," he stated, head jerked to the left. An avenue branched alongside the spiked wall, lined with the white pillars and neat courtyards of the quarter's pastel mansions. "This lot's for their excellencies o' the Light, under high town, an' they'll not tip me a penny for lateness."

The guard waved them on. The dray ground across the scored cobbles and passed the servants who polished the streetlamps. The air wore the syrupy scent of gardenias, tanged with the birch coals the wealthy preferred to brew their tea at midmorning. The corpulent carter reined his team beneath a raised gateway hung with a sunwheel emblem. Stopped, he placidly tied off his reins. Jumped down from the box, he strode to the painted doorway and banged to announce his arrival.

The liveried servant who cracked open the panel was displaced by an irritable head priest. "The kitchen entry is around the back," he began, then noticed the tailor, untying the tarps protecting a load of sparkling, damascened cloth.

"But this is a mistake!" the priest pronounced with asperity. "These are uncut bales of white silk you have brought. We expected to have finished vestments dispatched from the shops of the Capewell craft guild."

The carter returned a disinterested shrug. "Not my problem, your Splendid Eminence. Check the tags for yourself. The seals are Avenor's, and genuine."

The cleanly fellow with the tailor's kit stepped forward and bowed at the waist. He assured that his services had been procured to begin the initial fitting. A busy fellow, not minded to wait, he raked a glance of haughty contempt over the crude, ocher emblem painted over the chest of the florid priest's current tunic.

Plainly anxious to have his promised silk and gold thread, the religion's new envoy wrestled his irritation. "By grace of the Light," he complained, "This is bothersome! We've had our measurements taken once over, already."

The tailor backed down with a charming smile. "Then would your Excellency care to inscribe a clear statement canceling Avenor's commission?"

"No, no." The priest waved the man through the door. No help for the mishap, he directed his anxious servant to help carry the baled cloth inside. Meantime, the housemaid scuttled to retrieve the rest of the Light's enclave from their leisurely breakfast.

The emptied ox wain rolled on its way, while the tailor unpacked pins and measure. He had just set to with his shears and chalk when the eager acolytes jammed into the parlor to claim their promised new vestments.

They encountered, instead, their red-faced superior, draped like a ghost on a kitchen stool. Arms outstretched, he endured the stiff tedium of a first fitting, barely in progress. The garments just hacked from a raw bolt of silk draped his pink form like a tent.

Innish's devotees stopped short in dismay. "By the Light Everlasting!" cried one. "You look like my grandame's best tablecloth!"

"Must match the bias," mumbled the tailor around a mouthful of pins. His impatient beckon prompted the servant to procure additional stools. His Excellency's valet was commandeered to fold up each set of doffed clothes. Soon a pedestaled row of naked young men stood regaled in tucks of pearl silk. The tailor's shears clacked. The carpet lay strewn with a welter of clippings and scraps. While his victims posed in statuesque helplessness, raw hems and pinked seams stitched with pins, the tailor ransacked his satchel.

"I plead your forbearance," he murmured, contrite, "I'm afraid I've mislaid my thread." He bobbed with apology. The error would be rectified. On the promise of just a moment's delay, he nipped out through the back pantry.

The abandoned priests grumbled sour complaints. They ground their teeth, and waited. Stiff as draped fence posts, shiny with pins, they fidgeted in their welter of darts, while the Innish day heated toward noon.

The obsequious tailor never returned. Worse, their piles of shed clothing had been removed by the overly efficient housemaid. Plaintive shouts toward the kitchen failed to roust any servants to remedy their foolish predicament.

Incandescent, the head priest became first to crack. "How can the laziest servant we have be sleeping, amid all this noise?"

For in fact, the street beyond the dagged curtains suddenly seemed to be packed full of hooting revelers. The commotion masked worse: in brazen fact, the waylaid house staff had been tied up and gagged by a foray launched through the garden.

Cautious of his pins, a pudding-faced acolyte waddled onto the balcony. There, yanked up short and yowling with fury, he backpedaled, tripped, and sat on his unfinished hemline. Torqued around to nurse his stabbed arse, he yelped again as he skewered his armpit.

Through the subsequent stream of unlovely language, his fellows deduced that the lower-town whores had broken the record for outrage. The head priest ventured a tender descent from his perch. Trailing pale silk and a scatter of pins, he reached the casement and parted the curtains. The view dropped his jaw. Dancing on rouged feet, a parade of belled harlots regaled him with blown kisses and smiles. Covering each splendid, seductress's curves was a sunwheel robe, its emblem jiggling against unbound breasts, while the trade-quarter shopkeepers, reeling drunk, clapped and shouted to cheer on their antics.

One of the prostitutes screamed in delight. "Dharkaron bear witness, you fat, pious saint!" Bosom outthrust, her attire skirled above lissome thighs, she ran on, "Here's Ath's perfect justice! We're twins!"

The priest flushed puce and roared, indignation drowned under the roisterers' shrieks of hilarity.

There followed an infamous chase through the streets, in which eight naked priests in flapping silk held by pins bolted outside to fetch the town guard. Armed men were conscripted in the cause of the Light, then dispatched to wrestle the belled tarts of Innish to recover their desecrated sunwheel finery.

The ladies wore nothing but paint underneath. Amid the rough play and licentious jokes, all of Innish dropped prostrate with laughter.

From the safe seclusion of Fiark's locked warehouse, Kyrialt heard the wild tale of the fisticuffs to stand off the embarrassed town guard when the perfidious tailor came to report. Since the clansman ached too fiercely to roll on the floor, he buried his chuckles against his wife's neck until he was gasping and paralyzed.

This was the southcoast, where scandalous gossip was awarded the status of legend. Years might pass before any priest in white robes would escape being the butt of snide comments. The waterfront tarts would wage their mean feud. For the suppression of trained herbalists, they would seize the incentive to reenact the obscene celebration at each anniversary.

Early Summer 5671

Links

Arrived with all speed at the hidden encampment tucked in the Thaldein Peaks, and scarcely able to pause to acknowledge a homecoming deferred for sixteen years, Ianfar s'Gannley relates the urgent word sent by a Fellowship Sorcerer: "Forge an iron blade for a ritual death. A sunwheel priest rides the trade road from Erdane who's become the slaved shell for a necromancer…"

Late night, at Avenor, a breathless courier disembarks from an inbound ship and demands an immediate audience with the Blessed Prince; the sealed casket he bears holds the packet of dispatches rushed at speed from the far east, to be opened in private by no less than the hand of the avatar himself…

Awake in his chair under soft summer moonlight, Sethvir of Althain senses a wrongness with the pulse of the stone near Etarra, and *again* tastes the tang of an innocent's let blood; as a shudder of horror disturbs his gaunt frame, the adept by his side overhears his grim plea, "Let Asandir achieve his swift return from resetting the grimward at Scarpdale…

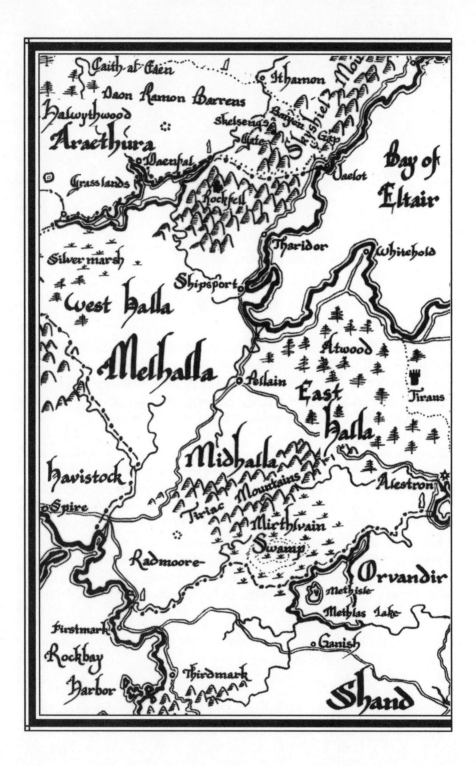

XI. Confrontations

Under the sheer blue sky of summer, the noon sunlight beat down, burnishing the raw gold of Lysaer s'Ilessid's blond hair. The black rag he wore tied over his eyes wicked up a darkening ring of perspiration.

"You look hot," Sulfin Evend observed, prepared to stand down and unstring the longbow gripped in his hand.

For answer, the Blessed Prince snapped his fingers in peremptory command to fire off another arrow.

No straw target had been set up on the greensward that sweltered beneath the gauze film of the midday haze. The shots dispatched throughout the morning had been random, each shaft launched to a different point of the compass. They hissed in flat arcs, or sailed into slow volleys, all directions including straight up.

"You've only missed eight out of ninescore and six," the lord commander pointed out with dry irony.

Lysaer's head turned. The bright hair that wrung longing sighs from the maidens lay wilted against the drenched blindfold. "That's eight times dead by some wretched clan marksman, should I show myself in the free wilds."

Sulfin Evend dutifully hefted the bow. He yanked a fresh arrow out of the sand bucket and set the fletched nock to the string. "You might not be tired; but the sweat and the blisters aren't serving a thing but your angry, perfectionist pride."

The sealed dispatches just arrived from the east an ongoing bone of contention between them, he drew and released. The shaft leaped out, its whining flight intercepted by a needle-thin flare of sent light. The wood lit incandescent and burned, trailing an acrid taint of scorched feathers on the sluggish stir of the sea breeze.

Today's show of inexhaustible accuracy gave Avenor's ranking war officer little cause for celebration. Not while his piercing inquiries kept on being deflected with oiled consistency. Years of experience in s'Ilessid service left Sulfin Evend ice-cold: he well knew when that charmed pattern of reticence brewed up the most wrenching campaign surprises.

Balked on one front, he turned his assault against the more volatile impasse. "If you won't restore trust with the Fellowship Sorcerers, or try other means to engage the latent talent passed down through your mother's lineage, trust me. The safest course would be to return to Hanshire and drive through a brutal bargain with the Koriathain."

"Filthy tactics!" Lysaer s'Ilessid declared. "You won't cozen me to soften my stance. The ladies can brood on their sour disappointment. I will not let them barter my sworn men for studs or play with lives as political bargaining chips."

His stilled pause served back as an ominous warning, Avenor's Lord Commander at Arms had made no move to string the next arrow.

Beneath the soaked rag, Lysaer's abrupt smile held a poignancy to seize mature heartstrings. He forewent his ill humor, aware that beguiling charisma could not soften resolve: the past months had proven he could not bend the will of his adamant, right-hand retainer.

Day upon day, they clashed verbal horns. The need to confront the incursive corruption that endangered the Light's governorship of Etarra also blazed into fierce disagreement between them. More than once, they had bruised themselves sparring when the sore issue edged onto the practice floor.

Now Lysaer unburdened, his honesty scathing. "I already gave you my word not to rush. We've agreed that Avenor's security must come first. I can't leave Tysan's capital exposed as it was, or have the trade road through Westwood left at sufferance of errant Khadrim."

"The last escaped predator has been recontained!" Unwilling to play coy with the least taint of falsehood, Sulfin Evend jettisoned tact. "That was Fellowship business, and better left to their knowledgeable hands and experience. If I can entrust them with my uncle's life, why can't you leave matters that are outside of your depth in the provenance of the Sorcerers?"

"Because I fear," Lysaer stated, reasonable. "The citizens of Etarra are my given charge. They cannot be abandoned to contend with the horrors that just cost you the lives of three officers. Nor will I knowingly cling to my safety. Not while a body of Sorcerers whose affairs are *all suspect* leave the common populace to live in ignorance. These people are wide-open to harrowing risk!"

Sulfin Evend bit back his urge to retread the same, tired arguments: that luck and surprise timing could not hope to prevail against a second incursion.

Not with the cult's secretive masters forewarned and still smarting from the resounding defeat given to the late cabal installed at Avenor. Etarra had no ancient Paravian circle to focus the force of the lane flux, a fact that eliminated the powerful backing once granted at need by Sethvir. Worn from the heat, chafed snappish with worry, Sulfin Evend left the next arrow untouched. Instead, his gaze measured the latest disturbance to impinge on the site of the tourney field.

A contingent of indignant figures marched across the hacked turf, resplendent with the flash of fine jewels and burdened down in state finery.

"Well, you can't deal with this matter blindfold," he said, caught aback by startled amusement.

For the dignitaries had abandoned their haughty decorum. Undaunted by the flyblown manure heaped by the cavalry's picket lines, they hiked up their ribbon-trimmed robes and pressed on like a covey of disgruntled quail. To judge by their militant strut and stiff chins, and the flush on their scowling faces, their pointed reception was going to make a close afternoon all the hotter.

"Could I guess?" Lysaer mused. "The seneschal's persnickety secretary has been overset by the justiciar's packet from Shand?" The firm line of his mouth also twitched with curbed laughter. "Bring the man on. Then just watch me."

Prodded by impulse and evil delight, Sulfin Evend notched a fresh shaft to his string. He pulled to full draw, then released.

The arrow arched out. An etched sliver under the broiling sun, the deadly missile whined upward. Slowed as the shaft reached the peak of its arc, the shot lost its impetus over the hats of the contingent of approaching councilmen. Sulfin Evend saw movement as one of them pointed. Several heads swiveled. Another peered skyward, eyes shaded by visored fingers.

The flustered officials were all male, in douce accord with the bias of town law, and the rigid practice of westlands propriety. No voice in Tysan would raise questions of gender. Yet Sulfin Evend was privy to Lysaer's private nightmares. He knew of the damage incurred by betrayal: a mother, a beloved wife, and now, Ellaine had abandoned this s'Ilessid prince. Since each one had crossed without shame to an enemy, Lysaer's distrust of women would not suffer the opening to tear at the deep-buried scars of such wounds.

Above the greensward, the trembling arrow tipped, then spun point down and rushed earthward.

"Should I presume you are also displeased?" Lysaer remarked with stripped humor. Awake to the prank just barely in time, he launched the razor-thin flash of his gift into the arrow's sped course. The shaft torched. Its residue puffed a roil of black smoke over the poleaxed councilmen.

Hazed to a sharp halt, Avenor's crown governance collectively bristled. Then, their state velvets snagging up dust, the shark pack regrouped, determined to vent scalded nerves on the grace of the divine presence.

The beak-faced trade minister shoved in first. "This storm of dissent that's inflamed the far south shows no sign of abating! There have been debauched acts—"

The surge of declaiming interruptions lost wind to the rotund minister of the treasury. Annoyed by the ruin of his best calfskin shoes, he elbowed in front, moist chins quivering. "My scribes are accounting our losses *twice weekly*. We've had recruiters' tents shredded by riots, stolen wine and mislaid stores, never mentioning the tally of damaged—"

"The missing white silk for the new priest initiates!" a ruddy crown acolyte burst in, at once shouted down by his beak-nosed superior, "Oh, that's scarcely the worst! Today we've had word that the gilded fittings for the new temple at Ishlir have gone missing. Every one of our inventoried wagons arrived filled by crates crammed with rocks! The stone for the marble facing's been lost under still more nefarious circumstances—"

"It sank, actually," the palace accountant upbraided in stuffy correction. "A bridge collapsed on the trade road. Four drays tumbled into the river. The carters were forced to go swimming to rescue their floundering oxen." He sniffed, then concluded, "Barbarian work, surely. Their pillaging raids have increased."

Sulfin Evend stayed poised behind Lysaer's shoulder, primed for the moment his blindfold liege would be hounded from regal complacency.

Lysaer snapped imperious fingers, instead. "Next arrow," he commanded.

Straight-faced, Sulfin Evend bent his yew bow, while the yammering councilmen stumbled awkwardly backward, still ticking off points on their fingers. "Four strayed shipments of gold, the tribute chests lifted from a company of guards, not to mention the pestilent scourge of indecent ballads and satire—why have we no edicts to curtail the bards? Their lying tongues are a galling obstruction!"

The bow cracked in release. Its launched shot sheared upward into the blue, where a snapped burst of brilliance destroyed it.

Coughing out the taint of singed fletching, Avenor's justiciar clung yet to the rags of diplomacy. "We have thefts going unpunished, and desertions applauded by riffraff."

Here, the gifted clairvoyant who trained for the high priesthood thrust forward to cite the fresh case. "Last fortnight, a temple's newly blessed floor was *defiled* by a crofter's escaped herd of swine! The doors were barred shut. No muddy pigs could have entered unless a malingerer herded them in."

The justiciar restrained the fuming priest by the shoulder, and strove to restore court decorum. "Our efforts to bring justice to bear on that incident turned your most competent officers into a laughingstock. Serious inquiries could not be held while jeering hecklers turned every magistrates' hearing into an act of low comedy! The dockside at Shaddorn foments open insurgency.

An outbreak of mudslinging begun by the whores was abetted when water-front craftsmen opened their shops and let the guilty escape the town watch."

Beneath the gleaming, fair hair and rag blindfold, Lysaer's mouth showed no change of expression. "Arrow," he stated in peremptory calm.

Sulfin Evend well knew when to follow an order. He nocked, drew, and released on demand, then observed to see how s'Ilessid ingenuity would field the mounting unpleasantness. There would be a design: Avenor's self-styled prince always played his tensioned lines with tenaciously brilliant resolve.

The next shaft whined aloft.

"How do you suggest the Light should respond?" Lysaer flicked his wrist. The seemingly casual gesture released a burst of ball lightning. The explosive energy consumed its frail mark, wisping another pall of spent carbon.

Avenor's shrewdest trade minister cleared his wattled throat. "Lord Exalted, your losses are happening. The longer we deliberate, the more chance we'll be faced with enforcing a drastic solution."

"Your Divine Grace." Avenor's crown steward ventured his case, his prudish, tucked hands ill at ease with the newfound mantle of his authority. "Since the spring, the holy treasury has been robbed of twenty-eight *thousand* gold royals. Thrice that in hard silver coin weight. That's not accounting for vandalized property or the fines that are, daily, being waived by south shore officials whose moral fiber has been swayed by malicious sabotage. We are losing hard-won support by the hour, and to what? Indecorous behavior, malign gossip, and life-sworn men-at-arms shamed into defection. I suggest that money and resource don't vanish by accident. Rumors on this scale do not sprout unsown. We know the bards who are singing the satires don't answer to the same description, however, the Spinner of Darkness has a most subtle hand. Surely this must be his work?"

"Arrow," said Lysaer. "A high, ranging arc, aimed for drift and wind, due southwest."

A cold-blooded order, most softly spoken: yet the crack of its emphasis cried challenge. Sulfin Evend stilled his pricked conscience, bent his powerful bow, and sighted the shot's angle above the flagged towers of the palace.

When he loosed, the shaft arced upward without interruption. It slowed, losing impetus at the height of its arc. A needle of sunlight glanced off varnished wood. Then the point turned, and gravity took charge. The missile plunged, aligned toward the heart of Avenor's inhabited court plaza.

As though no hapless bystander risked being skewered, Lysaer turned his masked face toward the cluster of dismayed councilmen. "You think I should act?"

The arrow whined earthward, its lethal broadhead a distant twinkle of steel nicked through the blanketing haze.

One fretful councilman moistened parched lips. "Your Blessed Grace, for the Light's justice, you must."

No one moved. The shaft's flight sped unchecked, raising stifled gasps from the onlookers.

"*Must?*" stated Lysaer s'Ilessid, and this time, his held fury lashed his governors a cringing step backward.

"Innocents are suffering!" The acolyte priest sank to his knees, broken to desperate pleading. "Intercede. I beg you, my lord. For wanton cruelty, would you chance an innocent's death as the price of our forward presumption?"

"You would not forget at the cost of a burial." Lysaer's forefinger flicked. Light erupted. The explosive blast slammed the dead air like a thunderclap. The descending arrow was annihilated, and more: the guildhall roof peak showed a smoking scar where melted lead had scoured through to expose the underlying support beams.

As dreadfully edged, the Divine Prince's restated question: "*How do you suggest that the Light should respond?*"

The acolyte swallowed. The trade ministers hedged. Hatted heads dipped, and pinned feathers nodded, while the egg-bald town gatekeeper peered at his toes as though his best shoes might sprout answers.

Sulfin Evend assessed the collective distress, silenced to burning contempt as no man of courage came forward.

Their blindfold avatar stood his unabashed ground. The soaked rag and the heat should have spoiled his grandeur: no sovereign majesty should rise above the wilted grass of a tourney field. Yet Lysaer's innate presence engaged his shocked dignitaries as though he sat enthroned, while the tension built higher, stretched to the bleak pitch of a storm front. When at last Lysaer chose to speak, his response only shocked for its mildness. "Ill-gotten, worse spent. The Master of Shadow shall receive the sour fruit of such petty conniving."

The gruff seneschal tripped over himself to chime in. "We have matched the creature's slinking ways often enough. All that is good, he will seek to desecrate. His works cloud the truth, defame and tear down."

Lysaer showed the untoward outburst his tolerance, then resumed with astringent dignity, "I have heard each insult, each injury, each death. I have not responded in anger. Never presume this has not been a choice! My restraint is not to be mistaken as fact, that I am resigned or complacent."

"Then guide us," entreated the harried Lord Treasurer. "How do you propose to redress rifled coffers? We require some tangible means to offset the depletions of theft and these constant, draining expenditures!"

Lysaer's imperious gesture enjoined his Lord Commander to unstring the longbow. Then he hooked off the blindfold, unveiling eyes turned steel-hard by the pain of experience. "The Spinner of Darkness has done naught but feint. He taunts. He withdraws. He wears at our flanks, not with lethal threat, but with laughter. What does he wish to provoke, but a cheap and undisciplined clamor for vengeance?"

The clipped pause was not gentle as Lysaer tossed his rag with the last, forlorn arrow in the sand bucket. "On your feet!" he cracked to his kneeling acolyte. "This cause we are bound to serve with our lives is not petty. It is not about anger, or antics, or a *little* rage, done to put down mean acts and desecrations. We are allied to serve the needs of a people and defend their born right to freedom. In our hands, the design must be shaped to liberate this world from the threat of tyrannical sorcery. You insist I should act."

Lysaer's drilling stare raked each face, as if searching for something found wanting. "Then where do I start? By hanging a false tailor? By arresting the dockside bawds of Innish for the crime of a naked priest's blushing embarrassment? Do I disrobe the trade council of Southshire because they succumbed to a fraud arranged by a covert conspiracy?"

"You risk an impotent image if you do nothing," the candidate for the high priesthood pointed out, while the treasurer's clutched list of deficits crackled between his nervous hands. "Injustice demands restitution."

Lysaer sighed, above rancor. "Would any such act reduce the threat imposed by the Master of Shadow? Would his *actual* strength be diminished? The degree to which we embroil ourselves will only debase our long-term credibility. Lose impetus to revenge, and we just defer the hour of lasting triumph. I will not rise! Nor will the Light stoop to the gutter over a skirmish of slanging and insults!"

"That's all very well." Shamed, but not cowed, the Minister of the Treasury drew breath to broach the issue of critical shortfalls.

The Blessed Prince cut him off. "This is my word, and your given will, as you cherish your grace under heaven. Gird yourselves for war. The conflict you desire is imminent. Forge weapons and raise arms in the name of Light. Recruit every able young man. Do your work well, without pause for effrontery. Never bow to outrage or embarrassment! For tomorrow, I shall sail east by fast ship and lay the groundwork for a true reckoning."

Lysaer unveiled his purpose, a flung stone amid the tense quiet. "I go to pursue two counts of rank treachery. Proof has reached my hand. My princess is at Spire in the hands of Ath's adepts, and Duke Bransian s'Brydion of Alestron has engaged in a treasonous collaboration with no less than the Master of Shadow."

"The fell demon's escaped Kewar!" someone gasped, shocked.

"For some months," Lysaer s'Ilessid avowed. "I had cautioned you all this would happen."

Amid reeling upset as Avenor's high councilors fought back the wind to regroup, the Blessed Prince closed with crisp force. "Let us see if the south can sustain its insurgency with my hand on the reins of Shand's politics."

Enraged to have been played in the dark alongside Avenor's fresh councilmen, Sulfin Evend did not scramble in stunned step to accommodate Lysaer's brazen announcement. Instead, he strode off the tourney field, placed the whirlwind muster of escort and honor guard in the hands of a competent officer, and returned to the royal suite. There, he ordered his crack team of sentries to retire into the anteroom. Still armed, and grimed with dusty sweat from his extended hours of archery, he bowled through the frantic servants who lugged trunks and scurried to pack the state wardrobe. Undaunted by protests, he shouldered past more attendants with towels and barged into the regent's bath chamber.

The Blessed Prince relaxed in the huge marble tub, sunk hip deep in the glass-tiled floor. His soaked head reclined on a sandbag of linen, while a manservant sponged lather over a torso sculpted with fit layers of muscle.

"Out!" snapped Sulfin Evend.

The manservant bristled, prepared to retort.

Yet Lysaer's genteel word affirmed the dismissal. The attendant waded out of the tub, his poisonous glare raking the vulgar intruder as he stalked through the doorway.

Undaunted, Sulfin Evend overshadowed the replete form of his liege. "You're not wearing your knife," he accused, while the steam whorled up in ghostly eddies between them.

Lysaer at last deigned to open his eyes. Surrounded by pristine white tile and set against bloodless, fair skin, the gaze burned with lapis intensity. Unspeaking, he raised a hand from the suds. The flint blade was clenched in his fist.

Which curt response did not disarm Sulfin Evend's combative mood. "You toy with good men," he attacked. "That disrespect shows a lack of trust that deeply shames and demeans them."

The Blessed Prince maintained his hard stare. "You're here to take issue? Then level the field. Strip off your armor and join me."

"I'm not here to play games!" Sulfin Evend cracked back.

Lysaer shoved up straight. He stretched his arm, hooked the cord for the knife sheath, and looped it back into place with the blade hung over his breastbone. "I don't play games. Nor will I argue with a man wearing a sword, itching in his rank sweat while he's irritable. If we're going to face off with honest intent, you'll sit just as naked beside me."

"Fair enough." Sulfin Evend removed his baldric and surcoat, then peeled off his chain mail and gambeson. His boots, his belt, then his breeches and hose were soon heaped on the bench by the towel rack. Stripped to his scars, and the uncanny pattern a Fellowship Sorcerer's touch had left impressed like a watermark over his heart, he slipped into the hot, scented water.

The bath was waist deep and sumptuous enough to admit his fighting man's brawn without crowding. He sank to his chest, doused his head under, then snatched the dropped sponge and sluiced into the grime ingrained from his bout on the practice field.

Too late, he recalled: his liege had never seen the protection bestowed on him at Althain Tower. The stilled pause took on weight as the mark came under Lysaer's probing survey. Seen through water, the warding became more pronounced, sparkling with glancing light at odd moments, or when direct vision drifted.

"Don't ever let my Lord Examiner discover the fact you've been spirit-marked," the Blessed Prince pronounced at last.

Sulfin Evend knew when not to rely on the passionless poise of the states-man. He submerged, then lounged back, while the fragrance of rare oils in-fused the steam that coiled over his collarbones. "You would stand silent and let your fanatics drag me to a sorcerer's death?"

"I would save the embarrassment," Lysaer said without heat. Then, "You didn't come here, or strip to the skin to retread the threats posed by necro-mancers. Nor have I given you reason to doubt my intent to stay clear of the morass surrounding Etarra. My recruiting will be confined to the south. Have I wakened suspicion to question this?"

"Not yet." A man not sworn to the cause of the land would have let matters rest, strongly warned. Sulfin Evend assessed the dangerous, male crea-ture whose innate majesty could not be trusted, then said, "You did not dis-close the contents of those dispatches. Your seneschal has not seen them either. If you want my backing, you will not conceal pertinent documents from your high council."

Lysaer's tempered poise kept its mildness. "You would dictate terms?"

Sulfin Evend sucked a reflexive, quick breath. "I would order the ship you board sunk at the dock before I set sail for a falsehood."

"A death warrant, for the men who obeyed you," said Lysaer. He did not seem perturbed, a signal red flag. "How dare you enact the presumption?"

"If you've nothing to hide, I don't have to." His courage a brazen act of imprudence, Sulfin Evend held firm. "Don't try me. If you win, the regret would become your destruction."

"How dramatic." Lysaer tipped back his soaked head, the picture of conge-nial amusement. "You would have applauded my guileless grace if I had exposed names for your uncle's close contacts?" Highly placed, inside officials employed by town mayors had sold themselves as Raiett's spies. "A self-righteous, clean breast on that score would have earned us some interesting enemies."

Mockery won no ground from Sulfin Evend. "How can you be sure that Raiett's contacts aren't compromised?"

Lysaer's indolent eyelids swept down, his careless posture as relaxed as his hands, laced at his knee under the waterline. "The dispatches included bonded copies of state documents from Kalesh and Adruin. As s'Brydion enemies, both towns detain inbound ships at the mouth of the inlet. Inven-tory in the holds, cross-checked against lading lists, shows an interesting trend of ore imports. The duke's foundries are busy. His shipyards have been building more vessels outfitted for war. The other significant news was sent from a clairvoyant who works out of Spire." The faint smile that followed showed a rancorous edge. "Apparently, your precious Fellowship Sorcerers have seen fit to install my wife under sanctuary inside Ath's hostel."

Sulfin Evend tested that ground like thin ice. "If so, they can't hold her against her will. The adepts will not sanction coercion."

Had those imperious eyes not been shut, their gleam would have been hardened enamel. "I will not accept your rote suppositions. Avenor's princess has forsaken her vows as my wife. I would hear that betrayal from her own lips, since judgment is rightfully mine to bestow should the charge of abandonment lead to a sentence of treason." Lysaer added, "No less than seven town mayors in Shand have petitioned the Light for an intercession. If I sail back home without granting their hearings, I should be accused of false cause, if not justly defamed as a covert clan sympathizer."

"That excuses Shand," Sulfin Evend allowed. "Perhaps. My gut says you haven't begun to come clean."

"My examiner should put you to trial for a rogue seer!" Lysaer retorted with venom. Eyes flicked open, unmoving, he counterthrust without pretense. "While we're in the south, you'll recruit in my name. Fail me there, and your officers could come to face your worst fear. For Etarra has been industriously training new troops since the losses were read for Daon Ramon. Your covert nest of necromancers stand to inherit a war host raised in support of the Light. Should your faith in a Fellowship intercession prove misplaced, we risk opposing our own banner on the field. What if our northern stronghold turns suspect? For all we know, their high command may already be swayed by the first taint of corruption."

The least chance that Shand's garrisons might be called to battle a troop turned by necromancy cast chills, even through the heat of the bath. "All right," Sulfin Evend was forced to concede. "I'll grant you Shand as a political necessity. But what do you have on Alestron? Your cited case of collusion with Shadow had better rest upon something more than lading lists and one renegade shipwright who fled for the chance to snatch amnesty."

"Cattrick?" Lysaer's reply held that lazy disinterest that set every instinct at guard point.

Sulfin Evend persisted, "The man is a valuable craftsman, enough that any shipbuilding ally would be tempted to overlook his past record. He's no cause for war. Not against clanblood holed up in a citadel designed on a scale that guts armies."

"Add treason," stated Lysaer, uncowed. "Misappropriation of funds. Let's not omit piracy, hand in glove with the Riverton sabotage, which also took lives acting in the Light's service."

A tactical commander could not afford to stay silent. "Challenge Alestron, you will stir a wasp's nest better off left unmolested. At least bide until your troop rolls are back to full strength and brought to the peak of their training."

"Wait," Lysaer said, "and we will face an insurgency under the sway of the Spinner of Darkness."

"Why now?" Sulfin Evend held out. "Cattrick's malfeasance was eighteen years back. I also know you've been hoarding sealed proofs of his perfidy since your priest reported last autumn!"

Lysaer arched his back, hands clasped at his nape. "Well, this news is fresh. The heart of all evil was admitted through the gates of the s'Brydion citadel only last night."

"You know this for certain? This wasn't a cult predator, deliberately baiting a hook to waylay you?" Too late, Sulfin Evend awoke to the danger: his query was seen as obstruction.

Already that hostile, fixed stare had hardened in glacial splendor upon him. "In nightmares, at times, I can hear the footsteps where my half brother treads on the ground."

Sulfin Evend ceased breathing. Confronted by the horrific change that presaged the Mistwraith's curse, he feared to move, feared to speak. The wrong word now could launch madness.

Yet fraught stillness compounded his deadly mistake. His alert tension itself framed resistance. Ungoverned insanity supplanted reason: Lysaer's sprawled frame recoiled and sprang.

Caught weaponless, Sulfin Evend snatched up the sponge. He hurled its soaped pulp into Lysaer's face and dodged the hands that grappled to throttle him. A wave slopped from the tub. The flood hissed across the tile mosaic, and slapped, echoing, into the benches.

Lysaer dropped his throat hold. On driven impetus, he plowed his shoulder into his liegeman's solar plexus.

Shot halfway out of the water, scrabbling to regain his feet, Sulfin Evend slammed into the rim of the pool. Impact knocked him windless and stunned nerves in his spine. As his body subsided back toward immersion, he recalled the stone knife. That redoubled threat spurred his desperate recovery. He rolled, spiked an elbow in useless evasion, unsure which peril would take him first, a drowning in soapy water, or a stab through the neck or the heart.

His hair was seized. A shove slammed him under. Still shocked by hazed pain, Sulfin Evend hit back without decency.

Lysaer scarcely flinched. A creature lashed into curse-bound rage, he lunged again, strikes with fists and knee aimed with feral violence.

Sulfin Evend submerged, let the water sap the force from the blows. Since the bruise to his back still impaired his reflex, he thrashed in retreat until the far wall of the bath held him at bay. This time, his groping heel met the stair. A hard thrust let him spring from the water.

Streaming, Lysaer surged after him.

The contest emerged onto the slippery tile, a battle closed in wet flesh and harsh breathing. Blow and counterblow were marked by the slap of clenched fists. Vicious grunts and gasped curses tagged each exchange, torn short by the bruising falls that pulped muscle, and smacked bone, and smeared blood like plumed dye in the puddles.

Sulfin Evend could not fight to kill. That sore disadvantage hampered each move. The holds that might cripple had to be tempered, where Lysaer's possessed fury sought murder. Hurled head over heels, kicked and slammed on splashed flooring, then pummeled against marble furnishings, Sulfin Evend wrestled in tortured evasion. His drive to win clear and snatch for his sword brought a club on the nape that dizzied his senses. Through a swelling bruise that slitted one eye, he sensed Lysaer loom over him. Fair features were racked into a rictus of nightmare. The driven intent in those glass-hard blue eyes exposed something worse than ferocity. Sulfin Evend struggled to throw off his numbing fear. This was no clash born of heated blood, but the cold-cast embrace of damnation: the same manic focus that had torched his shot arrows, one after the next on the practice field.

Not the knife, after all; Sulfin Evend cried out.

His shout raised the guards left behind in the anteroom and brought them pounding against the locked door.

Before they broke through, Lysaer's light burst and burned. The white-out levin bolt blinded sight and scalded wet tile to shrieking steam. Target of a blast that should scorch him to cinders, Sulfin Evend felt the wild strike slam his chest. Knocked off his feet and bowled over backward, he struck the wall, gasping and bruised, *but alive*; the awareness broke through, that *he had to be shielded. Lysaer's crazed attack was being intercepted by a starred pulse of silver-white* spellcraft.

Asandir's mark warded more than his spirit from necromancy. Its etheric imprint also bestowed an unlooked-for defense from the gifted powers suborned by Desh-thiere's curse. The working in fact had not transgressed free will.

'*How strong are you wanting to make these protections?*' the Sorcerer had inquired in due course of obtaining permission.

'*Strong as you know how to make them.*' Sulfin Evend had said, more than anxious to give the matter his brisk quittance. '*I'm no use to Lysaer if I should fall short. Just act as your wisdom sees fit.*'

Spared now by the grace of the Sorcerer's foresight, he had a scant instant to order his wits. The dire onslaught of light spent itself and snuffed out. The glass floor tiles were melted to smoking slag, with Lysaer's manic fury still rampant. Blows resounded: the diligent guardsmen were breaking the door. Their forced entry was going to happen too late. The s'Ilessid had finally drawn the stone knife. Assault followed with curse-bound ferocity.

Unlike the past trial on the dungeon stair set off by the meddling of necromancers, one man became the singular target for the raised bloodlust of Desh-thiere's curse. Talith's memory had lost any power to save. This time, a son's death could not be invoked to shift blame, or deflect the attack and wake reason.

Barehanded, Sulfin Evend fought for his life. The stabbing knife met his sharp parry. Once, twice, he fended the thrusts that darted to cripple and kill. The third barely missed opening his guarding forearm. Sulfin Evend scrambled backward, recovered, but lost his purchase upon the scorched tile. He skidded, lurching sideward to dodge as the razor-edged weapon bore in. Knapped flint scored his flesh, a shallow scratch.

Except wounding contact woke backlash: a blade that desert shamans had ritually fashioned to enact a warding defense drew blood through an act of unbridled hatred.

The virulent sting spurred Sulfin Evend to outcry as arcane forces whirled into recoil. The snarling confluence of violence and wronged spellcraft raised a wild burst of elemental Fire. The force that endowed both creation and destruction responded *in kind* to the fury that impelled the knife's wielder. Lysaer screamed as the red blaze of the handle seared the skin on his palm and fingers.

The spelled knife clattered out of his blistered grip, just as the roused guardsmen breached the lock and shouldered the burst panel inward.

Sulfin Evend barked out a command to hold hard. His grazed throat seized up. The shout he required came out mangled, barely louder than a scraped whisper. The men did not hear. Past recourse, their commander scrambled, found his feet, and slammed headlong into Lysaer. Since failure meant death, he rejected nicety. A clipped blow to the nape dropped the Blessed Prince in a senseless sprawl in the puddles. Sulfin Evend pounced and snatched the flint knife. One fist in gold hair, he clawed for the neck cord, then rammed the blade back into its soaked deerhide sheath.

Frantic shouting drowned out his string of voiced orders. Aware of the men charging past the sloshed bath, Sulfin Evend snapped his discarded belt from the bench. He had Lysaer's arms halfway noosed when the guards' disconcerted rush hammered into him.

Their mailed fists crashed him full length and pinned him facedownward on the splashed floor.

Lysaer was dragged clear, while merciless hands crushed Sulfin Evend prone, and a trio of swords pricked his neck. The wrecked room reeled and tilted. Steamed air reeked of blood, spilled scent, and spent carbon, which ripped battered senses to nausea. Worse, several towel boys already gaped at the view through the shattered doorway.

"Get them out." He ripped a hitched breath, forced clear thought, *tried again*. "By my life, which lies at your mercy," he gasped, "keep my liege restrained until he finds his way back to sane consciousness."

"And we should trouble to obey an assassin?" The guard sergeant jammed a boot in his prisoner's back and flattened Sulfin Evend's grazed chin to the floor tiles. "My lord, what fell working possessed you?"

The Lord Commander squeezed his eyes shut. Aching and bloody, seized by the throb of every blackening bruise, he spoke with adamant clarity. "As your titled officer, I ask for your trust. The scene you just witnessed was not an assault. No matter how grim the manifest evidence, my loyalty has not been compromised."

More steps pattered in through the splintered entry.

Sulfin Evend shifted a hand to arise. The jammed pressure of sword steel redoubled at once. His least movement was answered with vengeful zeal, while the boot on his back cramped his breathing. "Man that doorway, at once!" he snapped in hoarse rage. "At least spare the court from the sordid gossip that's going to be spread by the servants!"

"Not to fear," soothed a calm, older voice, just arrived. "I've sent the towel boys off to the kitchen with the promise they'll starve if they loosen their tongues."

Sulfin Evend peered askance at two frail, slippered feet, and gratefully recognized the sound sense of the royal valet.

Once again, the staid servant stood his brave ground before the armed fist of authority. "I beg you," he entreated. "Hear your Lord Commander. His intervention today was an act of necessity, called for through delicate circumstances. His Exalted Grace sometimes suffers from bouts of stressed nerves, a fact he prefers to keep shielded. Your senior officer knows the malady well. He's helped with such violent outbreaks before. By grace of your loyalty, let him up. You will do the Light's avatar no service at all if you don't cool your tempers and hear us."

The bared swords did not lift. Sulfin Evend forced patience. Listening with every strained sense he had left, he picked up a low moan, from the bench: already, Lysaer stirred out of his stupor, braced up by a stalwart sergeant.

"Leave us!" snapped the valet, fired desperate with outrage. "All of you. Now! Are you brutes, to so wound a man's dignity? Divinity walks among you in the flesh! But that privilege does not strengthen your ranks without cost. Such a prodigious gift must set strain on the vessel endowed beyond human frailty!"

"Prince Lysaer was born of a man and a woman joined in an ordinary marriage. He told me," Sulfin Evend backed up with scalded exasperation.

The grinding weight of the boot lifted off. The instant the bearing sword pressure wavered, Sulfin Evend rolled out from beneath the held points. Snarling obscenities for each fresh, gouging cut, he snapped to his knees and shoved upright.

Gasps met the sight of the mark on his chest. Like an uncertain swarm, the armed guardsmen closed in, unsure whether to skewer him as an unnatural creature touched by some unknown work of spellcraft.

Naked, near pulped, his balance unsure, their commander was too thrashed to care if their hysterical fear would see him run through. He turned his back on their weapons, propped a hand to the wall, then sent the valet for dry towels. "His Grace had a robe laid out for his bath? Then let's see about getting him into it."

Such care for the ordinary outfaced the raw threat. Sulfin Evend limped toward the confused guardsman who supported the Blessed Prince. "His Grace is unhurt? Then lay him down."

Bent, his scuffed fingers exploring the slack limbs for hot swelling or sign of snapped bones, Sulfin Evend glanced up as the towels arrived. He held Lysaer's wrists, while the valet rubbed him dry. Together they folded the sumptuous robe over his marked arms and shoulders. While his eyelids fluttered, they used the sash binding and secured his elbows in a gentle knot of restraint.

Sulfin Evend draped the used towel over his streaming neck. Then he bade the nervous sergeant to assist, since he could not trust his balance to hoist Lysaer's weight without help.

Hostile eyes watched him at every move. Whispers trailed after his footsteps. He sensed each leveled sword blade trained on him from behind, as he picked his way through the burst doorjamb. Across the carpet, with no sideward glance, he saw Lysaer installed on the bed. While the valet fussed over pillows and blankets, then soaked linen to make a cold compress, Sulfin Evend dragged up a brocade chair. He perched on the seat with complete disregard for the fact he was bloodied and breechless.

"You will all stay present," he commanded his guards. "I'll need you to bear witness as Lysaer awakes. For if this trip to Shand must go forward in state, there are going to be imposed limits. Given the hair-raising shambles today, you must see that I can't field my duties alone any longer."

The burly sergeant dispatched a man to secure the entry to the royal apartment. Still wrestling his conflicted loyalty, he said, "With due warning, my lord, I don't like what I see. That mark at your heart looks like spellcraft. If you've played us false as the agent of darkness, my blade takes your life straightaway."

Too sore to take issue with risks that no less than a Sorcerer's wisdom might argue, Sulfin Evend met the reproachful distrust of his elite sentries head-on. "No less than dire spellcraft can help against necromancy, and despite public faith, Lysaer's gift of light does not make him omnipotent."

"Blasphemy!" muttered the guard by the door.

Sulfin Evend stared the man down, then resumed, "Avenor required the bargain I struck. Watch as you please. Weigh what you see. For the sake of this realm, you had better judge fairly!"

Observed, every move, by that uneasy pack, no space could be snatched to spare dignity. Sulfin Evend faced his battered liege, now stirring awake, trussed like a roped fowl in the blankets.

Lysaer drew a shaken, sharp breath, then discovered his arms strapped immobile. His worn face turned anguished. No blinding grace of imperious majesty moved him to self-righteous rage. He apologized before his senses stopped spinning, or his opened eyes regained focus.

Then, in pained quiet, he addressed the stilled figure seated on vigil beside him. "That's you, Sulfin Evend? I should weep, except for the fact you're not dead. How close did I just come to killing you?"

Avenor's Lord Commander at Arms covered his disfigured face with his streaked fingers. Emotion strangled his throat. Nonetheless, he must speak. "Liege? If you can't remember, that's very bad news."

Bewildered blue eyes gazed vacantly upward, tracing the decorative patterns of vines twined in gilt on the vaulted ceiling. "That barbaric knife has blistered my hand."

"Had you not tried to kill, you'd be scatheless." Instead of relief that demanded his anger, Sulfin Evend felt nothing but scouring shame, that the wretched exchange must stay public.

As bruised as his own, that porcelain-fair skin; the contrite sorrow that ravaged the face on the pillow was all too woundingly genuine. Since care could not bind up that shattered nobility, he shouldered the gruff explanation. "The flint blade is a talisman wrought for arcane protection, not use as a weapon of murder. Had I been given the chance to cry warning, I doubt that you would have heard me."

"The Mistwraith's fell vengeance." Lysaer sounded torn. "You insist I am cursed? That my half brother's crimes are all innocent?"

Sulfin Evend was too wise to attempt a reply. Along with six horrified witnesses, he watched: as the warning, hard spark rekindled and canceled the soul-searching depths of a just man's innate awareness.

Lysaer's jaw tensed. He worked fevered hands in manic distress underneath the silk coverlet.

Not about to let silence betray him again, Sulfin Evend chose phrasing to placate. "I can't speak on matters of innocence or guilt. Too many have perished on both sides, my liege. I won't try to excuse that, or hide what has happened. I can't find my comfort in righteousness."

Lysaer turned away. With his face masked from sight, his fine, tangled hair lay like snarled gilt on damp linen. "Have you thrown away conscience?"

"Not yet." Sulfin Evend all but winced for the irony, that his bound oath made that virtue irrevocable. Empty-handed and aching, and pierced through the heart, he could not do less than speak honestly. "My service is given for friendship, not cause. If your burden comes to break you, my liege, remember it's going to take both of us."

The supine form in the blankets gave way. Hands bound up in ignominious cloth, Lysaer s'Ilessid turned his face into the pillow to silence his onslaught of weeping.

Sulfin Evend heard the soft scrape of steps. Unasked, the guard sergeant mustered his men, then slipped out, latching the door closed for privacy. The valet fetched out herbs to treat Lysaer's burns. He sat, mashing paste for a poultice, while Sulfin Evend wrapped himself in a spare sheet. Then he subsided back in the chair with his split knuckles loose in his lap.

"Don't go," Lysaer said. His plaintive tone might have been a lost child's, craving a world that was rinsed clean of blood and the specter of curse-driven nightmares.

Sulfin Evend saw further, and heard the stamped pain inflicted by repeated loss: first Diegan and Talith, then a young son, burned to death by the balefire of a Khadrim. He realized the question was not as it seemed, but pertained to a plea very different.

"You won't stop me," he murmured. "Go to Shand, or wage war, I will be the man standing steadfast next to your shoulder."

Lysaer flinched, cut to anguish. "By the grace of your name, save yourself. Please abandon me."

Yet when the valet came with dressings and remedy to succor the raw, blistered fingers, Sulfin Evend remained unmoved in the chair. He sat there still, but armed and reclothed, when Lysaer s'Ilessid relaxed his fraught nerves and drifted at last into sleep.

The valet did not speak, but returned the Lord Commander's pressed surcoat and shined boots. To such selfless valor, he awarded the same, unstinting service he had just granted to his royal master. Between the Lord Commander, with his baleful, hawk's carriage, and the servant, lined as an old hound, no banal words of hope were exchanged. No platitudes eased the regret.

On the morrow, the Light's Prince Exalted would sail, bound for the Kingdom of Shand. The stark challenge remained to forestall Lysaer's curse-ridden drive to assault the Duke of Alestron. War must be stopped, or at least averted until the Fellowship Sorcerers could curtail the Kralovir cult's vile workings. For an armed host was building behind friendly walls from a poisoned core at Etarra. Disaster loomed, if the sunwheel fanatics should march before the core incursion of necromancy could be exposed and routed.

Summer 5671

Stand Down

When the bard who was Master of Shadow gained entry to the guarded citadel at Alestron, he did not give his name or flaunt his sanctioned rank to be presented to the reigning duke. He played in the rough taverns by the barracks gate, until his provocative repertoire drew the shrewd notice of the indomitable s'Brydion matriarch.

Presented with a note by a liveried page whose inscription was velvet phrased over steel, Arithon Teir's'Ffalenn quashed the urge to laugh out loud for the bloodletting sport of sheer challenge. Since refusal would bring him a squad of armed men bearing an ultimatum, he accepted the clan dowager's invitation with the same style of combative grace. He did not change his clothes, or cut his hair, spilled in blond locks to his shoulders. Since Dakar had been dispatched ahead into Atwood, Rathain's prince stood at once and bade the young servant to guide him. Bearing no more than his lyranthe and sword, and a change of shirt in a knapsack, he entered the street and, with a nod to the footman, stepped into the waiting carriage.

The plush seats were crammed with mail-clad men-at-arms. Arithon displaced one to accommodate his instrument. His affable smile like the rose on the briar, he disarmed the rampant hostility that clenched their hardened fists to their weapons. "You aren't going to need the ring in the nose. For today, I've agreed to lead willingly."

The vehicle rolled uphill, its occupants disinclined to share conversation. Arithon tapped whistle tunes out on his forearms, until the matched team was reined to a halt. A lackey built like a retired drill sergeant opened the carriage door and ushered him out. Past the arch of a covered entry, Arithon glimpsed the buttressed walls that cradled the upper citadel. The conveyance had stopped in the midtown, in front of the palatial residence that housed the s'Brydion clan seat. He was chivvied inside. His escort clinked like mailed wolves at his heels, as the servant directed him through windowless corridors hung with shields like a barracks wardroom.

By contrast, Dame Dawr's apartment was a haven of sunlit comfort, tucked in a south-facing eyrie. Her taste ran to soft furnishings and saffron silk, with fine paintings preferred over the maces and edged weapons displayed on the paneled walls elsewhere. Led in by the servant, Arithon faced the formidable grandame herself. She had no attendants, but sat on a straight-backed, gryphon-carved couch, tucked like porcelain into an embroidered gown. White-haired, erect, she wore her ninety-eight years with paper-fine skin and distinguished character. If she walked with a stick, her rivet-bright eyes denounced her aged frailty with an air of emphatic impatience.

The lackey required no order to leave. The men-at-arms also remained in the anteroom, while the door panel clicked firmly shut.

Left alone, drab as blight in a garden, Arithon set his lyranthe down on the carpet. Expectant, he laced relaxed fingers.

"You may sit," said Dame Dawr.

A stool was left waiting, with squat lion feet and an embroidered heraldic cushion.

"I refuse the insult," denounced the Prince of Rathain. He shook back the deceiving, dandified ringlets and dropped off his masking glamour.

Shown seal-black hair and the face of s'Ffalenn royalty, Dame Dawr displayed no surprise. Long since, she had guessed his identity. "Wise man, to insist on no falsehood between us."

Arithon's smile displayed the joy of the tiger, peerlessly faced with its match. He came forward, bent his head and his knee, and with genuine grace, kissed her fingers. "Few are given the unlooked-for pleasure. My balladry caught your attention?"

Impressed by sheer mettle, Dame Dawr raised him. "Despite the license allowed a free singer, satires that ridicule Alestron's defenses are going to try someone's limits." Not put off one bit by the tavern reek from his clothes, or his raffishly insolent grooming, she locked his grasp in her brittle, ringed hand. "Charter law is not proof against s'Brydion temper."

"I feared as much," Prince Arithon said. "But reprisal is not what concerns me."

Reassured that he grasped her innuendo quite well, the grandame offered the stool once again, though this time with sharkish engagement. "I gather you've come to provoke as a warning?"

Arithon sat, flushed to naked relief. "By Ath, you're a gift that might save us a war. Shall I honestly tell you the reason?"

He spent the next several days closeted with Dame Dawr. She allowed him a room with a bath, and a bed, and had her seamstress redress his rough clothing. In return, he seemed willing enough to abide without testing the fact he was kept as her guarded prisoner. To the listening ears of the servants, he played as a bard for her private amusement. Between entertainment, he also engaged in piercingly deep conversation. If her verbal byplay stabbed for the viscera, his courtesy scarcely faltered. When the s'Brydion clan grandame dozed in her chair, he seized no ungallant advantage. At her invitation, he spent those intervals browsing through books and reading the ancient, hand-scripted accounts of her family's illustrious history.

Four days of her adroit quips and snide fencing failed to wear him to exhaustion. If her guileful traps at times forced him silent, she never unleashed his temper.

"You won't be dissuaded," she stated on the fifth morning, when, backed into a stand-down, she confronted him over breakfast.

Arithon passed her a toast point with jam. "You can't see the merit of lending support? Your hatched offspring are going to outnumber me."

Dame Dawr snorted, accepting the plate. Her glance could have cowed a starved jackal. "If the merit's past question, my spurred cockerels are full-grown. I'm too cagey to argue a cause I can't win. My grandsons aren't sensible on their home turf. Don't chance the mistake that might bait them."

Rathain's prince watched her, prepared in his way to match her disdain against his listening stillness.

Since mage training could outreach her caustic, crone's patience, she harried him, stubborn as pig iron. "The worthy opponent knows when he's outfaced."

His green eyes showed amusement. "I still have to try. The cynic alone claims to know all the answers. At least let me make my fool's bid worth your blessing."

"On my terms," said Dame Dawr. "Else I'll turn you out. I won't have your death on my conscience."

Arithon Teir's'Ffalenn inclined his head, his sable hair barbered back to trim elegance and his wit never less than hard-edged. "Asandir's gone before you. He holds my bound oath, sworn over a knife cut at Athir."

Dame Dawr rejected that protest, no matter how starkly he phrased his demand to be left his due right to autonomy. "You will go as a bard under shield of my patronage. I'll arrange for the wives to be present."

That won her his striking, spontaneous smile, which warmed for its depth of intensity. "'*Who spits against heaven, it falls in his face.*' I'll accept your offer of backing in skirts. Without women, how could a man triumph?"

"You would," the s'Brydion grandame replied, "though at far higher cost, and seldom without weapons and bloodshed."

* * *

Duke Bransian handled his grandmother's whims the way his hunting mastiff scratched fleas: by routing the itch with vigorous claws until the pest was scoured off his skin. To be rid of Dame Dawr, one acceded forthwith. The faster a man gave in to her wish, the sooner he could be done with her.

Tonight, the old tyrant demanded a family gathering, formally arranged with refined entertainment and cake. That meant doffing chain mail and sword, without which any s'Brydion male felt exposed as a babe on its birthday. Tricked out in velvet, Bransian glared at the boots with the pearl-stitched cuffs just offered to him by his wife. "I've got to wear *those*, for the sake of a singer who probably warbles in tremolo? No!" The Duke of Alestron folded his arms, hampered by his jingling cuff ties. "That pair has no hobnails, and besides, I already glitter and clink like some simpering maiden's court jewel box."

"Be glad I decided to leave out the hat," said his duchess with arid equanimity. A rawboned woman who fought like a ram, she plonked the reviled footwear into the hands of a servant. "Just get them on him." She tucked a fresh clove into her reticule, then smoothed her silk bodice, and added, "I'd rather be tortured for one day a month than hear more of your yapping complaints."

"My tongue's not so much to put up with," groused Bransian. "It's your snoring that drives me insane." Crammed into the boots, and flushed to black humor, he refused the pressed ribbons to pleat the silk sleeves that billowed over his elbows. "Too much like the prize bullock prinked for the fair. Keep at this, we're going to be late." Chin tucked in offense, he stalked toward the doorway, while the duchess's shrewd glance continued to bore unappeased holes in his back.

"You're not wearing that horrid old dagger again, strapped underneath your clean sleeve!"

"Damned well, I am!" Duke Bransian snapped. "Dawr's pet minstrel could be an assassin."

Since the towns of Kalesh and Adruin had been known to try murder by blowdart and poison, no s'Brydion lady who valued her marriage could argue the need to go armed. The stalemate quelled Liesse long enough to see both of them down to the hall.

There, Dawr's tame bard was installed by the dais on a stool of Paravian workmanship. Both sleeves and his knee breeches nipped tight with cord, he wore high court fashion with natural elegance. Despite his nondescript coloring, the duchess's hitched breath said plainly enough that the creature was matchlessly handsome. The Duke of Alestron spared him no second glance. Beside Dawr's upright posture, he seemed but a mouse, pretty hands too soft and refined to bear any serious weapons. If he carried poison, his dainty bones would be crushed. Even the wine steward's boy looked to be more than a match for him.

Liesse pressed a hand to her husband's elbow. "Your grandame will expect you to take the state chair."

Since grumbling now was a profitless waste, Bransian crossed the carpet, mincing in his tight boots, and mounted the low stair with his duchess. He assumed the carved seat of familial authority, though with Dawr on the muscle, better than any, he knew that assumption held pitfalls. Fiercely scowling, he watched his three younger brothers arrive. Each brought his glittering, combative wife, and their packs of direct offspring who were unrecognizable, done up in jewels and silk.

Only Mearn looked at ease, most likely because he had three poniards sewn into the seams of his doublet. Agile as a snake in new skin, he seated his pregnant wife, then surveyed the proceedings with slit-eyed suspicion. "Why's the old lady down there with the bard?"

"Who knows?" Parrien itched the burned skin left by a shave too hastily done with his dagger. "Like the south wind, she veers each time you try to read her."

"Trendsetting fashion?" suggested his wife, snatching his wrist with both hands before his irritable scraping drew blood. "Or else just her roustabout style of insisting on nonconformity."

Keldmar shook his head, snatched off the hat that made him look like a spaniel, and tossed the crushed velvet onto the table. "Old dame's getting deaf. About time, you ask me. She's got her stirring fingers poked altogether too far into the hot coals of politics."

"Deaf!" Bransian snorted.

"You wish in your dreams," added Mearn. "She's got something afoot, the conniving fiend." About to add more, he clamped his jaw shut and went suddenly silent.

"Has your wife kicked you under the table again?" asked Parrien with needling interest. "Mine tried that, once. Couldn't shut *my* trap. I roped her in bed and—" Shot stiff with a grunt, he glared at the petite brunette, all demure sweetness beside him.

"She's sharpened her hairpins," Liesse whispered in smiling response to Bransian's raised eyebrows.

Conjecture ceased as Dawr's stick banged the floor. Her punctilious serving man brought the lyranthe for the bard, while more liveried staff served cake, and a syrup-thick brandy in delicate snifters.

"That's drink for a toddler," Sevrand griped from his place down the table.

Dawr sat at last and arranged her severe skirts, while the overbred singer fussed his strings into tune with harmonics that stung for their clarity. Bransian poked at his cherry confection in distaste, shut his eyes, and prepared to be bored.

The first, ringing chord slashed the quiet like a sword, whetted to gleaming temper. All question of faulty hearing aside, Dawr possessed stringent taste. Her patronage had delivered a master. The choice of ballad was no effete romance, but a martial tale styled in clarion phrasing. Parrien shot straight. All but stretched across Liesse's lap, he badgered to say something urgent.

The duke shoved him off. "Douse your sniping cant! Let me listen."

After that, the tapestry of woven sound stole the breath for its power of raw captivation. The brothers s'Brydion ceased their clamor, drawn in, while the singer wielded voice and string with an artistry to storm the spirit. His matchless rendering described a war host that built on two fronts, then marched to besiege an isolate citadel. The story carried two posited endings: in one, the defenders died—woman, child, and man overwhelmed by relentless numbers. The other told of a triumph through courage and loss as the fortress's ruler ordered his own stronghold torn down and destroyed. Stone was pulled from stone; battlements were tumbled; the massive defense-works and timber gates burned. The invaders were ceded a field of wracked rubble, while their quarry stole away in unvanquished survival to enact a subversive campaign that undermined and wore down, and at last claimed the victory through long-term engagement.

Incensed by the bald-faced effrontery that had bearded them in their own hall, the brothers s'Brydion fumed in stunned stillness. The music's wild force held them ruthlessly thralled. Compelled to hold out through the last, burning verse, they turned in lashed fury upon the bard, who had never been what he seemed: an itinerant stranger plying a free singer's art to scratch out his nondescript living.

Black-haired, green-eyed, and stripped clear of the mage's glamour that had masked him, Arithon s'Ffalenn laid aside the lyranthe. He stood and confronted the threat of dismemberment glaring at him from the dais.

"*I tried to tell you!*" cracked Parrien, incensed. "I heard his Grace play that way once, at Sanpashir. Such talent's uncanny, and keen as a weapon, and no trick to foist upon a clan holding sworn as a friend and an ally!"

Prince Arithon struck back with a truth that smashed rhetoric. "And had I tried to talk, you'd have heard my speech through?"

"Speech!" Keldmar ripped through his wife's fingers and shoved onto his feet, to a shattering crash of spilled plates. "The man who even *suggests* we should run gets no word. Just my sword thrust, straight through his liver!"

"By damn, forget blades! My bare fists will do," howled Parrien in savage rejoinder. "I don't sit still for the slangs of a coward!" Yet his combative lunge to arise became jolted short. Spun with a poleaxed, irate expression, he glared at his wife, who was not eating cake. Left-handed and deft, she waged her own style of assault beneath the lace edge of the tablecloth.

Primed to wicked interest, Mearn peered sideward to see what new tactic had flummoxed his brother. He already knew how the duke was roped down:

Liesse had his thigh pinned beneath her sleek leg. Draped like a vine over his shoulder and arm, she offered him brandy, while Bransian spluttered and roared, "*This* is how you suggest we defeat an invasion? By wrecking our gates, and demolishing our battlements, and toppling our trebuchets into the inlet?"

"We've seen no evidence there's to be a campaign," Mearn probed. Alone of the four brothers, he stood on his wiles. Before he decided to rile *his* wife, he would hear through the facts that provoked such a drastic argument.

On his feet, empty-handed, Arithon responded with chill provocation. "The smoke from your foundry has blown on the wind. You've been recognized in Avenor."

"You imply someone's sold us. Who?" thundered the duke. "Give us the name, and I'll unwind his guts for the pigs' trough!"

Liesse snagged his elbow with tacit restraint. "His Grace has received Dawr's ear on the matter. Perhaps we should listen before rushing to false conclusions?"

"Listen!" sneered Keldmar. "That's for mincing ambassadors. Mealymouthed words never settled a thing! You want to arrive at a lasting solution, a brangling fight's always quickest." He would have fetched his sword there and then, had his partridge-plump woman not clamped his wrist and hung on with the force of a lamprey.

"Your duke outranks you," she murmured in warning. Then her titanic yank sat him back down before the wide eyes of his children.

Given the floor like a morsel of bait tossed before bristling lions, Arithon Teir's'Ffalenn advanced toward the dais. "You don't need a leak. Etarra has ears within every town's walls, while the new batch of priests given charge at Avenor has been handpicked for talented prescience. Your alliance has served me with invaluable help. Beyond any doubt, Mearn's fast wits in Tysan saved uncounted clan lives, as well as the living name of s'Gannley. But then is not now. This armed religion's become too strongly entrenched. Keep on as you have, and your irreplaceable heritage is going to face extirpation."

"What are you suggesting?" Mearn twirled his brandy, his sharp features intrigued. "Let the Light's weasels slink in for tea, then scratch their backs and befriend them?"

"Ah, no, prince!" cracked Bransian. "My people won't have Lysaer's canting false priests! Ath's law will abide here, though we come to die for it."

"You will be killed," Arithon agreed, unequivocal. "You and Alestron's loyal inhabitants, down to the last babe in the arms of its mother. Never forget! I bear the aware gift, bred into the s'Ahelas lineage when the king's ancestry was crossed with s'Dieneval. My passage through Kewar has forced the latent traits of Dari's rogue legacy into full flower. Your defense at Alestron will be written in blood, *I foresee this!*"

While the storm on the dais threatened explosion, and Keldmar and Sevrand surged to kick down the trestle and launch an assault with bare hands, Dawr raised her stick. She rapped the sounding board of the lyranthe. The loud, booming knock broke across pandemonium, followed up by her scathing admonishment. "Are we sunk low as townsmen, or just ravening boors! Hear his Grace through! You don't have to like what he says. He's asked for naught beyond your fair hearing."

Arithon inclined his head and acknowledged her. He wore no jewels. Not so much as a clasp with a pin; his neat clothes bore no concealed weapons or knives. His close-fitted doublet and tie belt had no bosses for expediency to wrap his fine knuckles for infighting.

Not enamored of his weaponless alliance one bit, Duke Bransian pent back his rage until his locked fists bent his cake fork. Too wise to press Dawr, he turned his murderous contempt on the insolent crown prince before him. "What do you suggest beside flinging open our gates? Did my hearing deceive me? You actually *think* we should topple our defenses down the east cliff and choke off the inlet that leads to the ocean?"

Arithon delivered his point with taut clarity. "I am begging the clans to make peace with the towns."

Before Mearn could howl his savage rejoinder, the Master of Shadow plunged on. "The Light's religion is supported by feud. Break its line of support from the merchants, and the incentive to grow will lose impetus. Stop piracy, cease raiding, and within one generation, the need for armed conflict will wither."

"What! You say we should bend our necks to the *mayors?*" Parrien pealed in disbelief.

Keldmar's frustrated bellow defeated the rest. "Whose force will stop townsmen from violating the free wilds? And how will we maintain our bloodlines and culture if our tradition does not stay separate?"

Bransian stabbed his mangled fork into the tabletop. The clangor of silverware jounced against plates and underscored his distemper. "Are you *done* yet, prince?"

"Shortly," said Arithon. "I've already garnered Lord Erlien's backing. Tomorrow, I move on to Atwood to place my appeal before the chieftains of Melhalla. Once they're amenable, I'll move on to Halwythwood and lay my proposal before High Earl Barach and his sister, Jeynsa s'Valerient."

Aware of a persistent, disturbed rumor from that quarter, Parrien grinned. The crocodile tickled by minnows, he said, "What if your style of absentee charm fails to win over your vested *caithdein?*"

Arithon raised his eyebrows. "Then the final word rests. Rathain's clans by crown sovereignty have no choice but to answer to me."

Mearn sucked in a swift breath, forehead knit. "To achieve that, your Grace, you'd have to submit to all of your sanctioned inheritance. You'd let the Fellowship complete the arcane attunements of a high king's coronation?" Still staring with focused intensity, he added, "Dharkaron's aimed Spear! What under Ath's sky came to break your fixed will? Ask me, I'd have sworn that no power alive could have brought you to heel on that issue."

"No power alive," stated Arithon s'Ffalenn. Against the backdrop of arrested shock, his response held tortured simplicity. "At Kewar, I discovered the cost of shed blood upon a Paravian-wrought sword blade. That's tied to the matter of your threatened heritage. If Alestron shoulders the part I am asking, friendship would bind me to accede to that debt."

Duke Bransian folded his forearm across the concealed sheath of his dagger. "State your proposal," he told Rathain's prince. Since the prospect of a restored crown in the north would create needed safeguards, and shore up the clans' harried standing, he subsided to listen. "What part must s'Brydion take to press you to invoke such a personal sacrifice?"

Arithon Teir's'Ffalenn mounted the dais. Exposed to the risk of violent contact, he braced his hands upon the rucked tablecloth. He regarded the s'Brydion brothers and their wives. Then, each in turn, he acknowledged their gathered, grown children. "You must give up your home to the cause of Ath's peace. Dismantle each battlement, stone from set stone." As umbrage stirred, he pursued his case, speaking quickly. "Deny Lysaer s'Ilessid the target to strike and forbid him the victory that would cede these warded walls as a future Alliance stronghold. Then join your resource with the rest of the clans living in the free wilds. From that position of reinforced, mobile strength, marry your efforts with theirs."

While the savage offense in s'Brydion eyes raked him over without quarter, Arithon pressed through, unflinching. "Begin to rebuild the broken trust that has alienated the old bloodlines, and dismantle the long-standing bleeding of trade that keeps the headhunters' coffers funded against you."

"Never!" cried Keldmar, slammed to his feet as his gesture swept the vaulted hall. "These gates have never been breached in defeat. We've broken the heart and ripped the marrow and sinew from every armed host ever mustered against us!"

"Our ancestors bled and died on this ground!" Parrien added, incensed. "How *dare* you suggest we slink off like whipped dogs for the sake of a few prying priests!"

"For no priests at all," Prince Arithon responded. "We are talking of clanblood's role in the compact, your long-term survival, and the threatened foundation that sustains Athera's grand mysteries! I have *seen!* At full strength, bound to peace, you will have a future in which to rebuild every tower of your wrecked citadel. Deny the cause that supplies the Light's doctrine, and my half brother becomes a curse-driven fanatic without any footing to mount a resistance."

Shown shut faces, tight fists, and shouted down by the clamor of vicious objection, Arithon raised a masterbard's diction, pitched to raze through all deafening noise.

"Give me Havish, Melhalla, Shand, and Rathain, free from clan strife and predation, and Tysan becomes a backwater pocket. Her merchants will be helplessly landlocked by winter if High King Eldir will seal amity and join force with me, and impose a stiff policy of port sanctions!"

Mearn's time at Avenor as s'Brydion ambassador showed him the first glimmer of merit. He smashed his glass to call halt to the racket, then rammed sane debate through the breach. "The north doesn't have enough blue-water sail to slip through a determined blockade. Certainly, Havish could close the southcoast."

"He could arrest shipping, if Parrien's seamanship backs him," Prince Arithon was swift to point out. "My trained crews can bottleneck Instrell Bay, and deny access through North Ward and Anglefen. Move now, with Tysan caught at a standstill and reliant on its fleet of oared galleys, we ought be able to strangle their guild industry within a season. Scarce funds and choked trade will drive the Alliance into a bloodless submission."

"We could do as much without dismantling our citadel," Bransian declared, his inimical scowl stamped into place and his clenched hands like raw beef before him.

Arithon matched that grueling regard. "You could not," he said, honest. The sorrow of his empathic understanding ripped to the bone and arrested the duchess's breath. "Not with Kalesh and Adruin raised to arms on your doorstep, and Etarra mustering troops. The instant you're stripped of the pretense of your sunwheel alliance, Alestron becomes a fixed target. You can't abide. The hour's too late. Don't underestimate the affliction of Desh-thiere's curse! Though I may have found means to master its relentless drive to seek slaughter, let's not cloud the facts! The geas still coils its hate through my vitals. For Lysaer, that urge has become overpowering, and I tell you now: subversive unrest draws him to Shand. This was my intent. We must now pin him down, hold him here as the winter sets in! That leaves Tysan cut off and vulnerable. The head of the snake can be defanged in the south, *as long as there is no given cause, and no traitorous town, to serve the Alliance with the determined incentive to rally."*

But Bransian broke patience and shoved to menacing, full height, overshadowing the slight bard before him. "You count us cheap, prince! The might of my men-at-arms is no pittance, to dissolve at the first threat of conflict. We will not turn tail! How *dare* you suggest that we shrink from the battle that my captains have been bred and trained for?"

"Courage has no bearing," said Arithon s'Ffalenn. "Fate's dice have been cast. By next spring, mark my words! You'll face a rising you cannot win. The hard past notwithstanding, I'm disarming a war that is bound by cursed impetus to destroy you! My lord of Alestron, listen and live! Or believe me, I'll turn my back and walk out, and never once weep for your memory!"

Bransian received this in electrified silence. Aware of his quivering edge of leashed temper, Liesse looked on, afraid to speak, while Mearn, Parrien, Keldmar, and Sevrand awaited the hair-trigger move that would unsheathe killing steel against a Fellowship-sanctioned crown prince.

Before s'Brydion temper, a man would be foolishly mad to hold his firm ground while disarmed.

"Don't try me," said Arithon, his calm of a depth to strike warning.

Bransian sucked in a taxed breath, spoke at last. "You would spurn our amity, prince? Repudiate our resource, that has shouldered your cause, even stooped to spy on your enemy's lair at Avenor? We have provisioned your blue-water ships. Have harbored your fugitives, with no questions asked. Now you insist you should broker our surrender, based upon *fear* and the belief we're incompetent to defend on our own home ground?"

Uproar threatened. Bransian brandished his fist, quelling his wolf pack of brothers. "Go on, prince. Make yourself heard!"

"I prize your friendship." Torn to the thread of his honest desperation, Arithon sustained the duke's threat. "I value true honor, none better," he said. "But there, I must draw my firm line. Bear witness, Bransian, before the eyes of your family! I will not endorse suicide. I refuse to back pride that will bring children to slaughter under the name of my birthright!"

No bard, now, but a sorcerer clothed in his assurance as initiate master, the Prince of Rathain bowed to acknowledge the duke. No man stirred. None served him with violence as he gave his salute to Dame Dawr, tucked erect in her chair. Last, his back turned, standing vulnerable to the uncivilized might wrapped in rage and fine silk on the dais, he pronounced his formal release. "On my word as Teir's'Ffalenn! The alliance is severed, that once was sworn upon the high ground at Vastmark."

There and then, Arithon descended the stair and walked off. Across the barren stone to the doorway, his footstep stayed firm in resolve. The men-at-arms the grandame had stationed gave him way without question. He passed through with no blade raised in challenge, and never a pause to look back.

The oak panel boomed shut and cut off his departure as he let himself into the street.

Left with ringing silence, nobody moved. As though glued in the draft-fluttered spill of the candles and the sickly-sweet reek of spilled brandy, the moment hung in suspended, high-strung disbelief.

Then Liesse stirred. Pearls clicked as she leaned forward and unstuck the fork her husband had jammed through the tablecloth. "His Grace meant every word," she ventured, shocked pale. "Mercy upon us! That was not any show of performer's theatrics."

Bransian's icy regard never shifted from Dawr's drawn face, where she sat, discomposed and erect in defiance. "You promised him *this?*" The duke's wounded gesture encompassed the keep's walls, hung with their faded array of war trophies: over five thousand years of proud history reflected in dented shields, commemorative swords, and sun-faded antique banners. Sick with grief, he accosted the grandame whose harsh wisdom had never so cruelly savaged his charge to carry his forefathers' heritage. "You think you'd survive your first winter living in a freezing hide lodge on jerked meat, and suffering harsh conditions and privation?"

"I'm not ruling, as duchess," Dame Dawr pointed out. She arose, leaning heavily on her silver-bossed stick. While her manservant collected the abandoned lyranthe, she smoothed her skirts, squared trim shoulders, and for the first time, refused to meet anyone's eyes. "My youngest grandchild is a grown man, while yours are still suckling at breast. I gave Rathain's prince his chance to be heard. Nothing more, since your decision will change the span of my days very little. It's your children's future," the s'Brydion dowager said. The weight of her years wrung her to a sorrow that battered her to exhaustion. "Either way, I won't be faced with bending my neck to that upstart popinjay and his false religion."

Mearn regarded his older brother, bemused. "I don't like the taste of what's happened. Not one bit. Arithon had the brute power to coerce us. Both as Masterbard, and as an initiate sorcerer, he could have enforced our compliance."

"Why didn't he?" Adrift without any target, Bransian crashed his balked fist on the table. "His Grace lives and breathes by his twisty wiles! Would he play fickle and turn on his heel if he truly foresaw our defeat?"

"He would not disabuse himself of Ath's law," Dawr stated. "Remember, each day, that he hasn't. His doings henceforward are not your concern. You have but one task ahead of you now: take arms. Yours is to make certain the cost of his seer's vision does not ever come home to roost."

Summer 5671

Atwood

Three days later, by nightfall amid drenching rain, the Prince of Rathain met the small party of clansmen posted to intercept him at the border of Atwood. He came on foot. From Alestron, he carried no more than his sword and a cerecloth cloak bestowed by a charitable stranger. The lyranthe from Selkwood remained in Dawr's chamber, its silent strings his undying reminder of the integrity that forced his renouncement.

The finery that she had gifted in turn had been soaked to sad rags by the downpour. Two nights on the road by a caravan's fire had grimed the silk ribbons and voile cuffs. Folded shivering into the anxious press of the scouts assigned charge of his safety and welfare, Arithon allowed them to hasten him into the cover of their rough-hewn shelter.

There, the Mad Prophet pushed through to greet him, his brosy face worried, and his jerkin redolent of the birch coals that made up their scant, woodsman's fire.

"You're earlier than we'd hoped." Attuned to Arithon's dispirited quiet and distressed beyond care for exposure, Dakar raised the dripping panes of the candle lamp. Mottled light showed him the haunted face of a man set stalking for lethal quarry. "You've lost your vital backing at Alestron, I see."

"Give the wives time," came the wearied response. While the scouts gave them space and helpfully dug through their packs to scrounge a spare change of clothing, Arithon knelt and warmed his chilled hands. "Alestron's women are unlikely to view the issue as settled. If I lost my first move to dissolve troop morale by sowing uncertainty in the barracks, I did gain Dawr's backing. Although she wasn't entirely convinced, she did not close her mind. My word of unequivocal severance, set against the hard buildup of enemy troops may be all we have left to shift Bransian's rock-stubborn pride."

"An outside hope." Dakar sighed. "You knew failure was likely."

Arithon's swift upward glance held the pain a fellow seer recognized all too well. "That's a mean comfort, isn't it?"

Dakar's preferred remedy, to seek refuge in drink, was not going to succor the cruel edge of this man's initiate awareness. The scouts also kept their respectful distance. No one need mention the outright disaster: that lacking the support of Alestron's ships, its stockpiled weapons and armed strength, with the discipline of its field-trained captains, no peace with the towns was going to be possible. Unequally matched, the forest-based clans could never risk the long-term price of a coexistence that might erode their vital heritage by assimilation.

A gust battered the wood, whisking a barrage of soaked leaves under the flimsy hide shelter. Arithon shook out his sodden sleeves, swiped back his wet hair, and stood. Under the close scrutiny of Melhalla's scouts, he refused the last word in defeat. "If your *caithdein* will hear me, I'll present my case. We're not lost, as they say, until bloodshed."

That moment, the oddly strained air of expectancy ruffled his mage-trained awareness. "What's wrong?"

The scout nearest blurted, "Your Grace, we have a Sorcerer already here to meet you on Fellowship business."

"Which one?" asked Arithon, attentively stilled. The return of poached crystals would never merit the pitched urgency that now surrounded him.

"Traithe was the only one they could spare," Dakar admitted with dismal reluctance. "This isn't about amethysts, though the news could have waited until you were dry and had a chance to snatch something to eat."

"We have horses waiting," the lead scout persisted, relentlessly scornful of pauses for comforts that could be expedited, astride. His skeptical distaste measured the pleated sleeves and crushed velvet that remained of the fancy court clothing. "Your liegemen gave us their word of assurance that your Grace required no coddling."

"Vhandon and Talvish? They're not my keepers, and Dame Dawr's taste in cloth was designed to please women, not handle the elements in the free wilds." Arithon stripped his rich dress and allowed their solicitude to replace doublet and knee breeches with dry leathers for riding, and a suitable oilcloth rain cloak. He was rested enough, and could eat on the move, he pronounced with clipped irritation. Then, just as sharply, "Does anyone know what bad business has come to demand a Fellowship audience?"

"Traithe would not say," the scout captain replied. "He awaits your presence twenty leagues from this place, under the roof of the *caithdein's* lodge tent."

If Arithon Teir's'Ffalenn preferred not to present himself before Melhalla's royal steward on the edge of defeated exhaustion, he had the resilience to manage the setback. He followed the scouts' lead and ducked into the rain, prepared to ride through the night.

The storm worsened. Scouring wind lashed the downpour in cold torrents, blinding the scouts and draping their path with a barrage of wet-laden branches. The oak forest of Atwood drowned them in dark like spilled ink at every miserable stage of the journey. Without lanterns, the riders could not make speed. Wet to the skin and chafed by drenched saddles, they reached the most guarded encampment in East Halla in the dismal hour before dawn.

Helping hands caught the reins of their steaming mounts in the flare of torchlight that rinsed the black trees. Arithon misliked the disquieting precedent, that unshielded flame had been kindled to greet him. Nor had dousing weather or hard travel dulled the curious scouts who delivered him. Their critical eyes followed him into the hands of the spry old earl who presented state visitors to Melhalla's *caithdein*.

Whatever that taciturn worthy expected, the slight, bundled form arrived at the lodge failed to match the appalling freight of renown. "Arithon Teir's'Ffalenn?"

The shadowed face under the cloak hood inclined, the barest grant of acknowledgment. The prince's neat step and unassuming poise might have belonged to any forest-bred clan scout, except that Dakar's slipshod manners reflected a resharpened respect in his presence.

Arithon himself was too weary to temper the misconceptions already engendered by his two liegemen's sealed discretion, and the volatile storms Fionn Areth's hot-tempered comments were wont to provoke. "As you see, I don't bring the fair winds the open heart might have hoped for. Bad news comes in batches. By the busy reception, I've gathered a Sorcerer's wanting an audience?"

Thrown such scalding directness, the High Earl of Atwood was pleased to abandon the forms of state courtesy. He leaned through drumming torrent and parted the sodden door flap. "Without fanfare, then, would your Grace go within?"

Arithon entered the dry comfort of Melhalla's clan lodge tent, redolent of soaked horse and pattering droplets off his borrowed leathers. Caught in the flare of the lamps, he took pause, braced for a seated array of proud chieftains, and the piercing regard of a Fellowship Sorcerer. The moment might have been torn from his past: another bleak rainstorm in Strakewood had brought him before an invested *caithdein*, exhausted and beset by the wounded horror inflicted by Desh-thiere's curse.

Yet in place of inimical strangers, he was greeted by an immense woman whose warm hands presumed and peeled the soaked wrap from his shoulders. "Sit, at once," she urged with melodic welcome. "You should have rested before this encounter. I would send you to bed, if all that is right and true in this world was not being set on its ear."

Her caring defused every instinct to bristle. Badgered onto a hassock, his tired frame already yielded. Arithon raised his face to the *caithdein* of Melhalla, overcome by speechless relief.

His glance met blue eyes and a brosy face. A clan braid fastened with intricate knots spilled like ripe corn across the colored shawl draped over her ample shoulders, and her beautiful smile warmed him straight through.

Arithon captured her pillow-soft hand, wrestling irreverent laughter. "My dear lady! You are Teiren's'Callient? What have I done to receive such delight?"

"Need you ask?" The power that stewarded a realm left bereft by the death of the last s'Ellestrion high king returned a chuckle of mischievous pleasure. "As though your fractious handling of s'Brydion belligerence all these years has not been an Ath-given gift." She beckoned. "Here, child. Come ahead. I swear, he won't bite."

Her shy youngest entered, perhaps seven years of age. Small steps, and uncertain fingers bore in a tray with hot food, and mulled wine sweetened with raisins. A raven swooped down, hard on the girl's heels, intent upon snatching a morsel. The child startled, then jerked short as Arithon's unthinking reflex shielded her face.

Hand still outstretched, the Prince of Rathain spoke a phrase in actualized Paravian and intercepted the thieving bird on his wrist.

"What did you say to him?" The child placed the tray on a chest by his knee. "Your way of speech made my ears ring." Eyes round, she glared at the bird, between bashful survey to see if the visitor was nice or forbidding.

"That the rascal could take whatever he wished, if he waited for due invitation." The dark stranger steadied the querulous bird. Green eyes enchanted, he added, "You do have a name?"

The child flushed, recalled her courtesy, and murmured, "Maretha. I was told you were to be called by 'your Grace.'"

"Address me as you please, Maretha. On my promise, nobody's going to mind." Arithon maintained his unthreatening smile, chafed though he was by the unsettled awareness that the *caithdein* was not the sole form in attendance. Reflex had set one hand to the hassock. His surge to arise met his hostess's palms, bearing down on his shoulders.

The raven fluttered, off-balance, as the huge woman pinned her royal visitor in place. "You will not rise, worn as you are, and too guarded to use formal titles."

Yet Arithon failed to be set at ease. "Ath's grace on earth, what affair will not wait, that I might need to ride out before dawnlight?"

"I did warn you, lady." The Sorcerer Traithe emerged from the deep shadow beyond the pricket holding the tallow dip. A snap of his scarred fingers recalled the inquisitive raven.

"*Quork!*" the bird said.

"You can't shelter me, friend." Prince Arithon tossed the bird off. Ignoring Traithe's shoulder, the creature flew and perched on the hide frame stretching a scraped pelt in the corner. There, dark bill flashing, the raven hackled his ruff and started to preen.

Traithe's softened smile capped the apology, now directed between Melhalla's *caithdein* and the state of taut nerves vised immobile on her best hassock. "No cosseting care in your generous heart can blunt the acuity of an initiate awareness."

"Dakar already knows, doesn't he?" Arithon accosted, while his intrepid benefactress let go at last and steered the charming child out of his presence. Unswerving, the crown prince's regard now tracked only the Fellowship Sorcerer. "The spellbinder was tight as a clam with respect to complaints. I wondered what else he kept from me."

Clipped silver hair, and a clean-shaven face scored with laugh lines: Traithe had changed little in the thirty-four years since their first encounter at Althain Tower. Another, more recent, was no boon to dignity. Yet the echo of intimacy sharpened the moment, while brown eyes with their melting, unshakable calm completed an unhurried assessment. "Sethvir warned me that you have fully unleashed Dari s'Ahelas's heritage of prismatic conscience. The burden's no boon, at such moments."

Arithon engaged his trained discipline to relax. "I didn't need Sight to notice the mulled wine was laced full of restoratives." To checkrein his temper, he waited upon the *caithdein*'s attendance before he spoke further. "Since the late round of s'Brydion recalcitrance could also have rested till morning, I have to ask why an armed party of scouts dragged Dakar out of shelter to meet me. Did you fear I would not have come on my own?"

"No." Traithe crossed the lodge tent. Troubled by his stiff limp, he eased himself into a seat by a trestle piled with a parchment map, stuck flat with a set of bone-handled daggers. "The Mad Prophet chose to go out of kindness."

Arithon sucked a short breath. "I'm remiss. By all means, let us chastise my dearth of gratitude, since the recovery of a few Tiriac amethysts *never required my presence.*"

Where Sethvir would have met the attack with a bracing reprimand, followed by softening care, Traithe kept his peace. Pensively silent, he folded scarred hands, while the raven spread wings and flew to his wrist, chortling to be stroked. The Sorcerer obliged the impertinent creature, while the scalding quiet extended. Trapped still on the sidelines, Melhalla's *caithdein* watched her offered hot meal steam, untouched. She had been too well counseled to try intervention, no matter how her nurturing instincts ached to relieve the pitched tension.

Arithon finally buried his face in taut fingers. The apology he would not utter became his shocking, sharp cry for release.

"What more could our Fellowship ask of you?" Traithe gently ventured, over the hiss of the tallow dips. "Would you feel better if we came with hot bricks and knelt to massage your sore feet?"

The shuttered hands moved. Arithon smiled with such startling sweetness, the woman who watched lost her breath. "I would have preferred to sing a balm to soothe your bad joints, but the lyranthe I last played was abandoned. I left her to resurrect a killed hope in Alestron. You can't want to be here. The sting of my setback becomes yours as well."

"More than you know, friend." Traithe made no mention of the Black Rose Prophecy, brought so near to the aching verge of fulfillment. Though tonight's demand must relinquish that future—would plunge this crown prince's willing accession to Rathain's throne all the more into jeopardy—the Sorcerer's bleak thought stayed shielded. Deliberately, Arithon Teir's'Ffalenn had never been told how his choices affected the Fellowship's hope of reunity.

Dauntlessly, Traithe pressed ahead. "Davien had his purpose for luring you to Kewar and granting the key to his library."

"A fool would suppose that he had no agenda." Arithon broke the loaf of flat bread, then scooped the torn edge into the thick stew. "The price has come due? Then speak, and let it be simple."

"Anything but." Traithe broke his news with savage clarity. "Asandir is immersed in a grimward, past reach, and Sethvir lies ill at Althain Tower, burning his own life force to bind the unstable leaks from two others. Those straits have allowed dire factions the loose rein to act without our constraint. Necromancers have seized a foothold within the Light's initiate priesthood. Darkling's diviner's affected, and Jaelot's, and worse, the cabal extant at Etarra. That branch is now lying poised to swallow the heart of Lysaer's delegate government."

There, the Sorcerer waited, as Arithon paled and laid down his morsel. A charged interval passed while that impacting news became marked and measured: the virulent, rogue gift of prismatic farsight must unveil the array of wide-ranging implication. Traithe endured throughout that vicious, slow agony, watched the defiant plan of a future resistance wither, unplucked, on the vine. At one terrible stroke, his stark fact cast its shadow to crush every effort now set in play to dissociate the clans from the havoc caused by Desh-thiere's curse.

"Which cult?" Arithon asked at scraped length.

"The nastiest." Traithe had no balm to mitigate grief. "Gray Kralovir, they are called." He need not elaborate. The devastation in those widened green eyes showed that Arithon already knew of that faction's horrific practice. A cult incursion within the Alliance would not just claim a handful of innocent lives. The blighting danger would spread, masked under the false covenant of Lysaer's religion. Unsuspecting, undefended, the towns' entire populations could come to be enslaved through an orgy of blood rites. Such hideous corruption outlasted death. Its coercive power could unleash a rabid war host no natural armed company could withstand.

"Darkling and Jaelot will pose little threat," Traithe resumed in the same candid vein. "Kharadmon and Luhaine can move in concert and clear the few trapped in corruption without undue fuss. But the newly raised battlements at Etarra are warded. As you have probably already realized, besides me, our Fellowship has no one else."

Arithon swiftly digested the gist. "Your other two colleagues are not corporate," he broke in, then, as perception leaped further, "*You need me to quell this?*" His piercing whisper ripped to the heart. No kindness might spare him. Initiate master, he was too dreadfully cognizant of the ghastly price should he falter. "How long do I have?"

Traithe answered quickly to shorten distress. "Enough time to plan wisely, since the first incursion has been successfully put down at Avenor."

That appalling, near miss was enough to choke speech. Before listening further, Arithon raised his raw will. First act of acceptance, he picked up his dropped meal and started to eat with methodical focus. The warm food was neither tasted, nor savored. He swallowed sustenance as no less than an act of bald-faced necessity. Melhalla's *caithdein* observed that staunch courage and fought brimming eyes in pent silence.

For an interval, no sound interrupted the pound of the rain or the whispered hiss of the tallow dips. The saucy raven held itself still, a coal figure stamped out of the air by Traithe's wrist, with eyes like piercing jet buttons. At length, the Sorcerer flicked his scarred fingers, urging the Teiren's'Callient to sit down. She found a chair, while a prince whose exhaustion should have found solace regrouped hammered wits and responded.

"If my half brother was touched, there will be complications. I think I'd do better to hear out the list."

"Lysaer was wrested clear," the Sorcerer reaffirmed. "You'll hear details, later. The time constraint stems from the fact that our Fellowship has no clear permission to ward him. He currently bears a ceremonial knife, wrought by the Sanpashir tribes' heritage. The talisman lends him a measure of defense. But the esoteric properties have distinct limits and won't guard him from exposure indefinitely."

Yet again, the fierce speed of unreeling prescience let Arithon grasp the raw irony: that an active entanglement would force his half brother to reject the enspelled knife's protection. "The blade's wardings are not compatible with the workings of Desh-thiere's curse?" Now sick to his core, Rathain's prince abandoned his effort to force down the last of his meal. "Why did no one inform me?"

The implied betrayal stung deepest since, at any time before Lysaer sailed south, the added threat posed by a curse-driven encounter might have been deferred, or averted.

Traithe ceded no ground for that lost opportunity. "Sethvir held out hope Asandir would return. The issue need never have touched you. Your effort to secure lasting peace for the clans was beyond all price, and remains so. We still hold out for the chance of reprieve. The torn grimward at Scarpdale could be settled and done, up until the last moment."

"How long do I have?" Prince Arithon repeated, and this round, no distraction availed him.

"The first warning's already behind us. Lysaer suffered an incident on the moment when you first set foot in Alestron. The curse aroused, and the knife burned his hand. He's at sea, and quiescent, but depending on weather, he might make a landfall at South Strait inside of ten days."

"And we know from my disastrous affray at Riverton that the curse can be raised through the use of a fetch." Arithon winced. "Played that way, my half brother would cast the knife off as black sorcery and not realize he had stripped his defenses. But Jaelot's corrupt priest is a long way from the southcoast. Surely that leaves a wide margin to act?"

Traithe shook his head. "Sadly, not. You have three weeks before a messenger bearing a sunwheel seal calls upon Jaelot to muster. The Kralovir's influence must be routed out before next month's new moon. The afflicted in all three of Rathain's towns will need to be cleared and destroyed simultaneously. Luhaine and Kharadmon can time their strike to match yours. That intervention must happen ahead of the cult's opportunistic bid for expansion."

And again, with cruel sorrow, the Sorcerer watched prismatic farsight impel the Teir's'Ffalenn to absorb the next shattering setback: that no time could be spared for his planned stop at Tirans. His chance was lost, to enact the divisive subversion designed to sweep disorder through the Alliance's entrenched hold across the East Halla peninsula. The awful truth dawned, that the Light's sway in Melhalla was going to be left all too disastrously well organized. Twelve towns would be chafing for Lysaer's divine word, dry tinder stacked for the inevitable spark when the call came to raise arms for the cause.

"This will doom Alestron," Rathain's prince concluded. "If the duke maintains his firm stand in refusal and will not abandon a futile defense, his citadel could face the ruinous consequence well ahead of next spring."

As Arithon's tortured awareness also encompassed the *caithdein*'s distraught state, she addressed him with brusque directness. "Whether the s'Brydion come through or not, you must go forward assured, your royal Grace. My clan chieftains will gather to shoulder what's left to be salvaged."

"My brave lioness!" Arithon exclaimed, fraught. "Given the choice, I should have forgone the presumption of crossing your threshold. Surely you realize?

409

This intervention to scour three strongholds of necromancy must incite another wave of raw fear. My hopes are as ashes. This act will force bloodshed. Etarra will be handed spectacular evidence. No matter how subtle the Fellowship's backing, the wholesale destruction of Rathain's corrupt priests is going to launch misguided fervor into explosion."

The Teiren's'Callient drew herself up straight, her dignity set into bedrock. "We will field this danger before facing worse."

Traithe intervened, before the flash-point tension incited more protesting argument. "Your Grace! I will need to teach you the keys to work the Paravian circle that stands in the ruin of old Tirans. From there, you and Dakar will cross latitude to reach the focus at Caith-al-Caen." Keen understanding acknowledged Arithon's speechless, swift gratitude, that he need not abandon his bound obligation to Jieret's widow at Halwythwood. "Your crown right to clan backing will speed your journey northward through Daon Ramon from there."

Three days ride to the trade road, a tight disguise, and a string of fast post-horses could see him through to the gates of Etarra. He must be there before the next dark moon, when Lysaer's curse-driven summons to arms would spur the cult's dedicates to bind its next string of picked victims.

Arithon gathered himself to arise, then checked short, aware that Traithe's raven as yet made no move to return to the Sorcerer's shoulder. Stilled as carved onyx, the bird watched with jet eyes, chill affirmation that this devastating audience *had not yet drawn to an end.* "We don't ride tonight for a lane transfer at dawn?" Now more than nettled, Arithon seized on the tepid wine cup left untasted at the edge of the supper tray. "That fails to explain the need for restoratives!"

Traithe matched that edged challenge with sorrow. Since the harsh pain of his tidings could not be assuaged, he had nothing to offer but pity. "Within Davien's library, you once refused to study the rites written inside the black grimoires."

Arithon stiffened. Pale before, now his skin drained utterly white. "For the soundest of reasons." Aghast horror lashed him onto his feet. Face on, he confronted the dark-clad Sorcerer, who wore the scars of a terrible sacrifice with a humility that burned for its seamless acceptance.

Much younger, more volatile for the raw depth of vision that inflamed his innate compassion, Arithon pleaded. "Such knowledge in my hands could be turned! Have you forgotten the reach of Desh-thiere's curse? Some risks," he paused, cringing scared, and braced his fists on the trestle as the winds of probability whipped and screamed through his mind. Anguished seconds passed one into the next, while the horrific images of a thousand posited massacres tore him to flinching ribbons. Arithon shuddered. "Some risks run outside of all sanity. Spare me this burden! I beg not to bear the dread form of this knowledge."

"You do have a counterweight," Traithe said with velvet-clad tenderness. "Your royal gift grants you the soundest of safeguards."

Arithon raised his eyebrows. "Not enough! The Mistwraith's works made short shrift of the s'Ilessid endowment of justice!"

"Lysaer had flaws of character to support that distortion," Traithe argued back, unequivocal.

"And I have none?" Arithon pealed. "That's blind arrogance! No more and no less, I am human, just as prone to make errant mistakes!"

"Free will!" cracked Traithe, sharp as adamant steel. "Go in without knowledge and dare the alternative: a half brother bound by geas, worshipped as a false avatar, and drawn under the abomination of the Kralovir's practice. His officers will fall first, then next month, or next year, such breeding horror will run rampant throughout the hapless ranks of the faithful. You face the choice, prince, for more than one kingdom, and *for more than Athera's grand mysteries*: to take your informed stand now, at the forefront, or to recoil and find yourself overtaken. I need not say what you already know. Only one of those paths is the master's!"

"The mercy that kills!" Incensed, Arithon shoved off and paced. "The Betrayer has hobbled your compact quite neatly."

Yet release was past reach. Having once touched the presence of a centaur guardian, he did not stand blind: the profound awakening of Paravian grace had changed his awareness forever. The flame born of that one glimpse of expansive love now seared mind and heart almost beyond self-preservation.

To Melhalla's *caithdein*, whose tradition was maintained by rote, the yawning chasm of this prince's conflict could not be grappled. Her limited view would see nothing beyond the appeal to a crown prince's sworn duty. Yet the Fellowship Sorcerer, and the eyes of the raven, perceived what was actual and real: that no living experience could supersede the importance of preserving a greater beacon of truth, untarnished and free on Athera.

No matter how clear the choice, or how shining the view revealed to the awakened visionary, the break with human ties could not be painless.

Arithon wrestled the hurt of that severance. Entrapped between the dimmed frame of his past and the limitless light that posed all the hope of the future, he appealed, "Who will explain to the brothers s'Brydion as the enemy rams their front gates? What about Erlien s'Taleyn of Alland? His clans are exposed, and already committed!" Since no answer met him, he flung out his hands, spurred by his flash-point frustration. "Had Lysaer *ever* received the bare basics of training, he would have been given the fair means to stand guard for his birth-born right to autonomy!"

Traithe sighed. "So the Fellowship's augury foresaw, and I tried. Any one of us would have granted such learning. Yet Lysaer never asked. On the hour I snatched the opening to broach the first question, he gave me no foothold, not even the opportune grace of ambiguity. By choice and free will, your half brother denied us the leave to pursue the first step toward a guided initiation."

"He was not proud," Prince Arithon insisted. "Lysaer had a strict father who taught him, too early, that only a shameful king asks for help."

"Said is done," Traithe said softly, while the raven looked on, black as a starless midnight.

Three sets of eyes shared the harrowing interval, as no less than Paravian survival swung in the trembling balance. While a desolate man wrestled to reconcile the decision laid onto his overtaxed shoulders, the woman charged to rule as *caithdein* of Melhalla was made to measure a dread that pressed caring resilience to the brink of rebellious, insane rejection. She found, after all, she could not bear to witness the force and breadth of such agony.

Head bent, she stared without sight at her realm, reduced to inked lines on the map.

Only the Sorcerer in his dark robes sustained the unbearable moment. Silver hair to tucked feet, Traithe held Arithon's eyes, as piercingly still as his raven.

Rathain's prince spoke at last. At bay in the shadows, arms crossed at his breast, he found his Masterbard's poise inadequate. "Fatemaster's fury! I swore a promise to young Fionn Areth regarding Tal Quorin's survivors." The ache of his grief tore through his voice and his bearing as he accosted Melhalla's *caithdein*. "Where is he? I'll need to explain."

Words failed her, then. As the stout woman lost her nerve, unable to spare the least of the blows that fell in her presence that night, Dakar responded, unasked and unnoticed, arrived in silence through the flapped entry.

"The task must be left to Vhandon and Talvish. I'm sorry. The north is too volatile. Fionn Areth's better off kept here, inside clan protection in Atwood."

Summer 5671

Changes

Beset by rain, a drifter woman kneels in soaked grass, attending a foaling mare; shown two tiny front hooves, she peels the caul from a coal-black head and reveals a ghost eye, pale as aquamarine glass in the lanternlight, "Isfarenn!" she gasps through the drumming downpour, "Merciful grace! Asandir's horse has sired his successor…"

At sunrise in Atwood, Vhandon and Talvish receive word from Melhalla's *caithdein* that the s'Brydion alliance has been dissolved by Prince Arithon, with his Grace departed at speed for the north without sending summons or word; stunned by the wrecked plan to disarm East Halla, the forsaken liegemen depart to stand with their duke, and outraged to be served with a broken pledge, Fionn Areth leaves with them…

At sea off the coast of Carithwyr, Lysaer s'Ilessid states the emphatic terms of his disputed landfall at Spire to his recalcitrant Lord Commander: "I will not be seen to strike my banner or skulk for the sake of a high king's crown edict! If Eldir has disbarred my sunwheel standard, we'll put into a cove on the coast of Radmoore, and finish the journey to Ath's hostel by land…"

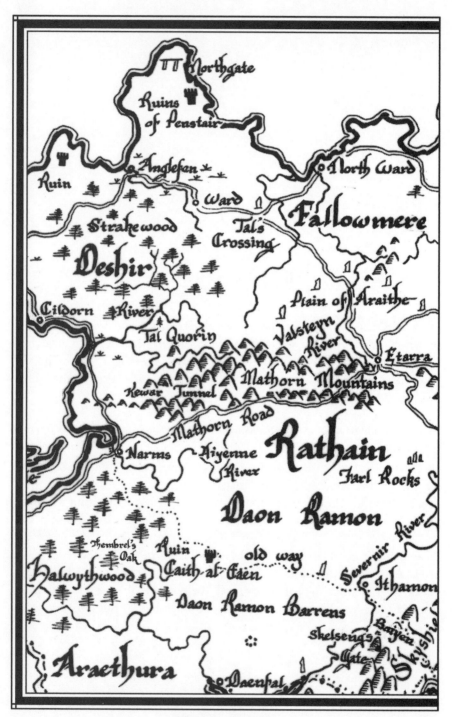

Western Rathain

XII. Halwythwood

The clan enclave deep inside the free wilds of Halwythwood was forewarned of the royal arrival about to occur at Caith-al-Caen. News came with the Koriani enchantress who had just finished a term of sanctuary at Ath's hostel. She had left Eastwall and crossed the free wilds of Daon Ramon Barrens on foot, without asking the auspice of clan escort. The connection she claimed to Prince Arithon, and her relayed word, that his Grace meant to fulfill his belated acknowledgment of the past winter's harsh losses, prompted Barach, as Earl of the North, to grant her the crown's hospitality. At Feithan's insistence, Elaira accepted guest welcome under the roof of the s'Valerient lodge tent.

Yet when the fated arrival drew nigh, the enchantress announced her decision to make herself scarce. "Your crown prince is going to ride in exhausted, and in raw straits from a harsh setback. Let him unburden himself, first. My near presence would only place strain on his focus, no boon to the delicate handling he'll need through the course of his feal obligations."

"Such love as you bear him should back his male strength," Feithan felt moved to point out. Insistently busy, she rammed her awl punch through a new set of leathers, and bestowed a wise smile upon the bronze-haired enchantress who helped split the sinew for lacing.

Elaira set down her sharp knife and blushed. "Not this time." Her wry grin threatened laughter. "Believe me! I know him. When Arithon's heart is clear of his sworn duty, I will be at hand to receive him."

"You can't know what you're missing." Feithan winked back. "Sure as rain falls, if my Jieret were living, I could not greet him with such virtuously staunch restraint!"

Yet no man alive trod the thicket of thorns imposed on the Prince of Rathain. Few women allowed him the space for his needs, and none with Elaira's perception. She chose to slip off and joined an outbound party of hunters on the excuse to replenish her herb stores. The scouts did not forbid her outsider's presence. Her time with Ath's adepts had graced her with an inner knowing tuned into accord with the land's voice. Left to fare as she pleased, this enchantress could be trusted to respect the ancient ground of the dancers' glade and its spring beneath Thembrel's Oak. Her successful traverse of Daon Ramon Barrens already had proven she knew not to intrude on those sites where the great mysteries abided in solitude.

Against Eriegal's complaints that the rough gaits of ponies chafed his shorter legs raw, he, Sidir, and Braggen, as the Companions at hand, rode out to the Paravian circle to meet their returning prince.

The *caithdein*'s successor, who should have gone with them, remained in the camp by the Willowbrook. Jeynsa's flagrant rebellion had not softened. She would not back down and accept her investiture, despite Braggen's exhaustive exoneration of the prince she had been Named to serve. Since her rejection was still flaunted by her bristle of close-cropped hair, her brother's direct order disbarred her from joining the welcoming party.

Too proud not to live by her heart, Jeynsa rejoiced in her banishment. First, she renewed the fletching on her deer arrows. Then she whetted her favorite skinning knife, and tested the edge by carving a decorative relief into a strip of boiled hide.

Mourning the loss of her father, each breath, she cursed the name of the Sorcerer who had marked her as *caithdein*'s heir within days of her birth. Soon to confront the uncanny creature whose defense had divided her family, she awaited her inevitable clash with crown protocol in combative anticipation.

The journey to Caith-al-Caen and back to the secure encampment in Halwythwood required three days, unless pressured circumstance demanded speed. Jeynsa's hostility kept her uninformed of the crisis that hastened the timing. The lapse came at high cost. She was not absent stalking, as she had planned, on the hour of the prince's arrival.

Instead, the event caught her drowsing behind the great trestle at the back of the s'Valerient lodge tent. Inbound voices aroused her, Eriegal's, raised to an untoward pitch of excitement, and Braggen's, dour with sarcasm. Jeynsa started awake where she slouched, propped against a grass-stuffed hassock. She was still seated cross-legged on the packed-dirt floor, well sprinkled with shavings of leather. A lowered light burned past the privacy flap. Her mother was wakeful, although the hour was well after nightfall.

The tallow dip on the bench had gone out. Lapped in dense shadow, the Teiren's'Valerient groped in her scrip for her flint. Dame fortune betrayed her: the darkened wick proved to be already spent, too short for her to rekindle.

Jeynsa swore. Caught at odds while the fast-moving band of Companions strode up to the curtained entry, she recognized Sidir's bass tone, giving guest welcome.

The ritual reply was delivered in a stranger's exquisitely cadenced Paravian.

She was trapped in the lodge. Furious that her brother had left her unwarned, and blindsided to face this encounter, Jeynsa froze. To bolt now would seem the act of a craven. She dared *not* slink into her mother's quarters. Feithan would just dress her down like a child, then march her back out on the force of parental authority. Denied every option to salvage her gaffe, unable to shed rage for diplomacy, Jeynsa gave rein to her mannerless impulse. She scrunched herself into the bulk of the hassock, entrusting the shadows to hide her.

The door flap slung back. Sidir poised at the threshold, his tall frame half-turned, the sable gleam of his braid and white temples distinct against starry darkness. "Come in. Take your ease."

While another mantled form filed past, too short to reveal a clear silhouette, Sidir ducked under the lintel, still speaking. "I'll strike a fresh light. Once you're both settled with cups and a flask, we'll bring Feithan to greet you."

Moving through gloom with the ease of a woodsman, Sidir flipped open the lodge tent's stores chest, while the others entered behind him: a stout man with thumping steps and a wheeze, hard followed by Eriegal's clipped stride. Braggen came last, his muscular tread picked out by the gleam of his weapons. Then the hide flap slapped shut. In the dark, the heavyset newcomer advanced with intent to park at the trestle.

Too late, Jeynsa realized her fateful mistake: the spellbinder Dakar accompanied the prince. No cover of darkness was going to withstand the talented range of his mage-sight.

Nor were his keen attributes blunted by drink: he had needed to assist with the lane transfer. The scouring, strong forces had left him honed sharp, if disgruntled from hours of hard riding. "My throat's parched enough to cure bacon," he grumped. Plonked down to a squealing creak of stressed wood, the Mad Prophet encountered Jeynsa's tucked boot, then her shrinking presence, jammed into the shadow.

No slacker, he ventured a warning, "We're not alone."

The other's light tread had crept up undetected: the response came back all but on top of her.

"I was aware." The sorcerer who was the Crown Prince of Rathain added with slicing contempt, "We won't know, now, will we, what measure of welcome eavesdrops in the crannies to meet me?"

The insult whipped Jeynsa onto her feet. The razor-edged knife lately used to incise decorations slithered out of her lap. She snatched, recaptured the dropped steel by reflex, while the cumbersome strap of boiled hide thumped to earth at her feet, wrapped her ankles, and tripped her.

She crashed into the trestle. Her left-handed grab saved her from a fall. But no timely reaction could salvage her livid humiliation.

Sidir's exclamation, "She's a rash adolescent!" clashed outright with Arithon's jabbing mockery. "Is she, by Ath? I'd have pegged her age at five years younger!"

Civility snapped. Jeynsa lunged. In the dark, her tormenter was a slight, faceless stranger, despoiling her home with his cruel jibes and his ungrateful, insupportable arrogance. Rage impelled her. She forgot the small dagger clenched in her fist.

Her royal nemesis was not taken off guard. His hard, agile parry caught the keen steel in the rain cloak bunched over his forearm.

Shocked to outcry, Jeynsa felt her well-tended blade stab into shielding cloth. Her recoil failed. His advance jammed her strike. Though her grip had gone slack, the dirk pierced the folds and snicked into flesh. She felt the horrific, slick gush of a wounding. Then the heavy, oiled fabric yanked back and jerked the snared weapon out of her grasp.

Sidir's effort at last sparked a flame. As his pine torch flared into dazzling light, Jeynsa was caught aback yet again: the whirled cloak dropped from nowhere and battened her face. Her ruthless royal adversary reeled her in. Then his wrenching tug spun her. Left forearm pinned under his bleeding wrist, hard against his unlaced shirtfront, Jeynsa sensed the warm skin at his breast, and far worse, the beat of his heart, that *did not race*. Arithon displayed no sign of startlement, a sure sign her hostility had been expected.

"Dharkaron's Black Spear!" Eriegal gasped in struck shock. He shoved forward, prepared to pull Jeynsa away. As Braggen's rough fist caught him back by the shoulder, he pealed on in shamed disbelief, "She's the Fellowship's marked choice as *caithdein*'s heir, and Ath save us, she's just tried to kill you!"

"Nothing like!" came the prince's granite response. "Braggen, shut him up. Sidir, no questions. Clear everyone out. You all have just witnessed the start of an oath sharing. Leave now. I would finish in privacy."

Choked under oilcloth, outraged to be served this unwanted excuse that would bestow an unequivocal exoneration, Jeynsa struggled. His firm grip clamped down. Her entrapped arm became savaged by a locked hold that was going to leave bruises, later.

"Go, *now!*" lashed the prince, no doubt pushed to speak twice because the Companions distrusted her temper. Yet they would not gainsay a royal command.

The cloth impaired hearing; masked footsteps and movement; but not the squealing creak of the bench or the muffled slap of the door flap. The prince's excruciating grasp scarcely slackened. Although Jeynsa had never intended to fight, her shivering rancor betrayed her. He sensed her core hatred, kept her immovably pinned as a wrestler. Then his expert hold shifted. He did not sit her down. Her left hand and forearm stayed clamped to his chest, slick with the let warmth of his blood.

Beyond resentful, still livid with anger, Jeynsa felt his quick breath. She closed her eyes, braced.

Yet Arithon Teir's'Ffalenn did not scorn her with reprimand. Instead, he invoked the Paravian rune of beginning. Then, centered in calm, he began the ritual of a mage's sworn bond of protection. *"Your self: as my own. Your breath: twined with mine. Two bodies: one flesh for this lifetime.'"*

Jeynsa shivered, struck helpless. Daughter of s'Valerient, she had the born talent to sense the bright power as his initiate oath wove about her.

"'Your spirit to my heart: bound unto death.'"

Whirled beyond protest, Jeynsa could not move, could not shout, could not recoup her resistance. Lifted to a sudden spinning euphoria, enclosed in shining warmth, she sensed the currents of mage-bonded light as they stitched themselves over, and through her. The moment commanded: she shared Arithon's heart. The gift he bestowed gloved her being in tenderness, undid her like water, and cradled her form as though precious.

Then the closure rang down and locked his sealed will into irrevocable finality. *"Dharkaron as my dark witness, my Word as sealed by my Name in Ath's light, none to sunder. Yours to call, mine to answer, until the Wheel of Fate grants one of us crossing. Anient,'"* he said. "Done."

Already, Jeynsa felt his rigid clasp opening. Half-unmoored, she scarcely noticed the tactful support as Rathain's prince sat her down within saving reach of the trestle. After that, mercy moved him. His touch retreated. Left veiled in the cloak, she could endure the desperate tears that streamed over her cheekbones.

Jeynsa wept out the storm. Outside the muffling shelter of cloth, the lodge tent seemed to be empty. Yet she dared not presume that her sovereign had left or called an end to his spontaneous audience. Therefore, she held out until her eyes dried before she relinquished the pretense of privacy.

When she tossed off the cloak, her suspicions proved true: the insufferable prince had not left her. He sat on the other side of the trestle, stilled enough that even her forest-bred senses could have overlooked his immediate presence. A tallow dip burned, *lit by craft and not striker:* the scrape of a flint would have broken the silence. The offending knife rested next to her hand, its cleaned blade a cold gleam in the dimness. Busy presumption had not ended there. Arithon had helped himself and fetched the flask of spirits from Feithan's provisions. Two cups waited, empty, between them, a mute invitation to seed amity.

Jeynsa refused to look at his face. Her antagonized nerves remained too disjointed. The unbearable care she had sensed in his oath would not let her encounter him fully.

Sight of his hands could not be avoided, cast into relief by the pooled spill of flame. The scarred right rested loose on the trestle before her, while the left pressed the shredded wreck of his sleeve to stanch the red seep of the knife cut.

The brutal fingers that had rendered her helpless were exquisitely fine, though ringless as any clan scout's. Jeynsa noted their mirrored imprint gouged into the skin of her wrist. The more searing memory would outlast abused flesh. Her fresh anger accosted the crown figure whose absence had shadowed her life, and whose errant doings had destroyed her father. "I will not be cozened to lean on your grand oath. Nor will I ever reciprocate."

The words satisfied for their perfect, chill ring.

"I hear you." The velvet tone that had shown its trust first picked up again after a moment. "Your preference is honored."

But that promise mocked, set against another that demanded her iron devotion. "You would gainsay the Fellowship's choosing?" Jeynsa stiffened, affronted. "Or are you afraid that in cold-blooded *fact* I might take my next chance, and backstab you?"

His stark pause affirmed that a *caithdein*'s vested power would endow her with the lawful right to stand as his judge and condemn him. Arithon's response showed his razor-edged care. "You are Jieret s'Valerient's daughter."

No fool, he had not poured the brandy.

Wrung breathless by her resurgent pain, Jeynsa seized the cup on her half of the trestle and placed it onto its side. In case he failed to recognize that symbolic rejection, she said, "Craven! How *dare* you invoke my sire's good name to beg surety!"

When Arithon ventured no token response, she hooked up the dropped cloak and scoured off the smeared trace of his blood from each of her quivering fingers. On her feet before thought, she glared downward. In vivid impression, the insightful awareness: that he was *small*—light-boned as a cat before her taller stature and hardened fitness. The immediate recall cracked her equilibrium: of his expert, sharp handling, that had just imposed a demeaning submission with an ease that had made her seem childish.

"I *saw* how my father died!" Jeynsa exploded. "Wielding sorcery as your proxy, he choked out his last breath with your half brother's sword through his heart. He was tortured. Crippled! Spat on by enemies before their unblessed fire destroyed his torn carcass."

Arithon regarded her. Unwashed from his ride, with his lean face unshaven and his dark hair tousled by weather, he should have seemed raffish. A renegade reduced to his seamy humanity, flawed, and beneath her contempt: except the intensity of his focus would not dismiss. He showed no pity; did not denigrate her tear-stained cheeks or broach the outrageous precedent of her shorn hair.

His eyes spoke, all too eloquent in the whipped spill of flame light.

Jeynsa watched him back, hardened, aching to receive the brisk quittance that his crown rank entitled through protocol.

Instead, Arithon elected to treat without artifice. "You did not cut off your hair to spite me. You did that for grief, to acknowledge the shame that your father endured. Your act reminded you not to forget the harsh price he paid for my life, that his dying act left as a bartered legacy."

Such relentless insight tore past *all* pretense. The bereft beheld her deep agony, *mirrored*.

"Don't ever forget, Jeynsa," urged Arithon Teir's'Ffalenn. "Grow back your clan braid. Let me stand in this world as your steadfast reminder *for as long as I live to draw breath*."

His tactful correction struck like a slap: that the span of his days could extend beyond hers. The Master of Shadow might seem untouched by time. Yet his actual age was older than Feithan; his birth had preceded the Companions. A Sorcerer's working imposed a longevity that was going to bind him for centuries.

Stung by his poignant censure, Jeynsa scoured his features. At close quarters, she yearned to unearth the glib falsehood: the facile mask that would catch him short and lay bare underlying insincerity.

No subterfuge met her. Only the clarity of an initiate mind, voluntarily stripped of defenses.

Arithon laid open his mage-sense, and *touched*, and the talented prompt of s'Valerient Sight arose to that calling, and *answered*.

Jeynsa sensed herself falling, awareness unreeled through the vaulting reach of a sorcerer's lucent experience. She was left ungrounded. *Even as her father, years before this, bore the horror of Tal Quorin's massacre, she knew the encounter would not leave her unchanged.* No foothold existed to save shattered balance. She could not disown Arithon's value. Shocked by the scope of his inward devastation, Jeynsa realized: the crown prince's desolate hurt outmatched hers. Jieret's death had once reft him beyond hope of healing. He still carried the scar of that crippling despair. A severance that damaged both will and integrity had left behind an unassuaged longing that, if Arithon escaped the trap of Desh-thiere's curse, must outlast her own grief for untold generations to come.

Yet unlike her, he had not yielded to pain. The unearthly calm posed by his acceptance itself was the cry that challenged her wound and pressed her for endurance to match him.

"How have you survived?" Jeynsa blurted.

"I nearly didn't." The admission stayed level. Before her anguished, peeling regard, Arithon held himself naked. "The crossing came hard, but need not have. In Kewar's maze, when I shared the grace of a centaur's presence, I saw Jieret's choice reconfigured by light as an act of exultant triumph. His love superseded my limitation. I could reject him, and die. Or I could embrace the gift as he meant: not as the dutiful burden of heritage, but done as an accolade, without condition."

Jeynsa slammed the bared boards. *This*, she could not endure. No prince, but a man, and a stranger, offered up his core self, all the while aware that he must fall short. *All that he was* could never replace the father—the friend—whose courageous heart and generous strength dealt a priceless loss, shared between them.

She suffered because her father had set *this one spirit* ahead of a safe return to his family. Nor was Jieret's hideous death rendered empty, or foolish, or in any way the mistake of a devalued sacrifice.

Arithon had not tried to console, or excuse. He did not demean by apology. That seamless humility shaped a force too unnervingly whole to withstand.

Jeynsa clawed back her dagger. Goaded on by her ungoverned denial, she dashed the two cups aside. A second blow smashed the decanter. Shards flew. Brandy gushed and spilled. Doused by the flood, Rathain's prince never flinched, though his lost calm revealed the fresh hurt her rejection tore through him.

Past her, he saw Steiven, and Dania, and Jieret, and the hacked bodies of four daughters, violated. Through Jeynsa, his ghosts spoke, a gale wind from a storm that scattered the hope he might reach her.

"Go on!" whispered Jeynsa. "Admit how I hate you, before your ripped flesh has stopped bleeding."

Silent, *he held*, while she quivered and broke, spirit dashed on the wrong side of quietude.

"I can't drink," she snarled, bitter. "Can't swear you a welcome. I look at your face, and I hear father screaming. His burned eyes and cut tongue were the cost of your lineage. The sound of your name is accursed in my ears. The shame of his degradation will not find redress for as long as you live."

Arithon Teir's'Ffalenn inclined his head, a small move made in resignation. The tension of contact snapped in release.

Unstrung, Jeynsa bolted, heedless as a hazed deer. Hard and fast as she left him, *she could not escape*. In life, her father had never denied the depth of Prince Arithon's compassion. At her core, Jeynsa *knew:* Earl Jieret had written his own fate, that dreadful hour upon Daon Ramon Barrens. He had crossed Fate's Wheel by a choice that was given, for a love that was both right and true.

The lie did not hold. Pretense gave no shelter. The crown prince whose oath bonded her in protection remained, then and now, everything else but unworthy. No breathing creature should burn with such grace, to eclipse the ache of her abandonment.

Outside, Jieret's daughter careened into Eriegal's stout arms and howled until she was emptied.

* * *

Arithon remained within the lodge tent, his face masked behind his braced hands. The winnowed flame of a tallow dip circled his motionless person in light. His torn, unlaced sleeve sopped up the spilled brandy amid scattered slivers, and two overset cups whose promise had failed to forge amity.

If his undressed wrist had ceased bleeding, the small wound kept its venomous sting.

And already, the tenor of the fallen quiet drew someone's inquiring notice: Sidir had not left the lodge tent. Beside Feithan throughout the turmoil of young Jeynsa's royal audience, he cracked the flap that divided the sleeping quarters, then gently dared a step through. Since service in Vastmark, he held to wise limits. His undisguised footfall volunteered the tact that signaled an invasion of privacy.

"You've come to inform me that Feithan's heard everything." The phrase was split rock, for its brevity. When Arithon stirred, his glance showed disgust for the sordid mess on the trestle. He arose, sharply fast. His snatch caught the heaped cloak from the bench, then cast its folds over the wreckage. He blotted the sopped mess, raked up cloth and fragments, and thrust the disaster into the Companion's capable grasp. "Get rid of this!"

His rushed gesture happened scarcely in time.

Behind Sidir's stance, the curtain trembled, then moved. Illumination spilled from beyond and slashed across the cleared trestle. No help for small details: the close air still wore the sickly tang of splashed brandy. Arithon could do nothing about his wrecked shirt, or the wound, which would smart like fell vengeance if he tried to mask it under his spirit-soaked sleeve.

Unable to effect kindly subterfuge, he stepped forward, all grace. Before Earl Jieret's widow, he bent his dark head, then knelt on bare earth at her feet. "My Lady Feithan, don't speak." He raised his upturned palms and caught the rough hands of the woman come forward to meet him. "My condolence is too little, done far too late, and your daughter is already forgiven."

Masterbard, he had been well schooled to rise to a difficult passage. Direct words availed little: the moment hung, anyway. Feithan was caught looking down at the disordered black hair that fronded his opened collar, and past that, to a knife cut placed with a precision that left his wrist unimpaired. This could not be chance. Feithan trembled. Upright, she encountered the prince she had never met, while the tears she wished she could have kept from him flooded her eyes.

"You already knew," she accused. "About Jeynsa."

Arithon nodded. His touch, upon hers, said all that words could not: that he had fielded her daughter's hatred, prepared, and provoked his slashed arm by design.

Sidir's sharp wits stayed unfazed by the gallantry. "Who broke our silence?"

"No," Feithan murmured, as Arithon bridled, his grasp locked to hers with fresh tension. "You have done enough, your Grace." Her narrow grip raised him.

He came to his feet with a seamless speed that *almost* avoided the flame light. But the weariness scored into his face showed grim endurance, not hackled anger.

Sidir nonetheless pressed his inquiry. "Among ourselves, we had agreed to spare you from Jeynsa's misconduct, at least until Feithan or Earl Barach could give you a suitable welcome."

"Well, don't dress down your scouts." Arithon flashed Jieret's widow the ghost of a smile as he watched an unflappable man stung to a rare burst of outrage. "Sit down, Sidir. The brangle killed no one. You thought to strangle the loose tongue of rumor?"

Arithon's attention flicked back to Feithan. Her leashed-back tears did not mislead him: her vital strength possessed the bold nerve to address his racked state of exhaustion. He thwarted her scolding, hooked the hassock, and perched, then tucked his slashed arm in his lap. "Two warnings reached me. Dame Dawr was specific. Melhalla's *caithdein*, kind soul, was concerned I'd be served with a public embarrassment. The snag I foresaw, and the sole point that mattered was to make Jeynsa draw my blood willingly."

Rasped hoarse at last, Arithon included the steadfast Companion, whose reliable insight had never once fallen short under pressure. "I promised her father," he informed Sidir. "My oath was the last thing he asked, by the Aiyenne. The girl's free to hate me. I frankly don't care. Keep her clear! She'll stay living. Whatever should come to befall me hereafter, my bond of protection will try no one's poise."

"Eriegal could mistake you," Sidir pointed out. "He may condemn your unkind provocation."

Arithon recoiled, flicked to impatience. "Let him! Don't you think I'd prefer my autonomy?" Caught aback by his overstrung nerves, he shut his teeth, fast, and stood up.

Feithan watched his approach, no less trapped by constraint. His haunted quietude suggested an urgency: he wanted the dance steps of etiquette done, as decently fast as compassionate care would permit.

Unwilling to burden his Grace with her need, she made her brave bid to release him. "Your enchantress was mistaken. She need not have been absent. Surely the onus of crown duty, and I, might have waited this once on your pleasure?"

But that heartfelt supposition proved to be wrong. Past resource to argue, Arithon rejected her saving excuse. He embraced the encounter, regardless. Though he wore his borrowed leathers with natural elegance, their fit was too large. Up close, he was no taller than she. That fine build deceived. His determined strength shocked through his touch as, again, he gathered her hands in his own and shouldered the force of her agony. "Jieret was the brother I always lacked. Ask, lady. My passage through the maze under Kewar has made me far more than eyewitness."

Her eyes searched his, stripped by grief, then with unruly sorrow, spilled over. "I need no more than this. Did my husband suffer?"

Arithon squeezed her fingers. His sight locked with hers, he pressed her knuckles against the beat of his heart, that she could measure his unflinching sincerity. "Jieret supported no more than he chose. His will prevailed, to the end. Had my orders been followed, he would be still living beside you, and Braggen's death would have burdened my conscience. The void that is left is too high a price. No victory, ever, can replace him."

Feithan shuddered, braced straight. "I have no more brandy," she lamented, her desolation as much for the stranger before her as for the absence inflicted by loss.

Arithon smiled, a brilliance of spirit that showed her a bittersweet glimpse of the humor her husband had shared through the sacrosanct bonds of deep fellowship.

"Jieret wouldn't mind," said the Crown Prince of Rathain, not as royalty, but as he might have chaffed a friend's sister. "We weren't in the habit of maudlin bouts of drinking, and Dakar's all too quick to suck down raw spirits until he's a prostrate nuisance."

Feithan shut her eyes, all at once overcome. The prince drew her in. His resilient frame was not massive, like Jieret's. She did not feel as though she leaned on the mountain that weathered all storms, immovable, until the last. Yet beyond any question, Feithan understood that Arithon's support would extend for as long as she asked for the bastion of his solace.

Yet the loss of the brandy had to be remedied, after all. The last hurdle facing the Crown Prince of Rathain was the Earl of the North's oath of fealty. Other unsworn clansfolk might come forward tomorrow. But Barach, as the inheriting chieftain, must acknowledge his sovereign ahead of them. Since clan custom also demanded the traditional cup and guest welcome, Arithon was required to maintain his poise through the course of another state obligation.

His tacit assurance reached the Koriani enchantress where she sat, immersed in light trance, in an oak grove not far from the camp. *'Soon, beloved. Dawr's word said Barach is reasonable.'*

Elaira's lips turned in the faintest of smiles. Nestled in comfort against a shagged tree, she touched back, sending him patience. As well as he masked his worn nerves in the flesh, the etheric connection between them was transparent. She sensed the deepest ache of his need, overlaid by the medicinal scald of the compress that someone well-meaning had bound over his cut arm.

'*Soon enough,*' Elaira returned. She would dress the gash more comfortably, later; in the moment, she sustained her caress within Arithon's mind, sweetened by the exquisite thrill of a partnered anticipation.

Around her, the midnight stars burned serene through the filigree patterns of greenery. Frogs croaked from a spring in the rocks, and the dew-soaked air smelled of jasmine. Wrapped in the peace of the woodland glade, Elaira tracked the ongoing flurry of activity inside the chieftain's lodge tent.

Dakar had entered, bearing the requisite flask. His rotund bulk was trailed by Braggen's chopped stride, with the self-conscious Companion red-faced and tongue-tied to find himself asked to stand vigil in place of Rathain's absent *caithdein*. His hand would bear the naked sword to safeguard his crown prince's back. At one stroke, that honor exorcised the unresolved ghost of distrust instilled by his past misjudgments in Daon Ramon.

The broad-shouldered man who entered behind would be Barach, second son born to s'Valerient, and risen to title as Earl of the North in the year before he reached his majority. Now twenty, he carried a fighting man's muscle under his fringed, buckskin leathers. His rough-cut good looks were made striking by his sire's hazel eyes, and the glossy clan braid, brown as walnut dipped into lacquer.

His affable nature had already won him Elaira's spontaneous friendship. She sent that reassurance across the twined link: knowing the serious young man who came to pledge loyalty must encounter his sovereign, sore with the outrage of his younger sister's uncivil behavior. His determined poise could make him seem forbidding as he stepped up to offer his unsheathed blade for the ritual.

A light breeze brushed the leaves. The springwaters burbled; flame hissed in the distant lodge tent. Immersed in the warmth of Elaira's sent peace, Arithon permitted Dakar's greater bulk to eclipse his immediate presence. Stilled at the center of purposeful movement, he shoved down the black wall of his tiredness. He had not slept beyond catnaps for days. Scoured sick by a course of malevolent study, left taxed from the use of strong magecraft, he needed, each moment, to marshal his bearing. Every second of respite was valued.

'*Soon,*' he affirmed, while the guest cup was brought, and brandy was poured for the welcoming.

Then Braggen crossed his fists at his heart. Handed the black sword, he moved into position at his liege's left shoulder.

The young earl stepped forward, and Rathain's prince beheld him, revealed in the flood of the tallow dip.

He looked so like Steiven! The resemblance jarred, cracking the last of Arithon's hard-set equanimity. Beset by a sorrow that laced him with dizziness, he pushed to his feet. The sharp motion failed to curb his wild talent. He stood erect, though harassed by that difficulty, striving for poise to bestow the respect that Deshir's new chieftain should merit. But the rote words he uttered felt distant and dim. Colors and noise came through muted as bygone memories sparked the vivid array of multiple unwritten futures. Their insistent pressure slammed through and broke over him.

Elaira sensed the frenetic wave as it crashed: *that this man might have been Jieret's father, reborn to an unscarred youth. The fresh glow of his presence did not blaze with hatred. No gouging burns disfigured his face, and no vicious hunt to pursue townborn reivers yet hardened the set of his mouth. Upcoming events at Etarra would change that. The required foray to curb practicing necromancy could not help but re-kindle the fire and storm to launch more butchering headhunters into the field. The ache was too much, that the unspoiled nobility of the next generation must come to reap the hideous price of that cleansing.*

Arithon shut his eyes, swayed, his stance salvaged by Braggen, who braced him with a touch from behind.

Then Barach uttered the formal greeting, clan chieftain to sanctioned crown prince. The contact that bridged Arithon's subtle link with the grove ripped into sparkles and drowned, slashed apart by a burst of raw prescience.

Heart pounding, peace destroyed, Elaira snapped out of trance. She was breathing too fast. Her frame was still pressed to the ancient tree. She enacted due courtesy: acknowledged its calm, and whispered swift thanks to the elements. Then she surged to her feet, as *soon* became *now* with a cry of exigent urgency.

Elaira ran. Her step trampled no underbrush. Inside the guarded bounds of the free wilds, the forest itself was aware; no matter how rushed, one did not fare heedlessly. She made haste with the delicate sense of a tracker, ducking beneath branches and runners of vine and easing her way through the thickets. Her tread did not crush the green moss in the hollows, but touched over stone, root, and hummock at speed, scattering only dew. Between strides, she snagged the impression: *of Arithon, once again kneeling.* The oath taking had started.

Now entangled by time-honored etiquette, the prince must turn his back to demonstrate his trust for the liegeman about to swear service. Elaira caught snatches of the opening affirmation, declaring Braggen's appointment as guard-ian, then the metallic ring as the Paravian sword was drawn and poised over-head as impeccable surety. Then came Arithon's wretched tremor of chill, *as the past wove its thread, warp through weft with the present:* now, Steiven's grandson would be bending his neck beneath that bared blade to give his edged weapon to seal pledge of loyalty.

The moments flowed one into the next: *she sensed the cold crossguard of Barach's dagger, clasped between unsteady hands. Against the cruel flare of prescient imagery, through the crosscurrents of battered awareness, Arithon raised his response on the strength of his Masterbard's training. "For the gift of feal duty, Barach s'Valerient..."*

Over a shallow brook, scored by the faint gleam of starlight, the enchantress raced for the lodge tent. The scouts on the outer perimeter had already detected her rapid approach. They closed, weapons lowered. One glimpse at her face, and they listened. She was waved through. A signal arrow sped from somebody's bow, forewarning the next defense cordon that she was inbound, and acknowledged to pass without challenge.

Under the wavering flame of the tallow dip, the crown's spoken oath was just barely ending. "Dharkaron witness," Arithon stated.

His equilibrium was still shattered. Elaira sensed his reeling distress. As he locked eyes with the clansman standing above, swept faint by the riptide of Sight, the metered phrase of the ritual sustained him. He laid one word after the next with precision to carry him through the abyss. *'Take back this blade as token of my trust, and with your true steel, my royal blessing.'*

He rose, as he must, without Braggen's help. On the trestle, he discovered the cup for the guest oath. There, the too-earnest help of his friends had done his worn condition no favors. Arithon stifled his flare of dismay for the Mad Prophet's relentless bad habits: the reprobate had naturally brought the heftiest vessel to be found in the Halwythwood camp...

"Damn the man!" Elaira gasped, angry. She sprinted flat out, with no pause for rest, through the damp summer foliage. A few minutes would bring her to Arithon's side. The interval yawned like eternity.

Barach affirmed the clan's welcome first.

'Speak,' Elaira prompted, driven by need to maintain a clear contact. To avoid affront, Arithon should respond with the time-honored invocation. Wrung breathless, she encouraged and cued his next phrase through the shearing web of his awareness. *'To this house, its earl, and his sworn companions, I pledge friendship...'*

The flame light was too brilliant, and the close air, too dense. Arithon battled his ripped concentration. The next line, and the next, he neared the end. He pronounced the last, ceremonial words as a man who fought for wind, drowning. 'Dharkaron witness.'

Elaira dashed welling moisture out of her eyes. Racing against time, she plunged through the dark wood, while the ongoing ritual proceeded: Barach would now lift the tankard and consume his half share of the brandy. Custom demanded: in declaration of amity, the guest of the lodge must drain the vessel and replace it rim down on the trestle. There, the affront set by Jeynsa's late tantrum left no ambiguous grace. Arithon had little choice but to finish. Fail, and he risked seeding the flawed implication of a fatal distrust of the clans.

He grasped the huge tankard, somehow without fumbling. Though the reeling rush as the s'Ahelas gift racked his mind in the smoke of ungovernable, overlaid futures, he hefted the vessel. There came a small shock, as the unsteady rim collided against his locked teeth.

'*Drink*,' Elaira begged as she broke through screening evergreen, sprang over split rocks, and plunged into a narrow ravine. At the draw, the inner line of clan sentries stood back and let her pass through without slacking. '*Drink, beloved!*'

Arithon could not afford carelessness. The last drop of brandy would have to be drained.

Well aware that an incident might launch disaster, Arithon propped his bandaged wrist on the trestle. The sting scarcely cleared his stressed senses. Elaira felt his deep breath, then the brutal will that caught back the dropped reins of his talent: for the hard complication could not be helped. His gift left him desperately sensitive. As the raw spirits seared down his throat, the potent kick scalded, racing through his rushed blood. He paused, though racking weariness and the incipient fever caused by a virulent backlash hobbled the trained skills he required to transmute the effects of the alcohol.

Gut roiling, Arithon tipped up the tankard and swallowed the volatile contents. Fire upon fire, he could scarcely stand up. The ground spun under his planted feet.

Elaira watched, caught helplessly distant, as his besieged control slipped his grasp, and his tenuous bearings upended.

No light glimmered ahead. Clan encampments were kept darkened for safety. Elaira pounded through the closed circle of tents, leaping pegged ropes to reach the lodge at the center. Already, Sidir heard her inbound step. Infallible guardian, he kept watch to avert an untoward intrusion. Since the enchantress's presence would *not* be gainsaid, he moved aside and lifted the flap for her entry.

Elaira burst through into flickering light. She arrived the same moment the tankard was banged, rim downward onto the boards. No spill marred that closure. As she rounded the trestle, too stressed for relief, she noticed that Braggen was weeping. His massive grasp closed, caught his liege as he folded. Young Barach proved to be just as quick. He had already turned at his sovereign's side, shifting the bench underneath him. Joined in evident conspiracy, he helped the Companion lower his prince and settle him onto the seat.

No fool, Elaira glared in censure at Dakar, hanging on the sidelines like a whipped hound in an attempt to stay inconspicuous.

"We all agreed!" the Mad Prophet exclaimed in defense. "The large cup was chosen by us in advance." Fat though he was, he could move lightning fast when singed by a wrathful woman. As Elaira brushed past, he rushed his excuses. "You weren't here! The prince was not biddable. He was burning his reserves like a creature possessed, and what else could his closest friends do for him?"

"Ask!" snapped Elaira.

She closed the last step, all but staggered as the explosive resurgence of vision whipped distress like balefire through Arithon's aura. Her hand closed on his shoulder. She felt damp, heated skin through the textures of leather and linen.

Despite masking clothes, her live touch jarred through him, a piercing arrow of sensation that raked him from head to feet. He ached, he burned, and he bled, that the brandy's cheap numbness undid him. Elaira sank down on the bench, close behind. She wound her arms around Arithon's shoulders and rested her cheek at the base of his neck.

"Never mind," she murmured. She resharpened her inward focus, the better to reach through disorder and lend a more intimate edge to the contact. *'You can let go in peace. Your friends meant you well, though they failed to realize their trick set no safety net under you.'*

Initiate talent infallibly sped the body's responses to volatile drink, a vulnerability exploited with vicious intent to ensure that the victim was flattened. The effect hazed the prince under with demeaning speed. Past question, Arithon was already beyond the grace of coherent response. Her giving nature begged him to release and fall the rest of the way into darkness.

'I'll be at your side when you waken.' Her promise sang through him, a weaving of water to quench unchecked Sight and snuff the live embers of prescience.

The Prince of Rathain stirred under her, anyway. Lifted his head; clasped his fingers to hers, then twisted. Eyes open, he beheld the sight of her fully. She saw his face, then his change of expression as he drank in each treasured detail.

The dark auburn hair, spilled loose from its tie, and gray eyes that met his, exquisite in their attentiveness. Her aware being would have changed, since her time at Ath's hostel: Elaira saw her heightened state of self-assurance mirrored back in his drowning regard. She felt his melting pleasure for her flushed skin, and the woods scents of jasmine and leaves brought in with her clothing. She shivered, in tune with his boundless delight, as the warmth that rushed through her vibrant touch resharpened the linkage between them.

The shock as his clasp tightened caught short her breath and forged a kinetic expansion. *There would be no boundary.* Scarcely able to separate which sensation was hers, and which current was sourced within Arithon, Elaira realized the brandy was not acting fast enough. *He was going to weep.* Not as the result of exhaustion, or stress, but from the unbridled joy that soared upward and burned toward exaltation. With that purest ecstasy came wild rage, that he could not command the least of his faculties. The gift of her presence spilled through his grasp, falling away like dropped pearls in a deluge.

Elaira felt the helpless surge of his anguish. He would have had no watching eyes mar their union. Though desperately tired, he should have received her solace without interruption. His explosive emotion ripped through him like storm, that she was also compelled to crush back the blaze of her unshielded welcome.

"Privacy! Now!" she cried in appeal.

But Sidir had already acted. Braggen and Barach were pressured to leave, while Dakar took charge of Alithiel. Feithan made the gift of the bed in her quarters. The curtain at the rear of the lodge tent was already open and waiting.

"Here," Sidir offered. "I'll bear him up. It's all right. You can trust. Our history extends back to Vastmark."

Summer 5671

Twining

Indomitable will could not break all limits. Arithon succumbed to the brandy. Elaira felt the thinned trace of his awareness slip away before Sidir set his liege down. His Grace of Rathain was laid, quite unconscious, onto a pine-stuffed mattress thrown over with softened deerhide.

"Do you wish my assistance?" the Companion inquired, his courtesy dauntless as he ascertained the candle was fresh, with spares close at hand, that the enchantress would not require the later indignity of asking.

"Thank you, no," said Elaira. "I need only two errands. My satchel, which I left by the spring on the north bank of the Willowbrook, and a bucket and basin for washing."

Sidir straightened and faced her. His tall frame loomed over her, shadowing the auburn spill of her hair, torn loose from her sprint through the brush. He measured her eyes, of a rain-washed gray that just now bordered on lilac, then her wrists, with the workaday scrapes from her herb-gathering. Koriani sister, oathbound to her prime, she might pose the realm's prince an unknown measure of danger. Sidir weighed her presence, not willing to hurry. His clan lineage carried the true talent for insight. As a man, he prized listening and honesty.

Discernment showed him a woman whose desire was forthright: every line of her wished his departure. Nonetheless, his grave survey held out until his peerless assessment was satisfied. "I will get what you need." Then he smiled, head tipped toward his prostrate liege. "He is in the best hands. You shall not be disturbed. I'll drive the pack off until daybreak."

"He's going to need longer." Elaira sank down on the pine-needle bed, fingers clasped to Arithon's wrist. "The brandy was a foolish mistake. He was

431

already run to the edge and verging on backlash from the handling of unre-
fined lane flux."

Sidir knelt, touched her sleeve till she faced him. His pale eyes stayed level,
unfired to rage by the animosity that accused him. "The brandy was not the best
tactic, perhaps. But without it, we couldn't have bought him an hour. Half the
men in the camp, and most of the women, have yet to meet their crown prince
in person. We don't have closed doors here, unless someone's sick. Our children
come and go as they please. They greet strangers by climbing all over them."

"I hadn't noticed," Elaira said, crisp.

Again, Sidir stood to full height and gazed down at her. "You wouldn't,"
he answered, his caution unmasked. "Enchantress, they were afraid of you."

Gone on that word, he shut the privacy flap. Elaira was left alone at long
last. Hers, the task to salvage the damage that exhaustion and strong drink
had wrought with a barely tamed gift of raw prescience. Arithon Teir's'Ffalenn
lay senseless beneath the glow of the candle. Though his numbed state was
brought on by alcohol, his pulse was too fast, and his skin held the flush of
a borderline fever.

Those symptoms stemmed from an imbalanced aura. Elaira attended them
first. She loosened his clothing, stripped off his leathers, his boots and breeches,
then slipped the stained shirt off his shoulders. Unwilling to impinge upon his
helpless dignity, she left him the modesty of his smallclothes. His body was
adjusted for comfort, faceup, with each of his limbs laid out straight.

Lean as fine sculpture, he was beautifully made, except for the scar where
the light bolt had struck, and the older marks left by shackles. Where the woman
might linger, admiring, the healer dared not show indulgence. Elaira combed
her fingertips just above his bared skin. She tracked the kinetic flow of his life
force and sounded the snarled energies left by overplayed talent and ragged
distress. Though her skills could have righted his traumatized shock within a
matter of moments, she dared not incur the risk. Not when the price of her
order's knowledge might bind him into an oath of debt.

Denied stronger remedies, she relied upon touch, lightly stroking to re-
settle the flux points that sustained the flow of his vitality. Release came in
stages. As she coaxed subtle energies back into alignment, his strung sinews
warmed through and relaxed. The heartbeat slowed down, and the breath
became regular. She checked his eyes, often. By the time her fresh water and
herbals arrived, Arithon's pupils had lost their blackened state of dilation.

The nightmare waves of prescience would be subsiding. If Arithon
dreamed, he was no longer hagridden to shock by the uncontained burst of
wild talent.

Only then did Elaira stir from his side. She recovered her satchel, then the
bucket and basin already brought in and left within reach of the curtain. Constrained to simple remedies, she used oil of lavender to scent the wax candle.

Then she made a compress of cold water and herbs, and laid the cloth over Arithon's closed eyes.

A sigh shuddered through him, relief as cool darkness soothed his taxed senses.

While the subtle blending of fragrance transformed the enclosure into a haven of quietude, Elaira made an infusion of hot water, chamomile, and wintergreen for a bracing tonic. With gentle care, she sponged off the dirt left ingrained from his overland journey. Inch by cherished inch, she explored his stilled form, an acquaintance enacted in a flame-lit silence unmatched for its vulnerable intimacy.

More than once, Elaira sat back on her heels, overcome: her beloved was *here*, in the care of her hands. Yet the spirit she held as close as life itself ranged too deep to respond. He was present, but unaware of her. The odd thought occurred, that their roles had reversed. Arithon must have felt much as she did now, when she had been undone by a difficult healing in a cottage in Merior twenty-six years ago. The desperate length of her wait to be near him let her savor the interval for its peace. Her contentment unfolded, moment by moment, now that he moved out of danger.

Brought to the last detail, Elaira stripped the compress off Arithon's arm. She rinsed away the medicinal salves, since they only posed a further hindrance. Ath's adepts had guided her to a deeper awareness. Where once, she would have used sigils and force, now she invoked by harmonic intent, and a partnered rapport with the elements. The wound healed. Not invisibly, not all at once: Elaira eschewed applied use of her talent. Her connection stayed sourced within Arithon's innate balance, until the gash closed to a hairline scab. From there, the tissues would knit without pain, clear of any scarring infection.

Sleep must finish the rest. As his weariness lifted, Arithon would recover the use of his arcane faculties. Since the soporific effect of the brandy would not hold him under for long, Elaira stripped down to the loosened strings of her shirt, then tucked in on the mattress beside him. In the warm, summer air, wrapped in fragrance of lavender, she indulged herself, and let the low candle burn. While her heartbeat twined into rhythm with his, she drifted asleep to the sight of his dark hair, nestled amid a pillow of balsam-stuffed deerhide.

Near dawn, she awoke to the change in his presence. The candle had extinguished, and the herbal compress was gone, tossed who knew where in the darkness. Arithon's eyes were wide-open. Chin propped on his closed fist, he was alert: regarding her with an almost desperate care, as though the gift of her at his side was a dream, inclined to shatter at the least movement. By his tenuous, pinched frown, she gathered the fact the camp's brandy flask packed a sharp wallop.

Elaira grinned. "If I stir, your head might tip over and fall off?" The words raised a thrilled shiver of anticipation that invited his touch, or his voice. "Are you very sore?"

"The hair of the dog would not be a blessing." Arithon reached out, stroked a strayed wisp from her cheek, then threaded an arm overtop of her shirt, and insistently drew her in close. "We had a promise?"

Pressed full length against his wiry strength, Elaira murmured the phrase he had said, from a memory shared within Kewar. " 'Kiss under the moon till the stars fall?' "

"No moon," said Arithon. "Don't expect me to wait." His hands moved, cupped full of her tumbled bronze hair, and paused for one glorious moment. Then his questing fingers slid upward and cradled the back of her head.

Ruffled to the barest chill of alarm, Elaira sucked in a swift breath.

"I know," he said. "Trust me fully, beloved." The tender brush of his lips against hers bloomed into a whisper-light contact.

She trembled and burned to that melting touch. Felt him tauten like an overstrung bow. His fiercely leashed will and careful restraint reassured her beyond need for protest. He respected her fear: that she was Prime Selidie's bait for a trap designed to tear down his autonomy. A stark folly, should they become swept away and fall into a heedless union. The approach toward completion must be watched for the unforeseen pitfall, which meant an arduous course of advance and retreat, with each intimacy sounded to its core response through the use of talented mage-sight.

Now that desire lay within reach, Elaira choked back blinding terror. The unconscionable dread, that she might cause his downfall, seized her numb and all but made her heart stop. Here, in his arms, where no care should intrude, there were agonies too dark to contemplate.

Arithon cradled her shivering against his clothed loins, and the warmth of his unabashed confidence. "We have all day, and all night, as need be," he whispered into the crown of her hair. "And the next night, or however many it takes." He moved, shifted grip, let her unquiet form mold against the stripped heat of his chest. Delight raced his heart. His breathing had quickened. Yet his hands upon her showed no urgency. "The bait is too sweet, though I promise not to explore you in earnest until we know for certain your Prime's vow of freedom holds true."

"You can't do that hungover!" Elaira accused. "You might be rested, but I am a healer. Plain as daylight, you know that your subtle awareness has not yet achieved full recovery."

He smiled, his mental touch a bit ragged, and his cheek against hers in mild need of a razor. "The drink hasn't quite lifted," he agreed in douce grace. "The shortfall ends there. Rauven's mages taught me the skills of restraint. Year upon year of practicing abstinence, you're likely to find I have far less experience releasing myself to indulgence." His bent knuckle stroked her cheek, trailed down her neck, then played over the skin underneath of her drawstring collar.

"Trust me. You must. Or else Selidie wins. The cold ache of her game will just as thoroughly ruin us."

Arithon cradled her chin in his palm. The resharpened sense of his presence let her know he looked with stripped earnest into her eyes. "If there are limits, beloved, let us find where they are."

The unwritten corollary of the initiate master, instilled by strict training at Rauven: that the fear never faced would let in the danger that stalked and destroyed from behind. Elaira clung to him, aware he was right. The snare first must be known, to disarm it.

Surrounded in tender warmth, ringed inside of a guarded protection that made her being an inseparable part of him, Elaira laid down the knot of her jangling unease. She matched his embrace. Their lips met again, and softly, so softly, tested the uncertain waters. She felt the depth of her care shock straight through him. Then the *almost* undetectable catch of his breath, as he engaged his schooled reflex and deflected response, and allowed the kindling conflagration to flow into him without resistance. The current streamed through the core of his body, and out, passed back to the realms of the infinite as an etheric wind through his aura. His expertise was an unerring shield that reconfigured the explosion of sexual response and stepped the flame down to a glowing, banked ember. Reduced, but complete, he sampled her with an exquisite constraint that surpassed pleasure and heightened the dance of expectation to a force that begged dissolution.

Terror fled in that moment. Elaira leaned into him, safe. She sank into his embrace, then spread her starved fingers over his skin and let go in suspended surrender. The connection between them closed and flowered, as the presence of spirit joined that of the flesh.

And light bloomed: a rolling charge of unspent, subtle energy that brightened and flared to a burst of actinic static. The confined quarters blazed. The close air belled, then sang, gathering tone to arrive at a pealing note of wild triumph. The vibration never fully awoke as heard sound: Arithon already damped down the contact and snuffed the errant explosion back into battening darkness.

"What—!" gasped Elaira.

He brushed her lips, shaking with rueful laughter. "No work of your Prime's, but the price of my heritage." He shivered, not with distress, but in wonderment. "My crown prince's tie to the realm, don't you see? An event in the Mathorns, and a centaur within Kewar, and the practice of a Fellowship attunement at the time I was sanctioned for right of succession have combined to spin us a startling tangle. Our union of spirit is raising a joy that invokes my sovereign tie to Rathain. We spark that much light. We're in the free wilds—too near Ithamon, bang over the ley that runs through Thembrel's Oak and flows across Caith-al-Caen. The flux has to respond. Your talent and mine are that strongly matched. Anywhere within leagues of this place, we are going to enact a completion of the land's higher mysteries."

The lane forces would be fired to a spontaneous consummation on no less than the love shared between them.

"We can't do that here!" Elaira shoved onto her elbow, appalled to a flush of embarrassment. "Mercy on us, we'd shake down this tent! Arouse every sleeper, and have the entire camp grinning as though they'd been shocked by the ripple of a grand confluence."

"Patience. You're right. We can't do that here, or hold out the least hope of commanding our privacy." Arithon soothed her down. A sprawled cat at her side, he let his hand play, rearranging her hair and grazing a feather-light fingertip over her shirtfront. Most carefully, he checked any heedless contact with bare skin through the moments as her touch responded. Posed a challenge to try even his mage-trained endurance, he shared his conclusion in the scented darkness. "We'll need night, and a spring, and a sourced connection with the earth. I know how to configure a gentle stay. If you don't mind open sky, and a bed in the moss, we can allow the flood to disperse and ground into the tides of the lane flux."

"Nightfall!" gasped Elaira. "Ath's own grace. That's a torment outside what is natural!"

"My dear, you are right." Arithon buried his cheek into her hair, still rocked by his wry amusement. "We'll surmount piquant torture. Though by the Fatemaster's list! There had better not be another setback, or any more confounding complications! As things stand, this predicament is bound to create the most damnably endless day."

Summer 5671

Severance

On the first occasion when Lysaer had visited an inhabited hostel maintained by the Brotherhood of Ath's adepts, he had set off without the least notion that their esoteric ways might inconvenience him or come to disturb his lasting peace of mind. He had approached with a foreigner's ignorance and collided headlong with their uncanny, beguiling powers.

This time forewarned, he did not arrive mounted. Nor did he lead an armed troop to the gate. The party of ten who guarded his back were told to wait at the head of the vale. Sulfin Evend alone stayed by his sovereign's side. Unarmed, they strode toward the carved plinths demarking the entrance through the tumbledown dry wall, which enclosed an overgrown, circular courtyard.

Under noon sunlight, the grass grew waist high. Seed heads tapped the Lord Commander's empty scabbard. Flowering vines draped the old, lichened field-stones and smothered the granite portal in verdant profusion. Such riotous growth was not due to neglect. The adepts' blameless code let the earth attend to her own, a celebration of life without boundary. Their orchards and gardens nurtured weeds, birds, and insects with equal-handed, burgeoning plenty.

Sited at the shoreline just east of Spire, the grass prairie of Havistock spread like baked ocher beneath a flawless sky. Trees tangled the hollows in thickets of shade, nestled between the low, rolling hills, whose crests shimmered under the scouring glare. Lysaer surveyed the solitary, cruik-built turret, its massive, beamed sides and gabled roof upheld by the shaped boughs of living trees.

The shagged trunks were ancient. Interlaced branches braced the king beam, which was smothered in stone-weighted thatch. The structure had no discernible windows, and no chimney to vent a kitchen fire or hearth. Those oddities failed to serve adequate warning, that the space inside was unlikely to conform to the limits implied by its unassuming, outside appearance.

Ath's adepts consorted with uncanny forces that linked with the mysteries outside the veil. Reason enough to approach their abode with taut nerves and trepidation; Sulfin Evend stood under the blazing sun, clammy with dread and unable to gage the course of the coming encounter. Lysaer came dressed in state. The panoply of his glittering finery included a sashed tabard, emblazoned with the sunwheel in gold. His right sleeve bore the badge of the regency claimed with town backing for sovereignty over Tysan. That statement alone was a dangerous overture. His embassy impinged upon territory subject to Havish, yet had not paused at Telmandir to acknowledge High King Eldir or receive a visiting ruler's credentials. Lysaer claimed sole authority to stand on his case: an outright demand for return of his princess, set under his autonomous right to declare her status as traitor or abducted victim.

Today's precipitate demand for a verdict might launch anything from a war to a diplomatic breach of crown protocol.

Not least of the unknown factors at play were the principles of Ath's adepts. A hurried, deep study had yielded little more by way of hard facts. The white brotherhood did not influence politics. Their wisdom inducted no following. Folk requested their blessing to marry, or to lay a benison over sown fields. They might visit a hostel to ask for knowledge or healing, or to leave gifts to commemorate good fortune. The adepts took no coin for their acts of service. Reputation insisted their ways eschewed violence. Their sojourns abroad were made empty-handed, and no record existed to say what occurred if they should be accosted by force. Scholar's theory on that subject claimed that prescient mystery kept Ath's initiates from showing themselves in the presence of conflict.

"You were the one who insisted I needed a man at my shoulder." Lysaer said into the teeth of his Lord Commander's discomfort.

"I would not be elsewhere," Sulfin Evend declared, too wise or too foolish to yield before truth, that his adamant stance was unwanted. No stripping glance sideward might crack his liege's facade of state poise. Yet behind the impervious mask, the human thread spun wrenching tragedy. Today's confrontation with Princess Ellaine must revisit the death of a fifteen-year-old son.

Lysaer s'Ilessid confronted the plinths at the hostel gateway, his ice-cut profile without vestige of feeling to reveal which force might rule the moment: the geas-bound hate that sought reason to kill, or the grief, born of love, Sulfin Evend had witnessed on one bitter night in Daon Ramon.

"The adepts won't approach unless you pass inside," he stated into the lengthening pause. "Their code demands that you take the first step."

"Let this speak instead." Lysaer extended a finger and engaged his gift.

Before Sulfin Evend could raise a stunned outcry, the shot ray leaped toward the gate, aimed straight for the cruik building's doorway.

A note sang on the air. The carved pillars seemed to shimmer bright silver. Lysaer's shaft of light did not pass through, but *disappeared*, erased from existence as it sliced across the stone portal.

At shocking risk, Sulfin Evend reached out and jerked down his liege's wrist. "Are you mad?" he gasped with outraged astonishment. "Ath's adepts are against all forms of coercion. If you want to parley, you aren't going to win any favors through bullying threats!"

"They are holding my wife!" snapped Lysaer, unmoved. "Best that we make things clear at the outset that I have not come to negotiate."

"But your wife is not held," an unperturbed voice announced from directly behind them. "Ellaine did not cross any of our three thresholds by less than her own free will."

Lysaer spun about, Sulfin Evend beside him. Together they beheld the white-robed apparition dispatched from the hostel to meet them. Not female, as gentle custom demanded, but a slender young man, his shining presence hazed in an ethereal glow, silvery as moonbeams that *could not exist* under the full glare of midday.

"I am your response," he stated without rancor. "Our gates are a boundary. Inside, our way serves the precepts of harmony. Outside, we match distortion with truth. Your aggressive overture is not sourced in balance. Therefore, the guidance that answers you past the stone markers cannot be other than male."

"That's no living man," Sulfin Evend was fast to point out. "His presence does not bend the grass or cast any visible shadow."

"I am a thought sending," the apparition agreed. "A focused intent, dispatched as a projection by the one who stands watch and guard on our portals."

"The particular bent of your sorceries is meaningless," Lysaer declared. "Nor will I waste time over rhetoric. I've traveled here for no other reason except to learn why Princess Ellaine abandoned her home, and whose influence parted her Grace from my secure palace at Avenor. If force was involved, then my light will answer, and your vaunted haven will burn."

"The fire of will both creates and destroys," the watcher's sending agreed. Wrapped in shining brilliance, he inclined his head toward the hostel enclosure. "S'Ilessid! Your wife, now informed of your coming, has determined to hear your petition. Speak wisely and address her with due respect since she stands on her birth-born right to determine her destiny."

"She is Princess of Avenor," Lysaer rebutted. "Her wedding vow binds her to Tysan."

The uncanny sending did not rise to argue, but vanished away without riffling the air.

Ahead, the sun-washed courtyard was no longer empty. Two additional figures advanced toward the upright plinths of the gateway. These cast a shadow and rustled the grass. Lysaer s'Ilessid confronted his wife, clad in a gown of unadorned linen and wearing no jewel as artifice. Ellaine was accompanied by a single, white-robed adept. Too tall for a desertman, his carriage graced by a striking calm, he held back with loosely clasped hands. Old or young, no eye could discern. His features stayed obscured by the scintillant glare thrown off the ciphers stitched into his hood.

If Sulfin Evend kept his field warrior's habit of assessing all points of resistance, Lysaer acknowledged no presence but Ellaine's. Yet there, without warning, his lordly bearing broke down. The instant, unfolding, held too sore a betrayal. Ringed by the uncanny powers that attended Ath's adepts, the woman who crossed the gold flood of day became both mother and wife. She woke Lysaer's ghosts and reopened the sting of each unrequited pain from his past.

His regal face lost its impervious shielding. Rampant need, and raw longing, and hurt smashed his poise at one shattering blow. Lysaer reeled. Stripped woundingly naked, he recoiled, hurled outside of torn pride and the blaze of unspent animosity.

Then the moment's shock passed. He found his recovery. Between heartbeats, all sign of emotion dispersed. Sulfin Evend, observing, could scarcely believe the display had been more than a wishful illusion.

Except Ellaine herself was not left untouched: that fleeting second of vulnerability crystallized her recollection of all she had left: the dazzling majesty of Lysaer's state dress, the gleam of his hair—the stunning impact of his virile allure displayed with untarnished splendor. Limned in the noon brilliance, he was power and strength. Yet the briefly glimpsed human heart underneath arrested all reasoned thought. The natural cry to nurture and heal tugged at her to forsake stern resolve and let go in abandoned surrender: to embrace the grand wake of a sovereign's life, set ablaze with reflected glory.

"Why, Ellaine?" asked Lysaer with sincere regret. "What drew you away from Avenor?"

The woman stopped her uncertain approach with only the gateway between them. Her eyes were doe brown, but not soft. Her trembling and her threatened tears were not weak, but the courage of stark desperation. "You once told me, my lord, that I was a piece set on a political game board." She tipped up her chin and pressed on. "My life, tied to yours, was worth nothing more than my value to give you an heir. Later, I found that you did not want a live son, but a bargaining chip to raise armies."

A short pause ensued. Lysaer made no plea. He did not offer excuses. Attentively rapt, he regarded his wife, prepared through strapped turmoil to listen.

Ellaine forged ahead. "I left on my own. No other hands helped me until I was outside of Tysan's crown territory. You may keep your sworn officers with their cold eyes. Their doings are above suspicion. Realm law would declare them no less than loyal. But to the eyes of a mother, they are nothing else but gutless jackals and murderers."

Lysaer received that accusation, unflinching. "Every last jackal, and all fourteen murderers have been condemned by my seal of crown justice." Vised to self-contained calm, he said gently, "For the unclean conspiracy that bought Kevor's death, every man of Avenor's high council has already faced execution. Come home, Ellaine. The realm shares your grief. Foreign exile cannot ease the loss of a son. But your place at my side can strengthen a people, and see honor is done in his memory."

"Kevor's memory requires nothing!" Ellaine declared, flushed. "If, as you say, the kingdom is grieving, the crown's ruling regent might have done better to value his gifts in the first place!" As though steadied by the silent, robed figure beside her, the princess pronounced her decision. "Leave," she told Lysaer. "Wherever you're going in the wide world, I will not return as the figurehead piece to complete the charade that you call a marriage."

"If I were to grant you the rule of Avenor?" The white-and-gold image of patient authority, Lysaer showed her the dazzling honesty that could shred the most steadfast intention. Then, as though shaken, he broke that clear gaze. Again, his pose of sovereignty ruffled: the scorching glimmer of jewels and gold recorded his unsteady breath. "Ellaine. I did not know our son. Can you imagine his loss held no meaning? Who other than you could restore the lost chance of setting a name and a face to the sorrow a father must bear at his passing?"

Sulfin Evend felt all his brazen nerves peeled. He heard that note; knew his liege: saw beneath the veneer of false arrogance. The threadbare appeal was forthright, *and genuine*. Lysaer stood at Ath's hostel, his true self exposed, begging an estranged wife to forgive the flaws instilled by a curse-driven geas.

Yet pride could not shape the words.

Ellaine failed to see past the cold gleam of ribbon and diamonds. Too long held as chattel, her response addressed only the image imposed by vested state rank and authority. "The men who taught Kevor, and those you commanded to raise him will have known him best! They are the same ones who sent him to die, and the same that your vaunted *justice* dispatched. Tell me if you dare, Blessed Prince! Whose heart more deserves to stay empty? I will never return. Seek your requital in your grand cause. Stand or fall by the swords you have paid blood to raise to tear at the throats of your enemies!"

Lysaer s'Ilessid did not crumble. His imperious calm as he heard her rejection all but blistered the thick, summer air.

Then he answered.

"Alestron," he pronounced with razor-edged clarity. "My allies turned enemy, who gave you their covert escort to Methisle and delivered you into the hands of a Fellowship Sorcerer. The price of your defiance shall be written in lives, through the downfall of the s'Brydion citadel. Your choice, Princess Ellaine! Your choice alone. Upon your loyalty rides the duke's name and family, and my forbearant trust that Alestron still serves in good faith!"

The moment had no chance to hang in suspension. Perhaps knowing how Desh-thiere's curse reforged pain to serve the destructive drive of its purpose, the white-robed adept touched Ellaine aside and spoke out for the first time. "Your choices are yours. The lady is blameless. Go from this place. You are done here."

Lysaer's presence blazed. "What gives you the right to come between me and the woman I've married as princess?"

"A law beyond man's," the adept stated clearly. "Relinquish your claim. You are done here."

"You revere all life?" Lysaer snapped, unmoved. "The child she bore me, has his slaughter meant nothing? If her case for abandonment rides on the accusation of a crown conspiracy to commit murder, the charge fails. I am innocent. No order of mine arranged my son's death."

"No murder was committed," the adept rebuked gently. "Since your son stands here, living, before you." The robed brother pushed off his hood.

Sulfin Evend gasped outright.

Across the ephemeral line of the gateway, amid humid greenery and relentless noon heat, he watched the father behold his lost offspring, without joy and past tears of redemption. What stood unveiled in the blaze of the sunlight shattered the bounds of all precedent.

"You are not Kevor!" Lysaer whispered, afraid.

Nor was he; the child born into crown title in Avenor had been refigured by the exalted currents that danced past the veil. Those burning, pale eyes had explored vistas beyond sight. Kevor might wear the raiment of breathing flesh. Yet the mantle of silent power upon him transcended the bounds of mortality. The being who upheld Princess Ellaine's free choice had walked through the grand chord of the mysteries. He had touched the wellspring of undying creation and embraced the awareness that sourced his true Name.

"Step forward," said Kevor. "Your wife will receive you. Your peace does not lie on the field of war, or in your brick walls at Avenor." He held out his hand and offered forgiveness, ablaze in the light of the infinite. The moment seemed an image, snap-frozen on glass, flooded with poignant longing that burned, and a sweetness that beckoned like agony.

Locked speechless, Sulfin Evend yearned for the miracle that cried beyond words for release.

Blue eyes that were clear met sapphire eyes that were troubled; and the shadow of doubt claimed its conquest. Of two men on either side of a gateway, Lysaer s'Ilessid became the one diminished, then undone by the harsh weight of shame. Folded to his knees by excoriating misery, he shouted aloud, lost as though plunged into blindness. The shoulder that braced him up from prostration was not offered by the son, or the wife.

Lysaer s'Ilessid was shielded, then raised, and borne from the site by his steadfast Lord Commander.

"I am sorry," Kevor said from behind. "Take your liege from this place. You are done here."

Sunset brought no relief from the heat. Its leaden calm hazed the untenanted cove where Avenor's state galley lay anchored. Beneath burning lamps, her banners hung limp as rags in the breezeless twilight. Moths off the marshes pattered and died against the hot glass of the gimbaled light at her chart desk. Though the sultry air settled like glue belowdecks, Lysaer did not venture outside. Hands braced against the sill in the stern cabin, he stared over the darkening scrub that hemmed the Havistock coast in petticoat layers of bullgrass and tidal marshes. The whine of midges sawed against the calls of foraging ducks and the boom of an unseen bittern.

"We should leave these waters without further delay," Sulfin Evend suggested. Perched on a locker with one casual boot propped on the frame of the bulkhead, he used a rag soaked in goose grease to treat the ingrained salt that threatened to rot through good leather. "With active unrest already plaguing the southcoast, the last thing you need is a diplomatic brangle involving the crown might of Havish."

Still clad in the ghostly white silk of his finery, Lysaer did not turn his head. "The Light does not recognize either sovereignty or borders."

By which oblique statement, the Alliance Lord Commander was left to presume that the queer wardings defending the gateway to Ath's hostel now posed something more than a sore irritation.

Skirting that delicate issue with tact, Sulfin Evend allowed, "Perhaps not."

The immaculate set to those white-clad shoulders still ruffled the worst of his instincts. All afternoon, his liege's hagridden mood had skirted the razor's edge. Tossed between blazing rage and the balked hurt of rejection, a man in his state would be wise to drink, if only to dull the flash-point pain of impact.

This one eschewed sense. A fool dared not guess which direction the discharge might strike for requital.

Gently, again, Sulfin Evend tried reason. "The Mayor of Forthmark was told to expect you."

Lysaer did not answer.

As the stalled silence prickled his nape, Sulfin Evend shot straight. "No!" He cast down his rag, but too late.

Either strain, or distress, or the intrigues played out by a perfidious ally had tipped the unseen, fragile balance. The creature who spun from the opened casement wore the face of curse-ridden conviction.

"No," Sulfin Evend repeated, much louder. When Lysaer kept coming, he slammed to his feet and blocked the companionway to the deck. "Liege," he said quickly. "What are you thinking? *Lysaer!* You can't launch an attack on the adepts of Ath's hostel. Not in the sovereign territory of *Havish!* Land on the wrong side of a high king's wrath, and you risk intervention by Fellowship Sorcerers."

"Clear my path," Lysaer s'Ilessid insisted. Eyes like blue diamond burned with a light that reflected no trace of humanity. "Move aside."

"No." Sulfin Evend held out in raw fear. He was as good as dead, whether he acted now or fell later to the insane repercussions touched off by a foray sent to assault the peace of a Brotherhood sanctuary. "There are men on this ship who have families at home. I won't let you launch a disaster."

Yet words had lost meaning. The avatar continued his stalker's advance. Now posed as obstruction, Sulfin Evend wedged himself into the doorjamb and shouted a desperate order to the posted watch abovedecks. "Captain! Weigh anchor! Out oars! Drive this vessel at speed toward Shand!"

He managed no more. Lysaer closed his raised fist. The bolt he unleashed struck his Lord Commander a battering blow to the chest. Sulfin Evend lost wind to scream. Spirit-marked by a Sorcerer, his flesh did not burn. But the force of concussion hammered him backward against bolted oak, and his head struck against the strapped hinge.

Knocked dizzy, collapsed to his knees, and coughing the fumes of his smoldering surcoat, Sulfin Evend saw an answering dazzle of light singe through the white-and-gold breast of the silk tabard, under which his liege hung the Biedar knife. Then he heard Lysaer's cry.

The snatched breath the commander forced into seized lungs to answer brought him the ghastly taint of seared flesh. "Don't," he gasped, desperate. "Lysaer! Don't throw off the flint blade!"

Yet hope already died. Sulfin Evend measured his length. As darkness roared over his reeling senses, he heard the distanced clatter of flint as the warding virtue of the stone blade was clawed off its thong and discarded.

Summer 5671

Resolves

Immersed in the labor of stemming the summer migration at Methisle, the Sorcerer Kharadmon receives urgent word from Sethvir: *'You will need to go north, once you're done helping Verrain. We have no more grace to wait on Asandir. As I feared, the Mistwraith's curse forces our hand. Fast couriers bear dispatches for the muster of Jaelot, and Lysaer s'Ilessid can no longer endure the Biedar knife's stay of protection...'*

Surfaced to dull pain and nausea, Sulfin Evend thrashes off a chill compress, his struggle to rise cut short by the galley's staunch captain, who assures, "Lie easy! Our Prince Exalted saw reason. Your first order still stands. We are now rowing east toward the mouth of the Ettin, where the avatar will debark and ride for East Halla. We'll face a hard siege. Divine word has decreed the s'Brydion must fall for abetting the corruption of Princess Ellaine, and your course will be to raise arms for the Light across the southcoast of Shand..."

Sent a seeress's message concerning an unusual shimmer of resonance striking down the fourth lane, Prime Selidie stifles a secretive smile, then appoints Lirenda to fetch the wrapped box from Highscarp containing Elaira's wrapped crystal...

Thembrel's Oak in Halwythwood

XIII. Confluence

If the Mad Prophet had not been blissed prostrate on brandy, the onset of prescient talent would not have taken him unaware. Sprawled in a dimmed corner of the clan chieftain's lodge tent while two of the Companions sat in subdued conference, his walrus bulk passed unnoticed all day. He stayed unmolested, until his resounding snores drew smiles and raised eyebrows from the scouts who arrived to deliver the sundown report to Sidir. The novel amusement also was discovered by an inquisitive boy, which started a bout of giggling mimicry from the camp's younger children.

When a sturdy toddler decided to bounce on the spellbinder's chest, Feithan gave the offender a scolding and ran the young rascals outside. They whooped as they scuttled. Such wild noise was unwise. Despite the unaccustomed excitement surrounding the return of crown-sanctioned royalty, a mindful adolescent shoved his gangling frame up from the trestle and ducked through the flap to correct them.

Only Sidir's relentless alertness tracked the gist of Dakar's sotted mumbling. A fragmented phrase snapped him onto his feet with the speed of a dart-shot wolf.

Across the tent at a bound, with his hardened grasp shaking the befuddled spellbinder by the collar, he demanded, *"What did you say?"*

Riled to rattled teeth, Dakar squeezed his eyes shut. His complaining grumble was ripped short by a belch. For that, he received Sidir's grip on his chin. Iron fingers twisted his face toward the tallow dip, snatched in fierce haste off the trestle.

"Damn you, speak clearly! What sight? Which vision?"

"Pesk you with lice!" Dakar stated, thick. "Douse that fiends-plaguing light in a bucket."

Sidir's response was to shove the flame close, within risk of singeing clamped lashes. "Talk," he insisted, while Braggen uncoiled from his seat and offered to help torch some hair.

Aware he was not going to wrest back his peace, the Mad Prophet dredged through his splintering hangover and coughed up his fast-fading augury. "The babe will be a girl child."

Braggen's bearded face split into a grin. "Whose?" he asked, laughing, while Sidir's ruthless fingers threatened to tear skin from bone on the force of resharpened impatience.

Dakar rolled spaniel eyes. Sullen and already sliding toward stupor to escape his galvanic headache, he slurred, "Whose do you think?" His mumble trailed off as he succumbed to turned senses. "Arithon's; Elaira's; conceived on this night."

The racketing cheers from the scouts at the trestle put the children's rash outburst to shame.

When Feithan strode over to quiet their foolishness, she was indignantly told of the posited chance there might be an heir for Rathain. She did not celebrate, but shouted for silence, and rushed to Sidir with expostulation.

"The prophet's all wrong. This is premature nonsense." Instantly flustered to jagged distress, she backed up her claim with bleak evidence. "No one planned for childbirth. I helped the enchantress prepare the decoction to prevent a conception myself."

"So I thought, also." Self-possessed and steel calm, Sidir fetched the small bucket kept to soak whetstones and doused the contents across Dakar's face. "Where's his Grace? Speak quickly! We haven't got time to wait out your miserable stupor."

Dakar spluttered, rammed erect, and coughed through the streaming droplets. Spurred by Feithan's glower, he declared with offense, "By Daelion Fatemaster's immortal bollocks! Did you have to soak me to perdition?"

"He'll do it again," threatened Braggen. "Talk quickly. We've got to find Arithon."

"Find him yourself," Dakar grumbled, peevish. "Your liege will have potent defenses laid down." He slapped off restraint, rolled clear of the puddle, and cursed until stopped by a hiccough. Since no Companion ever backed down, and Feithan's ire promised far worse than a cold-water bath from a bucket, the Mad Prophet let his unsteady frame be hauled upright. "Don't you think your liege should be private? His enchantress is not going to thank you for meddling."

Feithan lost patience. "She'll thank us less should your foresight prove true, and her gift of virginity brings her a birth that hasn't been of her devising!"

"She's under life vows to a childless order," groused Dakar with planted complacency. "Stop fretting. We have an accord. Arithon's not intending to father—"

Sidir recaptured soaked cloth in both fists and braced the Mad Prophet's swayed balance. "Well, vaunted seer, you've just stated otherwise!"

Dakar squirmed in discomfort. "I've forecast a *child?*" He broke off, brow furrowed, and ransacked his memory once more. Whatever mislaid image the concept recalled, his brosy cheeks drained. "Dharkaron, black angel of vengeance! Not this way!"

"How?" Feithan cracked, in no mood for maundering. "I would have sworn by Ath's grace that Elaira had no deceit in her."

"She doesn't." Dakar swallowed. "Damn her Prime for creating a blindsided noose." Sickness notwithstanding, he did not argue as the pair of Companions chose action and hauled him headlong past the trestle. While Braggen rousted the stupefied scouts, the Mad Prophet exposed the bleak fallacy. "We all thought Prime Selidie intended to snare Rathain's prince by means of the order's practice of debt." Shin barked on a footstool, he yelped as Sidir forced his stride to careening haste. "Instead, the devious witch has seeded an inactive string of spelled ciphers. She's hidden that spring trap within the ephemeral energy of Elaira's aura."

"She didn't notice?" said Feithan, a half pace ahead and clearing obstructions away from the drunkard's stumbling feet.

Dakar shook his head, by now rallied enough to sweat himself green with distress. "Elaira's will is bound into enslavement. Her Prime's master sigil would have been used, set over a powerful cipher to hide the awareness the craftmark was ever there. Since the working knots through her initiate's oath, Arithon himself can't detect its presence. He won't foresee any pending entrapment. He can't, while the spell chain's inactive. Its directive isn't going to engage until the lovers reach union. The release that completes tonight's consummation will trigger a fertile conception."

"Dharkaron avenge!" Braggen swore with scraped anguish. "By now, we could be too damned late."

The sundown report reaffirmed that assessment. Since the eager couple had slipped past the encampment's defenses before dusk, the off-watch scouts found themselves shamefaced. Despite dire stakes, they could not name the path their liege had taken to ensure his privacy.

"He'll have been running wards," the Mad Prophet gasped, wretchedly nauseous as his bulk was manhandled out of the lodge tent. He snatched a gulped breath, enfolded in sultry darkness, dense with the scents of white oak and pine resin. Against the fierce pressure of expectation, he could give only bad news.

"Arithon's a talent with initiate mastery! You must realize he outmatches my utmost trained strength. I hold your liege's bond of permission in trust for emergency use in defense. But skintight on spirits, my vested knowledge is going to be little use."

The acute pause clipped short as Sidir took charge. "Then your gift of prophecy needs must suffice. We'll augment your powers by means of a weakened infusion of seersweed."

Unsympathetic for the dismal result, that even a dilute dose of the toxic herb would inflame dissolute sickness into a wrenching state of torment, Sidir assigned Braggen to dispatch the scouts. Feithan rushed back for the treated tobacco, while the lodge sentry sprinted to summon a man whose lineage carried the inborn gift for subtle tracking.

Too swiftly for his tender condition, Dakar found himself clutching his spinning head, while his filled lungs stung from the volatile smoke. Still reeling on brandy, he succumbed all at once. His mind upended at plunging speed and hurtled him into tranced vision.

"Find Arithon Teir's'Ffalenn!"

The relentless demand smashed his unmoored awareness and dropped him headlong, into a starlit clearing...

...where, surrounded by silence, and ringed by a sentinel circle of oaks, Arithon Teir's'Ffalenn paused on the bank of a stream. His arm rested over Elaira's tucked shoulder, and his firm grasp was twined with her hands. The ground underfoot seemed newmade for lovers, a kindly hollow of green grass and mosses. While their pulses beat to the most primal desire and excitement raced through shared awareness, he smiled.

"My dear, my beloved, let it be here."

Mage-sight unveiled the moment in all of its rarefied splendor: Elaira's acquiescent reply unleashed an anticipation that flared like pearlescent mist through the stilled summer clearing.

Arithon stepped back. Pleased speechless, he bowed to her. Then, a slight tremble marring his touch, he slipped his cuff laces and peeled off his shirt. The cloth was let fall with abandon...

Dakar coughed out the bitter stream of pent smoke. His disjointed perception met a strong, weathered face, set into the night's humid darkness.

"What did you see?" Sidir's voice demanded.

The sound slashed through sensitized ears like a blade. Ripped witless with nausea, the Mad Prophet caught the Companion's forearm and tugged. "That way. Go north. There's a freshet with a pool. Hurry." Yanked into a stumbling run, Dakar was aware of the tracker's arrival and of someone talking with urgency. Then all solid sensation plunged away, folded into a dance wrought of light, laced into an eddying circle...

...a crown prince's soft, yet imperative phrasing asked for a line of permission. The trust he received was granted, then renewed with each of his unshod steps. His reverent progression caressed the land and called forth a synchronous balance. His enchantress looked on from the center of the gyre, aware of the spellcraft his presence enacted through talented sight and crown-sanctioned integrity. Heart and mind braided with water and air; stone and starlight framed a linked partnership with human bone and the fire of will. Naked, the man walked the bounds of the glen. His step stitched in and out of the streambed, and over the verdant ground. His wholeness of being fashioned the instrument that stroked the ephemeral flux into a spiraling vortex...

Dakar shuddered, wrenched away from the vista of dream by hard fingers, bracing him upright. He sensed Sidir, bent close to hear his torn phrases. He snatched cognizance out of the wheeling haze, spun from the dangerous blend of raw alcohol and a poisoned, narcotic trance. "Arithon's invoked his sovereign tie to the land to lay down a stay of protection."

Despair threaded through. The crushing impact of enhanced emotion doubled him over with dry heaves. Before Dakar recovered, Sidir had the clay pipe repacked, with the bowl ignited to serve him.

Shocked by the imperative behind such demand, the spellbinder gasped a strained protest. "Ath on earth! Even sober, I couldn't breach a ward of such power and strength."

"Then get Fellowship backing," Sidir snapped, terse. "You cannot do less! A birth of the blood royal in Koriani hands would unleash a certain disaster."

The pipe stem was jammed between Dakar's teeth. He sucked deep. The intake of smoke flensed him out of his flesh and scattered him, skin, bones, and viscera...

Far distant, tucked in his chair by the open casement at Althain Tower, Sethvir glanced up, alert. The tingling spill of fine energies set off by the grand warding enacted in Halwythwood already touched the strung web of his earth-sense. He knew what transpired. Though he could have invoked Athera's awareness and arrested the stayspell's completion, he held. His choice was firm, to guard the depleted reserves that secured the cracked seals that contained the last damaged grimwards. While sundown in Atainia stained the western sky crimson, he also received a concerned thought from Luhaine: specific facts tagged to a crystal that changed hands, plucked from a locked coffer at Forthmark.

The next moment brought him the ragged alarm dispatched by Dakar's distress call.

Since the wind's transmission would be far too slow, the Warden of Althain called on a risen star. Light from its vortex became the willing carrier for his intent and relayed his need to another point lying south; and then on again, bearing his message farther east, across the swept downs of Radmoore...

*   *   *

...while, deep under the steaming black mire of Mirthlvain, a needle of self-contained indigo light paused on its hunting course.

"What's wrong?" Verrain queried out of the dark, where he leaned on his stave by a sinkpool. Touched aware by a star that crossed the misted zenith, then invited to share in ephemeral communion, he shivered. Splashed mantle tugged close, he listened with care as a far-distant crisis was revealed to the discorporate Sorcerer immersed in the bog.

"I will manage," he stated in firm reassurance. "Return as you can. A few escaped migrants are not going to threaten a major breach of the compact."

The light in the waters died off as though pinched, and an icy breeze riffled the sedges. "Even one is too many," Kharadmon said. "Who will console a mother who wakens to find her slain child, bitten to death in its blankets?"

Yet Prime Selidie's plot to enslave the unborn heir to a crown prince demanded remedial action. The Sorcerer abandoned his labor of lancing the warped larvae burrowed into the mud flats. He unfurled from the sediment in the marsh and departed on a blast of scorched haste...

Dakar drifted. He saw stars like salt, and minnows like sequins, darting amid black-pearl current. Nearby, a scout's hurried phrases described a glen carved out by a curve in the Willowbrook. A pipe coal glowed red. Smoke plumed into his lungs. The pungent bite hit and unraveled his gut, then scattered his mind to oblivion. He did not stay lost. Drawn as to a beacon, his expanded awareness was gathered into a gyre, spun like a glorious coil of ribbon through the matrix of unseen light. The weaving stirred the undying flow of the mysteries, interlacing a Named thread into the subtle pattern that sustained Athera's firmament. Dakar tumbled into the winding drift. Softly, he eased through the stay that a crown prince had spun to bridle the lane flux...

...and there, Arithon stepped naked out of a pool, dripping under pale starlight. Water streamed from his obsidian hair. Droplets trickled over his skin, then scattered as lit sparks and diamonds. Unabashed, the spirit whose heritage embodied the realm stood for his enchantress's inspection.

She, a queen in her own right, surveyed him. Fully clothed, stilled as the earth's hidden mystery, Elaira awaited his invitation on the mossy rise of the bank.

Her beloved laughed and offered his hand.

Elaira stepped forward to meet him, gowned in the unadorned cloth of her shift and a cascade of auburn hair. Her smile was radiance, and her eyes were gray dusk, lit as though caught by moonlight.

Wild as storm amid sultry heat, beneath the crowned oaks of high summer, Arithon enfolded her into his arms. Breath lost, she sighed her contentment. Cool as the brook that had lately embraced him, he nestled against the linen that draped her. His damp lips brushed hers. Against him, she trembled, her eager warmth blossomed. The land underneath their partnered, bare feet received the thrill of that sensuous contact. A sparkle of light flared above their bent heads. Then Arithon's clasp tightened. A whisper of tension thrummed the night air, prelude to the first, struck note of a song that had languished for long generations...

Dakar cried out, wrenched back into his ungainly flesh by the frantic bite of Sidir's fingers.

"What do you see?" The demand shot glass-edged echoes through his gapped mind and sliced across his stripped senses.

The seer lost his vision. Weeping and sick from the tienelle's influence, Dakar sagged against the Companion whose dauntless strength kept him upright.

"No more seersweed," he mumbled. The acidic tang of ash on his tongue revolted his sensitized nerves. "Drive me under too far, I'll pass out and succumb to the deadly effects of the toxins."

"The decoction's too weak," someone remarked, to his left. "The wastrel's a slinking coward."

"He was drunk," Sidir stated. "Never make the mistake of believing Asandir would apprentice a fool."

"North," Dakar gasped. "They are farther upstream."

If the mazing effect of the gentle stay obscured the couple's location, the whirlpool kink in the natural flux might as well have been a lit compass. Its pulsing course tugged the dense flow of the blood. To overstrung talent, the chord of plucked energies rang and shimmered like lightning-struck bells.

The beckoning call pulled, then wound shattered vision into its revolving matrix...

Arithon's fingers slipped under dry linen and eased the shift off Elaira's shoulders. Under dappling shade, her unexplored flesh glimmered satin, alive to his stroking touch. She melted. When the cloth, unattended, slithered down to her hips, then dropped at her feet, she stepped free. The dew in the grass lapped her ivory ankles. She heard his breath catch in wonder, and smiled.

"Yours," murmured Elaira. "You can plunder at will. The day's lasted too long. If you were intending to bind me through abstinence, don't think for one second I'll bear it."

Arithon laughed. He refused to be hurried. His eyes savored the unveiled gift of her beauty. Then his hands moved again and, with sweet abandon, gathered the lush fall of her hair. He reeled her in. Then he laid claim to her parted mouth with a flooding, passionate tenderness.

Light fired and burned, as bared skin met and touched. One spark jumped, then another as the flux points of their auras interfaced, and entwined. At each connection, a frisson of pleasure shocked through. That tingling, effervescent tonic of joy spun out shining tendrils of energy. These wove themselves into the lattice of sound and light sustained by the primal chord. Harmony rippled a glittering wave through the myriad stream of creation...

Dakar surfaced, weeping. "I can't do this," he whispered. "It's a straight viola-tion." The desecration of such primordial beauty surely touched on the realm of the sacred.

"You have to." Sidir's urgent push shoved him onward, while the tracker who knelt at the verge of the Willowbrook surveyed a tussock of moss.

Relentless, he pointed. "This way. We're close. They can't have gone very much farther. There's a falls and a stretch of white water, ahead."

Yet the gifts of the prophet, fired by tienelle, could sense the deep draw of the lane flux. The glen where the consummate act was unfolding lay well beyond those thrashed rapids. A guarded spirit who treasured his privacy, Arithon had challenged the reach of his talent to provide a setting of pristine peace.

"Ath, please! I can't do this," the spellbinder begged, while Sidir crouched over him, adamant. The loyal Companion dared not bend for mercy. The clay pipe was relit, then the stem forced between the spellbinder's chattering teeth.

The smoke was inducted, its bitter astringency stripping the spirit out of the flesh...

Savored like wine in her lover's embrace, Elaira encountered each layer of Arithon's mage-taught defenses. The stilled points of power that shielded his core were unmasked by her touch, then surrendered, the keys to their opening set into her hands.

"Yours," he affirmed.

Her fingers explored and trailed down his breast. Where she stroked, those seamless protections gave way. Opened, the vulnerable heartline was freed to stream into partnered connection.

Her being responded. Fine energies interlaced between them. Ancient in renewal as the dance between sun and tide, the rarified flux of the ley burst and burned, then blazed in meteoric splendor about them.

The shower of ecstasy shuddered through flesh: in caught breath, in raced pulse, and in spurts of electrical tingles that ravished the nerves like a tonic.

Elaira clung to her beloved's sure strength. "Earth and sky, Arithon! Where are you taking me?"

His kiss brushed her ear. While his reverent clasp cradled her, he let her down onto the shift, left tumbled amid dew-drenched grasses. "Athlieria, beloved," her Teir's'Ffalenn an-swered. "We'll sail through the realms of pure light, past the veil. Where else would such grandeur be fitting?"

"You need no such setting," Elaira replied. "The oaks and the air by themselves frame your rightness. Your being requires no adornment."

"By myself, I am not enough." His inner longing verged upon desolate, as starving, he settled, and tenderly drew her against him...

*   *   *

Ripped blind and deaf, Dakar cried out. He felt shaken and shattered in pieces. Sidir's rough fists grasped him. The hold pinched his shoulders and harried his flesh, while he raked back his scattered awareness.

"Which way?" the Companion exhorted the scout. The white hair at his temples gleamed like thrown salt in the green-scented muddle of darkness. Dakar peered, but lost view of the man's looming face. He spun, slipped his grounding, then dissolved as pure sound, back into the coiling vortex...

She lay, tucked in sublime contact against his scorching flesh, while desire built like a storm front within her. Touch answered, a courtship that advanced and retreated, a fractional step shy of requital. His hair brushed her cheek. The loose ends drank the tears of unalloyed pleasure that welled through her gently closed lashes. As her form took fire, then blazed to match the explosive need channeled through him, he called to her spirit. His phrases in lyric Paravian chiseled their empathy into exquisite refinement. Led past inexperience, Elaira traced his taut flesh. Another access point snapped like silk thread. Resistance dissolved and poured forth his light. His bright, silver ribbons of essence met hers, weaving the warp and the weft. The tension unleashed by their building union meshed into the subtle lattice interlaced through the soil beneath them.

Twined energies sang and locked into connection. A harmonic resonance forged out of love, the match of crown prince to paired mate was acknowledged amid the grand tapestry as their living geometry conjoined with the flux. The land's mysteries welcomed their wholeness and set seal to their cadenced courtship.

Wild light soared into expansion as their fervor awakened the upper registers that extended beyond the senses. The pattern spilled outward, each unfurling ray netted into a spiral by Arithon's worked protection. The surge also pierced downward, ranging into the deeps of the earth, each crystalline tone beneath hearing.

Suspended; sustained; simultaneously lifted, man and woman awoke to themselves.

The unquiet male spirit understood his pure silence; while Elaira's laughter ran from her like water, pure as the child's, fulfilled as the mother's, and wise as the transcendent crone's...

...hurled off his feet, his sighted eyes dazzled, Dakar crashed to his knees in the streambed. Sharp stones bruised his shins. Chill water purled over his knuckles, and chased liquid ice through frail bone and taut sinew. "I can't," he protested.

Rude hands caught his wrists. Slung back to his feet, dragged ahead like a carcass, he shivered in agonized trauma. "They are raising a grand confluence," he gasped to Sidir. "If we break the warding set over their presence, the roused energies reined into a tempered eddy will run to ground with the charge of a levin bolt. The effects will excite the entire fourth lane. The cresting wave will carry for leagues, and doubtless smash glasswork in Falgaire."

"You forecast a birth!" Sidir shouted, unmoved. "Can we permit such a damaging risk? Who shoulders the price if a crown prince's child should fall to the usage of Koriathain?"

Hauled, dripping, onto the Willowbrook's shore, Dakar panted while the scout stretched his talent to coax portents out of the game trails. A whippoorwill called through the darkened leaves. A bullfrog's bass chorus answered. The Mad Prophet crouched with his ringing head in his hands, while trembling misery wrung him to nausea. Fragments of vision scored him like rain, etching across the transparent frame that demarked his frail hold on mortality...

"Elaira, beloved. Elaira..."

The spellbinder clapped his palms over his ears. Shamed as the eavesdropper caught by the scruff, he ripped out his savage rebuttal. "No reason holds meaning before such a breach!"

Against the unfolding pavane of the mysteries, pounding against his mazed senses, the strivings of men and the warped practice of witches fell away as noise without meaning.

"More smoke," Sidir commanded.

Dakar coughed, wretched. No liegeman's persistence was going to matter. As mage or as prophet, he could not be sure the pending completion could be stopped by anyone's act of profane intervention.

The pipe stem touched his lips. Too beaten to argue, the spellbinder sucked in the harsh blend of tienelle and tobacco. The fumes racked his lungs. His stabbed brain took fire.

Far distant, he heard Sidir's urgent voice, exhorting the tracker to hurry....

She touched, and another access point joined. Current unleashed through the near-complete tapestry, with only a strand left remaining. Arithon gasped. Already the shocking, bright current of pleasure streamed toward the moment of confluence. At one in mind and emotion since Merior, now, their dimensional contact merged through the etheric and sounded the downstepped octaves of physical frequency. The cresting resonance rocked the last, imposed stay of a master's initiate restraint.

A cascading shudder thrilled his aroused flesh. Riven through by the deluge, Arithon fought to brake the sweet, sliding rush toward unraveling ecstasy. Now, when precaution became a torment, and every faculty lay under siege by the drive toward sensual explosion, the potential for ruin was heightened.

If Prime Matriarch Selidie had placed a hook, this would be the moment to trap him.

He had entreated Elaira to trust him, a promise he held as sacrosanct. Adamant where he would have preferred to ease into the peace of full union, he held. Arithon summoned his mage-sense. He swept through the singing bands of fine energies that comprised their interlocked auras.

Nothing. The flux fields that wrapped them burned clean at each layering, their shimmering colors untainted.

Elaira drew in a shivering breath. Tucked securely beneath her love's cosseting warmth, she measured every rigorous step he entrained in safeguard. Leashed, unwilling, upon the rarified pinnacle that presaged the plunge toward enraptured surrender, she met Arithon's opened eyes, unconcerned.

"Beloved," she whispered. "Your care is unmatched."

Her drowning gaze held him, as language could not, and the crystalline flood of her gratitude threatened the gossamer seal on the final barrier between them...

Vision dissolved into stuttering static, undone by Sidir's rousting shake, followed up by the scout tracker's cry of dismay.

"I have lost them!" The trail his exacting talent discerned faded into the tangle of undergrowth. The subtle eddies left traced on the flux where a man and a woman had trodden, first diminished, then vanished away.

Dakar shut his eyes. Defeat made no difference. Rampant vision induced by drugged smoke ran outside of the body's five senses. Around and above him, life teemed beyond form. Aware of the night-flying moths as uncounted, jittering pinpoints, and of the black well of the underground springs, overlaid by the knit webwork of roots underpinning a mystical forest, the spellbinder had little choice but to rely upon Sidir's support. That, or else fall unconscious. To lose himself into an unbridled trance would be exceedingly dangerous. The insane mix of tienelle combined with strong brandy had already sapped his equilibrium. He felt himself tossed like a chip in a storm, without any anchor or mooring. He might easily dream himself out of his skin, to tumble amid the beguiling dark where the sublime chord of the star song keened in limitless harmony.

At the dissolute verge, Dakar wrestled his unruly senses. The coiling spin of the lane flux resisted. His need to ground back into cognizant reason became flayed like a rag in a shredder. Belated chagrin touched through inchoate chaos: he divined *why* the tracker was blinded. The pursuit trail had cut off for a crown prince's stay of protection. The ward had been spun with such seamless finesse, the land's subtle nature would appear serene and unruffled.

Yet, in fact, the flowed energies turned into a spiral that beguiled birth-born talent and mage-sense alike.

That conclusion must have been mumbled aloud, with Sidir prompted to exclamation. "Ath preserve! We've no choice." Appalled, he insisted, "You're going to have to break through."

"My powers are hobbled," Dakar stated, thick. Use of language encumbered him. Adrift as he was, he could scarcely explain: the line of permission garnered from Arithon might pass between the ribbon-thin dance of the flux. But the boundary itself was forged by aware partnership, through a sanctioned prince's link with the land. Raw forces engendered by oathsworn attunement had invoked an inviolate well of protection. "I can't gainsay the vested powers of guardianship bound over to Rathain's blood heritage!"

"You can't," interjected an astringent voice, just arrived on a chill blast of air. "But our Fellowship underpins all charter law. We are the source of crown sovereignty."

"Kharadmon!" the spellbinder gasped, overwhelmed as the Sorcerer's presence unfurled. Unshielded vision rinsed blind by that shearing vortex of spirit light, Dakar shrank, sweaty fingers jammed over his face. "Mercy on us, we're desperate! If you've come to help, I fear that the crisis has already passed beyond saving."

"No." Kharadmon's certainty excited the flux, and tripped off a fresh spate of imagery...

...of Arithon, with Elaira pressed full length against him. The white pitch of their tension lay poised between heartbeats, as one final time, he wielded his disciplined focus. While earth and air blazed to the rising flame that was going to unleash a grand confluence, he curbed his fierce passion and went still. Dauntless in his care, restrained at the tremulous edge of completion, the Teir's'Ffalenn scoured their auric fields for any spoiling taint of wrong spellcraft.

For that drawn second the balance swung, hanging, the spirit tie to integrity stamped over the consuming drive of the flesh...

"Dakar! Get ready," cracked Kharadmon. "When the ward falls, you will use the permission that Arithon gave into your hands."

A razing force clear as an arctic wind peeled the dross from the Mad Prophet's mind. Snapped back to clarity by Kharadmon's touch, he *saw* with the Sorcerer's perception...

...song, that unfurled in a cresting shimmer that was sourced in a dynamic joy. At the center, written in light, upon light, Arithon s'Ffalenn smiled upon his beloved. "Nothing," he murmured. "Your radiance is untarnished."

He gathered her nape in his interlaced hands, bent his head; kissed her mouth as she opened beneath him. She caught him close, then pressed into his warmth, embracing the tender pain of the thrust that would bind their ecstatic completion...

"Too late!" Dakar cried. "Ath preserve, we're already too late!"

He sensed the last access point, tearing free. Then the shattering flare, as the land's flux responded. Skin burning, mage-sight deluged, he felt the flickering glow that presaged the electrified union. Through his bones, through his being, the rarified note of a cascading harmony peaked toward exaltation. The well of Athera's grand mystery quivered, its silver-point matrix tuned to resound with the spark of explosive release.

Except Kharadmon acted.

Utterly ruled by his binding directive, he did not entrain the gentled grace of the elements, woven by free-will permission. Nor, as the Paravian dancers shaped power, in summons that called down the paean of glory sourced in the grand harmony beyond the veil. The Sorcerer wielded the initiate magic, bestowed by the will of the dragons.

The force he unleashed was a double edged flame, forged from the raw stuff of paradox. Its nature encompassed the interlaced hoop of creative birth and rampant destruction. The conjury hammered down as a scouring *Fire!*

Earth quaked to the shuddering impact. As lane flux tied into balance gave way, raw gusts lashed the trees, out of season. The gentle stay fashioned by Arithon's singing tore apart with a bang like a thunderclap.

Ahead, in the glen, prince and lady entwined: most cruelly exposed as they reached their long-sought requital.

The weaving between them was too fierce to sunder. No spoken warning might curb the impetus already set into motion. As the last check on Arithon's mage-taught restraint yielded into replete consummation, Kharadmon intervened. At one stroke, he razed through. His fierce grip caught short and arrested the expanding flare of the crown prince's subtle aura.

Shorn defenseless, Arithon had no chance to recoil. Ripped blind and deaf, wrested wholly numb, he did not hear Elaira's shocked outcry. Nor could he react as Dakar jerked the leash of his oathbound permission. Necessity abrogated all mercy.

The wrought cipher of severance sheared in like cut glass, straight down to his unguarded heart. The effect dropped the victim in senseless collapse. Bound in an uncompromised noose of tight spellcraft, Arithon s'Ffalenn tumbled limp inside of Elaira's clasped arms.

She keened as his conscious awareness snapped from her. Wrung to tears as his slackened weight sprawled onto her shoulder, she railed at the source of intrusion. "No. Damn you, no! I don't care what disaster. He would have our joy unmolested."

Dakar jerked short, panting. "A child would come of your union! Dare you proceed without his free consent?"

A step behind, Sidir knelt in the grass. He unlaced and peeled off his jerkin. Eyes averted, contrite, he tossed the shed garment. His gesture masked the half-coupled nakedness left stunned by their brute intervention. He retreated quickly. But the wounding could not be erased, that naught could be done beneath Ath's wide sky to restore the enchantress's raped privacy.

Kharadmon had no moment to spare for regret. His chill presence moved in, and with exigent ruthlessness, sliced every tie of etheric connection. Granted his right by Torbrand's founding oath, which bound every s'Ffalenn descendant, the Sorcerer disarmed the sprung coils of entrapment. He stopped off subtle access and kept the Prime's lurking sigil from snaring the fate of Rathain's hapless prince.

"The babe would be a daughter," Dakar explained, breathless. "Your Prime meant to recall you back to cloistered service, with your unborn child claimed as Koriani property. Royal get would be bound to initiate service, through your prior tie to the order."

"Except that I know herb lore," Elaira said, tart. She flinched, as the Sorcerer's swift ministrations raised chills across her damp skin. "Did you think I would so viciously serve a man that I love more than my very life?"

Wrapped in her indignant, sheltering arms, Arithon's unconscious form shuddered in recoil from Kharadmon's stringent safeguards. Painfully conscious, Elaira sensed the jarring sting of each break, as the energetic cords so tenderly forged in delight became sliced off, then capped, unrequited.

Even pressed down into witless oblivion, Arithon's body protested the shock of that intrusive working. Elaira cradled his senseless weight. With his mind and emotions cleaved from her awareness, she suffered the throes of a physical contact still living and seamlessly intimate. Her beloved's rushed breathing feathered her cheek. She sensed, by the rapid pound of his heartbeat, the ache of his sundered need, ripped from the torrent of her own state of frustrated arousal.

Her anger burned too sudden and sharp. "I find your manners without human grace, and your roughshod handling inexcusable."

Kharadmon fielded her acrimony, silent. Absorbed beyond pity, pressed to ruthless speed, he razed through each layer of the crown prince's aura. He had surgical skill. His ranging power was most careful to honor the integrity of the enchantress. As well, he respected the active currents that still married the Teir's'Ffalenn to the land's flux. The Sorcerer proceeded without striking the least quiver of primal disharmony.

Which set Rathain's crown prince, arrested, adrift, in the torment of isolate solitude.

"You can't leave him like this!" Elaira protested. "Not without breaking his health!"

"We won't," the Fellowship Sorcerer agreed. "But I can't reverse fate. Looping time would be folly. The flux lines have already crested too high. They must be let down, or else risk this forest to brush fires and drought. The backlash would seed disasters far worse, which could ravage the southern territories." His command to Elaira rebutted all argument. "You will not interfere! If you try, the Prime's plotted spring trap cannot do other than trigger and bind him."

Kharadmon's next order was issued to Dakar. "Toss off that jerkin. Then do as you must. I can't help, disembodied. The lane flux is inducted. His Grace is still ritually fused to the land, and you'll have to unleash the grand confluence."

"I can't touch him!" the Mad Prophet cried in dismay. "Ath wept, that's a rank desecration!"

"You'll have to!" the Fellowship Sorcerer snapped. "Else the heat of the summer will linger too long. Dry winds will scorch a year's harvest to ruin. Worse, you'll see massive storms that will tear the southcoast to wrack and destruction."

"Don't fail him, Dakar." Undone by sorrow, Elaira enfolded her dearest beloved against her unabashed breast. She tugged off Sidir's blanketing jerkin, then twined her fingers through Arithon's hair. Just as bravely, she extended herself to salve the spellbinder's appalled shock and excoriating misery. "You know your liege well. He is going to be nettled. But if as you say there's a child's fate at risk, he can't hold necessity against you."

"Stand by me, then," Dakar pleaded, stricken. "I daren't attempt this without your support."

He bent, unwilling. She, as reluctant, shifted aside, then released her embrace and let Dakar gather the Teir's'Ffalenn's tumbled weight from her arms. She did understand. No tactful care on his part could defuse the impact of this betrayal. Dakar laid his liege on the grass. More than gentle: his harrowed devotion was reverent.

"You cannot delay," Kharadmon pointed out. "The earth flux is charged. Its coil will backflow, not dissipate. For each second you hesitate, the lane force burns hotter. You must lift the prince back to surface sensation or risk damage to his aware cognizance."

"Daelion Fatemaster's heart! This is cruelty," Dakar gritted in useless protest. He braced himself, cringing, then murmured, "Forgive."

Then, as Elaira laced her fingers through Arithon's hands, the spellbinder moved, and slackened one stay from his set of locked bindings.

Arithon's lids fluttered. Held in a cloud-cotton state of suspension, he regained aware feeling, and thought, but not any freedom of movement. The spark that ignited deep in his eyes evinced no ambiguous doubt: he understood his demeaning condition. His fury was clear, and fueled white-hot by the well of his unresolved passion.

Elaira's breath caught, as his torn hurt flared across the restored link between them. She spoke at once to deflect his distress, though the admission shamed her past reason. "My Prime spun a trap, which your friends have disarmed. If you wish to weep, I will bear it."

His glance shifted, alarmed, then discerned Dakar's pending intention. Cold ferocity became rage: towering; wild; and caged beyond reach of all recourse.

The Mad Prophet stayed armored against crippling remorse. There could be no sanity, otherwise. While Elaira averted her glance in raw grief, he proceeded. A deft stroke here, a flicked finger there, each measured sensation designed to unstring a sacrosanct self-integrity. He found his way, swiftly. Five hundred years of feckless dalliance delivered the expertise into his hand.

Nor was the Fellowship Sorcerer withdrawn behind his adamant authority. Kharadmon held the lane's poised forces in balance. Throughout the hanging, volatile second, as the crux of the moment unfolded, he enclosed Rathain's crown prince within the charge of his limitless caring. Enveloped outside of that tender shield, Elaira cried out, forsaken.

Arithon's body arched and released. His seed jetted over the grasses.

Light flared, then burned, and a pealing note sounded. The summer air shimmered, while the pent-back ley burst and fired, and sorrow keened like desolation. While Kharadmon tempered the flash-point surge of energies, and downstepped the spike in the lane flux, Dakar yanked back as though singed.

"Necessity," he said into those furious eyes, driven with the helpless pain of violation. "Look carefully. See for yourself. Use my eyesight, if you don't believe me."

His reply held a subtlety of response, unexpected: Elaira sensed Dakar's revealing, quick gesture that opened a line of discernment.

Along with Arithon, she beheld how Selidie Prime had engaged her high art for manipulation. The master sigil of her initiate's oath had been used to conceal an inexcusable meddling. Stamped into the aura just inside her hip, the enchantress was shown the planted sigil that would enact a conception, then the wound barb of the spring lock intended to transfer to Arithon, that would plant a child upon any woman he might ever engage in the future. The ugly chain had been arrested just shy of enacting its malicious intent.

Elaira went white. Then she shuddered, turned her face into Arithon's hair, and wept in outraged desolation. Dakar rallied enough to react, draped her crushed mantle over her, then supported her bowed shoulders. Nobody spoke. No word could ease heartbreak. While Arithon languished, undone in forced sleep, Kharadmon resumed work with immaculate care. He cleared the entangling cords strung by sexual contact until the crown prince's aura burned clean, restored to astringent tidiness.

When the Fellowship Sorcerer's presence stood down, it was Dakar who retrieved the dropped shirt and covered the unconscious crown prince.

"I didn't know," Elaira murmured, wrung sick.

"Your Prime altered your memory," Kharadmon said, precise. "Luhaine did the back-trace, at Sethvir's request. The sigil would have been planted before last winter, in the course of your summons for audience."

She recalled the hour, clearly enough. A quartz sphere had changed hands within the Prime's presence, one fateful morning at Highscarp. Yet Elaira recollected no trace of the burn, as those vile, spelled ciphers had transferred. "Ath preserve us both, I never suspected."

"You can't dwell on such misery," Dakar entreated. "Tonight's threat is disarmed, and you now hold an informed awareness. We need to be done, here. Let me call Sidir. With least offense, he should be asked to bear his sworn liege off to bed."

"On whose permission?" the Sorcerer demanded. "Your wish is well-meant, but disrespectful. We're cosseting an embarrassment, not a bleeding trauma!"

Elaira pushed straight and responded at once. "Let Sidir retire. Leave Arithon to me. My instinct will know what to do for him."

"Your Prime Matriarch could still take coercive action!" Kharadmon warned. "Luhaine's on station, watching the enclave your order maintains at Forthmark. He's alerted Sethvir that we have complications. Elaira, did you know that Prime Selidie has taken charge of your personal crystal?"

"Ath's pity!" cried Dakar, stunned by the weight of wide-ranging implication. "Is there no ending? Such power has granted a clear line of reach into *everything* we have just done here!"

"We can't mend that." The discorporate Sorcerer's nettlesome nature poised back into contained cogitation. "Ath's adepts were the ones who took charge of that quartz. Nobody knows what prompted their choice, since it's not in their nature to dispatch a crystal back into domination."

"But I do know." Wrung pale, Elaira restated the facts as she remembered them. "The adept who came honored the crystal's clear preference. He told me the quartz wished to serve by free choice."

"A riddle!" fumed Kharadmon, out of patience. Unlike Luhaine, he found the esoterics of minerals a morass of vexing frustration. "One day, perhaps, we'll pursue the answer. Quartz crystals perceive us in ways we can't fathom. Somewhere, there will be a future that's hidden from Sethvir's extended awareness. Tonight, we can't settle for blind speculation. A piquant mystery cannot avert the immediate possibility of an attack."

"Then set seals of safeguard!" the enchantress appealed, at last stung to desolation. Frail as milk glass, now subject to shatter, she appealed to Dakar's humanity. "You're still holding Arithon's oath of permission! Lay down wards to ensure his defense. I'll handle his subsequent anger. Hurt and humiliation can be assuaged. But heed what I say for this hour, at least. You will drive us mad if you force us to separate."

While Dakar braced to protest, Kharadmon intervened. "It's *Prime Selidie's* character that can't be trusted. On that score, Elaira, accept my sworn word. Arithon Teir's'Ffalenn stays in your charge. I will guard your space for him, personally."

The Fellowship Sorcerer upheld that promise.

Under soft starlight, circled in peace, no mind on Athera saw what transpired as Dakar's crude stays of binding dissolved. No outsider stood witness. Alone with his beloved, Rathain's prince regained his shorn right to autonomy and received the sad shreds of the night's consolation.

Summer 5671

Loyalties

Sunrise burned coal-red through a cotton-thick mist that did not lift off, which presaged a drizzle by eventide. Huddled on the bank of the Willowbrook with her knees tucked up to her chin, Jeynsa swore to herself and tossed another rebellious pebble into the streambed. Shining ripples fled, shattering a reflection enveloped in streaming whiteness. Trees, rocks, and underbrush appeared cut adrift, their silhouettes snipped out of shadow. The morning seemed wrapped in a hush like held breath. Even the birdsong rang muffled.

"Still there?" Eriegal strode out of the brush, clad in dew-streaked leathers and bearing his bow and bone-handled hunting knives. His stout frame as ever moved without sound, a surprise that often dismayed the young boys, who thought they might take advantage of his apparent clumsiness. "If I'd sat there moping without supper all night, I'd be in a sore mood as well."

Another insolent stone struck the shallows. The splash frightened birds, and a squirrel scuttled, scolding. Jeynsa stirred, the ends of her cropped hair tipped with moisture and her doeskin tunic littered with clinging pine needles. "I slept sound in a thicket, no thanks for your noise. And I was thinking, not moping."

"Guilty on one count, at least." Eriegal knelt. He offered a brace of wriggling trout slung from a thong in his fist. "If you choose a site and build us a fire, I'll overlook your bad temper and cook."

Jeynsa uncurled from her tight-laced crouch. She laid the last pebble back down on the streambank, then stood, stretched cramped limbs, and regarded the Companion who brought something more than an offer of fish. "I didn't need you to stand guard at my back."

Eriegal raised his quizzical brows. That innocuous grin on his rounded face always masked convoluted intentions. "I didn't. That's true. Not if you stayed out here for thinking."

A corner of Jeynsa's mouth crept up. The spark of challenge softened out of her eyes, which were a pale green flecked with silver when she was not angry. "I suppose I owe our crown prince an apology. Damn him."

"His Grace doesn't want your contrition," Eriegal agreed. He crouched with his skinning knife and began gutting his catch. "Sidir always warned that our prince would be difficult."

"Not so much if you knew him." Prepared by her innate honesty to be fair, Jeynsa rubbed her bruised arm, which had stiffened during her solitary retreat. "Father once told me his Grace acted vicious those times when he was most vulnerable."

Eriegal met that opinion with silence. His blade remained busy. Blood streaked his short fingers as he sliced into rainbow-scaled bellies, and tossed the offal aside for the foxes. As the pause stretched, expectant, he finally shrugged. "I didn't serve in the campaign at Vastmark. Sidir would know better than I."

Nor had Eriegal fought in Daon Ramon; the remembered argument still stung, of the bitter hour when the past high earl had enforced his last orders. Eriegal's shrewd gift for tactics had tied him to the camp to advise Barach's inexperience as war captain. "I was too young to swear when our liege first took his crown oath before Steiven in Strakewood." In fact, Eriegal had been an observant, shy boy. One who still recalled a sickly and temperamental prince, carving whistles to fascinate toddlers.

What Caolle and Sidir had seen in the same man, neither one ever cared to discuss. Now, except for Braggen, and Deith, who maintained the understaffed watch in Deshir, all of the other Companions were dead.

"We can talk as we eat," Eriegal admonished, "which can't happen if there's no fire."

This was the heartcore of Halwythwood, and close enough to the well-springs where the mysteries held resonance that no spark could be struck without ritual. Jeynsa moved off to sound for a suitable site and invoke the due steps to establish permission.

Soon enough, she had a small blaze set against a flat boulder, and Eriegal had the fish roasting. Jeynsa sat to one side, nervously smoothing the fletching on the Companion's arrows, their filled quiver laid down with the recurve bow he had not yet warmed to unstring. The points were flanged war tips, and not the hunter's broadheads used to take deer. Under dank mist, while crows called, and the crowns of the trees dripped fizzling drops on the coals, Jeynsa broached the thorny subject that had tormented more than her for two nights.

"When did you stop fully trusting his Grace?"

Eriegal started. His fresh skin, pale eyes, and tarnished tousle of hair made his face seem transparently innocent. Yet the cunning that made him a deadly tactician never displayed open thoughts. "Even for you, Jeynsa, that's a bit specious. Arithon is Fellowship-sanctioned as crown prince!"

The Teiren's'Valerient did not back down. She stroked a striped cock feather into a razor's edge, then twirled the shaft, uncomplacent. "Well, who else would you have been guarding against? Sidir's had the sentry scouts tripled since the day his Grace was brought into camp."

Head bent, Eriegal speared a hot fillet on a stick and extended the offering to Jeynsa. "Are you asking as Jieret's bereaved daughter, or as the realm's chosen *caithdein?*"

"Should there be a difference?" Too taut-nerved to eat, Jeynsa ignored the fish. Thrown a tart glance, she insisted, "You're the one who said you were ravenous."

Yet Eriegal was never so easily deterred. "Oh, there's a difference," he stated. "One's a clear-cut act of crown treason. The other, a point of charter law I would be oathbound to answer." His steely glance nailed her, an unsparing assessment of the freshly shorn hair that *even still*, repudiated the ritual braid that denoted her rank and clan heritage.

Jeynsa flushed. Only *Arithon s'Ffalenn* had grasped the true reason behind her emphatic renouncement.

Yet if, like the rest, Eriegal presumed that her motive was no more than the pique of rebellion, he was not insensitive. The hard blink, then the tears that brightened her eyes were correctly acknowledged as grief. Wrapped in drifting mist, hot-blooded youth and staid Companion shared a moment of kindred distress.

A man grown since the slaughter that reddened Tal Quorin, Eriegal could never forget. He, too, knew the horror of losing close family to Arithon's feal defense. Childhood friends, siblings, his parents and cousins: all had been lost to Etarra's war host in the course of a single day. Of his generation, only fourteen young boys had survived, named by Jieret as his Companions. Through the years following, the unbearable losses had mounted. Indomitable, irreplaceable, Caolle had fallen. His wounding on Arithon's drawn blade at Riverton had been acquitted by Earl Jieret's bound inquiry. Of the nine slain the past winter on Daon Ramon Barrens, the tenth had been Red-beard himself. Deaths even Braggen's iron disposition had forgiven, though no one still living had been eyewitness to the ruthless sorceries that Arithon had spun; that had, at such inconceivable cost, broken the death grip of the cordon closed down by Lysaer's fanatics.

Eriegal was first to break the locked glance with his fallen chieftain's wayward daughter. "His Grace accepted my oath upon his arrival at the circle in Caith-al-Caen."

Yet Jeynsa's birth-born talent was Sight, that could sense where the heart's crosscurrents twisted. She voiced the chilling thought, while the silver mist ghosted between them. "He's also a master sorcerer. One who has accepted guest welcome from Davien the Betrayer. How much more of our precious clanblood will be spilled, you are thinking, before someone dares put the question? Whom do we have who has the main strength to examine that deadly connection?"

Eriegal sucked a sharp breath, while three trout fillets burned, and another one cooled, staked through by a sharpened stick. "Go back," he said, firm. "Accept your position as Asandir's choice and shoulder your charge as the realm's *caithdein*. Then, if you decide to open an inquiry, I'll be there to stand at your shoulder."

A frown pinched Jeynsa's brows, which were dark like her mother's. The war-tipped arrow was restored to its quiver, then returned, still hooked to its owner's antler-bossed belt. The stout Companion accepted the burden, then doused the fire and took up his bow.

Yet Jeynsa could not so easily reconcile her morass of conflicted thoughts. Against all she heard, through her desolate pain, she could not dismiss the impact of her royal audience.

The prince had attempted to treat with her fairly. Though stripped by exhaustion that overset tact, he had not belittled her vicious hostility. Nor had his initiate training been used to mask the most private core of his being: the oath of protection sworn on his blood had invoked the unimpeachable clarity of her Sighted perception. In that exposed moment, the reach and strength of his commitment had unmasked his inherent sincerity.

Jeynsa had beheld her lost father in Prince Arithon's eyes. The pain of shared love within that encounter had held nothing of falsehood: no burden of crown duty, no tarnish of sly scheming, and no trace of shallow, political platitude.

Reconciled to the weight of her obligation, she agreed to embrace her Named fate. But the young pride so brutally overturned would not easily bend before her s'Valerient integrity. She needed Eriegal's shrewd mind and anguished uncertainty as her counterstay, lest she shame her tattered dignity beyond salvage by begging forbearance at her crown prince's feet.

Under mist that still clung like a cloying blanket, Jeynsa approached the clan chieftain's lodge tent. Disheveled, her leathers and arms smeared with sap from two nights spent bedded in pine needles, she flushed, caught aback by Eriegal's suggestion that she amend her neglected appearance.

"*Caithdein*, you must. Your office demands the semblance of propriety."

"Dharkaron's almighty bollocks!" she exclaimed, raised to a self-conscious flush. "After putting an unsheathed dagger to royalty? If I run into Mother or Barach beforehand, they'll peel the last inch of hide off me!"

To evade that brangling brush with authority, she entreated Eriegal to divert the sharp eyes of the sentries. Stalker's skills let her skulk through the perimeter and worm her way under the back of the lodge tent. Breathless, now muddy, she reached the shelter of her personal quarters without being seen.

The shut cubicle was dark. Jeynsa dared not strike a light, lest the glow should alert the closed meeting in progress on the other side of the curtain. Moving by touch, she could not avoid overhearing the talk exchanged at the trestle.

"Where in Sithaer's black pit has Eriegal got to?" Braggen's expostulation ran on unchecked, through Feithan's placating murmur. "Well, he's overdue back! We're going to need hours to catch him up with yesterday's round of bad news."

"...can't be helped," Sidir stated, unmoved. "Sit down and stop pacing, will you?"

The trestle board creaked, through the slide of a bench, and the clunk as a weapon banged wood. "What's his Grace doing, anyway?"

"Still with his woman, far as we know," said the muted voice of the night's watch scout.

Since that particular man was renowned for sharp ears, and Sidir's keen perceptions too often sparked his talent for piercing insight, Jeynsa crept on cat feet. She stripped her soiled clothing, then scrounged through her satchel and hooked out her spare shirt. A hesitation, as her groping fingers encountered the weave of the garment beneath: the black tabard that once had belonged to her father, its folds already recut to fit for the investiture she had refused.

Jeynsa clenched her fist. Her apparent recalcitrance had sparked off her elders' exasperation, for months. Entangled in hurt and loss, driven inside herself, she had never shouldered the responsible burden by asking for their adult understanding. Only Arithon had exposed her deep grief, and beneath that, cracked the mask hiding her desperate fear. All her young life, she had never felt adequate to stand in her father's shoes. As Asandir's choice, she had *no* excuse to shirk her hard fate, or back down. Nor could she expect to be coddled through shame, as she surrendered her final resistance.

The aware recognition in her prince's eyes would be all she had to sustain the sting of a public humiliation.

Nerve steeled, teeth clenched, Jeynsa tugged the black tabard free of the satchel; while beyond the masking screen of the curtain, Braggen's combative tone sliced above the murmur of conversation.

"I'd have expected his Grace would show up by now, given the blood-bath that's bound to erupt when this wretched affray breaks wide open. After all that Alestron has done in his name? Who could *ever* believe that his Grace could disown the sworn alliance of the Teir's'Brydion!"

Shocked still, Jeynsa overheard Barach's snapped phrase, bidding Braggen to lower his voice.

As ever, the Companion's fierce temper prevailed. "Well then, where's your sister? More than anything his Grace will require a *caithdein*'s support at his back!"

"No!" Sidir objected. "Let things stand as they are. You'll not drag Jieret's daughter into this!"

Dakar's gruff remonstrance held out in support. "Your prince does not wish her to know right away. The girl cannot stay the horrific course! Damn pride, will you listen? His Grace's coming work at Etarra is altogether uncanny. No, Braggen, believe me, you have no idea! The dark practice of necromancy is unclean, and by far too deadly dangerous."

Jeynsa let the dark tabard fall from her nerveless hands. Chilled to clammy sweat, she scarcely dared breathe. While the acrimonious debate surged ahead, her quick, silent hands gathered up her tossed leathers. Shaking, distressed, she groped for her weapons, then unhooked her storm cloak and baldric.

"...naught else to do but prepare," Sidir was insisting. "Melhalla's been warned. We must secure the north. When this ugly news reaches the sunwheel Alliance, Alestron will wake with its walls under siege. The clans have *no choice* but to face that grim hour. We must act now to brace for persecution such as no chapter of history has ever foreseen."

Wrung white, Jeynsa dropped flat and skinned under the wall of the lodge tent. Unseen, she sprinted, then slammed into Eriegal, who had left the scout sentries and crossed the camp to find out what had delayed her.

"Cover for me!" she gasped in his ear. "Don't ask. I can't face the clan elders with this. Not right away. Let them think I've run off to go hunting."

Eriegal untangled himself from the wrack of storm cloak, flapping leathers, and baldric. He eyed the sheathed knives and sword; then the bow in her unsteady hand. "You'll need my quiver," he stated, nonplussed. "I don't think you're going to want deer tips."

Jeynsa shut her eyes. All but ready to weep for the gift of his understanding, she accepted the horn bow and quiver. Straightened up, now possessed of her sire's iron heart, she said, tense, "I'm not shirking my charge to safeguard the realm."

Eriegal gathered her trembling fingers, his eyes cool slate as he measured her. "If you answer the call to test Arithon's character, that is not running away." Since her inquiry concerned a devious man who was an initiate sorcerer, the Companion slipped her the heirloom amulet he carried, whose virtues were fiend bane and concealment. "Be steadfast and safe, girl. Remember your background. You are as dear as a daughter to every father in this encampment."

Jeynsa shifted her burden. She let Eriegal's solicitude slip the thong over her head and tuck the worn metal amulet beneath her shirt. Still too frightened to speak, she gripped his hard wrists, then bolted headlong into the misted murk of the greenwood.

Hours passed, while the fog lifted to a pewter overcast that spat drizzle and finally spun veils of fine rainfall. The harried gathering inside the lodge tent acquired the presence of Halwythwood's three titled elders. Barach's authority became freshly tried, as the assembly accosted the risky exposure now facing the reduced remnants of Rathain's armed strength. Since a third of the war band had been cut down in Daon Ramon, too few hands remained for the hazards of guarding the free wilds. The redoubled fervor as Alliance politics fanned the coals of townbred persecution could only bring more death and hardship.

Resharpened contention was already ongoing when Eriegal sauntered in through the door flap.

His tardy appearance was given short shrift by Sidir, whose place, with increasing, unabashed familiarity, was at the side of Earl Jieret's widow.

"Where's Jeynsa?" she asked.

"Hunting." Soaked from the rainfall, and predictably curt, Eriegal declined to drip at the crowded trestle. Instead, he tucked his stout frame on the floor, his back braced against the tent's center pole. "The quarry she's stalking scarcely requires the attentive eye of an adult."

"Her bratty behavior never needed anyone's shepherding in the first place," her brother said, chafed. "After two nights of sulking, we should applaud her initiative to supply the camp with *provisions?*"

Since Eriegal had spent all of those thankless hours standing watch in the open, Feithan was not unappreciative. She stirred from beneath Sidir's tucked arm, unhooked a grass basket, and bestowed the bundle of bread and dark sausage held for the Companion's return.

"No one will complain if you rest where you sit," she told Eriegal. Distressed for his scars, that would ache with the rain, she refused his contrary insistence. "We'll catch you up on the detailed news later. Barach's short-tempered because we've seen setbacks that force him to face some harsh choices. We all agreed, earlier: Jeynsa's too brittle. Until she's done grieving, she's better off gone on whatever errand she's chosen."

Eriegal reviewed the shut faces of Halwythwood's elders, their rancor offset by Barach's clamped jaw and Braggen's hunched glare and clenched fist. Since Sidir's steady glance begged forbearance, the younger Companion opted not to announce that Arithon's character was the targeted quarry that Jeynsa had left to pursue.

The omission would spare the crown prince's dignity, or so Eriegal thought at the time. Jieret's daughter was trustworthy. She would rise to wear her *caithdein*'s black with increased confidence, given the experience. Whether or not today's initiative determined Arithon's fitness to rule, someone needed to wrest the feckless creature away from his amorous dalliance.

Shrewdly practical, Eriegal finished his overdue meal. Then he dragged up a hassock, folded his arms, and nodded off, while the council's discussion droned in the background above him.

By midafternoon the rain fell in torrents. The trail scouts reported, wet to the skin. Then the foragers returned, complaining. They snacked on jerked meat, since the kindling outside was as uselessly soaked as their bowstrings, and game could not be tracked in a downpour. Only the sentries maintained their strict schedule, swathed in oiled leather, while the outlying patrols sheltered as they could under the wind battered oaks.

No one fretted that Jeynsa did not reappear. As discussion closed, and the elders arose to retire to the tents of their relatives, sly comments disparaged the Prince of Rathain's steamy passion, beyond doubt holed up in some piss-reeking den in a rock ledge claimed from a forest cat.

Twilight's gloom had dissolved into pitch-dark when the Koriani enchantress finally came in.

She had been gathering cattail roots in the mires, to judge by the mud drawn up in rings at her hemline and sleeves. Her sopped hair was tied back like a cart horse's mane, and his Grace of Rathain was not with her.

Before Feithan could address her need for dry clothes, she was accosted by Dakar's jagged state of suspended torment. "What did he say?"

Elaira surveyed the close-knit party of six, orange-lit by the flare of a pine knot: Sidir, seated with grave attention, a chart of the kingdom inked on rolled deerhide under his sensitive fingers; and beside him, Feithan, her dark lashes downcast. She, at least, displayed aching discomfort for the past night's inconsolable handling.

Braggen leaned his bull frame by the doorpost, great sword set aside and arms folded. If his fixed scowl wore a flush of embarrassment, High Earl Barach's candid stare implied that he might not yet know what had occurred in the glen by the Willowbrook. Also oblivious, Eriegal lay in a tucked heap by the center pole, sleeping against a scrunched hassock.

The dearth of privacy scarcely troubled clan custom; Dakar's stricken glance refused to release her. "Elaira, I beg you. What did his Grace say?"

The enchantress regarded him, eyes sparked to cold fire. "That you should have trusted him to protect me."

Braggen broke in with hot incredulity. "Over Selidie's possession of your personal crystal and a babe of his lineage, defenseless?"

"Even so." Her resharpened censure raked the huge clansman over, not sparing him the cut-glass state of her anguish. "His friends could have let him attend his own fate."

"That doesn't allow for the crux of the crisis," Sidir stated without remonstrance. "You imply that we should have permitted the lane flux to recoil and hurl the weal of two kingdoms to imbalance?"

Elaira just stared at him, while her bedraggled hems dripped, and her hands locked tight on her bundled roots, collected through her hours of cathartic foraging.

"What else under Ath's sky could we have done?" Dakar cried at last in stripped anguish.

Elaira stirred. She glanced sideward at Feithan, who nodded. Given that tacit leave against the sensitive uncertainty, that her Prime's meddling had not reneged the lodge tent's grant of guest welcome, the enchantress finally stepped into the light thrown by the flickering brand. There, shoulders bowed, she sat down. "You could have allowed Arithon the gift of respect for what was held sacred between us."

Earl Barach proved not to be uninformed: his steady calm much too old for his years, his comment cut through without passion. "You would have set your man's dignity above the land's health and the critical need for a bountiful harvest to redress the west's blight and famine?"

Elaira said nothing, but covered her face with chilled hands. By the tenor of their silence, the men did not see: except for Sidir, who lifted the burden of roots from her lap and delivered his whispered apology.

"I don't understand," Braggen insisted, his nerves sawed as the tension extended.

Feithan's unstinting spirit spared the enchantress the wretched need to explain. "She means you to know that Prince Arithon would have chosen the child before he left the lane's kindled forces imbalanced or the land's needs unrequited."

Dakar stood, shocked white. "That would have set him, and you, against the unleashed might of your order! *You're saying we should have left him such a risk?* Dharkaron's black vengeance, lady! Where are the sane limits? For a Teir's'Ffalenn's arrogance and his gift of rogue talent, we should turn our backs on all consequence? You tell us we ought to have sanctioned his ruin!"

The Koriani enchantress uncovered her face and regarded the prophet whose ungovernable Sight had entangled too many lives in fast knots. "I ask what you and your Fellowship will not give, in trust. Leave Arithon willing to fail on his merits!" Elaira's leashed temper gave way. "What could have happened?"

"Arithon's child—" began Dakar.

"And mine!" cracked Elaira. "His and mine! Not yours. Or your Fellowship's, or Prime Selidie's, despite what she thinks! We could have been left with the chance to look after our own, as a risk shouldered squarely between us."

When the spellbinder's heated stance failed to buckle, Elaira lashed back in raw shame. "Ath's mercy! He was helpless, and I lack the power to stand down a Fellowship Sorcerer! *How would you feel?*"

The Mad Prophet flushed. "Lady, on that score, I daresay I have cause to know!"

That forced her acknowledgment: he did not practice vice. The burden he bore from the glen was no pittance; was made worse, in chill fact, since as the free agent, he *could have* refused Kharadmon's ruthless expedient.

Dakar faced away. If the humid scents of wet leather, oiled steel, and pine smoke clogged an atmosphere grown too close, there remained unavoidable details to discuss. Despite his stripped nerves and Elaira's reft heartbreak, he stiffened resolve and pressed forward. "I have to ask, lady. Has his Grace abrogated the permissions I held?"

"No." Elaira knotted her fingers, scarcely aware as Feithan slipped off to fetch her mulled wine and a blanket. "That says far more for Arithon's grace of forgiveness than for the regard given a crown prince's *sanctioned* integrity."

"And now?" Language did not encompass the delicate words; Dakar could *not* frame the question, though she must know he could not leave that excoriating, last query unanswered: *whether or not the Crown Prince of Rathain had willfully chosen to go forward and make her entangled love consummate.*

Elaira replied, now shaking as the flushed hare pressed at bay by a wolf pack. "He would not have me endangered, he said."

She wept then, the silenced tears tracking down her already rain-soaked face.

Then Feithan arrived and wrapped her cold, huddled form into an heirloom blanket. "My dear, you're exhausted. Let's see you to bed with a cup of spiced wine and a posset."

Elaira did not protest the kindness and allowed the insistent clanswoman to guide her onto her feet. Checked as she stood by Sidir's tacit touch, she paused only to answer his last, gentle question.

"Your prince consulted with Kharadmon long enough to reach an accord for the timing to enact their planned purge of the Kralovir. Just before daybreak, Arithon left. If the Aiyenne's in flood, he'll ford at Narms, and ride post down the Mathorn Road. In fair weather or foul, ten days should see his Grace through to the gates of Etarra." For the anxiety on the Mad Prophet's face, she added, "He said you could abandon his service, or else catch up with him as you chose. He left an address for the purpose."

"A trapper's relation?" Dakar shivered, then nodded, if not relieved, at least reassured he would not be shunned out of rancor. "That makes sense. His Grace owes the man's sister a promise concerning a call of condolence." Yesterday's fulfilled obligation to a surviving clanborn uncle had provided the information. The woman's husband had closed his cooper's shop in Eastwall and reestablished his trade where the bounty of Alliance funding made business more lucrative.

Much later, when Elaira was settled and sleeping, Eriegal stirred from his extended catnap. First informed of Prince Arithon's precipitous departure, then given the round of ill news he had missed by his choice to guard Jeynsa, he heard out the grim scale of the upset served by the Alliance's taint of cult necromancy. Sidir's account did not finish until the pine knot had burned to a coal.

Under thin, bloody light, Eriegal rubbed at his balding head, the first uneasy sign he was troubled. "Jeynsa went after Prince Arithon," he admitted to Barach point-blank.

No one worried. The girl was well able to look after herself anywhere in the free wilds. Burdened down by far weightier concerns, Barach shrugged. "If my sister tried to follow his Grace, the rain will have spoiled her tracking."

"So she catches him up?" said Braggen, amused. "Our liege is no fool. He'll shred her dignity, raise every hackle she's got, then send her young backside packing."

Lumped onto a hassock in jellied exhaustion, Dakar dismissed, "If he doesn't, I'll knife him, believe it."

For what lay in the north was an unresolved danger cold-bloodedly vicious, and beyond the pale of any clansman's mortal imagining.

Summer 5671

Bait

Fast as Arithon could cross the wilds of Halwythwood, then engage the travelers' amenities for a swift passage by way of the trade road, the Mad Prophet could maintain no such scorching pace. He lacked the stamina to make speed on foot. Post-horses tired beneath his stout bulk, even if his slipshod balance astride did not scour him to raw blisters. Beyond mundane discomforts, he found himself loath to meet Arithon s'Ffalenn face-to-face.

The spellbinder who had enacted a Fellowship directive had not stood, heart or mind, as a friend.

A fortnight and two days granted too brief an interval to reconcile the hurt, or ease the fresh brunt of remorse. Hot sun, and dust, and the seasonal scourge of night-feeding insects could not eclipse the dread or distance the hollow eyes of the enchantress now left to keep desolate vigil in Halwythwood.

But the shadow thrown by the dark practice of necromancy posed a crisis too bleak to defer. Too soon, Dakar crossed the Mathorn foothills. First wrapped in the resin-thick taint of the firs that blackened the steepening slopes, then folded under the blanketing shade thrown by the flint-crowned rims of the peaks, he cleared the last notch, while his hack puffed and lagged underneath him.

Spread under dusty haze, amid the creak of spoked wheels and the lowing of the teamed oxen, the overlook exposed the last, rolling downs, where the wilds of Daon Ramon lapped against the furrowed pass that bisected the spurs of two ranges. All traffic bound northward funneled up through the gap, while the diminishing ruts of the eastbound trade road wound away toward the opposite coast. The snake-twist approach to Etarra had always dizzied, for the switched-back curves that rose in ascent to the southern gate.

Yet today, the brassy fall of noon sunlight lit the sweeping changes made since the year of Prince Arithon's failed coronation.

Dakar reined up with caught breath at the sight.

The wedged muddle of square-cut brick battlements and knobbed towers still straddled the cleft of the pass. But the forested vales he remembered had been razed to stripped clay and bare rock. Above loomed the bleak, fitted walls of an outer array of defense-works, newly constructed by conscript labor under the arcane expertise of Elssine's masons.

With Lysaer s'Ilessid now the ratified mayor, a westlands-bred chancellor had been appointed to govern, his experience and temperament a sharp match for the town's stew of pedigree arrogance and cutthroat politics. Etarra's influence lay at the hotbed center of the sunwheel Alliance. Onto that template, Raiett Raven's directive had stamped its pejorative imprint, transforming the north's most prosperous trade hub into the seat of command for its burgeoning war host.

The scorched scrub and broom grass at the foot of the notch were now trampled to dirt by a soldiers' camp, pavilions and tents sprawled out in picketed squares. Recruits drilled on the gouged turf of the practice fields, where wild orchards once ripened apples. Flag standards parted the tenuous breeze, smoke-hazed by the fires in the ramshackle armory sheds that scabbed the vale like a canker. The burdened air bore its tang of hot steel, the composting reek of the middens, the fly-swarming latrines, the stock pens, and the bustling cookshacks.

Thought stalled. The heart faltered. Nowhere was the Master of Shadow more hated and feared than here, in the heart of Rathain. Inside this wasp's nest of zealous fanatics, there walked that single, marked man, his flesh made the target for every fletched arrow; his blood the sought prize for each pennoned lance, and down to the last sharpened sword. To curb a deadly incursion of necromancy, Arithon Teir's'Ffalenn had entered Etarra, unsupported, bereft, and alone.

A whip cracked, close by. "Get along, you fat jackass!" An incensed driver shook his fist and shouted over the milling grind of the drays. "I'm not paid to park here for the view! Bedamned if your nag hasn't jammed the whole road while you nod off like a daisy!"

Dakar snapped from the throes of unpleasant reverie and reined his blown hack downhill. Before long, he steered through the warren of freebooting whore's cribs and craft shacks, where inquiry found him the cooper's shop appointed for Arithon's rendezvous.

The meeting he dreaded did not await him. Dismounted before the open, board shed, he was welcomed as a traveler tired from the road, well spoken for, and expected. A lanky boy led his horse off to the livery. Set at ease in the shade, Dakar was served currant bread and tepid tea by a muscular matron, who then hustled off to stoke the flame for the steam box. While he munched to the din of the cooper's apprentice, hammering steel into barrel hoops, the plank trestle was shared by an inquisitive old man whose pouched eyes were clouded by cataracts.

Dakar gave back all the news from the road, on request recounting the blazons of the dispatch riders inbound from the towns lying west. Such interest was ordinary, the routine queries any sight-impaired elder might ask, whose shelter relied on the fortune of a nephew's craft, or grandson's. Yet as the meal finished, the untidy fellow did not settle into his wicker chair for a nap. Instead, he delved into a box at his feet and pulled forth a folded document. The wrapper was tied with gilt ribbon and a genuine sunwheel seal.

Dakar shot erect as though pinked with an awl.

The man's milky eyes stared ahead, quite oblivious to the irregularity. "You will take this into Etarra, my friend. Deliver it to the proprietor of Simshane's House of Exotic Delights."

Dakar clicked his mouth shut. "But that's the brothel that sells—"

The old man had a cutting, ironic smile. "Did you come here to help? Then you'll say you're eager to sample his wares. Since this document offers him lavish reward, he'll fall over himself to oblige you. Is the bargain so dreadful? You'll have a comfortable bath. A softer bed than this abode can offer a guest who's a stranger. At breakfast, you'll tell the fat pimp that two hired carriages will arrive the next night to collect the young flowers he peddles. If you find them sweet, and yielding, and clean, you'll promise delivery of gold on these terms and seal a clandestine transaction."

The Mad Prophet slammed his fists on the trestle.

Plates, crumbs, and tea mugs jounced, lost under the din from the craftyard. The blind elder did not twitch an eyelash. "You don't like such instructions? They grate on your character?"

On his feet before thought, Dakar snatched the scroll from the man's idle hand. "Don't ask," he retorted through his clenched teeth. "If the conniving bastard who left me these orders comes back here to ask for more favors, you can tell him from me: he's got a vicious hand with a grudge, not to mention a sick touch for backstabbing cruelty."

The old man blinked. "I'll say you're not going?"

"Oh, I'll go!" Dakar shoved off the trestle, the ache in his spine like a heated steel rod and his eyes pinched to slits of hazed anger. "If only to say to the mountebank's face what I think of his vindictive temperament!"

The old man raised white eyebrows, and Dakar, beyond words, turned his back and stamped out.

Red-faced, and scorching in merciless sunlight, he was forced to beg transport uptown, cheek by jowl with a chatterbox boy who drove for the kiln that baked mud bricks. The urchin pattered through the day's seamy gossip in guttersnipe accents, while the rattletrap vehicle rumbled uphill, and the straining oxen dropped steaming manure. They crept past the tight bends. Stopped for the laden drays, paused to breathe draft teams, the spellbinder huddled in simmering fury until the odd phrase in the boy's busy tongue snatched his cogitation up short. "What did you just say?"

The filthy child flipped him a grin, snaggled with broken front teeth. "Which? The pedigree spinster who dropped stone dead in her plate while porking down snails at the banquet?"

"Not that," Dakar said, canny enough to cool his sharp interest.

"Oh!" The boy's puzzlement cleared. "The bit before that one. You weren't aware of the blind bard's bet with the city's appointed High Chancellor?"

"That one," the disgruntled spellbinder affirmed, and then heard in remarkable depth of the cloudy-eyed free singer who was winning enraptured acclaim through the vibrancy of his playing.

"There's this wager afoot," the waif ran on, switching his oxen around the last hairpin curve. High overhead a hawk sliced the sky, while the war camp sank into the bruise-colored shade that mantled the lower vale. "Word goes the High Chancellor can't sleep at night. The bard's posed a challenge, and promised hard proof. Inside of three days, he's claimed he will show that his music can free any man living from the affliction."

As the burdened cart ground up to the gate, Dakar chewed over the fresh pill of rancor: *that the encounter he dreaded had come and gone in the noisy murk of the craft shed.* In hindsight, that unassuming old man had been much too suave; not to mention the suspect, official parchment was sealed with a sunwheel blazon. The very same fiendish bent for conniving would mean that two birds must fall to one stone. This errand to visit an unsavory brothel promised more than an underhand stab to retaliate.

Which revelation stuck in the craw like the scrape of a fish bone, jammed sideward. "Damn you to the plague of a thousand fiends!" Dakar rasped under his breath as the wagon was reined up for the routine inspection at the town entry. Although he was dressed as an unkempt tradesman, unlikely to raise probing questions, the nefarious dispatch he carried now might see him condemned for seditious treason. Dakar swore with invention, forced to spin a diversion to defer the armed guards and gain free admittance through the paired brick keeps.

Simshane's House of Exotic Delights was an oasis of lavish, bad taste set amid the soot-grimed rows of the oldest, trade-quarter tenements. Dakar arrived streaming sweat, and nerve-jangled from the vituperative slang served out by

Etarra's carters. The narrow escapes as he missed being run down, and the contempt raised by pedigree snobbery had not changed one whit with Alliance rule. The brothel was a nestled confection of pink-brick walls and expensive quiet. A wrought-iron grille let into its compound, softened by a trellis of climbing roses. There, a huge eunuch who reeked of spiced oils unbolted the locks with a ring of ornate, gilded keys.

An obsequious touch, a secretive smile, and the client was ushered inside. Within lay a courtyard with fountains and a hidden alcove that echoed with flutes. A lithe youth with shaved hair, painted eyes, and a voice of mellow soprano came forward and steered Dakar to a bench beneath spouting satyrs. He was given a cool drink, while sensuous hands removed his crusted boots and washed his feet in a basin of lily water. Reshod in unguents and white-rope sandals, he was expected to smile, while an urchin wearing little but gold jewelery attended his unkempt footwear. Another blond boy led him on a meandering stroll through shade trees and flower beds, then into a doorway hung with glass beads. There, ankle deep in a costly carpet and nauseated from breathing perfume, he was greeted by the establishment's rotund proprietor.

Olive-skinned, sporting ringlets, and hanging emerald pendants in each powdered earlobe, the creature had carmine lips and the glittering eyes of a snake. "How shall Simshane's offer the gentleman ease?"

No pause, and no disparaging glance at the visitor's drab clothes: the wealthy who patronized this house's wares quite often disguised themselves as nondescript commoners. Still sickened with shame from the clinging touch of the *prandey* dispatched to sponge his sore feet, Dakar jammed his right hand in the crook of his arm lest he slam a fist in the simpering whoremonger's face. Unable to muster civilized words, he turned over the sunwheel-sealed parchment.

Bangled wrists jingled as the august seal was cracked and dismissed with no visible flicker of interest. Discretion would be stock-in-trade in this place. Yet any demand made by the priests of the Light would risk scandal beyond even Simshane's vicarious experience.

The proprietor fluttered the parchment closed with scarcely a blink and no break from solicitous servitude. "Quite an order. Of course, the immense compensation allows for all needs and contingencies. I'm pleased that your masters have entrusted our house to shoulder the requisite details."

Dakar need not guess the transaction at hand required the incentive of payment, at premium. His biting quiet would no doubt be mistaken for worldly impatience.

"You've asked proof in advance that the wares will be genuine," the proprietor resumed, his smile laid on thick as syrup.

The spellbinder forced a nod. Still too riled for speech, he watched his acquiescence change his unctuous reception to avaricious enthusiasm. The pimp clapped his soft hands.

A bevy of bath servants answered, each one male and exquisitely made, with hair dark, and auburn, and golden fair braided with jewels and scent.

"Simshane's finest, at your least command." The proprietor bowed. Already gloating, he waved for his pack of trained puppets to attend the rich client's comfort.

Dakar survived the bath, barely. Stripped, steaming mad, and worn-out by the need to repel the barrage of professional advances, he was soon installed in an airy chamber appointed with mirrors and silk sheets. In line with Etarran taste, the enameled furnishings and throw rugs had the gaudy opulence wealthy patrons expected of love nests. One glance made a man want to shield aching eyes.

By then, the day's afterglow streamed through the pierced metal screens inset in the louvered shutters. Dakar kept the sheer robe, despite torpid heat. Alone, at least until he received the live flesh imposed by the parchment, he made the best of a bad situation, locked the door, and settled to sleep.

The servant who called with fruit juice and supper was dispatched with one surly word. Dakar rolled over and subsided to dreams as night flooded the gilt tassels, poufed quilts, and overstuffed couches in shadow. Hours passed. He forgot where he was, until a knock at his door rousted him back to logy awareness.

Since his chamber was locked, no servant had come to light the lamps or crack the latched shutters. Dakar freed his ankles from the miring sheets and blundered between the grotesque, padded stools used for who knew what obscene purpose.

He shot back the bar, too disgruntled to curse, and encountered a gagged and bound coffle of children. Boys; still wet from the bath, and reeking of perfume. Above twisted cloth, knotted cruelly tight, their cleaned faces were flushed with fight and fear, or streaming tears of heart-wrenching terror.

Dakar's dumbfounded expression must have shown rage, for the escorting eunuch bearing the lamp blocked the corridor and snapped his fingers. Two muscular heavies pushed forward to flank him. These carried cudgels, and proffered no smile, their purpose being to eliminate trouble in cases where customers chose to be difficult.

"Your high priest's detailed order, as written," the eunuch pronounced with cold courtesy. "Two dozen young males, entire and unspoiled, with the spirit not yet broken out of them. As detailed, they are presented for your inspection and, Simshane's trusts, your subsequent word of approval."

Dakar burned. Locked by the fury that pounded his blood, he was unable to speak.

His silence posed danger. Already, the hardened attendants' regard shifted toward murderous suspicion. The parchment brought under the sunwheel seal could in fact pose them a trap. If the Light's priests chose to seed moral outrage and rout out the warrens of vice, they might tear down a long-standing, lucrative business, established with painstaking attention to delicacy.

Awake to his peril, Dakar felt his hair rise. This was Etarra, where disputes over trade were resolved by hired assassins. The inlaid tin shutters were not kept for privacy, but would be barred shut to discourage prying officials *and* keep the brothel's victimized wares from escaping.

Since the doorway was blocked by two heavyset thugs all too primed to use garrotes and knives, the spellbinder sent by the Master of Shadow stepped aside and let the bound children be herded into the room.

"You will be locked in," the eunuch explained, his honeyed tone masking threat. "House rules demand that the lamps stay unlit. With wildlings, we can't risk a fire. Naturally, if you find yourself compromised, we will have help stationed outside."

"I'll need no assistance," Dakar said, amazed he could manage even the semblance of calm. "In fact, I will sate my indulgence alone. Your attendants can take themselves elsewhere."

The eunuch bowed to a chink of gold chain. "Indulge as you wish. I suggest as precaution, you might be unwise to unbind such as these. The handlers who managed them in the baths said Simshane's would be negligent not to warn you."

As the last of the children was prodded past, Dakar said with chill dignity, "My masters have paid well enough for this night. Mine to choose how I'll use what they've asked for."

The eunuch returned an obscene, knowing smile, then mustered his escort and retired into the corridor. He took the lamp with him. Left in darkness, surrounded by the boys' panicked breathing, Dakar listened, while the fastening of chains, bolts, and bars went on for what seemed a long time.

He needed trained discipline to curb his riled nerves. Through the reek of jasmine, gardenia, and rose, he noticed the nauseating reek of seared flesh.

"My beauties," he greeted with ominous calm. "Can it be that you have been branded?"

No sound; only the thick, muffled whimpers of children whose quaking dread found no requital.

Dakar stepped forward. Mage-sight let him see. He bent to the tow-headed waif by his knee, examined an arm, and before the mite flinched away from his touch, felt the hot, swollen flesh where the iron had seared into young skin. "Easy."

Etarrans meted out such abuse to captive clanborn to mark them as criminal labor.

The kick launched at the spellbinder's kneecap missed, only because he expected a desperate move to retaliate. As Dakar dodged, he flipped off the child's gag.

"Stinking pervert!" the boy gasped through puffed lips, then added a vicious torrent of curses, snapping with forest-bred accents.

"Wise up!" Dakar cracked. "Don't force me to beat you." A risk within walls, since subtle knowledge of clan ways could see him staked out for a maiming, he ventured, "You have been well taught?"

As he hoped, that precise turn of phrase was recognized.

Chastened to have judged a man by appearances, the child glared back in mutinous silence.

"Good boy," Dakar crooned. For the sake of the watchful observers outside, he added, "Let's agree to be seen, but not heard." Fast and low, in Paravian, he whispered the rest. "I'll put the question to you just once. I know you were born to old families in Fallowmere. Did Simshane's purchase the lot of you?"

"Not the girls," the boy murmured. "They were already sold. Gone to the four winds and sad destiny. Why have you had us brought here?"

"To discover sweet pleasure," Dakar answered aloud, "until you sing out with joy and discover good manners and willing compliance. We have until dawn to achieve this." He sat on the bed, because his knees failed him. The tears welled thick and hot through his lashes. "Act pleased," he insisted. "You won't be made *prandey*. But our bargain with Simshane's depends on the quality of your performance." He added the Paravian term for "strict patience," masked as a murmured endearment.

The boy's return glare held white rage and murder. He spat upon the fine carpet.

"That's a start." Aware the flimsy silk robe on his back was no asset to his good character, Dakar hurled himself across the bed. "Mind carefully. Here's how we'll proceed." While the children stared, sullen, he kicked at the footboard. His terrified audience stared with huge eyes as he rolled and panted, and creaked frame and mattress with gusto. Then he added the flourish, tore the silk sheets, and cried out in breathless abandon, "Go on! Nip my fingers. Shout. You don't fight, I'll presume that your parents were sheep."

That comment raised from the lips of the child an insult straight out of the gutter.

Dakar whooped. "Again!" he encouraged. He tossed a pillow, then pounded until a snagged seam let out a blizzard of feathers. "That, for your savage, rank insolence!" A belting slap against his own thigh gave the remark a cruel punctuation. "Cry, damn you!" he gasped, while he gestured to cue the towheaded child who still stood with tied hands on the carpet.

A wide-eyed look met him, then a convincing whimper, more due to fright than playacting.

Dakar nodded. He finished his jouncing charade on the bed, then covered his movement with heavy breathing as he rose, and eased the rope binding the first child's wrists. "On the bed. Go to sleep," he encouraged in Paravian. "You won't be touched. I am trained as spellbinder, by Asandir. On my life, you shall have your freedom returned. But the plan for escape can't go forward until I've wrecked the room and faked the gamut of convincing appearances."

And so the night passed, with no suspicious attendant from Simshane's the wiser. When at last a red sunrise spilled through the screens, it lit the racked sheets, splintered stools, and frayed ends of rope knotted onto the posts of the bed. The restraints still left fastened to the older boys' limbs showed crusted traces of blood.

The breeze wafted eddies through the loose down and dried the degenerate stains marring rucked carpets and floor tiles.

On the bed, huddled into an exhausted, bruised heap, the boys who were wakeful glared at the eunuch who unbarred the door to the corridor. Among them, Dakar snored replete, naked, and scratched, and flushed pink in the sweat of indulgence. The beaten, raw circles under his eyes were not feigned, to the eunuch's professional eye. Nor was the brisk shake required to restore him back to his overslaked senses.

"Splendid entertainment," Dakar murmured, thick. "Exquisitely violent. Clean them up in the bath. Over breakfast, we'll seal the terms on your gold and arrange the hour for the coaches to come and collect them."

Noon broiled the craft shacks by the drill field. In the dusty, thick air, the sun blazed like lye, and heat trembled, redolent of baked earth, goose-greased leather, and horse sweat. The crossbuck doors of the cooper's shed were propped open to scoop the weak breeze, when Dakar blundered over the threshold.

The blind man who was no common craftsfolk's relation arose from the shadows to meet him. "They scratch?" he said gently.

A hand far too steady to be an old man's eased the spellbinder into a seat at the trestle. There, plain fare waited, and a pitcher of water that was cold and clean, and not tainted with exotic aphrodisiacs.

"I could fake bruises by sleight-of-hand spells and illusion. Not the blood, or the fluids, which were mine. And for that, damn your secretive viciousness!" Too distraught to do more than sip at the mug shoved into his shaken fingers, Dakar settled his damp head in a bitten hand that throbbed with an angry swelling. He was scarcely aware of the other fresh scabs, caused by an older boy too riddled with terror to listen, or trust him.

When Arithon did not speak, the silence hurt worse. Dakar could not suffer the poisonous ache or sustain the frayed thread of detachment. "They are all under ten, and out of their natural minds, frightened. *Why in Ath's sweet name didn't you tell me?*"

"You never inquired," came the soft-spoken reply.

Movement, to his left, then the chink of a crock; a cool compress that smelled of an astringent herb was pressed over the festering wound on his thumb.

"Just as well," stated Arithon, braced as his healer's touch was slapped off. He caught the wad of soaked rag just sent flying and tossed it within easy reach on the trestle. "Given the muddled state you were in, I didn't think you would listen."

The unfriendly truth pinched. Dakar expelled a racked breath. "That letter I delivered to Simshane's proprietor—it will in fact arrange for those branded clan children to recover their freedom from conscript captivity?"

"Merciful grace, Dakar! *You have to ask?*" A pause ensued. In the yard, the cooper's mallets banged on, while the matron harangued an apprentice for indecent language. Then, the lash of resentment *too* seamlessly masked, "For a thousand gold coin weight, sunwheel-stamped, we get all twenty-four—"

"How!" Dakar interrupted. "You couldn't arrange that—"

A raised hand jerked him down, while the Masterbard finished, "—complete with a signed bill of sale. You can burn that, once the children are back in safe custody. At this time tomorrow, if all goes well, they'll be on the way home to their families. Untouched. Unless, last night, you couldn't restrain yourself?"

Another pause, this one drivingly vicious. Dakar managed to choke his galled rage, *just barely*.

Rathain's crown prince resumed against censuring silence. "Simshane's was vying to purchase them, anyway." In that sharp change of course that *always* drowned fury beneath the moil of deeper waters, he added, "The girls went last week. To an unknown client who made his transactions by night and refused to receive their delivery in daylight."

Cold fear shot a jolt straight through a seized heart. Dakar raised his head. "Dharkaron avert!" Somehow, he forced his hazed wits to respond. "You think the females were purchased for *necromancy?*"

"I don't think. I know," stated Arithon s'Ffalenn, motionless in his disguise. Kewar had deepened him. The veiling illusion cast over his form was not visible, even to the extended awareness of a Fellowship-trained spellbinder's mage-sight. "After all, I have been in Etarra five days, pursuing the purpose that brought me."

"Enough!" cracked Dakar. "I suppose I deserved that. Though when all's said and done, I don't feel the least scrap of need to grovel and beg your forgiveness."

Arithon stared back through milky white eyes that might, or might not, cloud his vision. A sorcerer cloaked in a stilled well of mastery, he would not be blinded to resource. "Should you feel sorry? That was, after all, an inflicted, *unconscious* sacrifice." Almost no stain of rancor darkened the words of a man whose private will had been torn wholesale from the grasp of his dignity. "I gave the permission that granted you power in trust. What use to blame, that you and Kharadmon saw fit to use what you held for expediency? Apologize to Elaira," Prince Arithon said. "It is she who should grant absolution."

Dakar stood, furious. Fresh sweat stung his eyes. Between them, the crockery jug was a weapon he refrained from using, but only out of civil respect for a stranger's hospitality. "In my shoes, you would have risked walking away? You would have *dared* the dread consequence? Athera may have come to suffer the price! How much worse, had you shouldered the failure?"

Eyes locked, Arithon turned away first. "What is our experience, but the reflected truth of our misapprehensions and shortfalls? And also the grace of our beauty and strength, and the wise choices that make up our character?" He laid his slender, musician's hands out flat on the battered board trestle. Then gave his last line with the vulnerable quiet that stripped beyond grief to the core of him. "We'll never know, will we?"

Dakar swallowed. He cursed his own tears, which welled down his face in remorse and raw pain and stung sympathy. "You love her that much, that the whole world should burn?"

"You don't," said Arithon. "The world has stayed whole. Everyone else can rejoice for the fact. But not me." He moved at last, too scalded to stay still or contain the bright blaze of his anguish. "Without her, what else in my life keeps its meaning? We may as well stop this and just be ourselves. Plans set in motion must be carried through. Or Simshane's will be gelding your innocent boys, while their sisters get sacrificed to necromancy."

Summer 5671

Lines

In the *caithdein*'s lodge deep in Atwood, scouts from the forest's fringe outpost report the latest grim news: that, after scorching the road to reach Shipsport, Lysaer s'Ilessid has just raised the sunwheel standard for war and boarded a galley for Jaelot; now, northbound messengers bear sealed word to the garrisoned towns across the East Halla peninsula to call on their strength to take the field against Shadow in Alestron…

Bearing his orders to muster the south, Sulfin Evend delivers the dispatches that leave Ithish and Innish seething with the command to take arms, and as the sunwheel flagship dips her oars back to sea, the charge of a flint dagger left in his possession turns her prow toward the forbidding headland of Sanpashir…

Eriegal sweats under Feithan's cold eye, just made aware of the word arrived from the watch camp at the ford by the Arwent: that young Jeynsa never intended to confront the Teir's'Ffalenn directly, but instead has bolted southward to launch her formal inquiry from the clan seat in Melhalla; and though Sidir and Elaira leave on the hour in pursuit, the girl's lead may well be too wide for closure…

Overlook at Etarra

XIV. Sinkers and Hooks

The Mad Prophet chose to sulk by going to sleep. Because the night's efforts had left him tired, he snored through the upheaval that arose when the delegation of sunwheel priests arrived from the east and preempted the use of the practice field. Above protesting officers and cursing men, their sealed requisitions commandeered the Light's recruits to erect their elaborate pavilion.

Dakar's nap broke when the balding cooper stumbled in and collapsed, pounding the boards of the trestle, while his whooping journeymen roared with helpless hilarity alongside him.

Uncurled from the blankets where he had passed out, the Mad Prophet arose. Yawning, he shuffled past the stack of planed staves and plonked himself down on the bench between a spaniel-faced craftsman and a dandified boy, sporting tooled-leather bracers.

"What's funny?" he asked.

The bland inquiry redoubled the explosion of mirth, until the blond apprentice across the boards caught the glower shot off by the cooper's wife. Cheeks already packed, he shoved the crock of fresh cream and the basket of biscuits across to be shared with the wakened guest. Between gasping chuckles, the yard's workers explained that some Shadow-touched mountebank had rifled the Light's chests of tribute.

"Rocks!" The breathless cooper wheezed out. "The coffers came off the wagons chock-full of lichen-stained Skyshiel granite."

"No one knows where the strayed bullion's gone," said the grinning young man with the bracers. "The drivers claim that their mule train wasn't raided. Hide nor hair, they saw no trace of barbarians. That leaves the frocked priests, who swear by the avatar's name that they're clean and not lining the nests of their relatives."

Inquiries and accusations were still flying. Since no one seemed able to finger a culprit, suspicion had started fisticuffs.

The cooper clutched his aching ribs, ruefully shaking his head. "The Light's faithful got off with no worse than black eyes, once the bard used his lyranthe to calm them."

Caught tipping the cream jug, Dakar froze outright. "The free singer was there?"

"Oh, aye. The whole time." The apprentice swallowed his mouthful, then shot out an arm to right the pitcher and salvage the fat guest's inundated biscuit. "The fellow's still out there, impressing the faithful with sanctimonious ballads."

Dakar all but choked. Stunned by the breakneck speed of events, he pretended amusement by asking after the ballast.

"What became of the rocks?" The cooper swiped tears off his streaming chin. "Who knows? Who cares? Why not ask the singer? He'll have witnessed the whole thing. The priests are already so infatuated with his warbling, they've engaged him for their night's entertainment."

As Dakar braced to shove to his feet, the adjacent journeyman reached sideward and jammed his bulk back down on the bench. "Man, sit easy. You've no need to scuttle. The singer comes back here for supper each day. Our errand boy's got the cart horse already harnessed to fetch him."

In accord with the shop mistress's solicitous care, the blind singer was shortly led in by the child. The lyranthe he unslung from his shoulder was a nondescript instrument bearing a crudely etched sunwheel on the soundboard.

"The rocks?" he responded. His blade-thin features tracked only the food, as the beamy matron laid a filled plate and a mug between his supple hands. "They were sold for a pittance to a mason who said he wanted to chip them for curbstone. He brought in slave muscle to haul them away." The singer dug in, and the finish, disinterested, came muffled through mastication. "Two conscript barbarians, recently collared, and nursing the scabs of fresh brands."

Dakar suddenly found the bread sops and cream not settling well in his gut. Since the cooper's wife had a clanblood grandparent, the laborers' rowdiness staggered across a brief silence and discomfortably changed the subject. The bard devoted himself to his meal without comment. Shortly, the craftsmen scraped their plates, and grumbled their way to the work yard.

The matron departed to boil more glue. The instant she passed the threshold, Dakar accosted the singer's complacency. "That gold was masked under a powerful glamour! Else the resonance of conjury would have never gone past Lysaer's twitchy examiners. You had help for that sleight of hand, or I'm dead, and those conscripts weren't shackled, or branded."

Turbid eyes stayed trained straight ahead, unperturbed by badgering anxiety. "They were, in fact. But parents who have cherished offspring at risk won't balk at necessity to save them."

"Who is the mason?" Dakar said, wrung to shaking as the high-stakes course of Arithon's effrontery shredded his last, cringing nerve. "Dare I suppose? I'm to wander across for a social call before I engage two hack teams and a pair of closed carriages?" The lethal surmise remained beyond speech: *that the hot gold purloined from the tribute chests now would be destined for Simshane's, as barter for captive flesh.*

"Don't flare up in smoke," the bard stated, nonplussed. "I still have some friends from my travels as Medlir. Traithe also left me some trustworthy names. The mason's family was first on the list."

Dakar's queasy stomach failed to unclench. "You could still be sold out." The allure of the tribute, or the excessive bounty Avenor's edict had set upon Arithon's head, might tempt the most reliable acquaintance to turn coat.

The bard shrugged, unconcerned.

Which gesture raised Dakar to more anxious sweat. "You plan to expose Simshane's?" Then, impelled into terrified disbelief, *"Disenfranchise the priests?"*

"Watch and see," said Arithon Teir's'Ffalenn. The daylight reflected off those white eyes glinted cold as a headsman's axe blade. "Since the Light left its game pieces all in a row, do you trust they'll stay planted for gravity?"

That glib statement veiled more than Dakar cared to know: had, at Jaelot, and Riverton, and Dier Kenton Vale, tripped a balance that launched off a massacre. Wrong step or right move, one bold action might rend the whole web; and Etarra was tinder, primed for the torch to ignite a broadscale disaster. "If I'm to masquerade as the pimp, what part are you playing to back me?"

"The merry measures that whirl all the dancers to hell." One languid finger plucked a taut string. The struck note speared across trembling air and rang like the shine on a promise. "I'll be the performance out in plain sight, singing pap that will blindfold the priests." A damping thumb left the counterpoint thunder of mallets against the dauntless conclusion. "The stonemason has your instructions, my friend. All told, the outcome relies upon luck, subtle cues, and a clockwork array of stage timing."

Yet how daring the reel, and how giddy the pace, Dakar failed to anticipate. Not until after the sunwheel gold was unveiled in the dusty glare of the stone yard. The mason cocked back his filthy, slouch hat and related the audacious scope of Prince Arithon's planned machinations.

Much too late, the sane man found the sense to refuse. In the stifling sheds, helped by an anxious wife and three boys, the shop's craftsmen packed their tools and belongings in preparation for swift flight. They were townbred and upholding a choice that would see their home and livelihood abandoned against certain charges of treason. The spellbinder regarded the two close-mouthed clansmen, for whose sake these stout folk offered sacrifice. The strapping fellows were half-stripped to load wagons, and collared, if not actually captive. The price of their ruse had been paid all the same. Both sweated in pain from the heated iron that had disfigured their muscular forearms.

"Why are these people doing this?" Dakar asked point-blank, as the displaced family bustled around him.

Both clansmen stopped work. One replied in Paravian. "They act for what's right. It's an ironic twist out of history."

When Dakar's distrustful glower stayed fixed, the other posed conscript explained. "Apparently their mother was once taken prisoner by Earl Jieret's war captain, Caolle. He'd slaughtered her brother during a caravan raid to save the secret of our liege's whereabouts. But the sister was weaponless. She had two weans. Stuck holding the knife, Caolle lost his nerve. Since he couldn't slit three helpless throats in cold blood, the bunch was held in Daon Ramon, then released when their news lost its value. The old lady's stayed bitter. Still funds the league's bounties. But her older boy had seen through the lies that drive townsmen to kill for our differences. The mason who helps us is that man, grown, and now it's our children he's saving."

Dakar mopped his face, seized clammy with dread. Having heard tonight's plans in their damning entirety, he found no assurance to allay the fear that still leached at his shrinking resolve. "We're not just effecting a rescue," he challenged. "Follow this through, and you set your young sons at worse risk than gelding abuse by a brothel."

Both of the clanborn fathers stared back. The one with the bruised look around his eyes said, "For all the bodily harm they might see, their lost sisters stand to lose more than their lives. As a Fellowship spellbinder sent here to curb necromancy, if you can't find the gall to lead these coaches uptown, then charter law binds us to force you."

Dakar mounted the driver's box with shaking knees. The reins of the team weighed like lead in his sweating grasp. He rousted the horses, set the front vehicle rolling, not by choice, not for courage or duty, but for the lives of twenty-four boys, and for the friend whose unreserved trust relied on a flawless deception at Simshane's.

By then, the Master of Shadow was installed at the sunwheel pavilion, strings tuned for the priests, with the first set already in motion.

The most infamous night in Etarran history since the renegade prince's failed accession began with a murmur, as the reddened sun dipped into the haze of a fair-weather twilight. The routine, written summary that detailed the Light's vanished tribute gold had cleared the torpid delay of officialdom and reached the Lord Marshal's desk. A dispatch runner was bearing the customary sealed copy to Raiett Raven, when the closed coaches led by a grim-faced, fat driver reined up at the rear entrance of Simshane's House of Exotic Delights.

There, two massive chests were unloaded by eunuchs. The lids were pried open, and what had worn the semblance of plain, Skyshiel granite chimed through the proprietor's covetous hands. His nod to his staff tied up the exchange: two dozen young boys clad in bangles and paint were loaded and sent on their way. The packed coaches that bore them ground through darkening streets, wheel spokes glinting by lamplight. A bribe ensured that they cleared the south gate. More coin, and a discreet, spelled deception circumvented the routine inspection. The draft teams lumbered slowly downhill, while inside the town, a tip-off enclosed in a sealed affidavit was slipped into the Etarran Lord Magistrate's evening docket.

By then, the news of the infamous gold theft had been sorted by Raiett Raven's secretary. Since the High Chancellor now changed his state robes for his customary light supper, and given that he preferred to reflect in solitude as he dined on his private balcony, his staff withheld the interruption until the steward brought the dessert wine.

Across town, the anonymous affidavit planted with the magistrate encountered a different frame of delay: it was readdressed and turned into the hands of the acting officer of Etarra's garrison. The parchment arrived at the watch change, as the Lord Marshal departed for home. His night sergeant signed in, a gaunt creature known for blunt fists and a vicious temper. His ambitious, hard eyes perused the sealed statement, and widened. "Dharkaron's trampling Five Horses avenge!" he exclaimed. "Will you *look* where those thieving priests cashed their tribute?" Seasoned troops were rushed off to ransack Simshane's brothel before its pervert staff could snatch time to melt down the critical evidence.

Dakar's rented coaches, by then, were reined up by the verge, apparently stalled by the failure of one wheel's linchpin. When a passing carter pulled over to offer assistance, the livery barn's borrowed driver agreed to shoulder the nuisance of the repair. The fat lackey's live cargo was transferred to the volunteered vehicle, bound and gagged, and bundled from sight under blankets. More coin changed hands. Slightly mussed, and reeking of scent, the boys rolled on their way in a slatted dray crammed with hogsheads.

In the sunwheel pavilion, the Light's oblivious priesthood dined on roast swan and wine, their snowy raiment resplendent under candles and torchlight. If the loss of their gold left them with galled nerves, the skill of the bard was a tonic. Their rankled mood eased to his hand on the strings, and the honeyed gift of his singing. His talent raised no taint of distrust. Under the sighted acolytes' scrutiny, he had pressed his bare lips to the relic containing the Blessed Prince's plucked hair. That potent talisman should have unmasked any minion of Darkness. If free singers elsewhere were held in suspicion, this one had established his harmlessness. Since his repertoire extolled the Light's glory with every sincere sign of reverence, by the hour the picked bones were cleared from the boards, his credentials were taken as sterling.

Uptown, the High Chancellor's repast enjoyed no such felicitous tranquillity: the belatedly delivered official parchment caused the decanted wine to be abandoned beside a fluttering candle. Black-clad and grim, Raiett Raven raced from his balcony, shouting for spurs and boots, to be followed by an armed company of light horse to escort him at speed through the gate.

Across town at Simshane's, beside the gutted wreck of his desk, the distressed proprietor now pleaded in irons, alongside his weeping head eunuch. The purchase document bearing the sunwheel seal was being read off by an astonished equerry. Given the two chests of Alliance-stamped gold as firm evidence, Etarra's night sergeant realized he was in over his head. He dispatched two men, who rushed word of the horrific scandal to the senior ear of the offduty Lord Marshal.

That errand zigzagged from the man's private house to the packed doors of the uptown theater. There, a snobbish refusal to let in the uniformed watch created more fuming delay. The shouting cut through the players' performance. The Lord Marshal left his seat in his formal attire, to the tittering amusement of Etarra's pedigree society. Whispered talk swept the boxes throughout the last act, while the grooms' gossip also chewed over the stir as two liveried lackeys were sent at a run to the governor's mansion. For all their haste, they failed to inform the High Chancellor. His lordship's rattled butler opened the door in the wake of his master's precipitous departure. The stalwart attempt to intercept him at the stable proved a wasted effort. Raiett had already mounted and gone.

"Valley bound," grumped the grizzled master of horse. "Whipped his best mare in a towering fury, which isn't his usual, believe me."

The stableboy's scandalized comment was ripe. "Old Raven swore he'd rip gizzards for negligence before he ever licks arse for a bunch of disgruntled priests." Not convinced any lump sum in bullion had slipped through the Light's obsequious fingers, Raiett was bound to have somebody's blood, just for the stinging effrontery. "Aye so, wait and see. He'll force satisfaction. That upright, brass tack won't bury a victimized theft on his orderly turf at Etarra."

Night deepened, with the uptown propriety moiled through by an ever-widening dissonance. More messengers clattered down torchlit, brick streets. The armed squads of the Lord Marshal's horsemen rammed their purposeful way past the idle rakes seeking sport. Cries for right of way detained the elderly rich, jaunting on social calls in their glittering, lacquered carriages. In small knots, the bored and the curious abandoned their engagements to investigate. Soon the shakedown at Simshane's drew a titilated crowd, while on the roadway below the south gate, the town guard, with warrants, surrounded the parked hulks of two suspect coaches.

The bartered, live cargo had vanished long since. The rental hack's driver knew nothing. Brisk questions devolved into fist-shaking threats that unraveled to frustrated shouting.

The burgeoning fracas launched echoes uphill. Errant sparks to stacked fuel: Etarra's pedigree elite relished a social gaffe as nowhere else on the continent.

Meantime, the hotly sought children were safely sequestered in the darkened gloom of a harness shop. There, the erstwhile mason's two conscript clansmen settled their terrified tears. They assessed with soft questions, bolstered flagged spirits, and selected eight boys who possessed the audacious nerve to score a courageous revenge.

Dakar watched those small warriors straighten cowed spines. Sly grins became snickers. The most determined of the child volunteers was no less than the panicky sprite who had landed the festering bite on his thumb.

"You don't have to prove your young manhood to me," he assured, as the boy stepped up to the mark.

"It's those priests who should worry," the wee demon pronounced.

Dakar laughed, at last shaken loose by the chance to spit in the teeth of self-righteous authority. Granted the pluck displayed by last night's captives, he would see the snide viciousness driving Arithon's ploy orchestrated into a command performance. Committed, he saluted the determined clan parents and loaded the chosen contingent of boys back into the empty hogsheads. The barrels now carried a vintner's guild brand, with the wagon currently bearing the load painted to match the conveyance owned by Etarra's best winery.

Dakar tucked another sunwheel-sealed requisition into the breast of his shirt. Now whistling, he leaped on the driver's box, then rolled the laden vehicle from the shed, attended by two apprentice masons reclad as lackeys. On schedule, the mule team was reined toward the lit tents of the Light's frocked evangelists.

As the wine cart creaked from the darkened warren of craft shops, the looping road from the town wall was not quiet. Above slope, in meshed timing, the paired torches of the High Chancellor's outriders blinked through the gate piercing the lower barbicans.

"Dharkaron! We're slicker than butter on bread," enthused the young man to the Mad Prophet's left.

No chuckles emerged from his sober companion. "Too easy, perhaps. Mind your back. We're sure to be gutted as heretic dissenters if we get cocky and careless."

Dakar hushed the stray talk and soon pulled the team to a stop at the verge of the practice field. While the bored sentries who manned the priests' checkpoint arose from their dice to verify clearance, he easily tracked the whipped flare of the cressets, where the second armed company from the Lord Marshal's garrison now escorted the pair of stalled coaches. They had turned downhill, zealously chasing the trail of Simshane's execrable bargain. Paused at the hack stable, they would grill the head hostler. The geezer was deaf, and would also know nothing, since the rental fee had been paid with clean silver, under false name and employment. They were not going to get as far as the mason's, whose compound was already emptied.

The wine shipment to the priests being expected, Dakar's burdened cart was waved through. He rolled his load up to the central pavilion, conferred with its polished sunwheel steward, and received a signature on his receipt. A fox grin and a wave stirred his idling henchmen. "Let down the tailboard. No dedicate wants to dirty their linen, so they've asked us to pile their shipment inside."

More sentries admitted them through the back flap.

The sweet-ringing shower of music from the bard affirmed a finale now smoothly in progress.

"We're spot on target," Dakar informed the men. Since he dared not try magecraft in a sunwheel encampment endowed with a gifted examiner, the party masquerading as vintners had to plug their ears with soft wax. Dakar thumped a barrel in prearranged signal, and inside the tent, the blind singer's fingers configured a deft change in tempo and key. The music acquired an unearthly strain. Unaffected by an uncanny harmony that tugged mind and heart toward oblivion, the fake wine broker's men proceeded to unload their wagon.

One by one, the casks were hefted inside the pavilion and stacked behind the laid tables, with their extravagant flood of cinnabar candlelight. All the while, the bard plied his glittering strings. His spelled song wove light into a subliminal web. Peace settled, soft as air itself. The fluttering moths stilled pale wings and alighted. The trill of night insects went silent. Bound into a settling, eerie calm, the sunwheel priests nodded off on their couches. They snored, while the glassy-eyed guards at their threshold lost focus and drifted, then collapsed at the knees, fast asleep. Dakar and his henchmen grasped their slack wrists. Shielded behind the bulk of the wine cart, they hauled the recumbent soldiers inside. Throughout, the bard's milky gaze never wavered. The lyranthe notes struck and soared, bright as gilt, bedazzling all within listening range into soporific delight. Dakar and his apprentices closed the door flap. Fast as men with a grievance, they bent to the task of unbreeching the prostrate priests.

Fat and thin, well-muscled or soft, the creatures were stripped of their smallclothes. Then the eight sleeping boys were removed from the casks. Each one was arranged, in their paint and perfume, in pliant repose alongside.

Meantime, the lyranthe's spellbinding measures were brought to a masterful close. The bard arose smiling and gladly agreed to accept a lift home in the wine cart. Dakar and his accomplices slipped back outside, the last one guiding the free singer's step as he was helped over the tailboard. The stamped paper bearing the steward's mark saw the vehicle clear of the camp and into the dense summer darkness.

Between shed rows, another driver appeared, took over the reins, and turned the wagon with the mason's apprentices onto the eastbound road. Dakar and the blind bard parted ways with them there, melted into the nettles and wild scrub that bordered the edge of the tourney field. A short way upslope, they were rejoined by the skulking pair of branded clansmen. Only now the conscript collars were gone, replaced by soft leathers and weapons.

"We left the stage set to perfection," Dakar said, on fire with nerves as he crouched into the covering thicket.

The vantage permitted an untrammeled view: of the sunwheel pavilions, with gilt trappings agleam under the pale fall of starlight; of the weaving torches that demarked the site where two Etarran armed companies dispatched from uptown were presently jammed nose to nose. Arrived on level ground by the livery barns, and the ramshackle maze of the craft shacks, the High Chancellor and his outriders encountered the garrison's contingent and exchanged their incredulous news. The venue became lamentably public: loiterers lured out of the recruit camp's wineshops overheard the raised voices. The Lord Marshal's exodus from the theater had also attracted a loftier trail of coaches and lampmen, mounted rakes, and the idle curious: thrill seekers drawn by the promise of sport and an insatiable nose for fresh scandal.

"End game," whispered Arithon with satisfied glee. His swift fingers stayed busy, unwinding the lyranthe's tuning pegs. The moment he had the bass courses loosened, he slipped his hand inside the instrument's soundhole.

"Get ready," he murmured as he groped inside. "Mind you don't piss yourselves laughing."

The unsmiling clansmen checked the hang of their knives. They stood watch and guard as the free singer produced a shining collection of *iyats*. A soft flow of Paravian, a neat turn of talent, and Arithon imposed his directive. The fiends were unleashed to wreak vindictive mayhem, just as Raiett Raven's smart horsemen formed ranks and spurred on to descend upon the encampment of priests.

The peace lasted as long as an intaken breath. Then a wisp of dust puffed across the parched ground. Movement rustled the central pavilion's stainless expanse of taut canvas. A guyline supporting the ridgepole popped loose and slithered, dragging its uprooted sliver of stake. Another knot gave. A third rope came unraveled. The massive tent shimmied a moment, its golden sunwheel billowing. Then a spark bloomed from nowhere and fell. It settled downward like a hellish red star upon the religion's cloth emblem. Gilt glimmered a moment in crimson reflection. Then flame kindled, fanned into a whooshing blaze, as the unstable canvas ignited into conflagration.

Upslope, a wall sentry yelled. The watchkeep's alarm bells shattered the night. Downslope, the slumbering war camp erupted. Men seethed from their tents. Hopping and yanking on clothes, they snatched up their armor and weapons. Crushed into the forefront, Raiett Raven's contingent of riders reined up by the wildfire, chased by their straggle of thrill-seeking, pedigree gawkers.

The carriages parked. Mounted dandies milled in obstructive fascination, while the High Chancellor and the armed company's field sergeants seized charge and barked irritable commands to set cordons. The heaving press sorted itself like stirred glue. While rescuers stormed the collapsing tents, a bucket brigade formed, and the first naked priests sprinted out of their torched pavilion.

They were not alone. Each had a boy child clamped to his neck. Coughing and shrieking with tearful hysteria, the mites wore naught but greasepaint and perfume, and the sparkling gleam of paste jewelry.

Surprised fingers pointed. A shocked matron shrieked. Upright citizens recoiled. Hard-bitten campaign officers jeered. While veteran troops whooped in mocking laughter, the recruit infantrymen under their orders hurled down their filled buckets in poleaxed disgust. The frightened boys released their bellowing clients, then bolted, streaking like hares through the crowd. Catching them paled beside watching the Light's high priest, nakedly protesting his innocence. Raiett Raven reined in his plunging horse. While the onlookers jostled to snatch the best view, his lashing contempt carried through wind and smoke and the racket of outraged catcalls.

"I am sickened!" Poised at the forefront of political disaster, he had to distance himself to avoid getting mobbed. "Shame on us all, that honest funds were allotted to raise a temple for scum! Spare us! The vice masquerading behind the seal of our Prince Exalted is worse than a shaming fraud! In the name of the blessed avatar himself, I will see each wretched malingerer stripped. Justice will be served for abusing the public trust to support lewd acts and depraved habits!"

While the soldiers rounded up the buff miscreants, and the bucket brigade surged to toss mud clods, the breathless children pelted into the brush, met by the arms of their kinsmen.

"Time to go," said the bard. He asked one of the boys to guide his sightless step through the rapid retreat to the craft quarter. Dakar himself was too crazed with relief to question the need for that ruse. Breathlessly rushed toward shelter and safety, then panting to catch his lost wind, he crouched in a noisome cranny between sheds. There, he measured the public outcry, and the course of the fire, fast reducing the Light's wrecked encampment to ashes. He cleared a throat stinging from laughter and smoke and realized he owed an apology for the ignominy suffered at Simshane's. Turned in redress, he encountered a shock: the blind bard no longer accompanied them.

"Where's the singer?" he blurted.

Fast as thought, a scout clamped a hand to his lips. Armed men from the war camp now fanned out on patrol, enforcing the need for strict silence.

Dakar had to wait till their threatened straits eased before he dared press for an answer. Too late, he learned that Arithon had returned to the cooper's shop to face down the official inquiry.

"He's a free singer, and blind," allowed the brusque clansman. He shrugged off lathered worry, wary fingers poised on his knives and his eyes like chipped flint as the children were bedded down under sacking in a sympathizer's fusty warehouse. "The man can't be held responsible for what he couldn't see. Since the cooper's kinfolk know nothing at all, he had to stay. No way else could he prove out their innocence."

Dakar caught his breath, wrung by visceral dread. Fast as he dodged through the warren of shanties and burst into the ramshackle craft shack, he came too late. The cooper's distraught wife let him know that the bard's steady answers had satisfied no one.

Arithon Teir's'Ffalenn had been taken uptown in the custody of Raiett Raven's personal guard.

Left behind without means to slip through the security set over the governor's mansion, Dakar blotted fresh sweat and questioned the desolate craftsfolk. "Did the singer resist?"

"In fact, he went smiling." The burly cooper shook his bald head, unsettled a bit by the question. "We all understood the arrest was a farce. The fellow had nothing dishonest to hide. Even the soldiers showed him due respect. They led him off on the back of a horse and allowed the lyranthe to go with him."

"He'll be back by morning," Dakar was assured by the towhead who sharpened the adze blades.

Except for one suspect, insidious fact, recollected too late for avoidance. The Mad Prophet remembered the insouciant stakes lately placed on a public wager. The free singer's boast would be delivered tonight with a twist of excoriating arrogance: *that the brilliant allure of his music could enact a palliative cure for insomnia.*

"By the rank breath of Dharkaron's Black Horses!" Dakar swore, pressed to frightened exasperation. No belated rescue might follow; no impromptu act of fast salvage. Rathain's crown prince had gone to the adder's den, with six hours of darkness left before dawn and no man at his shoulder to back him. "My blind idiot, you are setting the hare on the fox! *What in Daelion's name were you thinking?*"

*   *   *

Etarra's High Chancellor himself stayed on edge since his return from the priesthood's debacle. The recurrent nightmares that ravaged his sleep meant his sixty-five years no longer rode his frame kindly. Ascetically thin before he had deserted his family interests at Hanshire to assume the mantle of s'Ilessid service, Raiett, still called Raven, now wore the semblance of a nerve-racked hawk, gaunt-cheeked, and beak-nosed, and craggy. His magnetic presence and keen intelligence wielded ruling authority with unimpaired prowess. The peridot eyes still burned like chill flame in the cavernous frame of deep sockets. Scorched by his impatience, the servants saw him divested of leathers and arms, freshly shaven, and reclad in the comfort of house clothes.

He was up and pacing the unadorned closet he kept for debriefing spies before his burdened outriders could dismount and escort the suspect free singer upstairs.

"My Lord, your instructions?" the liveried butler inquired.

The trailing hem of Raiett's belted robe whispered on tile as he spun between strides. "Have my armed men bring the prisoner in. Drag up the oak chair."

At the butler's raised eyebrows, Etarra's High Chancellor snapped outright, "You think I'm uncivil? Too bad. Keep him bound. I'll want cord, as well, for his ankles."

Raiett was poised still when the guardsmen arrived. Behind him, the tall candelabra were lit. A log on the hearth threw off cloying heat. The combined glare rendered his motionless form as a mirrored reflection. His preferred black velvet was flecked with shell clasps, and his silver hair combed, shoulder length. Lean hands laced together, he watched the prisoner dragged in with a viper's drilling intensity.

If the singer had faked blindness, his act was unflawed. The guard leading him guided each diffident step. When his heel hooked on the threshold, the white eyes stayed fixed, and never once flickered downward. The aged face displayed no telltale creases of crow's-feet, and the mismatched, cast-off clothing was ineptly patched at elbow and knee. The instrument borne by the trailing guard was nondescript, a likely find in a jumble stall.

The bard seemed as harmlessly ancient and worn. Pressed into a seat in the unpadded chair, then bound hand and foot for rough questioning, the odd creature seemed submissive enough. Except those sensitive, showman's hands showed not a quiver of nervous distress.

Raiett was not wont to miss a detail. Further, as the rumpled white head tipped his way, cued by the sound of his breathing, the expressive mouth curved with the insolent suggestion of cynical forbearance.

All effrontery, in fact, the bard chose to speak first. "The lyranthe of herself cannot frame words. Is this an interrogation?"

Caught setting the instrument on a tasseled couch, the trailing man-at-arms blushed.

Raiett replied in time to forestall the soft idiot's contrite apology. "The lyranthe of herself does not cut down pitched tents. Or set them aflame to unveil a staged scandal. Confess why you came to discredit our priests, and we can begin with a round of polite conversation." He waved the guard back to assume position in the hallway outside the closed door. By established custom, a taciturn pair of veterans remained on station behind the strapped captive.

"I didn't come for polite conversation." The bard shifted his shoulders, to no avail. His aged wrists were affixed to the chair back, tight enough to cause him discomfort.

Raiett edged a step closer. "Did you not?"

Blind eyes never wavered, but the weather-lined face lit up with engaging amusement. "I came to sing. You're not carefree?"

The High Chancellor was no sorcerer. His measure of born talent could not pierce through the audacious layers of wrought subterfuge. Yet the keen prompt of instinct made him sure of his hunch: *this man was the Master of Shadow.* Lifetime connoisseur of intrigue, Raiett Raven savored his moment to challenge the peril placed at his private disposal.

"Nor am I your enemy," said the man in the chair, "the shame to your upstart priests notwithstanding."

Which declaration was a slap without parallel, a taunting dare to unmask the bold sleight of hand, or expose the arcane trick and prove the Light's defamed delegates had been victimized. No, Raiett acknowledged: the damage was done. Tonight's display of vice could not be eclipsed. This frail singer's arraignment could never appease the contempt of a thousand outraged, sober witnesses.

"Our summer campaign's defanged, nonetheless," Raiett declared with stripped irritation. "Give me a reason why you should not bleed without trial for your malicious act of live sabotage."

The mirth that dogged the bard's lips disappeared. "Because no one's died *yet.* I am here, as I promised, to offer a *permanent* cure for the nightmares that cause your insomnia." The old singer's eyebrows, perhaps, showed the faintest tuck of impatience. "Release my hands. Send your guardsmen away. You cannot dismiss the harsh facts in this case. Dare you afford to misjudge my appeal? If you fail here, what fate for Etarra? *Can your misguided faith save the people you govern?* You have rats in your *cellar.* By all means, let them breed. Ignore their insidious pestilence, while you scour my empty carcass for fleas."

Blind eyes bored straight ahead, but no flawless performance could defer the fraught crux: now the hands in their bindings were rigid.

Raiett Raven measured that first sign of stress. Then, stung incredulous, he also divined the blistering courage behind the urgent appeal. "You were *Fellowship*-sent?"

The guards stirred, behind. The burly one with the unquiet eyes closed his fist and unsheathed his belt knife. The blind singer would know by the dissonant ring that the drawn steel bore a lethal temper. If he did not flinch for the blade at his back, he was not impervious, after all.

Springing sweat striped down his temples. "Does that matter, my friend?"

Raiett returned a clipped headshake, cranked to a strained note of sorrow. "My choice holds no sway anymore, my bold lark. Your offer comes far too late to spare anyone. Bid farewell to the sun. For you, the bad dreams won't be ending at daybreak."

"No execution in public?" said the bard to his captor with taut grief. "I won't have my clean passage across Fate's Wheel?"

Anguish infused the cat-gleam of Raiett's eyes. "You won't. I can't free you. Why didn't you see? You're the new prize the cultists will seize to finish their plot to snare Lysaer."

The bard closed his eyes. "Then for my sake, rest my appeal with Ath's grace."

The guard's heavy hand closed upon his bound wrist. Brought to defeat, he did not engage sorcery. Nor did he call on his wild gift of shadow. Such restraint brooked no logic. Raiett frowned for the lapse. Yet his flare of unease died without analysis. Though the blade was plain steel, its cold edge bit deep as the guard's lightning stroke sliced the prisoner's forearm from elbow to wrist.

The singer's frame shuddered. Shock parted his lips. The air left his lungs in a gasping rush, while his blood ran and splashed on the floor tiles.

Raiett lost all color, his sleeve pressed to his mouth to stem a sharp uprush of sickness. The knife *was not bone*. It bore no binding spellcraft. The bleak burn of dark sorcery would come later. But the High Chancellor of Etarra understood how the gushing wound felt, as the Kralovir bled a victim with talent to sap the mind and weaken the sinews. Each night, he dreamed of the hard, spinning rush, then the panting need to draw air to stave off the feeling of incipient suffocation. Too well, he recalled the nauseous faintness that came as the mind spun down into darkness.

The memory of what would occur after that framed the terror that wakened him, screaming.

"Grace," the bard whispered as consciousness failed him. His head tipped, chin forward, while his torso slumped, and the cord on his arms strained his tendons.

The cultist behind him wiped off the fouled blade. He sheathed his cleared steel, and waited. His dour-faced henchman looked on, unmoved, while in the oak chair, the victim's soaked fingers splashed a pattering red stream in the firelight. If a glamour had wrought his disguise, the white hair failed to shift coloring. Raiett stared, disbelieving, but observed no change. Even under the swift encroachment of death, the aged skin kept its wrinkles. No signs of royal identity emerged. The singer's slack flesh turned blanched as a corpse. His slumped frame convulsed, then loosened.

The heavyset guard snatched a fistful of hair. He raised the bowed head, peeled a fluttering eyelid, then swore for the inconvenience. Cataracts still fogged the pupil beneath.

Raiett Raven edged backward to spare his fine hem. "Look at the wretch, will you? He's no one's prized prince. My guess was mistaken. We've dealt with a lackey, and you have just butchered a free singer sent as a sanctioned Fellowship agent." Regret resurged, charged by vindictive hope, that the bard's strained bequest might be answered.

But the gray cult's initiates knew their macabre trade in the barter of spirit and flesh. Undeterred, they fingered the vein in the neck until they detected a pulse. The raced heartbeat let them measure the bard's ebbing vitality. Practiced experience made no mistakes.

"Enough. Strap his arm," the burly guard snapped. His spattered fist clamped down to stem flowing blood, while his taciturn henchman slipped off his belt and wound the strap into a tourniquet. "Blind victim or spy, he's no use to us, dead."

The surly guard also stripped off the rope manacles, while the knife-bearing brute freed the knots binding the unconscious prisoner's ankles.

"Lordship!" he barked, as though Raiett was a servant. "Fetch out some linen for dressings, and blankets. The spirit must not slip from the husk beforetime. Can't risk a chill that might start him shivering before we've got him down to the cellar."

"Should we bother to stir for this night's paltry take?" the man wrapping the savaged arm grumbled. "Could be he's naught but a decrepit old bird who carols for coin, after all."

"Who knows? Who cares?" The ringleader licked a slicked, scarlet knuckle, then smiled and mopped his smeared palms on the singer's patched shirt. "At least the tang of fresh blood never lies. The essence of him reeks of talent."

A last glance, shot off in piercing contempt, caught Raiett Raven's masked strain and gray pallor. "Still shrinking squeamish? Don't worry. We've bled your spy white. He won't be able to gather his wits, far less find the strength to recover his grip should he ever regain lucid consciousness."

While the litter bearing the blanket-wrapped bard was transferred to the crypt underneath the governor's mansion, the clan children whisked into hiding remained at risk of forced search and exposure. Around them, Etarra continued to seethe with the intensity of a stirred anthill. Torches streamed down the bends in the road, as the night's flagrant scandal sparked lights up and down the town battlements. The sunwheel tents smoldered to cinders and smoke, attended by grudging recruits who labored to thread buckets between the obstructive press of a mob stung to violence by moral betrayal.

Horns wailed. Harried officers shouted. Hecklers hurled mud at their white surcoats as they struggled to bind the naked offenders into locked custody.

The overwhelming noise drowned the priests' protestations as the on-looking crowd catcalled and fed on the rage of betrayal. More mounted patrols were dispatched from the garrison. Fast as they broke up the fist-shaking knots, angered citizens poured into the fringes and gathered in subversive clusters between the craft sheds.

More soldiers bore in. Since the entrenched canker of Etarran oppression bred hysterical fear of revolt, the troops were rough men who preferred to break heads and sort out with questioning later. Dakar dared not rely on glamours to mask old blood fugitives seeking escape. Not tonight, when any cloaked figure bearing a child was hell-bound to spark vengeful inquiry.

Just prior to dawn, as the ground mists rolled in, the unrest burned down to a sullen distrust of the motives of sunwheel priests. Before the daybreak change in the guard could revitalize the patrols, Dakar pushed aside his concern and fatigue, and wove the subtle protections that allowed the threatened clansmen to slip past the sentries. Dawn light saw the boy children safely away.

Dakar at long last found himself free to act. Past view of the town, tucked in the parched brush where the barrens of Daon Ramon lapped against the bleached ruts of the trade road, the misted air smelled of manure and dew and the packed clay soon to raise clouds of dust in the swelter of daylight. Dakar tipped a pebble out of his boot. Alone with bad thoughts, his apprehension intensified, raising the aching throb at his temples that often foreran the onset of prescience. Every ruffled instinct he owned made him chafe over Arithon's detainment.

No spellbinder's resource might obviate risk: not since the High Chancellor's court rooted the seat of the gray cult's machinations.

"Damn your secretive nature to Sithaer's deepest pit!" Dakar groused. The next instant, he hopped as a needling pain stabbed into his exposed ankle. He glanced down, discovered his foot in an anthill, and spouted off with more venom. Since cursing did the absent prince little good, the Mad Prophet brushed off the insects and snarled an apology. Limping a respectful distance away, he sat down on a boulder and seized his first chance to conjure a shielded scrying.

No need, at this pass, to invoke an elaborate ritual. The past crisis at Rockfell and a merging with Kharadmon's power had reconfigured Dakar's rapport with his talent. Less than a league from Etarra's defenses, he elected to channel his sight through Arithon's Named grant of permission. The view he received would arise from *within* the Teir's'Ffalenn's private being. That purposeful subtlety must suffice to forestall any hostile source from broaching the integrity of the connection.

Dakar closed his eyes. He settled his limbs. One deep breath, two, he released the distraction of his outer senses. Immersed in black calm, he configured the primary energy needed to shape his crafting: the heart-deep, clean flow of affectionate regard he held for the Prince of Rathain. To that, he linked the line of consent held under Arithon's given Name.

"Ath preserve," Dakar breathed as his set construct flamed against etheric darkness. Braced for a fight, resolved to withstand the lash of an initiate master's inner defenses, he dissolved the seal that demarked his privacy.

His delicate summons blazed forth, unshielded, but tuned with such precision that only one living spirit might answer...

...awareness swooped downward, sucked into a spin that dragged him beyond reach of sunlight. The air smelled of dank brick and mold. High and thin, as though distanced by fever, two echoing voices conversed. Whether they argued, or gloated, or simply passed time, the racked thread of awareness Dakar encountered could not track the meaning of words. He sensed the ache of bound hands. Then the bite of more cord, looped around knees and ankles. Not just set in constraint, his limbs felt encased by a leaden lassitude. He was cold. A leaching weakness infused his flesh, and a raging thirst parched his throat. He breathed, but felt dizzy, as though starved for air...

"Arithon?"

A wisp of awareness answered his call.

A ghost touch so tenuous, Dakar at first thought the sensation was errant, shaped out of frantic anxiety. *Never* had anyone managed to cross the Teir's'Ffalenn's inner boundaries without a defensive challenge. Even unconscious, the prince had been known to rise to invasive intrusion. *This* yielding helplessness felt utterly wrong. Though Dakar's impulse was to dismiss the faint contact, he sounded deeper, persisted, until he all but dissolved the connection to his own flesh.

No good news came back.

The throbbing sensation of cut muscle ran the full length of his left forearm...

The pain was *too real*. Shocked, Dakar recalled Sethvir's bleak assertion, that cultists who preyed on trained talent bled such victims to the brink of death to weaken their innate protection. The rampant horror stopped thought: the Teir's'Ffalenn languished in the hands of the Kralovir, preserved for their rite at the dark of the moon, with no friend at hand to defend him.

Fury shattered Dakar's tranced calm. Cast back into his shivering frame, he shoved to his feet, only to find himself checked up short.

A tall figure confronted him, arrived without sound. Male, but not mortal, he blocked Dakar's path, his flame-colored tunic embroidered with patterns too fine for a jaunt in the brush. His piercing regard viewed the spellbinder's flushed haste with intelligent, poisonous irony. "Sit back down, foolish man. You're not going anywhere."

Startled halfway out of his skin, Dakar panicked. The attack spell he started was slapped aside with demeaning ease.

"Sit," the frightening creature repeated. "I am not a cultist. Grab hold, take my counsel, you're not going to faint. If you keel over and crack your fool head, suit yourself. I haven't appeared here to harm you."

Thumped on the chest by the fellow's spread hand, Dakar overbalanced. Sent reeling backward, he encountered the rock, then dropped on his rump, enraged and huffed breathless.

"You!" he gasped, strangled.

Davien raised his eyebrows. His smile was a tiger's, fierce with bright teeth. "You're perishing quick to assign me the blame, that Arithon lies in Raiett Raven's cellar at risk of induction by necromancers."

"If Kharadmon knew you had shown yourself here, he would abandon his vigil at Darkling forthwith and rip out your oily guts." Dakar rubbed his chest, which evinced no scar from the Sorcerer's peremptory touch. But the ignominy burned like a wound cleaned with salt. "Restore my free will. Allow me to pass. Or better, say why you obstruct me."

"Leave your friend to his fate," the Betrayer responded. "He has not asked for rescue and needs none of your blundering assistance. For all of your mis-placed philanthropy, trust me, you have never seen to the core of him."

Dakar gasped, incredulous "You're claiming he'd send himself in there *as bait?* That offends me."

Davien stood unruffled, the citrine ring on his hand a hot spark in the sunlight. "I beg your pardon. Your prince went informed. He re-jected my grant to peruse the black grimoires, but Traithe caught the breach in Melhalla. Your Teir's'Ffalenn knows *in depth* how the Kralovir work. Since then, he requested, and received my direct help. No one's free will has been compromised."

"Except mine, of course," Dakar gritted, half-speechless. "You've been involved with this farce from the start?"

Davien did not respond: the reason was plain. Dakar bit back a curse, for his idiot blindness. *What else but a Sorcerer's hand could have masked a crown prince's etheric identity, or even, changed gold into stone, then back again?* "Why did you come here?" the Mad Prophet repeated. "Don't say you could not have shouldered this risk and spared Rathain's lineage from a lethal exposure!"

Again, still opaque, the Betrayer refused answer.

Dakar suppressed his headstrong tongue. He sustained spiteful silence, against precedent. For unless the Sorcerer allowed him to pass, no protest would make any difference.

"Not a whimper of argument?" Davien's needling shifted to laughter. "I see you've outgrown drowning setbacks in drink. That's unfortunate. You'll have to weather your rages, awake. The finale won't play for another two days, before midnight at the dark moon."

Dakar found his lost nerve. "Don't expect me to wait."

Amused, Davien watched him. Those obsidian eyes could absorb all the light in creation before an opponent could read him. "Arithon once told me the wish of his heart. Would you deny him the tempering experience he needs to achieve his most cherished desire?"

"Lies!" cracked Dakar, reduced to bravado. "You can't rightfully keep me. Nor would Sethvir allow you the blood of another crown prince as a sacrifice."

Davien's whimsy vanished. "Spare me your tangle of trite accusations!"

"Trite? *Accusations?*" Dakar lost his wits. "Your bluster's no better than piss in a windstorm!" Infused by a courage he had never possessed, he lashed out. "Alone, and drained to the verge of oblivion, Arithon lies at dreadful risk! He will succumb to the Kralovir's snare. Don't trouble to claim you'll act to spare him. Your double-dealing might make me toss breakfast."

"The risks lie outside of your limited grasp," the renegade Sorcerer rebutted. No muscle moved. Yet his patience was spent. "Don't even think you can try to imagine! Move one inch, and depend on the fact I will take forceful measures to prevent you."

Breathing hard, Dakar rose. "Do that, by Ath! I refuse to lie down and cringe like a dog while you toy with more royal lives. Your chess match to see a crown lineage cut dead cannot meet the same end as Melhalla's."

Davien wasted no word. His poised form stayed motionless. The spellcraft he deployed struck Dakar's awareness, and darkness welled up without form and dropped him unconscious.

Summer 5671

Catch

The galley the Prince Exalted engaged for fast transport reached port in Jaelot just prior to sunset at the dark of the moon. Caught aback, since the pennant that streamed from her masthead was the only forewarning received, the town's flustered Lord Mayor jumped, scrambling. Rushed orders saw an escort assembled. A cordon cleared space through the press at the harbor, while commerce ground to a stupefied halt, and a breathless fanfare of trumpets heralded the blessed arrival. The ranking burghers had assembled beneath the town banners by the time the august vessel tied up to the bollards. She had been run at speed. Her oarsmen panted in prostrate exhaustion, and her brightwork wore crusts of dried salt. The curious craned. Flushed in their finery, the guild ministers cheered while the gangway set down, and the gleaming embassy from Avenor stepped onto the carpet spread over the dock.

Amid the excited explosion of talk and the galvanic rumor of war, the royal arrival was welcomed with dazed speculation and obsequious, open arms.

Foremost among Jaelot's dignitaries was the clairvoyant high priest whose suspect appointment had originated under the auspice of the corrupt high priest, Cerebeld. Abroad in full daylight, the rotund little man displayed no sign he might share the vile taint of a binding instilled by the Kralovir.

Yet Lysaer s'Ilessid was taking no chances. His person stayed guarded ever since the debacle that had flushed the treasonous ring of Avenor's turned councilmen. A fresh-faced young man wearing the collared mantle of a crown examiner preceded the sunwheel guard, his tuned sensitivity entrusted to screen for signs of errant spellcraft.

While the town mayor was stalled by an opportune speech, the oathsworn talent gave the shining figure of the Blessed Prince his tacit signal of clearance. By his arcane assessment, the priest's presence was harmless. No lead-foil ripple of bound shades entangled the living stream of his aura.

Lysaer s'Ilessid smiled his relieved acknowledgment. A diamond in sunlight in his white and gold, he loosened the fist he had held in tense readiness to wield light for a summary execution. Assured of Jaelot's loyalty, his retinue gathered about him, and his guard captain signaled the drumroll to march.

The Blessed Prince stepped into the glare of late day, ablaze in the pomp of state trappings. His blond head was bare, a fair beacon amid his cowled clerks, and the enameled helms of his officers. As his personal guard and his bannerbearers formed ranks to proceed to the mayor's palace, the florid form of the resident priest was tucked into their glittering company.

Jaelot's aged mayor followed, leading his cluster of bedazzled councilmen. Surrounding, the cheers of the onlooking crowd swelled into a deafening roar. As the procession swept away from the bayside and arrowed through the packed streets, aproned craftsmen left work, and balcony windows banged open. If Lysaer did not pause to touch outstretched hands, he smiled with gracious acknowledgment. The shouts went from noisy to deafening. Matrons waved, and young girls with ribboned baskets showered a riot of flower petals. Man, woman, and child, all of Jaelot rejoiced for the avatar's visitation. Lysaer's cameo beauty and majestic grace captivated their adulation. Aged men lost their breath. Gawking boys pressed the cordon and clamored to enlist, starry-eyed with eagerness to bear arms for the cause of humankind's deliverance from Darkness.

In such august presence, the plump priest was outshone. His innocuous stride bobbed unremarked amid blinding white cloth and inspired charisma.

But to the shade of the Fellowship Sorcerer who lurked unseen, that man's innocent appearance was not harmless. A latent potential for threat lay embedded in the ephemeral stream of the priest's outer aura. Its pattern was dormant. Insidious as a shard of transparent glass suspended in flowing water, the minute fluctuation in density snagged barely a ripple across fine perception. Yet Luhaine detected that shimmer of subtle disharmony, however far it lay past the range of visible light.

His aware foreboding would not be dismissed. He stalked the circle of fervent disciples attached to the sunwheel banner, a purposeful current that stitched between the carved signboards and threaded through the stone finials of ivy-clad buildings. His eavesdropping raised no trace of disturbance. If years of sly practice had taught him to hoodwink the Koriani Council, that expertise did not ease his inherent distaste for skulking.

His caustic complaint spanned over distance and ruffled his colleague, on stationed surveillance in Darkling. *This pursuit is rank madness! Sethvir was insane to believe Rathain's prince should have risked the least part of our charge to purge the Kralovir from the Alliance.'*

'*So what's wrong with blood sport in front of the chase?*' Kharadmon flipped back in double entendre. Ensconced like a wisp of caught shade in a crack in the mountain-based citadel's curtain wall, he tracked a ferrety sunwheel devotee, as well. This one's mettlesome clairvoyance had once launched an armed company to hunt down the Master of Shadow. Since the disastrous outcome had left the Barrens littered with the bones of both horses and men, the reminder should have squelched Luhaine's grumbling dissatisfaction.

Yet today the scholarly spirit posted at Jaelot harbored a foreboding too jagged to still. '*Davien. That's what's wrong. He's juggled the stakes. Without his inveigling, do you truly think Arithon would have dared—*'

'*We're past second options,*' Kharadmon flared back. The surprise change in planning could not be undone. The Betrayer's hand had already meddled, with Arithon's life immutably thrown into jeopardy. '*Best stop wafting loose wind and mind the fat priest that you came for. If that latent sigil he carries turns active, we'll be in the proverbial muckheap over our heads.*'

Never less than meticulous, Luhaine huffed. '*Lose Rathain's prince, your revolting point's moot.*' The burnished procession he followed now arrived on Jaelot's palace stair. As Lysaer commanded the predictable pause to address the fawning crowd, the watchful Sorcerer blended his essence into the wood grain of a lamppost. '*No sanctioned crown heir should have been asked to redress Etarra's cult pestilence in the first place.*'

Kharadmon could never resist casting bait. '*You'd rather watch the prince speared on the run by the swords of a corrupted army? That's scarcely fair play. One against twelve makes far better odds than one set against fifteen thousand.*'

Yet Luhaine in pursuit of a chokehold concern could outlast the clamped jaws of a bulldog. '*Your charge is asleep?*'

'*Behind darkened shutters inside a locked keep, and sitting a clutch of ominous portents,*' Kharadmon allowed on a rankled shift into wariness. '*Don't rush to commiserate, or better still, volunteer to exchange places.*' Unlike the priest counterpart with Lysaer in Jaelot, his own charge bore the lead-foil haze that demarked a fully consecrated practitioner. Past question, the bad lot resided in Darkling. The inequity left all too little tolerance for the woolgathering indulgence of worry as the crucial hour approached.

Moment to moment, the crept line of shadow engulfed the surrounding slate rooftops. Alpenglow briefly burnished the Skyshiel peaks, then dimmed into featureless gloom. As night followed sundown on the dark of the moon, the pair of discorporate Sorcerers held their vigilant ground: one immersed in the speeches and pomp of a state celebration in Jaelot, and the other, standing guard in the dour, walled town that straddled the notched pass on the road to the Eltair coast. There, as cold dewfall pewtered the cobbles and dripped from the gargoyle gutters, the priest immured in the closed keep stirred awake.

Servants regaled him in his gold chain and sunwheel mantle behind his latched door and bronze shutters. Moments later, their helping hands were dismissed. The cult minion emerged alone. The terraced courtyard he chose to enact his dire sacrament was enclosed by thick walls, and bordered by tended flower beds. Around him, lavender and foxglove and phlox shed their fragrance in earthbound silence. From the street, far below, the grind of a dray and the dicers' whoops from a packed tavern seemed a life set apart. Under black sky and glittering starlight, the corrupt priest stepped onto swept stone and invoked his ritual circle.

'*They've started,*' Kharadmon signaled to Luhaine.

Still nestled into his niche in the masonry, the Fellowship Sorcerer watched the Kralovir cultist strike a spark to a stinking grease candle. Sullen red, the lit wick hissed and spat. As if ill-set flame resented its tether of string, it took hold and burned as though feeding on light. The priest drew a bone knife. He whispered in monotone, then pressed the point to his arm. One drop of let blood, a last guttural word, and the dark birthed a host of capering, unclean shadows.

These, the priest breathed in like perfume.

Kharadmon coiled in readiness...

At Jaelot, the first harbinger did not seem momentous. Beneath the waxlights of the sumptuous banquet given to honor Prince Lysaer, the smiling, fat priest accepted a seat with his fellows at the Lord Mayor's high table. Yet where any latent sigil of necromancy seeded potential for threat, the Sorcerer keeping watch in concealment knew not to place trust in appearances. Luhaine lurked with taut patience, prepared, as Sethvir's tacit contact came through and revealed the events in lockstep, at Etarra...

Darkness shot through with the smell of damp stone infused the glimmer of returned awareness. Arithon swallowed. His scraped throat was dry. Somewhere, forlorn, a child was crying. Befogged by lassitude, he realized her wailing had troubled him for some time. His disturbed effort to rise was caught short by fixed rope: *a wrongness.* Bound at ankles and wrists, he was splayed naked across a stone slab. The taut cords stretched his joints and pulled at his throbbing left forearm. The hurt arose from a scabbed-over cut; *more wrongness.*

He did not remember receiving the wound.

Arithon wrestled his spinning senses to sort meaning from febrile chaos. Shadows moved, near him. Male voices were chanting in scratched whispers that conjured; *a worse wrongness still.* A sullen flicker of flame burned nearby. He lay enclosed by a circle of candles, breathing in grease-stinking smoke. The pall burdened his lungs and shot queer, leaden murk through his mage-sight. Lids cracked as he peered through the whirling haze, Arithon made out the forms of his captors.

Their heads wore an unpleasant aureole of dull mercury, streaming in shadows above him. Each face was cowled. Bare arms were circled with inscribed copper bracelets, and drenched, ringless fingers touched, coated bright red. While the crying child wailed, Arithon felt them stroke his strapped flesh. The whispered chant rose and fell in the background as his person was painted over with uncanny symbols, rendered in blood.

Arithon wrenched. Ripped by gagging nausea, he found no relief. His gut was long emptied. Choked by the burn of heaved bile, he racked with dry heaves until he sank, wrung limp by wheeling vertigo. The nightmare of abusive practice continued. A soaked finger traced over his brow, while the metallic tang of fresh slaughter savaged his mind and his senses.

The phosphor shine of animal magnetism whirled away like blown dust, and trained mage-sense exploded with knowing: *the blood was a child's.* The odd, sucking sound he had struggled to place was her slashed-open heart, still beating in convulsive reflex.

Arithon cried aloud. Overcome by revulsion, he blacked out as his hammering pulse rushed him giddy, then drained his head.

Sensation returned in shimmering patches. He had to fight for each breath. Whirled by a roiling riptide of faintness, he clawed his way back to cognizance. A cold weight burdened his unsettled stomach. Someone had rested a clay bowl on the flat muscle beneath his rib cage. The rim was inscribed with baleful ciphers. Their power glared as a coal in the night, shedding ripples like miasmic blight. The emanation laced into the gravid dark and combed streaks through the vapor from drug-scented candles.

The child sacrifice had ceased her tormented crying. A gulf of unnatural quiet remained. Amid the fraught singing of blood in his ears, through the rags of his disjointed vision, Arithon saw the nacreous flicker of ghosts: children bearing the lead-foil seals that bridled the spirit beyond death. Snared shades had no voice. Without sinew to scream, their desperate, mute writhing became rendered in graphic silence.

Arithon strained at the knots on his wrists until exhaustion threatened oblivion. He could not pull free. Eyes shut, lips parted, he sought the dropped threads of his mastery. *How had he come to be here?* Swimming senses ravaged all cohesive thought. The harsh ciphers written at chest, throat, and brow stained the clarity of his mage-sense.

Through dizziness, he felt heavy fingers close on his bare arm, followed fast by the sting of sliced skin.

Shocking pain ripped a gasp from his throat. Though shallow, the cut hurt like the jab of a hornet. Arithon thrashed, yanked up short. The ties pinned him, utterly helpless. His attempt to turn his head was clamped fast. More voices whispered. Smoke and black robes swirled at the edges of vision as someone raised a ceremonial candle. Heated wax dripped across his fresh wound. The scald was followed by the imprint of a seal and given closure by lines of cold conjury.

Arithon howled as a sleeting needle of ice shot into the bones of his wrist. The sensation ripped through nerves, bones, and viscera, then stabbed as a spike through his heart. The left upper quadrant of his body went numb, more void than a sucking vacuum. As though flesh had vanished, Arithon was no longer aware of his arm. Worse, the hand still roped to the slab remained oddly unaffected. By the trickle of warmth tracing over his palm, he still felt the inflicted gash, copiously bleeding.

Something coiled as though alive through thick smoke. Its dull silver cloudiness made the burdened air seem too dense to draw into his chest. Raced pulse, panted breath, Arithon shuddered. The cowled figures moved a step widdershins. Scarlet fingers rose overhead. They clasped the hilt of the dripping blade, now streamered like flame with blued phosphor.

The horror broke Arithon to shivering sweat. Initiate sight recognized the effervescent stain unleashed by the act of blood sacrifice.

More hushed incantation; the gleaming bone blade was consecrated by the black art of necromancy, then rinsed in the bowl on his abdomen. The liquid inside captured the resonant imprint. Sigils inscribed in the vessel's clay rim entrapped Arithon's individual signature. Named consciousness recoiled. An invasive spider dropped onto a web, the thrust of warped conjury lanced a shard of ice through the victim's exposed navel.

Arithon screamed.

This, his first experience of dark sorcery: a separation from the stream of grand harmony that shattered the hoop of his being. The fissure expanded. His innate wholeness felt sundered in ways that left him no grasp to recover. The abyss sucked him *down*. Plunged into a gulf of imprisoning fear, shown helplessness beyond imagining, he howled. Initiate mastery could not reconcile the tear. He bled energy through the rent at his wrist; drowned in the dire void in his belly.

More voices muttered. A clammy touch handled him. A necromancer's spell infused the wax seal set over his bleeding wrist. The arcane closure fixed into the wound solidified the dissociated feeling. His torpid hand now felt cast in lead. Skin and joints were alive, but now sheared from the command of his natural reflex.

The rift hurled disarray through Arithon's aura. Racked, he could not shed the shackling weight as the binding laid foul hold upon him.

Nor could his desperate tears be contained, as once again, he found himself reft from the use of his birth-gifted talent. To extend his awareness beyond the veil, he must first cross through the ring of a necromancer's sigils of binding. There, his striving blundered like a winged bird wrapped in felt. His bard's mastery of sound became warped into dissonance. His innate awareness of light did not sing. A prison conjured of cruelty and domination held him as captive inside of his flesh.

Now the streaked hands bore down on his right arm. The bone blade bit again. Its virulent sting touched his nerves to dipped acid. Arithon writhed. Again, the flame of his beingness flickered, and *again* came the punch as the force of wrong conjury skewered his heart. But for his two hands, his torso went dead. A torrent of harsh words, and the wet knife was dipped. The swirl of stirred fluid unleashed its forced seal, and fell power lashed into his solar plexus.

The blow thrashed the breath from stunned lungs. Arithon's gasp was a moan of stark agony. "Mercy," he pleaded through hammering pain.

But the guttural voices over his head called only despair from the darkness. The whirlpool of grim force tugged him down, and down, while the fingers that tapped and prodded and stroked moved on and clamped his right ankle.

The next knife cut came, and ripped frost through his groin, and hurled him further into imprisonment.

Light-headed, Arithon drifted. The pain that intruded in scintillant flashes leached his being into gapped fragments. Relentless, its current scoured through hollowed bone, and dissolved the firm ties to identity. Foursquare, the seals with their haltering sigils bore into his suffering flesh. The inexorable drag of the filled bowl soaked him in, until he felt snuffed in silk batting. The suffocating numbness spread inward, leaving his hands and his feet as islands of truncated feeling. Unmoored, he could not track the self-aware life that drove his reflex for breathing. As an unraveled yarn from a knit, his spirit became drawn out of the gravid shell of his trunk.

Grace died, by dread increments. Awareness of light left his eyes. His hearing frayed into silence. The clay bowl on his stomach bore down like poured stone, absorbing his flickering consciousness.

Vertigo spun him as the vessel was raised. Cowled figures leaned over him, chanting. The print of spread hands that he could not feel froze the streaming sweat on his abdomen. Oblivion beckoned. The shrill warning of instinct whirled away.

Then the bone knife nicked into Arithon's navel.

Pain entered him, newborn. Its drilling force reawakened nerve, bone, and sinew, a molten lava that flensed him, spirit from tormented flesh.

This was not the kindly crossing known to the bard. No natural death, where the life-conscious essence gathered itself and in gentle parting, cast away mortal ties and slipped free. Instead, Arithon experienced a forced separation, a tearing of continuity that despoiled right order and savaged all rhythmic relinquishment. His husked body shuddered. Wrenched by the throes of that merciless backlash, the knotted ropes strained, while the incised bowl held above his splayed form wound in the peeled stream of his consciousness and plunged him, drowning in blood-murky broth.

Arithon fought the induction, to no avail. As though his life cord was reeled onto a spool, the dominant imprint infused in the vessel dragged him headlong into bondage.

He could not burst free. The refined shift in resonance that would buy his clear passage across Fate's Wheel could not rise into completion. His essence stayed tethered. The nailing spells fixed by the wax seals locked him into etheric connection. The auric remnant anchored in his extremities pinned him yet to his brutalized flesh. Constrained as a bead upon a plucked thread, Arithon's imprint became seized into a liquid-filled bowl for a diabolical sacrifice.

A cult parasite of the Kralovir would drink him down.

No action might save him. The black grimoires told over the hideous fate of human prey taken by necromancy. Their lost spirits became a fused part of the creature who partook of the vile sacrament. Hung in crossing between death and life, the immutable aspect of Arithon's being would remain enslaved. Like the children before him, his bound shade would be tapped, tormented, and wrung as emotional fuel for a cult host's unnatural immortality.

A last invocation would frame the ritual. Arithon felt cased in harrowing cold. The spells in the bowl were as knives, fencing his signature presence. His still-quickened hands and feet would not let him tear loose, though the suspension that shackled him to his dying flesh lashed his psyche to untold distress.

Then came the horrible, sloshing tilt, as the clay bowl was given over to the warped creature who would absorb him. Stopped lungs could not scream. A stilled tongue raised no utterance. The cult master's hissed recitation reached full closure, unchallenged. Arithon felt his consciousness pour into dark, a bright current spilled out of a jar.

Agony milled him. He became a thousand hurled shards of remembrance, vivid as light through stained glass. Wrenched from trued flight by wrists and sealed ankles, he felt *stretched*. A wire filament cranked to the verge of release, he was unable to let go, or snap, but could only be *drawn* and pulled under.

The spirit granted existence within Ath's creation was *of itself* too immutably real to rend from the span of the infinite.

Far off, so far, the Warden of Althain heard the shrill cry of vibration struck off by Arithon's ordeal in Etarra. He listened, knowing the moment was nigh. Anxious, he awaited the word of appeal to enable his Fellowship to react…in Jaelot, drawn tense, Luhaine watched a smiling priest tuck into the banquet on Lysaer's table…while in Darkling, under the dark of the moon, Kharadmon fretted out the delay, tracking another priest who shuddered on his knees, eyes closed for the jolt that presaged an addictive ecstasy…

* * *

Falling...falling...falling...the crux of one instant extended beyond bearing as seizing forces spun their vortex about him. Arithon dwindled into the clutching embrace of the host who inducted him. Strung out of body, stripped of physical senses, only mage-sight recorded his transit as the filament of his essence streamed through the mazing sigils stamped into the bowl. He could not break their grasp. The higher octaves of his awareness had become torn beyond reach.

Below him, the dark chains wrought of symbols and blood, that tethered him to his quivering husk: the naked form strapped to cold stone, now beyond help to release. He existed in terror, suspended, while the weave in spilled liquid winnowed him away, making him as a stranger unto himself.

Arithon fought to recall his beloved. Her features came to him faded, cheeks streaked with reproachful tears. *'Above anyone living, I trust you...'*

Not real: her voice was no more than an echo from memory. His heart's flame stayed shackled. Even Elaira could not reach him, here. No tie to the living might rip him clear: not his grant of permission to Dakar, nor the blood bonding, enacted by oath, made to a Fellowship Sorcerer. All aspects were lashed into subjugation. The imperative seal of Davien's longevity imposed by the Five Centuries Fountain did little more than prolong the dragging torment of transition.

Regret raised still more cries in scalding protest. Most wrenching of these, the death wish of Earl Jieret's deceased war captain: *"Say to Prince Arithon, when the Fellowship Sorcerers crown a s'Ffalenn descendant as Rathain's high king at Ithamon, on that hour, he will not have failed me..."*

Caolle's accusation was hard followed by Jieret's: *'Make me one promise, that after my death you honor my daughter with the same pact you gave me as a child in Strakewood...'*

Swallowed away with the ingested potion, Arithon still sensed the tug of that oathsworn commitment. His grant of protection to Jeynsa s'Valerient remained intact. Initiate master, he *had* set his intent in clean form. His binding cord to her must dissolve on the moment his mangled flesh perished. The incised wax ciphers holding him to the body would be broken once the collection of life force was finished. The necromancer would go on to burn the left husk, or else call forfeit the robbed power he sought to exploit.

Though Jieret's young daughter would escape without taint, no kindly reprieve might erase the ripping trauma of dissolution. First link in a seeded chain of disasters, the fate of the Teir's'Ffalenn at Etarra brushed against her clanbred gift for true vision...

Asleep in the prow of a waterman's craft in swift passage across Daenfal Lake, Jeynsa shocked awake, screaming. The prophetic dream that had broken her rest continued to rake her with gooseflesh. As the boatman's son tried to ease her discomfort, she swiped back her ruffled hair, panting to the raced pound of her pulse.

"No, you can't help me." Arms tucked to her breast, stunned to horrified fury, she shot a glance toward the northern horizon.

No shadow pursued her.

Only white needles of reflected starlight scribed the boat's foaming wake. Terror rode her, regardless. The scene exposed by her clanbred talent had been all too graphically damning: of her realm's crown prince, ringed by the rippling presence of ghosts. Girls, women, and boys, each had been entrapped by the black craft of necromancy.

The kindly boatman importuned her to sleep.

Jeynsa refused. She feared to close her eyes. The crushing dread rode her, that the nightmare just glimpsed in the crypt at Etarra would return to harrow her further. "Just row! Save us from evil, I must reach the shores of West Halla at speed."

Her Sighted dream had laid bare the hideous concern, half-suspected since the clandestine conversation overheard in the camp lodge tent. Past all question, Prince Arithon of Rathain had become seduced by a practicing cultist. Caithdein's successor, Jeynsa's office was plain: charter law forbade unclean works. The gravity of her errand now carried extreme stakes and a desperate urgency…

Lost, Arithon tumbled. Jerked under, then drowned, he thrashed, entangled within his captor's aura. He tasted despair, revolted by the corrupted taint of a life preserved from the grave. The future promised no hope, only desolate suffering to breed madness. Noosed tight, he howled alongside the innocents chained into bondage before him. Immersed in their agony, he could scarcely feel the ephemeral string of connection that linked him to his dying flesh. The actualized thread of selfhood that streamed from the infinite whole and rooted the seat of his being had been drawn too far beyond reach. The shackling hoop invoked by the bowl dismembered every harmonic alignment with the prime life chord. Ensnared by that garrote, he could not cross the gate through the veil, or access the higher mysteries.

Grace was absent. Dignity died. Light dimmed, and joy became a dumb figment. All that he was now existed for naught but to feed a blighting corruption.

Vile wretchedness claimed him: Arithon saw through the black cultist's eyes. He spoke with the creature's rough voice. In words that engendered no music, he recited more lines of ritual. He *was* the pale hand gripping the sacrificial knife to enact the final stroke over the heart. He slavered along with the diseased awareness that would shortly destroy the wax ciphers dribbled over the husk's bleeding limbs on the altar…

At Althain Tower, Sethvir masked his face, while a weeping adept braced his shoulder. Her steady question could not mask her dread, that no earthly recourse might salvage the balance of Athera's signature resonance. "You fear that your crown prince has crossed into irrevocable jeopardy?"

In the mountains of Darkling, observing the enraptured priest, Kharadmon clamped a fierce grip on himself to contain his scalding distress. 'Teir's'Ffalenn! The time to remember your training is now!'

While at Jaelot, a pinpoint vortex of cold nestled inside a candle sconce, even Luhaine's staid temperament cracked. 'Arithon's left his resistance too late! Show us all mercy! The drakes' charge is broken, and we're left foursquare in the breach of a grievous disaster!'

Beyond thought, the shared dread, that the bright weave of the world stood at risk if the heart seed of the last s'Ffalenn prince became severed past reach of a Fellowship intervention…

The bone blade touched the breast of the bard, then scribed the last of the dread ciphers. No whisper rose from stilled lips in protest. The incision seeped, nearly bloodless. By now, the victim's heartbeat had stopped. His nerves ceased to register feeling. Residual sensation had drained out of fingers and toes, though the wax seals still conserved the trapped trace of etheric connection.

Commingled as captive within the gray cultist's aura, Arithon sensed the corpse chill of his abandoned flesh as the creature whose foul practice had stripped him of will laid a splayed palm over the wound on his sternum. Forced symbiote, he shared the chant to unhook the heart spark of his being: the foundational core that guarded his earthly awareness.

Darkness beyond cognizance crushed his self-contained thought, as chant and cipher made contact. The necromancer's power closed in as a prisoning fist. Pinned at the crux, then dragged past the bleak threshold, Arithon melted into the array of knotted sigils that joined every Kralovir necromancer into energetic communion. His suborned shade would suckle the cult in an initiate order of hierarchy: from established master, to consecrate initiate, down to the least servant held under compulsion, and even unto the planted sigils that marked others, hooking them to an unconscious state of potential. The surge as his induction completed was going to recharge the whole web.

Arithon felt the pull of that sucking, dark hunger. Cultists whose practice spanned over millennia yearned toward that moment of sublime euphoria. They hungered to indulge in their forbidden fruit, as piercingly sweet as addiction.

The Kralovir master poised over his conquest with the heart's energy fluttering beneath his spread hand. "Ready yourselves." Anticipation thrilled through him. "Tonight's feast is a rare talent. All my years, I've tasted none like him!"

While Luhaine despaired, and Kharadmon raged, the Warden of Althain braced to enact an outcome of tragic necessity. Yet Arithon's failure foreclosed every planned option. To forestall the corruption of Etarra's armed company, Sethvir would have no choice but to free all the bound shades, and thereby invoke a crown lineage's ending…

The Kralovir master capped his incantation. His claim opened up the linked channel that married him to his brethren, then breached the innermost seal defining his victim's identity. The pent reservoir of the essence streamed forth, the linkage of interlocked sigils blazing with the burgeoning influx of power. Across the continent, in their secretive enclaves, or kneeling alone before ceremonial candles by starlight, his colleagues gasped, caught up, then enveloped in collective surrender as the fresh charge of the induction wrung them dizzy. The flux lit their shared weave as a lyrical bolt, wrought of tuned sound and bright lightning. The sensation burned, a whirling explosion that crested toward climax.

And there, at the crux, struck in fire and light, one word unfurled from a calyx of wardings and invoked the appeal for release:

GRACE!

At Althain Tower, Sethvir cried out. The adept at his side caught his shoulder, then gasped, brought to her knees in winded astonishment. "When did your s'Ffalenn prince touch Paravian presence? Ath's blessing on earth, how did we not notice?"

In Darkling, Kharadmon froze between seconds in time, while Luhaine, in Jaelot, all but ignited the palace on the levin bolt force of struck shock...

For Arithon had not wrought the predicted defense, or drawn on his rights as a crown prince. Instead of the expected, straightforward plea for a Fellowship intercession, this Teir's'Ffalenn had leaned in trust on the victory snatched from his trial within Kewar's maze.

There, on the hour he claimed absolution from the weight of his mortal failings, he had owned his true self in the presence of a living centaur guardian. His cry pealed out now, affirming that heritage, rightfully his by Ath's law.

Aware presence responded. While his defeated will of itself could not cross, or burst through the closed ring of sigils, *he was more than a spirit-tied mote of identity.* Sourced in the infinite, his true Name spanned the arc of creation. The embedded knowing could not be revoked: or the memory, once lifted to knowledge through the gift of Earl Jieret's sacrifice. *He was the land, and the land was his very self.* The prime chord acknowledged no physical boundary: the same forces that knit Athera *herself* underwrote his unencumbered autonomy.

Rock and air, flame and water confirmed the free gift of an unconditional deliverance.

The clay bowl exploded. Spattered dregs splashed the symbols on defiled flesh, breaking gaps in their wrought continuity. The very air burned with sound and light, scalding with a purity to remake the sea tides and the dense span of the firmament.

The master cultist shrieked and dropped his bone knife. Stunned witless, he staggered and fell as the bursting influx reamed through him. Its clean force unraveled all chains of dark sigils. Harmonic resonance snapped the warped ties that forged his parasitic longevity. Unstoppable, the wave surged throughout the cult's web, reaping each far-off member of the Kralovir through the whirlwind of immolation.

Chained spirits winnowed free. Stone and mountain resounded. Water shimmered and rebounded to joy. Stars blazed in exaltation, while the night's breezes laughed in rebirth. Across the five kingdoms, sleepers smiled in dreams. Unicorns flung up their horned heads and tossed their floss manes in astonishment. Within Ath's hostels, stone rang like bronze chimes, as every white-robed adept stood their ground as sounding board for the light.

No cranny or crypt might shelter the Kralovir from the reach of the prime vibration called down. No incursion survived. Across the continent of Paravia, the gray cult's coerced servants broke, weeping, cut free of unwilling bondage. The initiate masters' corrupted flesh crumpled, razed clear of surrogate domination.

While the strapped prince on the stone slab shuddered and breathed, the turning world chimed to the sound of his Name and drew him back into himself.

Summer 5671

Catalyst

The incandescent shout that swept the grand chord lasted for only an instant. Its shimmering deluge of sound and light keyed a rainbow shower of harmonics, then faded. No mortal mind might encompass the infinite arc of its imprint. Yet *every* aware mote of existence responded. All spirit expressed in form and in flesh underwent a moment of blackout, ecstatic reaction.

As the pealing reverberations subsided, initiate talent was first to recover full cognizance. Ath's adepts understood how to access such mystery and spin the exalted stream down into the beauty of manifest dreams. Their circle of peace embraced the influx of dimensional harmony. They channeled the resonance through their sacred groves and captured its pure essence in shimmering form as tree and leaf; as mystery, that welled in the sacred springs; and as the silent movement of animals, knit from the living fabric of dark beyond sight.

From hedge talent to the offspring of old blood clan lineage, whether healer, or seer, or clairvoyant, the spontaneous uprush dazzled the subtle senses. The event shocked the heart to inexpressible joy, then passed like a blanketing plunge from blinding sunshine into deep shade.

Highest in rank, the Koriani Seniors also sensed the burning harmonics, as the mighty crest struck a note of keening sorrow off the wardings that guarded their focus stones. While sisterhouse peeresses demanded an inquiry, distraught sisters scrambled to fill basins, or snatch veiling silk off their dormant crystals to enact an investigative scrying. Caution ruled as they sank into disciplined trance. This riddle's pursuit called for stringent protections, since the hapless lane-watchers, caught by surprise, had all crumpled into an unconscious faint.

An order whose wisdom extended beyond artifice, the Fellowship Sorcerers lived and worked past the bounds of the limited senses. The charge of the dragons forced their choice at the crux: to uphold the compact and guard the parameters essential to Paravian survival. The purge of the Kralovir achieved by Torbrand's descendant demanded a scouring cleanse for completion.

If the windfall gift came at punishing cost, the benefit must not be spurned. Sethvir's earth-sense recorded the site of each fallen cultist, tucked in their hidden crypts and in secretive enclaves across the continent. His appeal summoned both of his discorporate colleagues and assigned them the rigorous list. Before dawn, those husks of corrupt flesh must be burned. White magefire must destroy their scattered remains, down to the least sliver of bone. The ash must be immolated, leaving no trace for some power-blind fool whose ignorance might lead into dabbling.

Kharadmon answered, and streaked out of the cloistered courtyard in Darkling. Behind him, the actinic blast of raw power he unleashed sheared through the breezeless night. Corpse and candles flared up, consumed at one stroke. The slamming report of heat-shocked air showered dew from the flower beds, whose blossoms shivered, unsinged. Though concussion shot cracks through capstones and mortar, not so much as a single loose block tumbled from the mountain citadel's outer curtain wall.

Alarmed sentries shouted, regardless. The ram's horn sounded a blast from the gate keep. While the terrified garrison scurried to take arms, the night watch guarding the central plaza barricaded the guildhall doors. Convinced that their town was beset by dark sorcery, dispatch runners raced through the streets to summon the town's panicked mayor.

In distant Jaelot, before the candles at the avatar's formal banquet stopped shivering, the plump priest touched his breast, overcome by a faint rush of dizziness. His auric field swirled, rearranged by release as the dormant cult sigil burned off in the blaze of harmonic forces. Rocked through a moment of unsteady balance, the man suffered raced pulse and bursting sweat, then a shivering surge of clairvoyance. *Sight unveiled an image of blood in a crypt, and five cowled figures struck down by a burst of uncanny conjury; further, he beheld Raiett Raven and three of Etarra's ranked councilmen killed in their chairs where they met in closed conference...*

If Luhaine was able to damp down the reverberations of aftershock, and arrest the spurious vision's unfolding, he could not prevent the man's horrified shout. Nor could he avert the impact unleashed by the Prince of Rathain's surprise tactic. The Named affirmation of Arithon's being strung through the weft of the world's weave had struck off the inevitable spark from poised flint: the Mistwraith's geas of violence ignited and flared into ungovernable flame.

Lysaer's impassioned cry exhorting a vigorous retaliation against Shadow pealed across the shocked gap in the guests' conversation. "I bring no good news, and tonight's bizarre portent affirms this! The Spinner of Darkness has survived Kewar's mazes! My priest corroborates my affirmation: the creature now works in league with other fell powers to fracture our sworn ties of alliance. Heed my word well! If you fear for your lives, your dread is too small. If you think that your gates and the garrison on your walls can defend, beware! Your striving is as the needle raised against the poised axe. I speak this truth, not to dishearten, nor to raise terror or despair, but to guard your back gate! An ally I held in my highest esteem has been suborned into vile betrayal! For your well-being, for your children's safety, stand with me as I raise my standard to march in redress on the enemy who has turned coat against you…"

Galled by the rising tumult, Luhaine held his ground long enough to ascertain the fat priest's aura had burned clean. Naught else could be tried, short of cold-blooded murder. The backlash damage was already done. The smashed cabal at Etarra, and Darkling's vanished priest, would now inflame the muster already in progress. No salvage might defang the wrathful campaign or disarm the force now hell-bound to descend on the citadel at Alestron.

In accord with Sethvir, and in keeping with the tenets of free will posed by the Major Balance, Luhaine whirled out of Jaelot. Time demanded. He must join forces with his discorporate colleague to uphold the honor of Arithon's accomplishment and eradicate the emptied cadavers left at large by the demise of the Kralovir.

Luhaine arrived on-site at Etarra a split second behind Kharadmon. There, the Light's armed encampment already seethed. Frantic men and shouting officers raced to douse the outbreak of fires set to cleanse the cult's corrupted offshoots. Grooms scrambled to calm panicked horses and uproot the picket lines, while scared foot troops hauled sloshing buckets out of the cistern. Three officer's tents were already ablaze. Their crackling ferocity still sang of the arcane permission that had kindled the wild element. Another blaze smoldered in the palace precinct. Since his colleague's expedient entry had already shorn through the warded stone wall, Luhaine followed suit and nipped through the tumbled gap still showering fragments and dust over the gate keep's breached southern battlement.

'You've never liked stays on your freedom, I realize, but that mannerless assault will scarcely win you the next generation's endearments,' Luhaine accosted. Cold as arctic wind, he threaded through the hysterical servants who rushed toward Raiett Raven's torched audience chamber. The tainted remains of the four men inside were already reduced beyond reach of a meddler's recovery. Though Kharadmon always moved with the speed of a jackal where risk of cult practice ran rampant, tonight's unrestrained touch broke all precedent.

'You'd stall for Davien?' his shade fired back, already arrowed on direct course for the crypt hidden under the cellar. *'Is there a live chick in the henhouse besides? One dead, or twenty, the fox still gets chased.'*

For tonight's upset ran the gamut: *all* of Etarra's Alliance authority was either struck dead, or already reduced to discredited shame at the outset. No roughshod act of additional sabotage could hammer the hornet's nest any harder.

'And anyway,' Kharadmon cracked, before Luhaine huffed in to bore him with a trying lecture, *'if a rank upset here could slow down the Alliance assault on Alestron, I'd wave as many red flags as it took. Turn the bull's charge, we could let savage weather defang any maniac's march through the Skyshiels.'*

Luhaine acceded that grudging point. He kept pace with his colleague's scorching rush, whistling through a locked succession of doors and swooping through the gyre of dust raised in breezed passage down the wine cellar's turnpike stairwell.

No dissembling cover was possible, now. The Kralovir's inroads left too many dead. Each damning account of Etarra's plight would be sent on to Lysaer s'Ilessid. As governor elect, he was lawful authority. His cursed hand would be free to reap chaos. The order forged from the outbreak of mayhem would align hearsay and evidence to further Desh-thiere's design.

'It's the sad case of the pest who harries the pessimist,' Kharadmon stated, morose. *'The prank works too well, and the backfire flattens the starry-eyed spectators caught in between.'*

For the crypt, blasted open, proved empty of life. The stone slab was bare, the burst ropes singed away. Both the Kralovir corpses and the wrenching remains of nine children slaughtered in sacrifice had been scoured from the face of Athera by mage-fire. Arithon Teir's'Ffalenn was gone without trace, since Davien the Betrayer had already acted.

Far under the roots of the Mathorns, beneath the labyrinthine caverns of Kewar, a spark of light sprang into existence inside a parabolic dome of smoothed stone. The mote fell, drifting in airborne descent through the sealed chamber beneath. The vault existed without entry or exit. Its space was a sealed well of silence. But not empty: the glimmer of illumination rinsed the spare face, the silver-and-cinnamon spill of loose hair, then the gold-stitched patterns on the elegant clothes of the Sorcerer whose exhaustive labor had fashioned the uncanny creation.

Davien stood with hands braced on the rim of the reflecting pool that centered the floor underneath. Across his lean fingers and trefoil seal ring, the virgin, black waters welled from the earth's deeps and sheeted over the intricately carved pattern inscribed in the living granite. Opalescent light sprang like flame from the electromagnetic release as the flowing current crossed the mapwork array of linked ciphers.

"Where will you go, Teir's'Ffalenn?" he inquired.

The falling spark shimmered, a stinging imperative.

The Sorcerer sighed. "Could the outcome be different? You knew, once your signature presence responded. The release through the land must unleash Desh-thiere's curse. The muster you feared is already in motion. For better or worse, there's a future. Your half brother won't risk a repeat of the last campaign's tactical blunders. He will smash a fixed target and wring victory from ashes. Alestron and East Halla will salve the pride torn by his former defeat in Daon Ramon."

'No horrors will walk,' the light mote cracked, bitter. *'What choice could have been? You set the stage, knowing: I would author a course that offers clean death, before suffering the spread of a Kralovir abomination.'*

Davien bowed his head. His sleeve rustled as he raised a wet hand. The captive star drifted and settled into his shining, soaked palm. As though contact bit, the Sorcerer's mouth tightened. "Your triumph is written. Whether *or not* you could have saved bloodshed, those fallen now shall receive their clear passage. Daelion's Wheel claims *all* earthly life. Ath's law brooks no exceptions, Teir's'Ffalenn, no matter how savaged your heart."

'Tell the s'Brydion widows, if any survive! You say I have choice?' The held spark bristled challenge. *'Then dispatch me to Alland. I have obligations to allies who swore me a commitment that has been wrecked beyond salvage.'*

The Sorcerer raised his peaked eyebrows. "Healing first, my wild falcon. Fly south, as you wish. Chase your errand in Selkwood, though I warn, you won't find what you seek there."

Davien tipped his cupped hand. The adamant spark of a crown prince's being winnowed free and descended. Falling, it met the black well of the rock pool and winked out of ephemeral existence.

A rainbow shimmer burst forth, streaming a flare of incandescence more brilliant than midwinter's boreal light. The spring's surface gave birth to an image, exact as a mirrored reflection: *of Arithon Teir's'Ffalenn, sprawled naked in starlight on windswept black sand, inside the grand focus ring at Sanpashir.*

Summer 5671

Aftershocks

Sunrise at Jaelot sees the flying departure of six trade galleys, oars driving up spray to speed the Light's redoubled muster of the Alliance towns to raise arms for war against Shadow at Alestron; and while the discovery of unexplained deaths and portentous fires sparks unease across the rest of the continent, Lysaer s'Ilessid boards ship for Varens, to raise his standard upon the East Halla peninsula...

Dakar the Mad Prophet awakens from Davien's enspelled sleep to find Etarra driven to rage over the uncanny fires that have murdered three captains at arms, High Chancellor Raiett Raven, and his highest-ranking town ministers; since no more clan children survive to be saved, and the aged bard has suspiciously vanished, he contacts Sethvir, then hires a post-horse to scorch the road to bear warning back to the clans in Melhalla...

Shown the captured lane imprint of a crown prince's sweeping defeat of the Kralovir, Selidie Prime closets herself for a prescient augury, then rejects the Forthmark peeress's pleading request, that initiate Elaira should be recalled: "No change in her orders. She may resume her lapsed practice of healing only after she meets the terms of her current assignment..."

Story Time Line
What Has Gone Before

Third Age Year:

5637—The half brothers Arithon s'Ffalenn, Master of Shadow, and Lysaer s'Ilessid, gifted with Light, exiled through West Gate, are met as they arrive on Athera by the Fellowship Sorcerer Asandir and Dakar, the Mad Prophet, whose West Gate Prophecy forecast the defeat of the Mistwraith, Desh-thiere, and return of the sunlight that had been lost to Athera for five hundred years.

Arithon meets his beloved, Elaira, who is under a life vow of service to the celibate order of the enchantresses of the Koriathain.

5638—The Mistwraith is contained at Ithamon by Lysaer and Arithon and driven into captivity through their combined powers of light and shadow.

The Fellowship Sorcerers' effort to crown Arithon as High King, and reinstate Rathain's monarchy fails when the Mistwraith places the half brothers under its curse: they will be enemies, bent upon each other's destruction until one or the other lies dead.

War follows. Lysaer, whose cardinal virtue is the s'Ilessid gift of justice, leads a war host ten thousand strong from Etarra against Arithon, who is backed by the clansmen in Strakewood Forest. Lysaer and Etarra lose eight thousand men, and the clans suffer the Massacre at Tal Quorin, when Etarran headhunters destroy their women and children to draw the fighting men into the open. To spare his allies, Arithon is forced to use his mage talent to kill. And in the aftermath of this massive insult to his royal gift of compassion, he loses access to all facets of his trained mastery. Survivors of the debacle made possible by his sacrifice include fourteen young boys, named as Companions, and Earl Jieret, twelve years of age, who becomes Arithon's "shadow behind the throne"—or *caithdein*.

Lysaer returns to Etarra to begin the alliance of town forces against Arithon and court his beloved, Talith.

Arithon apprentices himself to the Masterbard, Halliron, and takes on the disguised persona of Medlir to deny his half brother, and the directive of the curse, a fixed target.

5643—The Fellowship Sorcerers reinstate crown rule in Havish, under High King Eldir. In redress for irresponsible conduct, Dakar the Mad Prophet is assigned to Arithon's protection.

5644—Dakar tries to escape his charge and links up with Halliron and "Medlir" on the westshore, whereupon his scapegrace behavior with town authorities in Jaelot leads to Halliron's death and Arithon's breaking his disguise as Medlir, then achieving the title of Masterbard of Athera.

Arithon relocates down the southcoast, with Dakar's escapades earning him the enmity of the powerful clan family of Duke Bransian s'Brydion of Alestron.

Elaira receives her longevity from the Koriani Order for the purpose of keeping track of Arithon, since the sisterhood considers him a danger.

Lysaer solidifies his alliance of town interests, rebuilds the ruined citadel at Avenor, marries Talith, and begins his maneuvers to claim ancestral title to rulership of Tysan.

Against the climate of building war, Arithon founds a shipyard in the fishing village of Merior, where he constructs blue-water sailing vessels with intent to escape to sea. He meets and befriends two fatherless twin children, Fiark and Feylind. He encounters Elaira, under orders from her Prime to involve herself in Arithon's affairs. Their affection deepens when a joint attempt to heal an injured fisherman creates an empathic link between them.

5645—Lysaer leads a war host to Rathain, with intent to sail south and crush Arithon in the fishing village of Merior. But Arithon hears, and uses wiles and shadow to trigger the Mistwraith's curse beforetime. Inflamed to insane rage, Lysaer burns the fleet he intended to transport his war host, leaving his campaign stranded and delaying his assault through the winter.

Arithon's escape plan suffers a setback when a rancorous, displaced field captain from Alestron burns his shipyard at Merior, with only one vessel left fit to be salvaged.

5646—On the run as war builds, Arithon takes refuge in the strategically difficult terrain in Vastmark. Faced by a war host and impossible odds, he takes Lysaer's wife Talith captive to stall the onset of open war.

5647—Talith is ransomed by Lysaer, under auspice of the Fellowship Sorcerers and High King Eldir. Although she is safely returned, the experience leaves an irreparable rift in her marriage.

Lysaer masses his war host, thirty-five thousand strong, and marches on Arithon's smaller force in Vastmark. Arithon resorts to desperate measures to turn them, including the Massacre at the Havens, in which five hundred of Lysaer's men are killed outright. The tactic fails, and is followed by the main engagement at Dier Kenton Vale, in which twenty thousand Alliance troops die in one day in a shale slide.

The campaign fails at the onset of winter, with Duke Bransian s'Brydion of Alestron changing sides and forging a covert alliance with Arithon.

Faced with a ruinous defeat, Lysaer decides to create a faith-based following and cast Arithon as evil incarnate.

Arithon escapes to sea to search for the lost Paravian races, who, as Ath's gift to redeem the world, offer hope he might break the Mistwraith's curse. Feylind sails as his navigator, and Fiark is apprenticed with a merchant factor in the town of Innish.

The Prime Matriarch of the Koriani Order casts an augury showing that Arithon will cause her downfall. Since she is aging and has only one flawed candidate in line for her succession, and her death will cause an irreparable loss of the sisterhood's knowledge, she becomes Arithon's inveterate enemy.

Still in love with Arithon, Elaira saves the life of an infant during childbirth in the grasslands of Araethura. Named Fionn Areth, he owes her a life debt, and a prophecy entangles him with Arithon's fate.

Back at Avenor to rebuild his following, Lysaer sets the clanborn who refuse to join his alliance to eradicate the Master of Shadow under a decree of slavery. His estrangement with Talith leads to her incarceration.

5648—9—For endorsing slave labor, Lysaer is cast out of the Fellowship's compact, which allows Mankind the right to inhabit Athera.

5649—The Prime Matriarch of the Koriathain confronts the Fellowship Sorcerers to lift restrictions imposed on her sisterhood and the use of their grand focus in their Waystone. The petition meets with refusal, sealing her determination to take Arithon captive and use him as leverage to force the Sorcerers to accede to her order's demands.

5652—Arithon fails in his search for the Paravians. He returns to the continent and discovers Lysaer is enslaving the clanborn. This leads him to infiltrate Lysaer's shipyard at Riverton, to steal vessels and assist the clansmen in their effort to escape the persecution of Lysaer's Alliance by fleeing to sanctuary in Havish.

5652—3—The Prime Matriarch of the Koriathain sets a trap to take Arithon by suborning his covert colleagues at the Riverton shipworks, only to have her grand plan undone by ambitious meddling on the part of her sole candidate for succession, Lirenda. The trap springs, but Arithon escapes into a grimward, chased by a company of men allied with Lysaer, under the captaincy of Sulfin Evend.

5653—Lysaer's wife Talith is murdered by a covert conspiracy in his own council, with her death made to appear as a suicide. Sulfin Evend survives the grimward and is appointed to the rank of Alliance Commander at Arms.

The Koriathain fail to forge an alliance with Lysaer against Arithon, and in disgrace for her meddling, Lirenda decides to use the life debt owed by Fionn Areth to Elaira. The child is shapechanged to mature as Arithon's double, to be used as bait in a second, more elaborate trap to achieve his capture.

5654—Of their own accord, the Duke's s'Brydion brothers, against Arithon's better judgment, decide to avenge the mishap at Riverton. When their argument leads to injury, Arithon is awarded the service of two trusted s'Brydion retainers, Vhandon and Talvish.

5654—Lysaer marries Lady Ellaine as a political expedient. On the day of the wedding, the s'Brydion vengeance plan destroys Lysaer's fleet and his shipyard at Riverton. Sulfin Evend's uncle, Raiett Raven, joins

Alliance service as Lysaer's advisor and is eventually appointed as High Chancellor of Etarra.

5655—Lysaer and Ellaine's child, Prince Kevor, is born.

5667—Ellaine learns that her predecessor, Princess Talith, died as a victim of murder, arranged by Lysaer's council at Avenor.

5669—The Koriani plot to trap Arithon using Fionn Areth sends the boy into the town of Jaelot, where he is taken and condemned to death, mistaken for the Master of Shadow. Arithon is drawn ashore to prevent the death of an innocent accused in his stead. On winter solstice day, Fionn Areth is snatched from the scaffold. The Koriani conspiracy fails, with Lirenda disgraced and Elaira exonerated.

Now desperate and dying, with no available successor, the Prime Matriarch seizes her moment and distracts the Fellowship Sorcerers by inciting a sweeping upset of the energetic balance of the world. Although she fails to take Arithon captive, she successfully resolves her predicament by taking over a younger candidate, Selidie, in possession. As "Selidie" assumes the mantle of Prime power, the Sorcerers' hands are tied. The upset has left the Mistwraith itself on the verge of escaping from containment, and other, equally dangerous predators left by the absent Paravian races pose further perils.

As the terrifying portents unleashed by Morriel's meddling cause sweeping panic, young Prince Kevor settles the riot that erupts in Lysaer's absence at Avenor. The brilliant statesmanship earns the young prince the love of the populace and the undying enmity of Lysaer's High Priest, Cerebeld.

5670—Fionn Areth's idealistic belief that Arithon is a criminal spoils the free escape from Jaelot. Alone, under pursuit by Alliance troops and Koriathain, Arithon is set to flight over the mountains and into Daon Ramon Barrens.

Young Prince Kevor is entrapped by the machinations of High Priest Cerebeld, and although he survives to become an adept of Ath's Brotherhood, his presumed death sends his mother Ellaine into flight to escape Lysaer's corrupt council at Avenor.

While Dakar and Fionn Areth are diverted to Rockfell Peak to assist the shorthanded Fellowship Sorcerers' recontainment of the Mistwraith, the clans of Rathain, under Jieret, are left to face the combined Alliance war host, under command of Lysaer and Sulfin Evend. With their help, Arithon escapes the troop cordon that has closed to take him, but at cost of seven Companions' lives and Jieret's capture and execution by Lysaer.

To evade capture, Arithon is driven into the dread maze under Kewar cavern, built by the Sorcerer Davien the Betrayer, whose hand originally caused the uprising that unseated the high kings and heated the conflict between town and clanborn. Arithon survives the arduous challenge of the maze, achieves mastery over the Mistwraith's curse, and recovers his mage talent. He takes sanctuary there, under guest welcome of Davien.

Defeated, since none dare follow Arithon's passage through the maze, Lysaer and the disheartened remains of his troop depart for Avenor.

After the successful reconfiguration of the wards containing the Mistwraith, Dakar and Fionn Areth resume their trip south to rendezvous with Feylind's ship, with intent to sail and rejoin Arithon's retainers, Vhandon and Talvish, who await them at Duke Bransian's citadel at Alestron. The year is Third Age Year 5670.

Appendix

Blood Heritage of the Royal Families

The five royal lines of Athera were originally selected by the Paravians, with each of the original founders chosen for a dominant gift of character.

> Torbrand s'Ffalenn, High King of Rathain—Compassion
> Halduin s'Ilessid, High King of Tysan—Justice
> Cindra s'Ahelas, High Queen of Shand—Farsight
> Bwin Evoc s'Lornmein, High King of Havish—Temperance
> Rondeil s'Ellestrion, High King of Melhalla—Wisdom

Each of these individuals gave their willing consent to accept the directive to rule, both for themselves, and for all of their future offspring for as long as their lineage should survive in participation with Athera's destiny. No distinction was made between matrilineal or patrilineal lines of descent; both were equally favored. The Fellowship Sorcerers used the initiate magic acquired from the dragons to fix these traits of character as an imperative geas, transferable through all subsequent issue. The prominence of this endowment was not passed on in a linear fashion. The gifts manifest in a "spread" that seeks outlet through all available blood descendents of the original forebear. Heritability does not pass in equal measure, but flows forward like water, seeking the easiest channel for expression. Descendents who display a natural leaning in character will "inherit"—or more correctly enact—the gift more intensely than others whose personalities bend in opposing directions. The wider the pool of descendents, the more "choice" of channel the royal gift will have to seek outlet. For this reason, direct blood descent is never the determinant factor, but rather, which descendant portrays the most emphatic stamp of the progenitor's qualities.

The more descendents there are, the less predetermined the course of the inheritance. Some individuals may show predominance. Others might show little trace, or even none, although all living offspring within the lineage will carry the latent range of the geas' fullest potential.

Where a lineage is sparse, or only one descendent remains, the full force of the royal gift will flow through that individual, and be expressed with indelible emphasis.

This is why the line of descent varies, and may move freely between cousins, or skip generations, and why, without exception, the Fellowship Sorcerers are charged to Name and sanction each crown successor.

To conclude, the degree to which a royal gift expresses is twofold: inherited potency (how many descendents are living to "carry" the trait) combined with the factor of personal choice, that arises as personal character: how each individual is inclined toward their particular forebear's gift in the first place.

In the case of a lone descendent born with a personality not favorably inclined, the gift must still express. That individual would struggle, at odds with the inborn drive, and threshed by internal conflict. For this reason, many offspring and a wide extended family became an imperative preference for royal lines.

The High Kings who ruled during Paravian times had shorter reigns, provided there were sufficient progeny to support an early retirement. Crown office was extremely rigorous—many died young. Some reigned only a month or a year or two—others for a matter of days. A few hardy individuals held the throne for several decades, all dependent on how well, or how many times, they sustained the call to enact a direct liaison with the Paravians. Their perceptions were often dramatically altered after such encounter(s). The strength by which each individual king could surmount the changes varied widely.

Succession of Crown Candidates and *Caithdeinen*

By terms of the compact, the Fellowship of Seven must Name a crown candidate. Any one Sorcerer's innate perception is deep enough, and wide enough, to make such an assessment based upon probability. The task is most often handled by Asandir, as his natural aptitude for executive action makes him the preeminent Sorcerer to serve in the field.

The Crown Prince's appointment is never automatic, and does not pass by direct descent. Nor do kings or any other office decreed by crown charter hold their seats until death—(Unlike town mayors, who are elected or selected by town council, but then rule for life term.) Royal lineages are not replaceable. They cannot be transplanted from another kingdom's bound line of descent, as the Paravians matched each forebear in resonant accord with the needs of the specific crown territories.

Provided that there are multiple blood relations, including cousins, to select from, the choice follows two factors: first, individual strength of character; and second, the quality of "natural calling"—this being any candidate (without bias toward male or female)—who displays the best aptitude for the post. Thus, if Arithon s'Ffalenn had possessed more than one relative, he may have passed the character requirement, but his natural calling as musician and initiate master may not have been deemed harmonious to the post. A cousin or relation of strong character, but who displayed more aptitude for the throne (by personal preference finding fulfillment and contentment in the position of arbitration) may have been chosen instead.

The heritable traits of Athera's crown lineages do not *ever* transfer to *caithdeinen* if a last royal linebearer should die without issue. *Caithdeinen* do administer crown justice in the absence of the king, and this may be an ongoing responsibility if crown rule has passed into a permanent state of stewardship. In this novel's historical setting, this only occurred in Melhalla since the last s'Ellestrion heir died childless. In such a case, succession of that realm's *caithdeinen* will now become Fellowship chosen.

Caithdeinen, or crown stewards, who stand behind a living royal heir are selected for character and for the ability to think independently. In times of peace, under a crowned High King, they would have been selected from a picked lineage, which could change with times and circumstance. The candidate would be suited to know their crown ruler well, and have the courage to draw clear and honest conclusions. This post would not suit a sycophantic personality, for example.

Proposed successors for *caithdeinen*, and other charter seats are usually 'designate.' This term denotes a conditional appointment, bestowed by a council of elders. (Kyrialt s'Taleyn was designate for Shand, as Ianfar s'Gannley now is to Tysan.) An heir designate will inherit *unless* the choice is overruled upon proven grounds of incapacity. The appointment also can be upset by either a crowned High King (who would possess the requisite power of insight acquired through four attuned initiations) or a Fellowship Sorcerer's direct word. Such a ruling would occur prior to, or during the ceremony of investiture, where such an authority would be present. An heir chosen by Fellowship auspice automatically becomes invested without question. The investment ceremony then becomes a formality, wherein oath is sworn to uphold the post. Jeynsa s'Valerient, therefore, owns the power of her office by default—she has but to claim the responsibility.

A Fellowship Sorcerer only executes the selection of a *caithdein* if the existing royal lineage should be actively threatened. In this manner, if the crown succession fails, that *caithdein* would stand steward for the throne in fact.

Particulars of Clan Heritage

All old blood lineages were determined by the Paravians at the time Mankind accepted the terms of the compact, yet the "system" was not closed, and not every family assumed the same function. Some lineages stood for land rule—these guarded the interface between humanity and the Paravians. These individuals possessed Sighted vision or natural talent enough to be charged with protection and preservation of the boundaries of the free wilds.

Other family lines were selected for adamant traits of character. These generally governed a town-based seat, and administered directly to human affairs in those areas where Mankind was free to live with least oversight. Sometimes land rule and town governance were held as dual functions. Checks and balances within the charter system were designed to thwart private concerns and blind ambition from degrading the compact's intent: to hold Athera's great mysteries, which are essential to Paravian survival, in balance with human activity.

Clan seats held solely for governance would rule from a keep town without a focus circle—these were not located within the designate bounds of the free wilds, and were the backbone of charter law before the uprising incited by Davien. They administered the king's justice in accord with those lineages holding the land rule.

The crown was the voice of land rule, and governance, under the charter written by the Fellowship Sorcerers. The sanctioned High Kings enacted the firsthand liaison with the Paravians, and were the protectorate for the free wilds. They presented the petitions to the Centaur guardians, then executed the final arbitration, as the agents of the Fellowship's compact. They appealed, and enacted Paravian decree, concerning what could and could not be altered to preserve the overall harmony of the land's mysteries.

Each child born into clan lineage was subject to testing at each generation through the trial of Paravian presence. This testing could be refused, in which case, the candidate would revoke his charge to interact with the free wilds. A town born individual could undergo the same test by free will choice. In rare cases this would occur, and a new lineage might arise from one candidate—just as an older, established lineage might become degraded, weaken and fail. Lacking Paravian presence, in recent generations the determinant factor has blurred. By the time of this novel's setting, the range of human talent cannot be identified with such definitive accuracy. Those individuals with latent or weakened talent are no longer able to prove out the direct function of heritable lineage. Thus, a "talent deaf" town born will see no apparent reason why the free wilds should not be considered another ripe acre of earth, ready for exploitation. Nor would such a person recognize why the old blood traits were not arbitrary politics.

The prolonged absence of the Paravians now has created a schism that is growing increasingly difficult for each side to reconcile. The non-talented individuals do not discern the wider perceptions of their clan born fellows. They see no convincing case left for the restraints imposed by the lapsed system of charter law. There is no such division of interests between the old blood lines and those who still follow charter law, since the underlying reason for the Fellowship's restrictions is still actively recognized.

The Designate Free Wilds, and Execution of the Compact

At the forming of the compact, which defined the terms for Mankind's permission to take sanctuary on Athera, the Fellowship Sorcerers had dispatched or contained the worst of the drake spawn. Paravians were in fact leaving their Second Age fortifications, which were tied to the web of Athera's mysteries by means of the focus circles. These structures are intersect points—connections that link the resonant flow between sites that comprise Athera's most exquisitely sensitive ground. The human families required immediate shelter. Those arrivals who already possessed the requisite awareness to inhabit a fortified circle, or who had talent that could be heightened to flower in proximity to such places were appointed charge of them.

The initial grants named in Third Age Year One went to individuals with the strongest heritable family traits—those born talents already able to perceive within the necessary range to handle the guiding purpose of their guardianship. These rulers also were charged to hold sacrosanct the high resonance land that could not be disturbed by any human activity. These areas were designated as sacrosanct areas deep inside the free wilds. Markers were set forth by the Centaur guardians delineating sectors where Mankind was not entitled to trespass.

Other acreage was not so critically reactive. There, new towns were built for those who had less natural "tolerance" for the higher resonance state of the original Second Age sites. Such land was given over to agriculture and roads in allotments generous enough to allow Mankind to raise children and survive. The governing seats for these settlements had an elected council, presided over by a family lineage chosen for tenacity of character more than aware talent. These seats were appended following Third Age Year One. Here, humanity had license to keep their affairs as they wished, based upon certain precepts laid down by charter right to inhabit that territory. Alestron fell into this category. So did Hanshire. A mixed population lived in these subsidiary towns. The least sensitive people found most comfort in the smaller villages and tended to choose areas furthest from the free wilds.

Therefore, to a certain degree, acclimation to the higher resonance sites determined who came to live where, and who was comfortable setting down roots in each particular locale. This tended to isolate the older lineages to a degree—with marriages evolving with the need to raise a next generation of children able to manage the duties defined by the compact. Mixed bloodlines tended to fail more often, and parents were understandably protective of their offspring's chances of a successful 'testing' against the Paravian presence. Records were kept to track the tried lineages, and note the most favorable crosses.

While the general population in the towns were not inclined toward the traits of expanded awareness, it must be noted: the intuitive propensity to perceive is inherent in all of Mankind. Whether the quality remains latent depends upon how each individual aligns their focus and lifestyle.

Latent gifts of any kind can be awakened. Dormant awareness can be raised through training and initiation. Few town born voluntarily choose such a course, unless pushed by circumstance to change. Most might view the arduous study, and the disorientation of learning to adjust to such an expansion an uncomfortable process. Encounter with a living Paravian was powerful enough to incite an accelerated shift by resonance. Yet the change could shove human perception too far, too fast, and leave what appeared to be a husk with a broken mind. Living amid the free wilds also enhances perception—as would time spent in close proximity to a focus circle, provided that buildings and the life patterns of the surrounding inhabitants did not interfere too much with the delicate frequency of the lane flow.

Throughout the course of the early Third Age, mankind tended to clump into enclaves of greater or lesser sensitivity. Over time, this caused the old lines to strengthen their innate talent, while the less gifted ones devolved to a lower threshold of sensitivity. As centuries passed, half the population came to view the precepts defined by the Fellowship's compact as rote rules without meaning. The factual foundation was forgotten, then lost, lying outside the range of sensory awareness the town born population understood.

For this reason, most Second Age sites fell to ruin after the uprising. (Jaelot being a rare exception). Town born alive now avoid such places, since crossing the free wilds, or traveling the forbidden ways, or spending time within an old ruins, will alter human perception by resonance.

Throughout Third Age history, there was no social strata, or concept of "nobility" attached to any old lineage gift. Nor was there any stigma attached to the town born without access to active talent. The cultural boundaries were not fixed, but fluid, defined case by case through choice and perceptual awareness. Blood inheritance is not a predetermined prerequisite. Yet without risking comparative insanity, a town born who set out to develop such enhanced sensitivity would require a gradual initiation to assimilate the shift.

GLOSSARY

A'BREND'AIA—the polite word for making love "the lyrical dance."

> pronounced: a-bren-day-ee-yah
>
> root meaning: *a'brend'aia*—the dynamic balance of yin and yang

ADRUIN—coastal city located in East Halla, Melhalla. Enemy of Alestron, usually over the issue of blockades at the harbor mouth leading to the Cildein Ocean.

> pronounced: add-ruin
>
> root meaning: *al*—over; *duinn*—hand

AIYENNE—river located in Daon Ramon, Rathain, rising from an underground spring in the Mathorn Mountains, and coming above ground south of the Mathorn Road.

> pronounced: eye-an
>
> root meaning: *ai'an*—hidden one

ALESTRON—city located in Midhalla, Melhalla. Ruled by Duke Bransian, Teir's'Brydion, and his three brothers. This city did not fall to merchant townsmen in the Third Age uprising that threw down the high kings, but is still ruled by its clanblood heirs.

> pronounced: ah-less-tron
>
> root meaning: *alesstair*—stubborn; *an*—one

ALITHIEL—one of twelve Blades of Isaer, forged by centaur Ffereton s'Darian from metal taken from a meteorite. Passed through Paravian possession, acquired the secondary name Dael-Farenn, or Kingmaker, since its owners tended to succeed the end of a royal line. Eventually was awarded to Kamridian s'Ffalenn for his valor in defense of the princess Taliennse, early Third Age. Currently in the possession of Arithon.

> pronounced: ah-lith-ee-el
>
> root meaning: *alith*—star; *iel*—light/ray

ALLAND—principality located in southeastern Shand. Ruled by the Lord Erlien s'Taleyn, High Earl, and appointed *caithdein* of Shand.

> pronounced: all-and
>
> root meaning: *a'lind*—pine glen

ALTHAIN TOWER—spire built at the edge of the Bittern Desert, beginning of the Second Age, to house records of Paravian histories. Third Age, became repository for the archives of all five royal houses of men after rebellion, overseen by the Fellowship Sorcerer, Sethvir, named Warden of Althain since Third Age Year 5100.

> pronounced: all-thay-in
>
> root meaning: *alt*—last; *thein*—tower, sanctuary
>
> original Paravian pronunciation: alt-thein

ANGLEFEN—marsh located in Deshir, Rathain. Also a port town that links the sea routes to Etarra.

>pronounced: angle fen

>root meaning not from the Paravian

ANIENT—Paravian invocation for unity.

>pronounced: an-ee-ent

>root meaning: *an*—one; *ient*—suffix for "most"

ARAETHURA—grass plains in southwest Rathain; principality of the same name in that location. Largely inhabited by Riathan Paravians in the Second Age. Third Age, used as pastureland by widely scattered nomadic shepherds. Fionn Areth's birthplace.

>pronounced: ar-eye-thoo-rah

>root meaning: *araeth*—grass; *era*—place, land

ARITHON—son of Avar, Prince of Rathain, 1,504th Teir's'Ffalenn after founder of the line, Torbrand in Third Age Year One. Also Master of Shadow, the Bane of Desh-thiere, and Halliron Masterbard's successor.

>pronounced: ar-i-thon

>root meaning: *arithon*—fate-forger; one who is visionary

ARWENT—river in Araethura, Rathain, that flows from Daenfal Lake through Halwythwood to empty in Instrell Bay.

>pronounced: are-went

>root meaning: *arwient*—swiftest

ASANDIR—Fellowship Sorcerer. Secondary name, Kingmaker, since his hand crowned every High King of Men to rule in the Age of Men (Third Age). After the Mistwraith's conquest, he acted as field agent for the Fellowship's doings across the continent. Also called Fiend-quencher, for his reputation for quelling iyats; Storm-breaker and Change-bringer for his past actions when Men first arrived upon Athera.

>pronounced: ah-san-deer

>root meaning: *asan*—heart; *dir*—stone "heartrock"

ATAINIA—northeastern principality of Tysan.

>pronounced: ah-tay-nee-ah

>root meaning: *itain*—the third; *ia*—suffix for "third domain" original Paravian, *itainia*

ATCHAZ—town located in Alland, Shand. Famed for its silk.

>pronounced: at-chaz

>root meaning: *atchias*—silk

ATH CREATOR—prime vibration, force behind all life.

>pronounced: ath

>root meaning: *ath*—prime, first (as opposed to an, one)

ATHERA—name for the world which holds the Five High Kingdoms; four Worldsend Gates; formerly inhabited by dragons, and current home of the Paravian races.

pronounced: ath-air-ah

root meaning: *ath*—prime force; *era*—place "Ath's world"

ATHIR—Second Age ruin of a Paravian stronghold, located in Ithilt, Rathain. Site of a seventh lane power focus; also where Arithon Teir's'Ffalenn swore his blood oath to survive to the Fellowship Sorcerer, Asandir.

pronounced: ath-ear

root meaning: *ath*—prime; *i'er*—the line/edge

ATHLIEN PARAVIANS—sunchildren. Small race of semimortals, pixielike, but possessed of great wisdom/keepers of the grand mystery.

pronounced: ath-lee-en

root meaning: *ath*—prime force; *lien*—to love "Ath-beloved"

ATHLIERIA—equivalent of heaven/actually a dimension removed from physical time/space, or the exalted that lies past the veil.

pronounced: ath-lee-air-ee-ah

root meaning: *ath*—prime force; *li'eria*—exalted place, with suffix for "beyond the veil."

AVENOR—Second Age ruin of a Paravian stronghold. Traditional seat of the s'Ilessid High Kings. Restored to habitation in Third Age 5644. Became the ruling seat of the Alliance of Light in Third Age 5648. Located in Korias, Tysan.

pronounced: ah-ven-or

root meaning: *avie*—stag; *norh*—grove

BAIYEN GAP—the trail built by the centaur guardians through the pass that crosses the Skyshiel Mountains, connecting the Eltair coast to Daon Ramon Barrens. Twice the site of a drake battle, once between rivals in the Age of Dragons, and again, in the First Age, against a pack of greater drake spawn. One of the old rights of way, not open to mankind's use.

pronounced: bye-yen

root meaning: *bayien*-slag

BARACH—second son of Jieret s'Valerient, and older brother of Jeynsa. Successor to the title, Earl of the North.

pronounced: bar-ack

root meaning: *baraich*-linchpin

BARISH—town located just north of the border of Tysan, on the coast of Mainmere Bay.

pronounced: bar ish

root meaning: *bar*-half; *ris*-way

BIEDAR—desert tribe living in Sanpashir, Shand. Also known as the Keepers of the Prophecy. Their sacred weaving at the well produced the conception of Dari s'Ahelas, which crossed the old *caithdein*'s lineage of s'Dieneval with the royal line of s'Ahelas, combining the gifts of prophetic clairvoyance with the Fellowship-endowed penchant for farsight.

> pronounced: bee-dar
>
> root meaning: *biehdahrr*—ancient desert dialect for "lore keepers"

BITTERN DESERT—waste located in Atainia, Tysan, north of Althain Tower. Site of a First Age battle between the great drakes and the Seardluin, permanently destroyed by dragonfire.

> pronounced: bittern
>
> root meaning: *bityern*—to sear or char

BRAGGEN—one of the fourteen Companions, who were the only children to survive the battle fought between Deshir's clansmen and the war host of Etarra beside the River Tal Quorin in Third Age Year 5638.

> pronounced: brag-en
>
> root meaning: *briocen*-surly

BRANSIAN s'BRYDION—Teir's'Brydion, ruling Duke of Alestron.

> pronounced: bran-see-an
>
> root meaning: *brand*-temper; *s'i'an*—suffix denoting "of the one"/the one with temper

CAINFORD—town located in Taerlin, Tysan.

> pronounced: cane-ford
>
> root meaning: *caen*-vale

CAITH-AL-CAEN—vale where Riathan Paravians (unicorns) celebrated equinox and solstice to renew the *athael*, or life-destiny of the world. Also the place where the Ilitharis Paravians first Named the winter stars—or encompassed their vibrational essence into language. Corrupted by the end of the Third Age to Castlecain.

> pronounced: cay-ith-al-cay-en, musical lilt, emphasis on second and last syllables; rising note on first two, falling note on last two.
>
> root meaning: *caith*—shadow; *al*—over; *caen*—vale "vale of shadow"

CAITHDEIN—(alternate spelling *caith'd'ein*, plural form *caithdeinen*) Paravian name for a high king's first counselor; also, the one who would stand as regent, or steward, in the absence of the crowned ruler. By heritage, the office also carries responsibility for oversight of crown royalty's fitness to rule.

> pronounced: kay-ith-day-in
>
> root meaning: *caith*—shadow; *d'ein*—behind the chair "shadow behind the throne"

CAITHWOOD—forest located in Taerlin, southeast principality of Tysan.

> pronounced: kay-ith-wood

root meaning: *caith*—shadow—shadowed wood

CALUM KINCAID—the individual who invented the great weapon that destroyed the worlds of humanity and caused the refugee faction, including the Koriathain, to seek sanctuary on Athera.

    pronounced: calum kin-cade

    not from an Atheran language

CAMRIS—north-central principality of Tysan. Original ruling seat was the city of Erdane.

    pronounced: cam-ris

    root meaning: *caim*—cross; *ris*—way "crossroad"

CAOLLE—past war captain of the clans of Deshir, Rathain. First raised by, and then served under, Lord Steiven, Earl of the North and *caithdein* of Rathain. Planned the campaign at Vastmark and Dier Kenton Vale for the Master of Shadow. Served Jieret Red-beard, and was feal liegeman of Arithon of Rathain; died of complications from a wound received from his prince while breaking a Koriani attempt to trap his liege in Third Age Year 5653.

    pronounced: kay-all-eh, with the "e" nearly subliminal

    root meaning: *caille*—stubborn

CAPEWELL—town located on the south shore of Korias, Tysan. Home of a major Koriani sisterhouse.

CARITHWYR—principality in Havish, once a grasslands breeding ground for the Riathan Paravians. Now produces grain, cattle, fine hides, and also wine.

    pronounced: car-ith-ear

    root meaning: *ci'arithiren*—forgers of the ultimate link with prime power. An old colloquialism for unicorn.

CASCAIN ISLANDS—rugged chain of islands off the coast of Vastmark, Shand.

    pronounced: cass-canes

    root meaning: *kesh kain*—shark's teeth

CATTRICK—master joiner hired to run the royal shipyard at Riverton; once in Arithon's employ at Merior by the Sea, now shipwright for Duke Bransian s'Brydion at Alestron.

    pronounced: cat-rick

    root meaning: *ciattiaric*—a knot tied of withies that has the magical property of confusing enemies

CEREBELD—Avenor's High Priest of the Light, formerly Lord Examiner of Avenor.

    pronounced: cara-belld

    root meaning: *ciarabeld*—ashes

CIENN—clan scout and Companion in Earl Jieret s'Valerient's war band, smith who shod their horses; died in the battle on Daon Ramons, Third Age

Year 5670.

> pronounced: kee-in
>
> root meaning: *cian*—spark

CIANOR SUNLORD—born at Caith-al-Caen, First Age Year 615. Crowned High King of Athera in Second Age Year 2545, until his death when a rise of Khadrim called him to war in Second Age 3651. He is the only Paravian in history to have a namesake, more properly termed a *tiendar'shayn'd* or "reborn." Cianor Moonlord was birthed at the darkest hour of the Second Age. He was still at hand in Third Age Year One to assist when the Fellowship Sorcerers wrote the compact that enabled Mankind to receive sanctuary on Athera. It was his hand that bestowed the sword Alithiel upon Kamridian s'Ffalenn.

CILADIS THE LOST—Fellowship Sorcerer who left the continent in Third Age 5462 in search of the Paravian races after their disappearance following the rebellion.

> pronounced: kill-ah-dis
>
> root meaning: *cael*—leaf; *adeis*—whisper, compound; *cael'adeis* colloquialism for "gentleness that abides"

CILDEIN OCEAN—body of water lying off Athera's east coast.

> pronounced: kill-dine
>
> root meaning: *cailde*—salty; *an*—one

CILDORN—city famed for carpets and weaving, located in Deshir, Rathain. Originally a Paravian holdfast, situated on a node of the third lane.

> pronounced: kill-dorn
>
> root meaning: *cieal*—thread; *dorn*—net "tapestry"

CORITH—island west of Havish in the Westland Sea. Site of an old drake lair, and a ruined First Age foundation. Here the council of Paravians convened during seige, and their appeal brought the Second Dreaming by dragons, which enacted the summoning of the seven who became the Fellowship Sorcerers.

> pronounced: core-ith
>
> root meaning: *cori*—ships, vessels; *itha*—five

CRUIK—an old form of architecture, wherein living trees are molded to become structural support for a building, which is constructed around them.

DAELION FATEMASTER—"entity" formed by set of mortal beliefs, which determine the fate of the spirit after death. If Ath is the prime vibration, or life force, Daelion is what governs the manifestation of free will.

> pronounced: day-el-ee-on
>
> root meaning: *dael*—king, or lord; *i'on*—of fate

DAELION'S WHEEL—cycle of life and the crossing point that is the transition into death.

> pronounced: day-el-ee-on

root meaning: *dael*—king or lord; *i'on*—of fate

DAENFAL LAKE—located on the northern lakeshore that bounds the southern edge of Daon Ramon Barrens in Rathain.

pronounced: dye-en-fall

root meaning: *daen*—clay; *fal*—red

DAKAR THE MAD PROPHET—apprentice to Fellowship Sorcerer, Asandir, during the Third Age following the Conquest of the Mistwraith. Given to spurious prophecies, it was Dakar who forecast the fall of the Kings of Havish in time for the Fellowship to save the heir. He made the Prophecy of West Gate, which forecast the Mistwraith's bane, and also, the Black Rose Prophecy, which called for reunification of the Fellowship. At this time, in the service of Arithon, Prince of Rathain.

pronounced: dah-kar

root meaning: *dakiar*—clumsy

DANIA—wife of Rathain's former *caithdein*, Steiven s'Valerient. Died by the hand of Pesquil's headhunters in the Battle of Strakewood, Third Age 5638; Jieret Red-beard's mother.

pronounced: dan-ee-ah

root meaning: *deinia*—sparrow

DAON RAMON BARRENS—central principality of Rathain. Site where Riathan Paravians (unicorns) bred and raised their young. Barrens was not appended to the name until the years following the Mistwraith's conquest, when the River Severnir was diverted at the source by a task force under Etarran jurisdiction.

pronounced: day-on-rah-mon

root meaning: *daon*—gold; *ramon*—hills/downs

DARI S'AHELAS—crown heir of Shand who was sent to safety through West Gate to preserve the royal lineage. Born following the death of the last Crown Prince of Shand, subsequently raised and taught by Sethvir to manage the rogue talent of a dual inheritance. Her mother was Meiglin s'Dieneval, last survivor of the old *caithdein*'s lineage of Melhalla, which was widely believed to have perished during the massacre at Tirans. However the pregnant widow of Egan s'Dieneval had escaped the uprising and survived under a false name in a Durn brothel.

pronounced: dar-ee

root meaning: *daer*—to cut

DARKLING—city located on the western side of the Skyshiel Mountains in the Kingdom of Rathain.

pronounced: dark-ling

root meaning: *dierk-linng*—drake eyrie

DAVIEN THE BETRAYER—Fellowship Sorcerer responsible for provoking the great uprising in Third Age Year 5018, that resulted in the fall of the high kings after Desh-thiere's conquest. Rendered discorporate by the Fellowship's judgment in Third Age 5129. Exiled since, by personal choice. Davien's works included the Five Centuries Fountain near Mearth on the splinter world of the Red Desert through West Gate; the shaft at Rockfell Peak, used by the Sorcerers to imprison harmful entities; the Stair on Rockfell Peak; and also, Kewar Tunnel in the Mathorn Mountains.

pronounced: dah-vee-en

root meaning: *dahvi*—fool; *an*—one "mistaken one"

DAWR s'BRYDION—grandmother of Duke Bransian of Alestron, and his brothers Keldmar, Parrien, and Mearn.

pronounced: dour

root meaning: *dwyiar*—vinegar wine

DEITH—clansman of Rathain, and the youngest of Jieret's Companions, who were the fourteen child survivors of the massacre of Tal Quorin in Third Age Year 5638. Currently among the group of scouts guarding the free wilds in Deshir.

pronounced: dee-ith

root meaning: *d'*—prefix for behind; *ieth*—to stand, to plant, to fix in place

DESH-THIERE—Mistwraith that invaded Athera from the splinter worlds through South Gate in Third Age 4993. Access cut off by Fellowship Sorcerer, Traithe. Battled and contained in West Shand for twenty-five years, until the rebellion splintered the peace, and the high kings were forced to withdraw from the defense lines to attend their disrupted kingdoms. Confined through the combined powers of Lysaer s'Ilessid's gift of light and Arithon s'Ffalenn's gift of shadow. Currently imprisoned in a warded flask in Rockfell Pit.

pronounced: desh-thee-air-e (last "e" mostly subliminal)

root meaning: *desh*—mist; *thiere*—ghost or wraith

DESHIR—northwestern principality of Rathain.

pronounced: desh-eer

root meaning: *deshir*—misty

DHARKARON AVENGER—called Ath's Avenging Angel in legend. Drives a chariot drawn by five horses to convey the guilty to Sithaer. Dharkaron as defined by the adepts of Ath's Brotherhood is that dark thread mortal men weave with Ath, the prime vibration, that creates self-punishment, or the root of guilt.

pronounced dark-air-on

root meaning: *dhar*—evil; *khiaron*—one who stands in judgment

DHIRKEN—lady captain of the contraband runner, *Black Drake*. Reputed to have taken over the brig's command by right of arms following her father's death at sea. Died at the hands of Lysaer's allies on the charge of liaison with Arithon s'Ffalenn, Third Age Year 5647.

pronounced: dur-kin

root meaning: *dierk*—tough; *an*—one

DIARIN s'GANNLEY—daughter of the *caithdein*'s lineage of Tysan, handfasted to marry a Westwood clan chieftain when she was abducted and forced to marriage by the Mayor of Hanshire.

> pronounced: die-are-in
>
> root meaning: *diarin*—a precious, or coveted object

DIEGAN—once Lord Commander of Etarra's garrison; given over by his mayor to serve as Lysaer s'Ilessid's Lord Commander at Avenor. Titular commander of the war host sent against the Deshans to defeat the Master of Shadow at Tal Quorin; high commander of the war host mustered at Werpoint. Also brother of Lady Talith. Died of a clan arrow in the Battle of Dier Kenton Vale in Vastmark, Third Age 5647.

> pronounced: dee-gan
>
> root meaning: *diegan*—trinket a dandy might wear/ornament

DIER KENTON VALE—a valley located in the principality of Vastmark, Shand, where Lysaer's war host, thirty-five thousand strong, fought and lost to the Master of Shadow in Third Age 5647, largely decimated in one day by a shale slide. The remainder were harried by a small force of Vastmark shepherds and clan scouts from Shand, under Caolle, who served as Arithon's war captain, until supplies and loss of morale broke the Alliance campaign.

> pronounced: deer ken-ton
>
> root meaning: *dier'kendion*—a jewel with a severe flaw that may result in shearing or cracking

DURN—town located in Orvandir, Shand.

> pronounced: dern
>
> root meaning: *diern*—a flat plain

DYSHENT—town on the west coast of Instrell Bay in Atainia, Tysan.

> pronounced: die-shent
>
> root meaning: *dyshient*—cedar

EAST HALLA—principality in Melhalla.

> pronounced: east hall-ah
>
> root meaning: *hal'lia*—white light

EASTWALL—city located in the Skyshiel Mountains, Rathain.

EDAN—boy recruit for the Light, chosen for talent.

> pronounced: eh-dan
>
> root meaning: *e'dian*—the clay

EI'AN IST'THALIENT—a stingingly pointed colloquial insult, and a warning; roughly "a particularly rock-headed fool bound for disaster."

> pronounced: ee-eh-an eest-thal-ee-ent
>
> root meaning: ei—"a" in the specific form; *an*—one; *ist'thal*—closed, hard or stubborn head, contrary-minded - *ient*—suffix that indicates a state of fullest evolution, or "the most."

EILISH—Lord Minister of the Treasury at Avenor.

> pronounced: eye-lish
>
> root meaning: *eyalish*—fussy

ELAIRA—initiate enchantress of the Koriathain. Originally a street child, taken on in Morvain for Koriani rearing. Arithon's beloved.

> pronounced: ee-layer-ah
>
> root meaning: *e*—prefix, diminutive for small; *laere*—grace

ELDIR s'LORNMEIN—King of Havish and last surviving scion of s'Lornmein royal line. Raised as a wool-dyer until the Fellowship Sorcerers crowned him at Ostermere in Third Age 5643 following the defeat of the Mistwraith.

> pronounced: el-deer
>
> root meaning: *eldir*—to ponder, to consider, to weigh

ELKFOREST—free wilds located in Carithwyr, Havish.

ELLAINE—daughter of the Lord Mayor of Erdane, became Princess of Avenor when she married Lysaer s'Ilessid, mother of the heir apparent, Kevor, who is believed to be deceased.

> pronounced: el-lane
>
> not from the Paravian

ELSSINE—town on the coast of Alland, Shand.

> pronounced: el-seen
>
> root meaning: *elssien*—small pit

ELTAIR BAY—large bay off Cildein Ocean and east coast of Rathain; where the River Severnir was diverted following the Mistwraith's conquest.

> pronounced: el-tay-er
>
> root meaning: *al'tieri*—of steel/a shortening of original Paravian name; *dascen al'tieri*—which meant "ocean of steel," which referred to the color of the waves

EMRIC s'GANNLEY—former *Caithdein* of Tysan, and father of Diarin s'Gannley who was once handfasted to the clan chieftain of Westwood.

> pronounced: em-rick
>
> root meaning: *am'ric*—plenty, "state of wealth"

ENITHEN TUER—seeress living in the town of Erdane. Originally a Koriani sister who was freed from her initiate's vow of service by Fellowship Sorcerer Asandir's intervention.

> pronounced: en-ith-en too-er
>
> root meaning: *en'wethen*—farsighted; *tuer*—crone

ENNA—girl child who was once a weaver's apprentice.

> pronounced: enn-na
>
> not from the Paravian.

ERDANE—old Paravian city, later taken over by Men. Seat of old princes of Camris until Desh-thiere's conquest and rebellion. Erdani—meaning, from

Erdane.
>   pronounced: er-day-na with the last syllable almost subliminal
>   root meaning: *er'deinia*—long walls

ERIEGAL—second youngest of the fourteen child survivors of the Tal Quorin massacre known as Jieret's Companions. Renowned as a shrewd tactician, he was ordered to serve Jieret's son Barach as war captain in the Halwythwood camp rather than fight Lysaer's war host in Daon Ramon Barrens in Third Age Year 5670.
>   pronounced: air-ee-gall
>   root meaning: *eriegal*—snake

ERLIEN s'TALEYN—High Earl of Alland; *caithdein* of Shand, chieftain of the forest clansmen of Selkwood. Once fought Arithon s'Ffalenn at sword point over an issue of law bound over by Melhalla's *caithdein* and also as a trial of a sanctioned crown prince's honest character.
>   pronounced: er-lee-an
>   root meaning: *aierlyan*—bear; *tal*—branch; *an*—one/first "of first branch"

ETARRA—trade city built across the Mathorn Pass by townsfolk after the revolt that cast down Ithamon and the High Kings of Rathain. Nest of corruption and intrigue, and policy maker for the North. Lysaer s'Ilessid was ratified as mayor upon Morfett's death in Third Age Year 5667. Raiett Raven subsequently appointed as ruling High Chancellor. Also the seat of the Alliance armed forces.
>   pronounced: ee-tar-ah
>   root meaning: *e*—prefix for small; *taria*—knots

ETTIN—river that empties into Rockbay Harbor at the border between Shand and Havish.
>   pronounced: et-tin
>   root meaning: *e'tennd*—the slow

EVENSTAR—first brig stolen from Riverton's royal shipyard by Cattrick's conspiracy with Prince Arithon. Currently of Innish registry, running merchant cargoes under joint ownership of Fiark and his sister Feylind, who is acting captain.

FALGAIRE—coastal city on Instrell Bay, located in Araethura, Rathain, famed for its glassworks.
>   pronounced: fall-gair—to rhyme with "air"
>   root meaning: *fal'mier*—to sparkle or glitter

FALLOWMERE—northeastern principality of Rathain.
>   pronounced: fal-oh-meer
>   root meaning: *fal'ei'miere*—literally, tree self-reflection, colloquialism for "place of perfect trees"

FATE'S WHEEL—see Daelion's Wheel.

FELLOWSHIP OF SEVEN—sorcerers bound to Athera by the summoning dream of the dragons and charged to secure the mysteries that enable Paravian survival. Achieved their redemption from Cianor Sunlord, under the Law of the Major Balance in Second Age Year One. Originators and keepers of the covenant of the compact, made with the Paravian races, to allow Mankind's settlement on Athera in Third Age Year One. Their authority backs charter law, upheld by crown justice and clan oversight of the free wilds.

FEITHAN—widow of Jieret s'Valerient, Earl of the North, and *caithdein* of Rathain.

> pronounced: faith-an
>
> root meaning: *feiathen*—ivy

FEYLIND—daughter of a Scimlade fisherman and Jinesse, twin sister of Fiark, currently master of *Evenstar,* a merchant brig of Innish registry.

> pronounced: fay-lind
>
> root meaning: *faelind'an*—outspoken or noisy one

FIARK—son of a Scimlade fisherman and Jinesse, twin brother of Feylind, currently a merchant factor at Innish, also handles all of Arithon's covert shoreside affairs.

> pronounced: fee-ark
>
> root meaning: *fyerk*—to throw or toss

FIONN ARETH CAID'AN—goatherd's child born in Third Age 5647; fated by prophecy to leave home and play a role in the Wars of Light and Shadow. Laid under Koriani spellcraft to mature as Arithon's double, then used as the bait in the order's conspiracy to trap the s'Ffalenn prince. Rescued from execution in Jaelot in 5669-70. Currently in the protective custody of the Prince of Rathain, held through Dakar's binding promise.

> pronounced: fee-on-are-eth cayed-ahn
>
> root meaning: *fionne arith caid an*—one who brings choice

FORTHMARK—city in Vastmark, Shand. Once the site of a hostel of Ath's Brotherhood. By Third Age 5320, the site was abandoned and taken over by the Koriani Order as a healer's hospice.

> root meaning not from the Paravian

FREYARD—elderly servant in Hanshire.

> pronounced: free-ard
>
> not from the Paravian.

GACE STEWARD—Palace Steward of Avenor.

> pronounced: gace-to rhyme with "race"
>
> root meaning: *gyce*—weasel

GANISH—trade city located south of Methlas Lake in Orvandir, Shand.

> pronounced: gan-eesh

root meaning: *gianish*—a halfway point, a stopping place

GARDE—Lord Mayor of Hanshire, father of Sulfin Evend, brother of Raiett Raven.

> pronounced: guard
>
> not from the Paravian.

GLENDIEN—a Shandian clanswoman handfasted to Kyrialt s'Taleyn, heir designate of the High Earl of Alland.

> pronounced: glen-dee-en
>
> root meaning: *glyen*—sultry; *dien*—object of beauty

GRAY BOOK OF OLVEC—an old genealogy that listed clan lineages and recorded the inheritable talents of each family.

> pronounced: oll-veck
>
> root meaning: *olvec*—record

GREAT WAYSTONE—see entry for Waystone.

GRIMWARD—a circle of spells of Paravian making that seal and isolate the dire dreams of dragon haunts, a force with the potential for mass destruction. With the disappearance of the old races, the defenses are maintained by embodied Sorcerers of the Fellowship of Seven. There are seventeen separate sites listed at Althain Tower.

HALDUIN s'ILESSID—founder of the line that became High Kings of Tysan since Third Age Year One. The attribute he passed on, by means of the Fellowship's geas, was justice.

> pronounced: hal-dwin
>
> root meaning: *hal*—white; *duinne*—hand

HALWYTHWOOD—forest located in Araethura, Rathain. Current main campsite of High Earl Barach's band, predominantly survivors of the Battle of Strakewood and Daon Ramon's late war.

> pronounced: hall-with-wood
>
> root meaning: *hal*—white; *wythe*—vista

HANHAFFIN—river running through Selkwood in Alland and emptying into the Cildein Ocean.

> pronounced: han-haf-fin
>
> root meaning: *hanha*—evergreen; *affein*—a dance step

HANSHIRE—port city on the Westland Sea, coast of Korias, Tysan; reigning official Lord Mayor Garde, father of Sulfin Evend; opposed to royal rule at the time of Avenor's restoration.

> pronounced: han-sheer
>
> root meaning: *hansh*—sand; *era*—place

HASPASTION—ghost of the dragon contained in the grimward located in Radmoore.

> pronounced: has-past-ee-on

root meaning: *hashpashdion*—Drakish for black thunder

HAVENS—an inlet on the northeastern shore of Vastmark, Shand, now known as the site of the massacre enacted by the Spinner of Darkness, preceding the Battle of Dier Kenton Vale, Third Age Year 5647.

HAVISH—one of the Five High Kingdoms of Athera as defined by the charters of the Fellowship of Seven. Ruled by Eldir s'Lornmein. Crown heritage: temperance. Device: gold hawk on red field.

> pronounced: hav-ish
>
> root meaning: *havieshe*—hawk

HAVISTOCK—southeast principality of Kingdom of Havish.

> pronounced: hav-i-stock
>
> root meaning: *haviesha*—hawk; *tiok*—roost

HELFIN—Lord Mayor of Erdane, father of Princess Ellaine.

> pronounced: hell-fin
>
> root meaning: *hal*—white; *fiomn'd*—a fib

HIGHSCARP—city sited near the stone quarries on the coast of the Bay of Eltair, located in Daon Ramon, Rathain. Also contains a sisterhouse of the Koriani Order.

IAMINE s'GANNLEY—woman who founded the *caithdein's* lineage for Tysan.

> pronounced: ee-ahm-meen-e
>
> root meaning: *iamine*—amethyst

IANFAR s'GANNLEY—cousin and heir designate of Lord Maenol s'Gannley, *caithdein* of Tysan, sent to fosterage with High King Eldir of Havish in Third Age Year 5652.

> pronounced: ee-an-far
>
> root meaning: *ianfiar*—birch tree

ILITHARIS PARAVIANS—centaurs, one of three semimortal old races; disappeared after the Mistwraith's conquest, the last guardian's departure by Third Age Year 5100. They were the guardians of the earth's mysteries.

> pronounced: i-li-thar-is
>
> root meaning: *i'lith'earis*—the keeper/preserver of mystery

INNISH—city located on the southcoast of Shand at the delta of the River Ippash. Birthplace of Halliron Masterbard. Formerly known as "the Jewel of Shand," this was the site of the high king's winter court, prior to the time of the uprising.

> pronounced: in-ish
>
> root meaning: *inniesh*—a jewel with a pastel tint

INSTRELL BAY—body of water off the Gulf of Stormwell, separates principality of Atainia, Tysan, from Deshir, Rathain.

> pronounced: in-strell
>
> root meaning: *arin'streal*—strong wind

IPPASH—river that originates in the southern spur of the Kelhorns and flows into the South Sea by the city of Innish, southcoast, Shand.

> pronounced: ip-ash
>
> root meaning: *ipeish*—crescent

ISFARENN—etheric Name for the black stallion ridden by Asandir.

> pronounced: ees-far-en
>
> root meaning: *is'feron*—speed maker

ISHLIR—town on the eastshore of Orvandir, Shand.

> pronounced: ish-leer
>
> root meaning: *ieshlier*—sheltered place

ITHAMON—Historically significant in the First Age, site of a Paravian focus, a Second Age Paravian stronghold, and a Third Age ruin; built on a fifth lane power-node in Daon Ramon Barrens, Rathain, and inhabited until the year of the uprising. Site of the Compass Point Towers, or Sun Towers. Became the seat of the High Kings of Rathain during the Third Age and in Third Age Year 5638 was the site where Princes Lysaer s'Ilessid and Arithon s'Ffalenn battled the Mistwraith to confinement.

> pronounced: ith-a-mon
>
> root meaning: *itha*—five; *mon*—needle, spire

ITHISH—city located at the edge of the principality of Vastmark, on the southcoast of Shand. Where the Vastmark woolfactors once shipped fleeces.

> pronounced: ith-ish
>
> root meaning: *ithish*—fleece or fluffy

IYAT—energy sprite, and minor drake spawn inhabiting Athera, not visible to the eye, manifests in a poltergeist fashion by taking temporary possession of objects. Feeds upon natural energy sources: fire, breaking waves, lightning.

> pronounced: ee-at
>
> root meaning: *iyat*—to break

JAELOT—city located on the coast of Eltair Bay at the southern border of the Kingdom of Rathain. Once a Second Age power site, with a focus circle. Now a merchant city with a reputation for extreme snobbery and bad taste. Also the site where Arithon s'Ffalenn played his eulogy for Halliron Masterbard, which raised the powers of the Paravian focus circle beneath the mayor's palace. The forces of the mysteries and resonant harmonics caused damage to city buildings, watchkeeps, and walls, which has since been repaired. Site where Fionn Areth was arraigned for execution, as bait in a Koriani conspiracy that failed to trap Arithon s'Ffalenn.

> pronounced: jay-lot
>
> root meaning: *jielot*—affectation

JERIAYISH—sixth-rank initiate priest of the Light who had a seer's talent. Died of madness during the Alliance war host's invasion of Daon Ramon

Barrens in Third Age Year 5670.

> pronounced: jeer-ee-ah-yish
>
> root meaning: *jier'yaish*—unclean magic

JEYNSA—daughter of Jieret s'Valerient and Feithan, born Third Age 5653; appointed successor for her father's title, *Caithdien* of Rathain.

> pronounced: jay-in-sa
>
> root meaning: *jieyensa*—garnet

JIERET s'VALERIENT—former Earl of the North, clan chief of Deshir; *caithdein* of Rathain, sworn liegeman of Prince Arithon s'Ffalenn. Also son and heir of Lord Steiven. Blood pacted to Arithon by sorcerer's oath prior to the battle of Strakewood Forest. Came to be known by headhunters as Jieret Red-beard. Father of Jeynsa and Barach. Husband to Feithan. Died by Lysaer s'Ilessid's hand in Daon Ramon Barrens, Third Age Year 5670.

> pronounced: jeer-et
>
> root meaning: *jieret*—thorn

KALESH—town at the mouth of the harbor inlet from the Cildein Ocean, enemy of Alestron.

> pronounced: cal-esh
>
> root meaning: *caille'iesh*—stubborn hold

KAMRIDIAN s'FFALENN—Crowned High King of Rathain, a tragic figure who died of his conscience under the fated influence of the maze in Kewar Caverns, built by Davien the Betrayer under the Mathorn Mountains.

> pronounced: cam-rid-ee-an
>
> root meaning: *kaim'riadien*—thread cut shorter

KELDMAR s'BRYDION—younger brother of Duke Bransian of Alestron, older brother of Parrien and Mearn.

> pronounced: keld-mar
>
> root meaning: *kiel'd'maeran*—one without pity

KEVOR—son and heir of Lysaer s'Ilessid and Princess Ellaine; born at Avenor in Third Age 5655. At age fourteen, in his father's absence, he exercised royal authority and averted a riot by the panicked citizenry of Avenor. Commonly held to have died by Khadrim fire in Westwood, but in fact was spared by an interaction with Ath's Brotherhood. Became an adept in Third Year 5670, at the hostel in Northerly, Tysan.

> pronounced: kev-or
>
> root meaning: *kiavor*—high virtue

KEWAR TUNNEL—cavern built beneath the Mathorn Mountains by Davien the Betrayer; contains the maze of conscience, which caused High King Kamridian s'Ffalenn's death.

> pronounced: key-wahr

root meaning: *kewiar*—a weighing of conscience

KHADRIM—drake-spawned creatures, flying, fire-breathing reptiles that were the scourge of the Second Age. By the Third Age, they had been driven back and confined in the Sorcerers' Preserve in the volcanic peaks in north Tysan.

pronounced: kaa-drim

root meaning: *khadrim*—dragon

KHARADMON—Sorcerer of the Fellowship of Seven; discorporate since rise of Khadrim and Seardluin leveled Paravian stronghold at Ithamon in Second Age 3651. It was by Kharadmon's intervention that the survivors of the attack were sent to safety by means of transfer from the fifth lane power focus. Currently working the wardings to defer a minor invasion of wraiths from Marak.

pronounced: kah-rad-mun

root meaning: *kar'riad en mon*—phrase translates to mean "twisted thread on the needle" or colloquialism for "a knot in the works"

KHETIENN—name for a brigantine built at Merior and owned by Arithon; also a small spotted wildcat native to Daon Ramon Barrens that became the s'Ffalenn royal device.

pronounced: key-et-ee-en

root meaning: *kietienn*—small leopard

KIELING TOWER—one of the four compass points, or Sun Towers, standing at ruin of Ithamon, Daon Ramon Barrens, in Rathain. The warding virtue that binds its stones is compassion.

pronounced: key-eh-ling

root meaning: *kiel'ien*—root for pity, with suffix for "lightness" added, translates to mean "compassion"

KORIANI—possessive and singular form of the word "Koriathain"; see entry.

pronounced: kor-ee-ah-nee

KORIAS—southwestern principality of Tysan.

pronounced: kor-ee-as

root meaning: *cor*—ship, vessel; *i'esh*—nest, haven

KORIATHAIN—order of enchantresses ruled by a circle of Seniors, under the power of one Prime Enchantress. They draw their talent from the orphaned children they raise, or from daughters dedicated to service by their parents. Initiation rite involves a vow of consent that ties the spirit to a power crystal keyed to the Prime's control.

pronounced: kor-ee-ah-thain—to rhyme with "main"

root meaning: *koriath*—order; *ain*—belonging to

KOSHLIN—influential trade minister from Erdane, renowned for his hatred of the clans and his support of the headhunters' leagues.

pronounced: kosh-lynn

root meaning: *kioshlin*—opaque

KRALOVIR—term for a sect of necromancers, also called the gray cult.
> pronounced: kray-low-veer
> root meaning: *krial*—name for the rune of crossing; *oveir*—abomination

KYRIALT s'TALEYN—heir designate and youngest son of the High Earl of Alland, Lord Erlien s'Taleyn, *Caithdein* of Shand.
> pronounced: key-ree-alt
> root meaning: *kyrialt*—word for the rune of crossing with the suffix for "last," which is the name for the rune of ending.

LANSHIRE—northernmost principality in the Kingdom of Havish. Name taken from the wastes at Scarpdale, site of First Age battles with Seardluin that blasted the soil to slag.
> pronounced: lahn-sheer-e
> root meaning: *lan'hansh'era*—place of hot sands

LAW OF THE MAJOR BALANCE—founding order of the powers of the Fellowship of Seven, as taught by the Paravians. The primary tenet is that no force of nature should be used without consent, or against the will of another consciousness.

LEYNSGAP—a narrow pass in the Mathorn Mountains in the Kingdom of Rathain.
> pronounced: lay-ens-gap
> root meaning: *liyond*—corridor

LIESSE s'BRYDION—Duchess of Alestron and wife of Duke Bransian.
> pronounced: lee-ess
> root meaning: *liesse*—state of accord, based from the word "a note in harmony"

LIRENDA—former First Senior Enchantress to the Prime, Koriani Order; failed in her assignment to capture Arithon s'Ffalenn for Koriani purposes. Currently under the Prime Matriarch's sentence of punishment.
> pronounced: leer-end-ah
> root meaning: *lyron*—singer; *di-ia*—a dissonance—the hyphen denotes a glottal stop

LITHMERE—principality located in the Kingdom of Havish.
pronounced: lith-mere
> root meaning: *lithmiere*—to preserve intact, or keep whole; maintain in a state of harmony

LOS MAR—a city located on the westshore of Carithwyr, Havish, best known for its libraries and scholars.
> pronounced: loss-mar
> root meaning: *liosmar*—letters, written records

LUHAINE—Sorcerer of the Fellowship of Seven—discorporate since the fall of Telmandir in Third Age Year 5018. Luhaine's body was pulled down by the mob while he was in ward trance, covering the escape of the royal heir to Havish.

> pronounced: loo-hay-ne
>
> root meaning: *luirhainon*—defender

LYRANTHE—instrument played by the bards of Athera. Strung with four-teen strings, tuned to seven tones (doubled). Two courses are "drone strings" set to octaves. Five are melody strings, the lower three courses being octaves, the upper two, in unison.

> pronounced: leer-anth-e (last "e" being nearly subliminal)
>
> root meaning: *lyr*—song, *anthe*—box

LYSAER s'ILESSID—prince of Tysan, 1497th in succession after Halduin, founder of the line in Third Age Year One. Gifted at birth with control of Light, and Bane of Desh-thiere. Also known as Blessed Prince since he de-clared himself avatar.

> pronounced: lie-say-er
>
> root meaning: *lia*—blond, yellow or light, *saer*—circle

MACHIEL—*caithdein* of the realm of Havish. In service under High King Eldir at Telmandir.

> pronounced: mak-ee-el
>
> root meaning: *mierkiel*—post, pillar

MAENELLE s'GANNLEY—former steward and *caithdein* of Tysan; put on trial for outlawry and theft on the trade roads; executed by Lysaer s'Ilessid at Isaer, Third Age 5645.

> pronounced: may-nahl-e (last "e" is near subliminal)
>
> root meaning: *maeni*—to fall, disrupt; *alli*—to save or preserve/collo-quial translation: "to patch together"

MAENOL—heir, after Maenalle s'Gannley, Steward and *caithdein* of Tysan.

> pronounced: may-nall
>
> root meaning: *maeni'alli*—to patch together

MAINMERE—town at the head of the Valenford River in Taerlin, Tysan.
pronounced: main-meer

> root meaning: *maeni*—to fall, disrupt; *miere*—reflection, colloquial trans-lation, "to disrupt continuity"

MARAK—splinter world, cut off beyond South Gate, left lifeless after cre-ation of the Mistwraith. The original inhabitants were men exiled by the Fel-lowship from Athera for beliefs or practices that were incompatible with the compact sworn between the Sorcerers and the Paravian races, which permit-ted human settlement on Athera.

> pronounced: maer-ak
>
> root meaning: *m'era'ki*—a place held separate

MARETHA s'CALLIENT—daughter of the *caithdein* of Melhalla.

pronounced: mar-ee-tha

root meaning: *mier'atha*—kindly

MATHIELL GATE—last gate to the inner citadel in Alestron, Paravian built to withstand the fires of dragons. It was the Mathiell garrison who secured the span guarding incursion from the Wyntok Gate during the uprising that threatened clan rule in Third Age Year 5018.

pronounced: math-ee-ell

root meaning: *mon'thiellen*—sky spires

MATHORN MOUNTAINS—range that bisects the Kingdom of Rathain east to west.

pronounced: math-orn

root meaning: *mathien*—massive

MATHORN ROAD—way passing to the south of the Mathorn Mountains, leading to the trade city of Etarra from the west.

pronounced: math-orn

root meaning: *mathien*—massive

MEARN s'BRYDION—youngest brother of Duke Bransian of Alestron. Former ducal emissary to Lysaer s'Ilessid's Alliance of Light.

pronounced: may-arn

root meaning: *mierne*—to flit

MEDLIR—name used by Arithon when he traveled incognito with Halliron Masterbard as apprentice in Third Age Years 5638 through 5647.

pronounced: med-leer

root meaning: *midlyr*—phrase of melody

MELHALLA—High Kingdom of Athera once ruled by the line of s'Ellestrion. The last prince died in the crossing of the Red Desert.

pronounced: mel-hall-ah

root meaning: *maelhallia*—grand meadows/plain—also word for an open space of any sort.

MERIOR BY THE SEA—small seaside fishing village on the Scimlade peninsula in Alland, Shand. Once the temporary site of Arithon's shipyard.

pronounced: mare-ee-or

root meaning: *merioren*—cottages

METHISLE—small body of land in Methlas Lake, site of Methisle Fortress in Orvandir.

pronounced: meth

root meaning: *meth*—hate

METHSPAWN—an animal descended from a host warped by possession by a methuri, an *iyat*-related parasite that infested live hosts. Though the Methuri were destroyed by the Third Age, their crossbred, aberrated descendants continue to breed mutant offspring in Mirthlvain Swamp.

pronounced: meth

root meaning: *meth*—hate

METHURI—METHURIEN (plural form) an *iyat*-related parasite that infested live hosts and altered them for the purpose of creating new hosts. Extinct by the Third Age.

    pronounced: meth-you-ree

    root meaning: *meth'thieri*—hate wraith

MIRTHLVAIN SWAMP—boglands located in Midhalla, Melhalla; filled with dangerous crossbreeds engendered from drake spawn. Guarded by the Master Spellbinder, Verrain.

    pronounced: mirth-el-vain

    root meaning: *myrthl*—noxious; *vain*—bog, mud

MISTWRAITH—see Desh-thiere.

MORNOS—town on the westshore of Lithmere, Havish.

    pronounced: more-nos

    root meaning: *moarnosh*—a coffer where the greedy store valuables.

MORRIEL—Prime Enchantress of the Koriathain since the Third Age 4212. Instigated the plot to upset the Fellowship's compact which upset the seven magnetic lanes on the continent. Her death on winter solstice 5670 left an irregular succession, resolved by the elevation of an incompetent initiate, Selidie, who had been chosen to facilitate an unprincipled act of possession by Morriel that had usurped the young woman's body.'

    pronounced: more-real

    root meaning: *moar*—greed; *riel*—silver

NARMS—city on the coast of Instrell Bay, built as a craft center by Men in the early Third Age. Best known for dyeworks.

    pronounced: narms

    root meaning: *narms*—color

NAYLA—young girl taken in by the Koriani Order as a child candidate for initiation.

    pronounced: nay-lah

    root meaning: *nayl*—lack

ODREY—a merchant courtier and member of the regent's council in Avenor.

    pronounced: oh-dree

    not from the Paravian

ORLAN—pass through the Thaldein Mountains, also location of the Camris's clans hidden outpost, located in Camris, Tysan.

    pronounced: or-lan

    root meaning: *irlan*—ledge

ORVANDIR—principality located in northeastern Shand.

    pronounced: or-van-deer

root meaning: *orvein*—crumbled; *dir*—stone

PARAVIAN—name for the three old races that inhabited Athera before Mankind. Including the centaurs, the sunchildren, and the unicorns, these races never die unless mishap befalls them; they are the world's channel, or direct connection, to Ath Creator.

>   pronounced: par-ai-vee-ans
>   root meaning: *para*—great; *i'on*—fate or great mystery

PARRIEN s'BRYDION—younger brother of Duke Bransian s'Brydion of Alestron, Keldmar, and older brother of Mearn. Broke Arithon's leg in Third Age Year 5654, and in restitution awarded Rathain's prince the service of two s'Brydion retainers, Talvish and Vhandon.

>   pronounced: par-ee-on
>   root meaning: *para ient*—great dart

PRANDEY—term for gelded pleasure boy.

>   pronounced: pran-dee
>   not from the Paravian

QUAIDE—trade town in Carithwyr, Havish, lying inland along the trade road from Los Mar to Redburn. Famous for fired clay and brick.

>   pronounced: qu-wade
>   root meaning: *cruaid*—a clay used for brickmaking.

QUARN—town on the trade road that crosses Caithwood in Taerlin, Tysan.

>   pronounced: kwarn
>   root meaning: *quarin*—ravine, canyon

QUINOLD—Lord Chancellor of Avenor and a member of Lysaer's regent's council.

>   pronounced: kwin-old
>   root meaning: *quen*—one who is narrow-minded

RADMOORE DOWNS—meadowlands in Midhalla, Melhalla.

>   pronounced: rad-more
>   root meaning: *riad*—thread; *mour*—carpet, rug

RAIETT RAVEN—brother of the Mayor of Hanshire; uncle of Sulfin Evend. Considered a master statesman and a bringer of wars. Currently serving as High Chancellor of Etarra, ruling in the absence of the ratified mayor.

>   pronounced: rayett
>   root meaning: *raiett*—carrion bird

RATHAIN—High Kingdom of Athera ruled by descendants of Torbrand s'Ffalenn since Third Age Year One. Device: black-and-silver leopard on green field. Arithon Teir's'Ffalenn is sanctioned crown prince, by the hand of Asandir of the Fellowship, in Third Age Year 5638 at Etarra.

pronounced: rath-ayn

root meaning: *roth*—brother; *thein*—tower, sanctuary

RAUVEN TOWER—home of the s'Ahelas mages who brought up Arithon s'Ffalenn and trained him to the ways of power. Located on the splinter world, Dascen Elur, through West Gate.

pronounced: raw-ven

root meaning: *rauven*—invocation

REDBURN—town located in a deep inlet in the northern shore of Rockbay Harbor in Havistock, Havish.

pronounced: red-burn

root meaning not from the Paravian

RIATHAN PARAVIANS—unicorns, the purest, most direct connection to Ath Creator; the prime vibration channels directly through the horn.

pronounced: ree-ah-than

root meaning: *ria*—to touch; *ath*—prime life force; *an*—one; *ri'athon*—one who touches divinity

RIVERTON—trade town at the mouth of the Ilswater River, in Korias, Tysan; once the site of Lysaer's royal shipyard, before the site burned in Third Age Year 5654.

ROCKBAY HARBOR—body of water located on the southcoast, between Shand and West Shand.

ROCKFELL PEAK—mountain containing Rockfell Pit, used to imprison harmful entities throughout all three Ages. Located in West Halla, Melhalla; became the warded prison for Desh-thiere.

pronounced: rock-fell

root meaning not from the Paravian

s'AHELAS—family name for the royal line appointed by the Fellowship Sorcerers in Third Age Year One to rule the High Kingdom of Shand. Gifted geas: farsight.

pronounced: s'ah-hell-as

root meaning: *ahelas*—mage-gifted

s'BRYDION—ruling line of the Dukes of Alestron. The only old blood clansmen to maintain rule of a fortified city through the uprising that defeated the rule of the high kings.

pronounced: s-bry-dee-on

root meaning: *baridien*-tenacity

s'CALLIENT—lineage of the *caithdeinen* of Melhalla, Fellowship chosen to succeed s'Dieneval after the fall of Tirans.

pronounced: scal-lee-ent

root meaning: *caillient*—most extreme form of "fixed" or stubborn—"immovable"

SANPASHIR—desert waste on the southcoast of Shand. Home to the desert tribes.

> pronounced: sahn-pash-eer
>
> root meaning: *san*—black or dark; *pash'era*—place of grit or gravel

SANSHEVAS—town on the south shore in Alland, Shand, known for citrus, sugar, and rum.

> pronounced: san-shee-vas
>
> root meaning: *san*—black; *shievas*—flint

SCARPDALE—waste in Lanshire, Havish, created by a First Age war with Seardluin. Site of the Scarpdale grimward.

> pronounced: scarp-dale
>
> not from the Paravian

SCIMLADE TIP—peninsula at the southeast corner of Alland, Shand.

> pronounced: skim-laid
>
> root meaning: *scimlait*—curved knife or scythe

SECOND AGE—Marked by the arrival of the Fellowship of Seven at Crater Lake, their called purpose to fight the drake spawn.

s'DIENEVAL—lost lineage of the *caithdeinen* of Melhalla, the last to carry the title being Egan, who died at the side of his high king in the battle to subdue the Mistwraith. The bloodline carried strong talent for prophecy, and was decimated during the sack of Tirans in the uprising in Third Age Year 5018, with Egan's pregnant wife the sole survivor. Her daughter, Meiglin was mother of Dari s'Ahelas, crown heir of Shand.

> pronounced: s-dee-in-ee-vahl
>
> root meaning: *dien*—large; *eval*-endowment, gifted talent

SELIDIE—young woman initiate appointed by Morriel Prime as a candidate in training for succession. Succeeded to the office of Prime Matriarch after Morriel's death on winter solstice in Third Age Year 5670, at which time an unprincipled act of possession by Morriel usurped the young woman's body.

> pronounced: sell-ih-dee
>
> root meaning: *selyadi*—air sprite

SELKWOOD—forest located in Alland, Shand.

> pronounced: selk-wood
>
> root meaning: *selk*—pattern

s'ELLESTRION—lineage of the High Kings of Melhalla, died out in the course of the uprising in Third Age Year 5018. Gifted geas: wisdom.

> pronounced: sell-ess-tree-on
>
> root meaning: *eliestrion*—inspiration, from the word *elya*—air

SETHVIR—Sorcerer of the Fellowship of Seven, also trained to serve as Warden of Althain since Third Age 5100, when the last centaur guardian departed after the Mistwraith's conquest.

> pronounced: seth-veer

root meaning: *seth*—fact; *vaer*—keep

SEVRAND s'BRYDION—heir designate of Duke Bransian of Alestron.

    pronounced: sev-rand

    root meaning: *sevaer'an'd*—one who travels behind, a follower

s'FFALENN—family name for the royal line appointed by the Fellowship Sorcerers in Third Age Year One to rule the High Kingdom of Rathain. Gifted geas: compassion/empathy.

    pronounced: s-fal-en

    root meaning: *ffael*—dark, *an*—one

s'GANNLEY—lineage of the Earls of the West, once the Camris princes, now bearing the heritage of *caithdein* of Tysan. Iamine s'Gannley was the woman founder.

    pronounced: sgan-lee

    root meaning: *gaen*—guide; *li*—exalted or in harmony

SHADDORN—town located on the Scimlade Tip in Alland, Shand.

    pronounced: shad-dorn

    root meaning: *shaddiern*—sea turtle

SHAND—High Kingdom on the southeast corner of the Paravian continent, originally ruled by the line of s'Ahelas. Current device, purple-and-gold chevrons, since the adjunct kingdom of West Shand came under high crown rule. The old device was a falcon on a crescent moon, sometimes still showed, backed by the more recent purple-and-gold chevrons.

    pronounced: shand—as in "hand"

    root meaning: *shayn* or *shiand*—two/pair

SHIPSPORT—city located on the Bay of Eltair in the principality of West Halla, Melhalla.

SIDIR—one of the Companions, who were the fourteen boys to survive the Battle of Strakewood. Served Arithon at the Battle of Dier Kenton Vale, and the Havens. Second-in-command of Earl Jieret's war band.

    pronounced: see-deer

    root meaning: *i'sid'i'er*—one who has stood at the verge of being lost.

s'ILESSID—family name for the royal line appointed by the Fellowship Sorcerers in Third Age Year One to rule the High Kingdom of Tysan. Gifted geas: justice.

    pronounced: s-ill-ess-id

    root meaning: *liessiad*—balance

SIMSHANE'S HOUSE OF EXOTIC DELIGHTS—disreputable brothel located in Etarra, renowned for vice and peddling *prandeys*.

    pronounced: sim-shane

    not from the Paravian

SITHAER—mythological equivalent of hell, halls of Dharkaron Avenger's judgment; according to Ath's adepts, that state of being where the prime vibration is not recognized.

pronounced: sith-air

root meaning: *sid*—lost; *thiere*—wraith/spirit

SKYRON FOCUS—large aquamarine focus stone, used by the Koriani Senior Circle for their major magic after the loss of the Great Waystone during the rebellion.

pronounced: sky-run

root meaning: *skyron*—colloquialism for shackle; *s'kyr'i'on*—literally "sorrowful fate"

SKYSHIELS—mountain range that runs north and south along the eastern coast of Rathain.

pronounced: sky-shee-ells

root meaning: *skyshia*—to pierce through; *iel*—ray

SOUTHSHIRE—town on the southcoast of Alland, Shand, known for shipbuilding.

pronounced: south-shire

not from the Paravian

SPIRE—town with a hostel of Ath's Brotherhood, located on the southcoast in Havistock, Havish.

s'TALEYN—lineage of the *Caithdeinen* of Shand.

pronounced: stall-ay-en

root meaning: *tal*—branch; *an*—one/first "of the first branch"

STEIVEN—Earl of the North, *caithdein* and regent to the Kingdom of Rathain at the time of Arithon Teir's'Ffalenn's return. Chieftain of the Deshans until his death in the battle of Strakewood Forest in Third Year 5638. Jieret Red-beard's father. Barach and Jeynsa's grandfather.

pronounced: stay-vin

root meaning: *steiven*—stag

STORLAINS—mountains dividing the Kingdom of Havish.

pronounced: store-lanes

root meaning: *storlient*—largest summit, highest divide

STORMWELL—Gulf of Stormwell, body of water off the northcoast of Tysan.

STRAKEWOOD—forest in the principality of Deshir, Rathain; site of the battle of Strakewood Forest, where the garrison from Etarra marched against the clans under Steiven s'Valerient and Prince Arithon, in Third Age Year 5638.

pronounced: strayk-wood similar to "stray wood"

root meaning: *streik*—to quicken, to seed

SULFIN EVEND—son of the Mayor of Hanshire who holds the post of Alliance Lord Commander under Lysaer s'Ilessid.

pronounced: sool-finn ev-end

root meaning: *suilfinn eiavend*—colloquialism, diamond mind "one who is persistent"

s'VALERIENT—family name for the Earls of the North, regents and *caithdein* for the High Kings of Rathain.

> pronounced: val-er-ee-ent
>
> root meaning: *val*—straight; *erient*—spear

TAERLIN—southwestern principality of Kingdom of Tysan. Also a lake, Taerlin Waters located in the southern spur of Tornir Peaks. Halliron taught Arithon a ballad of that name, which is of Paravian origin and commemorates the First Age slaughter of a unicorn herd by Khadrim.

> pronounced: tay-er-lin
>
> root meaning: *taer*—calm; *lien*—to love

TAL QUORIN—river formed by the confluence of watershed on the southern side of Strakewood, principality of Deshir, Rathain, where traps were laid for Etarra's army in the battle of Strakewood Forest, and where the rape and massacre of Deshir's clan women and children occurred under Lysaer and headhunters under Pesquil's command in Third Age Year 5638.

> pronounced: tal quar-in
>
> root meaning: *tal*—branch; *quorin*—canyons

TALITH—Etarran princess; former wife of Lysaer s'Ilessid. Died of a fall from Avenor's tower of state.

> pronounced: tal-ith—to rhyme with "gal with"
>
> root meaning: *tal*—branch; *lith*—to keep/nurture

TALVISH—a clanborn retainer in sworn service to s'Brydion at Alestron who was sworn into the service of Prince Arithon as a point of honor.

> pronounced: tall-vish
>
> root meaning: *talvesh*—reed

TANUIN—a clansman of Shand who died in defense of noncombatant families during the campaign at Vastmark in Third Age Year 5647, father of Glendien.

> pronounced: tan-oo-win
>
> root meaning: *tanuin*—swift, or swallow

TEIR—masculine form of a title fixed to a name denoting heirship.

> pronounced: tayer
>
> root meaning: *teir's*—successor to power

TEIREN—feminine form of Teir.

TEIVE—first mate of the merchant brig *Evenstar* and father of Feylind's two children.

> pronounced: tee-ev
>
> root meaning: *tierve*—reliable

TELLESEC—guild minister in Avenor, and one of the regent's council of Tysan.

> pronounced: tell-i-sec

root meaning: *tellisec*—a small spider

TELMANDIR—seat of the High Kings of Havish in Lithmere, Havish. Ruined during the uprising in Third Age Year 5018, rebuilt by High King Eldir s'Lornmein after his coronation in Third Age Year 5643.

pronounced: tell-man-deer

root meaning: *telman'en*-leaning; *dir*-rock

TELZEN—town on the eastshore of Alland, Shand.

pronounced: tell-zen

root meaning: *tielsen*—to saw wood

THEMBREL'S OAK—tree by the sacred spring in the heart of Halwythwood, Rathain, where the Athlien dancers once enacted the rites of renewal. Site of the grand mysteries, off-limits to humankind.

pronounced: them-brel

root meaning: *thembrel*—acorn

THALDEINS—mountain range that borders the principality of Camris, Tysan, to the east. Site of the Camris clans' west outpost. Site of the raid at the Pass of Orlan.

pronounced: thall-dayn

root meaning: *thal*—head; *dein*—bird

THARIDOR—trade city on the shores of the Bay of Eltair in Melhalla.

pronounced: thar-i-door

root meaning: *tier'i'dur*—keep of stone

THARRICK—former captain of the guard in the city of Alestron assigned charge of the duke's secret armory; now married to Jinesse and working as a gentleman mercenary guard at Innish.

pronounced: thar-rick

root meaning: *thierik*—unkind twist of fate

TIDEPORT—a coastal town in Korias, Tysan.

not from the Paravian

TIENELLE—high-altitude herb valued by mages for its mind-expanding properties. Highly toxic. No antidote. The leaves, dried and smoked, are most potent. To weaken its powerful side effects and allow safer access to its vision, Koriani enchantresses boil the flowers, then soak tobacco leaves with the brew.

pronounced: tee-an-ell-e ("e" mostly subliminal)

root meaning: *tien*—dream; *iel*—light/ray

TIRANS—trade town located on the East Halla peninsula in Melhalla, also a Second Age ruin, seat of the High Kings of Melhalla, sacked during the uprising in Third Age Year 5018. Site of a Paravian focus circle.

pronounced: tee-rans

root meaning: *tier*—to hold fast, to keep, or to covet

TIRIACS—mountain range to the north of Mirthlvain Swamp, in Midhalla, Melhalla.

pronounced: tie-ree-axe

root meaning: *tieriach*—alloy of metals

TORBRAND s'FFALENN—founder of the s'Ffalenn line appointed by the Fellowship of Seven to rule the High Kingdom of Rathain in Third Age Year One.

pronounced: tor-brand

root meaning: *tor*—sharp, keen; *brand*—temper

TORNIR PEAKS—mountain range on western border in Camris, Tysan. Northern half is actively volcanic, and there the last surviving packs of Khadrim are kept under ward.

pronounced: tor-neer

root meaning: *tor*—sharp, keen; *nier*—tooth

TRAITHE—Sorcerer of the Fellowship of Seven. Solely responsible for the closing of South Gate to deny further entry to the Mistwraith. Traithe lost most of his faculties in the process and was left with a limp. Since it is not known whether he can make the transfer into discorporate existence with his powers impaired, he has retained his physical body.

pronounced: tray-the

root meaning: *traithe*—gentleness

TYSAN—one of the Five High Kingdoms of Athera as defined by the charters of the Fellowship of Seven. Ruled by the s'Ilessid royal line. Device: gold star on blue field.

pronounced: tie-san

root meaning: *tiasen*—rich

VAE—mother of a young boy, recruited by Lysaer s'Ilessid.

root meaning not from the Paravian.

VARENS—trade town on the shore of Eltair Bay in East Halla, Melhalla.

pronounced: var-ens

root meaning: *var'uens*—keep safe, or lock

VARRUN—Lord High Justiciar of Avenor, one of Lysaer's regent's council of Tysan.

pronounced: var-run

root meaning: *vaer'ruann*—eyrie

VASTMARK—principality located in southwestern Shand. Highly mountainous and not served by trade roads. Its coasts are renowned for shipwrecks. Inhabited by nomadic shepherds and wyverns, non-fire-breathing, smaller relatives of Khadrim. Site of the grand massacre of Lysaer's war host in Third Age 5647.

pronounced: vast-mark

root meaning: *vhast*—bare; *mheark*—valley

VERRAIN—master spellbinder, trained by Luhaine; stood as Guardian of Mirthlvain when the Fellowship of Seven was left shorthanded after the conquest of the Mistwraith.

pronounced: ver-rain

root meaning: *ver*—keep; *ria*—touch; *an*—one original Paravian: *verria'an*

Biography

Janny Wurts is the author of fourteen novels, a collection of short stories, and the internationally best selling Empire trilogy written in collaboration with Raymond E. Feist.

A central focus of her career, the latest in her ongoing Wars of Light and Shadow series, *Peril's Gate* and *Traitor's Knot*, are the culmination of more than thirty years of carefully evolved ideas. The cover images on the books, both in the US and abroad, are her own paintings, depicting her vision of characters and setting.

Through her combined talents as a writer/illustrator, Janny has immersed herself in a lifelong ambition: to create a seamless interface between words and pictures that will lead reader and viewer beyond the world we know. Her lavish use of language lures the mind into a crafted realm of experience, with characters and events woven into a complex tapestry, and drawn with an intensity to leave a lasting impression. Her research includes a range of direct experience, lending her fantasy a gritty realism, and her scenes involving magic an almost visionary credibility. A self–taught painter, she draws directly from the imagination, creating scenes in a representational style that blurs the edges between dream and reality. She makes no preliminary sketches, but envisions her characters and the scenes that contain them, then executes the final directly from the initial pencil drawing.

The seed idea for the Wars of Light and Shadow series occurred, when, in the course of researching tactics and weapons, she viewed a documentary film on the Battle of Culloden Moor. This was the first time she had encountered that historical context of that brutal event, with the embroidery of romance stripped from it. The experience gave rise to an awakening, which became anger, that so often, our education, literature and entertainment slant history in a manner that equates winners and losers with moral right and wrong, and the prevalent attitude, that killing wars can be seen as justifiable solutions when only one side of the picture is presented.

Her series takes the stance that there are two sides to every question, and follows two characters who are half brothers. One a bard trained as a master of magecraft, and the other a born ruler with a charismatic passion for justice, have become cursed to lifelong enmity. As one sibling raises a devoted mass following, the other tries desperately to stave off defeat through solitary discipline and cleverness. The conflict sweeps across an imaginary world, dividing land and people through an intricate play of politics and the inborn prejudices of polarized factions already set at odds. Readers are led on a journey that embraces both viewpoints. The story explores the ironies of morality which often confound our own human condition—that what appears right and just, by one side, becomes reprehensible when seen from the opposite angle. What is apprently good for the many, too often causes devastating suffering to the nonconformist minority. Through the interactions between the characters themselves, the reader is left to their own descretion to interpret the moral impact of events.

Says Janny of her work, "I chose to frame this story against a backdrop of fantasy because I could handle even the most sensitive issues with the gloves off—explore the myriad angles of our troubled times with the least risk of offending anyone's personal sensibilities. The result, I can hope, is an expanding journey of the spirit that explores the grand depths, and rises to the challenge of mapping the ethereal potential of an evolving planetary consciousness."

Beyond writing, Janny's award winning paintings have been showcased in exhibitions of imaginative artwork, among them a commemorative exhibition for NASA's 25th Anniversary; the Art of the Cosmos at Hayden Planetarium in New York; and two exhibits of fantasy art, at both the Delaware Art Museum, and Canton Art Museum.